A selection of translations from the Russian by
CONSTANCE GARNETT

LEO TOLSTOY
War and Peace
Anna Karenina

IVAN TURGENEV
Rudin
A House of Gentlefolk
On the Eve
The Torrents of Spring
Selected Stories

FYODOR DOSTOEVSKY
The Brothers Karamazov
The Idiot
The Possessed
Crime and Punishment
The House of the Dead
The Insulted and Injured
A Raw Youth
The Eternal Husband and other stories
The Gambler and other stories
White Nights and other stories
An Honest Thief and other stories
The Friend of the Family and another story

To my dearest Darling Linda,
the most beautiful woman in
the world,

lo [illegible] dying

Jack (xxxxxx)

ANNA KARENINA

LEO TOLSTOY

ANNA KARENINA

Translated from the Russian by
CONSTANCE GARNETT

'Vengeance is mine
and I will repay'

HEINEMANN: LONDON

William Heinemann Ltd

15 Queen St, Mayfair, London W1X 8BE

LONDON MELBOURNE TORONTO
JOHANNESBURG AUCKLAND

First published in 1901
in Library Edition (*two volumes*)
Colonial Edition (*one volume*) 1901
Popular Edition (*one volume*) 1911
Nine impressions 1912–1954
Reprinted (re-set) 1960
Re-set in this edition 1972
Reissued 1977
434 78755 8

Printed and bound in Great Britain by
Hazell Watson & Viney Ltd,
Aylesbury, Bucks

NOTE

The first edition of this translation carried a note by Constance Garnett, dated August 1901, explaining that she did not adopt the form 'Anna Karenina' 'since such a preservation of the feminine form of the surname is unparalleled in English.' Since that time, however, the feminine form of Russian names has become far more familiar to English readers. Although 'Karenin' remains unchanged throughout the text of the novel the universally-recognised 'Anna Karenina' is now used on the title-page, binding and jacket of this edition.

PART I

I

HAPPY families are all alike; every unhappy family is unhappy in its own way.

Everything was in confusion in the Oblonskys' house. The wife had discovered that the husband was carrying on an intrigue with a French girl, who had been a governess in their family, and she had announced to her husband that she could not go on living in the same house with him. This position of affairs had now lasted three days, and not only the husband and wife themselves, but all the members of their family and household, were painfully conscious of it. Every person in the house felt that there was no sense in their living together, and that the stray people brought together by chance in any inn had more in common with one another than they, the member of the family and household of the Oblonskys. The wife did not leave her own room, the husband had not been at home for three days. The children ran wild all over the house; the English governess quarrelled with the housekeeper, and wrote to a friend asking her to look out for a new situation for her; the man-cook had walked off the day before just at dinner-time; the kitchen-maid and the coachman had given warning.

Three days after the quarrel, Prince Stepan Arkadyevitch Oblonsky —Stiva, as he was called in the fashionable world—woke up at his usual hour, that is, at eight o'clock in the morning, not in his wife's bedroom, but on the leather-covered sofa in his study. He turned over his stout, well-cared-for person on the springy sofa, as though he would sink into a long sleep again; he vigorously embraced the pillow on the other side and buried his face in it; but all at once he jumped up, sat up on the sofa, and opened his eyes.

'Yes, yes, how was it now?' he thought, going over his dream. 'Now, how was it? To be sure! Alabin was giving a dinner at Darmstadt; no, not Darmstadt, but something American. Yes, but then, Darmstadt was in America. Yes, Alabin was giving a dinner on glass tables, and the tables sang, *Il mio tesoro*—not *Il mio tesoro* though, but something better, and there were some sort of little decanters on the table, and they were women too,' he remembered.

Stepan Arkadyevitch's eyes twinkled gaily, and he pondered with a smile. 'Yes, it was nice, very nice. There was a great deal more that was delightful, only there's no putting it into words, or even expressing it in one's thoughts awake.' And noticing a gleam of light peeping in beside one of the serge curtains, he cheerfully dropped his feet over the edge of the sofa, and felt about with them for his slippers, a present on his last birthday, worked for him by his wife on gold-coloured morocco. And, as he had done every day for the last nine years, he stretched out his hand, without getting up, towards the place where his dressing-gown always hung in his bedroom. And thereupon he suddenly remembered that he was not sleeping in his wife's room, but in his study, and why: the smile vanished from his face, he knitted his brows.

'Ah, ah, ah! Oo! . . .' he muttered, recalling everything that had happened. And again every detail of his quarrel with his wife was present to his imagination, all the hopelessness of his position, and worst of all, his own fault.

'Yes, she won't forgive me, and she can't forgive me. And the most awful thing about it is that it's all my fault—all my fault, though I'm not to blame. That's the point of the whole situation,' he reflected. 'Oh, oh, oh!' he kept repeating in despair, as he remembered the acutely painful sensations caused him by this quarrel.

Most unpleasant of all was the first minute when, on coming, happy and good-humoured, from the theatre, with a huge pear in his hand for his wife, he had not found his wife in the drawing-room, to his surprise had not found her in the study either, and saw her at last in her bedroom with the unlucky letter that revealed everything in her hand.

She, his Dolly, for ever fussing and worrying over household details, and limited in her ideas, as he considered, was sitting perfectly still with the letter in her hand, looking at him with an expression of horror, despair, and indignation.

'What's this? this?' she asked, pointing to the letter.

And at this recollection, Stepan Arkadyevitch, as is so often the case, was not so much annoyed at the fact itself as at the way in which he had met his wife's words.

There happened to him at that instant what does happen to people when they are unexpectedly caught in something very disgraceful. He did not succeed in adapting his face to the position in which he was placed towards his wife by the discovery of his fault. Instead of being hurt, denying, defending himself, begging forgiveness, instead of remaining indifferent even—anything would have been better than what he did do—his face utterly involuntarily (reflex spinal action, reflected Stepan Arkadyevitch, who was fond of physiology)—utterly involuntarily assumed its habitual, good-humoured, and therefore idiotic smile.

This idiotic smile he could not forgive himself. Catching sight of that smile, Dolly shuddered as though at physical pain, broke out with her characteristic heat into a flood of cruel words, and rushed out of the room. Since then she had refused to see her husband.

'It's that idiotic smile that's to blame for it all,' thought Stepan Arkadyevitch.

'But what's to be done? What's to be done?' he said to himself in despair, and found no answer.

II

STEPAN ARKADYEVITCH was a truthful man in his relations with himself. He was incapable of deceiving himself and persuading himself that he repented of his conduct. He could not at this date repent of the fact that he, a handsome, susceptible man of thirty-four, was not in love with his wife, the mother of five living and two dead children, and only a year younger than himself. All he repented of was that he had not succeeded better in hiding it from his wife. But he felt all the difficulty of his position and was sorry for his wife, his children, and himself. Possibly he might have managed to conceal his sins better from his wife if he had anticipated that the knowledge of them would have had such an effect on her. He had never clearly thought out the subject, but he had vaguely conceived that his wife must long ago have suspected him of being unfaithful to her, and shut her eyes to the fact. He had even supposed that she, a worn-out woman no longer young or good-looking, and in no way remarkable or interesting, merely a good mother, ought from a sense of fairness to take an indulgent view. It had turned out quite the other way.

'Oh, it's awful! oh dear, oh dear! awful!' Stepan Arkadyevitch kept repeating to himself, and he could think of nothing to be done. 'And how well things were going up till now! how well we got on! She was contented and happy in her children; I never interfered with her in anything; I let her manage the children and the house just as she liked. It's true it's bad *her* having been a governess in our house. That's bad! There's something common, vulgar, in flirting with one's governess. But what a governess!' (He vividly recalled the roguish black eyes of Mlle. Roland and her smile.) 'But after all, while she was in the house, I kept myself in hand. And the worst of it all is that she's already . . . it seems as if ill-luck would have it so! Oh, oh! But what, what is to be done?'

There was no solution, but that universal solution which life gives to all questions, even the most complex and insoluble. That answer is: one must live in the needs of the day—that is, forget oneself. To forget himself in sleep was impossible now, at least till night-time; he could not go back now to the music sung by the decanter-women; so he must forget himself in the dream of daily life.

'Then we shall see,' Stepan Arkadyevitch said to himself, and getting up he put on a grey dressing-gown lined with blue silk, tied the tassels in a knot, and, drawing a deep breath of air into his broad, bare chest, he walked to the window with his usual confident step, turning out his feet that carried his full frame so easily. He pulled up the blind and rang the bell loudly. It was at once answered by the appearance of an old friend, his valet Matvey, carrying his clothes, his boots, and a telegram. Matvey was followed by the barber with all the necessaries for shaving.

'Are there any papers from the office?' asked Stepan Arkadyevitch, taking the telegram and seating himself at the looking-glass.

'On the table,' replied Matvey, glancing with inquiring sympathy at his master; and, after a short pause, he added with a sly smile, 'They've sent from the carriage-jobbers.'

Stepan Arkadyevitch made no reply, he merely glanced at Matvey in the looking-glass. In the glance, in which their eyes met in the looking-glass, it was clear that they understood one another. Stepan Arkadyevitch's eyes asked: 'Why do you tell me that? don't you know?'

Matvey put his hands in his jacket pockets, thrust out one leg, and gazed silently, good-humouredly, with a faint smile, at his master.

'I told them to come on Sunday, and till then not to trouble you or themselves for nothing,' he said. He had obviously prepared the sentence beforehand.

Stepan Arkadyevitch saw Matvey wanted to make a joke and attract attention to himself. Tearing open the telegram, he read it through, guessing at the words, misspelt as they always are in telegrams, and his face brightened.

'Matvey, my sister Anna Arkadyevna will be here tomorrow,' he said, checking for a minute the sleek, plump hand of the barber, cutting a pink path through his long, curly whiskers.

'Thank God!' said Matvey, showing by this response that he, like his master, realised the significance of this arrival—that is, that Anna

Arkadyevna, the sister he was so fond of, might bring about a reconciliation between husband and wife.

'Alone, or with her husband?' inquired Matvey.

Stepan Arkadyevitch could not answer, as the barber was at work on his upper lip, and he raised one finger. Matvey nodded at the looking-glass.

'Alone. Is the room to be got ready upstairs?'

'Inform Darya Alexandrovna: where she orders.'

'Darya Alexandrovna?' Matvey repeated, as though in doubt.

'Yes, inform her. Here, take the telegram; give it her, and then do what she tells you.'

'You want to try it on,' Matvey understood, but he only said, 'Yes, sir.'

Stepan Arkadyevitch was already washed and combed and ready to be dressed, when Matvey, stepping deliberately in his creaky boots, came back into the room with the telegram in his hand. The barber had gone.

'Darya Alexandrovna told me to inform you that she is going away. Let him do—that is you—do as he likes,' he said, laughing only with his eyes, and putting his hands in his pockets, he watched his master with his head on one side. Stepan Arkadyevitch was silent a minute. Then a good-humoured and rather pitiful smile showed itself on his handsome face.

'Eh, Matvey?' he said, shaking his head.

'It's all right, sir; she will come round,' said Matvey.

'Come round?'

'Yes, sir.'

'Do you think so? Who's there?' asked Stepan Arkadyevitch, hearing the rustle of a woman's dress at the door.

'It's I,' said a firm, pleasant woman's voice, and the stern, pock-marked face of Matrona Philimonovna, the nurse, was thrust in at the doorway.

'Well, what it it, Matrona?' queried Stepan Arkadyevitch, going up to her at the door.

Although Stepan Arkadyevitch was completely in the wrong as regards his wife, and was conscious of this himself, almost everyone in the house (even the nurse, Darya Alexandrovna's chief ally) was on his side.

'Well, what now?' he asked disconsolately.

'Go to her, sir; own your fault again. Maybe God will aid you. She is suffering so, it's sad to see her; and besides, everything in the house is topsy turvy. You must have pity, sir, on the children. Beg her forgiveness, sir. There's no help for it! One must take the consequences . . .'

'But she won't see me.'

'You do your part. God is merciful; pray to God, sir, pray to God.'

'Come, that'll do, you can go,' said Stepan Arkadyevitch, blushing suddenly. 'Well now, do dress me.' He turned to Matvey and threw off his dressing-gown decisively.

Matvey was already holding up the shirt like a horse's collar, and, blowing off some invisible speck, he slipped it with obvious pleasure over the well-groomed body of his master.

III

WHEN he was dressed, Stepan Arkadyevitch sprinkled some scent on himself, pulled down his shirt-cuffs, distributed into his pockets his cigarettes, pocket-book, matches, and watch with its double chain and seals, and shaking out his handkerchief, feeling himself clean, fragrant, healthy, and physically at ease, in spite of his unhappiness, he walked with a slight swing on each leg into the dining-room, where coffee was already waiting for him, and beside the coffee, letters and papers from the office.

He read the letters. One was very unpleasant, from a merchant who was buying a forest on his wife's property. To sell this forest was absolutely essential; but at present, until he was reconciled with his wife, the subject could not be discussed. The most unpleasant thing of all was that his pecuniary interests should in this way enter into the question of his reconciliation with his wife. And the idea that he might be led on by his interests, that he might seek a reconciliation with his wife on account of the sale of the forest—that idea hurt him.

When he had finished his letters, Stepan Arkadyevitch moved the office-papers close to him, rapidly looked through two pieces of business, made a few notes with a big pencil, and pushing away the papers, turned to his coffee. As he sipped his coffee, he opened a still damp morning paper, and began reading it.

Stepan Arkadyevitch took in and read a liberal paper, not an extreme one, but one advocating the views held by the majority. And in spite of the fact that science, art, and politics had no special interest for him, he firmly held those views on all these subjects which were held by the majority and by his paper, and he only changed them when the majority changed them—or, more strictly speaking, he did not change them, but they imperceptibly changed of themselves within him.

Stepan Arkadyevitch had not chosen his political opinions or his views; these political opinions and views had come to him of themselves, just as he did not choose the shapes of his hat and coat, but simply took those that were being worn. And for him, living in a certain society—owing to the need, ordinarily developed at years of discretion, for some degree of mental activity—to have views was just as indispensable as to have a hat. If there was a reason for his preferring liberal to conservative views, which were held also by many of his circle, it arose not from his considering liberalism more rational, but from its being in closer accordance with his manner of life. The liberal party said that in Russia everything is wrong, and certainly Stepan Arkadyevitch had many debts and was decidedly short of money. The liberal party said that marriage is an institution quite out of date, and that it needs reconstruction; and family life certainly afforded Stepan Arkadyevitch little gratification, and forced him into lying and hypocrisy, which was so repulsive to his nature. The liberal party said, or rather allowed it to be understood, that religion is only a curb to keep in check the barbarous classes of the people; and Stepan Arkadyevitch could not get through even a short service without his legs aching from standing up, and could never make out what was the object of all the terrible and high-flown language about another world when life might be so very amusing in this world. And with all this, Stepan Arkadyevitch, who liked a joke, was fond of puzzling a plain man by saying that if he prided himself on his origin, he ought not to stop at Rurik and disown the first founder of his family—the monkey. And so liberalism had become a habit of Stepan Arkadyevitch's, and he liked his newspaper, as he did his cigar after dinner, for the slight fog it diffused in his brain. He read the leading article, in which it was maintained that it was quite senseless in our day to raise an outcry that radicalism was threatening to swallow up all conservative elements, and that the government ought to take measures to crush the revolutionary hydra; that, on the contrary, 'in our opinion the danger lies not in that fantastic revolutionary hydra, but in the obstinacy of traditionalism clogging progress,' etc. etc. He read another article too, a financial one, which alluded to Bentham and Mill, and dropped some innuendoes reflecting on the ministry. With his characteristic quick-wittedness he caught the drift of each innuendo, divined whence it came, at whom and on what ground it was aimed, and that afforded him, as it always did, a certain satisfaction. But today that satisfaction was embittered by Matrona Philimonovna's advice and the unsatisfactory state of the household. He read, too, that Count Beist was rumoured to have left for Wiesbaden, and that one need have no more grey hair, and of the sale of a light carriage, and of a young person seeking a situation; but these items of information did not give him, as usual, a quiet, ironical gratification. Having finished the paper, a second cup of coffee and a roll and butter, he got up, shaking the crumbs of the roll off his waistcoat; and, squaring his broad chest, he smiled joyously: not because there was anything particularly agreeable in his mind—the joyous smile was evoked by a good digestion.

But this joyous smile at once recalled everything to him, and he grew thoughtful.

Two childish voices (Stepan Arkadyevitch recognised the voices of Grisha, his youngest boy, and Tanya, his eldest girl) were heard outside the door. They were carrying something, and dropped it.

'I told you not to sit passengers on the roof,' said the little girl in English; 'there, pick them up!'

'Everything's in confusion,' thought Stepan Arkadyevitch; 'there are the children running about by themselves.' And going to the door, he called them. They threw down the box, that represented a train, and came in to their father.

The little girl, her father's favourite, ran up boldly, embraced him, and hung laughingly on his neck, enjoying as she always did the smell of scent that came from his whiskers. At last the little girl kissed his face, which was flushed from his stooping posture and beaming with tenderness, loosed her hands, and was about to run away again; but her father held her back.

'How is mamma?' he asked, passing his hand over his daughter's smooth, soft little neck. 'Good morning,' he said, smiling to the boy, who had come up to greet him. He was conscious that he loved the boy less, and always tried to be fair; but the boy felt it, and did not respond with a smile to his father's chilly smile.

'Mamma? She is up,' answered the girl.

Stepan Arkadyevitch sighed. 'That means that she's not slept again all night,' he thought.

'Well, is she cheerful?'

The little girl knew that there was a quarrel between her father and mother, and that her mother could not be cheerful, and that her father must be aware of this, and that he was pretending when he asked about it so lightly. And she blushed for her father. He at once perceived it, and blushed too.

'I don't know,' she said. 'She did not say we must do our lessons, but she said we were to go a walk with Miss Hoole to grandmamma's.'

'Well, go, Tanya, my darling. Oh, wait a minute, though,' he said, still holding her and stroking her soft little hand.

He took off the mantelpiece, where he had put it yesterday, a little box of sweets, and gave her two, picking out her favourites, a chocolate and a fondant.

'For Grisha?' said the little girl, pointing to the chocolate.

'Yes, yes.' And still stroking her little shoulder, he kissed her on the roots of her hair and neck, and let her go.

'The carriage is ready,' said Matvey; 'but there's some one to see you with a petition.'

'Been here long?' asked Stepan Arkadyevitch.

'Half an hour.'

'How many times have I told you to tell me at once?'

'One must let you drink your coffee in peace, at least,' said Matvey, in the affectionately gruff tone with which it was impossible to be angry.

'Well, show the person up at once,' said Oblonsky, frowning with vexation.

The petitioner, the widow of a staff captain Kalínin, came with a request impossible and unreasonable; but Stepan Arkadyevitch, as he generally did, made her sit down, heard her to the end attentively without interrupting her, and gave her detailed advice as to how and to whom to apply, and even wrote her, in his large, sprawling, good and legible hand, a confident and fluent little note to a personage who might be of use to her. Having got rid of the staff captain's widow, Stepan Arkadyevitch took his hat and stopped to recollect whether he had forgotten anything. It appeared that he had forgotten nothing except what he wanted to forget—his wife.

'Ah, yes!' He bowed his head, and his handsome face assumed a harassed expression. 'To go, or not to go!' he said to himself; and an inner voice told him he must not go, that nothing could come of it but falsity; that to amend, to set right their relations was impossible, because it was impossible to make her attractive again and able to inspire love, or to make him an old man, not susceptible to love. Except deceit and lying nothing could come of it now; and deceit and lying were opposed to his nature.

'It must be some time, though: it can't go on like this,' he said, trying to give himself courage. He squared his chest, took out a cigarette, took two whiffs at it, flung it into a mother-of-pearl ash-tray, and with rapid steps walked through the drawing-room, and opened the other door into his wife's bedroom.

IV

DARYA ALEXANDROVNA, in a dressing-jacket, and with her now scanty, once luxuriant and beautiful hair fastened up with hairpins on the nape of her neck, with a sunken, thin face and large, startled eyes, which looked prominent from the thinness of her face, was standing among a litter of all sorts of things scattered all over the room, before an open bureau, from which she was taking something. Hearing her husband's steps, she stopped, looking towards the door, and trying assiduously to give her features a severe and contemptuous expression. She felt she was afraid of him, and afraid of the coming interview. She was just attempting to do what she had attempted to do ten times already in these last three days—to sort out the children's things and her own, so as to take them to her mother's—and again she could not bring herself to do this; but now again, as each time before, she kept saying to herself, 'that things cannot go on like this, that she must take some step' to punish him, put him to shame, avenge on him some little part at least of the suffering he had caused her. She still continued to tell herself that she should leave him, but she was conscious that this was impossible; it was impossible because she could not get out of the habit of regarding him as her husband and loving him. Besides this, she realised that if even here in her own house she could hardly manage to look after her five children properly, they would be still worse off where she was going with them all. As it was, even in the course of these three days, the youngest was unwell from being given unwholesome soup, and the others had almost gone without their dinner the day before. She was conscious that it was impossible to go away; but, cheating herself, she went on all the same sorting out her things and pretending she was going.

Seeing her husband, she dropped her hands into the drawer of the bureau as though looking for something, and only looked round at him when he had come quite up to her. But her face, to which she tried to give a severe and resolute expression, betrayed bewilderment and suffering.

'Dolly!' he said in a subdued and timid voice. He bent his head towards his shoulder and tried to look pitiful and humble, but for all that he was radiant with freshness and health. In a rapid glance she scanned his figure that beamed with health and freshness. 'Yes, he is happy and content!' she thought; 'while I . . . And that disgusting good nature, which everyone likes him for and praises—I hate that good nature of his,' she thought. Her mouth stiffened, the muscles of the cheek contracted on the right side of her pale, nervous face.

'What do you want?' she said in a rapid, deep, unnatural voice.

'Dolly!' he repeated, with a quiver in his voice. 'Anna is coming today.'

'Well, what is that to me? I can't see her!' she cried.

'But you must, really, Dolly. . . .'

'Go away, go away, go away!' she shrieked, not looking at him, as though this shriek were called up by physical pain.

Stepan Arkadyevitch could be calm when he thought of his wife, he could hope that she would *come round*, as Matvey expressed it, and could quietly go on reading his paper and drinking his coffee; but when he saw her tortured, suffering face, heard the tone of her voice, submissive to fate and full of despair, there was a catch in his breath and a lump in his throat, and his eyes began to shine with tears.

'My God! what have I done? Dolly! For God's sake! . . . You know . . .' He could not go on; there was a sob in his throat.

She shut the bureau with a slam, and glanced at him.

'Dolly, what can I say? . . . One thing: forgive . . . Remember, cannot nine years of my life atone for an instant . . .'

She dropped her eyes and listened, expecting what he would say, as it were beseeching him in some way or other to make her believe differently.

'—instant of passion?' . . . he said, and would have gone on, but at that word, as at a pang of physical pain, her lips stiffened again, and again the muscles of her right cheek worked.

'Go away, go out of the room!' she shrieked still more shrilly, 'and don't talk to me of your passion and your loathsomeness.'

She tried to go out, but tottered, and clung to the back of a chair to support herself. His face relaxed, his lips swelled, his eyes were swimming with tears.

'Dolly!' he said, sobbing now; 'for mercy's sake, think of the children; they are not to blame! I am to blame, and punish me, make me expiate my fault. Anything I can do, I am ready to do anything! I am to blame, no words can express how much I am to blame! But, Dolly, forgive me!'

She sat down. He listened to her hard, heavy breathing, and he was unutterably sorry for her. She tried several times to begin to speak, but could not. He waited.

'You remember the children, Stiva, to play with them; but I remember them, and know that this means their ruin,' she said—obviously one of the phrases she had more than once repeated to herself in the course of the last three days.

She had called him 'Stiva,' and he glanced at her with gratitude, and moved to take her hand, but she drew back from him with aversion.

'I think of the children, and for that reason I would do anything in the world to save them; but I don't myself know how to save them. By taking them away from their father, or by leaving them with a vicious father—yes, a vicious father. . . . Tell me, after what . . . has happened, can we live together? Is that possible? Tell me, eh, is it possible?' she repeated, raising her voice, 'after my husband, the father of my children, enters into a love-affair with his own children's governess?'

'But what could I do? what could I do?' he kept saying in a pitiful voice, not knowing what he was saying, as his head sank lower and lower.

'You are loathsome to me, repulsive!' she shrieked, getting more and more heated. 'Your tears mean nothing! You have never loved me; you have neither heart nor honourable feeling! You are hateful to me, disgusting, a stranger—yes, a complete stranger!' With pain and wrath she uttered the word so terrible to herself—*stranger*.

He looked at her, and the fury expressed in her face alarmed and amazed him. He did not understand how his pity for her exasperated her. She saw in him sympathy for her, but not love. 'No, she hates me. She will not forgive me,' he thought.

'It is awful! awful!' he said.

At that moment in the next room a child began to cry; probably it had fallen down. Darya Alexandrovna listened, and her face suddenly softened.

She seemed to be pulling herself together for a few seconds, as though she did not know where she was, and what she was doing, and getting up rapidly, she moved towards the door.

'Well, she loves my child,' he thought, noticing the change of her face at the child's cry, 'my child: how can she hate me?'

'Dolly, one word more,' he said, following her.

'If you come near me, I will call in the servants, the children! They may all know you are a scoundrel! I am going away at once, and you may live here with your mistress!'

And she went out, slamming the door.

Stepan Arkadyevitch sighed, wiped his face, and with a subdued tread walked out of the room. 'Matvey says she will come round; but how? I don't see the least chance of it. Ah, oh, how horrible it is! And how vulgarly she shouted,' he said to himself, remembering her shriek and the words—'scoundrel' and 'mistress.' 'And very likely the maids were listening! Horribly vulgar! horrible!' Stepan Arkadyevitch stood a few seconds alone, wiped his face, squared his chest, and walked out of the room.

It was Friday, and in the dining-room the German watch-maker was winding up the clock. Stepan Arkadyevitch remembered his joke about this punctual, bald watchmaker, 'that the German was wound up for a whole lifetime himself, to wind up watches,' and he smiled. Stepan Arkadyevitch was fond of a joke. 'And maybe she will come round! That's a good expression, "*come round*,"' he thought. 'I must repeat that.'

'Matvey!' he shouted. 'Arrange everything with Marya in the sitting-room for Anna Arkadyevna,' he said to Matvey when he came in.

'Yes, sir.'

Stepan Arkadyevitch put on his fur coat and went out on to the steps.

'You won't dine at home?' said Matvey, seeing him off.

'That's as it happens. But here's for the housekeeping,' he said, taking ten roubles from his pocket-book. 'That'll be enough.'

'Enough or not enough, we must make it do,' said Matvey, slamming the carriage door and stepping back on to the steps.

Darya Alexandrovna meanwhile having pacified the child, and knowing from the sound of the carriage that he had gone off, went back again to her bedroom. It was her solitary refuge from the household cares which crowded upon her directly she went out from it. Even now, in the short time she had been in the nursery, the English governess and Matrona Philimonovna had succeeded in putting several questions to her, which did not admit of delay, and which only she could answer: 'What were the children to put on for their walk? Should they have any milk? Should not a new cook be sent for?'

'Ah, let me alone, let me alone!' she said, and going back to her bedroom she sat down in the same place as she had sat when talking to her husband, clasping tightly her thin hands with the rings that slipped down on her bony fingers, and fell to going over in her memory all the conversation. 'He has gone! But has he broken it off with her?' she thought. 'Can it be he sees her? Why didn't I ask him! No, no, reconciliation is impossible. Even if we remain in the same house, we are strangers—strangers for ever!' She repeated again with special significance the word so dreadful to her. 'And how I loved him! my God, how I loved him! . . . How I loved him! And now don't I love him? Don't I love him more than before? The most horrible thing is,' she began, but did not finish her thought, because Matrona Philimonovna put her head in at the door.

'Let us send for my brother,' she said; 'he can get a dinner any way, or we shall have the children getting nothing to eat till six again, like yesterday.'

'Very well, I will come directly and see about it. But did you send for some new milk?'

And Darya Alexandrovna plunged into the duties of the day, and drowned her grief in them for a time.

V

STEPAN ARKADYEVITCH had learned easily at school, thanks to his excellent abilities, but he had been idle and mischievous, and therefore was one of the lowest in his class. But in spite of his habitually dissipated mode of life, his inferior grade in the service, and his comparative youth, he occupied the honourable and lucrative position of president of one of the government boards at Moscow. This post he had received through his sister Anna's husband, Alexey Alexandrovitch Karenin, who held one of the most important positions in the ministry to whose department the Moscow office belonged. But if Karenin had not got his brother-in-law this berth, then through a hundred other personages—brothers, sisters, cousins, uncles, and aunts—Stiva Oblonsky would have received this post, or some other similar one, together with the salary of six thousand absolutely needful for him, as his affairs, in spite of his wife's considerable property, were in an embarrassed condition.

Half Moscow and Petersburg were friends and relations of Stepan Arkadyevitch. He was born in the midst of those who had been and are the powerful ones of this world. One-third of the men in the government, the older men, had been friends of his father's, and had known him in petticoats; another third were his intimate chums, and the remainder were friendly acquaintances. Consequently the distributors of earthly blessings in the shape of places, rents, shares, and such, were all his friends, and could not overlook one of their own set; and Oblonsky had no need to make any special exertion to get a lucrative post. He had only not to refuse things, not to show jealousy, not to be quarrelsome or take offence, all of which from his characteristic good nature he never did. It would have struck him as absurd if he had been told that he would not get a position with the salary he required, especially as he expected nothing out of the way; he only wanted what the men of his own age and standing did get, and he was no worse qualified for performing duties of the kind than any other man.

Stepan Arkadyevitch was not merely liked by all who knew him for his good-humour, his bright disposition, and his unquestionable honesty. In him, in his handsome, radiant figure, his sparkling eyes, black hair and eyebrows, and the white and red of his face, there was something which produced a physical effect of kindliness and good-humour on the people who met him. 'Aha! Stiva! Oblonsky! Here he is!' was almost always said with a smile of delight on meeting him. Even though it happened at times that after a conversation with him it seemed that nothing particularly delightful had happened, the next day, and the next, every one was just as delighted at meeting him again.

After filling for three years the post of president of one of the government boards at Moscow, Stepan Arkadyevitch had won the respect, as well as the liking, of his fellow-officials, subordinates, and superiors, and all who had had business with him. The principal qualities in Stepan Arkadyevitch which had gained him this universal respect in the service consisted, in the first place, of his extreme indulgence for others, founded on a consciousness of his own shortcomings; secondly, of his perfect liberalism—not the liberalism he read of in the papers, but the liberalism that was in his blood, in virtue of which he treated all men perfectly equally and exactly the same, whatever their fortune or calling might be; and thirdly—the most important point—his complete indifference to the business in which he was engaged, in consequence of which he was never carried away, and never made mistakes.

On reaching the offices of the board, Stepan Arkadyevitch, escorted by a deferential porter with a portfolio, went into his little private room, put on his uniform, and went into the board-room. The clerks and copyists all rose, greeting him with good-humoured deference. Stepan Arkadyevitch moved quickly, as ever, to his place, shook hands with his colleagues, and sat down. He made a joke or two, and talked just as much as was consistent with due decorum, and began work. No one knew better than Stepan Arkadyevitch how to hit on the exact line between freedom, simplicity, and official stiffness necessary for the agreeable conduct of business. A secretary, with the good-houmoured deference common to every one in Stepan Arkadyevitch's office, came up with papers, and began to speak in the familiar and easy tone which had been introduced by Stepan Arkadyevitch.

'We have succeeded in getting the information from the government department of Penza. Here, would you care? . . .'

'You've got them at last?' said Stepan Arkadyevitch, laying his finger on the paper. 'Now, gentlemen. . . .'

And the sitting of the board began.

'If they knew,' he thought, bending his head with a significant air as he listened to the report, 'what a guilty little boy their president was

A.K.—2

half an hour ago.' And his eyes were laughing during the reading of the report. Till two o'clock the sitting went on without a break, and at two o'clock there would be an interval and luncheon.

It was not yet two, when the large glass doors of the boardroom suddenly opened and some one came in.

All the officials sitting on the further side under the portrait of the Tsar and the eagle, delighted at any distraction, looked round at the door; but the doorkeeper standing at the door at once drove out the intruder, and closed the glass door after him.

When the case had been read through, Stepan Arkadyevitch got up and stretched, and by way of tribute to the liberalism of the times took out a cigarette in the board-room and went into his private room. Two of the members of the board, the old veteran in the service, Nikitin, and the *kammer-yunker* Grinevitch, went in with him.

'We shall have time to finish after lunch,' said Stepan Arkadyevitch.

'To be sure we shall!' said Nikitin.

'A pretty sharp fellow this Fomin must be,' said Grinevitch of one of the persons taking part in the case they were examining.

Stepan Arkadyevitch frowned at Grinevitch's word, giving him thereby to understand that it was improper to pass judgment prematurely, and made him no reply.

'Who was that came in?' he asked the doorkeeper.

'Someone, your excellency, crept in without permission directly my back was turned. He was asking for you. I told him: when the members come out, then....'

'Where is he?'

'Maybe he's gone into the passage, but here he comes anyway. That is he,' said the doorkeeper, pointing to a strongly built, broad-shouldered man with a curly beard, who, without taking off his sheepskin cap, was running lightly and rapidly up the worn steps of the stone staircase. One of the members going down—a lean official with a portfolio—stood out of his way and looked disapprovingly at the legs of the stranger, then glanced inquiringly at Oblonsky.

Stepan Arkadyevitch was standing at the top of the stairs. His good-naturedly beaming face above the embroidered collar of his uniform beamed more than ever when he recognised the man coming up.

'Why, it's actually you, Levin, at last!' he said with a friendly mocking smile, scanning Levin as he approached. 'How is it you have deigned to look me up in this den?' said Stepan Arkadyevitch, and not content with shaking hands, he kissed his friend. 'Have you been here long?'

'I have just come, and very much wanted to see you,' said Levin, looking shyly and at the same time angrily and uneasily around.

'Well, let's go into my room,' said Stepan Arkadyevitch, who knew his friend's sensitive and irritable shyness, and, taking his arm, he drew him along, as though guiding him through dangers.

Stepan Arkadyevitch was on familiar terms with almost all his acquaintances, and called almost all of them by their Christian names: old men of sixty, boys of twenty, actors, ministers, merchants, and adjutant-generals, so that many of his intimate chums were to be found at the extreme ends of the social ladder, and would have been very much surprised to learn that they had, through the medium of Oblonsky, something in common. He was the familiar friend of everyone with whom he took a glass of champagne, and he took a glass of champagne with everyone, and when in consequence he met any of his *disreputable* chums, as he used in joke to call many of his friends, in the presence of his subordinates, he well knew how, with his characteristic tact, to diminish the disagreeable impression made on them. Levin was not a disreputable chum, but Oblonsky, with his ready tact, felt that Levin fancied he might not care to show his intimacy with him before his subordinates, and so he made haste to take him off into his room.

Levin was almost of the same age as Oblonsky; their intimacy did not rest merely on champagne. Levin had been the friend and companion of his early youth. They were fond of one another in spite of the difference of their characters and tastes, as friends are fond of one another who have been together in early youth. But in spite of this, each of them—as is often the way with men who have selected careers of different kinds—though in discussion he would even justify the other's career, in his heart despised it. It seemed to each of them that the life he led himself was the only real life, and the life led by his friend was a mere phantasm. Oblonsky could not restrain a slight mocking smile at the sight of Levin. How often he had seen him come up to Moscow from the country where he was doing something, but what precisely Stepan Arkadyevitch could never quite make out, and indeed he took no interest in the matter. Levin arrived in Moscow always excited and in a hurry, rather ill at ease and irritated by his own want of ease, and for the most part with a perfectly new, unexpected view of things. Stepan Arkadyevitch laughed at this, and liked it. In the same way Levin in his heart despised the town mode of life of his friend, and his official duties, which he laughed at, and regarded as trifling. But the difference was that Oblonsky, as he was doing the same as every one did, laughed complacently and good-humouredly, while Levin laughed without complacency and sometimes angrily.

'We have long been expecting you,' said Stepan Arkadyevitch, going into his room and letting Levin's hand go as though to show that here all danger was over. 'I am very, very glad to see you,' he went on. 'Well, how are you? Eh? When did you come?'

Levin was silent, looking at the unknown faces of Oblonsky's two companions, and especially at the hand of the elegant Grinevitch, which had such long white fingers, such long yellow filbert-shaped nails, and such huge shining studs on the shirt-cuff, that apparently they absorbed all his attention and allowed him no freedom of thought. Oblonsky noticed this at once, and smiled.

'Ah, to be sure, let me introduce you,' he said. 'My colleagues: Philip Ivanitch Nikitin, Mihail Stanislavitch Grinevitch'—and turning to Levin—'a district councillor, a modern district council man, a gymnast who lifts thirteen stone with one hand, a cattle-breeder and sportsman, and my friend, Konstantin Dmitrievitch Levin, the brother of Sergey Ivanovitch Koznishev.'

'Delighted,' said the veteran.

'I have the honour of knowing your brother, Sergey Ivanovitch,' said Grinevitch, holding out his slender hand with its long nails.

Levin frowned, shook hands coldly, and at once turned to Oblonsky. Though he had a great respect for his half-brother, an author well known to all Russia, he could not endure it when people treated him not as Konstantin Levin, but as the brother of the celebrated Koznishev.

'No, I am no longer a district councillor. I have quarrelled with them all, and don't go to the meetings any more,' he said, turning to Oblonsky.

'You've been quick about it!' said Oblonsky with a smile. 'But how? why?'

'It's a long story. I will tell you some time,' said Levin, but he began telling him at once. 'Well, to put it shortly, I was convinced that nothing was really done by the district councils, or ever could be,' he began, as though someone had just insulted him. 'On one side it's a plaything; they play at being a parliament, and I'm neither young enough nor old enough to find amusement in playthings; and on the other side' (he stammered) 'it's a means for the coterie of the district to make money. Formerly they had wardships, courts of justice, now they have the district council—not in the form of bribes, but in the form of unearned salary,' he said, as hotly as though some one of those present had opposed his opinion.

'Aha! You're in a new phase again, I see—a conservative,' said Stepan Arkadyevitch. 'However, we can go into that later.'

'Yes, later. But I wanted to see you,' said Levin, looking with hatred at Grinevitch's hand.

Stepan Arkadyevitch gave a scarcely perceptible smile.

'How was it you used to say you would never wear European dress again?' he said, scanning his new suit, obviously cut by a French tailor. 'Ah! I see: a new phase.'

Levin suddenly blushed, not as grown men blush, slightly, without being themselves aware of it, but as boys blush, feeling that they are ridiculous through their shyness, and consequently ashamed of it and blushing still more, almost to the point of tears. And it was so strange to see this sensible, manly face in such a childish plight, that Oblonsky left off looking at him.

'Oh, where shall we meet? You know I want very much to talk to you,' said Levin.

Oblonsky seemed to ponder.

'I'll tell you what: let's go to Gurin's to lunch, and there we can talk. I am free till three.'

'No,' answered Levin, after an instant's thought, 'I have got to go on somewhere else.'

'All right, then, let's dine together.'

'Dine together? But I have nothing very particular, only a few words to say, and a question I want to ask you, and we can have a talk afterwards.'

'Well, say the few words, then, at once, and we'll gossip after dinner.'

'Well, it's this,' said Levin; 'but it's of no importance, though.'

His face all at once took an expression of anger from the effort he was making to surmount his shyness.

'What are the Shtcherbatskys doing? Everything as it used to be?' he said.

Stepan Arkadyevitch, who had long known that Levin was in love with his sister-in-law, Kitty, gave a hardly perceptible smile, and his eyes sparkled merrily.

'You said a few words, but I can't answer in a few words, because . . . Excuse me a minute . . .'

A secretary came in, with respectful familiarity and the modest consciousness, characteristic of every secretary, of superiority to his chief in the knowledge of their business; he went up to Oblonsky with some papers, and began, under pretence of asking a question, to explain some objection. Stepan Arkadyevitch, without hearing him out, laid his hand genially on the secretary's sleeve.

'No, you do as I told you,' he said, softening his words with a smile, and with a brief explanation of his view of the matter he turned away from the papers, and said: 'So do it in that way, if you please, Zahar Nikititch.'

The secretary retired in confusion. During the consultation with the secretary Levin had completely recovered from his embarrassment. He was standing with his elbows on the back of a chair, and on his face was a look of ironical attention.

'I don't understand it, I don't understand it,' he said.

'What don't you understand?' said Oblonsky, smiling as brightly as ever, and picking up a cigarette. He expected some queer outburst from Levin.

'I don't understand what you are doing,' said Levin, shrugging his shoulders. 'How can you do it seriously?'

'Why not?'

'Why, because there's nothing in it.'

'You think so, but we're overwhelmed with work.'

'On paper. But, there, you've a gift for it,' added Levin.

'That's to say, you think there's a lack of something in me?'

'Perhaps so,' said Levin. 'But all the same I admire your grandeur, and am proud that I've a friend such a great person. You've not answered my question, though,' he went on, with a desperate effort looking Oblonsky straight in the face.

'Oh, that's all very well. You wait a bit, and you'll come to this yourself. It's very nice for you to have over six thousand acres in the Karazinsky district, and such muscles, and the freshness of a girl of twelve; still you'll be one of us one day. Yes, as to your question, there is no change, but it's a pity you've been away so long.'

'Oh, why so?' Levin queried, panic-stricken.

'Oh, nothing,' responded Oblonsky. 'We'll talk it over. But what's brought you up to town?'

'Oh, we'll talk about that, too, later on,' said Levin, reddening again up to his ears.

'All right. I see,' said Stepan Arkadyevitch. 'I should ask you to come to us, you know, but my wife's not quite the thing. But I tell you what: if you want to see them, they're sure now to be at the Zoological Gardens from four to five. Kitty skates. You drive along there, and I'll come and fetch you, and we'll go and dine somewhere together.'

'Capital. So good-bye till then.'

'Now mind, you'll forget, I know you, or rush off home to the country!' Stepan Arkadyevitch called out, laughing.

'No, truly!'

And Levin went out of the room, only when he was in the doorway remembering that he had forgotten to take leave of Oblonsky's colleagues.

'That gentleman must be a man of great energy,' said Grinevitch, when Levin had gone away.

'Yes, my dear boy,' said Stepan Arkadyevitch, nodding his head, 'he's a lucky fellow! Over six thousand acres in the Karazinsky district; everything before him; and what youth and vigour! Not like some of us.'

'You have a great deal to complain of, haven't you, Stepan Arkadyevitch?'

'Ah, yes, I'm in a poor way, a bad way,' said Stepan Arkadyevitch with a heavy sigh.

VI

WHEN Oblonsky asked Levin what had brought him to town, Levin blushed, and was furious with himself for blushing, because he could not answer, 'I have come to make your sister-in-law an offer,' though that was precisely what he had come for.

The families of the Levins and the Shtcherbatskys were old, noble Moscow families, and had always been on intimate and friendly terms. This intimacy had grown still closer during Levin's student-days. He had both prepared for the university with the young Prince Shtcherbatsky, the brother of Kitty and Dolly, and had entered at the same time with him. In those days Levin used often to be in the Shtcherbatskys' house, and he was in love with the Shtcherbatsky household. Strange as it may appear, it was with the household, the family that Konstantin Levin was in love, especially with the feminine half of the household. Levin did not remember his own mother, and his only sister was older than he was, so that it was in the Shtcherbtaskys' house that he saw for the first time that inner life of an old, noble, cultivated, and honourable family of which he had been deprived by the death of his father and mother. All the members of that family, especially the feminine half, were pictured by him, as it were, wrapped about with a mysterious poetical veil, and he not only perceived no defects whatever in them, but under the poetical veil that shrouded them he assumed the existence of the loftiest sentiments and every possible perfection. Why it was the three young ladies had one day to speak French, and the next English; why it was that at certain hours they played by turns on the piano, the sounds of which were audible in their brother's room above, where the students used to work; why they were visited by those professors of French literature, of music, of drawing, of dancing; why at certain hours all the three young ladies, with Mademoiselle Linon, drove in the coach to the Tversky boulevard, dressed in their satin cloaks, Dolly in a long one, Natalia in a half-long one, and Kitty in one so short that her shapely legs in tightly-drawn red stockings were visible to all beholders; why it was they had to walk about the Tversky boulevard escorted by a footman with a gold cockade in his hat – all this and much more that was done in their mysterious world he did not understand, but he was sure that everything that was done there was very good, and he was in love precisely with the mystery of the proceedings.

In his student-days he had all but been in love with the eldest, Dolly, but she was soon married to Oblonsky. Then he began being in love with the second. He felt, as it were, that he had to be in love with one of the sisters, only he could not quite make out which. But Natalia, too, had hardly made her appearance in the world when she married the diplomat Lvov. Kitty was still a child when Levin left the university. Young Shtcherbatsky went into the navy, was drowned in the Baltic, and Levin's relations with the Shtcherbatskys, in spite of his friendship with Oblonsky, became less intimate. But when early in the winter of this year Levin came to Moscow, after a year in the country, and saw the Shtcherbatskys, he realised which of the three sisters he was indeed destined to love.

One would have thought that nothing could be simpler than for him, a man of good family, rather rich than poor, and thirty-two years old, to make the young Princess Shtcherbatsky an offer of marriage; in all likelihood he would at once have been looked upon as a good match. But Levin was in love, and so it seemed to him that Kitty was so perfect in every respect, that she was a creature far above everything earthly; and that he was a creature so low and so earthly, that it could not even be conceived that other people and she herself could regard him as worthy of her.

After spending two months in Moscow in a state of enchantment, seeing Kitty almost every day in society, into which he went so as to meet her, he abruptly decided that it could not be, and went back to the country.

Levin's conviction that it could not be was founded on the idea that in the eyes of her family he was a disadvantageous and worthless match for the charming Kitty, and that Kitty herself could not love him. In her family's eyes he had no ordinary, definite career and position in society, while his contemporaries by this time, when he was thirty-two, were already, one a colonel, and another a professor, another director of a bank and railways, or president of a board like Oblonsky. But he (he knew very well how he must appear to others) was a country gentleman, occupied in breeding cattle, shooting game, and building barns; in other words, a fellow of no ability, who had not turned out well, and who was doing just what, according to the ideas of the world, is done by people fit for nothing else.

The mysterious, enchanting Kitty herself could not love such an ugly person as he conceived himself to be, and, above all, such an ordinary, in no way striking person. Moreover, his attitude to Kitty in the past—the attitude of a grown-up person to a child, arising from his friendship with her brother—seemed to him yet another obstacle of love. An ugly, good-natured man, as he considered himself, might, he supposed, be liked as a friend; but to be loved with such a love as that with which he loved Kitty, one would need to be a handsome and, still more, a distinguished man.

He had heard that women often did care for ugly and ordinary men, but he did not believe it, for he judged by himself, and he could not himself have loved any but beautiful, mysterious, and exceptional women.

But after spending two months alone in the country, he was convinced that this was not one of those passions of which he had had experience in his early youth; that this feeling gave him not an instant's rest; that he could not live without deciding the question, would she or would she not be his wife, and that his despair had arisen only from his own imaginings, that he had no sort of proof that he would be rejected. And he had now come to Moscow with a firm determination to make an offer, and get married if he were accepted. Or . . . he could not conceive what would become of him if he were rejected.

VII

ON arriving in Moscow by a morning train, Levin had put up at the house of his elder half-brother, Koznishev. After changing his clothes he went down to his brother's study, intending to talk to him at once about the object of his visit, and to ask his advice; but his brother was not alone. With him there was a well-known professor of philosophy, who had come from Harkov expressly to clear up a difference that had arisen between them on a very important philosophical question. The professor was carrying on a hot crusade against materialists. Sergey Koznishev had been following this crusade with interest, and after reading the professor's last article, he had written him a letter stating his objections. He accused the professor of making too great concessions to the materialists. And the professor had promptly appeared to argue the matter out. The point in discussion was the question then in vogue: Is there a line to be drawn between psychological and physiological phenomena in man? and if so, where?

Sergey Ivanovitch met his brother with the smile of chilly friendliness he always had for everyone, and introducing him to the professor, went on with the conversation.

A little man in spectacles, with a narrow forehead, tore himself from the discussion for an instant to greet Levin, and then went on talking without paying any further attention to him. Levin sat down to wait till the professor should go, but he soon began to get interested in the subject under discussion.

Levin had come across the magazine articles about which they were disputing, and had read them, interested in them as a development of the first principles of science, familiar to him as a natural science student at the university. But he had never connected these scientific deductions as to the origin of man as an animal, as to reflex action, biology, and sociology, with those questions as to the meaning of life and death to himself, which had of late been more and more often in his mind.

As he listened to his brother's argument with the professor, he noticed that they connected these scientific questions with those spiritual problems, that at times they almost touched on the latter; but every time they were close upon what seemed to him the chief point, they promptly beat a hasty retreat, and plunged again into a sea of subtle distinctions, reservations, quotations, allusions, and appeals to authorities, and it was with difficulty that he understood what they were talking about.

'I cannot admit it,' said Sergey Ivanovitch, with his habitual clearness, precision of expression, and elegance of phrase. 'I cannot in any case agree with Keiss that my whole conception of the external world has been derived from perceptions. The most fundamental idea, the idea of existence, has not been received by me through sensation; indeed, there is no special sense-organ for the transmission of such an idea.'

'Yes, but they—Wurt, and Knaust, and Pripasov—would answer that your consciousness of existence is derived from the conjunction of all your sensations, that that consciousness of existence is the result of your sensations. Wurst, indeed, says plainly that, assuming there are no sensations, it follows that there is no idea of existence.'

'I maintain the contrary,' began Sergey Ivanovitch.

But here it seemed to Levin that just as they were close upon the real point of the matter, they were again retreating, and he made up his mind to put a question to the professor.

'According to that, if my senses are annihilated, if my body is dead, I can have no existence of any sort?' he queried.

The professor, in annoyance, and as it were mental suffering at the interruption, looked round at the strange inquirer, more like a bargeman than a philosopher, and turned his eyes upon Sergey Ivanovitch, as though to ask: What's one to say to him? But Sergey Ivanovitch, who had been talking with far less heat and one-sidedness than the professor, and who had sufficient breadth of mind to answer the professor and at the same time to comprehend the simple and natural point of view from which the question was put, smiled and said—

'That question we have no right to answer as yet.'

'We have not the requisite data,' chimed in the professor, and he went back to his argument. 'No,' he said; 'I would point out the fact that if, as Pripasov directly asserts, perception is based on sensation, then we are bound to distinguish sharply between these two conceptions.'

Levin listened no more, and simply waited for the professor to go.

VIII

WHEN the professor had gone, Sergey Ivanovitch turned to his brother.

'Delighted that you've come. For some time, is it? How's your farming getting on?'

Levin knew that his elder brother took little interest in farming, and only put the question in deference to him, and so he only told him about the sale of his wheat and money matters.

Levin had meant to tell his brother of his determination to get married, and to ask his advice; he had indeed firmly resolved to do so. But after seeing his brother, listening to his conversation with the professor, hearing afterwards the unconsciously patronising tone in which his brother questioned him about agricultural matters (their mother's property had not been divided, and Levin took charge of both their shares), Levin felt that he could not for some reason begin to talk to him of his intention of marrying. He felt that his brother would not look at it as he would have wished him to.

'Well, how is your district council doing,' asked Sergey Ivanovitch, who was greatly interested in these local boards and attached great importance to them.

'I really don't know.'

'What! Why, surely you're a member of the board?'

'No, I'm not a member now; I've resigned,' answered Levin, 'and I no longer attend the meetings.'

'What a pity!' commented Sergey Ivanovitch, frowning.

Levin in self-defence began to describe what took place in the meetings in his district.

'That's how it always is!' Sergey Ivanovitch interrupted him. 'We Russians are always like that. Perhaps it's our strong point, really, the faculty of seeing our own shortcomings; but we overdo it, we comfort ourselves with irony which we always have on the tip of our tongues. All I say is, give such rights as our local self-government to any other European people—why, the Germans or the English would have worked their way to freedom from them, while we simply turn them into ridicule.'

'But how can it be helped?' said Levin penitently. 'It was my last effort. And I did try with all my soul. I can't. I'm no good at it.'

'It's not that you're no good at it,' said Sergey Ivanovitch, 'it is that you don't look at it as you should.'

'Perhaps not,' Levin answered dejectedly.

'Oh! do you know brother Nikolay's turned up again?' This brother Nikolay was the elder brother of Konstantin Levin, and half-brother of Sergey Ivanovitch; a man utterly ruined, who had dissipated the greater part of his fortune, was living in the strangest and lowest company, and had quarrelled with his brothers.

'What did you say?' Levin cried with horror. 'How do you know?'

'Prokofy saw him in the street.'

'Here in Moscow? Where is he? Do you know?' Levin got up from his chair, as though on the point of starting off at once.

'I am sorry I told you,' said Sergey Ivanovitch, shaking his head at his younger brother's excitement. 'I sent to find out where he is living, and sent him his I O U to Trubin, which I paid. This is the answer he sent me.'

And Sergey Ivanovitch took a note from under a paperweight and handed it to his brother.

Levin read in the queer, familiar handwriting: 'I humbly beg you to leave me in peace. That's the only favour I ask of my gracious brothers.—NIKOLAY LEVIN.'

Levin read it, and without raising his head stood with the note in his hands opposite Sergey Ivanovitch.

There was a struggle in his heart between the desire to forget his unhappy brother for the time, and the consciousness that it would be base to do so.

'He obviously wants to offend me,' pursued Sergey Ivanovitch; 'but he cannot offend me, and I should have wished with all my heart to assist him, but I know it's impossible to do that.'

'Yes, yes,' repeated Levin. 'I understand and appreciate your attitude to him; but I shall go and see him.'

'If you want to, do; but I shouldn't advise it,' said Sergey Ivanovitch. 'As regards myself, I have no fear of your doing so; he will not make you quarrel with me; but for your own sake, I should say you would do better not to go. You can't do him any good; still, do as you please.'

'Very likely I can't do any good, but I feel—especially at such a moment—but that's another thing—I feel I could not be at peace.'

'Well, that I don't understand,' said Sergey Ivanovitch. 'One thing I do understand,' he added, 'it's a lesson in humility. I have come to look very differently and more charitably on what is called infamous since brother Nikolay has become what he is . . . you know what he did . . .'

'Oh, it's awful, awful!' repeated Levin.

After obtaining his brother's address from Sergey Ivanovitch's footman, Levin was on the point of setting off at once to see him, but on second thoughts he decided to put off his visit till the evening. The first thing to do to set his heart at rest was to accomplish what he had come to Moscow for. From his brother's Levin went to Oblonsky's office, and on getting news of the Shtcherbatskys from him, he drove to the place where he had been told he might find Kitty.

IX

AT four o'clock, conscious of his throbbing heart, Levin stepped out of a hired sledge at the Zoological Gardens, and turned along the path to the frozen mounds and the skating-ground, knowing that he would certainly find her there, as he had seen the Shtcherbatskys' carriage at the entrance.

It was a bright, frosty day. Rows of carriages, sledges, drivers, and policemen were standing in the approach. Crowds of well-dressed people, with hats bright in the sun, swarmed about the entrance and along the well-swept little paths between the little houses adorned with carving in the Russian style. The old curly birches of the gardens, all their twigs laden with snow, looked as though freshly decked in sacred vestments.

He walked along the path towards the skating-ground, and kept saying to himself—'You musn't be excited, you must be calm. What's the matter with you? What do you want? Be quiet, stupid,' he conjured his heart. And the more he tried to compose himself, the more breathless he found himself. An acquaintance met him and called him by his name, but Levin did not recognise him. He went towards the mounds, whence came the clank of the chains of sledges as they slipped down or were dragged up, the rumble of the sliding sledges, and the sounds of merry voices. He walked on a few steps, and the skating-ground lay open before his eyes, and at once, amidst all the skaters, he knew her.

He knew she was there by the rapture and the terror that seized on his heart. She was standing talking to a lady at the opposite end of the ground. There was apparently nothing striking either in her dress or her attitude. But for Levin she was as easy to find in that crowd, as a rose among nettles. Everything was made bright by her. She was the smile that shed light on all around her. 'Is it possible I can go over there on the ice, go up to her?' he thought. The place where she stood seemed to him a holy shrine, unapproachable, and there was one moment when he was almost retreating, so overwhelmed was he with terror. He had to make an effort to master himself, and to remind himself that people of all sorts were moving about her, and that he too might come there to skate. He walked down, for a long while avoiding looking at her as at the sun, but seeing her, as one does the sun, without looking.

On that day of the week and at that time of day people of one set, all acquainted with one another, used to meet on the ice. There were crack skaters there, showing off their skill, and learners clinging to chairs with timid, awkward movements, boys, and elderly people skating with hygienic motives. They seemed to Levin an elect band of blissful beings because they were here, near her. All the skaters, it seemed, with perfect self-possession, skated towards her, skated by her, even spoke to her, and were happy, quite apart from her, enjoying the capital ice and the fine weather.

Nikolay Shtcherbatsky, Kitty's cousin, in a short jacket and tight trousers, was sitting on a garden seat with his skates on. Seeing Levin, he shouted to him—

'Ah, the first skater in Russia! Been here long? First-rate ice—do put your skates on.'

'I haven't got my skates,' Levin answered, marvelling at this boldness and ease in her presence, and not for one second losing sight of her, though he did not look at her. He felt as though the sun were coming near him. She was in a corner, and turning out her slender feet in their high boots with obvious timidity, she skated towards him. A boy in Russian dress, desperately waving his arms and bowed down to the ground, overtook her. She skated a little uncertainly; taking her hands out of the little muff, that hung on a cord, she held them ready for emergency, and looking towards Levin, whom she had recognised, she smiled at him and at her own fears. When she had got round the turn, she gave herself a push off with one foot, and skated straight up to Shtcherbatsky. Clutching at his arm, she nodded smiling to Levin. She was more splendid than he had imagined her.

When he thought of her, he could call up a vivid picture of her to himself, especially the charm of that little fair head, so freely set on the shapely girlish shoulders, and so full of childish brightness and good-humour. The childishness of her expression, together with the delicate beauty of her figure, made up her special charm, and that he fully realised. But what always struck him in her as something unlooked for, was the expression of her eyes, soft, serene, and truthful, and above all, her smile, which always transported Levin to an enchanted world, where he felt himself softened and tender, as he remembered himself in some days of his early childhood.

'Have you been here long?' she said, giving him her hand. 'Thank you,' she added, as he picked up the handkerchief that had fallen out of her muff.

'I? I've not long . . . yesterday . . . I mean today . . . I arrived,' answered Levin, in his emotion not at once understanding her question. 'I was meaning to come and see you,' he said; and then, recollecting with what intention he was trying to see her, he was promptly overcome with confusion and blushed.

'I didn't know you could skate, and skate so well.'

She looked at him earnestly, as though wishing to make out the cause of his confusion.

'Your praise is worth having. The tradition is kept up here that you are the best of skaters,' she said, with her little black-gloved hand brushing a grain of hoar-frost off her muff.

'Yes, I used once to skate with passion; I wanted to reach perfection.'

'You do everything with passion, I think,' she said, smiling. 'I should so like to see how you skate. Put on skates, and let us skate together.'

'Skate together! Can that be possible?' thought Levin, gazing at her.

'I'll put them on directly,' he said.

And he went off to get skates.

'It's a long while since we've seen you here, sir,' said the attendant, supporting his foot, and screwing on the heel of the skate. 'Except you, there's none of the gentlemen first-rate skaters. Will that be all right?' said he, tightening the strap.

'Oh, yes, yes; make haste, please,' answered Levin, with difficulty restraining the smile of rapture which would overspread his face. 'Yes,' he thought, 'this now is life, this is happiness! *Together*, she said; *let us skate together!* Speak to her now? But that's just why I'm afraid to speak—because I'm happy now, happy in hope, anyway. . . . And then? . . . But I must! I must! I must! Away with weakness!'

Levin rose to his feet, took off his overcoat, and scurrying over the rough ice round the hut, came out on the smooth ice and skated without effort, as it were by simple exercise of will increasing and slackening speed and turning his course. He approached with timidity, but again her smile reassured him.

She gave him her hand, and they set off side by side, going faster and faster, and the more rapidly they moved the more tightly she grasped his hand.

'With you I should soon learn; I somehow feel confidence in you,' she said to him.

'And I have confidence in myself when you are leaning on me,' he said, but was at once panic-stricken at what he had said, and blushed. And indeed, no sooner had he uttered these words, when all at once, like the sun going behind a cloud, her face lost all its friendliness, and Levin detected the familiar change in her expression that denoted the working of thought; a crease showed on her smooth brow.

'Is there anything troubling you?—though I've no right to ask such a question,' he said hurriedly.

'Oh, why so? . . . No, I have nothing to trouble me,' she responded coldly; and she asked immediately: 'You haven't seen Mlle. Linon, have you?'

'Not yet.'

'Go and speak to her, she likes you so much.'

'What's wrong? I have offended her. Lord help me!' thought Levin, and he flew towards the old Frenchwoman with the grey ringlets, who was sitting on a bench. Smiling and showing her false teeth, she greeted him as an old friend.

'Yes, you see we're growing up,' she said to him, glancing towards Kitty, 'and growing old. *Tiny bear* has grown big now!' pursued the Frenchwoman, laughing, and she reminded him of his joke about the three young ladies whom he had compared to the three bears in the English nursery-tale. 'Do you remember that's what you used to call them?'

He remembered absolutely nothing, but she had been laughing at the joke for ten years now, and was fond of it.

'Now, go and skate, go and skate. Our Kitty has learned to skate nicely, hasn't she?'

When Levin darted up to Kitty her face was no longer stern; her eyes looked at him with the same sincerity and friendliness, but Levin fancied that in her friendliness there was a certain note of deliberate composure. And he felt depressed. After talking a little of her old governess and her peculiarities, she questioned him about his life.

'Surely you must be dull in the country in the winter, aren't you?' she said.

'No, I'm not dull, I am very busy,' he said, feeling that she was holding him in check by her composed tone, which he would not have the force to break through, just as it had been at the beginning of the winter.

'Are you going to stay in town long?' Kitty questioned him.

'I don't know,' he answered, not thinking of what he was saying. The thought that if he were held in check by her tone of quiet friendliness he would end by going back again without deciding anything came into his mind, and he resolved to make a struggle against it.

'How is it you don't know?'

'I don't know. It depends upon you,' he said, and was immediately horror-stricken at his own words.

Whether it was that she had heard his words, or that she did not want to hear them, she made a sort of stumble, twice struck out, and hurriedly skated away from him. She skated up to Mlle. Linon, said something to her, and went towards the pavilion where the ladies took off their skates.

'My God! what have I done! Merciful God! help me, guide me,' said Levin, praying inwardly, and at the same time, feeling a need of violent exercise, he skated about, describing inner and outer circles.

At that moment one of the young men, the best of the skaters of the day, came out of the coffee-house in his skates, with a cigarette in his mouth. Taking a run, he dashed down the steps in his skates, crashing and bounding up and down. He flew down, and without even changing the position of his hands, skated away over the ice.

'Ah! that's a new trick!' said Levin, and he promptly ran up to the top to do this new trick.

'Don't break your neck! it needs practice!' Nikolay Shtcherbatsky shouted after him.

Levin went to the steps, took a run from above as best he could, and dashed down, preserving his balance in this unwonted movement with his hands. On the last step he stumbled, but barely touching the ice with his hand, with a violent effort recovered himself, and skated off laughing.

'How splendid, how nice he is!' Kitty was thinking at that time, as she came out of the pavilion with Mlle Linon, and looked towards him with a smile of quiet affection, as though he were a favourite brother. 'And can it be my fault, can I have done anything wrong? They talk of flirtation. I know it's not he that I love; but still I am happy with him, and he's so jolly. Only, why did he say that? . . .' she mused.

Catching sight of Kitty going away, and her mother meeting her at the steps, Levin, flushed from his rapid exercise, stood still and pondered a minute. He took off his skates, and overtook the mother and daughter at the entrance of the gardens.

'Delighted to see you,' said Princess Shtcherbatsky. 'On Thursdays we are at home, as always.'

'Today, then?'

'We shall be pleased to see you,' the princess said stiffly.

This stiffness hurt Kitty, and she could not resist the desire to smooth over her mother's coldness. She turned her head, and with a smile said—

'Good-bye till this evening.'

At that moment Stepan Arkadyevitch, his hat cocked on one side, with beaming face and eyes, strode into the garden like a conquering hero. But as he approached his mother-in-law, he responded in a mournful and crestfallen tone to her inquiries about Dolly's health. After a little subdued and dejected conversation with his mother-in-law, he threw out his chest again, and put his arm in Levin's.

'Well, shall we set off?' he asked. 'I've been thinking about you all this time, and I'm very, very glad you've come,' he said, looking him in the face with a significant air.

'Yes, come along,' answered Levin in ecstasy, hearing unceasingly the sound of that voice saying 'Good-bye till this evening,' and seeing the smile with which it was said.

'To the England or the Hermitage?'

'I don't mind which.'

'All right, then, the England,' said Stepan Arkadyevitch, selecting that restaurant because he owed more there than at the Hermitage, and consequently considered it mean to avoid it. 'Have you got a sledge? That's first-rate, for I sent my carriage home.'

The friends hardly spoke all the way. Levin was wondering what that change in Kitty's expression had meant, and alternately assuring himself that there was hope, and falling into despair, seeing clearly that his hopes were insane, and yet all the while he felt himself quite another man, utterly unlike what he had been before her smile and those words, 'Good-bye till this evening.'

Stepan Arkadyevitch was absorbed during the drive in composing the menu of the dinner.

'You like turbot, don't you?' he said to Levin as they were arriving.

'Eh?' responded Levin. 'Turbot? Yes, I'm *awfully* fond of turbot.'

X

WHEN Levin went into the restaurant with Oblonsky, he could not help noticing a certain peculiarity of expression, as it were a restrained radiance, about the face and whole figure of Stepan Arkadyevitch. Oblonsky took off his overcoat, and with his hat over one ear walked into the dining-room, giving directions to the Tatar waiters, who were clustered about him in evening coats, bearing napkins. Bowing to right and left to the people he met, and here as everywhere joyously greeting acquaintances, he went up to the sideboard for a preliminary appetiser of fish and vodka, and said to the painted Frenchwoman decked in ribbons, lace, and ringlets, behind the counter, something so amusing that even that Frenchwoman was moved to genuine laughter. Levin for his part refrained from taking any vodka simply because he felt such a loathing of that Frenchwoman, all made up, it seemed, of false hair, *poudre de riz*, and *vinaigre de toilette*. He made haste to move away from her, as from a dirty place. His whole soul was filled with memories of Kitty, and there was a smile of triumph and happiness shining in his eyes.

'This way, your excellency, please. Your excellency won't be disturbed here,' said a particularly pertinacious, white-headed old Tatar with immense hips and coat-tails gaping widely behind. 'Walk in, your excellency,' he said to Levin; by way of showing his respect to Stepan Arkadyevitch, being attentive to his guest as well.

Instantly flinging a fresh cloth over the round table under the bronze chandelier, though it already had a tablecloth on it, he pushed up velvet chairs, and came to a standstill before Stepan Arkadyevitch with a napkin and a bill of fare in his hands, awaiting his commands.

'If you prefer it, your excellency, a private room will be free directly; Prince Golitsin with a lady. Fresh oysters have come in.'

'Ah! oysters.'

Stepan Arkadyevitch became thoughtful.

'How if we were to change our programme, Levin?' he said, keeping his finger on the bill of fare. And his face expressed serious hesitation. 'Are the oysters good? Mind now.'

'They're Flensburg, your excellency. We've no Ostend.'

'Flensburg will do, but are they fresh?'

'Only arrived yesterday.'

'Well, then, how if we were to begin with oysters, and so change the whole programme? Eh?'

'It's all the same to me. I should like cabbage soup and porridge better than anything; but of course there's nothing like that here.'

'*Porridge à la Russe*, your honour would like?' said the Tatar, bending down to Levin, like a nurse speaking to a child.

'No, joking apart, whatever you choose is sure to be good. I've been skating, and I'm hungry. And don't imagine,' he added, detecting a look of dissatisfaction on Oblonsky's face, 'that I shan't appreciate your choice. I am fond of good things.'

'I should hope so! After all, it's one of the pleasures of life,' said Stepan Arkadyevitch. 'Well, then, my friend, you give us two—or better say three—dozen oysters, clear soup with vegetables. . . .'

'*Printanière*,' prompted the Tatar. But Stepan Arkadyevitch apparently did not care to allow him the satisfaction of giving the French names of the dishes.

'With vegetables in it, you know. Then turbot with thick sauce, then . . . roast beef; and mind it's good. Yes, and capons, perhaps, and then sweets.'

The Tatar, recollecting that it was Stepan Arkadyevitch's way not to call the dishes by the names in the French bill of fare, did not repeat them after him, but could not resist rehearsing the whole menu to himself according to the bill:—'*Soupe printanière, turbot, sauce Beaumarchais, poulard à l'estragon, macédoine de fruits* . . . etc.,' and then instantly, as though worked by springs, laying down one bound bill of fare, he took up another, the list of wines, and submitted it to Stepan Arkadyevitch.

'What shall we drink?'

'What you like, only not too much. Champagne,' said Levin.

'What! to start with? You're right though, I dare say. Do you like the white seal?'

'*Cachet blanc*,' prompted the Tatar.

'Very well, then, give us that brand with the oysters, and then we'll see.'

'Yes, sir. And what table wine?'

'You can give us Nuits. Oh no, better the classic Chablis.'

'Yes, sir. And *your* cheese, your excellency?'

'Oh yes, Parmesan. Or would you like another?'

'No, it's all the same to me,' said Levin, unable to suppress a smile.

And the Tatar ran off with flying coat-tails, and in five minutes darted in with a dish of opened oysters on mother-of-pearl shells, and a bottle between his fingers.

Stepan Arkadyevitch crushed the starchy napkin, tucked it into his waitcoat, and settling his arms comfortably, started on the oysters.

'Not bad,' he said, stripping the oysters from the pearly shell with a silver fork, and swallowing them one after another. 'Not bad,' he repeated, turning his dewy, brilliant eyes from Levin to the Tatar.

Levin ate the oysters indeed, though white bread and cheese would have pleased him better. But he was admiring Oblonsky. Even the Tatar, uncorking the bottle and pouring the sparkling wine into the delicate glasses, glanced at Stepan Arkadyevitch, and settled his white cravat with a perceptible smile of satisfaction.

'You don't care much for oysters, do you?' said Stepan Arkadyevitch, emptying his wine-glass, 'or you're worried about something. Eh?'

He wanted Levin to be in good spirits. But it was not that Levin was not in good spirits; he was ill at ease. With what he had in his soul, he felt sore and uncomfortable in the restaurant, in the midst of private rooms where men were dining with ladies, in all this fuss and bustle; the surroundings of bronzes, looking-glasses, gas, and waiters—all of it was offensive to him. He was afraid of sullying what his soul was brimful of.

'I? Yes, I am; but besides, all this bothers me,' he said. 'You can't conceive how queer it all seems to a country person like me, as queer as that gentleman's nails I saw at your place....'

'Yes, I saw how much interested you were in poor Grinevitch's nails,' said Stepan Arkadyevitch, laughing.

'It's too much for me,' responded Levin. 'Do try, now, and put yourself in my place, take the point of view of a country person. We in the country try to bring our hands into such a state as will be most convenient for working with. So we cut our nails; sometimes we turn up our sleeves. And here people purposely let their nails grow as long as they will, and link on small saucers by way of studs, so that they can do nothing with their hands.'

Stepan Arkadyevitch smiled gaily.

'Oh yes, that's just a sign that he has no need to do coarse work. His work is with the mind....'

'Maybe. But still it's queer to me, just as at this moment it seems queer to me that we country folks try to get our meals over as soon as we can, so as to be ready for our work, while here are we trying to drag out our meal as long as possible, and with that object eating oysters. . . .'

'Why, of course,' objected Stepan Arkadyevitch. 'But that's just the aim of civilisation—to make everything a source of enjoyment.'

'Well, if that's its aim, I'd rather be a savage.'

'And so you are a savage. All you Levins are savages.'

Levin sighed. He remembered his brother Nikolay, and felt ashamed and sore, and he scowled; but Oblonsky began speaking of a subject which at once drew his attention.

'Oh, I say, are you going tonight to our people, the Shtcherbatskys', I mean?' he said, his eyes sparkling significantly as he pushed away the empty rough shells, and drew the cheese towards him.

'Yes, I shall certainly go,' replied Levin; 'though I fancied the princess was not very warm in her invitation.'

'What nonsense! That's her manner. . . . Come, boy, the soup! . . . That's her manner—*grande dame*,' said Stepan Arkadyevitch. 'I'm coming too, but I have to go to the Countess Bonin's rehearsal. Come, isn't it true that you're a savage? How do you explain the sudden way in which you vanished from Moscow? The Shtcherbatskys were continually asking me about you, as though I ought to know. The only thing I know is that you always do what no one else does.'

'Yes,' said Levin, slowly and with emotion, 'you're right. I am a savage. Only, my savageness is not in having gone away, but in coming now. Now I have come . . .'

'Oh, what a lucky fellow you are!' broke in Stepan Arkadyevitch, looking into Levin's eyes.

'Why?'

' "I know a gallant steed by tokens sure,
And by his eyes I know a youth in love," '

declaimed Stepan Arkadyevitch. 'Everything is before you.'

'Why, is it over for you already?'

'No; not over exactly, but the future is yours, and the present is mine, and the present—well, it's not all that it might be.'

'How so?'

'Oh, things go wrong. But I don't want to talk of myself, and besides I can't explain it all,' said Stepan Arkadyevitch. 'Well, why have you come to Moscow, then? . . . Hi! take away!' he called to the Tatar.

'You guess?' responded Levin, his eyes like deep wells of light fixed on Stepan Arkadyevitch.

'I guess, but I can't be the first to talk about it. You can see by that whether I guess right or wrong,' said Stepan Arkadyevitch, gazing at Levin with a subtle smile.

'Well, and what have you to say to me?' asid Levin in a quivering voice, feeling that all the muscles of his face were quivering too. 'How do you look at the question?'

Stepan Arkadyevitch slowly emptied his glass of Chablis, never taking his eyes off Levin.

'I?' said Stepan Arkadyevitch, 'there's nothing I desire so much as that—nothing! It would be the best thing that could be.'

'But you're not making a mistake? You know what we're speaking of?' said Levin, piercing him with his eyes. 'You think it's possible?'

'I think it's possible. Why not possible?'

'No! do you really think it's possible? No, tell me all you think! Oh, but if . . . if refusal's in store for me! . . . Indeed I feel sure . . .'

'Why should you think that?' said Stepan Arkadyevitch, smiling at his excitement.

'It seems so to me sometimes. That will be awful for me, and for her too.'

'Oh, well, anyway there's nothing awful in it for a girl. Every girl's proud of an offer.'

'Yes, every girl, but not she.'

Stepan Arkadyevitch smiled. He so well knew that feeling of Levin's, that for him all the girls in the world were divided into two classes: one class—all the girls in the world except her, and those girls with all sorts of human weaknesses, and very ordinary girls; the other class—she alone, having no weaknesses of any sort and higher than all humanity.

'Stay, take some sauce,' he said, holding back Levin's hand as it pushed away the sauce.

Levin obediently helped himself to sauce, but would not let Stepan Arkadyevitch go on with his dinner.

'No, stop a minute, stop a minute,' he said. 'You must understand that it's a question of life and death for me. I have never spoken to anyone of this. And there's no one I could speak of it to, except you. You know we're utterly unlike each other, different tastes and views and everything; but I know you're fond of me and understand me, and that's why I like you awfully. But, for God's sake, be quite straightforward with me.'

'I tell you what I think,' said Stepan Arkadyevitch, smiling. 'But I'll say more: my wife is a wonderful woman . . .' Stepan Arkadyevitch sighed, remembering his position with his wife, and, after a moment's silence, resumed—'She has a gift of foreseeing things. She sees right through people; but that's not all, she knows what will come to pass, especially in the way of marriages. She foretold, for instance, that Princess Shahovskoy would marry Brenteln. No one would believe it, but it came to pass. And she's on your side.'

'How do you mean?'

'It's not only that she likes you—she says that Kitty is certain to be your wife.'

At these words Levin's face suddenly lighted up with a smile, a smile not far from tears of emotion.

'She says that!' cried Levin. 'I always said she was exquisite, your wife. There, that's enough, enough said about it,' he said, getting up from his seat.

'All right, but do sit down.'

But Levin could not sit down. He walked with his firm tread twice up and down the little cage of a room, blinked his eyelids that his tears might not fall, and only then sat down to the table.

'You must understand,' said he, 'it's not love. I've been in love, but it's not that. It's not my feeling, but a sort of force outside me has taken possession of me. I went away, you see, because I made up my mind that it could never be, you understand, as a happiness that does not come on earth; but I've struggled with myself, I see there's no living without it. And it must be settled.'

'What did you go away for?'

'Ah, stop a minute! Ah, the thoughts that come crowding on one! The questions one must ask oneself! Listen. You can't imagine what you've done for me by what you said. I'm so happy that I've become positively hateful; I've forgotten everything. I heard today that my brother Nikolay . . . you know, he's here . . . I had even forgotten him. It seems to me that he's happy too. It's a sort of madness. But one thing's awful. . . . Here, you've been married, you know the feeling . . . it's awful that we—old—with a past . . . not of love, but of sins . . . are brought all at once so near to a creature pure and innocent; it's loathsome, and that's why one can't help feeling oneself unworthy.'

'Oh, well, you've not many sins on your conscience.'

'Alas! all the same,' said Levin, 'when with loathing I go over my life, I shudder and curse and bitterly regret it. . . . Yes.'

'What would you have? The world's made so,' said Stepan Arkadyevitch.

'The one comfort is like that prayer, which I always liked: "Forgive me not according to my unworthiness, but according to Thy loving-kindness." That's the only way she can forgive me.'

XI

LEVIN emptied his glass, and they were silent for a while.

'There's one other thing I ought to tell you. Do you know Vronsky?' Stepan Arkadyevitch asked Levin.

'No, I don't. Why do you ask?'

'Give us another bottle,' Stepan Arkadyevitch directed the Tatar, who was filling up their glasses and fidgeting round them just when he was not wanted.

'Why you ought to know Vronsky is that he's one of your rivals.'

'Who's Vronsky?' said Levin, and his face was suddenly transformed from the look of childlike ecstasy which Oblonsky had just been admiring to an angry and unpleasant expression.

'Vronsky is one of the sons of Count Kirill Ivanovitch Vronsky, and one of the finest specimens of the gilded youth of Petersburg. I made his acquaintance in Tver when I was there on official business, and he came there for the levy of recruits. Fearfully rich, handsome, great connections, an aide-de-camp, and with all that a very nice, good-natured fellow. But he's more than simply a good-natured fellow, as I've found out here—he's a cultivated man too, and very intelligent; he's a man who'll make his mark.'

Levin scowled and was dumb.

'Well, he turned up here soon after you'd gone, and, as I can see, he's over head and ears in love with Kitty, and you know that her mother . . .'

'Excuse me, but I know nothing,' said Levin, frowning gloomily. And immediately he recollected his brother Nikolay and how hateful he was to have been able to forget him.

'You wait a bit, wait a bit,' said Stepan Arkadyevitch, smiling and touching his hand. 'I've told you what I know, and I repeat that in this delicate and tender matter, as far as one can conjecture, I believe the chances are in your favour.'

Levin dropped back in his chair; his face was pale.

'But I would advise you to settle the thing as soon as may be,' pursued Oblonsky, filling up his glass.

'No, thanks, I can't drink any more,' said Levin, pushing away his glass. 'I shall be drunk. . . . Come, tell me how you are getting on?' he went on, obviously anxious to change the conversation.

'One word more: in any case I advise you to settle the question soon. Tonight I don't advise you to speak,' said Stepan Arkadyevitch.

'Go round tomorrow morning, make an offer in due form, and God bless you. . . .'

'Oh, do you still think of coming to me for some shooting? Come next spring, do,' said Levin.

Now his whole soul was full of remorse that he had begun this conversation with Stepan Arkadyevitch. A feeling such as his was profaned by talk of the rivalry of some Petersburg officer, of the suppositions and the counsels of Stepan Arkadyevitch.

Stepan Arkadyevitch smiled. He knew what was passing in Levin's soul.

'I'll come some day,' he said. 'But women, my boy, they're the pivot everything turns upon. Things are in a bad way with me, very bad. And it's all through women. Tell me frankly now,' he pursued, picking up a cigar and keeping one hand on his glass; 'give me your advice.'

'Why, what is it?'

'I'll tell you. Suppose you're married, you love your wife, but you're fascinated by another woman. . . .'

'Excuse me, but I'm absolutely unable to comprehend how . . . just as I can't comprehend how I could now, after my dinner, go straight to a baker's shop and steal a roll.'

Stepan Arkadyevitch's eyes sparkled more than usual.

'Why not? A roll will sometimes smell so good one can't resist it.

"Himmlisch ist's, wenn ich bezwungen
  Meine irdische Begier;
Aber doch wenn's nicht gelungen
  Hatt' ich auch recht hübsch Plaisir!"'

As he said this Stepan Arkadyevitch smiled subtly. Levin too could not help smiling.

'Yes; but joking apart,' resumed Stepan Arkadyevitch, 'you must understand that the woman is a sweet, gentle, loving creature, poor and lonely, and has sacrificed everything. Now, when the thing's done, don't you see, can one possibly cast her off? Even supposing one parts from her, so as not to break up one's family life, still, can one help feeling for her, setting her on her feet, softening her lot?'

'Well, you must excuse me there. You know to me all women are divided into two classes . . . at least no . . . truer to say: there are women and there are . . . I've never seen exquisite fallen beings, and I never shall see them, but such creatures as that painted Frenchwoman at the counter with the ringlets are vermin to my mind, and all fallen women are the same.'

'But the Magdalen?'

'Ah, drop that! Christ would never have said those words if He had known how they would be abused. Of all the Gospel those words are the only ones remembered. However, I'm not saying so much what I think, as what I feel. I have a loathing for fallen women. You're afraid of spiders, and I of these vermin. Most likely you've not made a study of spiders and don't know their character; and so it is with me.'

'It's very well for you to talk like that; it's very much like that gentleman in Dickens who used to fling all difficult questions over his right shoulder. But to deny the facts is no answer. What's to be done—you tell me that, what's to be done? Your wife gets older, while you're full of life. Before you've time to look round, you feel that you can't love your wife with love, however much you may esteem her. And then all at once love turns up, and you're done for, done for!' Stepan Arkadyevitch said with weary despair.

Levin half smiled.

'Yes, you're done for,' resumed Oblonsky. 'But what's to be done?'

'Don't steal rolls.'

Stepan Arkadyevitch laughed outright.

'O moralist! But you must understand, there are two women: one insists only on her rights, and those rights are your love, which you can't give her; and the other sacrifices everything for you and asks for nothing. What are you to do? How are you to act? There's a fearful tragedy in it.'

'If you care for my profession of faith as regards that, I'll tell you that I don't believe there was any tragedy about it. And this is why. To my mind, love . . . both the sorts of love, which you remember Plato defines in his Banquet, serve as the test of men. Some men only understand one sort, and some only the other. And those who only know the non-platonic love have no need to talk of tragedy. In such love there can be no sort of tragedy. "I'm much obliged for the gratification, my humble respects"—that's all the tragedy. And in platonic love there can be no tragedy, because in that love all is clear and pure, because . . .'

At that instant Levin recollected his own sins and the inner conflict he had lived through. And he added unexpectedly—

'But perhaps you are right. Very likely. . . . I don't know, I don't know.'

'It's this, don't you see,' said Stepan Arkadyevitch, 'you're very much all of a piece. That's your strong point and your failing. You have a character that's all of a piece, and you want the whole of life to be of a piece too—but that's not how it is. You despise public official work because you want the reality to be invariably corresponding all the while with the aim—and that's not how it is. You want a man's work, too, always to have a defined aim, and love and family life always to be undivided—and that's not how it is. All the variety, all the charm, all the beauty of life is made up of light and shadow.'

Levin sighed and made no reply. He was thinking of his own affairs, and did not hear Oblonsky.

And suddenly both of them felt that though they were friends, though they had been dining and drinking together, which should have drawn them closer, yet each was thinking only of his own affairs, and they had nothing to do with one another. Oblonsky had more than once experienced this extreme sense of aloofness, instead of intimacy, coming on after dinner, and he knew what to do in such cases.

'Bill!' he called, and he went into the next room, where he promptly came across an aide-de-camp of his acquaintance and dropped into a conversation with him about an actress and her protector. And at once in the conversation with the aide-de-camp Oblonsky had a sense of relaxation and relief after the conversation with Levin, which always put him to too great a mental and spiritual strain.

When the Tatar appeared with a bill for twenty-six roubles and odd kopecks, beside a tip for himself, Levin, who would another time have been horrified, like anyone from the country, at his share of fourteen roubles, did not notice it, paid, and set off homewards, to dress and go to the Shtcherbatskys' there to decide his fate.

XII

THE young Princess Kitty Shtcherbatsky was eighteen. It was the first winter that she had been out in the world. Her success in society had been greater than that of either of her elder sisters, and greater even than her mother had anticipated. To say nothing of the young men who danced at the Moscow balls being almost all in love with Kitty, two serious suitors had already this first winter made their appearance: Levin and, immediately after his departure, Count Vronsky.

Levin's appearance at the beginning of the winter, his frequent visits, and evident love for Kitty, had led to the first serious conversations between Kitty's parents as to her future, and to disputes between them. The prince was on Levin's side; he said he wished for nothing better for Kitty. The princess for her part, going round the question in the manner peculiar to women, maintained that Kitty was too young, that Levin had done nothing to prove that he had serious intentions, that Kitty felt no great attraction to him, and other side issues; but she did not state the principal point, which was that she looked for a better match for her daughter, and that Levin was not to her liking, and she did not understand him. When Levin had abruptly departed, the princess was delighted, and said to her husband triumphantly: 'You see I was right.' When Vronsky appeared on the scene, she was still more delighted, confirmed in her opinion that Kitty was to make not simply a good, but a brilliant match.

In the mother's eyes there could be no comparison between Vronsky and Levin. She disliked in Levin his strange and uncompromising opinions and his shyness in society, founded, as she supposed, on his pride and his queer sort of life, as she considered it, absorbed in cattle and peasants. She did not very much like it that he, who was in love with her daughter, had kept coming to the house for six weeks, as though he were waiting for something, inspecting, as though he were afraid he might be doing them too great an honour by making an offer, and did not realise that a man, who continually visits at a house where there is a young unmarried girl, is bound to make his intentions clear. And suddenly, without doing so, he disappeared. 'It's as well he's not attractive enough for Kitty to have fallen in love with him,' thought the mother.

Vronsky satisfied all the mother's desires. Very wealthy, clever, of aristocratic family, on the highroad to a brilliant career in the army and at court, and a fascinating man. Nothing better could be wished for.

Vronsky openly flirted with Kitty at balls, danced with her, and came continually to the house, consequently there could be no doubt of the seriousness of his intentions. But, in spite of that, the mother had spent the whole of that winter in a state of terrible anxiety and agitation.

Princess Shtcherbatsky had herself been married thirty years ago, her aunt arranging the match. Her husband, about whom everything was well known beforehand, had come, looked at his future bride, and been looked at. The matchmaking aunt had ascertained and communicated their mutual impression. That impression had been favourable. Afterwards, on a day fixed beforehand, the expected offer was made to her parents, and accepted. All had passed very simply and easily. So it seemed, at least, to the princess. But over her own daughters she had felt how far from simple and easy is the business, apparently so commonplace, of marrying off one's daughters. The panics that had been lived through, the thoughts that had been brooded over, the money that had been wasted, and the disputes with her husband over marrying the two elder girls, Darya and Natalya! Now, since the youngest had come out, she was going through the same terrors, the same doubts, and still more violent quarrels with her husband than she had over the elder girls. The old prince, like all fathers indeed, was exceedingly punctilious on the score of the honour and reputation of his daughters. He was irrationally jealous over his daughters, especially over Kitty, who was his favourite. At every turn he had scenes with the princess for compromising her daughter. The princess had grown accustomed to this already with her other daughters, but now she felt that there was more ground for the prince's touchiness. She saw that of late years much was changed in the manners of society, that a mother's duties had become still more difficult. She saw that girls of Kitty's age formed some sort of clubs, went to some sort of lectures, mixed freely in men's society, drove about the streets alone, many of them did not curtsey, and, what was the most important thing, all of them were firmly convinced that to choose their husband was their own affair, and not their parents'. 'Marriages aren't made nowadays as they used to be,' was thought and said by all these young girls, and even by their elders. But how marriages were made now, the princess could not learn from anyone. The French fashion—of the parents arranging their children's future—was not accepted; it was condemned. The English fashion of the complete independence of girls was also not accepted, and not possible in Russian society. The Russian fashion of matchmaking by the offices of intermediate persons was for some reason considered unseemly; it was ridiculed by everyone, and by the princess herself. But how girls were to be married, and how parents were to marry them, no one knew. Everyone with whom the princess had chanced to discuss the matter said the same thing: 'Mercy on us, it's high time in our day to cast off all that old-fashioned business. It's the young people have to marry, and not their parents; and so we ought to leave the young people to arrange it as they choose.' It was very easy for anyone to say that who had no daughters, but the princess realised that in the process of getting to know each other, her daughter might fall in love, and fall in love with someone who did not care to marry her or who was quite unfit to be her husband. And, however much it was instilled into the princess that in our times young people ought to arrange their lives for themselves, she was unable to believe it, just as she would have been unable to believe that, at any time whatever, the most suitable playthings for children five years old ought to be loaded pistols. And so the princess was more uneasy over Kitty than she had been over her elder sisters.

Now she was afraid that Vronsky might confine himself to simply flirting with her daughter. She saw that her daughter was in love with him, but tried to comfort herself with the thought that he was an honourable man, and would not do this. But at the same time she knew how easy it is, with the freedom of manners of to-day, to turn a girl's head, and how lightly men generally regard such a crime. The week before, Kitty had told her mother of a conversation she had had with Vronsky during a mazurka. This conversation had partly reassured the princess; but perfectly at ease she could not be. Vronsky had told Kitty that both he and his brother were so used to obeying their mother that they never made up their minds to any important undertaking without consulting her. 'And just now, I am impatiently awaiting my mother's arrival in Petersburg, as peculiarly fortunate,' he told her.

Kitty had repeated this without attaching any significance to the words. But her mother saw them in a different light. She knew that the old lady was expected from day to day, that she would be pleased at her son's choice, and she felt it strange that he should not make his offer through fear of vexing his mother. However, she was so anxious for the marriage itself, and still more for relief from her fears, that she believed it was so. Bitter as it was for the princess to see the unhappiness of her eldest daughter, Dolly, on the point of leaving her husband, her anxiety over the decision of her youngest daughter's fate engrossed all her feelings. Today, with Levin's reappearance, a fresh source of anxiety arose. She was afraid that her daughter, who had at one time, as she fancied, a feeling for Levin, might, from extreme sense of honour, refuse Vronsky, and that Levin's arrival might generally complicate and delay the affair so near being concluded.

'Why, has he been here long?' the princess asked about Levin, as they returned home.

'He came today, mamma.'

'There's one thing I want to say . . .' began the princess, and from her serious and alert face, Kitty guessed what it would be.

'Mamma,' she said, flushing hotly and turning quickly to her, 'please, please don't say anything about that. I know, I know all about it.'

She wished for what her mother wished for, but the motives of her mother's wishes wounded her.

'I only want to say that to raise hopes . . .'

'Mamma, darling, for goodness' sake, don't talk about it. It's so horrible to talk about it.'

'I won't,' said her mother, seeing the tears in her daughter's eyes; 'but one thing, my love; you promised me you would have no secrets from me. You won't?'

'Never, mamma, none,' answered Kitty, flushing a little, and looking her mother straight in the face; 'but there's no use in my telling you anything, and I . . . I . . . if I wanted to, I don't know what to say or how . . . I don't know . . .'

'No, she could not tell an untruth with those eyes,' thought the mother, smiling at her agitation and happiness. The princess smiled that what was taking place just now in her soul seemed to the poor child so immense and so important.

XIII

AFTER dinner, and till the beginning of the evening, Kitty was feeling a sensation akin to the sensation of a young man before a battle. Her heart throbbed violently, and her thoughts would not rest on anything.

She felt that this evening, when they would both meet for the first time, would be a turning-point in her life. And she was continually picturing them to herself, at one moment each separately, and then both together. When she mused on the past, she dwelt with pleasure, with tenderness, on the memories of her relations with Levin. The memories of childhood and of Levin's friendship with her dead brother gave a special poetic charm to her relations with him. His love for her, of which she felt certain, was flattering and delightful to her; and it was pleasant for her to think of Levin. In her memories of Vronsky there always entered a certain element of awkwardness, though he was in the highest degree well-bred and at ease, as though there were some false note—not in Vronsky, he was very simple and nice, but in herself, while with Levin she felt perfectly simple and clear. But, on the other hand, directly she thought of the future with Vronsky, there arose before her a perspective of brilliant happiness; with Levin the future seemed misty.

When she went upstairs to dress, and looked into the looking-glass, she noticed with joy that it was one of her good days, and that she was in complete possession of all her forces,—she needed this so for what lay before her: she was conscious of external composure and free grace in her movements.

At half-past seven she had only just gone down into the drawing-room, when the footman announced, 'Konstantin Dmitrievitch Levin.' The princess was still in her room, and the prince had not come in. 'So it is to be,' thought Kitty, and all the blood seemed to rush to her heart. She was horrified at her paleness, as she glanced into the looking-glass. At that moment she knew beyond doubt that he had come early on purpose to find her alone and to make her an offer. And only then for the first time the whole thing presented itself in a new, different aspect; only then she realised that the question did not affect her only—with whom she would be happy, and whom she loved—but that she would have that moment to wound a man whom she liked. And to wound him cruelly. What for? Because he, dear fellow, loved her, was in love with her. But there was no help for it, so it must be, so it would have to be.

'My God! shall I myself really have to say it to him?' she thought. 'Can I tell him I don't love him? That will be a lie. What am I to say to him? That I love someone else? No, that's impossible. I'm going away, I'm going away.'

She had reached the door, when she heard his step. 'No! it's not honest. What have I to be afraid of? I have done nothing wrong. What is to be, will be! I'll tell the truth. And with him one can't be ill at ease. Here he is,' she said to herself, seeing his powerful, shy figure, with his shining eyes fixed on her. She looked straight into his face, as though imploring him to spare her, and gave her hand.

'It's not time yet; I think I'm too early,' he said, glancing round the empty drawing-room. When he saw that his expectations were realised, that there was nothing to prevent him from speaking, his face became gloomy.

'Oh no,' said Kitty, and sat down to the table.

'But this was just what I wanted, to find you alone,' he began, not sitting down, and not looking at her, so as not to lose courage.

'Mamma will be down directly. She was very much tired . . . Yesterday . . .'

She talked on, not knowing what her lips were uttering, and not taking her supplicating and caressing eyes off him.

He glanced at her; she blushed, and ceased speaking.

'I told you I did not know whether I should be here long . . . that it depended on you . . .'

She dropped her head lower and lower, not knowing herself what answer she should make to what was coming.

'That it depended on you,' he repeated. 'I meant to say . . . I meant to say . . . I came for this . . . to be my wife!' he brought out, not knowing what he was saying; but feeling that the most terrible thing was said, he stopped short and looked at her. . . .

She was breathing heavily, not looking at him. She was feeling ecstasy. Her soul was flooded with happiness. She had never anticipated that the utterance of love would produce such a powerful effect on her. But it lasted only an instant. She remembered Vronsky. She lifted her clear, truthful eyes, and seeing his desperate face, she answered hastily—

'That cannot be . . . forgive me.'

A moment ago, and how close she had been to him, of what importance in his life! And how aloof and remote from him she had become now!

'It was bound to be so,' he said, not looking at her.

He bowed, and was meaning to retreat.

XIV

BUT at that very moment the princess came in. There was a look of horror on her face when she saw them alone, and their disturbed faces. Levin bowed to her, and said nothing. Kitty did not speak nor lift her eyes. 'Thank God, she has refused him,' thought the mother, and her face lighted up with the habitual smile with which she greeted her guests on Thursdays. She sat down and began questioning Levin about his life in the country. He sat down again, waiting for other visitors to arrive, in order to retreat unnoticed.

Five minutes later there came in a friend of Kitty's, married the preceding winter, Countess Nordston.

She was a thin, sallow, sickly, and nervous woman, with brilliant black eyes. She was fond of Kitty, and her affection for her showed itself, as the affection of married women for girls always does, in the desire to make a match for Kitty after her own ideal of married happiness; she wanted her to marry Vronsky. Levin she had often met at the Shtcherbatskys' early in the winter, and she had always disliked him. Her invariable and favourite pursuit, when they met, consisted in making fun of him.

'I do like it when he looks down at me from the height of his grandeur, or breaks off his learned conversation with me because I'm a fool, or is condescending to me. I like that so; to see him condescending! I am so glad he can't bear me,' she used to say of him.

She was right, for Levin actually could not bear her, and despised her for what she was proud of and regarded as a fine characteristic—her nervousness, her delicate contempt and indifference for everything coarse and earthly.

The Countess Nordston and Levin had got into that relation with one another not seldom seen in society, when two persons, who remain externally on friendly terms, despise each other to such a degree that they cannot even take each other seriously, and cannot even be offended by each other.

The Countess Nordston pounced upon Levin at once.

'Ah! Konstantin Dmitrievitch! So you've come back to our corrupt Babylon,' she said, giving him her tiny, yellow hand, and recalling what he had chanced to say early in the winter, that Moscow was a Babylon. 'Come, is Babylon reformed, or have you degenerated?' she added, glancing with a simper at Kitty.

'It's very flattering for me, countess, that you remember my words so well,' responded Levin, who had succeeded in recovering his composure, and at once from habit dropped into his tone of joking hostility to the Countess Nordston. 'They must certainly make a great impression on you.'

'Oh, I should think so! I always note it all down. Well, Kitty, have you been skating again? . . .'

And she began talking to Kitty. Awkward as it was for Levin to withdraw now, it would still have been easier for him to perpetrate this awkwardness than to remain all the evening and see Kitty, who glanced at him now and then and avoided his eyes. He was on the point of getting up, when the princess noticing that he was silent, addressed him.

'Shall you be long in Moscow? You're busy with the district council, though, aren't you, and can't be away for long?'

'No, princess, I'm no longer a member of the council,' he said. 'I have come up for a few days.'

'There's something the matter with him,' thought Countess Nordston, glancing at his stern, serious face. 'He isn't in his old argumentative mood. But I'll draw him out. I do love making a fool of him before Kitty, and I'll do it.'

'Konstantin Dmitritch,' she said to him, 'do explain to me, please, what's the meaning of it. You know all about such things. At home in our village of Kaluga all the peasants and all the women have drunk up all they possessed, and now they can't pay us any rent. What's the meaning of that? You always praise the peasants so.'

At that instant another lady came into the room, and Levin got up.

'Excuse me, countess, but I really know nothing about it, and can't tell you anything,' he said, and looked round at the officer who came in behind the lady.

'That must be Vronsky,' thought Levin, and, to be sure of it, glanced at Kitty. She had already had time to look at Vronsky, and looked round at Levin. And simply from the look in her eyes, that grew unconsciously brighter, Levin knew that she loved that man, knew it as surely as if she had told him so in words. But what sort of man was he? Now, whether for good or for ill, Levin could not choose but remain; he must find out what the man was like whom she loved.

There are people who, on meeting a successful rival, no matter in what, are at once disposed to turn their backs on everything good in him, and to see only what is bad. There are people, on the other hand, who desire above all to find in that lucky rival the qualities by which he has outstripped them, and seek with a throbbing ache at heart only what is good. Levin belonged to the second class. But he had no difficulty in finding what was good and attractive in Vronsky. It was apparent at the first glance. Vronsky was a squarely built, dark man, not very tall, with a good-humoured, handsome, and exceedingly calm and resolute face. Everything about his face and figure, from his short-cropped black hair and freshly shaven chin down to his loosely fitting, brand-new uniform, was simple and at the same time elegant. Making way for the lady who had come in, Vronsky went up to the princess and then to Kitty.

As he approached her, his beautiful eyes shone with a specially tender light, and with a faint, happy, and modestly triumphant smile (so it seemed to Levin), bowing carefully and respectfully over her, he held out his small broad hand to her.

Greeting and saying a few words to everyone, he sat down without once glancing at Levin, who had never taken his eyes off him.

'Let me introduce you,' said the princess, indicating Levin. 'Konstantin Dmitritch Levin, Count Alexey Kirillovitch Vronsky.'

Vronsky got up and, looking cordially at Levin, shook hands with him.

'I believe I was to have dined with you this winter,' he said, smiling his simple and open smile; 'but you had unexpectedly left for the country.'

'Konstantin Dmitritch despises and hates town and us townspeople,' said Countess Nordston.

'My words must make a deep impression on you, since you remember them so well,' said Levin, and, suddenly conscious that he had said just the same thing before, he reddened.

Vronsky looked at Levin and Countess Nordston, and smiled.

'Are you always in the country?' he inquired. 'I should think it must be dull in the winter.'

'It's not dull if one has work to do; besides, one's not dull by oneself,' Levin replied abruptly.

'I am fond of the country,' said Vronsky, noticing, and affecting not to notice, Levin's tone.

'But I hope, count, you would not consent to live in the country always,' said Countess Nordston.

'I don't know; I have never tried for long. I experienced a queer feeling once,' he went on. 'I never longed so for the country, Russian country, with bast shoes and peasants, as when I was spending a winter with my mother in Nice. Nice itself is dull enough, you know. And indeed, Naples and Sorrento are only pleasant for a short time. And it's just there that Russia comes back to me most vividly, and especially the country. It's as though . . .'

He talked on, addressing both Kitty and Levin, turning his serene, friendly eyes from one to the other, and saying obviously just what came into his head.

Noticing that Countess Nordston wanted to say something, he stopped short without finishing what he had begun, and listened attentively to her.

The conversation did not flag for an instant, so that the princess, who always kept in reserve, in case a subject should be lacking, two heavy guns—the relative advantages of classical and of modern education, and universal military service—had not to move out either of them, while Countess Nordston had not a chance of chaffing Levin.

Levin wanted to, and could not, take part in the general conversation; saying to himself every instant, 'Now go,' he still did not go, as though waiting for something.

The conversation fell upon table-turning and spirits, and Countess Nordston, who believed in spiritualism, began to describe the marvels she had seen.

'Ah, countess, you really must take me, for pity's sake do take me to see them! I have never seen anything extraordinary, though I am always on the look-out for it everywhere,' said Vronsky, smiling.

'Very well, next Saturday,' answered Countess Nordston. 'But you, Konstantin Dmitritch, do you believe in it?' she asked Levin.

'Why do you ask me? You know what I shall say.'

'But I want to hear your opinion.'

'My opinion,' answered Levin, 'is only that this table-turning simply proves that educated society—so called—is no higher than the peasants. They believe in the evil eye, and in witchcraft and omens, while we . . .'

'Oh, then you don't believe in it?'

'I can't believe in it, countess.'

'But if I've seen it myself?'

'The peasant women too tell us they have seen goblins.'

'Then you think I tell a lie?'

And she laughed a mirthless laugh.

'Oh no, Masha, Konstantin Dmitritch said he could not believe in it,' said Kitty, blushing for Levin, and Levin saw this, and, still more exasperated, would have answered, but Vronsky with his bright frank smile rushed to the support of the conversation, which was threatening to become disagreeable.

'You do not admit the conceivability at all?' he queried. 'But why not? We admit the existence of electricity, of which we know nothing. Why should there not be some new force, still unknown to us, which . . .'

'When electricity was discovered,' Levin interrupted hurriedly, 'it was only the phenomenon that was discovered, and it was unknown from what it proceeded and what were its effects, and ages passed before its applications were conceived. But the spiritualists have begun with tables writing for them, and spirits appearing to them, and have only later started saying that it is an unknown force.'

Vronsky listened attentively to Levin, as he always did listen, obviously interested in his words.

'Yes, but the spiritualists say we don't know at present what this force is, but there is a force, and these are the conditions in which it acts. Let the scientific men find out what the force consists in. No, I don't see why there should not be a new force, if it . . .'

'Why, because with electricity,' Levin interrupted again, 'every time you rub tar against wool, a recognised phenomenon is manifested, but in this case it does not happen every time, and so it follows it is not a natural phenomenon.'

Feeling probably that the conversation was taking a tone too serious for a drawing-room, Vronsky made no rejoinder, but by way of trying to change the conversation, he smiled brightly, and turned to the ladies.

'Do let us try at once, countess,' he said; but Levin would finish saying what he thought.

'I think,' he went on, 'that this attempt of the spiritualists to explain their marvels as some sort of new natural force is most futile. They boldly talk of a spiritual force, and then try to subject it to material experiment.'

Everyone was waiting for him to finish, and he felt it.

'And I think you would be a first-rate medium,' said Countess Nordston; 'there's something enthusiastic in you.'

Levin opened his mouth, was about to say something, reddened, and said nothing.

'Do let us try table-turning at once, please,' said Vronsky. 'Princess, will you allow it?'

And Vronsky stood up, looking about for a little table.

Kitty got up to fetch a table, and as she passed, her eyes met Levin's. She felt for him with her whole heart, the more because she was pitying him for suffering of which she was herself the cause. 'If you can forgive me, forgive me,' said her eyes, 'I am so happy.'

'I hate them all, and you, and myself,' his eyes responded, and he took up his hat. But he was not destined to escape. Just as they were arranging themselves round the table, and Levin was on the point of retiring, the old prince came in, and after greeting the ladies, addressed Levin.

'Ah!' he began joyously. 'Been here long, my boy? I didn't even know you were in the town. Very glad to see you.' The old prince embraced Levin, and talking to him did not observe Vronsky, who had risen, and was serenely waiting till the prince should turn to him.

Kitty felt how distasteful her father's warmth was to Levin after what had happened. She saw, too, how coldly her father responded at last to Vronsky's bow, and how Vronsky looked with amiable perplexity at her father, as though trying and failing to understand how and why one could be hostilely disposed towards him, and she flushed.

'Prince, let us have Konstantin Dmitritch,' said Countess Nordston; 'we want to try an experiment.'

'What experiment? Table-turning? Well, you must excuse me, ladies and gentlemen, but to my mind it is better fun to play the ring game,' said the old prince, looking at Vronsky, and guessing that it had been his suggestion. 'There's some sense in that, anyway.'

Vronsky looked wonderingly at the prince with his resolute eyes, and, with a faint smile, began immediately talking to Countess Nordston of the great ball that was to come off next week.

'I hope you will be there?' he said to Kitty. As soon as the old prince turned away from him, Levin went out unnoticed, and the last impression he carried away with him of that evening was the smiling, happy face of Kitty answering Vronsky's inquiry about the ball.

XV

AT the end of the evening Kitty told her mother of her conversation with Levin, and in spite of all the pity she felt for Levin, she was glad at the thought that she had received an *offer*. She had no doubt that she had acted rightly. But after she had gone to bed, for a long while she could not sleep. One impression pursued her relentlessly. It was Levin's face, with his scowling brows, and his kind eyes looking out in dark dejection below them, as he stood listening to her father, and glancing at her and at Vronsky. And she felt so sorry for him that tears came into her eyes. But immediately she thought of the man for whom she had given him up. She vividly recalled his manly, resolute face, his noble self-possession, and the good-nature conspicuous in everything towards everyone. She remembered the love for her of the man she loved, and once more all was gladness in her soul, and she lay on the pillow, smiling happiness. 'I'm sorry, I'm sorry; but what could I do? It's not my fault,' she said to herself; but an inner voice told her something else. Whether she felt remorse at having won Levin's love, or at having refused him, she did not know. But her happiness was poisoned by doubts. 'Lord, have pity on us; Lord, have pity on us; Lord, have pity on us!' she repeated to herself, till she fell asleep.

Meanwhile there took place below, in the prince's little library, one of the scenes so often repeated between the parents on account of their favourite daughter.

'What? I'll tell you what!' shouted the prince, waving his arms, and at once wrapping his squirrel-lined dressing-gown round him again. 'That you've no pride, no dignity; that you're disgracing, ruining your daughter by this vulgar, stupid matchmaking!'

'But, really, for mercy's sake, prince, what have I done?' said the princess, almost crying.

She, pleased and happy after her conversation with her daughter, had gone to the prince to say good-night as usual, and though she had no intention of telling him of Levin's offer and Kitty's refusal, still she hinted to her husband that she fancied things were practically settled with Vronsky, and that he would declare himself so soon as his mother arrived. And thereupon, at those words, the prince had all at once flown into a passion, and began to use unseemly language.

'What have you done? I'll tell you what. First of all, you're trying to catch an eligible gentleman, and all Moscow will be talking of it, and with good reason. If you have evening parties, invite everyone, and don't pick out the possible suitors. Invite all the young bucks. Engage a piano-player, and let them dance, and not as you do things nowadays, hunting up good matches. It makes me sick, sick to see it, and you've gone on till you've turned the poor wench's head. Levin's a thousand times the better man. As for this little Petersburg swell, they're turned out by machinery, all on one pattern, and all precious rubbish. But if he were a prince of the blood, my daughter need not run after anyone.'

'But what have I done?'

'Why, you've . . .' The prince was crying wrathfully.

'I know if one were to listen to you,' interrupted the princess, 'we should never marry our daughter. If it's to be so, we'd better go into the country.'

'Well, and we had better.'

'But do wait a minute. Do I try and catch them? I don't try to catch them in the least. A young man, and a very nice one, has fallen in love with her, and she, I fancy . . .'

'Oh yes, you fancy! And how if she really is in love, and he's no more thinking of marriage than I am! . . . Oh, that I should live to see it! . . . Ah! spiritualism! Ah! Nice! Ah! the ball!' And the prince, imagining that he was mimicking his wife, made a mincing curtsey at each word. 'And this is how we're preparing wretchedness for Kitty; and she's really got the notion into her head . . .'

'But what makes you suppose so?'

'I don't suppose; I know. We have eyes for such things, though women-folk haven't. I see a man who has serious intentions, that's Levin; and I see a peacock, like this featherhead, who's only amusing himself.'

'Oh, well, when once you get an idea into your head! . . .'

'Well, you'll remember my words, but too late, just as with Dolly.'

'Well, well, we won't talk of it,' the princess stopped him, recollecting her unlucky Dolly.

'By all means, and good-night!'

And signing each other with the cross, the husband and wife parted with a kiss, feeling that they each remained of their own opinion.

The princess had at first been quite certain that that evening had settled Kitty's future, and that there could be no doubt of Vronsky's intentions, but her husband's words had disturbed her. And returning to her own room, in terror before the unknown future, she too, like Kitty, repeated several times in her heart, 'Lord, have pity; Lord, have pity; Lord, have pity!'

XVI

VRONSKY had never had a real home-life. His mother had been in her youth a brilliant society woman, who had had during her married life, and still more afterwards, many love-affairs notorious in the whole fashionable world. His father he scarcely remembered, and he had been educated in the Corps of Pages.

Leaving the school very young as a brilliant officer, he had at once got into the circle of wealthy Petersburg army men. Although he did go more or less into Petersburg society, his love-affairs had always hitherto been outside it.

In Moscow he had for the first time felt, after his luxurious and coarse life at Petersburg, all the charm of intimacy with a sweet and innocent girl of his own rank, who cared for him. It never even entered his head that there could be any harm in his relations with Kitty. At balls he danced principally with her. He was a constant visitor at their house. He talked to her as people commonly do talk in society—all sorts of nonsense, but nonsense to which he could not help attaching a special meaning in her case. Although he said nothing to her that he could not have said before everybody, he felt that she was becoming more and more dependent upon him, and the more he felt this, the better he liked it, and the tenderer was his feeling for her. He did not know that his mode of behaviour in relation to Kitty had a definite character, that it is courting young girls with no intention of marriage, and that such courting is one of the evil actions common amongst brilliant young men such as he was. It seemed to him that he was the first who had discovered this pleasure, and he was enjoying his discovery.

If he could have heard what her parents were saying that evening, if he could have put himself at the point of view of the family and have heard that Kitty would be unhappy if he did not marry her, he would have been greatly astonished, and would not have believed it. He could not believe that what gave such great and delicate pleasure to him, and above all to her, could be wrong. Still less could he have believed that he ought to marry.

Marriage had never presented itself to him as a possibility. He not only disliked family life, but a family, and especially a husband was, in accordance with the views general in the bachelor world in which he lived, conceived as something alien, repellent, and, above all, ridiculous.

But though Vronsky had not the least suspicion what the parents were saying, he felt on coming away from the Shtcherbatskys' that the secret spiritual bond which existed between him and Kitty had grown so much stronger that evening that some step must be taken. But what step could and ought to be taken he could not imagine.

'What is so exquisite,' he thought, as he returned from the Shtcherbatskys', carrying away with him, as he always did, a delicious feeling of purity and freshness, arising partly from the fact that he had not been smoking for a whole evening, and with it a new feeling of tenderness at her love for him—'what is so exquisite is that not a word has been said by me or by her, but we understand each other so well in this unseen language of looks and tones, that this evening more clearly than ever she told me she loves me. And how secretly, simply, and most of all, how trustfully! I feel myself better, purer. I feel that I have a heart, and that there is a great deal of good in me. Those sweet, loving eyes! When she said: "Indeed I do . . ."

'Well, what then? Oh nothing. It's good for me, and good for her.' And he began wondering where to finish the evening.

He passed in review the places he might go to. 'Club? a game of bezique, champagne with Ignatov? No, I'm not going. Château des Fleurs; there I shall find Oblonsky, songs, the cancan. No, I'm sick of it. That's why I like the Shtcherbatskys', that I'm growing better. I'll go home.' He went straight to his room at Dussots' Hotel, ordered supper, and then undressed, and as soon as his head touched the pillow, fell into a sound sleep.

XVII

NEXT day at eleven o'clock in the morning Vronsky drove to the station of the Petersburg railway to meet his mother, and the first person he came across on the great flight of steps was Oblonsky, who was expecting his sister by the some train.

'Ah! your excellency!' cried Oblonsky, 'whom are you meeting?'

'My mother,' Vronsky responded, smiling, as everyone did who met Oblonsky. He shook hands with him, and together they ascended the steps. 'She is to be here from Petersburg today.'

'I was looking out for you till two o'clock last night. Where did you go after the Shtcherbatskys'?'

'Home,' answered Vronsky. 'I must own I felt so well content yesterday after the Shtcherbatskys' that I didn't care to go anywhere.'

'"I know a gallant steed by tokens sure,
And by his eyes I know a youth in love,"'

declaimed Stepan Arkadyevitch, just as he had done before to Levin.

Vronsky smiled with a look that seemed to say that he did not deny it, but he promptly changed the subject.

'And whom are you meeting?' he asked.

'I? I've come to meet a pretty woman,' said Oblonsky.

'You don't say so!'

'*Honi soit qui mal y pense*! My sister Anna.'

'Ah! that's Madame Karenin,' said Vronsky.

'You know her, no doubt?'

'I think so. Or perhaps not . . . I really am not sure,' Vronsky answered heedlessly, with a vague recollection of something stiff and tedious evoked by the name Karenin.

'But Alexy Alexandrovitch, my celebrated brother-in-law, you surely must know. All the world knows him.'

'I know him by reputation and by sight. I know that he's clever, learned, religious somewhat . . . But you know that's not . . . *not in my line*,' said Vronsky in English.

'Yes, he's a very remarkable man; rather a conservative, but a splendid man,' observed Stepan Arkadyevitch, 'a splendid man.'

'Oh well, so much the better for him,' said Vronsky smiling. 'Oh, you've come,' he said, addressing a tall old footman of his mother's standing at the door; 'come here.'

Besides the charm Oblonsky had in general for everyone, Vronsky had felt of late specially drawn to him by the fact that in his imagination he was associated with Kitty.

'Well, what do you say? Shall we give a supper on Sunday for the *diva*?' he said to him with a smile, taking his arm.

'Of course. I'm collecting subscriptions. Oh, did you make the acquaintance of my friend Levin?' asked Stepan Arkadyevitch.

'Yes; but he left rather early.'

'He's a capital fellow,' pursued Oblonsky. 'Isn't he?'

'I don't know why it is,' responded Vronsky, 'in all Moscow people—present company of course excepted,' he put in jestingly, 'there's something uncompromising. They are all on the defensive, lose their tempers, as though they all want to make one feel something. . . .'

'Yes, that's true, it is so,' said Stepan Arkadyevitch, laughing good-humouredly.

'Will the train soon be in?' Vronsky asked a railway official.

'The train's signalled,' answered the man.

The approach of the train was more and more evident by the preparatory bustle in the station, the rush of porters, the movement of policemen and attendants, and people meeting the train. Through the frosty vapour could be seen workmen in short sheepskins and soft felt boots crossing the rails of the curving line. The hiss of the boiler could be heard on the distant rails, and the rumble of something heavy.

'No,' said Stepan Arkadyevitch, who felt a great inclination to tell Vronsky of Levin's intentions in regard to Kitty. 'No, you've not got a true impression of Levin. He's a very nervous man, and is sometimes out of humour, it's true, but then he is often very nice. He's such a true, honest nature, and a heart of gold. But yesterday there were special reasons,' pursued Stepan Arkadyevitch, with a meaning smile, totally oblivious of the genuine sympathy he had felt the day before for his friend, and feeling the same sympathy now, only for Vronsky. 'Yes, there were reasons why he could not help being either particularly happy or particularly unhappy.'

Vronsky stood still and asked directly: 'How so? Do you mean he made your *belle-sœur* an offer yesterday?'

'Maybe,' said Stepan Arkadyevitch. 'I fancied something of the sort yesterday. Yes, if he went away early, and was out of humour too, it must mean it . . . He's been so long in love, and I'm very sorry for him.'

'So that's it! . . . I should imagine, though, she might reckon on a better match,' said Vronsky, drawing himself up and walking about again, 'though I don't know him, of course,' he added. 'Yes, that is a hateful position! That's why most fellows prefer to have to do with Klaras. If you don't succeed with them it only proves that you've not enough cash, but in this case one's dignity's at stake. But here's the train.'

The engine had already whistled in the distance. A few instants later the platform was quivering, and with puffs of steam hanging low in the air from the frost, the engine rolled up, with the lever of the middle wheel ryhthmically moving up and down, and the stooping figure of the engine-driver covered with frost. Behind the tender, setting the platform more and more slowly swaying, came the luggage-van with a dog whining in it. At last the passenger carriages rolled in, oscillating before coming to a standstill.

A smart guard jumped out, giving a whistle, and after him one by one the impatient passengers began to get down: an officer of the guards, holding himself erect, and looking severely about him; a nimble little merchant with a satchel, smiling gaily; a peasant with a sack over his shoulder.

Vronsky, standing beside Oblonsky, watched the carriages and the passengers, totally oblivious of his mother. What he had just heard about Kitty excited and delighted him. Unconsciously he arched his chest, and his eyes flashed. He felt himself a conqueror.

'Countess Vronsky is in that compartment,' said the smart guard, going up to Vronsky.

The guard's words roused him, and forced him to think of his mother and his approaching meeting with her. He did not in his heart respect his mother, and without acknowledging it to himself, he did not love her, though in accordance with the ideas of the set in which he lived, and with his own education, he could not have conceived of any behaviour to his mother not in the highest degree respectful and obedient, and the more externally obedient and respectful his behaviour, the less in his heart he respected and loved her.

XVIII

VRONSKY followed the guard to the carriage, and at the door of the compartment he stopped short to make room for a lady who was getting out.

With the insight of a man of the world, from one glance at this lady's appearance Vronsky classified her as belonging to the best society. He begged pardon, and was getting into the carriage, but felt he must glance at her once more; not that she was very beautiful, not on account of the elegance and modest grace which were apparent in her whole figure, but because in the expression of her charming face, as she passed close by him, there was something peculiarly caressing and soft. As he looked round, she too turned her head. Her shining grey eyes, that looked dark from the thick lashes, rested with friendly attention on his face, as though she were recognising him, and then promptly turned away to the passing crowd, as though seeking someone. In that brief look Vronsky had time to notice the suppressed eagerness which played over her face, and flitted between the brilliant eyes and the faint smile that curved her red lips. It was as though her nature were so brimming over with something that against her will it showed itself now in the flash of her eyes, and now in her smile. Deliberately she shrouded the light in her eyes, but it shone against her will in the faintly perceptible smile.

Vronsky stepped into the carriage. His mother, a dried-up old lady with black eyes and ringlets, screwed up her eyes, scanning her son, and smiled slightly with her thin lips. Getting up from the seat and handing her maid a bag, she gave her little wrinkled hand to her son to kiss, and lifting his head from her hand kissed him on the cheek.

'You got my telegram? Quite well? Thank God.'

'You had a good journey?' said her son, sitting down beside her, and involuntarily listening to a woman's voice outside the door. He knew it was the voice of the lady he had met at the door.

'All the same I don't agree with you,' said the lady's voice.

'It's the Petersburg view, madame.'

'Not Petersburg, but simply feminine,' she responded.

'Well, well, allow me to kiss your hand.'

'Good-bye, Ivan Petrovitch. And would you see if my brother is here, and send him to me?' said the lady in the doorway, and stepped back again into the compartment.

'Well, have you found your brother?' said Countess Vronsky, addressing the lady.

Vronsky understood now that this was Madame Karenin.

'Your brother is here,' he said, standing up. 'Excuse me, I did not know you, and, indeed, our acquaintance was so slight,' said Vronsky bowing, 'that no doubt you do not remember me.'

'Oh no,' said she, 'I should have known you because your mother and I have been talking, I think, of nothing but you all the way.' As she spoke she let the eagerness that would insist on coming out show itself in her smile. 'And still no sign of my brother.'

'Do call him Alexey,' said the old countess. Vronsky stepped out on to the platform and shouted—

'Oblonsky! Here!'

Madame Karenin, however, did not wait for her brother, but catching sight of him she stepped out with her light, resolute step. And as soon as her brother had reached her, with a gesture that struck Vronsky by its decision and its grace, she flung her left arm round his neck, drew him rapidly to her, and kissed him warmly. Vronsky gazed, never taking his eyes from her, and smiled, he could not have said why. But recollecting that his mother was waiting for him, he went back again into the carriage.

'She's very sweet, isn't she?' said the countess of Madame Karenin. 'Her husband put her with me, and I was delighted to have her. We've been talking all the way. And so you, I hear . . . *vous filez le parfait amour. Tant mieux, mon cher, tant mieux.*'

'I don't know what you are referring to, maman,' he answered coldly. 'Come, maman, let us go.'

Madame Karenin entered the carriage again to say good-bye to the countess.

'Well, countess, you have met your son, and I my brother,' she said. 'And all my gossip is exhausted. I should have nothing more to tell you.'

'Oh no,' said the countess, taking her hand. 'I could go all round the world with you and never be dull. You are one of those delightful women in whose company it's sweet to be silent as well as to talk. Now please don't fret over your son; you can't expect never to be parted.'

Madame Karenin stood quite still, holding herself very erect, and her eyes were smiling.

'Anna Arkadyevna,' the countess said in explanation to her son, 'has a little son eight years old, I believe, and she has never been parted from him before, and she keeps fretting over leaving him.'

'Yes, the countess and I have been talking all the time, I of my son and she of hers,' said Madame Karenin, and again a smile lighted up her face, a caressing smile intended for him.

'I am afraid that you must have been dreadfully bored,' he said, promptly catching the ball of coquetry she had flung him. But apparently she did not care to pursue the conversation in that strain, and she turned to the old countess.

'Thank you so much. The time has passed so quickly. Good-bye, countess.'

'Good-bye, my love,' answered the countess. 'Let me have a kiss of your pretty face. I speak plainly, at my age, and I tell you simply that I've lost my heart to you.'

Stereotyped as the phrase was, Madame Karenin obviously believed it and was delighted by it. She flushed, bent down slightly, and put her cheek to the countess's lips, drew herself up again, and with the same smile fluttering between her lips and her eyes, she gave her hand to Vronsky. He pressed the little hand she gave him, and was delighted, as though at something special, by the energetic squeeze with which she freely and vigorously shook his hand. She went out with the rapid step, which bore her rather fully-developed figure with such strange lightness.

'Very charming,' said the countess.

That was just what her son was thinking. His eyes followed her till her graceful figure was out of sight, and then the smile remained on his face. He saw out of window how she went up to her brother, put her arm in his, and began telling him something eagerly, obviously something that had nothing to do with him, Vronsky, and at that he felt annoyed.

'Well, maman, are you perfectly well?' he repeated, turning to his mother.

'Everything has been delightful. Alexandre has been very good, and Marie has grown very pretty. She's very interesting.'

And she began telling him again of what interested her most—the christening of her grandson, for which she had been staying in Petersburg, and the special favour shown her elder son by the Tsar.

'Here's Lavrenty,' said Vronsky, looking out of window; 'now we can go, if you like.'

The old butler, who had travelled with the countess, came to the carriage to announce that everything was ready, and the countess got up to go.

'Come; there's not such a crowd now,' said Vronsky.

The maid took a handbag and the lapdog, the butler and a porter the other baggage. Vronsky gave his mother his arm; but just as they were getting out of the carriage several men ran suddenly by with panic-stricken faces. The stationmaster too ran by in his extraordinary coloured cap. Obviously something unusual had happened. The crowd who had left the train were running back again.

'What? ... What? ... Where? ... Flung himself! ... Crushed! ...' was heard among the crowd. Stepan Arkadyevitch, with his sister on his arm, turned back. They too looked scared, and stopped at the carriage door to avoid the crowd.

The ladies got in, while Vronsky and Stepan Arkadyevitch followed the crowd to find out details of the disaster.

A guard, either drunk or too much muffled up in the bitter frost, had not heard the train moving back, and had been crushed.

Before Vronsky and Oblonsky came back the ladies heard the facts from the butler.

Oblonsky and Vronsky had both seen the mutilated corpse. Oblonsky was evidently upset. He frowned and seemed ready to cry.

'Ah, how awful! Ah, Anna, if you had seen it! Ah, how awful!' he said.

Vronsky did not speak; his handsome face was serious, but perfectly composed.

'Oh, if you had seen it, countess,' said Stepan Arkadyevitch. 'And his wife was there. ... It was awful to see her! ... She flung herself on the body. They say he was the only support of an immense family. How awful!'

'Couldn't one do anything for her?' said Madame Karenin in an agitated whisper.

Vronsky glanced at her, and immediately got out of the carriage.

'I'll be back directly, maman,' he remarked, turning round in the doorway.

When he came back a few minutes later Stepan Arkadyevitch was already in conversation with the countess about the new singer, while the countess was impatiently looking towards the door, waiting for her son.

'Now let us be off,' said Vronsky coming in. They went out together. Vronsky was in front with his mother. Behind walked Madame Karenin with her brother. Just as they were going out of the station the stationmaster overtook Vronsky.

'You gave my assistant two hundred roubles. Would you kindly explain for whose benefit you intend them?'

'For the widow,' said Vronsky, shrugging his shoulders. 'I should have thought there was no need to ask.'

'You gave that?' cried Oblonsky behind, and, pressing his sister's hand, he added: 'Very nice, very nice! Isn't he a splendid fellow? Good-bye, countess.'

And he and his sister stood still, looking for her maid.

When they went out the Vronskys' carriage had already driven away. People coming in were still talking of what happened.

'What a horrible death!' said a gentleman, passing by. 'They say he was cut in two pieces.'

'On the contrary, I think it's the easiest—instantaneous,' observed another.

'How is it they don't take proper precautions?' said a third.

Madame Karenin seated herself in the carriage, and Stepan Arkadyevitch saw with surprise that her lips were quivering, and she was with difficulty restraining her tears.

'What is it, Anna?' he asked, when they had driven a few hundred yards.

'It's an omen of evil,' she said.

'What nonsense!' said Stepan Arkadyevitch. 'You've come, that's the chief thing. You can't conceive how I'm resting my hopes on you.'

'Have you known Vronsky long?' she asked.

'Yes. You know we're hoping he will marry Kitty.'

'Yes?' said Anna softly. 'Come now, let us talk of you,' she added, tossing her head, as though she would physically shake off something superfluous oppressing her. 'Let us talk of your affairs. I got your letter, and here I am.'

'Yes, all my hopes are in you,' said Stepan Arkadyevitch.

'Well, tell me all about it.'

And Stepan Arkadyevitch began to tell his story.

On reaching home Oblonsky helped his sister out, sighed, pressed her hand, and set off to his office.

XIX

WHEN Anna went into the room, Dolly was sitting in the little drawing-room with a white-headed fat little boy, already like his father, giving him a lesson in French reading. As the boy read, he kept twisting and trying to tear off a button that was nearly off his jacket. His mother had several times taken his hand from it, but the fat little hand went back to the button again. His mother pulled the button off and put it in her pocket.

'Keep your hands still, Grisha,' she said, and she took up her work, a coverlet she had long been making. She always set to work on it at depressed moments, and now she knitted at it nervously, twitching her fingers and counting the stitches. Though she had sent word the day before to her husband that it was nothing to her whether his sister came or not, she had made everything ready for her arrival, and was expecting her sister-in-law with emotion.

Dolly was crushed by her sorrow, utterly swallowed up by it. Still she did not forget that Anna, her sister-in-law, was the wife of one of the most important personages in Petersburg, and was a Petersburg *grandedame.* And, thanks to this circumstance, she did not carry out her threat to her husband—that is to say, she remembered that her sister-in-law was coming. 'And, after all, Anna is in no wise to blame,' thought Dolly. 'I know nothing of her except the very best, and I have seen nothing but kindness and affection from her towards myself.' It was true that as far as she could recall her impressions at Petersburg at the Karenins', she did not like their household itself; there was something artificial in the whole framework of their family life. 'But why should I not receive her? If only she doesn't take it into her head to console me!' thought Dolly. 'All consolation and counsel and Christian forgiveness, all that I have thought over a thousand times, and it's all no use.'

All these days Dolly had been alone with her children. She did not want to talk of her sorrow, but with that sorrow in her heart she could not talk of outside matters. She knew that in one way or another she would tell Anna everything, and she was alternately glad at the thought of speaking freely, and angry at the necessity of speaking of her humiliation with her, his sister, and of hearing her ready-made phrases of good advice and comfort. She had been on the look-out for her, glancing at her watch every minute, and, as often happens, let slip just that minute when her visitor arrived, so that she did not hear the bell.

Catching a sound of skirts and light steps at the door, she looked round, and her careworn face unconsciously expressed not gladness, but wonder. She got up and embraced her sister-in-law.

'What, here already!' she said as she kissed her.

'Dolly, how glad I am to see you!'

'I am glad too,' said Dolly, faintly smiling, and trying by the expression of Anna's face to find out whether she knew. 'Most likely she knows,' she thought, noticing the sympathy in Anna's face. 'Well, come along, I'll take you to your room,' she went on, trying to defer as long as possible the moment of confidences.

'Is this Grisha? Heavens, how he's grown!' said Anna; and kissing him, never taking her eyes off Dolly, she stood still and flushed a little. 'No, please, let us stay here.'

She took off her kerchief and her hat, and catching it in a lock of her black hair, which was a mass of curls, she tossed her head and shook her hair down.

'You are radiant with health and happiness!' said Dolly, almost with envy.

'I? . . . Yes,' said Anna. 'Merciful heavens, Tanya! You're the same age as my Seryozha,' she added, addressing the little girl as she ran in. She took her in her arms and kissed her. 'Delightful child, delightful! Show me them all.'

She mentioned them, not only remembering the names, but the years, months, characters, illnesses of all the children, and Dolly could not but appreciate that.

'Very well, we will go to them,' she said. 'It's a pity Vassya's asleep.'

After seeing the children, they sat down, alone now, in the drawing-room, to coffee. Anna took the tray, and then pushed it away from her.

'Dolly,' she said, 'he has told me.'

Dolly looked coldly at Anna; she was waiting now for phrases of conventional sympathy, but Anna said nothing of the sort.

'Dolly, dear,' she said, 'I don't want to speak for him to you, nor to try to comfort you; that's impossible. But, darling, I'm simply sorry, sorry from my heart for you!'

Under the thick lashes of her shining eyes tears suddenly glittered. She moved nearer to her sister-in-law and took her hand in her vigorous little hand. Dolly did not shrink away, but her face did not lose its frigid expression. She said—

'To comfort me's impossible. Everything's lost after what has happened, everything's over!'

And directly she had said this, her face suddenly softened. Anna lifted the wasted, thin hand of Dolly, kissed it and said—

'But, Dolly, what's to be done, what's to be done? How is it best to act in this awful position—that's what you must think of.'

'All's over, and there's nothing more,' said Dolly. 'And the worst of it all is, you see, that I can't cast him off: there are the children, I am tied. And I can't live with him; it's a torture to me to see him.'

'Dolly, darling, he has spoken to me, but I want to hear it from you: tell me all about it.'

Dolly looked at her inquiringly.

Sympathy and love unfeigned were visible on Anna's face.

'Very well,' she said all at once. 'But I will tell you it from the beginning. You know how I was married. With the education mamma gave us I was more than innocent, I was stupid. I knew nothing. I know they say men tell their wives of their former lives, but Stiva—'

she corrected herself—'Stepan Arkadyevitch told me nothing. You'll hardly believe it, but till now I imagined that I was the only woman he had known. So I lived eight years. You must understand that I was so far from suspecting infidelity, I regarded it as impossible, and then—try to imagine it—with such ideas to find out suddenly all the horror, all the loathsomeness . . . You must try and understand me. To be fully convinced of one's happiness, and all at once . . .' continued Dolly, holding back her sobs, 'to get a letter . . . his letter to his mistress, my governess. No, it's too awful!' She hastily pulled out her handkerchief and hid her face in it. 'I can understand being carried away by feeling,' she went on after a brief silence, 'but deliberately, slyly deceiving me . . . and with whom? . . . To go on being my husband together with her . . . it's awful! You can't understand . . .'

'Oh yes, I understand! I understand! Dolly, dearest, I do understand,' said Anna, pressing her hand.

'And do you imagine he realises all the awfulness of my position?' Dolly resumed. 'Not the slightest! He's happy and contented.'

'Oh no!' Anna interposed quickly. 'He's to be pitied, he's weighed down by remorse . . .'

'Is he capable of remorse?' Dolly interrupted, gazing intently into her sister-in-law's face.

'Yes. I know him. I could not look at him without feeling sorry for him. We both know him. He's good-hearted, but he's proud, and now he's so humiliated. What touched me most . . .' (and here Anna guessed what would touch Dolly most) 'he's tortured by two things: that he's ashamed for the children's sake, and that, loving you—yes, yes, loving you beyond everything on earth,' she hurriedly interrupted Dolly, who would have answered—'he has hurt you, pierced you to the heart. "No, no, she cannot forgive me," he keeps saying.'

Dolly looked dreamily away beyond her sister-in-law as she listened to her words.

'Yes, I can see that his position is awful; it's worse for the guilty than the innocent,' she said, 'if he feels that all the misery comes from his fault. But how am I to forgive him, how am I to be his wife again after her? For me to live with him now would be torture, just because I love my past love for him . . .'

And sobs cut short her words. But as though of set design, each time she was softened she began to speak again of what exasperated her.

'She's young, you see, she's pretty,' she went on. 'Do you know, Anna, my youth and my beauty are gone, taken by whom? By him and his children. I have worked for him, and all I had has gone in his service, and now of course any fresh, vulgar creature has more charm for him. No doubt they talked of me together, or, worse still, they were silent. Do you understand?'

Again her eyes glowed with hatred.

'And after that he will tell me . . . What! can I believe him? Never! No, everything is over, everything that once made my comfort, the reward of my work, and my sufferings. . . . Would you believe it, I was teaching Grisha just now: once this was a joy to me, now it is a torture. What have I to strive and toil for? Why are the children here? What's so awful is that all at once my heart's turned, and instead of love and tenderness, I have nothing but hatred for him; yes, hatred. I could kill him.'

'Darling Dolly, I understand, but don't torture yourself. You are so distressed, so overwrought, that you look at many things mistakenly.'

Dolly grew calmer, and for two minutes both were silent.

'What's to be done? Think for me, Anna, help me. I have thought over everything, and I see nothing.'

Anna could think of nothing, but her heart responded instantly to each word, to each change of expression of her sister-in-law.

'One thing I would say,' began Anna. 'I am his sister, I know his character, that faculty of forgetting everything, everything' (she waved her hand before her forehead), 'that faculty for being completely carried away, but for completely repenting too. He cannot believe it, he cannot comprehend now how he can have acted as he did.'

'No; he understands, he understood!' Dolly broke in. 'But I . . . you are forgetting me . . . does it make it easier for me?'

'Wait a minute. When he told me, I will own I did not realise all the awfulness of your position. I saw nothing but him, and that the family was broken up. I felt sorry for him, but after talking to you, I see it, as a woman, quite differently. I see your agony, and I can't tell you how sorry I am for you! But, Dolly, darling, I fully realise your sufferings, only there is one thing I don't know: I don't know . . . I don't know how much love there is still in your heart for him. That you know—whether there is enough for you to be able to forgive him. If there is, forgive him!'

'No,' Dolly was beginning, but Anna cut her short, kissing her hand once more.

'I know more of the world than you do,' she said. 'I know how men like Stiva look at it. You speak of his talking of you with her. That never happened. Such men are unfaithful, but their own home and wife are sacred to them. Somehow or other these women are still looked on with contempt by them, and do not touch on their feeling for their family. They draw a sort of line that can't be crossed between them and their families. I don't understand it, but it is so.'

'Yes, but he has kissed her . . .'

'Dolly, hush, darling. I saw Stiva when he was in love with you. I remember the time when he came to me and cried, talking of you, and all the poetry and loftiness of his feeling for you, and I know that the longer he has lived with you the loftier you have been in his eyes. You know we have sometimes laughed at him for putting in at every word: "Dolly's a marvellous woman." You have always been a divinity for him, and you are that still, and this has not been an infidelity of the heart. . . .'

'But if it is repeated?'

'It cannot be, as I understand it. . . .'

'Yes, but could you forgive it?'

'I don't know, I can't judge. . . . Yes, I can,' said Anna, thinking a moment; and grasping the position in her thought and weighing it in her inner balance, she added: 'Yes, I can, I can, I can. Yes, I could forgive it. I could not be the same, no; but I could forgive it, and forgive it as though it had never been, never been at all. . . .'

'Oh, of course,' Dolly interposed quickly, as though saying what she had more than once thought, 'else it would not be forgiveness. If one forgives, it must be completely, completely. Come, let us go; I'll take you to your room,' she said, getting up, and on the way she embraced Anna. 'My dear, how glad I am you came. It has made things better, ever so much better.'

XX

THE whole of that day Anna spent at home, that's to say at the Oblonskys', and received no one, though some of her acquaintances had already heard of her arrival, and came to call the same day. Anna spent the whole morning with Dolly and the children. She merely sent a brief note to her brother to tell him that he must not fail to dine at home. 'Come, God is merciful,' she wrote.

Oblonsky did dine at home: the conversation was general, and his wife, in speaking to him, addressed him as 'Stiva', as she had not done before. In the relations of the husband and wife the same estrangement still remained, but there was no talk now of separation, and Stepan Arkadyevitch saw the possibility of explanation and reconciliation.

Immediately after dinner Kitty came in. She knew Anna Arkadyevna, but only very slightly, and she came now to her sister's with some trepidation, at the prospect of meeting this fashionable Petersburg lady, whom every one spoke so highly of. But she made a favourable impression on Anna Arkadyevna—she saw that at once. Anna was unmistakably admiring her loveliness and her youth: before Kitty knew where she was she found herself not merely under Anna's sway, but in love with her, as young girls do fall in love with older and married women. Anna was not like a fashionable lady, nor the mother of a boy of eight years old. In the elasticity of her movements, the freshness and the unflagging eagerness which persisted in her face, and broke out in her smile and her glance, she would rather have passed for a girl of twenty, had it not been for a serious and at times mournful look in her eyes, which struck and attracted Kitty. Kitty felt that Anna was perfectly simple and was concealing nothing, but that she had another higher world of interests inaccessible to her, complex and poetic.

After dinner, when Dolly went away to her own room, Anna rose quickly and went up to her brother, who was just lighting a cigar.

'Stiva,' she said to him, winking gaily, crossing him, and glancing towards the door, 'go, and God help you.'

He threw down the cigar, understanding her, and departed through the doorway.

When Stepan Arkadyevitch had disappeared, she went back to the sofa where she was sitting, surrounded by the children. Either because the children saw that their mother was fond of this aunt, or that they felt a special charm in her themselves, the two elder ones, and the younger following their lead, as children so often do, had clung about their new aunt since before dinner, and would not leave her side. And it had become a sort of game among them to sit as close as possible to their aunt, to touch her, hold her little hand, kiss it, play with her ring, or even touch the flounce of her skirt.

'Come, come, as we were sitting before,' said Anna Arkadyevna, sitting down in her place.

And again Grisha poked his little face under her arm, and nestled with his head on her gown, beaming with pride and happiness.

'And when is your next ball?' she asked Kitty.

'Next week, and a splendid ball. One of those balls where one always enjoys oneself.'

'Why, are there balls where one always enjoys oneself?' Anna said, with tender irony.

'It's strange, but there are. At the Bobrishtchevs' one always enjoys oneself, and at the Nikitins' too, while at the Mezhkovs' it's always dull. Haven't you noticed it?'

'No, my dear, for me there are no balls now where one enjoys oneself,' said Anna, and Kitty detected in her eyes that mysterious world which was not open to her. 'For me there are some less dull and tiresome.'

'How can *you* be dull at a ball?'

'Why should not *I* be dull at a ball?' inquired Anna.

Kitty perceived that Anna knew what answer would follow.

'Because you always look nicer than anyone.'

Anna had the faculty of blushing. She blushed a little, and said—

'In the first place it's never so; and secondly, if it were, what difference would it make to me?'

'Are you coming to this ball?' asked Kitty.

'I imagine it won't be possible to avoid going. Here, take it,' she said to Tanya, who was pulling the loosely-fitting ring off her white, slender-tipped finger.

'I shall be so glad if you go. I should so like to see you at a ball.'

'Anyway, if I do go, I shall comfort myself with the thought that it's a pleasure to you. . . . Grisha, don't pull my hair. It's untidy enough without that,' she said, putting up a straying lock, which Grisha had been playing with.

'I imagine you at the ball in lilac.'

'And why in lilac precisely?' asked Anna, smiling. 'Now, children, run along, run along. Do you hear? Miss Hoole is calling you to tea,' she said, tearing the children from her, and sending them off to the dining-room.

'I know why you press me to come to the ball. You expect a great deal of this ball, and you want everyone to be there to take part in it.'

'How do you know? Yes.'

'Oh! what a happy time you are at,' pursued Anna. 'I remember, and I know that blue haze like the mist on the mountains in Switzerland. That mist which covers everything in that blissful time when childhood is just ending, and out of that vast circle, happy and gay, there is a path growing narrower and narrower, and it is delightful and alarming to enter the ballroom, bright and splendid as it is. . . . Who has not been through it?'

Kitty smiled without speaking. 'But how did she go through it? How I should like to know all her love-story!' thought Kitty, recalling the unromantic appearance of Alexey Alexandrovitch, her husband.

'I know something. Stiva told me, and I congratulate you, I liked him so much,' Anna continued. 'I met Vronsky at the railway station.'

'Oh, was he there?' asked Kitty, blushing. 'What was it Stiva told you?'

'Stiva gossiped about it all. And I should be so glad . . . I travelled yesterday with Vronsky's mother,' she went on; 'and his mother talked without a pause of him, he's her favourite. I know mothers are partial, but . . .'

'What did his mother tell you?'

'Oh, a great deal! And I know that he's her favourite; still one can see how chivalrous he is . . . Well, for instance, she told me that he had wanted to give up all his property to his brother, that he had done something extraordinary when he was quite a child, saved a woman out of the water. He's a hero, in fact,' said Anna, smiling and recollecting the two hundred roubles he had given at the station.

But she did not tell Kitty about the two hundred roubles. For some reason it was disagreeable to her to think of it. She felt that there was something that had to do with her in it, and something that ought not to have been.

'She pressed me very much to go and see her,' Anna went on; 'and I shall be glad to go to see her tomorrow. Stiva is staying a long while in Dolly's room, thank God,' Anna added, changing the subject, and getting up, Kitty fancied, displeased with something.

'No, I'm first! No, I!' screamed the children, who had finished tea, running up to their Aunt Anna.

'All together!' said Anna, and she ran laughing to meet them, and embraced and swung round all the throng of swarming children, shrieking with delight.

XXI

DOLLY came out of her room to the tea of the grown-up people. Stepan Arkadyevitch did not come out. He must have left his wife's room by the other door.

'I am afraid you'll be cold upstairs,' observed Dolly, addressing Anna; 'I want to move you downstairs, and we shall be nearer.'

'Oh, please, don't trouble about me,' answered Anna, looking intently into Dolly's face, trying to make out whether there had been a reconciliation or not.

'It will be lighter for you here,' answered her sister-in-law.

'I assure you that I sleep everywhere, and always like a marmot.'

'What's the question?' inquired Stepan Arkadyevitch, coming out of his room and addressing his wife.

From his tone both Kitty and Anna knew that a reconciliation had taken place.

'I want to move Anna downstairs, but we must hang up blinds. No one knows how to do it; I must see to it myself,' answered Dolly, addressing him.

'God knows whether they are fully reconciled,' thought Anna, hearing her tone, cold and composed.

'Oh, nonsense, Dolly, always making difficulties,' answered her husband. 'Come, I'll do it all, if you like . . .'

'Yes, they must be reconciled,' thought Anna.

'I know how you do everything,' answered Dolly. 'You tell Matvey to do what can't be done, and go away yourself, leaving him to make a muddle of everything,' and her habitual mocking smile curved the corners of Dolly's lips as she spoke.

'Full, full reconciliation, full,' thought Anna; 'thank God!' and rejoicing that she was the cause of it, she went up to Dolly and kissed her.

'Not at all. Why do you always look down on me and Matvey?' said Stepan Arkadyevitch, smiling hardly perceptibly, and addressing his wife.

The whole evening Dolly was, as always, a little mocking in her tone to her husband, while Stepan Arkadyevitch was happy and cheerful, but not so as to seem as though, having been forgiven, he had forgotten his offence.

At half-past nine o'clock a particularly joyful and pleasant family conversation over the tea-table at the Oblonskys' was broken up by an apparently simple incident. But this simple incident for some reason struck every one as strange. Talking about common acquaintances in Petersburg, Anna got up quickly.

'She is in my album,' she said; 'and by the way, I'll show you my Seryozha,' she added, with a mother's smile of pride.

Towards ten o'clock, when she usually said good-night to her son, and often before going to a ball put him to bed herself, she felt depressed at being so far from him; and whatever she was talking about, she kept coming back in thought to her curly-headed Seryozha. She longed to look at his photograph and talk of him. Seizing the first pretext, she got up, and with her light, resolute step went for her album. The stairs up to her room came out on the landing of the great warm main staircase.

Just as she was leaving the drawing-room, a ring was heard in the hall.

'Who can that be?' said Dolly.

'It's early for me to be fetched, and for anyone else it's late,' observed Kitty.

'Sure to be someone with papers for me,' put in Stepan Arkadyevitch. When Anna was passing the top of the staircase, a servant was running up to announce the visitor, while the visitor himself was standing under a lamp. Anna glancing down at once recognised Vronsky, and a strange feeling of pleasure and at the same time of dread of something stirred in her heart. He was standing still, not taking off his coat, pulling something out of his pocket. At the instant when she was just facing the stairs, he raised his eyes, caught sight of her, and into the expression of his face there passed a shade of embarrassment and dismay. With a slight inclination of her head she passed, hearing behind her Stepan Arkadyevitch's loud voice calling him to come up, and the quiet, soft, and composed voice of Vronsky refusing.

When Anna returned with the album, he was already gone, and Stepan Arkadyevitch was telling them that he had called to inquire about the dinner they were giving next day to a celebrity who had just arrived. 'And nothing would induce him to come up. What a queer fellow he is!' added Stepan Arkadyevitch.

Kitty blushed. She thought that she was the only person who knew why he had come, and why he would not come up. 'He has been at home,' she thought, 'and didn't find me, and thought I should be here, but he did not come up because he thought it late, and Anna's here.'

All of them looked at each other, saying nothing, and began to look at Anna's album.

There was nothing either exceptional or strange in a man's calling at half-past nine on a friend to inquire details of a proposed dinner-party and not coming in, but it seemed strange to all of them. Above all, it seemed strange and not right to Anna.

XXII

THE ball was only just beginning as Kitty and her mother walked up the great staircase, flooded with light, and lined with flowers and footmen in powder and red coats. From the rooms came a constant, steady hum, as from a hive, and the rustle of movement; and while on the landing between trees they gave last touches to their hair and dresses before the mirror, they heard from the ball-room the careful, distinct notes of the fiddles of the orchestra beginning the first waltz. A little old man in civilian dress, arranging his grey curls before another mirror, and diffusing an odour of scent, stumbled against them on the stairs, and stood aside, evidently admiring Kitty, whom he did not know. A beardless youth, one of those society youths whom the old Prince Shtcherbatsky called 'young bucks', in an exceedingly open waistcoat, straightening his white tie as he went, bowed to them, and after running by, came back to ask Kitty for a quadrille. As the first quadrille had already been given to Vronsky, she had to promise this youth the second. An officer, buttoning his glove, stood aside in the doorway, and, stroking his moustache, admired rosy Kitty.

Although her dress, her coiffure, and all the preparation for the ball had cost Kitty great trouble and consideration, at this moment she walked into the ballroom in her elaborate tulle dress over a pink slip as easily and simply as though all the rosettes and lace, all the minute details of her attire, had not cost her or her family a moment's attention, as though she had been born in that tulle and lace, with her hair done up high on her head, and a rose and two leaves on the top of it.

When, just before entering the ballroom, the princess, her mother, tried to turn right side out the ribbon of her sash, Kitty had drawn back a little. She felt that everything must be right of itself, and graceful, and nothing could need setting straight.

It was one of Kitty's best days. Her dress was not uncomfortable anywhere; her lace bertha did not droop anywhere; her rosettes were not crushed nor torn off; her pink slippers with high, hollowed-out heels did not pinch, but gladdened her feet; and the thick rolls of fair chignon kept up on her head as if they were her own hair. All the three buttons buttoned up without tearing on the long glove that covered her hand without concealing its lines. The black velvet of her locket nestled with special softness round her neck. That velvet was delicious; at home, looking at her neck in the looking-glass, Kitty had felt that that velvet was speaking. About all the rest there might be doubt, but the velvet was delicious. Kitty smiled here too, at the ball, when she glanced at it in the glass. Her bare shoulders and arms gave Kitty a sense of chill marble, a feeling she particularly liked. Her eyes sparkled, and her rosy lips could not keep from smiling from the consciousness of her own attractiveness. She had scarcely entered the ballroom and reached the throng of ladies, all tulle, ribbons, lace, and flowers, waiting to be asked to dance—Kitty was never one of that throng—when she was asked for a waltz, and asked by the best partner, the first star in the hierarchy of the ballroom, a renowned director of dances, a married man, handsome and well-built, Yegorushka Korsunsky. He had only just left the Countess Banin, with whom he had danced the first half of the waltz, and, scanning his kingdom—that is to say, a few couples who had started dancing—he caught sight of Kitty, entering, and flew up to her with that peculiar, easy amble which is confined to directors of balls. Without even asking her if she cared to dance, he put out his arm to encircle her slender waist. She looked round for someone to give her fan to, and their hostess, smiling to her, took it.

'How nice you've come in good time,' he said to her, embracing her waist; 'such a bad habit to be late.' Bending her left hand, she laid it on his shoulder, and her little feet in their pink slippers began swiftly, lightly, and rhythmically moving over the slippery floor in time to the music.

'It's a rest to waltz with you,' he said to her, as they fell into the first slow steps of the waltz. 'It's exquisite—such lightness, precision.' He said to her the same thing he said to almost all his partners whom he knew well.

She smiled at his praise, and continued to look about the room over his shoulder. She was not like a girl at her first ball, for whom all faces in the ballroom melt into one vision of fairyland. And she was not a girl who had gone the stale round of balls till every face in the ballroom was familiar and tiresome. But she was in the middle stage between these two: she was excited, and at the same time she had sufficient self-possession to be able to observe. In the left corner of the ballroom she saw the cream of society gathered together. There—incredibly naked—was the beauty Lidi, Kosunsky's wife; there was the lady of the house; there shone the bald head of Krivin, always to be found where the best people were. In that direction gazed the young men, not venturing to approach. There, too, she descried Stiva, and there she saw the exquisite figure and head of Anna in a black velvet gown. And *he* was there. Kitty had not seen him since the evening she refused Levin. With her long-sighted eyes she knew him at once, and was even aware that he was looking at her.

'Another turn, eh? You're not tired?' said Korsunsky, a little out of breath.

'No, thank you!'

'Where shall I take you?'

'Madame Karenin's here, I think . . . take me to her.'

'Wherever you command.'

And Korsunsky began waltzing with measured steps straight towards the group in the left corner, continually saying, 'Pardon, mesdames, pardon, pardon, mesdames'; and steering his course through the sea of lace, tulle, and ribbon, and not disarranging a feather, he turned his partner sharply round, so that her slim ankles, in light, transparent stockings, were exposed to view, and her train floated out in fan shape and covered Krivin's knees. Korsunsky bowed, set straight his open shirt-front, and gave her his arm to conduct her to Anna Arkadyevna. Kitty, flushed, took her train from Krivin's knees, and, a little giddy, looked round, seeking Anna. Anna was not in lilac, as Kitty had so urgently wished, but in a black, low-cut velvet gown, showing her full throat and shoulders, that looked as though carved in old ivory, and her rounded arms, with tiny, slender wrists. The whole gown was trimmed with Venetian guipure. On her head, among her black hair—her own, with no false additions—was a little wreath of pansies, and a bouquet of the same in the black ribbon of her sash among white lace. Her coiffure was not striking. All that was noticeable was the little wilful tendrils of her curly hair that would always break free about her neck and temples.

Kitty had been seeing Anna every day; she adored her, and had pictured her invariably in lilac. But now seeing her in black, she felt that she had not fully seen her charm. She saw her now as someone quite new and surprising to her. Now she understood that Anna could not have been in lilac, and that her charm was just that she always stood out against her attire, that her dress could never be noticeable on her. And her black dress, with its sumptuous lace, was not noticeable on her; it was only the frame, and all that was seen was she—simple, natural, elegant, and at the same time gay and eager.

She was standing, holding herself, as always, very erect, and when Kitty drew near the group she was speaking to the master of the house, her head slightly turned towards him.

'No, I don't throw stones,' she was saying, in answer to something, 'though I can't understand it,' she went on, shrugging her shoulders, and she turned at once with a soft smile of protection towards Kitty. With a flying, feminine glance she scanned her attire, and made a movement of her head, hardly perceptible, but understood by Kitty, signifying approval of her dress and her looks. 'You came into the room dancing,' she added.

'This is one of my most faithful supporters,' said Korsunsky, bowing to Anna Arkadyevna, whom he had not yet seen. 'The princess helps to make balls happy and successful. Anna Arkadyevna, a waltz?' he said, bending down to her.

'Why, have you met?' inquired their host.

'Is there anyone we have not met? My wife and I are like white wolves—everyone knows us,' answered Korsunsky. 'A waltz, Anna Arkadyevna?'

'I don't dance, when it's possible not to dance,' she said.

'But tonight it's impossible,' answered Korsunsky.

At that instant Vronsky came up.

'Well, since it's impossible tonight, let us start,' she said, not noticing Vronsky's bow, and she hastily put her hand on Korsunsky's shoulder.

'What is she vexed with him about?' thought Kitty, discerning that Anna had intentionally not responded to Vronsky's bow. Vronsky went up to Kitty, reminding her of the first quadrille, and expressing his regret that he had not seen her all this time. Kitty gazed in admiration at Anna waltzing, and listened to him. She expected him to ask for a waltz, but he did not, and she glanced wonderingly at him. He flushed slightly, and hurriedly asked her to waltz, but he had only just put his arm round her waist and taken the first step when the music suddenly stopped. Kitty looked into his face, which was so close to her own, and long afterwards—for several years after—that look, full of love, to which he made no response, cut her to the heart with an agony of shame.

'*Pardon! pardon!* Waltz! waltz!' shouted Korsunsky from the other side of the room, and seizing the first young lady he came across he began dancing himself.

XXIII

VRONSKY and Kitty waltzed several times round the room. After the waltz Kitty went to her mother, and she had hardly time to say a few words to Countess Nordston when Vronsky came up again for the first quadrille. During the quadrille nothing of any significance was said: there was disjointed talk between them of the Korsunskys, husband and wife, whom he described very amusingly, as delightful children at forty, and of the future town theatre; and only once the conversation touched her to the quick, when he asked her about Levin, whether he was here, and added that he liked him so much. But Kitty did not expect much from the quadrille. She looked forward with a thrill at her heart to the mazurka. She fancied that in the mazurka everything must be decided. The fact that he did not during the quadrille ask her for the mazurka did not trouble her. She felt sure she would dance the mazurka with him as she had done at former balls, and refused five young men, saying she was engaged for the mazurka. The whole ball up to the last quadrille was for Kitty an enchanted vision of delightful colours, sounds, and motions. She only sat down when she felt too tired and begged for a rest. But as she was dancing the last quadrille with one of the tiresome young men whom she could not refuse, she chanced to be *vis-à-vis* with Vronsky and Anna. She had not been near Anna again since the beginning of the evening, and now again she saw her suddenly quite new and surprising. She saw in her the signs of that excitement of success she knew so well in herself; she saw that she was intoxicated with the delighted admiration she was exciting. She knew that feeling and knew its signs, and saw them in Anna; saw the quivering, flashing light in her eyes, and the smile of happiness and excitement unconsciously playing on her lips, and the deliberate grace, precision, and lightness of her movements.

'Who?' she asked herself. 'All or one?' And not assisting the harassed young man she was dancing with in the conversation, the thread of which he had lost and could not pick up again, she obeyed with external liveliness the peremptory shouts of Korsunsky starting them all into the *grand rond*, and then into the *chaîne*, and at the same time she kept watch with a growing pang at her heart. 'No, it's not the admiration of the crowd has intoxicated her, but the admiration of one. And that one? can it be he?' Every time he spoke to Anna the joyous light flashed into her eyes, and the smile of happiness curved her red lips. She seemed to make an effort to control herself, not to show these signs of delight, but they came out on her face of themselves. 'But what of him?' Kitty looked at him and was filled with horror. What was pictured so clearly to Kitty in the mirror of Anna's face she saw in him. What had become of his always self-possessed resolute manner, and the carelessly serene expression of his face? Now every time he turned to her, he bent his head, as though he would have fallen at her feet, and in his eyes there was nothing but humble submission and dread. 'I would not offend you,' his eyes seemed every time to be saying, 'but I want to save myself, and I don't know how.' On his face was a look such as Kitty had never seen before.

They were speaking of common acquaintances, keeping up the most trivial conversation, but to Kitty it seemed that every word they said was determining their fate and hers. And strange it was that they were actually talking of how absurd Ivan Ivanovitch was with his French, and how the Eletsky girl might have made a better match, yet these words had all the while consequence for them, and they were feeling just as Kitty did. The whole ball, the whole world, everything seemed lost in fog in Kitty's soul. Nothing but the stern discipline of her bringing-up supported her and forced her to do what was expected of her, that is, to dance, to answer questions, to talk, even to smile. But before the mazurka, when they were beginning to rearrange the chairs and a few couples moved out of the smaller rooms into the big room, a moment of despair and horror came for Kitty. She had refused five partners, and now she was not dancing the mazurka. She had not even a hope of being asked for it, because she was so successful in society that the idea would never occur to anyone that she had remained disengaged till now. She would have to tell her mother she felt ill and go home, but she had not the strength to do this. She felt crushed. She went to the furthest end of the little drawing-room and sank into a low chair. Her light, transparent skirts rose like a cloud about her slender waist; one bare, thin, soft, girlish arm, hanging listlessly, was lost in the folds of her pink tunic; in the other she held her fan, and with rapid, short strokes fanned her burning face. But while she looked like a butterfly, clinging to a blade of grass, and just about to open its rainbow wings for fresh flight, her heart ached with a horrible despair.

'But perhaps I am wrong, perhaps it was not so?' And again she recalled all she had seen.

'Kitty, what is it?' said Countess Nordston, stepping noiselessly over the carpet towards her. 'I don't understand it.'

Kitty's lower lip began to quiver; she got up quickly.

'Kitty, you're not dancing the mazurka?'

'No, no,' said Kitty in a voice shaking with tears.

'He asked her for the mazurka before me,' said Countess Nordston, knowing Kitty would understand who were 'he' and 'her'. 'She said: "Why, aren't you going to dance it with Princess Shtcherbatsky?"'

'Oh, I don't care!' answered Kitty.

No one but she herself understood her position; no one knew that she had just refused the man whom perhaps she loved, and refused him because she had put her faith in another.

Countess Nordston found Korsunsky, with whom she was to dance the mazurka, and told him to ask Kitty.

Kitty danced in the first couple, and luckily for her she had not to talk, because Korsunsky was all the time running about directing the figure. Vronsky and Anna sat almost opposite her. She saw them with her long-sighted eyes, and saw them, too, close by, when they met in the figures, and the more she saw of them the more convinced was she that her unhappiness was complete. She saw that they felt themselves alone in that crowded room. And on Vronsky's face, always so firm and independent, she saw that look that had struck her, of bewilderment and humble submissiveness, like the expression of an intelligent dog when it has done wrong.

Anna smiled, and her smile was reflected by him. She grew thoughtful, and he became serious. Some supernatural force drew Kitty's eyes to Anna's face. She was fascinating in her simple black dress, fascinating were her round arms with their bracelets, fascinating was her firm neck with its thread of pearls, fascinating the straying curls of her loose hair, fascinating the graceful, light movements of her little feet and hands, fascinating was that lovely face in its eagerness, but there was something terrible and cruel in her fascination.

Kitty admired her more than ever, and more and more acute was her suffering. Kitty felt overwhelmed, and her face showed it. When Vronsky saw her, coming across her in the mazurka, he did not at once recognise her, she was so changed.

'Delightful ball!' he said to her, for the sake of saying something.

'Yes,' she answered.

In the middle of the mazurka, repeating a complicated figure, newly invented by Korsunsky, Anna came forward into the centre of the circle, chose two gentlemen, and summoned a lady and Kitty. Kitty gazed at her in dismay as she went up. Anna looked at her with drooping eyelids, and smiled, pressing her hand. But, noticing that Kitty only responded to her smile by a look of despair and amazement, she turned away from her, and began gaily talking to the other lady.

'Yes, there is something uncanny, devilish and fascinating in her,' Kitty said to herself.

Anna did not mean to stay to supper, but the master of the house began to press her to do so.

'Nonsense, Anna Arkadyevna,' said Korsunsky, drawing her bare arm under the sleeve of his dress coat, 'I've such an idea for a *cotillion*! *Un bijou!*'

And he moved gradually on, trying to draw her along with him. Their host smiled approvingly.

'No, I am not going to stay,' answered Anna, smiling, but in spite of her smile, both Korsunsky and the master of the house saw from her resolute tone that she would not stay.

'No; why, as it is, I have danced more at your ball in Moscow than I have all the winter in Petersburg,' said Anna, looking round at Vronsky, who stood near her. 'I must rest a little before my journey.'

'Are you certainly going tomorrow then?' asked Vronsky.

'Yes, I suppose so,' answered Anna, as it were wondering at the boldness of his question; but the irrepressible, quivering brilliance of her eyes and her smile set him on fire as she said it.

Anna Arkadyevna did not stay to supper, but went home.

XXIV

'YES, there is something in me hateful, repulsive,' thought Levin, as he came away from the Shtcherbatskys', and walked in the direction of his brother's lodgings. 'And I don't get on with other people. Pride, they say. No, I have no pride. If I had any pride, I should not have put myself in such a position.' And he pictured to himself Vronsky, happy, good-natured, clever, and self-possessed, certainly never placed in the awful position in which he had been that evening. 'Yes, she was bound to choose him. So it had to be, and I cannot complain of anyone or anything. I am myself to blame. What right had I to imagine she would care to join her life to mine? Who am I and what am I? A nobody, not wanted by anyone, nor of use to anybody.' And he recalled his brother Nikolay, and dwelt with pleasure on the thought of him. 'Isn't he right that everything in the world is base and loathsome? And are we fair in our judgment of brother Nikolay? Of course, from the point of view of Prokofy, seeing him in a torn cloak and tipsy, he's a despicable person. But I know him differently. I know his soul, and know that we are like him. And I, instead of going to seek him out, went out to dinner, and came here.' Levin walked up to a lamp-post, read his brother's address, which was in his pocket-book, and called a sledge. All the long way to his brother's, Levin vividly recalled all the facts familiar to him of his brother Nikolay's life. He remembered how his brother, while at the university, and for a year afterwards, had, in spite of the jeers of his companions, lived like a monk, strictly observing all religious rites, services, and fasts, and avoiding every sort of pleasure, especially women. And afterwards, how he had all at once broken out: he had associated with the most horrible people, and rushed into the most senseless debauchery. He remembered later the scandal over a boy, whom he had taken from the country to bring up, and, in a fit of rage, had so violently beaten that proceedings were brought against him for unlawfully wounding. Then he recalled the scandal with a sharper, to whom he had lost money, and given a promissory note, and against whom he had himself lodged a complaint, asserting that he had cheated him. (This was the money Sergey Ivanovitch had paid.) Then he remembered how he had spent a night in the lock-up for disorderly conduct in the street. He remembered the shameful proceedings he had tried to get up against his brother Sergey Ivanovich, accusing him of not having paid him his share of his mother's fortune, and the last scandal, when he had gone to a western province in an official capacity, and there had got into trouble for assaulting a village elder. . . . It was all horribly disgusting, yet to Levin it appeared not at all in the same disgusting light as it inevitably would to those who did not know Nikolay, did not know all his story, did not know his heart.

Levin remembered that when Nikolay had been in the devout stage, the period of fasts and monks and church services, when he was seeking in religion a support and a curb for his passionate temperament, everyone, far from encouraging him, had jeered at him, and he, too, with the others. They had teased him, called him Noah, and monk; and, when he had broken out, no one had helped him, but everyone had turned away from him with horror and disgust.

Levin felt that, in spite of all the ugliness of his life, his brother Nikolay, in his soul, in the very depths of his soul, was no more in the wrong than the people who despised him. He was not to blame for having been born with his unbridled temperament and his somehow limited intelligence. But he had always wanted to be good. 'I will tell him everything, without reserve, and I will make him speak without reserve too, and I'll show him that I love him, and so understand him,' Levin resolved to himself, as, towards eleven o'clock, he reached the hotel of which he had the address.

'At the top, 12 and 13,' the porter answered Levin's inquiry.

'At home?'

'Sure to be at home.'

The door of No. 12 was half open, and there came out into the streak of light thick fumes of cheap, poor tobacco, and the sound of a voice, unknown to Levin; but he knew at once that his brother was there; he heard his cough.

As he went in at the door, the unknown voice was saying—

'It all depends with how much judgment and knowledge the thing's done.'

Konstantin Levin looked in at the door, and saw that the speaker was a young man with an immense shock of hair, wearing a Russian jerkin, and that a pock-marked woman in a woollen gown, without collar or cuffs, was sitting on the sofa. His brother was not to be seen. Konstantin felt a sharp pang at his heart at the thought of the strange company in which his brother spent his life. No one had heard him, and Konstantin, taking off his goloshes, listened to what the gentleman in the jerkin was saying. He was speaking of some enterprise.

'Well, the devil flay them, the privileged classes,' his brother's voice responded, with a cough. 'Masha! get us some supper and some wine if there's any left; or else go and get some.'

The woman rose, came out from behind the screen, and saw Konstantin.

'There's some gentleman, Nikolay Dmitrich,' she said.

'Whom do you want?' said the voice of Nikolay Levin, angrily.

'It's I,' answered Konstantin Levin, coming forward into the light.

'Who's *I*?' Nikolay's voice said again, still more angrily. He could be heard getting up hurriedly, stumbling against something, and Levin saw, facing him in the doorway, the big scared eyes, and the huge, thin, stooping figure of his brother, so familiar, and yet astonishing in its weirdness and sickliness.

He was even thinner than three years before, when Konstantin Levin had seen him last. He was wearing a short coat, and his hands and big bones seemed huger than ever. His hair had grown thinner, the same straight moustaches hid his lips, the same eyes gazed strangely and naïvely at his visitor.

'Ah, Kostya!' he exclaimed suddenly, recognising his brother, and his eyes lighted up with joy. But the same second he looked round at the young man, and gave the nervous jerk of his head and neck that Konstantin knew so well, as if his neckband hurt him; and a quite different expression, wild, suffering, and cruel, rested on his emaciated face.

'I wrote to you and Sergey Ivanovitch both that I don't know you and don't want to know you. What is it you want?'

He was not at all the same as Konstantin had been fancying him. The worst and most tiresome part of his character, what made all relations with him so difficult, had been forgotten by Konstantin Levin when he thought of him, and now, when he saw his face, and especially that nervous twitching of his head, he remembered it all.

'I didn't want to see you for anything,' he answered timidly. 'I've simply come to see you.'

His brother's timidity obviously softened Nikolay. His lips twitched.

'Oh, so that's it?' he said. 'Well, come in; sit down. Like some supper? Masha, bring supper for three. No, stop a minute. Do you know who this is?' he said, addressing his brother, and indicating the gentleman in the jerkin: 'This is Mr. Kritsky, my friend from Kiev, a very remarkable man. He's persecuted by the police, of course, because he's not a scoundrel.'

And he looked round in the way he always did at everyone in the room. Seeing that the woman standing in the doorway was moving to go, he shouted to her, 'Wait a minute, I said.' And with the inability to express himself, the incoherence that Konstantin knew so well, he began, with another look round at everyone, to tell his brother Kritsky's story: how he had been expelled the university for starting a benefit society for the poor students and Sunday-schools; and how he had afterwards been a teacher in a peasant school, and how he had been driven out of that too, and had afterwards been condemned for something.

'You're of the Kiev university?' said Konstantin Levin to Kritsky, to break the awkward silence that followed.

'Yes, I was of Kiev,' Kritsky replied angrily, his face darkening.

'And this woman,' Nikolay Levin interrupted him, pointing to her, 'is the partner of my life, Marya Nikolaevna. I took her out of a bad house,' and he jerked his neck saying this; 'but I love her and respect her, and anyone who wants to know me,' he added, raising his voice and knitting his brows, 'I beg to love her and respect her. She's just the same as my wife, just the same. So now you know whom you've got to do with. And if you think you're lowering yourself, well, here's the floor, there's the door.'

And again his eyes travelled inquiringly over all of them.

'Why I should be lowering myself, I don't understand.'

'Then, Masha, tell them to bring supper: three portions, spirits and wine. . . . No, wait a minute. . . . No, it doesn't matter. . . . Go along.'

XXV

'So you see,' pursued Nikolay Levin, painfully wrinkling his forehead and twitching.

It was obviously difficult for him to think of what to say and do.

'Here, do you see?' . . . He pointed to some sort of iron bars, fastened together with strings, lying in a corner of the room. 'Do you see that? That's the beginning of a new thing we're going into. It's a productive association. . . .'

Konstantin scarcely heard him. He looked into his sickly, consumptive face, and he was more and more sorry for him, and he could not force himself to listen to what his brother was telling him about the association. He saw that this association was a mere anchor to save him from self-contempt. Nikolay Levin went on talking—

'You know that capital oppresses the labourer. The labourers with us, the peasants, bear all the burden of labour, and are so placed that however much they work they can't escape from their position of beasts of burden. All the profits of labour, on which they might improve their position, and gain leisure for themselves, and after that education, all the surplus values are taken from them by the capitalists. And society's so constituted that the harder they work, the greater the profit of the merchants and landowners, while they stay beasts of burden to the end. And that state of things must be changed,' he finished up, and he looked questioningly at his brother.

'Yes, of course,' said Konstantin, looking at the patch of red that had come out on his brother's projecting cheek-bones.

'And so we're founding a locksmith's association, where all the production and profit and the chief instruments of production will be in common.'

'Where is the association to be?' asked Konstantin Levin.

'In the village of Vozdrem, Kazan government.'

'But why in a village? In the villages, I think, there is plenty of work as it is. Why a locksmiths' association in a village?'

'Why? Because the peasants are just as much slaves as they ever were, and that's why you and Sergey Ivanovitch don't like people to try and get them out of their slavery,' said Nikolay Levin, exasperated by the objection.

Konstantin Levin sighed, looking meanwhile about the cheerless and dirty room. This sigh seemed to exasperate Nikolay still more.

'I know your and Sergey Ivanovitch's aristocratic views. I know that he applies all the power of his intellect to justify existing evils.'

'No; and what do you talk of Sergey Ivanovitch for?' said Levin, smiling.

'Sergey Ivanovitch? I'll tell you what for!' Nikolay Levin shrieked suddenly at the name of Sergey Ivanovitch. 'I'll tell you what for. . . . But what's the use of talking? There's only one thing. . . . What did you come to me for? You look down on this, and you're welcome to,—and go away, in God's name go away!' he shrieked, getting up from his chair. 'And go away, and go away!'

'I don't look down on it at all,' said Konstantin Levin timidly. 'I don't even dispute it.'

At that instant Marya Nikolaevna came back. Nikolay Levin looked round angrily at her. She went quickly to him, and whispered something.

'I'm not well; I've grown irritable,' said Nikolay Levin, getting calmer and breathing painfully; 'and then you talk to me of Sergey Ivanovitch and his article. It's such rubbish, such lying, such self-deception. What can a man write of justice who knows nothing of it? Have you read his article?' he asked Kritsky, sitting down again at the table, and moving back off half of it the scattered cigarettes, so as to clear a space.

'I've not read it,' Kritsky responded gloomily, obviously not desiring to enter into the conversation.

'Why not?' said Nikolay Levin, now turning with exasperation upon Kritsky.

'Because I didn't see the use of wasting my time over it.'

'Oh, but excuse me, how did you know it would be wasting your time? That article's too deep for many people—that's to say it's over their heads. But with me, it's another thing; I see through his ideas, and I know where its weakness lies.'

Everyone was mute. Kritsky got up deliberately and reached his cap.

'Won't you have supper? All right, good-bye! Come round tomorrow with the locksmith.'

Kritsky had hardly gone out when Nikolay Levin smiled and winked.

'He's no good either,' he said. 'I see, of course . . .'

But at that instant Kritsky, at the door, called him.

'What do you want now?' he said, and went out to him in the passage. Left alone with Marya Nikolaevna, Levin turned to her.

'Have you been long with my brother?' he said to her.

'Yes, more than a year. Nikolay Dmitritch's health has become very poor. Nikolay Dmitritch drinks a great deal,' she said.

'That is . . . how does he drink?'

'Drinks vodka, and it's bad for him.'

'And a great deal?' whispered Levin.

'Yes,' she said, looking timidly towards the doorway, where Nikolay Levin had reappeared.

'What were you talking about?' he said, knitting his brows, and turning his scared eyes from one to the other. 'What was it?'

'Oh, nothing,' Konstantin answered in confusion.

'Oh, if you don't want to say, don't. Only it's no good your talking to her. She's a wench, and you're a gentleman,' he said with a jerk of the neck. 'You understand everything, I see, and have taken stock of everything, and look with commiseration on my shortcomings,' he began again, raising his voice.

'Nikolay Dmitritch, Nikolay Dmitritch,' whispered Marya Nikolaevna, again going up to him.

'Oh, very well, very well! . . . But where's the supper? Ah, here it is,' he said, seeing a waiter with a tray. 'Here, set it here,' he added angrily, and promptly seizing the vodka, he poured out a glassful and drank it greedily. 'Like a drink?' he turned to his brother, and at once became better humoured.

'Well, enough of Sergey Ivanovitch. I'm glad to see you, anyway.

After all's said and done, we're not strangers. Come, have a drink. Tell me what you're doing,' he went on, greedily munching a piece of bread, and pouring out another glassful. 'How are you living?'

'I live alone in the country, as I used to. I'm busy looking after the land,' answered Konstantin, watching with horror the greediness with which his brother ate and drank, and trying to conceal that he noticed it.

'Why don't you get married?'

'It hasn't happened so,' Konstantin answered, reddening a little.

'Why not? For me now . . . everything's at an end! I've made a mess of my life. But this I've said, and I say still, that if my share had been given me when I needed it, my whole life would have been different.'

Konstantin made haste to change the conversation.

'Do you know your little Vanya's with me, a clerk in the counting-house at Pokrovsky.'

Nikolay jerked his neck, and sank into thought.

'Yes, tell me what's going on at Pokrovsky. Is the house standing still, and the birch-trees, and our schoolroom? And Philip the gardener, is he living? How I remember the arbour and the seat! Now mind and don't alter anything in the house, but make haste and get married, and make everything as it used to be again. Then I'll come and see you, if your wife is nice.'

'But come to me now,' said Levin. 'How nicely we could arrange it!'

'I'd come and see you if I were sure I should not find Sergey Ivanovitch.'

'You wouldn't find him there. I live quite independently of him.'

'Yes, but say what you like, you will have to choose between me and him,' he said, looking timidly into his brother's face.

This timidity touched Konstantin.

'If you want to hear my confession of faith on the subject, I tell you that in your quarrel with Sergey Ivanovitch I take neither side. You're both wrong. You're more wrong externally, and he inwardly.'

'Ah, ah! You see that, you see that!' Nikolay shouted joyfully.

'But I, personally, value friendly relations with you more because . . .'

'Why, why?'

Konstantin could not say that he valued it more because Nikolay was unhappy, and needed affection. But Nikolay knew that this was just what he meant to say, and scowling he took up the vodka again.

'Enough, Nikolay Dmitritch!' said Marya Nikolaevna, stretching out her plump, bare arm toward the decanter.

'Let it be! Don't insist! I'll beat you!' he shouted.

Marya Nikolaevna smiled a sweet and good-humoured smile, which was at once reflected on Nickolay's face, and she took the bottle.

'And do you suppose she understands nothing?' said Nikolay. 'She understands it all better than any of us. Isn't it true there's something good and sweet in her?'

'Were you never before in Moscow?' Konstantin said to her, for the sake of saying something.

'Only you mustn't be polite and stiff with her. It frightens her. No one ever spoke to her so but the justices of the peace who tried her for trying to get out of a house of ill-fame. Mercy on us, the senselessness in the world!' he cried suddenly. 'These new institutions, these justices of the peace, rural councils, what hideousness it all is!'

And he began to enlarge on his encounters with the new institutions.

Konstantin Levin heard him, and the disbelief in the sense of all public institutions, which he shared with him, and often expressed, was distasteful to him now from his brother's lips.

'In another world we shall understand it all,' he said lightly.

'In another world! Ah, I don't like that other world! I don't like it,' he said, letting his scared eyes rest on his brother's eyes. 'Here one would think that to get out of all the baseness and the mess, one's own and other people's, would be a good thing, and yet I'm afraid of death, awfully afraid of death.' He shuddered. 'But do drink something. Would you like some champagne? Or shall we go somewhere? Let's go to the Gypsies! Do you know I have got so fond of the Gypsies and Russian songs.'

His speech had begun to falter, and he passed abruptly from one subject to another. Konstantin with the help of Masha persuaded him not to go out anywhere, and got him to bed hopelessly drunk.

Masha promised to write to Konstantin in case of need, and to persuade Nikolay Levin to go and stay with his brother.

XXVI

IN the morning Konstantin Levin left Moscow, and towards evening he reached home. On the journey in the train he talked to his neighbours about politics and the new railways, and, just as in Moscow, he was overcome by a sense of confusion of ideas, dissatisfaction with himself, shame of something or other. But when he got out at his own station, when he saw his one-eyed coachman, Ignat, with the collar of his coat turned up; when, in the dim light reflected by the station fires, he saw his own sledge, his own horses with their tails tied up, in their harness trimmed with rings and tassels; when the coachman Ignat, as he put in his luggage, told him the village news, that the contractor had arrived, and that Pava had calved,—he felt that little by little the confusion was clearing up, and the shame and self-dissatisfaction were passing away. He felt this at the mere sight of Ignat and the horses; but when he had put on the sheepskin brought for him, had sat down wrapped up in the sledge, and had driven off pondering on the work that lay before him in the village, and staring at the side-horse, who had been his saddle-horse, past his prime now, but a spirited beast from the Don, he began to see what had happened to him in quite a different light. He felt himself, and did not want to be anyone else. All he wanted now was to be better than before. In the first place he resolved that from that day he would give up hoping for any extraordinary happiness, such as marriage must have given him, and consequently he would not so disdain what he really had. Secondly, he would never again let himself give way to love passion, the memory of which had so tortured him when he had been making up his mind to make an offer. Then remembering his brother Nikolay, he resolved to himself that he would never allow himself to forget him, that he would follow him up, and not lose sight of him, so as to be ready to help when things should go ill with him. And that would be soon, he felt. Then too his brother's talk of communism, which he had treated so lightly at the time, now made him think. He considered a revolution in economic conditions nonsense. But he always felt the injustice of his own abundance in comparison with the poverty of the peasants, and now he determined that so as to feel quite in the right, though he had worked hard and lived by no means luxuriously before, he would now work still harder, and would allow himself even less luxury. And all this seemed to him so easy a conquest over himself that he spent the whole drive in the pleasantest day-dreams. With a resolute feeling of hope in a new, better life, he reached home before nine o'clock at night.

The snow of the little quadrangle before the house was lit up by a light in the bedroom windows of his old nurse, Agafea Mihalovna, who performed the duties of housekeeper in his house. She was not yet asleep. Kouzma, waked up by her, came sidling sleepily out on to the steps. A setter bitch, Laska, ran out too, almost upsetting Kouzma, and whining, turned round about Levin's knees, jumping up and longing, but not daring, to put her forepaws on his chest.

'You're soon back again, sir,' said Agafea Mihalovna.

'I got tired of it, Agafea Mihalovna. With friends, one is well; but at home, one is better,' he answered, and went into his study.

The study was slowly lit up as the candle was brought in. The familiar details came out: the stag's horns, the bookshelves, the looking-glass, the stove with its ventilator, which had long wanted mending, his father's sofa, a large table, on the table an open book, a broken ash-tray, a manuscript-book with his handwriting. As he saw all this, there came over him for an instant a doubt of the possibility of arranging the new life, of which he had been dreaming on the road. All these traces of his life seemed to clutch him, and to say to him: 'No, you're not going to get away from us, and you're not going to be different, but you're going to be the same as you've always been; with doubts, everlasting dissatisfaction with yourself, vain efforts to amend, and falls, and everlasting expectation of a happiness which you won't get, and which isn't possible for you.'

This the things said to him, but another voice in his heart was telling him that he must not fall under the sway of the past, and that one can do anything with oneself. And hearing that voice, he went into the corner where stood his two heavy dumb-bells, and began brandishing them like a gymnast, trying to restore his confident temper. There was a creak of steps at the door. He hastily put down the dumb-bells.

The bailiff came in, and said that everything, thank God, was doing well; but informed him that the buckwheat in the new drying-machine had been a little scorched. This piece of news irritated Levin. The new drying-machine had been constructed and partly invented by Levin. The bailiff had always been against the drying-machine, and now it was with suppressed triumph that he announced that the buckwheat had been scorched. Levin was firmly convinced that if the buckwheat had been scorched, it was only because the precautions had not been taken, for which he had hundreds of times given orders. He was annoyed, and reprimanded the bailiff. But there had been an important and joyful event: Pava, his best cow, an expensive beast, bought at a show, had calved.

'Kouzma, give me my sheepskin. And you tell them to take a lantern. I'll come and look at her,' he said to the bailiff.

The cowhouse for the more valuable cows was just behind the house. Walking across the yard, passing a snowdrift by the lilac-tree, he went into the cowhouse. There was the warm, steamy smell of dung when the frozen door was opened, and the cows, astonished at the unfamiliar light of the lantern, stirred on the fresh straw. He caught a glimpse of the broad, smooth, black and piebald back of Hollandka. Berkoot, the bull, was lying down with his ring in his lip, and seemed about to get up, but thought better of it, and only gave two snorts as they passed by him. Pava, a perfect beauty, huge as a hippopotamus, with her back turned to them, prevented their seeing the calf, as she sniffed her all over.

Levin went into the pen, looked Pava over, and lifted the red and spotted calf on to her long, tottering legs. Pava, uneasy, began lowing, but when Levin put the calf close to her she was soothed, and sighing heavily, began licking her with her rough tongue. The calf, fumbling, poked her nose under her mother's udder, and stiffened her tail out straight.

'Here, bring the light, Fyodor, this way,' said Levin, examining the calf. 'Like the mother! though the colour takes after the father; but that's nothing. Very good. Long and broad in the haunch. Vassily Fedorovitch, isn't she splendid?' he said to the bailiff, quite forgiving him for the buckwheat under the influence of his delight in the calf.

'How could she fail to be? Oh, Semyon the contractor came the day after you left. You must settle with him, Konstantin Dmitritch,' said the bailiff. 'I did inform you about the machine.'

This question was enough to take Levin back to all the details of his work on the estate, which was on a large scale, and complicated. He went straight from the cowhouse to the counting-house, and after a little conversation with the bailiff and Semyon the contractor, he went back to the house and straight upstairs to the drawing-room.

XXVII

THE house was big and old fashioned, and Levin, though he lived alone, had the whole house heated and used. He knew that this was stupid, he knew that it was positively not right, and contrary to his present new plans, but this house was a whole world to Levin. It was the world in which his father and mother had lived and died. They had lived just the life that to Levin seemed the ideal of perfection, and that he had dreamed of beginning with his wife, his family.

Levin scarcely remembered his mother. His conception of her was for him a sacred memory, and his future wife was bound to be in his imagination a repetition of that exquisite, holy ideal of a woman that his mother had been.

He was so far from conceiving of love for woman apart from marriage, that he positively pictured to himself first the family, and only secondarily the woman who would give him a family. His ideas of marriage were, consequently, quite unlike those of the great majority of his acquaintances, for whom getting married was one of the numerous facts of social life. For Levin it was the chief affair of life, on which its whole happiness turned. And now he had to give up that.

When he had gone into the little drawing-room, where he always had tea, and had settled himself in his armchair with a book, and Agafea Mihalovna had brought him tea, and with her usual, 'Well, I'll stay a while, sir,' had taken a chair in the window, he felt that, however strange it might be, he had not parted from his day-dreams, and that he could not live without them. Whether with her, or with another, still it would be. He was reading a book, and thinking of what he was reading, and stopping to listen to Agafea Mihalovna, who gossiped away without flagging, and yet with all that, all sorts of pictures of family life and work in the future rose disconnectedly before his imagination. He felt that in the depth of his soul something had been put in its place, settled down, and laid to rest.

He heard Agafea Mihalovna talking of how Prohor had forgotten his duty to God, and with the money Levin had given him to buy a horse, had been drinking without stopping, and had beaten his wife till he'd half killed her. He listened, and read his book, and recalled the whole train of ideas suggested by his reading. It was Tyndall's *Treatise on Heat*. He recalled his own criticisms of Tyndall for his complacent satisfaction in the cleverness of his experiments, and for his lack of philosophic insight. And suddenly there floated into his mind the joyful thought: 'In two years' time I shall have two Dutch cows; Pava herself will perhaps still be alive, a dozen young daughters of Berkoot and the three others—how lovely!'

He took up his book again. 'Very good, electricity and heat are the same thing; but is it possible to substitute the one quantity for the other in the equation for the solution of any problem? No. Well then, what of it? The connection between all the forces of nature is felt instinctively. . . . It's particularly nice if Pava's daughter should be a red-spotted cow, and all the herd will take after her, and the other three, too! Splendid! To go out with my wife and visitors to meet the herd. . . . My wife says, "Kostya and I looked after that calf like a child." "How can it interest you so much?" says a visitor. "Everything that interests him, interests me." But who will she be?' And he remembered what had happened at Moscow. . . . 'Well, there's nothing to be done. . . . It's not my fault. But now everything shall go on in a new way. It's nonsense to pretend that life won't let one, that the past won't let one. One must struggle to live better, much better.' . . . He raised his head, and fell to dreaming. Old Laska, who had not yet fully digested her delight at his return, and had run out into the yard to bark, came back wagging her tail, and crept up to him, bringing in the scent of the fresh air, put her head under his hand, and whined plaintively, asking to be stroked.

'There, who'd have thought it?' said Agafea Mihalovna. 'The dog now . . . why, she understands that her master's come home, and that he's low-spirited.'

'Why low-spirited?'

'Do you suppose I don't see it, sir? It's high time I should know the gentry. Why, I've grown up from a little thing with them. It's nothing, sir, so long as there's health and a clear conscience.'

Levin looked intently at her, surprised at how well she knew his thought.

'Shall I fetch you another cup?' said she, and taking his cup she went out.

Laska kept poking her head under his hand. He stroked her, and she promptly curled up at his feet, laying her head on a hind-paw. And in token of all now being well and satisfactory, she opened her mouth a little, smacked her lips, and settling her sticky lips more comfortably about her old teeth, she sank into blissful repose. Levin watched all her movements attentively.

'That's what I'll do,' he said to himself; 'that's what I'll do! Nothing's amiss. . . . All's well.'

XXVIII

AFTER the ball, early next morning, Anna Arkadyevna sent her husband a telegram that she was leaving Moscow the same day.

'No, I must go, I must go'; she explained to her sister-in-law the change in her plans in a tone that suggested that she had to remember so many things that there was no enumerating them: 'no, it had really better be today!'

Stepan Arkadyevitch was not dining at home, but he promised to come and see his sister off at seven o'clock.

Kitty, too, did not come, sending a note that she had a headache. Dolly and Anna dined alone with the children and the English governess. Whether it was that the children were fickle, or that they had acute senses, and felt that Anna was quite different that day from what she had been when they had taken such a fancy to her, that she was not now interested in them,— but they had abruptly dropped their play with their aunt, and their love for her, and were quite indifferent that she was going away. Anna was absorbed the whole morning in preparations for her departure. She wrote notes to her Moscow acquaintances, put down her accounts, and packed. Altogether Dolly fancied she was not in a placid state of mind, but in that worried mood, which Dolly knew well with herself, and which does not come without cause, and for the most part covers dissatisfaction with self. After dinner, Anna went up to her room to dress, and Dolly followed her.

'How queer you are today!' Dolly said to her.

'I? Do you think so? I'm not queer, but I'm nasty. I am like that sometimes. I keep feeling as if I could cry. It's very stupid, but it'll pass off,' said Anna quickly, and she bent her flushed face over a tiny bag in which she was packing a nightcap and some cambric handkerchiefs. Her eyes were peculiarly bright, and were continually swimming with tears. 'In the same way I didn't want to leave Petersburg, and now I don't want to go away from here.'

'You came here and did a good deed,' said Dolly, looking intently at her.

Anna looked at her with eyes wet with tears.

'Don't say that, Dolly. I've done nothing, and could do nothing. I often wonder why people are all in league to spoil me. What have I done, and what could I do? In your heart there was found love enough to forgive . . .'

'If it had not been for you, God knows what would have happened! How happy you are, Anna!' said Dolly. 'Everything is clear and good in your heart.'

'Every heart has its own *skeletons*, as the English say.'

'You have no sort of *skeleton*, have you? Everything is so clear in you.'

'I have!' said Anna suddenly, and, unexpectedly after her tears, a sly, ironical smile curved her lips.

'Come, he's amusing, anyway, your *skeleton*, and not depressing,' said Dolly, smiling.

'No, he's depressing. Do you know why I'm going today instead of tomorrow? It's a confession that weighs on me; I want to make it to you,' said Anna, letting herself drop definitely into an armchair, and looking straight into Dolly's face.

And to her surprise Dolly saw that Anna was blushing up to her ears, up to the curly black ringlets on her neck.

'Yes,' Anna went on. 'Do you know why Kitty didn't come to dinner? She's jealous of me. I have spoiled . . . I've been the cause of that ball being a torture to her instead of a pleasure. But truly, truly, it's not my fault, or only my fault a little bit,' she said, daintily drawling the words 'a little bit.'

'Oh, how like Stiva you said that!' said Dolly, laughing.

Anna was hurt.

'Oh no, oh no! I'm not Stiva,' she said, knitting her brows. 'That's why I'm telling you, just because I could never let myself doubt myself for an instant,' said Anna.

But at the very moment she was uttering the words, she felt that they were not true. She was not merely doubting of herself, she felt emotion at the thought of Vronsky, and was going away sooner than she had meant, simply to avoid meeting him.

'Yes, Stiva told me you danced the mazurka with him, and that he . . .'

'You can't imagine how absurdly it all came about. I only meant to be matchmaking, and all at once it turned out quite differently. Possibly against my own will . . .'

She crimsoned and stopped.

'Oh, they feel it directly!' said Dolly.

'But I should be in despair if there were anything serious in it on his side,' Anna interrupted her. 'And I am certain it will all be forgotten, and Kitty will leave off hating me.'

'All the same, Anna, to tell you the truth, I'm not very anxious for this marriage for Kitty. And it's better it should come to nothing, if he, Vronsky, is capable of falling in love with you in a single day.'

'Oh, heavens, that would be too silly!' said Anna, and again a deep flush of pleasure came out on her face, when she heard the idea, that absorbed her, put into words. 'And so here I am going away, having made an enemy of Kitty, whom I liked so much! Ah, how sweet she is! But you'll make it right, Dolly? Eh?'

Dolly could scarcely suppress a smile. She loved Anna, but she enjoyed seeing that she too had her weaknesses.

'An enemy? That can't be.'

'I did so want you all to care for me, as I do for you, and now I care for you more than ever,' said Anna, with tears in her eyes. 'Ah, how silly I am today!'

She passed her handkerchief over her face and began dressing.

At the very moment of starting Stepan Arkadyevitch arrived, late, rosy and good-humoured, smelling of wine and cigars.

Anna's emotionalism infected Dolly, and when she embraced her sister-in-law for the last time, she whispered: 'Remember, Anna, what you've done for me,—I shall never forget. And remember that I love you, and shall always love you as my dearest friend!'

'I don't know why,' said Anna, kissing her and hiding her tears.

'You understood me, and you understand. Good-bye, my darling!'

XXIX

'COME, it's all over, and thank God!' was the first thought that came to Anna Arkadyevna, when she had said good-bye for the last time to her brother, who had stood blocking up the entrance to the carriage till the third bell rang. She sat down on her lounge beside Annushka, and looked about her in the twilight of the sleeping-carriage. 'Thank God! tomorrow I shall see Seryozha and Alexey Alexandrovitch, and my life will go on in the old way, all nice and as usual.'

Still in the same anxious frame of mind, as she had been all that day, Anna took pleasure in arranging herself for the journey with great care. With her little deft hands she opened and shut her little red bag, took out a cushion, laid it on her knees, and carefully wrapping up her feet, settled herself comfortably. An invalid lady had already lain down to sleep. Two other ladies began talking to Anna, and a stout elderly lady tucked up her feet, and made observations about the heating of the train. Anna answered a few words, but not foreseeing any entertainment from the conversation, she asked Annushka to get a lamp, hooked it on to the arm of her seat, and took from her bag a paper-knife and an English novel. At first her reading made no progress. The fuss and bustle was disturbing; then when the train had started, she could not help listening to the noises; then the snow beating on the left window and sticking to the pane, and the sight of the muffled guard passing by, covered with snow on one side, and the conversations about the terrible snowstorm raging outside, distracted her attention. Further on, it was continually the same again and again: the same shaking and rattling, the same snow on the window, the same rapid transitions from steaming heat to cold, and back again to heat, the same passing glimpses of the same figures in the twilight, and the same voices, and Anna began to read and to understand what she read. Annushka was already dozing, the red bag on her lap, clutched by her broad hands, in gloves, of which one was torn. Anna Arkadyevna read and understood; but it was distasteful to her to read, that is, to follow the reflection of other people's lives. She had too great a desire to live herself. If she read that the heroine of the novel were nursing a sick man, she longed to move with noiseless steps about the room of a sick man; if she read of a member of Parliament making a speech, she longed to be delivering the speech; if she read of how Lady Mary had ridden after the hounds, and had provoked her sister-in-law, and had surprised everyone by her boldness, she too wished to be doing the same. But there was no chance of doing anything; and twisting the smooth paper-knife in her little hands, she forced herself to read.

The hero of the novel was already almost reaching his English happiness, a baronetcy and an estate, and Anna was feeling a desire to go with him to the estate, when she suddenly felt that *he* ought to feel ashamed, and that she was ashamed of the same thing. But what had he to be ashamed of? 'What have I to be ashamed of?' she asked herself in injured surprise. She laid down the book and sank against the back of the chair, tightly gripping the paper-cutter in both hands. There was nothing. She went over all her Moscow recollections. All were good, pleasant. She remembered the ball, remembered Vronsky and his face of slavish adoration, remembered all her conduct with him: there was nothing shameful. And for all that, at the same point in her memories, the feeling of shame was intensified, as though some inner voice, just at the point when she thought of Vronsky, were saying to her, 'Warm, very warm, hot.' 'Well, what is it?' she said to herself resolutely, shifting her seat in the lounge. 'What does it mean? Am I afraid to look it straight in the face? Why, what is it? Can it be that between me and this officer boy there exists, or can exist, any other relations than such as are common with every acquaintance?' She laughed contemptuously and took up her book again; but now she was definitely unable to follow what she read. She passed the paper-knife over the window-pane, then laid its smooth, cool surface to her cheek, and almost laughed aloud at the feeling of delight that all at once without cause came over her. She felt as though her nerves were strings being strained tighter and tighter on some sort of screwing peg. She felt her eyes opening wider and wider, her fingers and toes twitching nervously, something within oppressing her breathing, while all shapes and sounds seemed in the uncertain half-light to strike her with unaccustomed vividness. Moments of doubt were continually coming upon her, when she was uncertain whether the train were going forwards or backwards, or were standing still altogether; whether it were Annushka at her side or a stranger. 'What's that on the arm of the chair, a fur cloak or some beast? And what am I myself? Myself or some other woman?' She was afraid of giving way to this delirium. But something drew her towards it, and she could yield to it or resist it at will. She got up to rouse herself, and slipped off her plaid and the cape of her warm dress. For a moment she regained her self-possession, and realised that the thin peasant who had come in wearing a long overcoat, with buttons missing from it, was the stoveheater, that he was looking at the thermometer, that it was the wind and snow bursting in after him at the door; but then everything grew blurred again . . . That peasant with the long waist seemed to be gnawing something on the wall, the old lady began stretching her legs the whole length of the carriage, and filling it with a black cloud; then there was a fearful shrieking and banging, as though someone were being torn to pieces; then there was a blinding dazzle of red fire before her eyes and a wall seemed to rise up and hide everything. Anna felt as though she were sinking down. But it was not terrible, but delightful. The voice of a man muffled up and covered with snow shouted something in her ear. She got up and pulled herself together; she realised that they had reached a station and that this was the guard. She asked Annushka to hand her the cape she had taken off and her shawl, put them on and moved towards the door.

'Do you wish to get out?' asked Annushka.

'Yes, I want a little air. It's very hot in here.' And she opened the door. The driving snow and the wind rushed to meet her and struggled with her over the door. But she enjoyed the struggle.

She opened the door and went out. The wind seemed as though lying in wait for her; with gleeful whistle it tried to snatch her up and bear her off, but she clung to the cold doorpost, and holding her skirt got down on to the platform and under the shelter of the carriages. The wind had been powerful on the steps, but on the platform, under the lee of the carriages, there was a lull. With enjoyment she drew deep breaths of the frozen, snowy air, and standing near the carriage looked about the platform and the lighted station.

XXX

THE raging tempest rushed whistling between the wheels of the carriages, about the scaffolding, and round the corner of the station. The carriages, posts, people, everything that was to be seen was covered with snow on one side, and was getting more and more thickly covered. For a moment there would come a lull in the storm, but then it would swoop down again with such onslaughts that it seemed impossible to stand against it. Meanwhile men ran to and fro, talking merrily together, their steps crackling on the platform as they continually opened and closed the big doors. The bent shadow of a man glided by at her feet, and she heard sounds of a hammer upon iron. 'Hand over that telegram!' came an angry voice out of the stormy darkness on the other side. 'This way! No. 28!' several different voices shouted again, and muffled figures ran by covered with snow. Two gentlemen with lighted cigarettes passed by her. She drew one more deep breath of the fresh air, and had just put her hand out of her muff to take hold of the doorpost and get back into the carriage, when another man in a military overcoat, quite close beside her, stepped between her and the flickering light of the lamp-post. She looked round, and the same instant recognised Vronsky's face. Putting his hand to the peak of his cap, he bowed to her and asked, 'Was there anything she wanted? Could he be of any service to her?' She gazed rather a long while at him without answering, and, in spite of the shadow in which he was standing, she saw, or fancied she saw, both the expression of his face and his eyes. It was again that expression of reverential ecstasy which had so worked upon her the day before. More than once she had told herself during the past few days, and again only a few moments before, that Vronsky was for her only one of the hundreds of young men, for ever exactly the same, that are met everywhere, that she would never allow herself to bestow a thought upon him. But now at the first instant of meeting him, she was seized by a feeling of joyful pride. She had no need to ask why he had come. She knew as certainly as if he had told her that he was here to be where she was.

'I didn't know you were going. What are you coming for?' she said, letting fall the hand with which she had grasped the doorpost. And irrepressible delight and eagerness shone in her face.

'What am I coming for?' he repeated, looking straight into her eyes. 'You know that I have come to be where you are,' he said, 'I can't help it.'

At that moment the wind, as it were surmounting all obstacles, sent the snow flying from the carriage roofs, and clanked some sheet of iron it had torn off, while the hoarse whistle of the engine roared in front, plaintively and gloomily. All the awfulness of the storm seemed to her more splendid now. He had said what her soul longed to hear, though she feared it with her reason. She made no answer, and in her face he saw conflict.

'Forgive me, if you dislike what I said,' he said humbly.

He had spoken courteously, deferentially, yet so firmly, so stubbornly, that for a long while she could make no answer.

'It's wrong, what you say, and I beg you, if you're a good man, to forget what you've said, as I forget it,' she said at last.

'Not one word, not one gesture of yours shall I, could I, ever forget. . . .'

'Enough, enough!' she cried, trying assiduously to give a stern expression to her face, into which he was gazing greedily. And clutching at the cold doorpost, she clambered up the steps and got rapidly into the corridor of the carriage. But in the little corridor she paused, going over in her imagination what had happened. Though she could not recall her own words or his, she realised instinctively that that momentary conversation had brought them fearfully closer; and she was panic-stricken and blissful at it. After standing still a few seconds, she went into the carriage and sat down in her place. The overstrained condition which had tormented her before did not only come back, but was intensified, and reached such a pitch that she was afraid every minute that something would snap within her from the excessive tension. She did not sleep all night. But in that nervous tension, and in the visions that filled her imagination, there was nothing disagreeable or gloomy: on the contrary there was something blissful, glowing, and exhilarating. Towards morning Anna sank into a doze, sitting in her place, and when she waked it was daylight and the train was near Petersburg. At once thoughts of home, of husband and of son, and the details of that day and the following came upon her.

At Petersburg, so soon as the train stopped and she got out, the first person that attracted her attention was her husband. 'Oh, mercy! why do his ears look like that?' she thought, looking at his frigid and imposing figure, and especially the ears that struck her at the moment as propping up the brim of his round hat. Catching sight of her, he came to meet her, his lips falling into their habitual sarcastic smile, and his big, tired eyes looking straight at her. An unpleasant sensation gripped at her heart when she met his obstinate and weary glance, as though she had expected to see him different. She was especially struck by the feeling of dissatisfaction with herself that she experienced on meeting him. That feeling was an intimate, familiar feeling, like a consciousness of hypocrisy, which she experienced in her relations with her husband. But hitherto she had not taken note of the feeling, now she was clearly and painfully aware of it.

'Yes, as you see, your tender spouse, as devoted as the first year after marriage, burned with impatience to see you,' he said in his deliberate, high-pitched voice, and in that tone which he almost always took with her, a tone of jeering at anyone who should say in earnest what he said.

'Is Seryozha quite well?' she asked.

'And is this all the reward,' said he, 'for my ardour? He's quite well....'

XXXI

VRONSKY had not even tried to sleep all that night. He sat in his armchair, looking straight before him or scanning the people who got in and out. If he had indeed on previous occasions struck and impressed people who did not know him by his air of unhesitating composure, he seemed now more haughty and self-possessed than ever. He looked at people as if they were things. A nervous young man, a clerk in a law-court, sitting opposite him, hated him for that look. The young man asked him for a light, and entered into conversation with him, and even pushed against him, to make him feel that he was not a thing, but a person. But Vronsky gazed at him exactly as he did at the lamp, and the young man made a wry face, feeling that he was losing his self-possession under the oppression of this refusal to recognise him as a person.

Vronsky saw nothing and no one. He felt himself a king, not because he believed that he had made an impression on Anna—he did not yet believe that,—but because the impression she had made on him gave him happiness and pride.

What would come of it all he did not know, he did not even think. He felt that all his forces, hitherto dissipated, wasted, were centred on one thing, and bent with fearful energy on one blissful goal. And he was happy at it. He knew only that he had told her the truth, that he had come where she was, that all the happiness of his life, the only meaning in life for him, now lay in seeing and hearing her. And when he got out of the carriage at Bologova to get some seltzer water, and caught sight of Anna, involuntarily his first word had told her just what he thought. And he was glad he had told her it, that she knew it now and was thinking of it. He did not sleep all night. When he was back in the carriage, he kept unceasingly going over every position in which he had seen her, every word she had uttered, and before his fancy, making his heart faint with emotion, floated pictures of a possible future.

When he got out of the train at Petersburg, he felt after his sleepless night as keen and fresh as after a cold bath. He paused near his compartment, waiting for her to get out. 'Once more,' he said to himself, smiling unconsciously, 'once more I shall see her walk, her face; she will say something, turn her head, glance, smile, maybe.' But before he caught sight of her, he saw her husband, whom the stationmaster was deferentially escorting through the crowd. 'Ah, yes! The husband.' Only now for the first time did Vronsky realise clearly the fact that there was a person attached to her, a husband. He knew that she had a husband, but had hardly believed in his existence, and only now fully believed in him, with his head and shoulders, and his legs clad in black trousers; especially when he saw this husband calmly take her arm with a sense of property.

Seeing Alexey Alexandrovitch with his Petersburg face and severely self-confident figure, in his round hat, with his rather prominent spine, he believed in him, and was aware of a disagreeable sensation, such as a man might feel tortured by thirst, who, on reaching a spring, should find a dog, a sheep, or a pig, who has drunk of it and muddied the water. Alexey Alexandrovitch's manner of walking, with a swing of the hips and flat feet, particularly annoyed Vronsky. He could recognise in no one but himself an indubitable right to love her. But she was still the same, and the sight of her affected him the same way, physically reviving him, stirring him, and filling his soul with rapture. He told his German valet, who ran up to him from the second-class, to take his things and go on, and he himself went up to her. He saw the first meeting between the husband and wife, and noted with a lover's insight the signs of slight reserve with which she spoke to her husband. 'No, she does not love him and cannot love him,' he decided to himself.

At the moment when he was approaching Anna Arkadyevna he noticed too with joy that she was conscious of his being near, and looked round, and seeing him, turned again to her husband.

'Have you had a good night?' he said, bowing to her and to her husband together, and leaving it to Alexey Alexandrovitch to accept the bow on his own account, and to recognise it or not, as he might see fit.

'Thank you, very good,' she answered.

Her face looked weary, and there was not that play of eagerness in it, peeping out in her smile and her eyes; but for a single instant, as she glanced at him, there was a flash of something in her eyes, and although the flash died away at once, he was happy for that moment. She glanced at her husband to find out whether he knew Vronsky. Alexey Alexandrovitch looked at Vronsky with displeasure, vaguely recalling who this was. Vronsky's composure and self-confidence here struck, like a scythe against a stone, upon the cold self-confidence of Alexey Alexandrovitch.

'Count Vronsky,' said Anna.

'Ah! We are acquainted, I believe,' said Alexey Alexandrovitch indifferently, giving his hand.

'You set off with the mother and you return with the son,' he said, articulating each syllable, as though each were a separate favour he was bestowing.

'You're back from leave, I suppose?' he said, and without waiting for a reply, he turned to his wife in his jesting tone: 'Well, were a great many tears shed at Moscow at parting?'

By addressing his wife like this he gave Vronsky to understand that he wished to be left alone, and, turning slightly towards him, he touched his hat; but Vronsky turned to Anna Arkadyevna.

'I hope I may have the honour of calling on you,' he said.

Alexey Alexandrovitch glanced with his weary eyes at Vronsky.

'Delighted,' he said coldly. 'On Mondays we're at home. Most fortunate,' he said to his wife, dismissing Vronsky altogether, 'that I should just have half an hour to meet you, so that I can prove my devotion,' he went on in the same jesting tone.

'You lay too much stress on your devotion for me to value it much,' she responded in the same jesting tone, involuntarily listening to the sound of Vronsky's steps behind them. 'But what has it to do with me?' she said to herself, and she began asking her husband how Seryozha had got on without her.

'Oh, capitally! Mariette says he has been very good, and . . . I must disappoint you . . . but he has not missed you as your husband has. But once more *merci*, my dear, for giving me a day. Our dear *Samovar* will be delighted.' (He used to call the Countess Lidia Ivanovna, well known in society, a samovar, because she was always bubbling over with excitement.) 'She has been continually asking after you. And, do you know, if I may venture to advise you, you should go and see her to-day. You know how she takes everything to heart. Just now, with all her own cares, she's anxious about the Oblonskys being brought together.'

The Countess Lidia Ivanovna was a friend of her husband's, and the centre of that one of the coteries of the Petersburg world with which Anna was, through her husband, in the closest relations.

'But you know I wrote to her?'

'Still she'll want to hear details. Go and see her, if you're not too tired, my dear. Well, Kondraty will take you in the carriage, while I go to my committee. I shall not be alone at dinner again,' Alexey Alexandrovitch went on, no longer in a sarcastic tone. 'You wouldn't believe how I've missed . . .' And with a long pressure of her hand and a meaning smile, he put her in her carriage.

XXXII

THE first person to meet Anna at home was her son. He dashed down the stairs to her, in spite of the governess's call, and with desperate joy shrieked: 'Mother! mother!' Running up to her, he hung on her neck.

'I told you it was mother!' he shouted to the governess. 'I knew!'

And her son, like her husband, aroused in Anna a feeling akin to disappointment. She had imagined him better than he was in reality. She had to let herself drop down to the reality to enjoy him as he really was. But even as he was, he was charming, with his fair curls, his blue eyes, and his plump, graceful little legs in tightly pulled-up stockings. Anna experienced almost physical pleasure in the sensation of his nearness, and his caresses, and moral soothing, when she met his simple, confiding, and loving glance, and heard his naïve questions. Anna took out the presents Dolly's children had sent him, and told her son what sort of a little girl was Tanya at Moscow, and how Tanya could read, and even taught the other children.

'Why, am I not so nice as she?' asked Seryozha.

'To me you're nicer than anyone in the world.'

'I know that,' said Seryozha, smiling.

Anna had not had time to drink her coffee when the Countess Lidia Ivanovna was announced. The Countess Lidia Ivanovna was a tall, stout woman, with an unhealthily sallow face and splendid, pensive black eyes. Anna liked her, but today she seemed to be seeing her for the first time with all her defects.

'Well, my dear, so you took the olive branch?' inquired Countess Lidia Ivanovna, as soon as she came into the room.

'Yes, it's all over, but it was all much less serious than we had supposed,' answered Anna. 'My *belle-sœur* is in general too hasty.'

But Countess Lidia Ivanovna, though she was interested in everything that did not concern her, had a habit of never listening to what interested her; she interrupted Anna—

'Yes, there's plenty of sorrow and evil in the world. I am so worried today?'

'Oh, why?' asked Anna, trying to suppress a smile.

'I'm beginning to be weary of fruitlessly championing the truth, and sometimes I'm quite unhinged by it. The Society of the Little Sisters' (this was a religiously-patriotic, philanthropic institution) 'was going splendidly, but with these gentlemen it's impossible to do anything,' added Countess Lidia Ivanovna in a tone of ironical submission to destiny. 'They pounce on the idea, and distort it, and then work it out so pettily and unworthily. Two or three people, your husband among them, understand all the importance of the thing, but the others simply drag it down. Yesterday Pravdin wrote to me . . .'

Pravdin was a well-known Panslavist abroad, and Countess Lidia Ivanovna described the purport of his letter.

Then the countess told her of more disagreements and intrigues against the work of the unification of the churches, and departed in haste, as she had that day to be at the meeting of some society and also at the Slavonic committee.

'It was all the same before, of course; but why was it I didn't notice it before?' Anna asked herself. 'Or has she been very much irritated today? It's really ludicrous; her object is doing good; she's a Christian, yet she's always angry; and she always has enemies, and always enemies in the name of Christianity and doing good.'

After Countess Lidia Ivanovna another friend came, the wife of a chief secretary, who told her all the news of the town. At three o'clock she too went away, promising to come to dinner. Alexey Alexandrovitch was at the ministry. Anna, left alone, spent the time till dinner in assisting at her son's dinner (he dined apart from his parents) and in putting her things in order, and in reading and answering the notes and letters which had accumulated on her table.

The feeling of causeless shame, which she had felt on the journey, and her excitement, too, had completely vanished. In the habitual conditions of her life she felt again resolute and irreproachable.

She recalled with wonder her state of mind on the previous day. 'What was it? Nothing. Vronsky said something silly, which it was easy to put a stop to, and I answered as I ought to have done. To speak of it to my husband would be unnecessary and out of the question. To speak of it would be to attach importance to what has no importance.' She remembered how she had told her husband of what was almost a declaration made her at Petersburg by a young man, one of her husband's subordinates, and how Alexey Alexandrovitch had answered that every woman living in the world was exposed to such incidents, but that he had the fullest confidence in her tact, and could never lower her and himself by jealousy. 'So then there's no reason to speak of it? And indeed, thank God, there's nothing to speak of,' she told herself.

XXXIII

ALEXEY ALEXANDROVITCH came back from the meeting of the ministers at four o'clock, but as often happened, he had not time to come in to her. He went into his study to see the people waiting for him with petitions, and to sign some papers brought him by his chief secretary. At dinner-time (there were always a few people dining with the Karenins) there arrived an old lady, a cousin of Alexey Alexandrovitch, the chief secretary of the department and his wife, and a young man who had been recommended to Alexey Alexandrovitch for the service. Anna went into the drawing-room to receive these guests. Precisely at five o'clock, before the bronze Peter the First clock had struck the fifth stroke, Alexey Alexandrovitch came in, wearing a white tie and evening coat with two stars, as he had to go out directly after dinner. Every minute of Alexey Alexandrovitch's life was portioned out and occupied.

And to make time to get through all that lay before him every day, he adhered to the strictest punctuality. 'Unhasting and unresting,' was his motto. He came into the dining-hall, greeted everyone, and hurriedly sat down, smiling to his wife.

'Yes, my solitude is over. You wouldn't believe how uncomfortable' (he laid stress on the word *uncomfortable*) 'it is to dine alone.'

At dinner he talked a little to his wife about Moscow matters, and, with a sarcastic smile, asked her after Stepan Arkadyevitch; but the conversation was for the most part general, dealing with Petersburg official and public news. After dinner he spent half an hour with his guests, and again, with a smile, pressed his wife's hand, withdrew, and drove off to the council. Anna did not go out that evening either to the Princess Betsy Tverskoy, who, hearing of her return, had invited her, nor to the theatre, where she had a box for that evening. She did not go out principally because the dress she had reckoned upon was not ready. Altogether, Anna, on turning, after the departure of her guests, to the consideration of her attire, was very much annoyed. She was generally a mistress of the art of dressing well without great expense, and before leaving Moscow she had given her dressmaker three dresses to transform. The dresses had to be altered so that they could not be recognised, and they ought to have been ready three days before. It appeared that two dresses had not been done at all, while the other one had not been altered as Anna had intended. The dressmaker came to explain, declaring that it would be better as she had done it, and Anna was so furious that she felt ashamed when she thought of it afterwards. To regain her serenity completely she went into the nursery, and spent the whole evening with her son, put him to bed herself, signed him with the cross, and tucked him up. She was glad she had not gone out anywhere, and had spent the evening so well. She felt so light-hearted and serene, she saw so clearly that all that had seemed to her so important on her railway journey was only one of the common trivial incidents of fashionable life, and that she had no reason to feel ashamed before anyone else or before herself. Anna sat down at the hearth with an English novel and waited for her husband. Exactly at half-past nine she heard his ring, and he came into the room.

'Here you are at last!' she observed, holding out her hand to him.

He kissed her hand and sat down beside her.

'Altogether then, I see your visit was a success,' he said to her.

'Oh yes,' she said, and she began telling him about everything from the beginning: her journey with Countess Vronsky, her arrival, the accident at the station. Then she described the pity she had felt, first for her brother, and afterwards for Dolly.

'I imagine one cannot exonerate such a man from blame, though he is your brother,' said Alexey Alexandrovitch severely.

Anna smiled. She knew that he said that simply to show that family considerations could not prevent him from expressing his genuine opinion. She knew that characteristic in her husband, and liked it.

'I am glad it has all ended so satisfactorily, and that you are back again,' he went on. 'Come, what do they say about the new act I have got passed in the council?'

Anna had heard nothing of this act, and she felt conscience-stricken at having been able so readily to forget what was to him of such importance.

'Here, on the other hand, it has made a great sensation,' he said, with a complacent smile.

She saw Alexey Alexandrovitch wanted to tell her something pleasant to him about it, and she brought him by questions to telling it. With the same complacent smile he told her of the ovations he had received in consequence of the act he had passed.

'I was very, very glad. It shows that at last a reasonable and steady view of the matter is becoming prevalent among us.'

Having drunk his second cup of tea with cream, and bread, Alexey Alexandrovitch got up, and was going towards his study.

'And you've not been anywhere this evening? You've been dull, I expect?' he said.

'Oh no!' she answered, getting up after him and accompanying him across the room to his study. 'What are you reading now?' she asked.

'Just now I'm reading Duc de Lille, *Poésie des Enfers*,' he answered. 'A very remarkable book.'

Anna smiled, as people smile at the weaknesses of those they love, and, putting her hand under his, she escorted him to the door of the study. She knew his habit, that had grown into a necessity, of reading in the evening. She knew, too, that in spite of his official duties, which swallowed up almost the whole of his time, he considered it his duty to keep up with everything of note that appeared in the intellectual world. She knew, too, that he was really interested in books dealing with politics, philosophy, and theology, that art was utterly foreign to his nature; but, in spite of this, or rather, in consequence of it, Alexey Alexandrovitch never missed over anything in the world of art, but made it his duty to read everything. She knew that in politics, in philosophy, in theology, Alexey Alexandrovitch often had doubts, and made investigations; but on questions of art and poetry, and, above all, of music, of which he was totally devoid of understanding, he had the most distinct and decided opinions. He was fond of talking about

Shakespeare, Raphael, Beethoven, of the significance of new schools of poetry and music, all of which were classified by him with very conspicuous consistency.

'Well, God be with you,' she said at the door of the study, where a shaded candle and a decanter of water were already put by his armchair. 'And I'll write to Moscow.'

He pressed her hand, and again kissed it.

'All the same he's a good man; truthful, good-hearted, and remarkable in his own line,' Anna said to herself going back to her room, as though she were defending him to someone who had attacked him and said that one could not love him. 'But why is it his ears stick out so strangely? Or has he had his hair cut?'

Precisely at twelve o'clock, when Anna was still sitting at her writing-table, finishing a letter to Dolly, she heard the sound of measured steps in slippers, and Alexey Alexandrovitch, freshly washed and combed, with a book under his arm, came in to her.

'It's time, it's time,' said he, with a meaning smile, and he went into their bedroom.

'And what right had he to look at him like that?' thought Anna, recalling Vronsky's glance at Alexey Alexandrovitch.

Undressing, she went into the bedroom; but her face had none of the eagerness which, during her stay at Moscow, had fairly flashed from her eyes and her smile; on the contrary, now the fire seemed quenched in her, hidden somewhere far away.

XXXIV

WHEN Vronsky went to Moscow from Petersburg, he had left his large set of rooms in Morskaia to his friend and favourite comrade Petritsky.

Petritsky was a young lieutenant, not particularly well-connected, and not merely not wealthy, but always hopelessly in debt. Towards evening he was always drunk, and he had often been locked up after all sorts of ludicrous and disgraceful scandals, but he was a favourite both of his comrades and his superior officers. On arriving at twelve o'clock from the station at his flat, Vronsky saw, at the outer door, a hired carriage familiar to him. While still outside his own door, as he rang, he heard masculine laughter, the lisp of a feminine voice, and Petritsky's voice. 'If that's one of the villains, don't let him in!' Vronsky told the servant not to announce him, and slipped quietly into the first room. Baroness Shilton, a friend of Petritsky's, with a rosy little face and flaxen-hair, resplendent in a lilac satin gown, and filling the whole room, like a canary, with her Parisian chatter, sat at the round table making coffee. Petritsky, in his overcoat, and the cavalry captain Kamerovsky, in full uniform, probably just come from duty, were sitting each side of her.

'Bravo! Vronsky!' shouted Petritsky, jumping up, scraping his chair. 'Our host himself! Baroness, some coffee for him out of the new coffee-pot. Why, we didn't expect you! Hope you're satisfied with the ornament of your study,' he said, indicating the baroness. 'You know each other, of course?'

'I should think so,' said Vronsky, with a bright smile, pressing the baroness's little hand. 'What next! I'm an old friend.'

'You're home after a journey,' said the baroness, 'so I'm flying. Oh, I'll be off this minute, if I'm in the way.'

'You're at home wherever you are, baroness,' said Vronsky. 'How do you do, Kamerovsky?' he added, coldly shaking hands with Kamerovsky.

'There, you never know how to say such pretty things,' said the baroness, turning to Petritsky.

'No; what's that for? After dinner I say things quite as good.'

'After dinner there's no credit in them! Well, then, I'll make you some coffee, so go and wash and get ready,' said the baroness, sitting down again, and anxiously turning the screw in the new coffee-pot. 'Pierre, give me the coffee,' she said, addressing Petritsky, whom she called Pierre as a contraction of his surname, making no secret of her relations with him. 'I'll put it in.'

'You'll spoil it!'

'No, I won't spoil it! Well, and your wife?' said the baroness suddenly, interrupting Vronsky's conversation with his comrade. 'We've been marrying you here. Have you brought your wife?'

'No, baroness. I was born a Bohemian, and a Bohemian I shall die.'

'So much the better, so much the better. Shake hands on it.'

And the baroness, detaining Vronsky, began telling him, with many jokes, about her last new plans of life, asking his advice.

'He persists in refusing to give me a divorce! Well, what am I to do?' (*He* was her husband.) 'Now I want to begin a suit against him. What do you advise? Kamerovsky, look after the coffee; it's boiling over. You see I'm engrossed with business! I want a lawsuit, because I must have my property. Do you understand the folly of it, that on the pretext of my being unfaithful to him,' she said contemptuously, 'he wants to get the benefit of my fortune.'

Vronsky heard with pleasure this light-hearted prattle of a pretty woman, agreed with her, gave her half-joking counsel, and altogether dropped at once into the tone habitual to him in talking to such women. In his Petersburg world all people were divided into utterly opposed classes. One, the lower class, vulgar, stupid, and, above all, ridiculous people, who believe that one husband ought to live with the one wife whom he has lawfully married; that a girl should be innocent, a woman modest, and a man manly, self-controlled, and strong; that one ought to bring up one's children, earn one's bread, and pay one's debts; and various similar absurdities. This was the class of old-fashioned and ridiculous people. But there was another class of people, the real people. To this class they all belonged, and in it the great thing was to be elegant, generous, plucky, gay, to abandon oneself without a blush to every passion, and to laugh at everything else.

For the first moment only, Vronsky was startled after the impressions of a quite different world that he had brought with him from Moscow. But immediately, as though slipping his feet into old slippers, he dropped back into the light-hearted, pleasant world he had always lived in.

The coffee was never really made, but spluttered over everyone, and boiled away, doing just what was required of it—that is, providing cause for much noise and laughter, and spoiling a costly rug and the baroness's gown.

'Well now, good-bye, or you'll never get washed, and I shall have on my conscience the worst sin a gentleman can commit. So you would advise a knife to his throat?'

'To be sure, and manage that your hand may be not far from his lips. He'll kiss your hand, and all will end satisfactorily,' answered Vronsky.

'So at the Français!' and, with a rustle of her skirts, she vanished.

Kamerovsky got up too, and Vronsky, not waiting for him to go, shook hands and went off to his dressing-room.

While he was washing, Petritsky described to him in brief outlines his position, as far as it had changed since Vronsky had left Petersburg. No money at all. His father said he wouldn't give him any and pay his debts. His tailor was trying to get him locked up, and another fellow, too, was threatening to get him locked up. The colonel of the regiment had announced that if these scandals did not cease he would have to leave. As for the baroness, he was sick to death of her, especially since she'd taken to offering continually to lend him money. But he had found a girl—he'd show her to Vronsky—a marvel, exquisite, in the strict Oriental style, 'genre of the slave Rebecca, don't you know.' He'd had a row, too, with Berkoshov, and was going to send seconds to him, but of course it would come to nothing. Altogether everything was supremely amusing and jolly. And, not letting his comrade enter into further details of his position, Petritsky proceeded to tell him all the interesting news. As he listened to Petritsky's familiar stories in the familiar setting of the rooms he had spent the last three years in, Vronsky felt a delightful sense of coming back to the careless Petersburg life that he was used to.

'Impossible!' he cried, letting down the pedal of the washing basin in which he had been sousing his healthy red neck. 'Impossible!' he cried, at the news that Laura had flung over Fertinghof and had made up to Mileev. 'And is he as stupid and pleased as ever? Well, and how's Buzulukov?'

'Oh, there is a tale about Buzulukov—simply lovely!' cried Petritsky. 'You know his weakness for balls, and he never misses a single court ball. He went to a big ball in a new helmet. Have you seen the new helmets? Very nice, lighter. Well, so he's standing. . . . No, I say, do listen.'

'I am listening,' answered Vronsky, rubbing himself with a rough towel.

'Up comes the Grand-Duchess with some ambassador or other, and, as ill-luck would have it, she begins talking to him about the new helmets. The Grand-Duchess positively wanted to show the new helmet to the ambassador. They see our friend standing there.' (Petritsky mimicked how he was standing with the helmet.) 'The Grand-Duchess asked him to give her the helmet; he doesn't give it her. What do you think of that? Well, everyone's winking at him, nodding, frowning—give it to her, do! He doesn't give it her. He's mute as a fish. Only picture it! . . . Well, the . . . what's his name, whatever he was . . . tries to take the helmet from him . . . he won't give it up! . . . He pulls it from him, and hands it to the Grand-Duchess. "Here, your Highness," says he, "is the new helmet." She turned the helmet the other side up, and—just picture it!—plop went a pear and sweetmeats out of it, two pounds of sweetmeats! . . . He'd been storing them up, the darling!'

Vronsky burst into roars of laughter. And long afterwards, when he was talking of other things, he broke out into his healthy laugh, showing his strong, close rows of teeth, when he thought of the helmet.

Having heard all the news, Vronsky, with the assistance of his valet, got into his uniform, and went off to report himself. He intended, when he had done that, to drive to his brother's, and to Betsy's, and to pay several visits with a view to beginning to go into that society where he might meet Madame Karenin. As he always did in Petersburg, he left home not meaning to return till late at night.

PART II

I

AT the end of the winter, in the Shtcherbatskys' house, a consultation was being held, which was to pronounce on the state of Kitty's health and the measures to be taken to restore her failing strength. She had been ill, and as spring came on she grew worse. The family doctor gave her codliver oil, then iron, then nitrate of silver, but as the first and the second and the third were alike in doing no good, and as his advice when spring came was to go abroad, a celebrated physician was called in. The celebrated physician, a very handsome man, still youngish, asked to examine the patient. He maintained, with peculiar satisfaction, it seemed, that maiden modesty is a mere relic of barbarism, and that nothing could be more natural than for a man still youngish to handle a young girl naked. He thought it natural because he did it every day, and felt and thought, as it seemed to him, no harm as he did it, and consequently he considered modesty in the girl not merely as a relic of barbarism, but also as an insult to himself.

There was nothing for it but to submit, since, although all the doctors had studied in the same school, had read the same books, and learned the same science, and though some people said this celebrated doctor was a bad doctor, in the princess's household and circle it was for some reason accepted that this celebrated doctor alone had some special knowledge, and that he alone could save Kitty. After a careful examination and sounding of the bewildered patient, dazed with shame, the celebrated doctor, having scrupulously washed his hands, was standing in the drawing-room talking to the prince. The prince frowned and coughed, listening to the doctor. As a man who had seen something of life, and neither a fool nor an invalid, he had no faith in medicine, and in his heart was furious at the whole farce, especially as he was perhaps the only one who fully comprehended the cause of Kitty's illness. 'Conceited blockhead!' he thought, as he listened to the celebrated doctor's chatter about his daughter's symptoms. The doctor was meantime with difficulty restraining the expression of his contempt for this old gentleman, and with difficulty condescending to the level of his intelligence. He perceived that it was no good talking to the old man, and that the principal person in the house was the mother. Before her he decided to scatter his pearls. At that instant the princess came into the drawing-room with the family doctor. The prince withdrew, trying not to show how ridiculous he thought the whole performance. The princess was distracted, and did not know what to do. She felt she had sinned against Kitty.

'Well, doctor, decide our fate,' said the princess. 'Tell me everything.'

'Is there hope?' she meant to say, but her lips quivered, and she could not utter the question. 'Well, doctor?'

'Immediately, princess. I will talk it over with my colleague, and then I will have the honour of laying my opinion before you.'

'So we had better leave you?'

'As you please.'

The princess went out with a sigh.

When the doctors were left alone, the family doctor began timidly explaining his opinion, that there was a commencement of tuberculous trouble, but . . . and so on. The celebrated doctor listened to him, and in the middle of his sentence looked at his big gold watch.

'Yes,' said he. 'But . . .'

The family doctor respectfully ceased in the middle of his observations.

'The commencement of the tuberculous process we are not, as you are aware, able to define; till there are cavities, there is nothing definite. But we may suspect it. And there are indications: malnutrition, nervous excitability, and so on. The question stands thus: in presence of indications of tuberculous process, what is to be done to maintain nutrition?'

'But, you know, there are always moral, spiritual causes at the back in these cases,' the family doctor permitted himself to interpolate with a subtle smile.

'Yes, that's an understood thing,' responded the celebrated physician, again glancing at his watch. 'Beg pardon, is the Yausky bridge done yet, or shall I have to drive round?' he asked. 'Ah! it is. Oh, well, then I can do it in twenty minutes. So we were saying the problem may be put thus: to maintain nutrition and to give tone to the nerves. The one is in close connection with the other, one must attack both sides at once.'

'And how about a tour abroad?' asked the family doctor.

'I've no liking for foreign tours. And take note: if there is an early stage of tuberculous process, of which we cannot be certain, a foreign tour will be of no use. What is wanted is means for improving nutrition, and not for lowering it.' And the celebrated doctor expounded his plan of treatment with Soden waters, a remedy obviously prescribed primarily on the ground that they could do no harm.

The family doctor listened attentively and respectfully.

'But in favour of foreign travel I would urge the change of habits, the removal from conditions calling up reminiscences. And then the mother wishes it,' he added.

'Ah! Well, in that case, to be sure, let them go. Only, those German quacks are mischievous. . . . They ought to be persuaded. . . . Well, let them go then.'

He glanced once more at his watch.

'Oh! time's up already,' and he went to the door. The celebrated doctor announced to the princess (a feeling of what was due from him dictated his doing so) that he ought to see the patient once more.

'What! another examination!' cried the mother, with horror.

'Oh no, only a few details, princess.'

'Come this way.'

And the mother, accompanied by the doctor, went into the drawing-room to Kitty. Wasted and flushed, with a peculiar glitter in her eyes, left there by the agony of shame she had been put through, Kitty stood in the middle of the room. When the doctor came in she flushed crimson, and her eyes filled with tears. All her illness and treatment struck her as a thing so stupid, ludicrous even! Doctoring her seemed to her as absurd as putting together the pieces of a broken vase. Her heart was broken. Why would they try to cure her with pills and powders? But she could not grieve her mother, especially as her mother considered herself to blame.

'May I trouble you to sit down, princess?' the celebrated doctor said to her.

He sat down with a smile, facing her, felt her pulse, and again began asking her tiresome questions. She answered him, and all at once got up furious.

'Excuse me, doctor, but there is really no object in this. This is the third time you've asked me the same thing.'

The celebrated doctor did not take offence.

'Nervous irritability,' he said to the princess, when Kitty had left the room. 'However, I had finished. . . .'

And the doctor began scientifically explaining to the princess, as an exceptionally intelligent woman, the condition of the young princess, and concluded by insisting on the drinking of the waters, which were certainly harmless. At the question: Should they go abroad? the doctor plunged into deep meditation, as though resolving a weighty problem. Finally his decision was pronounced: they were to go abroad, but to put no faith in foreign quacks, and to apply to him in any need.

It seemed as though some piece of good fortune had come to pass after the doctor had gone. The mother was much more cheerful when she went back to her daughter, and Kitty pretended to be more cheerful. She had often, almost always, to be pretending now.

'Really, I'm quite well, mamma. But if you want to go abroad, let's go!' she said, and trying to appear interested in the proposed tour, she began talking of the preparations for the journey.

II

SOON after the doctor, Dolly had arrived. She knew that there was to be a consultation that day, and though she was only just up after her confinement (she had another baby, a little girl, born at the end of the winter), though she had trouble and anxiety enough of her own, she had left her tiny baby and a sick child, to come and hear Kitty's fate, which was to be decided that day.

'Well, well?' she said, coming into the drawing-room, without taking off her hat. 'You're all in good spirits. Good news, then?'

They tried to tell her what the doctor had said, but it appeared that though the doctor had talked distinctly enough and at great length, it was utterly impossible to report what he had said. The only point of interest was that it was settled they should go abroad.

Dolly could not help sighing. Her dearest friend, her sister, was going away. And her life was not a cheerful one. Her relations with Stepan Arkadyevitch after their reconciliation had become humiliating. The union Anna had cemented turned out to be of no solid character, and family harmony was breaking down again at the same point. There had been nothing definite, but Stepan Arkadyevitch was hardly ever at home; money, too, was hardly ever forthcoming, and Dolly was continually tortured by suspicions of infidelity, which she tried to dismiss, dreading the agonies of jealousy she had been through already. The first onslaught of jealousy, once lived through, could never come back again, and even the discovery of infidelities could never now affect her as it had the first time. Such a discovery now would only mean breaking up family habits, and she let herself be deceived, despising him and still more herself for the weakness. Besides this, the care of her large family was a constant worry to her: first, the nursing of her young baby did not go well, then the nurse had gone away, now one of the children had fallen ill.

'Well, how are all of you?' asked the mother.

'Ah, mamma, we have plenty of troubles of our own. Lili is ill, and I'm afraid it's scarlatina. I have come here now to hear about Kitty, and then I shall shut myself up entirely, if—God forbid—it should be scarlatina.'

The old prince too had come in from his study after the doctor's departure, and after presenting his cheek to Dolly, and saying a few words to her, he turned to his wife—

'How have you settled it? you're going? Well, and what do you mean to do with me?'

'I suppose you had better stay here, Alexandre,' said his wife.

'That's as you like.'

'Mamma, why shouldn't father come with us?' said Kitty. 'It'll be nicer for him and for us too.'

The old prince got up and stroked Kitty's hair. She lifted her head and looked at him with a forced smile. It always seemed to her that he understood her better than anyone in the family, though he did not say much about her. Being the youngest, she was her father's favourite, and she fancied that his love gave him insight. When now her glance met his blue kindly eyes looking intently at her, it seemed to her that he saw right through her, and understood all that was not good that was passing within her. Reddening, she stretched out towards him expecting a kiss, but he only patted her hair and said—

'These stupid chignons! There's no getting at the real daughter, one simply strokes the bristles of dead women. Well, Dolinka,' he turned to his elder daughter, 'what's your young buck about, hey?'

'Nothing, father,' answered Dolly, understanding that her husband was meant. 'He's always out; I scarcely ever see him,' she could not resist adding with a sarcastic smile.

'Why, hasn't he gone into the country yet—to see about selling that forest?'

'No, he's still getting ready for the journey.'

'Oh, that's it!' said the prince. 'And so am I to be getting ready for a journey too? At your service,' he said to his wife, sitting down. 'And I tell you what, Katia,' he went on to his younger daughter, 'you must wake up one fine day and say to yourself: Why, I'm quite well, and merry, and going out again with father for an early morning walk in the frost. Hey?'

What her father said seemed simple enough, yet at these words Kitty became confused and overcome like a detected criminal. 'Yes, he sees it all, he understands it all, and in these words he's telling me that though I'm ashamed, I must get over my shame.' She could not pluck up spirit to make any answer. She tried to begin, and all at once burst into tears, and rushed out of the room.

'See what comes of your jokes!' the princess pounced down on her husband. 'You're always . . .' she began a string of reproaches.

The prince listened to the princess's scolding rather a long while without speaking, but his face was more and more frowning.

'She's so much to be pitied, poor child, so much to be pitied, and you don't feel how it hurts her to hear the slightest reference to the cause of it. Ah! to be so mistaken in people!' said the princess, and by the change in her tone both Dolly and the prince knew she was speaking of Vronsky. 'I don't know why there aren't laws against such base, dishonourable people.'

'Ah, I can't bear to hear you!' said the prince gloomily, getting up from his low chair, and seeming anxious to get away, yet stopping in the doorway. 'There are laws, madam, and since you've challenged me to it, I'll tell you who's to blame for it all: you and you, you and nobody else. Laws against such young gallants there have always been, and there still are! Yes, if there has been nothing that ought not to have been, old as I am, I'd have called him out to the barrier, the young dandy. Yes, and now you physic her and call in these quacks.'

The prince apparently had plenty more to say, but as soon as the princess heard his tone she subsided at once, and became penitent, as she always did on serious occasions.

'Alexandre, Alexandre,' she whispered, moving to him and beginning to weep.

As soon as she began to cry the prince too calmed down. He went up to her.

'There, that's enough, that's enough! You're wretched too, I know. It can't be helped. There's no great harm done. God is merciful . . . thanks . . .,' he said, not knowing what he was saying, as he responded to the tearful kiss of the princess that he felt on his hand. And the prince went out of the room.

Before this, as soon as Kitty went out of the room in tears, Dolly, with her motherly, family instincts, had promptly perceived that here a woman's work lay before her, and she prepared to do it. She took off her hat, and, morally speaking, tucked up her sleeves and prepared for action. While her mother was attacking her father, she tried to restrain her mother, so far as filial reverence would allow. During the prince's outburst she was silent; she felt ashamed for her mother, and tender towards her father for so quickly being kind again. But when her father left them she made ready for what was the chief thing needful—to go to Kitty and console her.

'I'd been meaning to tell you something for a long while, mamma: did you know that Levin meant to make Kitty an offer when he was here the last time? He told Stiva so.'

'Well, what then? I don't understand. . . .'

'So did Kitty perhaps refuse him? . . . She didn't tell you so?'

'No, she has said nothing to me either of one or the other; she's too proud. But I know it's all on account of the other.'

'Yes, but suppose she has refused Levin, and she wouldn't have refused him if it hadn't been for the other, I know. And then, he has deceived her so horribly.'

It was too terrible for the princess to think how she had sinned against her daughter, and she broke out angrily.

'Oh, I really don't understand! Nowadays they will all go their own way, and mothers haven't a word to say in anything, and then . . .'

'Mamma, I'll go up to her.'

'Well, do. Did I tell you not to?' said her mother.

III

WHEN she went into Kitty's little room, a pretty, pink little room, full of knick-knacks in *vieux saxe*, as fresh, and pink, and white, and gay as Kitty herself had been two months ago, Dolly remembered how they had decorated the room the year before together, with what love and gaiety. Her heart turned cold when she saw Kitty sitting on a low chair near the door, her eyes fixed immovably on a corner of the rug. Kitty glanced at her sister, and the cold, rather ill-tempered, expression of her face did not change.

'I'm just going now, and I shall have to keep in and you won't be able to come to see me,' said Dolly, sitting down beside her. 'I want to talk to you.'

'What about?' Kitty asked swiftly, lifting her head in dismay.

'What should it be, but your trouble?'

'I have no trouble.'

'Nonsense, Kitty. Do you suppose I could help knowing? I know all about it. And believe me, it's of so little consequence. . . . We've all been through it.'

Kitty did not speak, and her face had a stern expression.

'He's not worth your grieving over him,' pursued Darya Alexandrovna, coming straight to the point.

'No, because he has treated me with contempt,' said Kitty, in a breaking voice. 'Don't talk of it! Please, don't talk of it!'

'But who can have told you so? No one has said that. I'm certain he was in love with you, and would still be in love with you, if it hadn't . . .'

'Oh, the most awful thing of all for me is this sympathising!' shrieked Kitty, suddenly flying into a passion. She turned round on her chair, flushed crimson, and rapidly moving her fingers, pinched the clasp of her belt first with one hand and then with the other. Dolly knew this trick her sister had of clenching her hands when she was much excited; she knew, too, that in moments of excitement Kitty was capable of forgetting herself and saying a great deal too much, and Dolly would have soothed her, but it was too late.

'What, what is it you want to make me feel, eh?' said Kitty quickly. 'That I've been in love with a man who didn't care a straw for me, and that I'm dying of love for him? And this is said to me by my own sister, who imagines that . . . that . . . that she's sympathising with me! . . . I don't want these condolences and humbug!'

'Kitty, you're unjust.'

'Why are you tormenting me?'

'But I . . . quite the contrary . . . I see you're unhappy. . . .'

But Kitty in her fury did not hear her.

'I've nothing to grieve over and be comforted about. I am too proud ever to allow myself to care for a man who does not love me.'

'Yes, I don't say so either. . . . Only one thing. Tell me the truth,' said Darya Alexandrovna, taking her by the hand: 'tell me, did Levin speak to you? . . .'

The mention of Levin's name seemed to deprive Kitty of the last vestige of self-control. She leaped up from her chair, and flinging her clasp on the ground, she gesticulated rapidly with her hands and said—

'Why bring Levin in too? I can't understand what you want to torment me for. I've told you, and I say it again, that I have some pride, and never, *never* would I do as you're doing—go back to a man who's deceived you, who has cared for another woman. I can't understand it! You may, but I can't!'

And saying these words she glanced at her sister, and seeing that Dolly sat silent, her head mournfully bowed, Kitty, instead of running out of the room, as she had meant to do, sat down near the door, and hid her face in her handkerchief.

The silence lasted for two minutes: Dolly was thinking of herself. That humiliation of which she was always conscious came back to her with a peculiar bitterness when her sister reminded her of it. She had not looked for such cruelty in her sister, and she was angry with her. But suddenly she heard the rustle of a skirt, and with it the sound of heart-rending, smothered sobbing, and felt arms about her neck. Kitty was on her knees before her.

'Dolinka, I am so, so wretched!' she whispered penitently. And the sweet face covered with tears hid itself in Darya Alexandrovna's skirt.

As though tears were the indispensable oil, without which the machinery of mutual confidence could not run smoothly between the two sisters, the sisters after their tears talked, not of what was uppermost in their minds, but, though they talked of outside matters, they understood each other. Kitty knew that the word she had uttered in anger about her husband's infidelity and her humiliating position, had cut her poor sister to the heart, but that she had forgiven her. Dolly for her part knew all she had wanted to find out. She felt certain that her surmises were correct; that Kitty's misery, her inconsolable misery, was due precisely to the fact that Levin had made her an offer and she had rufused him, and Vronsky had deceived her, and that she was fully prepared to love Levin and to detest Vronsky. Kitty said not a word of that; she talked of nothing but her spiritual condition.

'I have nothing to make me miserable,' she said, getting calmer; 'but can you understand that everything has become hateful, loathsome, coarse to me, and I myself most of all? You can't imagine what loathsome thoughts I have about everything.'

'Why, whatever loathsome thoughts can you have?' asked Dolly, smiling.

'The most utterly loathsome and coarse; I can't tell you. It's not unhappiness, or low spirits, but much worse. As though everything that was good in me was all hidden away, and nothing was left but the most loathsome. Come, how am I to tell you?' she went on, seeing the puzzled look in her sister's eyes. 'Father began saying something to me just now. . . . It seems to me he thinks all I want is to be married. Mother takes me to a ball: it seems to me she only takes me to get me married off as soon as may be, and be rid of me. I know it's not the truth; but I can't drive away such thoughts. Eligible suitors, as they call them—I can't bear to see them. It seems to me they're taking stock of me and summing me up. In old days to go anywhere in a ball-dress was a simple joy to me, I admired myself; now I feel ashamed and awkward. And then! The doctor. . . . Then . . .' Kitty hesitated; she wanted to say further that ever since this change had taken place in her, Stepan Arkadyevitch had become insufferably repulsive to her, and that she could not see him without the grossest and most hideous conceptions rising before her imagination.

'Oh well, everything presents itself to me in the coarsest, most loathsome light,' she went on. 'That's my illness. Perhaps it will pass off.'

'But you mustn't think about it.'

'I can't help it. I'm never happy except with the children at your house.'

'What a pity you can't be with me!'

'Oh yes, I'm coming. I've had scarlatina, and I'll persuade mamma to let me.'

Kitty insisted on having her way, and went to stay at her sister's, and nursed the children all through the scarlatina, for scarlatina it turned out to be. The two sisters brought all the six children successfully through it, but Kitty was no better in health, and in Lent the Shtcherbatskys went abroad.

IV

THE highest Petersburg society is essentially one. In it everyone knows everyone else, everyone even visits everyone else. But this great set has its subdivisions. Anna Arkadyevna Karenin had friends and close ties in three different circles of this highest society. One circle was her husband's government, official set, consisting of his colleagues and subordinates, brought together in the most various and capricious manner, and belonging to different social strata. Anna found it difficult now to recall the feeling of almost awe-stricken reverence which she had at first entertained for these persons. Now she knew all of them as people know one another in a country town; she knew their habits and weaknesses, and where the shoe pinched each one of them. She knew their relations with one another and with the head authorities, knew who was for whom, and how each one maintained his position, and where they agreed and disagreed. But that circle of political, masculine interests had never interested her, in spite of Countess Lidia Ivanovna's influence, and she avoided it.

Another little set with which Anna was in close relations was the one by means of which Alexey Alexandrovitch had made his career. The centre of this circle was the Countess Lidia Ivanovna. It was a set made up of elderly, ugly, benevolent, and godly women, and clever, learned, and ambitious men. One of the clever people belonging to the set had called it 'the conscience of Petersburg society.' Alexey Alexandrovitch had the highest esteem for this circle; and Anna, with her special gift for getting on with everyone, had in the early days of her life in Petersburg made friends in this circle also. Now, since her return from Moscow, she had come to feel this set insufferable. It seemed to her that both she and all of them were insincere, and she felt so bored and ill at ease in that world that she went to see the Countess Lidia Ivanovna as little as possible.

The third circle with which Anna had ties was pre-eminently the fashionable world—the world of balls, of dinners, of sumptuous dresses, the world that hung on to the court with one hand, so as to avoid sinking to the level of the demi-monde. For the demi-monde the members of that fashionable world believed that they despised, though their tastes were not merely similar, but in fact identical. Her connection with this circle was kept up through Princess Betsy Tverskoy, her cousin's wife, who had an income of a hundred and twenty thousand roubles, and who had taken a great fancy to Anna ever since she first came out, showed her much attention, and drew her into her set, making fun of Countess Lidia Ivanovna's coterie.

'When I'm old and ugly I'll be the same,' Betsy used to say; 'but for a pretty young woman like you it's early days for that house of charity.'

Anna had at first avoided as far as she could Princess Tverskoy's world, because it necessitated an expenditure beyond her means, and besides in her heart she preferred the first circle. But since her visit to Moscow she had done quite the contrary. She avoided her serious-minded friends, and went out into the fashionable world. There she met Vronsky, and experienced an agitating joy at those meetings. She met Vronsky specially often at Betsy's, for Betsy was a Vronsky by birth and his cousin. Vronsky was everywhere where he had any chance of meeting Anna, and speaking to her, when he could, of his love. She gave him no encouragement, but every time she met him there surged up in her heart that same feeling of quickened life that had come upon her that day in the railway carriage when she saw him for the first time. She was conscious herself that her delight sparkled in her eyes and curved her lips into a smile, and she could not quench the expression of this delight.

At first Anna sincerely believed that she was displeased with him for daring to pursue her. Soon after her return from Moscow, on arriving at a soirée where she had expected to meet him, and not finding him there, she realised distinctly from the rush of disappointment that she had been deceiving herself, and that this pursuit was not merely not distasteful to her, but that it made the whole interest of her life.

The celebrated singer was singing for the second time, and all the fashionable world was in the theatre. Vronsky, seeing his cousin from his stall in the front row, did not wait till the *entr'acte*, but went to her box.

'Why didn't you come to dinner?' she said to him. 'I marvel at the second-sight of lovers,' she added with a smile, so that no one but he could hear; '*she wasn't there*. But come after the opera.'

Vronsky looked inquiringly at her. She nodded. He thanked her by a smile, and sat down beside her.

'But how I remember your jeers!' continued Princess Betsy, who took a peculiar pleasure in following up this passion to a successful issue. 'What's become of all that? You're caught, my dear boy.'

'That's my one desire, to be caught,' answered Vronsky, with his serene, good-humoured smile. 'If I complain of anything it's only that I'm not caught enough, to tell the truth. I begin to lose hope.'

'Why, whatever hope can you have?' said Betsy, offended on behalf of her friend. '*Entendons nous*. . . .' But in her eyes there were gleams of light that betrayed that she understood perfectly and precisely as he did what hope he might have.

'None whatever,' said Vronsky, laughing and showing his even rows of teeth. 'Excuse me,' he added, taking an opera-glass out of her hand, and proceeding to scrutinise, over her bare shoulder, the row of boxes facing them. 'I'm afraid I'm becoming ridiculous.'

He was very well aware that he ran no risk of being ridiculous in the eyes of Betsy or any other fashionable people. He was very well aware that in their eyes the position of an unsuccessful lover of a girl, or of any woman free to marry, might be ridiculous. But the position of a man pursuing a married woman, and, regardless of everything, staking his life on drawing her into adultery, has something fine and grand about it, and can never be ridiculous; and so it was with a proud and gay smile under his moustaches that he lowered the opera-glass and looked at his cousin.

'But why was it you didn't come to dinner?' she said, admiring him.

'I must tell you about that. I was busily employed, and doing what, do you suppose? I'll give you a hundred guesses, a thousand . . . you'd never guess. I've been reconciling a husband with a man who'd insulted his wife. Yes, really!'

'Well, did you succeed?'

'Almost.'

'You really must tell me about it,' she said, getting up. 'Come to me in the next *entr'acte*.'

'I can't; I'm going to the French theatre.'

'From Nilsson?' Betsy queried in horror, though she could not herself have distinguished Nilsson's voice from any chorus girl's.

'Can't help it. I've an appointment there, all to do with my mission of peace.'

'"Blessed are the peacemakers; theirs is the kingdom of heaven,"' said Betsy, vaguely recollecting she had heard some similar saying from someone. 'Very well, then, sit down, and tell me what it's all about.'

And she sat down again.

V

'THIS is rather indiscreet, but it's so good, it's an awful temptation to tell the story,' said Vronsky, looking at her with his laughing eyes. 'I'm not going to mention any names.'

'But I shall guess, so much the better.'

'Well, listen: two festive young men were driving——'

'Officers of your regiment, of course?'

'I didn't say they were officers,—two young men who had been lunching.'

'In other words, drinking.'

'Possibly. They were driving on their way to dinner with a friend in the most festive state of mind. And they beheld a pretty woman in a hired sledge; she overtakes them, looks round at them, and, so they fancy anyway, nods to them and laughs. They, of course, follow her. They gallop at full speed. To their amazement, the fair one alights at the entrance of the very house to which they were going. The fair one darts upstairs to the top storey. They get a glimpse of red lips under a short veil, and exquisite little feet.'

'You describe it with such feeling that I fancy you must be one of the two.'

'And after what you said, just now! Well, the young men go in to their comrade's; he was giving a farewell dinner. There they certainly did drink a little too much, as one always does at farewell dinners. And at dinner they inquire who lives at the top in that house. No one knows; only their host's valet, in answer to their inquiry whether any "young ladies" are living on the top floor, answered that there were a great many of them about there. After dinner the two young men go into their host's study, and write a letter to the unknown fair one. They compose an ardent epistle, a declaration in fact, and they carry the letter upstairs themselves, so as to elucidate whatever might appear not perfectly intelligible in the letter.'

'Why are you telling me these horrible stories? Well?'

'They ring. A maid-servant opens the door, they hand her the letter, and assure the maid that they're both so in love that they'll die on the spot at the door. The maid, stupefied, carries in their messages. All at once a gentleman appears with whiskers like sausages, as red as a lobster, announces that there is no one living in that flat except his wife, and sends them both about their business.'

'How do you know he had whiskers like sausages, as you say?'

'Ah, you shall see. I've just been to make peace between them.'

'Well, and what then?'

'That's the most interesting part of the story. It appears that it's a happy couple, a government clerk and his lady. The government clerk lodges a complaint, and I became a mediator, and such a mediator! . . . I assure you Talleyrand couldn't hold a candle to me.'

'Why, where was the difficulty?'

'Ah, you shall hear. . . . We apologise in due form: we are in despair, we entreat forgiveness for the unfortunate misunderstanding. The government clerk with the sausages begins to melt, but he, too, desires to express his sentiments, and as soon as ever he begins to express them, he begins to get hot and say nasty things, and again I'm obliged to trot out all my diplomatic talents. I allowed that their conduct was bad, but I urged him to take into consideration their heedlessness, their youth; then, too, the young men had only just been lunching together. "You understand. They regret it deeply, and beg you to overlook their misbehaviour." The government clerk was softened once more. "I consent, count, and am ready to overlook it; but you perceive that my wife—my wife's a respectable woman—has been exposed to the persecution, and insults, and effrontery of young upstarts, scoundrels . . ." And you must understand, the young upstarts are present all the while, and I have to keep the peace between them. Again I call out all my diplomacy, and again as soon as the thing was about at an end, our friend the government clerk gets hot and red, and his sausages stand on end with wrath, and once more I launch out into diplomatic wiles.'

'Ah, he must tell you this story!' said Betsy, laughing, to a lady who came into her box. 'He has been making me laugh so.'

'Well, *bonne chance*!' she added, giving Vronsky one finger of the hand in which she held her fan, and with a shrug of her shoulders she twitched down the bodice of her gown that had worked up, so as to be duly naked as she moved forward towards the footlights into the light of the gas, and the sight of all eyes.

Vronsky drove to the French theatre, where he really had to see the colonel of his regiment, who never missed a single performance there.

He wanted to see him, to report on the result of his mediation, which had occupied and amused him for the last three days. Petritsky, whom he liked, was implicated in the affair, and the other culprit was a capital fellow and first-rate comrade, who had lately joined the regiment, the young Prince Kedrov. And what was most important, the interests of the regiment were involved in it too.

Both the young men were in Vronsky's company. The colonel of the regiment was waited upon by the government clerk, Venden, with a complaint against his officers, who had insulted his wife. His young wife, so Venden told the story—he had been married half a year—was at church with her mother, and suddenly overcome by indisposition, arising from her interesting condition, she could not remain standing, she drove home in the first sledge, a smart-looking one, she came across. On the spot the officers set off in pursuit of her; she was alarmed, and feeling still more unwell, ran up the staircase home. Venden himself, on returning from his office, heard a ring at their bell and voices, went out, and seeing the intoxicated officers with a letter, he had turned them out. He asked for exemplary punishment.

'Yes, it's all very well,' said the colonel to Vronsky, whom he had invited to come and see him. 'Petritsky's becoming impossible. Not a week goes by without some scandal. This government clerk won't let it drop, he'll go on with the thing.'

Vronsky saw all the thanklessness of the business, and that there could be no question of a duel in it, that everything must be done to soften the government clerk, and hush the matter up. The colonel had called in Vronsky just because he knew him to be an honourable and intelligent man, and, more than all, a man who cared for the honour of the regiment. They talked it over, and decided that Petritsky and Kedrov must go with Vronsky to Venden's to apologise. The colonel and Vronsky were both fully aware that Vronsky's name and rank would be sure to contribute greatly to the softening of the injured husband's feelings.

And these two influences were not in fact without effect; though the result remained, as Vronsky had described, uncertain.

On reaching the French theatre, Vronsky retired to the foyer with the colonel, and reported to him his success, or non-success. The colonel, thinking it all over, made up his mind not to pursue the matter further, but then for his own satisfaction proceeded to cross-examine Vronsky about his interview; and it was a long while before he could restrain his laughter, as Vronsky described how the government clerk, after subsiding for a while, would suddenly flare up again, as he recalled the details, and how Vronsky, at the last half word of conciliation, skilfully manœuvred a retreat, shoving Petritsky out before him.

'It's a disgraceful story, but killing. Kedrov really can't fight the gentleman! Was he so awfully hot?' he commented, laughing. 'But what do you say to Claire today? She's marvellous,' he went on, speaking of a new French actress. 'However often you see her, every day she's different. It's only the French who can do that.'

VI

PRINCESS BETSY drove home from the theatre, without waiting for the end of the last act. She had only just time to go into her dressing-room, sprinkle her long, pale face with powder, rub it, set her dress to rights, and order tea in the big drawing-room, when one after another the carriages drove up to her huge house in Bolshaia Morskaia. Her guests stepped out at the wide entrance, and the stout porter, who used to read the newspapers in the mornings behind the glass door, to the edification of the passers-by, noiselessly opened the immense door, letting the visitors pass by him into the house.

Almost at the same instant the hostess, with freshly arranged coiffure and freshened face, walked in at one door and her guests at the other door of the drawing-room, a large room with dark walls, downy rugs, and a brightly lighted table, gleaming with the light of candles, white cloth, silver samovar, and transparent china tea-things.

The hostess sat down at the table and took off her gloves. Chairs were set with the aid of footmen, moving almost imperceptibly about the room; the party settled itself, divided into two groups; one round the samovar near the hostess, the other at the opposite end of the drawing-room, round the handsome wife of an ambassador, in black velvet, with sharply defined black eyebrows. In both groups conversation wavered, as it always does, for the first few minutes, broken up by meetings, greetings, offers of tea, and as it were feeling about for something to rest upon.

'She's exceptionally good as an actress; one can see she's studied Kaulbach,' said a diplomatic attaché in the group round the ambassador's wife. 'Did you notice how she fell down? . . .'

'Oh, please, don't let us talk about Nilsson! No one can possibly say anything new about her,' said a fat, red-faced, flaxen-headed lady, without eyebrows and chignon, wearing an old silk dress. This was Princess Myaky, noted for her simplicity and the roughness of her manners, and nicknamed *enfant terrible*. Princess Myaky, sitting in the middle between the two groups, and listening to both, took part in the conversation first of one and then of the other. 'Three people have used that very phrase about Kaulbach to me today already, just as though they had made a compact about it. And I can't see why they liked that remark so.'

The conversation was cut short by this observation, and a new subject had to be thought of again.

'Do tell me something amusing but not spiteful,' said the ambassador's wife, a great proficient in the art of that elegant conversation called by the English *small-talk*. She addressed the attaché, who was at a loss now what to begin upon.

'They say that that's a difficult task, that nothing's amusing that isn't spiteful,' he began with a smile. 'But I'll try. Get me a subject. It all lies in the subject. If a subject's given me, it's easy to spin something round it. I often think that the celebrated talkers of last century would have found it difficult to talk cleverly now. Everything clever is so stale . . .'

'That has been said long ago,' the ambassador's wife interrupted him, laughing.

The conversation began amiably, but just because it was too amiable it came to a stop again. They had to have recourse to the sure, never-failing topic—gossip.

'Don't you think there's something Louis Quinze about Tushkevitch?' he said, glancing towards a handsome, fair-haired young man, standing at the table.

'Oh yes! He's in the same style as the drawing-room, and that's why it is he's so often here.'

This conversation was maintained, since it rested on allusions to what could not be talked of in that room—that is to say, of the relations of Tushkevitch with their hostess.

Round the samovar and the hostess the conversation had been meanwhile vacillating in just the same way between three inevitable topics: the latest piece of public news, the theatre, and scandal. It, too, came finally to rest on the last topic, that is, ill-natured gossip.

'Have you heard the Maltishtchev woman—the mother, not the daughter—has ordered a costume in *diable rose* colour?'

'Nonsense! No, that's too lovely!'

'I wonder that with her sense—for she's not a fool, you know—that she doesn't see how funny she is.'

Everyone had something to say in censure or ridicule of the luckless Madame Maltishtchev, and the conversation crackled merrily, like a burning fagot-stack.

The husband of Princess Betsy, a good-natured fat man, an ardent collector of engravings, hearing that his wife had visitors, came into the drawing-room before going to his club. Stepping noiselessly over the thick rugs, he went up to Princess Myaky.

'How did you like Nilsson?' he asked.

'Oh, how can you steal upon anyone like that! How you startled me!' she responded. 'Please don't talk to me about the opera; you know nothing about music. I'd better meet you on your own ground, and talk about your maiolica and engravings. Come now, what treasure have you been buying lately at the old curiosity shops?'

'Would you like me to show you? But you don't understand such things.'

'Oh, do show me! I've been learning about them at those—what's their names? . . . the bankers . . . they've some splendid engravings. They showed them to us.'

'Why, have you been at the Schützburgs?' asked the hostess from the samovar.

'Yes, *ma chère*. They asked my husband and me to dinner, and told us the sauce at that dinner cost a hundred pounds,' Princess Myaky said, speaking loudly, and conscious everyone was listening; 'and very nasty sauce it was, some green mess. We had to ask them, and I made them sauce for eighteenpence, and everybody was very much pleased with it. I can't run to hundred-pound sauces.'

'She's unique!' said the lady of the house.

'Marvellous!' said someone.

The sensation produced by Princess Myaky's speeches was always unique, and the secret of the sensation she produced lay in the fact that though she spoke not always appropriately, as now, she said simple things with some sense in them. In the society in which she lived such plain statements produced the effect of the wittiest epigram. Princess Myaky could never see why it had that effect, but she knew it had, and took advantage of it.

As everyone had been listening while Princess Myaky spoke, and so the conversation around the ambassador's wife had dropped, Princess Betsy tried to bring the whole party together, and she turned to the ambassador's wife.

'Will you really not have tea? You should come over here by us.'

'No, we're very happy here,' the ambassador's wife responded with a smile, and she went on with the conversation that had been begun.

It was a very agreeable conversation. They were criticising the Karenins, husband and wife.

'Anna is quite changed since her stay in Moscow. There's something strange about her,' said her friend.

'The great change is that she brought back with her the shadow of Alexey Vronsky,' said the ambassador's wife.

'Well, what of it? There's a fable of Grimm's about a man without a shadow, a man who's lost his shadow. And that's his punishment for something. I never could understand how it was a punishment. But a woman must dislike being without a shadow.'

'Yes, but women with a shadow usually come to a bad end,' said Anna's friend.

'Bad luck to your tongue!' said Princess Myaky suddenly. 'Madame Karenin's a splendid woman. I don't like her husband, but I like her very much.'

'Why don't you like her husband? He's such a remarkable man,' said the ambassador's wife. 'My husband says there are few statesmen like him in Europe.'

'And my husband tells me just the same, but I don't believe it,' said Princess Myaky. 'If our husbands didn't talk to us, we should see the facts as they are. Alexy Alexandrovitch, to my thinking, is simply a fool. I say it in a whisper . . . but doesn't it really make everything clear? Before, when I was told to consider him clever, I kept looking for his ability, and thought myself a fool for not seeing it; but directly I said, *he's a fool*, though only in a whisper, everything's explained, isn't it?'

'How spiteful you are today!'

'Not a bit. I'd no other way out of it. One of the two had to be a fool. And, well, you know one can't say that of oneself.'

'"No one is satisfied with his fortune, and everyone is satisfied with his wit."' The attaché repeated the French saying.

'That's just it, just it,' Princess Myaky turned to him. 'But the point is that I won't abandon Anna to your mercies. She's so nice, so charming. How can she help it if they're all in love with her, and follow her about like shadows?'

'Oh, I had no idea of blaming her for it,' Anna's friend said in self-defence.

'If no one follows us about like a shadow, that's no proof that we've any right to blame her.'

And having duly disposed of Anna's friend, the Princess Myaky got up, and together with the ambassador's wife, joined the group at the table, where the conversation was dealing with the king of Prussia.

'What wicked gossip were you talking over there?' asked Betsy.

'About the Karenins. The princess gave us a sketch of Alexey Alexandrovitch,' said the ambassador's wife with a smile, as she sat down at the table.

'Pity we didn't hear it!' said Princess Betsy, glancing towards the door. 'Ah, here you are at last!' she said, turning with a smile to Vronsky, as he came in.

Vronsky was not merely acquainted with all the persons whom he was meeting here; he saw them all every day; and so he came in with the quiet manner with which one enters a room full of people from whom one has only just parted.

'Where do I come from?' he said, in answer to a question from the ambassador's wife. 'Well, there's no help for it, I must confess. From the *opera bouffe*. I do believe I've seen it a hundred times, and always with fresh enjoyment. It's exquisite! I know it's disgraceful, but I go to sleep at the opera, and I sit out the *opera bouffe* to the last minute, and enjoy it. This evening . . .'

He mentioned a French actress, and was going to tell something about her; but the ambassador's wife, with playful horror, cut him short.

'Please don't tell us about that horror.'

'All right, I won't, especially as everyone knows those horrors.'

'And we should all go to see them if it were accepted as the correct thing, like the opera,' chimed in Princess Myaky.

VII

STEPS were heard at the door, and Princess Betsy, knowing it was Madame Karenin, glanced at Vronsky. He was looking towards the door, and his face wore a strange, new expression. Joyfully, intently, and at the same time timidly, he gazed at the approaching figure, and slowly he rose to his feet. Anna walked into the drawing-room. Holding herself extremely erect, as always, looking straight before her, and moving with her swift, resolute, and light step, that distinguished her from all other society women, she crossed the short space to her hostess, shook hands with her, smiled, and with the same smile looked round at Vronsky. Vronsky bowed low and pushed a chair up for her.

She acknowledged this only by a slight nod, flushed a little, and frowned. But immediately, while rapidly greeting her acquaintances, and shaking the hands proffered to her, she addressed Princess Betsy—

'I have been at Countess Lidia's, and meant to have come here earlier, but I stayed on. Sir John was there. He's very interesting.'

'Oh, that's this missionary?'

'Yes; he told us about the life in India, most interesting things.'

The conversation, interrupted by her coming in, flickered up again like the light of a lamp being blown out.

'Sir John! Yes, Sir John; I've seen him. He speaks well. The Vlassiev girl's quite in love with him.'

'And is it true the younger Vlassiev girl's to marry Topov?'

'Yes, they say it's quite a settled thing.'

'I wonder at the parents! They say it's a marriage for love.'

'For love? What antediluvian notions you have! Can one talk of love in these days?' said the ambassador's wife.

'What's to be done? It's a foolish old fashion that's kept up still,' said Vronsky.

'So much the worse for those who keep up the fashion. The only happy marriages I know are marriages of prudence.'

'Yes, but then how often the happiness of these prudent marriages flies away like dust just because that passion turns up that they have refused to recognise,' said Vronsky.

'But by marriages of prudence we mean those in which both parties have sown their wild oats already. That's like scarlatina—one has to go through it and get it over.'

'Then they ought to find out how to vaccinate for love, like smallpox.'

'I was in love in my young days with a deacon,' said the Princess Myaky. 'I don't know that it did me any good.'

'No; I imagine, joking apart, that to know love, one must make mistakes and then correct them,' said Princess Betsy.

'Even after marriage?' said the ambassador's wife playfully.

'"It's never too late to mend."' The attaché repeated the English proverb.

'Just so,' Betsy agreed; 'one must make mistakes and correct them. What do you think about it?' She turned to Anna, who, with a faintly perceptible resolute smile on her lips, was listening in silence to the conversation.

'I think,' said Anna, playing with the glove she had taken off, 'I think . . . if so many men, so many minds, certainly so many hearts, so many kinds of love.'

Vronsky was gazing at Anna, and with a fainting heart waiting for what she would say. He sighed as after a danger escaped when she uttered these words.

Anna suddenly turned to him.

'Oh, I have had a letter from Moscow. They write me that Kitty Shtcherbatsky's very ill.'

'Really?' said Vronsky, knitting his brows.

Anna looked sternly at him.

'That doesn't interest you?'

'On the contrary, it does, very much. What was it exactly they told you, if I may know?' he questioned.

Anna got up and went to Betsy.

'Give me a cup of tea,' she said, standing at her table.

While Betsy was pouring out the tea, Vronsky went up to Anna.

'What is it they write to you?' he repeated.

'I often think men have no understanding of what's not honourable though they're always talking of it,' said Anna, without answering him. 'I've wanted to tell you so a long while,' she added, and moving a few steps away, she sat down at a table in a corner covered with albums.

'I don't quite understand the meaning of your words,' he said, handing her the cup.

She glanced towards the sofa beside her, and he instantly sat down.

'Yes, I have been wanting to tell you,' she said, not looking at him. 'You behaved wrongly, very wrongly.'

'Do you suppose I don't know that I've acted wrongly? But who was the cause of my doing so?'

'What do you say that to me for?' she said, glancing severely at him.

'You know what for,' he answered boldly and joyfully, meeting her glance and not dropping his eyes.

Not he, but she, was confused.

'That only shows you have no heart,' she said. But her eyes said that she knew he had a heart, and that was why she was afraid of him.

'What you spoke of just now was a mistake, and not love.'

'Remember that I have forbidden you to utter that word, that hateful word,' said Anna, with a shudder. But at once she felt that by that very word 'forbidden' she had shown that she acknowledged certain rights over him, and by that very fact was encouraging him to speak of love. 'I have long meant to tell you this,' she went on, looking resolutely into his eyes, and hot all over from the burning flush on her cheeks. 'I've come on purpose this evening, knowing I should meet you. I have come to tell you that this must end. I have never blushed before anyone, and you force me to feel to blame for something.'

He looked at her and was struck by a new spiritual beauty in her face.

'What do you wish of me?' he said simply and seriously.

'I want you to go to Moscow and ask for Kitty's forgiveness,' she said.

'You don't wish that?' he said.

He saw she was saying what she forced herself to say, not what she wanted to say.

'If you love me, as you say,' she whispered, 'do so that I may be at peace.'

His face grew radiant.

'Don't you know that you're all my life to me? But I know no peace, and I can't give it you; all myself—and love . . . yes. I can't think of you and myself apart. You and I are one to me. And I see no chance before us of peace for me or for you. I see a chance of despair, of wretchedness . . . or I see a chance of bliss, what bliss! . . . Can it be there's no chance of it?' he murmured with his lips; but she heard.

She strained every effort of her mind to say what ought to be said. But instead of that she let her eyes rest on him, full of love, and made no answer.

'It's come!' he thought in ecstasy. 'When I was beginning to despair, and it seemed there would be no end—it's come! She loves me! She owns it!'

'Then do this for me: never say such things to me, and let us be friends,' she said in words; but her eyes spoke quite differently.

'Friends we shall never be, you know that yourself. Whether we shall be the happiest or the wretchedest of people—that's in your hands.'

She would have said something, but he interrupted her.

'I ask one thing only: I ask for the right to hope, to suffer as I do. But if even that cannot be, command me to disappear, and I disappear. You shall not see me if my presence is distasteful to you.'

'I don't want to drive you away.'

'Only don't change anything, leave everything as it is,' he said in a shaky voice. 'Here's your husband.'

At that instant Alexey Alexandrovitch did in fact walk into the room with his calm, awkward gait.

Glancing at his wife and Vronsky, he went up to the lady of the house, and sitting down for a cup of tea, began talking in his deliberate, always audible voice, in his habitual tone of banter, ridiculing someone.

'Your Rambouillet is in full conclave,' he said, looking round at all the party; 'the graces and the muses.'

But Princess Betsy could not endure that tone of his—'sneering', as she called it, using the English word, and like a skilful hostess she at once brought him into a serious conversation on the subject of universal conscription. Alexey Alexandrovitch was immediately interested in the subject, and began seriously defending the new imperial decree against Princess Betsy, who had attacked it.

Vronsky and Anna still sat at the little table.

'This is getting indecorous,' whispered one lady, with an expressive glance at Madame Karenin, Vronsky, and her husband.

'What did I tell you?' said Anna's friend.

But not only those ladies, almost everyone in the room, even the Princess Myaky and Betsy herself, looked several times in the direction of the two who had withdrawn from the general circle, as though that were a disturbing fact. Alexey Alexandrovitch was the only person who did not once look in that direction, and was not diverted from the interesting discussion he had entered upon.

Noticing the disagreeable impression that was being made on everyone, Princess Betsy slipped someone else into her place to listen to Alexey Alexandrovitch, and went up to Anna.

'I'm always amazed at the clearness and precision of your husband's language,' she said. 'The most transcendental ideas seem to be within my grasp when he's speaking.'

'Oh yes!' said Anna, radiant with a smile of happiness, and not understanding a word of what Betsy had said. She crossed over to the big table and took part in the general conversation.

Alexey Alexandrovitch, after staying half an hour, went up to his wife and suggested that they should go home together. But she answered, not looking at him, that she was staying to supper. Alexey Alexandrovitch made his bows and withdrew.

The fat old Tatar, Madame Karenin's coachman, was with difficulty holding one of her pair of greys, chilled with the cold and rearing at the entrance. A footman stood opening the carriage door. The hall-porter stood holding open the great door of the house. Anna Arkadyevna, with her quick little hand, was unfastening the lace of her sleeve, caught in the hook of her fur cloak, and with bent head listening with rapture to the words Vronsky murmured as he escorted her down.

'You've said nothing, of course, and I ask nothing,' he was saying; 'but you know that friendship's not what I want: that there's only one happiness in life for me, that word that you dislike so . . . yes, love! . .'

'Love,' she repeated slowly, in an inner voice, and suddenly at the very instant she unhooked the lace, she added, 'Why I don't like the word is that it means too much to me, far more than you can understand,' and she glanced into his face. '*Au revoir!*'

She gave him her hand, and with her rapid, springy step she passed by the porter and vanished into the carriage.

Her glance, the touch of her hand, set him aflame. He kissed the palm of his hand where she had touched it, and went home, happy in the sense that he had got nearer to the attainment of his aims that evening than during the two last months.

VIII

ALEXEY ALEXANDROVITCH had seen nothing striking or improper in the fact that his wife was sitting with Vronsky at a table apart, in eager conversation with him about something. But he noticed that to the rest of the party this appeared something striking and improper, and for that reason it seemed to him too to be improper. He made up his mind that he must speak of it to his wife.

On reaching home Alexey Alexandrovitch went to his study, as he usually did, seated himself in his low chair, opened a book on the Papacy at the place where he had laid the paper-knife in it, and read till one o'clock, just as he usually did. But from time to time he rubbed his high forehead and shook his head, as though to drive away something. At his usual time he got up and made his toilet for the night. Anna Arkadyevna had not yet come in. With a book under his arm he went upstairs. But this evening, instead of his usual thoughts and meditations upon official details, his thoughts were absorbed by his wife and something disagreeable connected with her. Contrary to his usual habit, he did not get into bed, but fell to walking up and down the rooms with his hands clasped behind his back. He could not go to bed, feeling that it was absolutely needful for him first to think thoroughly over the position that had just arisen.

When Alexey Alexandrovitch had made up his mind that he must talk to his wife about it, it had seemed a very easy and simple matter. But now, when he began to think over the question that had just presented itself, it seemed to him very complicated and difficult.

Alexey Alexandrovitch was not jealous. Jealousy according to his notions was an insult to one's wife, and one ought to have confidence in one's wife. Why one ought to have confidence—that is to say complete conviction that his young wife would always love him—he did not ask himself. But he had had no experience of lack of confidence, because he had confidence in her, and told himself that he ought to have it. Now, though his conviction that jealousy was a shameful feeling, and that one ought to feel confidence, had not broken down, he felt that he was standing face to face with something illogical and irrational, and did not know what was to be done. Alexey Alexandrovitch was standing face to face with life, with the possibility of his wife's loving someone other than himself, and this seemed to him very irrational and incomprehensible because it was life itself. All his life Alexey Alexandrovitch had lived and worked in official spheres, having to do with the reflection of life. And every time he had stumbled against life itself he had shrunk away from it. Now he experienced a feeling akin to that of a man who, while calmly crossing a precipice by a bridge, should suddenly discover that the bridge is broken, and that there is a chasm below. That chasm was life itself, the bridge that artificial life in which Alexey Alexandrovitch had lived. For the first time the question presented itself to him of the possibility of his wife's loving someone else, and he was horrified at it.

He did not undress, but walked up and down with his regular tread over the resounding parquet of the dining-room, where one lamp was burning, over the carpet of the dark drawing-room, in which the light was reflected on the big new portrait of himself hanging over the sofa, and across her boudoir, where two candles burned, lighting up the portraits of her parents and woman friends, and the pretty knick-knacks of her writing-table, that he knew so well. He walked across her boudoir to the bedroom door, and turned back again. At each turn in his walk, especially at the parquet of the lighted dining-room, he halted and said to himself, 'Yes, this I must decide and put a stop to; I must express my view of it and my decision.' And he turned back again. 'But express what—what decision?' he said to himself in the drawing-room, and he found no reply. 'But after all,' he asked himself before turning into the boudoir, 'what has occurred? Nothing. She was talking a long while with him. But what of that? Surely women in society can talk to whom they please. And then, jealousy means lowering both myself and her,' he told himself as he went into her boudoir; but this dictum, which had always had such weight with him before, had now no weight and no meaning at all. And from the bedroom door he turned back again; but as he entered the dark drawing-room some inner voice told him that it was not so, and that if others noticed it that showed that there was something. And he said to himself again in the dining-room, 'Yes, I must decide and put a stop to it, and express my view of it. . . .' And again at the turn in the drawing-room he asked himself, 'Decide how?' And again he asked himself, 'What had occurred?' and answered, 'Nothing,' and recollected that jealousy was a feeling insulting to his wife; but again in the drawing-room he was convinced that something had happened. His thoughts, like his body, went round a complete circle, without coming upon anything new. He noticed this, rubbed his forehead, and sat down in her boudoir.

There, looking at her table, with the malachite blotting-case lying at the top and an unfinished letter, his thoughts suddenly changed. He began to think of her, of what she was thinking and feeling. For the first time he pictured vividly to himself her personal life, her ideas, her desires, and the idea that she could and should have a separate life of her own seemed to him so alarming that he made haste to dispel it. It was the chasm which he was afraid to peep into. To put himself in thought and feeling in another person's place was a spiritual exercise not natural to Alexey Alexandrovitch. He looked on this spiritual exercise as a harmful and dangerous abuse of the fancy.

'And the worst of it all,' thought he, 'is that just now, at the very moment when my great work is approaching completion' (he was thinking of the project he was bringing forward at the time), 'when I stand in need of all my mental peace and all my energies, just now this stupid worry should fall foul of me. But what's to be done? I'm not one of those men who submit to uneasiness and worry without having the force of character to face them.

'I must think it over, come to a decision, and put it out of my mind,' he said aloud.

'The question of her feelings, of what has passed and may be passing in her soul, that's not my affair; that's the affair of her conscience, and falls under the head of religion,' he said to himself, feeling consolation in the sense that he had found to which division of regulating principles this new circumstance could be properly referred.

'And so,' Alexey Alexandrovitch said to himself, 'questions as to her feelings, and so on, are questions for her conscience, with which I can have nothing to do. My duty is clearly defined. As the head of the family, I am a person bound in duty to guide her, and consequently, in part the person responsible; I am bound to point out the danger I perceive, to warn her, even to use my authority. I ought to speak plainly to her.' And everything that he would say tonight to his wife took clear shape in Alexey Alexandrovitch's head. Thinking over what he would say, he somewhat regretted that he should have to use his time and mental powers for domestic consumption, with so little to show for it, but, in spite of that, the form and contents of the speech before him shaped itself as clearly and distinctly in his head as a ministerial report.

'I must say and express fully the following points: first, exposition of the value to be attached to public opinion and to decorum; secondly, exposition of religious significance of marriage; thirdly, if need be, reference to the calamity possibly ensuing to our son; fourthly, reference to the unhappiness likely to result to herself.' And, interlacing his fingers, Alexey Alexandrovitch stretched them, and the joints of the fingers cracked. This trick, a bad habit, the cracking of his fingers, always soothed him, and gave precision to his thoughts, so needful to him at this juncture.

There was the sound of a carriage driving up to the front door. Alexey Alexandrovitch halted in the middle of the room.

A woman's step was heard mounting the stairs. Alexey Alexandrovitch, ready for his speech, stood compressing his crossed fingers, waiting to see if the crack would not come again. One joint cracked.

Already, from the sound of light steps on the stairs, he was aware that she was close, and though he was satisfied with his speech, he felt frightened of the explanation confronting him....

IX

ANNA came in with hanging head, playing with the tassels of her hood. Her face was brilliant and glowing; but this glow was not one of brightness, it suggested the fearful glow of a conflagration in the midst of a dark night. On seeing her husband, Anna raised her head and smiled, as though she had just waked up.

'You're not in bed? What a wonder!' she said, letting fall her hood, and, without stopping, she went on into the dressing-room. 'It's late, Alexey Alexandrovitch,' she said, when she had gone through the doorway.

'Anna, it's necessary for me to have a talk with you.'

'With me?' she said, wonderingly. She came out from behind the door of the dressing-room, and looked at him. 'Why, what is it? What about?' she asked, sitting down. 'Well, let's talk, if it's so necessary. But it would be better to get to sleep.'

Anna said what came to her lips, and marvelled, hearing herself, at her own capacity for lying. How simple and natural were her words, and how likely that she was simply sleepy! She felt herself clad in an impenetrable armour of falsehood. She felt that some unseen force had come to her aid and was supporting her.

'Anna, I must warn you,' he began.

'Warn me?' she said. 'Of what?'

She looked at him so simply, so brightly, that anyone who did not know her as her husband knew her could not have noticed anything unnatural, either in the sound or the sense of her words. But to him, knowing her, knowing that whenever he went to bed five minutes later than usual, she noticed it, and asked him the reason; to him, knowing that every joy, every pleasure and pain that she felt she communicated to him at once; to him, now, to see that she did not care to notice his state of mind, that she did not care to say a word about herself, meant a great deal. He saw that the inmost recesses of her soul, that had always hitherto lain open before him, were closed against him. More than that, he saw from her tone that she was not even perturbed at that, but as it were said straight out to him: 'Yes, it's shut up, and so it must be, and will be in future.' Now he experienced a feeling such as a man might have, returning home and finding his own house locked up. 'But perhaps the key may yet be found,' thought Alexey Alexandrovitch.

'I want to warn you,' he said in a low voice, 'that through thoughtlessness and lack of caution you may cause yourself to be talked about in society. Your too animated conversation this evening with Count

Vronsky' (he enunciated the name firmly and with deliberate emphasis) 'attracted attention.'

He talked and looked at her laughing eyes, which frightened him now with their impenetrable look, and, as he talked, he felt all the uselessness and idleness of his words.

'You're always like that,' she answered, as though completely misapprehending him, and of all he had said only taking in the last phrase. 'One time you don't like my being dull, and another time you don't like my being lively. I wasn't dull. Does that offend you?'

Alexey Alexandrovitch shivered, and bent his hands to make the joints crack.

'Oh, please, don't do that, I do so dislike it,' she said.

'Anna, is this you?' said Alexey Alexandrovitch, quietly, making an effort over himself, and restraining the motion of his fingers.

'But what is it all about?' she said, with such genuine and droll wonder. 'What do you want of me?'

Alexey Alexandrovitch paused, and rubbed his forehead and his eyes. He saw that instead of doing as he had intended—that is to say, warning his wife against a mistake in the eyes of the world—he had unconsciously become agitated over what was the affair of her conscience, and was struggling against the barrier he fancied between them.

'This is what I meant to say to you,' he went on coldly and composedly, 'and I beg you to listen to it. I consider jealousy, as you know, a humiliating and degrading feeling, and I shall never allow myself to be influenced by it; but there are certain rules of decorum which cannot be disregarded with impunity. This evening it was not I observed it, but judging by the impression made on the company, everyone observed that your conduct and deportment were not altogether what could be desired.'

'I positively don't understand,' said Anna, shrugging her shoulders.—'He doesn't care,' she thought. 'But other people noticed it, and that's what upsets him.'—'You're not well, Alexey Alexandrovitch,' she added, and she got up, and would have gone towards the door; but he moved forward as though he would stop her.

His face was ugly and forbidding, as Anna had never seen him. She stopped, and bending her head back and on one side, began with her rapid hand taking out her hairpins.

'Well, I'm listening to what's to come,' she said, calmly and ironically; 'and indeed I listen with interest, for I should like to understand what's the matter.'

She spoke, and marvelled at the confident, calm, and natural tone in which she was speaking, and the choice of the words she used.

'To enter into all the details of your feelings I have no right, and besides, I regard that as useless and even harmful,' began Alexey Alexandrovitch. 'Ferreting in one's soul, one often ferrets out something that might have lain there unnoticed. Your feelings are an affair of your own conscience; but I am in duty bound to you, to myself, and to God, to point out to you your duties. Our life has been joined, not by man, but by God. That union can only be severed by a crime, and a crime of that nature brings its own chastisement.'

'I don't understand a word. And, oh dear! how sleepy I am, unluckily,' she said, rapidly passing her hand through her hair, feeling for the remaining hairpins.

'Anna, for God's sake don't speak like that!' he said gently. 'Perhaps I am mistaken, but believe me, what I say, I say as much for myself as for you. I am your husband, and I love you.'

For an instant her face fell, and the mocking gleam in her eyes died away; but the word love threw her into revolt again. She thought: 'Love? Can he love? If he hadn't heard there was such a thing as love, he would never have used the word. He doesn't even know what love is.'

'Alexey Alexandrovitch, really I don't understand,' she said. 'Define what it is you find . . .'

'Pardon, let me say all I have to say. I love you. But I am not speaking of myself; the most important persons in this matter are our son and yourself. It may very well be, I repeat, that my words seem to you utterly unnecessary and out of place; it may be that they are called forth by my mistaken impression. In that case, I beg you to forgive me. But if you are conscious yourself of even the smallest foundation for them, then I beg you to think a little, and if your heart prompts you, to speak out to me. . . .'

Alexey Alexandrovitch was unconsciously saying something utterly unlike what he had prepared.

'I have nothing to say. And besides,' she said hurriedly, with difficulty repressing a smile, 'it's really time to be in bed.'

Alexey Alexandrovitch sighed, and, without saying more, went into the bedroom.

When she came into the bedroom, he was already in bed. His lips were sternly compressed, and his eyes looked away from her. Anna got into her bed, and lay expecting every minute that he would begin to speak to her again. She both feared his speaking and wished for it. But he was silent. She waited for a long while without moving, and had forgotten about him. She thought of that other; she pictured him, and felt how her heart was flooded with emotion and guilty delight at the thought of him. Suddenly she heard an even, tranquil snore. For the first instant Alexey Alexandrovitch seemed as it were appalled at his own snoring, and ceased; but after an interval of two breathings the snore sounded again, with a new tranquil rhythm.

'It's late, it's late,' she whispered with a smile. A long while she lay, not moving, with open eyes, whose brilliance she almost fancied she could herself see in the darkness.

X

FROM that time a new life began for Alexey Alexandrovitch and for his wife. Nothing special happened. Anna went out into society, as she had always done, was particularly often at Princess Betsy's, and met Vronsky everywhere. Alexey Alexandrovitch saw this, but could do nothing. All his efforts to draw her into open discussion she confronted with a barrier which he could not penetrate, made up of a sort of amused perplexity. Outwardly everything was the same, but their inner relations were completely changed. Alexey Alexandrovitch, a man of great power in the world of politics, felt himself helpless in this. Like an ox with head bent, submissively he awaited the blow which he felt was lifted over him. Every time he began to think about it, he felt that he must try once more, that by kindness, tenderness, and persuasion there was still hope of saving her, of bringing her back to herself, and every day he made ready to talk to her. But every time he began talking to her, he felt that the spirit of evil and deceit, which had taken possession of her, had possession of him too, and he talked to her in a tone quite unlike that in which he had meant to talk. Involuntarily he talked to her in his habitual tone of jeering at anyone who should say what he was saying. And in that tone it was impossible to say what needed to be said to her.

XI

THAT which for Vronsky had been almost a whole year the one absorbing desire of his life, replacing all his old desires; that which for Anna had been an impossible, terrible, and even for that reason more entrancing dream of bliss, that desire had been fulfilled. He stood before her, pale, his lower jaw quivering, and besought her to be calm, not knowing how or why.

'Anna! Anna!' he said with a choking voice, 'Anna, for pity's sake! . . .'

But the louder he spoke, the lower she dropped her once proud and gay, now shame-stricken head, and she bowed down and sank from the sofa where she was sitting, down on the floor, at his feet; she would have fallen on the carpet if he had not held her.

'My God! Forgive me!' she said, sobbing, pressing his hands to her bosom.

She felt so sinful, so guilty, that nothing was left her but to humiliate herself and beg forgiveness; and as now there was no one in her life but him, to him she addressed her prayer for forgiveness. Looking at him, she had a physical sense of her humiliation, and she could say nothing more. He felt what a murderer must feel, when he sees the body he has robbed of life. That body, robbed by him of life, was their love, the first stage of their love. There was something awful and revolting in the memory of what had been bought at this fearful price of shame. Shame at their spiritual nakedness crushed her and infected him. But in spite of all the murderer's horror before the body of his victim, he must hack it to pieces, hide the body, must use what he has gained by his murder.

And with fury, as it were with passion, the murderer falls on the body, and drags it and hacks at it; so he covered her face and shoulders with kisses. She held his hand, and did not stir. 'Yes, these kisses—that is what has been bought by this shame. Yes, and one hand, which will always be mine—the hand of my accomplice.' She lifted up that hand and kissed it. He sank on his knees and tried to see her face; but she hid it, and said nothing. At last, as though making an effort over herself, she got up and pushed him away. Her face was still as beautiful, but it was only the more pitiful for that.

'All is over,' she said; 'I have nothing but you. Remember that.'

'I can never forget what is my whole life. For one instant of this happiness . . .'

'Happiness!' she said with horror and loathing, and her horror unconsciously infected him. 'For pity's sake, not a word, not a word more.'

She rose quickly and moved away from him.

'Not a word more,' she repeated, and with a look of chill despair, incomprehensible to him, she parted from him. She felt that at that moment she could not put into words the sense of shame, of rapture, and of horror at this stepping into a new life, and she did not want to speak of it, to vulgarise this feeling by inappropriate words. But later too, and the next day and the third day, she still found no words in which she could express the complexity of her feelings; indeed, she could not even find thoughts in which she could clearly think out all that was in her soul.

She said to herself; 'No, just now I can't think of it; later on, when I am calmer.' But this calm for thought never came; every time the thought rose of what she had done and what would happen to her, and what she ought to do, a horror came over her and she drove those thoughts away.

'Later, later,' she said—'when I am calmer.'

But in dreams, when she had no control over her thoughts, her position presented itself to her in all its hideous nakedness. One dream haunted her almost every night. She dreamed that both were her husbands at once, that both were lavishing caresses on her. Alexey Alexandrovitch was weeping, kissing her hands, and saying, 'How happy we are now!' And Alexey Vronsky was there too, and he too was her husband. And she was marvelling that it had once seemed impossible to her, was explaining to them, laughing, that this was ever so much simpler, and that now both of them were happy and contented. But this dream weighed on her like a nightmare, and she awoke from it in terror.

XII

IN the early days after his return from Moscow, whenever Levin shuddered and grew red, remembering the disgrace of his rejection, he said to himself: 'This was just how I used to shudder and blush, thinking myself utterly lost, when I was plucked in physics and did not get my remove; and how I thought myself utterly ruined after I had mismanaged that affair of my sister's that was intrusted to me. And yet, now that years have passed, I recall it and wonder that it could distress me so much. It will be the same thing too with this trouble. Time will go by and I shall not mind about this either.'

But three months had passed and he had not left off minding about it; and it was as painful for him to think of it as it had been those first days. He could not be at peace because after dreaming so long of family life, and feeling himself so ripe for it, he was still not married, and was further than ever from marriage. He was painfully conscious himself, as were all about him, that at his years it is not well for man to be alone. He remembered how before starting for Moscow he had once said to his cowman Nikolay, a simple-hearted peasant, whom he liked talking to: 'Well, Nikolay! I mean to get married,' and how Nikolay had promptly answered, as of a matter on which there could be no possible doubt; 'And high time too, Konstantin Dmitrich.' But marriage had now become further off than ever. The place was taken, and whenever he tried to imagine any of the girls he knew in that place, he felt that it was utterly impossible. Moreover, the recollection of the rejection and the part he had played in the affair tortured him with shame. However often he told himself that he was in nowise to blame in it, that recollection, like other humiliating reminiscences of a similar kind, made him twinge and blush. There had been in his past, as in every man's, actions, recognised by him as bad, for which his conscience ought to have tormented him; but the memory of these evil actions was far from causing him so much suffering as those trivial but humiliating reminiscences. These wounds never healed. And with these memories was now ranged his rejection and the pitiful position in which he must have appeared to others that evening. But time and work did their part. Bitter memories were more and more covered up by the incidents—paltry in his eyes, but really important—of his country life. Every week he thought less often of Kitty. He was impatiently looking forward to the news that she was married, or just going to be married, hoping that such news would, like having a tooth out, completely cure him.

Meanwhile spring came on, beautiful and kindly, without the delays and treacheries of spring,—one of those rare springs in which plants, beasts, and man rejoice alike. This lovely spring roused Levin still more, and strengthened him in his resolution of renouncing all his past and building up his lonely life firmly and independently. Though many of the plans with which he had returned to the country had not been carried out, still his most important resolution—that of purity—had been kept by him. He was free from that shame, which had usually harassed him after a fall; and he could look everyone straight in the face. In February he had received a letter from Marya Nikolaevna telling him that his brother Nikolay's health was getting worse, but that he would not take advice, and in consequence of this letter Levin went to Moscow to his brother's, and succeeded in persuading him to see a doctor and to go to a watering-place abroad. He succeeded so well in persuading his brother, and in lending him money for the journey without irritating him, that he was satisfied with himself in that matter. In addition to his farming, which called for special attention in spring, in addition to reading, Levin had begun that winter a work on agriculture, the plan of which turned on taking into account the character of the labourer on the land as one of the unalterable data of the question, like the climate and the soil, and consequently deducing all the principles of scientific culture, not simply from the data of soil and climate, but from the data of soil, climate, and a certain unalterable character of the labourer. Thus, in spite of his solitude, or in consequence of his solitude, his life was exceedingly full. Only rarely he suffered from an unsatisfied desire to communicate his stray ideas to someone besides Agafea Mihalovna. With her indeed he not unfrequently fell into discussions upon physics, the theory of agriculture, and especially philosophy; philosophy was Agafea Mihalovna's favourite subject.

Spring was slow in unfolding. For the last few weeks it had been steadily fine frosty weather. In the daytime it thawed in the sun, but at night there were even seven degrees of frost. There was such a frozen surface on the snow that they drove the wagons anywhere off the roads. Easter came in the snow. Then all of a sudden, on Easter Monday, a warm wind sprang up, storm-clouds swooped down, and for three days and three nights the warm, driving rain fell in streams. On Thursday the wind dropped, and a thick grey fog brooded over the land as though hiding the mysteries of the transformations that were being wrought in nature. Behind the fog there was the flowing of water, the cracking and floating of ice, the swift rush of turbid, foaming torrents; and on the following Monday, in the evening, the fog parted, the storm-clouds split up into little curling crests of cloud, the sky cleared, and the real spring had come. In the morning the sun rose brilliant and quickly wore away the thin layer of ice that covered the water, and all the warm air was quivering with the steam that rose up from the quickened earth. The old grass looked greener, and the young grass thrust up its tiny blades; the buds of the guelder-rose and of the currant and the sticky birch-buds were swollen with sap, and an exploring bee was humming about the golden blossoms that studded the willow. Larks trilled unseen above the velvety green fields and the ice-covered stubble-land; peewits wailed over the low lands and marshes flooded by the pools; cranes and wild geese flew high across the sky uttering their spring calls. The cattle, bald in patches where the new hair had not grown yet, lowed in the pastures; the bow-legged lambs frisked round their bleating mothers. Nimble children ran about the drying paths, covered with the prints of bare feet. There was a merry chatter of peasant women over their linen at the pond, and the ring of axes in the yard, where the peasants were repairing ploughs and harrows. The real spring had come.

XIII

LEVIN put on his big boots, and, for the first time, a cloth jacket, instead of his fur cloak, and went out to look after his farm, stepping over streams of water that flashed in the sunshine and dazzled his eyes, and treading one minute on ice and the next into sticky mud.

Spring is the time of plans and projects. And, as he came out into the farmyard, Levin, like a tree in spring that knows not what form will be taken by the young shoots and twigs imprisoned in its swelling buds, hardly knew what undertakings he was going to begin upon now in the farm-work that was so dear to him. But he felt that he was full of the most splendid plans and projects. First of all he went to the cattle. The cows had been let out into their paddock, and their smooth sides were already shining with their new, sleek, spring coats; they basked in the sunshine and lowed to go to the meadow. Levin gazed admiringly at the cows he knew so intimately to the minutest detail of their condition, and gave orders for them to be driven out into the meadow, and the calves to be let into the paddock. The herdsman ran gaily to get ready for the meadow. The cowherd girls, picking up their petticoats, ran splashing through the mud with bare legs, still white, not yet brown from the sun, waving brushwood in their hands, chasing the calves that frolicked in the mirth of spring.

After admiring the young ones of that year, who were particularly fine—the early calves were the size of a peasant's cow, and Pava's daughter, at three months old, was as big as a yearling,—Levin gave orders for a trough to be brought out and for them to be fed in the paddock. But it appeared that as the paddock had not been used during the winter, the hurdles made in the autumn for it were broken. He sent for the carpenter, who, according to his orders, ought to have been at work at the thrashing-machine. But it appeared that the carpenter was repairing the harrows, which ought to have been repaired before Lent. This was very annoying to Levin. It was annoying to come upon that everlasting slovenliness in the farm-work against which he had been striving with all his might for so many years. The hurdles, as he ascertained, being not wanted in winter, had been carried to the cart horses' stable, and there broken, as they were of light construction, only meant for folding calves. Moreover, it was apparent also that the harrows and all the agricultural implements, which he had directed to be looked over and repaired in the winter, for which very purpose he had hired three carpenters, had not been put into repair, and the harrows were being repaired when they ought to have been harrowing the field. Levin sent for his bailiff, but immediately went off himself to look for him. The bailiff, beaming all over, like everyone that day, in a sheepskin bordered with astrachan, came out of a barn, twisting a bit of straw in his hands.

'Why isn't the carpenter at the thrashing-machine?'

'Oh, I meant to tell you yesterday, the harrows want repairing. Here it's time they got to work in the fields.'

'But what were they doing in the winter, then?'

'But what did you want the carpenter for?'

'Where are the hurdles for the calves' paddock?'

'I ordered them to be got ready. What would you have with those peasants!' said the bailiff, with a wave of his hand.

'It's not those peasants but this bailiff!' said Levin, getting angry. 'Why, what do I keep you for?' he cried. But, bethinking himself that this would not help matters, he stopped short in the middle of a sentence, and merely sighed. 'Well, what do you say? Can sowing begin?' he asked, after a pause.

'Behind Turkin tomorrow or next day they might begin.'

'And the clover?'

'I've sent Vassily and Mishka; they're sowing. Only I don't know if they'll manage to get through; it's so slushy.'

'How many acres?'

'About fifteen.'

'Why not sow all?' cried Levin.

That they were only sowing the clover on fifteen acres, not in all the forty-five, was still more annoying to him. Clover, as he knew, both from books and from his own experience, never did well except when it was sown as early as possible, almost in the snow. And yet Levin could never get this done.

'There's no one to send. What would you have with such a set of peasants? Three haven't turned up. And there's Semyon . . .'

'Well, you should have taken some men from the thatching.'

'And so I have, as it is.'

'Where are the peasants, then?'

'Five are making *compôte*' (which meant compost), 'four are shifting the oats for fear of a touch of mildew, Konstantin Dmitritch.'

Levin knew very well that 'a touch of mildew' meant that his English seed oats were already ruined. Again they had not done as he had ordered.

'Why, but I told you during Lent to put pipes,' he cried.

'Don't put yourself out; we shall get it all done in time.'

Levin waved his hand angrily, went into the granary to glance at the oats, and then to the stable. The oats were not yet spoiled. But the peasants were carrying the oats in spades when they might simply let them slide down into the lower granary; and arranging for this to be done, and taking two workmen from there for sowing clover, Levin got over his vexation with the bailiff. Indeed, it was such a lovely day that one could not be angry.

'Ignat!' he called to the coachman, who, with his sleeves tucked up, was washing the carriage wheels, 'saddle me . . .'

'Which, sir?'

'Well, let it be Kolpik.'

'Yes, sir.'

While they were saddling his horse, Levin again called up the bailiff, who was hanging about in sight, to make it up with him, and began talking to him about the spring operations before them, and his plans for the farm.

The wagons were to begin carting manure earlier, so as to get all done before the early mowing. And the ploughing of the further land to go on without a break so as to let it ripen lying fallow. And the mowing to be all done by hired labour, not on half-profits. The bailiff listened attentively, and obviously made an affort to approve of his employer's projects. But still he had that look Levin knew so well that always irritated him, a look of hopelessness and despondency. That look said: 'That's all very well, but as God wills.'

Nothing mortified Levin so much as that tone. But it was the tone common to all the bailiffs he had ever had. They had all taken up that attitude to his plans, and so now he was not angered by it, but mortified, and felt all the more roused to struggle against this, as it seemed, elemental force continually ranged against him, for which he could find no other expression than 'as God wills.'

'If we can manage it, Konstantin Dmitrich,' said the bailiff.

'Why ever shouldn't you manage it?'

'We positively must have another fifteen labourers. And they don't turn up. There were some here today asking seventy roubles for the summer.'

Levin was silent. Again he was brought face to face with that opposing force. He knew that however much they tried, they could not hire more than forty—thirty-seven perhaps or thirty-eight—labourers for a reasonable sum. Some forty had been taken on, and there were no more. But still he could not help struggling against it.

'Send to Sury, to Tchefirovka; if they don't come we must look for them.'

'Oh, I'll send, to be sure,' said Vassily Fedorovitch despondently. 'But there are the horses too, they're not good for much.'

'We'll get some more. I know, of course,' Levin added laughing, 'you always want to do with as little and as poor quality as possible; but this year I'm not going to let you have things your own way. I'll see to everything myself.'

'Why, I don't think you take much rest as it is. It cheers us up to work under the master's eye ...'

'So they're sowing clover behind the Birch Dale? I'll go and have a look at them,' he said, getting on to the little bay cob, Kolpik, who was led up by the coachman.

'You can't get across the streams, Konstantin Dmitrich,' the coachman shouted.

'All right, I'll go by the forest.'

And Levin rode through the slush of the farmyard to the gate and out into the open country, his good little horse, after his long inactivity, stepping out gallantly, snorting over the pools, and asking, as it were, for guidance. If Levin had felt happy before in the cattle-pens and farmyard, he felt happier yet in the open country. Swaying rhythmically with the ambling paces of his good little cob, drinking in the warm yet fresh scent of the snow and the air, as he rode through his forest over the crumbling, wasted snow, still left in parts, and covered with dissolving tracks, he rejoiced over every tree, with the moss reviving on its bark and the buds swelling on its shoots. When he came out of the forest, in the immense plain before him, his grassfields stretched in an unbroken carpet of green, without one bare place or swamp, only spotted here and there in the hollows with patches of melting snow. He was not put out of temper even by the sight of the peasants' horses and colts trampling down his young grass (he told a peasant he met to drive them out), nor by the sarcastic and stupid reply of the peasant Ipat, whom he met on the way, and asked, 'Well, Ipat, shall we soon be sowing?' 'We must get the ploughing done first, Konstantin Dmitritch,' answered Ipat. The further he rode, the happier he became, and plans for the land rose to his mind each better than the last; to plant all his fields with hedges along the southern borders, so that the snow should not lie under them; to divide them up into six fields of arable and three of pasture and hay; to build a cattle-yard at the further end of the estate, and to dig a pond and to construct movable pens for the cattle as a means of manuring the land. And then eight hundred acres of wheat, three hundred of potatoes, and four hundred of clover, and not one acre exhausted.

Absorbed in such dreams, carefully keeping his horse by the hedges, so as not to trample his young crops, he rode up to the labourers who had been sent to sow clover. A cart with the seed in it was standing, not at the edge, but in the middle of the crop, and the winter-corn had been torn up by the wheels and trampled by the horse. Both the labourers were sitting in the hedge, probably smoking a pipe together. The earth in the cart, with which the seed was mixed, was not crushed to powder, but crusted together or adhering in clods. Seeing the master, the labourer, Vassily, went towards the cart, while Mishka set to work sowing. This was not as it should be, but with the labourers Levin seldom lost his temper. When Vassily came up, Levin told him to lead the horse to the hedge.

'It's all right, sir, it'll spring up again,' responded Vassily.

'Please don't argue,' said Levin, 'but do as you're told.'

'Yes, sir,' answered Vassily, and he took the horse's head. 'What a sowing, Konstantin Dmitrich,' he said, hesitating; 'first-rate. Only it's a work to get about! You drag a ton of earth on your shoes.'

'Why is it you have earth that's not sifted?' said Levin.

'Well, we crumble it up,' answered Vassily, taking up some seed and rolling the earth in his palms.

Vassily was not to blame for their having filled up his cart with unsifted earth, but still it was annoying.

Levin had more than once already tried a way he knew for stifling his anger, and turning all that seemed dark right again, and he tried that way now. He watched how Mishka strode along, swinging the huge clods of earth that clung to each foot; and getting off his horse, he took the sieve from Vassily and started sowing himself.

'Where did you stop?'

Vassily pointed to the mark with his foot, and Levin went forward, as best he could, scattering the seed on the land. Walking was as difficult as on a bog, and by the time Levin had ended the row he was in a great heat, and he stopped and gave up the sieve to Vassily.

'Well, master, when summer's here, mind you don't scold me for these rows,' said Vassily.

'Eh?' said Levin cheerily, already feeling the effect of his method.

'Why, you'll see in the summer-time. It'll look different. Look you where I sowed last spring. How I did work at it! I do my best, Konstantin Dmitrich, d'ye see, as I would for my own father. I don't like bad work myself, nor would I let another man do it. What's good for the master's good for us too. To look out yonder now,' said Vassily, pointing, 'it does one's heart good.'

'It's a lovely spring, Vassily.'

'Why, it's a spring such as the old men don't remember the like of. I was up home; an old man up there has sown wheat too, about an acre of it. He was saying you wouldn't know it from rye.'

'Have you been sowing wheat long?'

'Why, sir, it was you taught us the year before last. You gave me two measures. We sold about eight bushels and sowed a rood.'

'Well, mind you crumble up the clods,' said Levin, going towards his house, 'and keep an eye on Mishka. And if there's a good crop you shall have half a rouble for every acre.'

'Humbly thankful. We are very well content, sir, as it is.'

Levin got on his horse and rode towards the field where was last year's clover, and the one which was ploughed ready for the spring corn.

The crop of clover coming up in the stubble was magnificent. It had survived everything, and stood up vividly green through the broken stalks of last year's wheat. The horse sank in up to the pasterns, and he drew each hoof with a sucking sound out of the half-thawed ground. Over the ploughland riding was utterly impossible; the horse could only keep a foothold where there was ice, and in the thawing furrows he sank deep in at each step. The ploughland was in splendid condition; in a couple of days it would be fit for harrowing and sowing. Everything was capital, everything was cheering. Levin rode back across the streams, hoping the water would have gone down. And he did in fact get across, and started two ducks. 'There must be snipe too,' he thought, and just as he reached the turning homewards he met the forest keeper, who confirmed his theory about the snipe.

Levin went home at a trot, so as to have time to eat his dinner and get his gun ready for the evening.

XIV

As he rode up to the house in the happiest frame of mind, Levin heard the bell ring at the side of the principal entrance of the house.

'Yes, that's someone from the railway station,' he thought, 'just the time to be here from the Moscow train. . . . Who could it be? What if it's brother Nikolay? He did say: "Maybe I'll go to the waters, or maybe I'll come down to you."' He felt dismayed and vexed for the first minute that his brother Nikolay's presence should come to disturb his happy mood of spring. But he felt ashamed of the feeling, and at once he opened, as it were, the arms of his soul, and with a softened feeling of joy and expectation, now he hoped with all his heart that it was his brother. He pricked up his horse, and riding out from behind the acacias he saw a hired three-horse sledge from the railway station, and a gentleman in a fur coat. It was not his brother. 'Oh, if it were only some nice person one could talk to a little!' he thought.

'Ah!' cried Levin joyfully, flinging up both his hands. 'Here's a delightful visitor! Ah, how glad I am to see you!' he shouted, recognising Stepan Arkadyevitch.

'I shall find out for certain whether she's married, or when she's going to be married,' he thought. And on that delicious spring day he felt that the thought of her did not hurt him at all.

'Well, you didn't expect me, eh?' said Stepan Arkadyevitch, getting out of the sledge, splashed with mud on the bridge of his nose, on his cheek, and on his eyebrows, but radiant with health and good spirits. 'I've come to see you in the first place,' he said, embracing and kissing him, 'to have some stand-shooting second, and to sell the forest at Ergushovo third.'

'Delightful! What a spring we're having! How ever did you get along in a sledge?'

'In a cart it would have been worse still, Konstantin Dmitritch,' answered the driver, who knew him.

'Well, I'm very, very glad to see you,' said Levin, with a genuine smile of childlike delight.

Levin led his friend to the room set apart for visitors, where Stepan Arkadyevitch's things were carried also—a bag, a gun in a case, a satchel for cigars. Leaving him there to wash and change his clothes, Levin went off to the counting-house to speak about the ploughing and clover. Agafea Mihalovna, always very anxious for the credit of the house, met him in the hall with inquiries about dinner.

'Do just as you like, only let it be as soon as possible,' he said, and went to the bailiff.

When he came back, Stepan Arkadyevitch, washed and combed, came out of his room with a beaming smile, and they went upstairs together.

'Well, I am glad I managed to get away to you! Now I shall understand what the mysterious business is that you are always absorbed in here. No, really, I envy you. What a house, how nice it all is! So bright, so cheerful!' said Stepan Arkadyevitch, forgetting that it was not always spring and fine weather like that day. 'And your nurse is simply charming! A pretty maid in an apron might be even more agreeable, perhaps; but for your severe monastic style it does very well.'

Stepan Arkadyevitch told him many interesting pieces of news; especially interesting to Levin was the news that his brother, Sergey Ivanovitch, was intending to pay him a visit in the summer.

Not one word did Stepan Arkadyevitch say in reference to Kitty and the Shtcherbatskys; he merely gave him greetings from his wife. Levin was grateful to him for his delicacy, and was very glad of his visitor. As always happened with him during his solitude, a mass of ideas and feelings had been accumulating within him, which he could not communicate to those about him. And now he poured out upon Stepan Arkadyevitch his poetic joy in the spring, and his failures and plans for the land, and his thoughts and criticisms on the books he had been reading, and the idea of his own book, the basis of which really was, though he was unaware of it himself, a criticism of all the old books on agriculture. Stepan Arkadyevitch, always charming, understanding everything at the slightest reference, was particularly charming on this visit, and Levin noticed in him a special tenderness, as it were, and a new tone of respect that flattered him.

The efforts of Agafea Mihalovna and the cook, that the dinner should be particularly good, only ended in the two famished friends attacking the preliminary course, eating a great deal of bread-and-butter, salt goose and salted mushrooms, and in Levin's finally ordering the soup to be served without the accompaniment of little pies, with which the cook had particularly meant to impress their visitor. But though Stepan Arkadyevitch was accustomed to very different dinners, he thought everything excellent: the herb-brandy, and the bread, and the butter, and above all the salt goose and the mushrooms, and the nettle soup, and the chicken in white sauce, and the white Crimean wine—everything was superb and delicious.

'Splendid, splendid!' he said, lighting a fat cigar after the roast. 'I feel as if, coming to you, I had landed on a peaceful shore after the noise and jolting of a steamer. And so you maintain that the labourer himself is an element to be studied and to regulate the choice of methods in agriculture. Of course, I'm an ignorant outsider; but I should fancy theory and its application will have its influence on the labourer too.'

'Yes, but wait a bit. I'm not talking of political economy, I'm talking of the science of agriculture. It ought to be like the natural sciences, and to observe given phenomena and the labourer in his economic, ethnographical . . .'

At that instant Agafea Mihalovna came in with jam.

'Oh, Agafea Mihalovna,' said Stepan Arkadyevitch, kissing the tips of his plump fingers, 'what salt goose, what herb-brandy! . . . What do you think, isn't it time to start, Kostya?' he added.

Levin looked out of window at the sun sinking behind the bare treetops of the forest.

'Yes, it's time,' he said. 'Kouzma, get ready the trap,' and he ran downstairs.

Stepan Arkadyevitch, going down, carefully took the canvas cover off his varnished gun-case with his own hands, and opening it, began to get ready his expensive new-fashioned gun. Kouzma, who already scented a big tip, never left Stepan Arkadyevitch's side, and put him on both his stockings and boots, a task which Stepan Arkadyevitch readily left him.

'Kostya, give orders that if the merchant Ryabinin comes . . . I told him to come today, he's to be brought in and to wait for me . . .'

'Why, do you mean to say you're selling the forest to Ryabinin?'

'Yes. Do you know him?'

'To be sure I do. I have had to do business with him, "positively and conclusively."'

Stepan Arkadyevitch laughed. 'Positively and conclusively' were the merchant's favourite words.

'Yes, it's wonderfully funny the way he talks. She knows where her master's going!' he added, patting Laska, who hung about Levin, whining and licking his hands, his boots, and his gun.

The trap was already at the steps when they went out.

'I told them to bring the trap round; or would you rather walk?'

'No, we'd better drive,' said Stepan Arkadyevitch, getting into the trap. He sat down, tucked the tiger-skin rug round him, and lighted a cigar. 'How is it you don't smoke? A cigar is a sort of thing, not exactly a pleasure, but the crown and outward sign of pleasure. Come, this is life! How splendid it is! This is how I should like to live!'

'Why, who prevents you?' said Levin, smiling.

'No, you're a lucky man! You've got everything you like. You like horses—and you have them; dogs—you have them; shooting—you have it; farming—you have it.'

'Perhaps because I rejoice in what I have, and don't fret for what I haven't,' said Levin, thinking of Kitty.

Stepan Arkadyevitch comprehended, looked at him, but said nothing.

Levin was grateful to Oblonsky for noticing, with his never-failing tact, that he dreaded conversation about the Shtcherbatskys, and so saying nothing about them. But now Levin was longing to find out what was tormenting him so, yet he had not the courage to begin.

'Come, tell me how things are going with you,' said Levin, bethinking himself that it was not nice of him to think only of himself.

Stepan Arkadyevitch's eyes sparkled merrily.

'You don't admit, I know, that one can be fond of new rolls when one has had one's rations of bread—to your mind it's a crime; but I don't count life as life without love,' he said, taking Levin's question in his own way. 'What am I to do? I'm made that way. And really, one does so little harm to anyone, and gives oneself so much pleasure . . .'

'What! is there something new, then?' queried Levin.

'Yes, my boy, there is! There, do you see, you know the type of Ossian's women . . . Women, such as one sees in dreams . . . Well, these women are sometimes to be met in reality . . . and these women are terrible. Woman, don't you know, is such a subject that however much you study it, it's always perfectly new.'

'Well, then, it would be better not to study it.'

'No. Some mathematician has said that enjoyment lies in the search for truth, not in the finding it.'

Levin listened in silence, and in spite of all the efforts he made, he could not in the least enter into the feelings of his friend and understand his sentiments and the charm of studying such women.

XV

THE place fixed on for the stand-shooting was not far above a stream in a little aspen copse. On reaching the copse, Levin got out of the trap and led Oblonsky to a corner of a mossy, swampy glade, already quite free from snow. He went back himself to a double birch-tree on the other side, and leaning his gun on the fork of a dead lower branch, he took off his full overcoat, fastened his belt again, and worked his arms to see if they were free.

Grey old Laska, who had followed them, sat down warily opposite him and pricked up her ears. The sun was setting behind a thick forest, and in the glow of sunset the birch-trees, dotted about in the aspen copse, stood out clearly with their hanging twigs, and their buds swollen almost to bursting.

From the thickest parts of the copse, where the snow still remained, came the faint sound of narrow winding threads of water running away. Tiny birds twittered, and now and then fluttered from tree to tree.

In the pauses of complete stillness there came the rustle of last year's leaves, stirred by the thawing of the earth and the growth of the grass.

'Imagine! One can hear and see the grass growing!' Levin said to himself, noticing a wet, slate-coloured aspen leaf moving beside a blade of young grass. He stood, listened, and gazed sometimes down at the wet mossy ground, sometimes at Laska listening all alert, sometimes at the sea of bare tree-tops that stretched on the slope below him, sometimes at the darkening sky, covered with white streaks of cloud.

A hawk flew high over a forest far away with a slow sweep of its wings; another flew with exactly the same motion in the same direction and vanished. The birds twittered more and more loudly and busily in the thicket. An owl hooted not far off, and Laska, starting, stepped cautiously a few steps forward, and putting her head on one side, began to listen intently. Beyond the stream was heard the cuckoo. Twice she uttered her usual cuckoo-call, and then gave a hoarse, hurried call and broke down.

'Imagine! the cuckoo already!' said Stepan Arkadyevitch, coming out from behind a bush.

'Yes, I hear it,' answered Levin, reluctantly breaking the stillness with his voice, which sounded disagreeable to himself. 'Now it's coming!'

Stepan Arkadyevitch's figure again went behind the bush and Levin saw nothing but the bright flash of a match, followed by the red glow and blue smoke of a cigarette.

'Tchk! tchk!' came the snapping sound of Stepan Arkadyevitch cocking his gun.

'What's that cry?' asked Oblonsky, drawing Levin's attention to a prolonged cry, as though a colt were whinnying in a high voice, in play.

'Oh, don't you know it? That's the hare. But enough talking! Listen, it's flying!' almost shrieked Levin, cocking his gun.

They heard a shrill whistle in the distance, and in the exact time, so well-known to the sportsman, two seconds later—another, a third, and after the third whistle the hoarse, guttural cry could be heard.

Levin looked about him to right and to left, and there, just facing him against the dusky blue sky above the confused mass of tender shoots of the aspens, he saw the flying bird. It was flying straight towards him; the guttural cry, like the even tearing of some strong stuff, sounded close to his ear; the long beak and neck of the bird could be seen, and at the very instant when Levin was taking aim, behind the bush where Oblonsky stood, there was a flash of red lightning: the bird dropped like an arrow, and darted upwards again. Again came the red flash and the sound of a blow, and fluttering its wings as though trying to keep up in the air, the bird halted, stopped still an instant, and fell with a heavy splash on the slushy ground.

'Can I have missed it?' shouted Stepan Arkadyevitch, who could not see for the smoke.

'Here it is!' said Levin, pointing to Laska, who with one ear raised, wagging the end of her shaggy tail, came slowly back as though she would prolong the pleasure, and as it were smiling, brought the dead bird to her master. 'Well, I'm glad you were successful,' said Levin, who, at the same time, had a sense of envy that he had not succeeded in shooting the snipe.

'It was a bad shot from the right barrel,' responded Stepan Arkadyevitch, loading his gun. 'Sh . . . it's flying!'

The shrill whistles rapidly following one another were heard again. Two snipe, playing and chasing one another, and only whistling, not crying, flew straight at the very heads of the sportsmen. There was the report of four shots, and like swallows the snipe turned swift somersaults in the air and vanished from sight.

The stand-shooting was capital. Stepan Arkadyevitch shot two more birds and Levin two, of which one was not found. It began to get dark. Venus, bright and silvery, shone with her soft light low down in the west behind the birch-trees, and high up in the east twinkled the red lights of Arcturus. Over his head Levin made out the stars of the Great Bear and lost them again. The snipe had ceased flying; but Levin resolved to stay a little longer, till Venus, which he saw below a branch of birch, should be above it, and the stars of the Great Bear should be perfectly plain. Venus had risen above the branch, and the car of the Great Bear with its shaft was now all plainly visible against the dark blue sky, yet still he waited.

'Isn't it time to go home?' said Stepan Arkadyevitch.

It was quite still now in the copse, and not a bird was stirring.

'Let's stay a little while,' answered Levin.

'As you like.'

They were standing now about fifteen paces from one another.

'Stiva!' said Levin unexpectedly; 'how is it you don't tell me whether your sister-in-law's married yet, or when she's going to be?'

Levin felt so resolute and serene that no answer, he fancied, could affect him. But he had never dreamed of what Stepan Arkadyevitch replied.

'She's never thought of being married, and isn't thinking of it; but she's very ill, and the doctors have sent her abroad. They're positively afraid she may not live.'

'What!' cried Levin. 'Very ill? What is wrong with her? How has she ...?'

While they were saying this, Laska, with ears pricked up, was looking upwards at the sky, and reproachfully at them.

'They have chosen a time to talk,' she was thinking. 'It's on the wing ... Here it is, yes it is. They'll miss it,' thought Laska.

But at that very instant both suddenly heard a shrill whistle which, as it were, smote on their ears, and both suddenly seized their guns and two flashes gleamed, and two bangs sounded at the very same instant. The snipe flying high above instantly folded its wings and fell into a thicket, bending down the delicate shoots.

'Splendid! Together!' cried Levin, and he ran with Laska into the thicket to look for the snipe.

'Oh yes, what was it that was unpleasant?' he wondered. 'Yes, Kitty's ill. ... Well, it can't be helped; I'm very sorry,' he thought.

'She's found it! Isn't she a clever thing!' he said, taking the warm bird from Laska's mouth and packing it into the almost full game-bag. 'I've got it, Stiva!' he shouted.

XVI

ON the way home Levin asked all details of Kitty's illness and the Shtcherbatskys' plans, and though he would have been ashamed to admit it, he was pleased at what he heard. He was pleased that there was still hope, and still more pleased that she should be suffering who had made him suffer so much. But when Stepan Arkadyevitch began to speak of the causes of Kitty's illness, and mentioned Vronsky's name, Levin cut him short.

'I have no right whatever to know family matters, and, to tell the truth, no interest in them either.'

Stepan Arkadyevitch smiled hardly perceptibly, catching the instantaneous change he knew so well in Levin's face, which had become as gloomy as it had been bright a minute before.

'Have you quite settled about the forest with Ryabinin?' asked Levin.

'Yes, it's settled. The price is magnificent; thirty-eight thousand. Eight straight away, and the rest in six years. I've been bothering about it for ever so long. No one would give more.'

'Then you've as good as given away your forest for nothing,' said Levin gloomily.

'How do you mean for nothing?' said Stepan Arkadyevitch with a good-humoured smile, knowing that nothing would be right in Levin's eyes now.

'Because the forest is worth at least a hundred and fifty roubles the acre,' answered Levin.

'Oh, these farmers!' said Stepan Arkadyevitch playfully. 'Your tone of contempt for us poor townsfolk! . . . But when it comes to business, we do it better than anyone. I assure you I have reckoned it all out,' he said, 'and the forest is fetching a very good price—so much so that I'm afraid of this fellow's crying off, in fact. You know it's not "timber",' said Stepan Arkadyevitch, hoping by this distinction to convince Levin completely of the unfairness of his doubts. 'And it won't run to more than twenty-five yards of fagots per acre, and he's giving me at the rate of seventy roubles the acre.'

Levin smiled contemptuously. 'I know,' he thought, 'that fashion not only in him, but in all city people, who, after being twice in ten years in the country, pick up two or three phrases and use them in season and out of season, firmly persuaded that they know all about it. "*Timber, run to so many yards the acre.*" He says those words without understanding them himself.'

'I wouldn't attempt to teach you what you write about in your office,' said he, 'and if need arose, I should come to you to ask about it. But you're so positive you know all the lore of the forest. It's difficult. Have you counted the trees?'

'How count the trees?' said Stepan Arkadyevitch, laughing, still trying to draw his friend out of his ill-temper. 'Count the sands of the sea, number the stars. Some higher power might do it.'

'Oh, well, the higher power of Ryabinin can. Not a single merchant ever buys a forest without counting the trees, unless they get it given them for nothing, as you're doing now. I know your forest. I go there every year shooting, and your forest's worth a hundred and fifty roubles an acre paid down, while he's giving you sixty by instalments. So that in fact you're making him a present of thirty thousand.'

'Come, don't let your imagination run away with you,' said Stepan Arkadyevitch piteously. 'Why was it none would give it, then?'

'Why, because he has an understanding with the merchants; he's bought them off. I've had to do with all of them; I know them. They're not merchants, you know; they're speculators. He wouldn't look at a bargain that gave him ten, fifteen per cent profit, but holds back to buy a rouble's worth for twenty copecks.'

'Well, enough of it! You're out of temper.'

'Not the least,' said Levin gloomily, as they drove up to the house.

At the steps there stood a trap tightly covered with iron and leather, with a sleek horse tightly harnessed with broad collar-straps. In the trap sat the chubby, tightly belted clerk who served Ryabinin as coachman. Ryabinin himself was already in the house, and met the friends in the hall. Ryabinin was a tall, thinnish, middle-aged man, with moustache and a projecting clean-shaven chin, and prominent muddy-looking eyes. He was dressed in a long-skirted blue coat, with buttons below the waist at the back, and wore high boots wrinkled over the ankles and straight over the calf, with big goloshes drawn over them. He rubbed his face with his handkerchief, and wrapping round him his coat, which sat extremely well as it was, he greeted them with a smile, holding out his hand to Stepan Arkadyevitch, as though he wanted to catch something.

'So here you are,' said Stepan Arkadyevitch, giving him his hand. 'That's capital.'

'I did not venture to disregard your excellency's commands, though the road was extremely bad. I positively walked the whole way, but I am here at my time. Konstantin Dmitritch, my respects'; he turned to Levin, trying to seize his hand too. But Levin, scowling, made as though he did not notice his hand, and took out the snipe. 'Your honours have been diverting yourselves with the chase? What kind of bird may it be pray?' added Ryabinin, looking contemptuously at the snipe: 'a great delicacy, I suppose.' And he shook his head disapprovingly, as though he had grave doubts whether this game was worth the candle.

'Would you like to go into my study?' Levin said in French to Stepan Arkadyevitch, scowling morosely. 'Go into my study; you can talk there.'

'Quite so, where you please,' said Ryabinin with contemptuous dignity, as though wishing to make it felt that others might be in difficulties as to how to behave, but that he could never be in any difficulty about anything.

On entering the study Ryabinin looked about, as his habit was, as though seeking the holy picture, but when he had found it, he did not cross himself. He scanned the bookcases and bookshelves, and with the same dubious air with which he had regarded the snipe, he smiled contemptuously and shook his head disapprovingly, as though by no means willing to allow that this game were worth the candle.

'Well, have you brought the money?' asked Oblonsky. 'Sit down.'

'Oh, don't trouble about the money. I've come to see you to talk it over.'

'What is there to talk over? But do sit down.'

'I don't mind if I do,' said Ryabinin, sitting down and leaning his elbows on the back of his chair in a position of the intensest discomfort to himself. 'You must knock it down a bit, prince. It would be too bad. The money is ready conclusively to the last farthing. As to paying the money down, there'll be no hitch there.'

Levin, who had meanwhile been putting his gun away in the cupboard, was just going out of the door, but catching the merchant's words, he stopped.

'Why, you've got the forest for nothing as it is,' he said. 'He came to me too late, or I'd have fixed the price for him.'

Ryabinin got up, and in silence, with a smile, he looked Levin down and up.

'Very close about money is Konstantin Dmitritch,' he said with a smile, turning to Stepan Arkadyevitch; 'there's positively no dealing with him. I was bargaining for some wheat of him, and a pretty price I offered too.'

'Why should I give you my goods for nothing? I didn't pick it up on the ground, nor steal it either.'

'Mercy on us! nowadays there's no chance at all of stealing. With the open courts and everything done in style, nowadays there's no question of stealing. We are just talking things over like gentlemen. His excellency's asking too much for the forest. I can't make both ends meet over it. I must ask for a little concession.'

'But is the thing settled between you or not? If it's settled, it's useless haggling; but if it's not,' said Levin, 'I'll buy the forest.'

The smile vanished at once from Ryabinin's face. A hawk-like, greedy, cruel expression was left upon it. With rapid, bony fingers he unbuttoned his coat, revealing a shirt, bronze waistcoat buttons, and a watch-chain, and quickly pulled out a fat old pocket-book.

'Here you are, the forest is mine,' he said, crossing himself quickly, and holding out his hand. 'Take the money; it's my forest. That's Ryabinin's way of doing business; he doesn't haggle over every half-penny,' he added, scowling and waving the pocket-book.

'I wouldn't be in a hurry if I were you,' said Levin.

'Come, really,' said Oblonsky in surprise, 'I've given my word, you know.'

Levin went out of the room, slamming the door. Ryabinin looked towards the door and shook his head with a smile.

'It's all youthfulness—positively nothing but boyishness. Why, I'm buying it, upon my honour, simply, believe me, for the glory of it, that Ryabinin, and no one else, should have bought the copse of Oblonsky. And as to the profits, why, I must make what God gives. In God's name. If you would kindly sign the title-deed . . .'

Within an hour the merchant, stroking his big overcoat neatly down, and hooking up his jacket, with the agreement in his pocket, seated himself in his tightly covered trap, and drove homewards.

'Ugh, these gentlefolks!' he said to the clerk. 'They—they're a nice lot!'

'That's so,' responded the clerk, handing him the reins and buttoning the leather apron. 'But can I congratulate you on the purchase, Mihail Ignatitch?'

'Well, well. . . .'

XVII

STEPAN ARKADYEVITCH went upstairs with his pocket bulging with notes, which the merchant had paid him for three months in advance. The business of the forest was over, the money in his pocket; their shooting had been excellent, and Stepan Arkadyevitch was in the happiest frame of mind, and so he felt specially anxious to dissipate the ill-humour that had come upon Levin. He wanted to finish the day at supper as pleasantly as it had been begun.

Levin certainly was out of humour, and in spite of all his desire to be affectionate and cordial to his charming visitor, he could not control his mood. The intoxication of the news that Kitty was not married had gradually begun to work upon him.

Kitty was not married, but ill, and ill from love for a man who had slighted her. This slight, as it were, rebounded upon him. Vronsky had slighted her, and she had slighted him, Levin. Consequently Vronsky had the right to despise Levin, and therefore he was his enemy. But all this Levin did not think out. He vaguely felt that there was something in it insulting to him, and he was not angry now at what had disturbed him, but he fell foul of everything that presented itself. The stupid sale of the forest, the fraud practised upon Oblonsky and concluded in his house, exasperated him.

'Well, finished?' he said, meeting Stepan Arkadyevitch upstairs. 'Would you like supper?'

'Well, I wouldn't say no to it. What an appetite I get in the country! Wonderful! Why didn't you offer Ryabinin something?'

'Oh, damn him!'

'Still, how you do treat him!' said Oblonsky. 'You didn't even shake hands with him. Why not shake hands with him?'

'Because I don't shake hands with a waiter, and a waiter's a hundred times better than he is.'

'What a reactionist you are, really! What about the amalgamation of classes?' said Oblonsky.

'Anyone who likes amalgamating is welcome to it, but it sickens me.'

'You're a regular reactionist, I see.'

'Really, I have never considered what I am. I am Konstantin Levin, and nothing else.'

'And Konstantin Levin very much out of temper,' said Stepan Arkadyevitch, smiling.

'Yes, I am out of temper, and do you know why? Because—excuse me—of your stupid sale. . . .'

Stepan Arkadyevitch frowned good-humouredly, like one who feels himself teased and attacked for no fault of his own.

'Come, enough about it!' he said. 'When did anybody ever sell anything without being told immediately after the sale, "It was worth much more"? But when one wants to sell, no one will give anything. . . . No, I see you've a grudge against that unlucky Ryabinin.'

'Maybe I have. And do you know why? You'll say again that I'm a reactionist, or some other terrible word; but all the same it does annoy and anger me to see on all sides the impoverishing of the nobility to which I belong, and, in spite of the amalgamation of classes, I'm glad to belong. And their impoverishment is not due to extravagance—that would be nothing; living in good style—that's the proper thing for noblemen: it's only the nobles who know how to do it. Now the peasants about us buy land, and I don't mind that. The gentleman does nothing, while the peasant works and supplants the idle man. That's as it ought to be. And I'm very glad for the peasant. But I do mind seeing the process of impoverishment from a sort of—I don't know what to call it—innocence. Here a Polish speculator bought for half its value a magnificent estate from a young lady who lives in Nice. And there a merchant will get three acres of land, worth ten roubles, as security for the loan of one rouble. Here, for no kind of reason, you've made that rascal a present of thirty thousand roubles.'

'Well, what should I have done? Count every tree?'

'Of course, they must be counted. You didn't count them, but Ryabinin did. Ryabinin's children will have means of livelihood and education, while yours maybe will not!'

'Well, you must excuse me, but there's something mean in this counting. We have our business and they have theirs, and they must make their profit. Anyway, the thing's done, and there's an end of it. And here come some poached eggs, my favourite dish. And Agafea Mihalovna will give us that marvellous herb-brandy. . . .'

Stepan Arkadyevitch sat down at the table and began joking with Agafea Mihalovna, assuring her that it was long since he had tasted such a dinner and such a supper.

'Well, you do praise it, anyway,' said Agafea Mihalovna, 'but Konstantin Dmitritch, give him what you will—a crust of bread—he'll eat it and walk away.'

Though Levin tried to control himself, he was gloomy and silent. He wanted to put one question to Stepan Arkadyevitch, but he could not bring himself to the point, and could not find the words or the moment in which to put it. Stepan Arkadyevitch had gone down to his room, undressed, again washed, and attired in a night-shirt with goffered frills, he had got into bed, but Levin still lingered in his room, talking of various trifling matters, and not daring to ask what he wanted to know.

'How wonderfully they make this soap,' he said, gazing at a piece of soap he was handling, which Agafea Mihalovna had put ready for the visitor but Oblonsky had not used. 'Only look; why, it's a work of art.'

'Yes, everything's brought to such a pitch of perfection nowadays,' said Stepan Arkadyevitch, with a moist and blissful yawn. 'The theatre, for instance, and the entertainments . . . a-a-a!' he yawned. 'The electric light everywhere . . . a-a-a!'

'Yes, the electric light,' said Levin. 'Yes. Oh, and where's Vronsky now?' he asked suddenly, laying down the soap.

'Vronsky?' said Stepan Arkadyevitch, checking his yawn; 'he's in Petersburg. He left soon after you did, and he's not once been in Moscow since. And do you know, Kostya, I'll tell you the truth,' he went on, leaning his elbow on the table, and propping on his hand his handsome ruddy face, in which his moist, good-natured, sleepy eyes shone like stars. 'It's your own fault. You took fright at the sight of your rival. But, as I told you at the time, I couldn't say which had the better chance. Why didn't you fight it out? I told you at the time that . . .' He yawned inwardly, without opening his mouth.

'Does he know, or doesn't he, that I did make an offer?' Levin wondered, gazing at him. 'Yes, there's something humbugging, diplomatic in his face,' and feeling he was blushing, he looked Stepan Arkadyevitch straight in the face without speaking.

'If there was anything on her side at that time, it was nothing but a superficial attraction,' pursued Oblonsky. 'His being such a perfect aristocrat, don't you know, and his future position in society, had an influence not with her, but with her mother.'

Levin scowled. The humiliation of his rejection stung him to the heart, as though it were a fresh wound he had only just received. But he was at home, and the walls of home are a support.

'Stay, stay,' he began, interrupting Oblonsky. 'You talk of his being an aristocrat. But allow me to ask what it consists in, that aristocracy of Vronsky or of anybody else, beside which I can be looked down upon? You consider Vronsky an aristocrat, but I don't. A man whose father crawled up from nothing at all by intrigue, and whose mother—God knows whom she wasn't mixed up with. . . . No, excuse me, but I consider myself aristocratic, and people like me, who can point back in the past to three or four honourable generations of their family, of the highest degree of breeding (talent and intellect, of course that's another matter), and have never curried favour with anyone, never depended on anyone for anything, like my father and my grandfather. And I know many such. You think it mean of me to count the trees in my forest, while you make Ryabinin a present of thirty thousand; but you get rents from your lands and I don't know what, while I don't, and so I prize what's come to me from my ancestors or been won by hard work. . . . We are aristocrats, and not those who can only exist by favour of the powerful of this world, and who can be bought for twopence halfpenny.'

'Well, but whom are you attacking? I agree with you,' said Stepan Arkadyevitch, sincerely and genially; though he was aware that in the class of those who could be bought for twopence halfpenny Levin was reckoning him too. Levin's warmth gave him genuine pleasure. 'Whom are you attacking? Though a good deal is not true that you say about Vronsky, but I won't talk about that. I tell you straight out, if I were you, I should go back with me to Moscow, and . . .'

'No; I don't know whether you know it or not, but I don't care. And I tell you—I did make an offer and was rejected, and Katerina Alexandrovna is nothing now to me but a painful and humiliating reminiscence.'

'What ever for? What nonsense!'

'But we won't talk about it. Please forgive me, if I've been nasty,' said Levin. Now that he had opened his heart, he became as he had been in the morning. 'You're not angry with me, Stiva? Please don't be angry,' he said, and smiling, he took his hand.

'Of course not; not a bit, and no reason to be. I'm glad we've spoken openly. And do you know, stand-shooting in the morning is usually good—why not go? I couldn't sleep the night anyway, but I might go straight from shooting to the station.'

'Capital.'

XVIII

ALTHOUGH all Vronsky's inner life was absorbed in his passion, his external life unalterably and inevitably followed along the old accustomed lines of his social and regimental ties and interests. The interests of his regiment took an important place in Vronsky's life, both because he was fond of the regiment, and because the regiment was fond of him. They were not only fond of Vronsky in his regiment, they respected him too, and were proud of him; proud that this man, with his immense wealth, his brilliant education and abilities, and the path open before him to every kind of success, distinction, and ambition, had disregarded all that, and of all the interests of life had the interests of his regiment and his comrades nearest to his heart. Vronsky was aware of his comrades' view of him, and in addition to his liking for the life, he felt bound to keep up that reputation.

It need not be said that he did not speak of his love to any of his comrades, nor did he betray his secret even in the wildest drinking bouts (though indeed he was never so drunk as to lose all control of himself). And he shut up any of his thoughtless comrades who attempted to allude to his connection. But in spite of that, his love was known to all the town; everyone guessed with more or less confidence at his relations with Madame Karenin. The majority of the younger men envied him for just what was the most irksome factor in his love—the exalted position of Karenin, and the consequent publicity of their connection in society.

The greater number of the young women, who envied Anna and had long been weary of hearing her called *virtuous*, rejoiced at the fulfilment of their predictions, and were only waiting for a decisive turn in public opinion to fall upon her with all the weight of their scorn. They were already making ready their handfuls of mud to fling at her when the right moment arrived. The greater number of the middle-aged people and certain great personages were displeased at the prospect of the impending scandal in society.

Vronsky's mother, on hearing of his connection, was at first pleased at it, because nothing to her mind gave such a finishing-touch to a brilliant young man as a *liaison* in the highest society; she was pleased, too, that Madame Karenin, who had so taken her fancy, and had talked so much of her son, was, after all, just like all other pretty and well-bred women,—at least according to the Countess Vronsky's ideas. But she had heard of late that her son had refused a position offered him of great importance to his career, simply in order to remain in the regiment, where he could be constantly seeing Madame Karenin. She learned that great personages were displeased with him on this account, and she changed her opinion. She was vexed, too, that from all she could learn of this connection it was not that brilliant, graceful, worldly *liaison* which she would have welcomed, but a sort of Werterish, desperate passion, so she was told, which might well lead him into imprudence. She had not seen him since his abrupt departure from Moscow, and she sent her elder son to bid him come to see her.

This elder son too was dipleased with his younger brother. He did not distinguish what sort of love his might be, big or little, passionate or passionless, lasting or passing (he kept a ballet-girl himself, though he was the father of a family, so he was not disposed to be severe on that score), but he knew that this love-affair was viewed with displeasure by those whom it was necessary to please, and therefore he did not approve of his brother's conduct.

Besides the service and society, Vronsky had another great interest—horses; he was passionately fond of horses.

That year races and a steeplechase had been arranged for the officers. Vronsky had put his name down, bought a thoroughbred English mare, and in spite of his love-affair, he was looking forward to the races with intense, though reserved, excitement. . . .

These two passions did not interfere with one another. On the contrary, he needed occupation and distraction quite apart from his love, so as to recruit and rest himself from the violent emotions that agitated him.

XIX

ON the day of the races at Krasnoe Selo, Vronsky had come earlier than usual to eat beefsteak in the common mess-room of the regiment. He had no need to be strict with himself, as he had very quickly been brought down to the required light weight; but still he had to avoid gaining flesh, and so he eschewed farinaceous and sweet dishes. He sat with his coat unbuttoned over a white waistcoat, resting both elbows on the table, and while waiting for the steak he had ordered he looked at a French novel that lay open on his plate. He was only looking at the book to avoid conversation with the officers coming in and out; he was thinking.

He was thinking of Anna's promise to see him that day after the races. But he had not seen her for three days, and as her husband had just returned from abroad, he did not know whether she would be able to meet him today or not, and he did not know how to find out. He had had his last interview with her at his cousin Betsy's summer villa. He visited the Karenins' summer villa as rarely as possible. Now he wanted to go there, and he pondered the question how to do it.

'Of course I shall say Betsy has sent me to ask whether she's coming to the races. Of course, I'll go,' he decided, lifting his head from the book. And as he vividly pictured the happiness of seeing her, his face lighted up.

'Send to my house, and tell them to have out the carriage and three horses as quick as they can,' he said to the servant, who handed him the steak on a hot silver dish, and moving the dish up he began eating.

From the billiard-room next door came the sound of balls knocking, of talk and laughter. Two officers appeared at the entrance-door: one, a young fellow, with a feeble, delicate face, who had lately joined the regiment from the Corps of Pages; the other, a plump, elderly officer, with a bracelet on his wrist, and little eyes, lost in fat.

Vronsky glanced at them, frowned, and looking down at his book as though he had not noticed them, he proceeded to eat and read at the same time.

'What? Fortifying yourself for your work?' said the plump officer, sitting down beside him.

'As you see,' responded Vronsky, knitting his brows, wiping his mouth, and not looking at the officer.

'So you're not afraid of getting fat?' said the latter, turning a chair round for the young officer.

'What?' said Vronsky angrily, making a wry face of disgust, and showing his even teeth.

'You're not afraid of getting fat?'

'Waiter, sherry!' said Vronsky, without replying, and moving the book to the other side of him, he went on reading.

The plump officer took up the list of wines and turned to the young officer.

'You choose what we're to drink,' he said, handing him the card, and looking at him.

'Rhine wine, please,' said the young officer, stealing a timid glance at Vronsky, and trying to pull his scarcely visible moustache. Seeing that Vronsky did not turn round, the young officer got up.

'Let's go into the billiard-room,' he said.

The plump officer rose submissively, and they moved towards the door.

At that moment there walked into the room the tall and well-built Captain Yashvin. Nodding with an air of lofty contempt to the two officers, he went up to Vronsky.

'Ah! here he is!' he cried, bringing his big hand down heavily on his epaulet. Vronsky looked round angrily, but his face lighted up immediately with his characteristic expression of genial and manly serenity.

'That's it, Alexey,' said the captain, in his loud baritone. 'You must just eat a mouthful, now, and drink only one tiny glass.'

'Oh, I'm not hungry.'

'There go the inseparables,' Yashvin dropped, glancing sarcastically at the two officers who were at that instant leaving the room. And he bent his long legs, swathed in tight riding-breeches, and sat down in the chair, too low for him, so that his knees were cramped up in a sharp angle.

'Why didn't you turn up at the Red Theatre yesterday? Numerova wasn't at all bad. Where were you?'

'I was late at the Tverskoys',' said Vronsky.

'Ah!' responded Yashvin.

Yashvin, a gambler and a rake, a man not merely without moral principles, but of immoral principles, Yashvin was Vronsky's greatest friend in the regiment. Vronsky liked him both for his exceptional physical strength, which he showed for the most part by being able to drink like a fish, and do without sleep without being in the slightest degree affected by it; and for his great strength of character, which he showed in his relations with his comrades and superior officers, commanding both fear and respect, and also at cards, when he would play for tens of thousands, and however much he might have drunk, always with such skill and decision, that he was reckoned the best player in the English Club. Vronsky respected and liked Yashvin particularly because he felt Yashvin liked him, not for his name and his money, but for himself. And of all men he was the only one with whom Vronsky would have liked to speak of his love. He felt that Yashvin, in spite of his apparent contempt for every sort of feeling, was the only man who could, so he fancied, comprehend the intense passion which now filled his whole life. Moreover, he felt certain that Yashvin, as it was, took no delight in gossip and scandal, and interpreted his feeling rightly, that is to say, knew and believed that this passion was not a jest, not a pastime, but something more serious and important.

Vronsky had never spoken to him of his passion, but he was aware that he knew all about it, and that he put the right interpretation on it, and he was glad to see that in his eyes.

'Ah! yes,' he said, to the announcement that Vronsky had been at the Tverskoys'; and his black eyes shining, he plucked at his left moustache, and began twisting it into his mouth, a bad habit he had.

'Well, and what did you do yesterday? Win anything?' asked Vronsky.

'Eight thousand. But three don't count; he won't pay up.'

'Oh, then you can afford to lose over me,' said Vronsky, laughing. (Yashvin had betted heavily on Vronsky in the races.)

'No chance of my losing. Mahotin's the only one that's risky.'

And the conversation passed to forecasts of the coming race, the only thing Vronsky could think of just now.

'Come along, I've finished,' said Vronsky, and getting up he went to the door. Yashvin got up too, stretching his long legs and his long back.

'It's too early for me to dine, but I must have a drink. I'll come along directly. Hi, wine!' he shouted, in his rich voice, that always rang out so loudly at drill, and set the windows shaking now.

'No, all right,' he shouted again immediately after. 'You're going home, so I'll go with you.'

And he walked out with Vronsky.

XX

VRONSKY was staying in a roomy, clean, Finnish hut, divided into two by a partition. Petritsky lived with him in camp too. Petritsky was asleep when Vronsky and Yashvin came into the hut.

'Get up, don't go on sleeping,' said Yashvin, going behind the partition and giving Petritsky, who was lying with ruffled hair and with his nose in the pillow, a prod on the shoulder.

Petritsky jumped up suddenly on to his knees and looked round.

'Your brother's been here,' he said to Vronsky. 'He waked me up, damn him, and said he'd look in again.' And pulling up the rug he flung himself back on the pillow. 'Oh, do shut up, Yashvin!' he said, getting furious with Yashvin, who was pulling the rug off him. 'Shut up!' He turned over and opened his eyes. 'You'd better tell me what to drink; such a nasty taste in my mouth, that . . .'

'Brandy's better than anything,' boomed Yashvin. 'Tereshtchenko!

brandy for your master and cucumbers,' he shouted, obviously taking pleasure in the sound of his own voice.

'Brandy do you think? Eh?' queried Petritsky, blinking and rubbing his eyes. 'And you'll drink something? All right then, we'll have a drink together! Vronsky, have a drink?' said Petritsky, getting up and wrapping the tiger-skin rug round him. He went to the door of the partition wall, raised his hands, and hummed in French, 'There was a king in Thule.' 'Vronsky, will you have a drink?'

'Go along,' said Vronsky, putting on the coat his valet handed him.

'Where are you off to?' asked Yashvin. 'Oh, here are your three horses,' he added, seeing the carriage drive up.

'To the stables, and I've got to see Bryansky, too, about the horses,' said Vronsky.

Vronsky had as a fact, promised to call at Bryansky's, some eight miles from Peterhof, and to bring him some money owing for some horses; and he hoped to have time to get that in too. But his comrades were at once aware that he was not only going there.

Petritsky, still humming, winked and made a pout with his lips, as though he would say: 'Oh yes, we know your Bryansky.'

'Mind you're not late!' was Yashvin's only comment; and to change the conversation: 'How's my roan? is he doing all right?' he inquired, looking out of window at the middle one of the three horses, which he had sold Vronsky.

'Stop!' cried Petritsky to Vronsky as he was just going out. 'Your brother left a letter and a note for you. Wait a bit; where are they?'

Vronsky stopped.

'Well, where are they?'

'Where are they? That's just the question!' said Petritsky solemnly, moving his forefinger upwards from his nose.

'Come, tell me; this is silly!' said Vronsky smiling.

'I have not lighted the fire. Here somewhere about.'

'Come, enough fooling! Where is the letter?'

'No, I've forgotten really. Or was it a dream? Wait a bit, wait a bit! But what's the use of getting in a rage. If you'd drunk four bottles yesterday as I did you'd forget where you were lying. Wait a bit, I'll remember!'

Petritsky went behind the partition and lay down on his bed.

'Wait a bit! This was how I was lying, and this was how he was standing. Yes—yes—yes. . . . Here it is!'—and Petritsky pulled a letter out from under the mattress, where he had hidden it.

Vronsky took the letter and his brother's note. It was the letter he was expecting—from his mother, reproaching him for not having been to see her—and the note was from his brother to say that he must have a little talk with him. Vronsky knew that it was all about the same thing. 'What business is it of theirs!' thought Vronsky, and crumpling up the letters he thrust them between the buttons of his coat so as to read them carefully on the road. In the porch of the hut he was met by two officers; one of his regiment and one of another.

Vronsky's quarters were always a meeting-place for all the officers.

'Where are you off to?'

'I must go to Peterhof.'

'Has the mare come from Tsarskoe?'

'Yes, but I've not seen her yet.'

'They say Mahotin's Gladiator's lame.'

'Nonsense! But however are you going to race in this mud?' said the other.

'Here are my saviours!' cried Petritsky, seeing them come in. Before him stood the orderly with a tray of brandy and salted cucumbers. 'Here's Yashvin ordering me to drink a pick-me-up.'

'Well, you did give it to us yesterday,' said one of those who had come in; 'you didn't let us get a wink of sleep all night.'

'Oh, didn't we make a pretty finish!' said Petritsky. 'Volkov climbed on to the roof and began telling us how sad he was. I said: "Let's have music, the funeral march!" He fairly dropped asleep on the roof over the funeral march.'

'Drink it up; you positively must drink the brandy, and then seltzer water and a lot of lemon,' said Yashvin, standing over Petritsky like a mother making a child take medicine, 'and then a little champagne—just a small bottle.'

'Come, there's some sense in that. Stop a bit, Vronsky, we'll all have a drink.'

'No; good-bye all of you. I'm not going to drink today.'

'Why, are you gaining weight? All right, then we must have it alone. Give us the seltzer water and lemon.'

'Vronsky!' shouted someone when he was already outside.

'Well?'

'You'd better get your hair cut, it'll weigh you down, especially at the top.'

Vronsky was in fact beginning, prematurely, to get a little bald. He laughed gaily, showing his even teeth, and pulling his cap over the thin place, went out and got into his carriage.

'To the stables!' he said, and was just pulling out the letters to read them through, but he thought better of it, and put off reading them so as not to distract his attention before looking at the mare. 'Later!'

XXI

THE temporary stable, a wooden shed, had been put up close to the racecourse, and there his mare was to have been taken the previous day. He had not yet seen her there.

During the last few days he had not ridden her out for exercise himself, but had put her in the charge of the trainer, and so now he positively did not know in what condition his mare had arrived yesterday and was today. He had scarcely got out of his carriage when his groom, the so-called 'stable-boy', recognising the carriage some way off, called the trainer. A dry-looking Englishman, in high boots and a short jacket, clean shaven, except for a tuft below his chin, came to meet him, walking with the uncouth gait of a jockey, turning his elbows out and swaying from side to side.

'Well, how's Frou-Frou?' Vronsky asked in English.

'All right, sir,' the Englishman's voice responded somewhere in the inside of his throat. 'Better not go in,' he added, touching his hat. 'I've put a muzzle on her, and the mare's fidgety. Better not go in, it'll excite the mare.'

'No, I'm going in. I want to look at her.'

'Come along, then,' said the Englishman, frowning, and speaking with his mouth shut, and, with swinging elbows, he went on in front with his disjointed gait.

They went into the little yard in front of the shed. A stable-boy, spruce and smart in his holiday attire, met them with a broom in his hand, and followed them. In the shed there were five horses in their separate stalls, and Vronsky knew that his chief rival, Gladiator, a very tall chestnut horse, had been brought there, and must be standing among them. Even more than his mare, Vronsky longed to see Gladiator, whom he had never seen. But he knew that by the etiquette of the racecourse it was not merely impossible for him to see the horse, but improper even to ask questions about him. Just as he was passing along the passage, the boy opened the door into the second horse-box on the left, and Vronsky caught a glimpse of a big chestnut horse with white legs. He knew that this was Gladiator, but, with the feeling of a man turning away from the sight of another man's open letter, he turned round and went into Frou-Frou's stall.

'The horse is here belonging to Mak . . . Mak . . . I never can say the name,' said the Englishman, over his shoulder, pointing his big finger and dirty nail towards Gladiator's stall.

'Mahotin? Yes, he's my most serious rival,' said Vronsky.

'If you were riding him,' said the Englishman, 'I'd bet on you.'

'Frou-Frou's more nervous; he's stronger,' said Vronsky, smiling at the compliment to his riding.

'In a steeplechase it all depends on riding and on pluck,' said the Englishman.

Of pluck—that is, energy and courage—Vronsky did not merely feel that he had enough; what was of far more importance, he was firmly convinced that no one in the world could have more of this 'pluck' than he had.

'Don't you think I want more thinning down?'

'Oh no,' answered the Englishman. 'Please, don't speak loud. The mare's fidgety,' he added, nodding towards the horse-box, before which they were standing, and from which came the sound of restless stamping in the straw.

He opened the door, and Vronsky went into the horse-box, dimly lighted by one little window. In the horse-box stood a dark bay mare, with a muzzle on, picking at the fresh straw with her hoofs. Looking round him in the twilight of the horse-box, Vronsky unconsciously took in once more in a comprehensive glance all the points of his favourite mare. Frou-Frou was a beast of medium size, not altogether free from reproach, from a breeder's point of view. She was small-boned all over; though her chest was extremely prominent in front, it was narrow. Her hind-quarters were a little drooping, and in her fore-legs, and still more in her hind-legs, there was a noticeable curvature. The muscles of both hind and fore legs were not very thick; but across her shoulders the mare was exceptionally broad, a peculiarity specially striking now that she was lean from training. The bones of her leg below the knees looked no thicker than a finger from in front, but were extraordinarily thick seen from the side. She looked altogether, except across the shoulders, as it were pinched in at the sides and pressed out in depth. But she had in the highest degree the quality that makes all defects forgotten: that quality was *blood*, the blood *that tells*, as the English expression has it. The muscles stood up sharply under the network of sinews, covered with the delicate, mobile skin, as soft as satin, and they were hard as bone. Her clean-cut head, with prominent, bright, spirited eyes, broadened out at the open nostrils, that showed the red blood in the cartilage within. About all her figure, and especially her head, there was a certain expression of energy, and, at the same time, of softness. She was one of those creatures, which seem only not to speak because the mechanism of their mouth does not allow them to.

To Vronsky, at any rate, it seemed that she understood all he felt at that moment, looking at her.

Directly Vronsky went towards her, she drew in a deep breath, and, turning back her prominent eye till the white looked bloodshot, she stared at the approaching figures from the opposite side, shaking her muzzle, and shifting lightly from one leg to the other.

'There, you see how fidgety she is,' said the Englishman.

'There, darling! There!' said Vronsky, going up to the mare and speaking soothingly to her.

But the nearer he came, the more excited she grew. Only when he stood by her head, she was suddenly quieter, while the muscles quivered under her soft, delicate coat. Vronsky patted her strong neck, straightened over her sharp withers a stray lock of her mane that had fallen on the other side, and moved his face near her dilated nostrils, transparent as a bat's wing. She drew a loud breath and snorted out through her tense nostrils, started, pricked up her sharp ear, and put out her strong, black lip towards Vronsky, as though she would nip hold of his sleeve. But remembering the muzzle, she shook it and again began restlessly stamping one after the other her shapely legs.

'Quiet, darling, quiet!' he said, patting her again over her hindquarters; and with a glad sense that his mare was in the best possible condition, he went out of the horse-box.

The mare's excitement had infected Vronsky. He felt that his heart was throbbing, and that he too, like the mare, longed to move, to bite; it was both dreadful and delicious.

'Well, I rely on you, then,' he said to the Englishman; 'half-past six on the ground.'

'All right,' said the Englishman. 'Oh, where are you going, my lord?' he asked suddenly, using the title 'my lord', which he had scarcely ever used before.

Vronsky in amazement raised his head, and stared, as he knew how to stare, not into the Englishman's eyes, but at his forehead, astounded at the impertinence of his question. But realising that in asking this the Englishman had been looking at him not as an employer, but as a jockey, he answered—

'I've got to go to Bryansky's; I shall be home within an hour.'

'How often I'm asked that question today!' he said to himself, and he blushed, a thing which rarely happened to him. The Englishman looked gravely at him; and, as though he, too, knew where Vronsky was going, he added—

'The great thing's to keep quiet before a race,' said he; 'don't get out of temper or upset about anything.'

'All right,' answered Vronsky, smiling; and jumping into his carriage, he told the man to drive to Peterhof.

Before he had driven many paces away, the dark clouds that had been threatening rain all day broke, and there was a heavy downpour of rain.

'What a pity!' thought Vronsky, putting up the roof of the carriage. 'It was muddy before, now it will be a perfect swamp.' As he sat in solitude in the closed carriage, he took out his mother's letter and his brother's note, and read them through.

Yes, it was the same thing over and over again. Everyone, his mother, his brother, everyone thought fit to interfere in the affairs of his heart. This interference aroused in him a feeling of angry hatred—a feeling he had rarely known before. 'What business is it of theirs? Why does everybody feel called upon to concern himself about me? And why do they worry me so? Just because they see that this is something they can't understand. If it were a common, vulgar, worldly intrigue, they would have left me alone. They feel that this is something different, that this is not a mere pastime, that this woman is dearer to me than life. And this is incomprehensible, and that's why it annoys them. Whatever our destiny is or may be, we have made it ourselves, and we do not complain of it,' he said, in the word *we* linking himself with Anna. 'No, they must needs teach us how to live. They haven't an idea of what happiness is; they don't know that without our love, for us there is neither happiness nor unhappiness—no life at all,' he thought.

He was angry with all of them for their interference just because he felt in his soul that they, all these people, were right. He felt that the love that bound him to Anna was not a momentary impulse, which would pass, as worldly intrigues do pass, leaving no other traces in the life of either but pleasant or unpleasant memories. He felt all the torture of his own and her position, all the difficulty there was for them, conspicuous as they were in the eye of all the world, in concealing their love, in lying and deceiving; and in lying, deceiving, feigning, and continually thinking of others, when the passion that united them was so intense that they were both oblivious of everything else but their love.

He vividly recalled all the constantly recurring instances of inevitable necessity for lying and deceit, which were so against his natural bent. He recalled particularly vividly the shame he had more than once detected in her at this necessity for lying and deceit. And he experienced the strange feeling that had sometimes come upon him since his secret love for Anna. This was a feeling of loathing for something—whether for Alexey Alexandrovitch, or for himself, or for the whole world, he could not have said. But he always drove away this strange feeling. Now, too, he shook it off and continued the thread of his thoughts.

'Yes, she was unhappy before, but proud and at peace; and now she cannot be at peace and feel secure in her dignity, though she does not show it. Yes, we must put an end to it,' he decided.

And for the first time the idea clearly presented itself that it was essential to put an end to this false position, and the sooner the better. 'Throw up everything, she and I, and hide ourselves somewhere alone with our love,' he said to himself.

XXII

THE rain did not last long, and by the time Vronsky arrived, his shaft-horse trotting at full speed, and dragging the trace-horses galloping through the mud, with their reins hanging loose, the sun had peeped out again, the roofs of the summer villas and the old lime-trees in the gardens on both sides of the principal streets sparkled with wet brilliance, and from the twigs came a pleasant drip and from the roofs rushing streams of water. He thought no more of the shower spoiling the racecourse, but was rejoicing now that—thanks to the rain—he would be sure to find her at home and alone, as he knew that Alexey Alexandrovitch, who had lately returned from a foreign watering-place, had not moved from Petersburg.

Hoping to find her alone, Vronsky alighted, as he always did, to avoid attracting attention, before crossing the bridge, and walked to the house. He did not go up the steps to the street door, but went into the court.

'Has your master come?' he asked a gardener.

'No, sir. The mistress is at home. But will you please go to the front door; there are servants there,' the gardener answered. 'They'll open the door.'

'No, I'll go in from the garden.'

And feeling satisfied that she was alone, and wanting to take her by surprise, since he had not promised to be there today, and she would certainly not expect him to come before the races, he walked, holding his sword and stepping cautiously over the sandy path, bordered with flowers, to the terrace that looked out upon the garden. Vronsky forgot now all that he had thought on the way of the hardships and difficulties of their position. He thought of nothing but that he would see her directly, not in imagination, but living, all of her, as she was in reality. He was just going in, stepping on his whole foot so as not to creak, up the worn steps of the terrace, when he suddenly remembered what he always forgot, and what caused the most torturing side of his relations with her, her son with his questioning—hostile, as he fancied—eyes.

This boy was more often than anyone else a check upon their freedom. When he was present, both Vronsky and Anna did not merely avoid speaking of anything that they could not have repeated before everyone; they did not even allow themselves to refer by hints to anything the boy did not understand. They had made no agreement about this, it had settled itself. They would have felt it wounding themselves to deceive the child. In his presence they talked like acquaintances. But in spite of this caution, Vronsky often saw the child's intent, bewildered glance fixed upon him, and a strange shyness, uncertainty, at one time friendliness, at another, coldness and reserve, in the boy's manner to him; as though the child felt that between this man and his mother there existed some important bond, the significance of which he could not understand.

As a fact the boy did feel that he could not understand this relation, and he tried painfully, and was not able to make clear to himself what feeling he ought to have for this man. With a child's keen instinct for every manifestation of feeling, he saw distinctly that his father, his governess, his nurse,—all did not merely dislike Vronsky, but looked on him with horror and aversion, though they never said anything about him, while his mother looked on him as her greatest friend.

'What does it mean? Who is he? How ought I to love him? If I don't know, it's my fault; either I'm stupid or a naughty boy,' thought the child. And this was what caused his dubious, inquiring, sometimes hostile, expression, and the shyness and uncertainty which Vronsky found so irksome. This child's presence always and infallibly called up in Vronsky that strange feeling of inexplicable loathing which he had experienced of late. This child's presence called up both in Vronsky and in Anna a feeling akin to the feeling of a sailor who sees by the compass that the direction in which he is swiftly moving is far from the right one, but that to arrest his motion is not in his power, that every instant is carrying him further and further away, and that to admit to himself his deviation from the right direction is the same as admitting his certain ruin.

This child, with his innocent outlook upon life, was the compass that showed them the point to which they had departed from what they knew, but did not want to know.

This time Seryozha was not at home, and she was completely alone.

She was sitting on the terrace waiting for the return of her son, who had gone out for his walk and been caught in the rain. She had sent a manservant and a maid out to look for him. Dressed in a white gown, deeply embroidered, she was sitting in a corner of the terrace behind some flowers, and did not hear him. Bending her curly black head, she pressed her forehead against a cool watering-pot that stood on the parapet, and both her lovely hands, with the rings he knew so well, clasped the pot. The beauty of her whole figure, her head, her neck, her hands, struck Vronsky every time as something new and unexpected. He stood still, gazing at her in ecstasy. But, directly he would have made a step to come nearer to her, she was aware of his presence, pushed away the watering-pot, and turned her flushed face towards him.

'What's the matter? You are ill?' he said to her in French, going up to her. He would have run to her, but remembering that there might be spectators, he looked round towards the balcony door, and reddened a little, as he always reddened, feeling that he had to be afraid and be on his guard.

'No; I'm quite well,' she said, getting up and pressing his outstretched hand tightly. 'I did not expect . . . thee.'

'Mercy! what cold hands!' he said.

'You startled me,' she said. 'I'm alone, and expecting Seryozha; he's out for a walk; they'll come in from this side.'

But, in spite of her efforts to be calm, her lips were quivering.

'Forgive me for coming, but I couldn't pass the day without seeing you,' he went on, speaking French, as he always did to avoid using the stiff Russian plural form, so impossibly frigid between them, and the dangerously intimate singular.

'Forgive you? I'm so glad!'

'But you're ill or worried,' he went on, not letting go her hands and bending over her. 'What were you thinking of?'

'Always of the same thing,' she said, with a smile.

She spoke the truth. If ever at any moment she had been asked what she was thinking of, she could have answered truly: of the same thing, of her happiness and her unhappiness. She was thinking, just when he came upon her, of this: why was it, she wondered, that to others, to Betsy (she knew of her secret connection with Tushkevitch) it was all easy, while to her it was such torture? Today this thought gained special poignancy from certain other considerations. She asked him about the races. He answered her questions, and, seeing that she was agitated, trying to calm her, he began telling her in the simplest tone the details of his preparations for the races.

'Tell him or not tell him?' she thought, looking into his quiet, affectionate eyes. 'He is so happy, so absorbed in his races that he won't understand as he ought, he won't understand all the gravity of this fact to us.'

'But you haven't told me what you were thinking of when I came in,' he said, interrupting his narrative; 'please, tell me!'

She did not answer, and, bending her head a little, she looked inquiringly at him from under her brows, her eyes shining under their long lashes. Her hand shook as it played with a leaf she had picked. He saw it, and his face expressed that utter subjection, that slavish devotion, which had done so much to win her.

'I see something has happened. Do you suppose I can be at peace, knowing you have a trouble I am not sharing? Tell me, for God's sake,' he repeated imploringly.

'Yes; I shan't be able to forgive him if he does not realise all the gravity of it. Better not tell; why put him to the proof?' she thought, still staring at him in the same way, and feeling the hand that held the leaf was trembling more and more.

'For God's sake!' he repeated, taking her hand.

'Shall I tell you?'

'Yes, yes, yes . . .'

'I'm with child,' she said, softly and deliberately. The leaf in her hand shook more violently, but she did not take her eyes off him, watching how he would take it. He turned white, would have said something, but stopped; he dropped her hand, and his head sank on his breast. 'Yes, he realises all the gravity of it,' she thought, and gratefully she pressed his hand.

But she was mistaken in thinking he realised the gravity of the fact as she, a woman, realised it. On hearing it, he felt come upon him with tenfold intensity that strange feeling of loathing of someone. But at the same time, he felt that the turning-point he had been longing for had come now; that it was impossible to go on concealing things from her husband, and it was inevitable in one way or another that they should soon put an end to their unnatural position. But, besides that, her emotion physically affected him in the same way. He looked at her with a look of submissive tenderness, kissed her hand, got up, and, in silence, paced up and down the terrace.

'Yes,' he said, going up to her resolutely. 'Neither you nor I have looked on our relations as a passing amusement, and now our fate is sealed. It is absolutely necessary to put an end'—he looked round as he spoke—'to the deception in which we are living.'

'Put an end? How put an end, Alexey?' she said softly.

She was calmer now, and her face lighted up with a tender smile.

'Leave your husband and make our life one.'

'It is one as it is,' she answered, scarcely audibly.

'Yes, but altogether; altogether.'

'But how, Alexey, tell me how?' she said in melancholy mockery at the hopelessness of her own position. 'Is there any way out of such a position? Am I not the wife of my husband?'

'There is a way out of every position. We must take our line,' he said. 'Anything's better than the position in which you're living. Of course, I see how you torture yourself over everything—the world and your son and your husband.'

'Oh, not over my husband,' she said, with a quiet smile. 'I don't know him, I don't think of him. He doesn't exist.'

'You're not speaking sincerely. I know you. You worry about him too.'

'Oh, he doesn't even know,' she said, and suddenly a hot flush came over her face; her cheeks, he brow, her neck crimsoned, and tears of shame came into her eyes. 'But we won't talk of him.'

XXIII

VRONSKY had several times already, though not so resolutely as now, tried to bring her to consider their position, and every time he had been confronted by the same superficiality and triviality with which she met his appeal now. It was as though there were something in this which she could not or would not face, as though directly she began to speak of this, she, the real Anna, retreated somehow into herself, and another strange and unaccountable woman came out, whom he did not love, and whom he feared, and who was in opposition to him. But today he was resolved to have it out.

'Whether he knows or not,' said Vronsky, in his usual quiet and resolute tone, 'that's nothing to do with us. We cannot . . . you cannot stay like this, especially now.'

'What's to be done, according to you?' she asked with the same frivolous irony. She who had so feared he would take her condition too lightly was now vexed with him for deducing from it the necessity of taking some step.

'Tell him everything, and leave him.'

'Very well, let us suppose I do that,' she said. 'Do you know what the result of that would be? I can tell you it all beforehand,' and a wicked light gleamed in her eyes, that had been so soft a minute before. '"Eh, you love another man, and have entered into criminal intrigues with him?"' (Mimicking her husband, she threw an emphasis on the word 'criminal', as Alexey Alexandrovitch did.) '"I warned you of the results in the religious, the civil, and the domestic relation. You have not listened to me. Now I cannot let you disgrace my name,—"' and my son, she had meant to say, but about her son she could not jest,— '"disgrace my name, and"—and more in the same style,' she added. 'In general terms, he'll say in his official manner, and with all distinctness and precision, that he cannot let me go, but will take all measures in his power to prevent scandal. And he will calmly and punctually act in accordance with his words. That's what will happen. He's not a man, but a machine, and a spiteful machine when he's angry,' she added, recalling Alexey Alevandrovitch as she spoke, with all the peculiarities of his figure and manner of speaking, and reckoning against him every defect she could find in him, softening nothing for the great wrong she herself was doing him.

'But, Anna,' said Vronsky, in a soft and persuasive voice, trying to soothe her, 'we absolutely must, anyway, tell him, and then be guided by the line he takes.'

'What, run away?'

'And why not run away? I don't see how we can keep on like this. And not for my sake—I see that you suffer.'

'Yes, run away, and become your mistress,' she said angrily.

'Anna,' he said, with reproachful tenderness.

'Yes,' she went on, 'become your mistress, and complete the ruin of . . .'

Again she would have said 'my son', but she could not utter that word.

Vronsky could not understand how she, with her strong and truthful nature, could endure this state of deceit, and not long to get out of it. But he did not suspect that the chief cause of it was the word—*son*, which she could not bring herself to pronounce. When she thought of her son, and his future attitude to his mother, who had abandoned his father, she felt such terror at what she had done, that she could not face it; but, like a woman, could only try to comfort herself with lying assurances that everything would remain as it always had been, and that it was possible to forget the fearful question of how it would be with her son.

'I beg you, I entreat you,' she said suddenly, taking his hand, and speaking in quite a different tone, sincere and tender, 'never speak to me of that!'

'But, Anna . . .'

'Never. Leave it to me. I know all the baseness, all the horror of my position; but it's not so easy to arrange as you think. And leave it to me, and do what I say. Never speak to me of it. Do you promise me? . . . No, no, promise! . . .'

'I promise everything, but I can't be at peace, especially after what you have told me. I can't be at peace, when you can't be at peace . . .'

'I?' she repeated. 'Yes, I am worried sometimes; but that will pass, if you will never talk about this. When you talk about it—it's only then it worries me.'

'I don't understand,' he said.

'I know,' she interrupted him, 'how hard it is for your truthful nature to lie, and I grieve for you. I often think that you have ruined your whole life for me.'

'I was just thinking the very same thing,' he said; 'how could you sacrifice everything for my sake? I can't forgive myself that you're unhappy.'

'I unhappy?' she said, coming closer to him, and looking at him with an ecstatic smile of love. 'I am like a hungry man who has been given food. He may be cold, and dressed in rags, and ashamed, but he is not unhappy. I unhappy? No, this is my happiness. . . .'

She could hear the sound of her son's voice coming towards them, and, glancing swiftly round the terrace, she got up impulsively. Her eyes glowed with the fire he knew so well; with a rapid movement she raised her lovely hands, covered with rings, took his head, looked a long look into his face, and, putting up her face with smiling, parted lips, swiftly kissed his mouth and both eyes, and pushed him away. She would have gone, but he held her back.

'When?' he murmured in a whisper, gazing in ecstasy at her.

'Today, at one o'clock,' she whispered, and, with a heavy sigh, she walked with her light, swift step to meet her son.

Seryozha had been caught by the rain in the big garden, and he and his nurse had taken shelter in an arbour.

'Well, *au revoir*,' she said to Vronsky. 'I must soon be getting ready for the races. Betsy promised to fetch me.'

Vronsky, looking at his watch, went away hurriedly.

XXIV

WHEN Vronsky looked at his watch on the Karenins' balcony, he was so greatly agitated and lost in his thoughts that he saw the figures on the watch's face, but could not take in what time it was. He came out on to the high road and walked, picking his way carefully through the mud, to his carriage. He was so completely absorbed in his feeling for Anna, that he did not even think what o'clock it was, and whether he had time to go to Bryansky's. He had left him, as often happens, only the external faculty of memory, that points out each step one has to take, one after the other. He went up to his coachman, who was dozing on the box in the shadow, already lengthening, of a thick lime-tree; he admired the shifting clouds of midges circling over the hot horses, and, waking the coachman, he jumped into the carriage, and told him to drive to Bryansky's. It was only after driving nearly five miles that he had sufficiently recovered himself to look at his watch, and realise that it was half-past five, and he was late.

There were several races fixed for that day: the Mounted Guards' race, then the officers' mile-and-a-half race, then the three-mile race, and then the race for which he was entered. He could still be in time for his race, but if he went to Bryansky's he could only just be in time, and he would arrive when the whole of the court would be in their places. That would be a pity. But he had promised Bryansky to come, and so he decided to drive on, telling the coachman not to spare the horses.

He reached Bryansky's, spent five minutes there, and galloped back. The rapid drive calmed him. All that was painful in his relations with Anna, all the feeling of indefiniteness left by their conversation, had slipped out of his mind. He was thinking now with pleasure and excitement of the race, of his being, anyhow, in time, and now and then the thought of the blissful interview awaiting him that night flashed across his imagination like a flaming light.

The excitement of the approaching race gained upon him as he drove further and further into the atmosphere of the races, overtaking carriages driving up from the summer villas or out of Petersburg.

At his quarters no one was left at home; all were at the races, and his valet was looking out for him at the gate. While he was changing his clothes, his valet told him that the second race had begun already, that a lot of gentlemen had been to ask for him, and a boy had twice run up from the stables. Dressing without hurry (he never hurried himself, and never lost his self-possession), Vronsky drove to the sheds. From the sheds he could see a perfect sea of carriages, and people on foot, soldiers surrounding the racecourse, and pavilions swarming with people. The second race was apparently going on, for just as he went into the sheds he heard a bell ringing. Going towards the stable, he met the white-legged chestnut, Mahotin's Gladiator, being led to the racecourse in a blue forage horsecloth, with what looked like huge ears edged with blue.

'Where's Cord?' he asked the stable-boy.

'In the stable, putting on the saddle.'

In the open horse-box stood Frou-Frou, saddled ready. They were just going to lead her out.

'I'm not too late?'

'All right! All right!' said the Englishman; 'don't upset yourself!'

Vronsky once more took in in one glance the exquisite lines of his favourite mare, who was quivering all over, and with an effort he tore himself from the sight of her, and went out of the stable. He went towards the pavilions at the most favourable moment for escaping attention. The mile-and-a-half race was just finishing, and all eyes were fixed on the horse-guard in front and the light hussar behind, urging their horses on with a last effort close to the winning-post. From the centre and outside of the ring all were crowding to the winning-post, and a group of soldiers and officers of the horse-guards were shouting loudly their delight at the expected triumph of their officer and comrade. Vronsky moved into the middle of the crowd unnoticed, almost at the very moment when the bell rang at the finish of the race, and the tall, mud-spattered horse-guard who came in first, bending over the saddle, let go the reins of his panting grey horse that looked dark with sweat.

The horse, stiffening out its legs, with an effort stopped its rapid course, and the officer of the horse-guards looked round him like a man waking up from a heavy sleep, and just managed to smile. A crowd of friends and outsiders pressed round him.

Vronsky intentionally avoided that select crowd of the upper world, which was moving and talking with discreet freedom before the pavilions. He knew that Madame Karenin was there, and Betsy, and his brother's wife, and he purposely did not go near them for fear of something distracting his attention. But he was continually met and stopped by acquaintances, who told him about the previous races, and kept asking him why he was so late.

At the time when the racers had to go to the pavilion to receive the prizes, and all attention was directed to that point, Vronsky's elder brother, Alexander, a colonel with heavy fringed epaulets, came up to him. He was not tall, though as broadly built as Alexey, and handsomer and rosier than he; he had a red nose, and an open, drunken-looking face.

'Did you get my note?' he said. 'There's never any finding you.'

Alexander Vronsky, in spite of the dissolute life, and in especial the drunken habits, for which he was notorious, was quite one of the court circle.

Now, as he talked to his brother of a matter bound to be exceedingly disagreeable to him, knowing that the eyes of many people might be fixed upon him, he kept a smiling countenance, as though he were jesting with his brother about something of little moment.

'I got it, and I really can't make out what *you* are worrying yourself about,' said Alexey.

'I'm worrying myself because the remark has just been made to me that you weren't here, and that you were seen in Peterhof on Monday.'

'There are matters which only concern those directly interested in them, and the matter you are so worried about is . . .'

'Yes, but if so, you may as well cut the service. . . .'

'I beg you not to meddle, and that's all I have to say.'

Alexey Vronsky's frowning face turned white, and his prominent lower jaw quivered, which happened rarely with him. Being a man of very warm heart, he was seldom angry; but when he was angry, and when his chin quivered, then, as Alexander Vronsky knew, he was dangerous. Alexander Vronsky smiled gaily.

'I only wanted to give you mother's letter. Answer it, and don't worry about anything just before the race. *Bonne chance*,' he added, smiling, and he moved away from him. But after him another friendly greeting brought Vronsky to a standstill.

'So you won't recognise your friends! How are you, *mon cher*?' said Stepan Arkadyevitch, as conspicuously brilliant in the midst of all the Petersburg brilliance as he was in Moscow, his face rosy, and his whiskers sleek and glossy. 'I came up yesterday, and I'm delighted that I shall see your triumph. When shall we meet?'

'Come tomorrow to the mess-room,' said Vronsky, and squeezing him by the sleeve of his coat, with apologies, he moved away to the centre of the racecourse, where the horses were being led for the great steeplechase.

The horses who had run in the last race were being led home, steaming and exhausted, by the stable-boys, and one after another the fresh horses for the coming race made their appearance, for the most part English racers, wearing horse-cloths, and looking with their drawn-up bellies like strange, huge birds. On the right was led in Frou-Frou, lean and beautiful, lifting up her elastic, rather long pasterns, as though moved by springs. Not far from her they were taking the rug off the lop-eared Gladiator. The strong, exquisite, perfectly correct lines of the stallion, with his superb hind-quarters and excessively short pasterns almost over his hoofs, attracted Vronsky's attention in spite of himself. He would have gone up to his mare, but he was again detained by an acquaintance.

'Oh, there's Karenin!' said the acquaintance with whom he was chatting. 'He's looking for his wife, and she's in the middle of the pavilion. Didn't you see her?'

'No,' answered Vronsky, and without even glancing round towards the pavilion where his friend was pointing out Madame Karenin, he went up to his mare.

Vronsky had not had time to look at the saddle, about which he had to give some direction, when the competitors were summoned to the pavilion to receive their numbers and places in the row at starting. Seventeen officers, looking serious and severe, many with pale faces, met together in the pavilion and drew the numbers. Vronsky drew the number seven. The cry was heard: 'Mount!'

Feeling that with the others riding in the race, he was the centre upon which all eyes were fastened, Vronsky walked up to his mare in that state of nervous tension in which he usually became deliberate and composed in his movements. Cord, in honour of the races, had put on his best clothes, a black coat buttoned up, a stiffly starched collar, which propped up his cheeks, a round black hat, and top-boots. He was calm and dignified as ever, and was with his own hands holding Frou-Frou by both reins, standing straight in front of her. Frou-Frou was still trembling as though in a fever. Her eye, full of fire, glanced sideways at Vronsky. Vronsky slipped his finger under the saddle-girth. The mare glanced aslant at him, drew up her lip, and twitched her ear. The Englishman puckered up his lips, intending to indicate a smile that anyone should verify his saddling.

'Get up; you won't feel so excited.'

Vronsky looked round for the last time at his rivals. He knew that he would not see them during the race. Two were already riding forward to the point from which they were to start. Galtsin, a friend of Vronsky's and one of his more formidable rivals, was moving round a bay horse that would not let him mount. A little light hussar in tight riding-breeches rode off at a gallop, crouched up like a cat on the saddle, in imitation of English jockeys. Prince Kuzovlev sat with a white face on his thoroughbred mare from the Gabrovsky stud, while an English groom led her by the bridle. Vronsky and all his comrades knew Kuzovlev and his peculiarity of 'weak nerves' and terrible vanity. They knew that he was afraid of everything, afraid of riding a spirited horse. But now, just because it was terrible, because people broke their necks, and there was a doctor standing at each obstacle, and an ambulance with a cross on it, and a sister of mercy, he had made up his mind to take part in the race. Their eyes met, and Vronsky gave him a friendly and encouraging nod. Only one he did not see, his chief rival, Mahotin on Gladiator.

'Don't be in a hurry,' said Cord to Vronsky, 'and remember one thing: don't hold her in at the fences, and don't urge her on; let her go as she likes.'

'All right, all right,' said Vronsky, taking the reins.

'If you can, lead the race; but don't lose heart till the last minute, even if you're behind.'

Before the mare had time to move, Vronsky stepped with an agile, vigorous movement into the steel-toothed stirrup, and lightly and firmly seated himself on the creaking leather of the saddle. Getting his right foot in the stirrup, he smoothed the double reins, as he always did, between his fingers, and Cord let go.

As though she did not know which foot to put first, Frou-Frou started, dragging at the reins with her long neck, and as though she were on springs, shaking her rider from side to side. Cord quickened his step, following him. The excited mare, trying to shake off her rider first on one side and then the other, pulled at the reins, and Vronsky tried in vain with voice and hand to soothe her.

They were just reaching the dammed-up stream on their way to the starting-point. Several of the riders were in front and several behind, when suddenly Vronsky heard the sound of a horse galloping in the mud behind him, and he was overtaken by Mahotin on his white-legged, lop-eared Gladiator. Mahotin smiled, showing his long teeth, but Vronsky looked angrily at him. He did not like him, and regarded him now as his most formidable rival. He was angry with him for galloping past and exciting his mare. Frou-Frou started into a gallop, her left foot forward, made two bounds, and fretting at the tightened reins, passed into a jolting trot, bumping her rider up and down. Cord too scowled, and followed Vronsky almost at a trot.

XXV

THERE were seventeen officers in all riding in this race. The race-course was a large three-mile ring of the form of an ellipse in front of the pavilion. On this course nine obstacles had been arranged: the stream, a big and solid barrier five feet high, just before the pavilion, a dry ditch, a ditch full of water, a precipitous slope, an Irish barricade (one of the most difficult obstacles, consisting of a mound fenced with brushwood, beyond which was a ditch out of sight for the horses, so that the horse had to clear both obstacles or might be killed); then two more ditches filled with water, and one dry one; and the end of the race was just facing the pavilion. But the race began not in the ring, but two hundred yards away from it, and in that part of the course was the first obstacle, a dammed-up stream, seven feet in breadth, which the racers could leap or wade through as they preferred.

Three times they were ranged ready to start, but each time some horse thrust itself out of line, and they had to begin again. The umpire who was starting them, Colonel Sestrin, was beginning to lose his temper, when at last for the fourth time he shouted 'Away!' and the racers started.

Every eye, every opera-glass, was turned on the brightly coloured group of riders at the moment they were in line to start.

'They're off! They're starting!' was heard on all sides after the hush of expectation.

And little groups and solitary figures among the public began running from place to place to get a better view. In the very first minute the close group of horsemen drew out, and it could be seen they were approaching the stream in twos and threes and one behind another. To the spectators it seemed as though they had all started simultaneously, but to the racers there were seconds of difference that had great value to them.

Frou-Frou, excited and over-nervous, had lost the first moment, and several horses had started before her, but before reaching the stream, Vronsky, who was holding in the mare with all his force as she tugged at the bridle, easily overtook three, and there were left in front of him Mahotin's chestnut Gladiator, whose hind-quarters were moving lightly and rhythmically up and down exactly in front of Vronsky, and in front of all, the dainty mare Diana, bearing Kuzovlev more dead than alive.

For the first instant Vronsky was not master either of himself or his mare. Up to the first obstacle, the stream, he could not guide the motions of his mare.

Gladiator and Diana came up to it together and almost at the same instant; simultaneously they rose above the stream and flew across to the other side; Frou-Frou darted after them, as if flying; but at the very moment when Vronsky felt himself in the air, he suddenly saw almost under his mare's hoofs Kuzovlev, who was floundering with Diana on the further side of the stream. (Kuzovlev had let go the reins as he took the leap, and the mare had sent him flying over her head). Those details Vronsky learned later; at the moment all he saw was that just under him, where Frou-Frou must alight, Diana's legs or head might be in the way. But Frou-Frou drew up her legs and back in the very act of leaping, like a falling cat, and, clearing the other mare, alighted beyond her.

'O the darling!' thought Vronsky.

After crossing the stream Vronsky had complete control of his mare, and began holding her in, intending to cross the great barrier behind Mahotin, and to try to overtake him in the clear ground of about five hundred yards that followed it.

The great barrier stood just in front of the imperial pavilion. The Tsar and the whole court and crowds of people were all gazing at them —at him, and Mahotin a length ahead of him, as they drew near the 'devil', as the solid barrier was called. Vronsky was aware of those eyes fastened upon him from all sides, but he saw nothing except the ears and neck of his own mare, the ground racing to meet him, and the back and white legs of Gladiator beating time swiftly before him, and keeping always the same distance ahead. Gladiator rose, with no sound of knocking against anything. With a wave of his short tail he disappeared from Vronsky's sight.

'Bravo!' cried a voice.

At the same instant, under Vronsky's eyes, right before him flashed the palings of the barrier. Without the slightest change in her action his mare flew over it; the palings vanished, and he heard only a crash behind him. The mare, excited by Gladiator's keeping ahead, had risen too soon before the barrier, and grazed it with her hind hoofs. But her pace never changed, and Vronsky, feeling a spatter of mud in his face, realised that he was once more the same distance from Gladiator. Once more he perceived in front of him the same back and short tail, and again the same swiftly moving white legs that got no further away.

At the very moment when Vronsky thought that now was the time to overtake Mahotin, Frou-Frou herself, understanding his thoughts, without any incitement on his part, gained ground considerably, and began getting alongside of Mahotin on the most favourable side, close to the inner cord. Mahotin would not let her pass that side. Vronsky had hardly formed the thought that he could perhaps pass on the outer side, when Frou-Frou shifted her pace and began overtaking him on the other side. Frou-Frou's shoulder, beginning by now to be dark with sweat, was even with Gladiator's back. For a few lengths they moved evenly. But before the obstacle they were approaching, Vronsky began working at the reins, anxious to avoid having to take the outer circle, and swiftly passed Mahotin just upon the declivity. He caught a glimpse of his mud-stained face as he flashed by. He even fancied that he smiled. Vronsky passed Mahotin, but he was immediately aware of him close upon him, and he never ceased hearing the even-thudding hoofs and the rapid and still quite fresh breathing of Gladiator.

The next two obstacles, the watercourse, and the barrier, were easily crossed, but Vronsky began to hear the snorting and thud of Gladiator closer upon him. He urged on his mare, and to his delight felt that she easily quickened her pace, and the thud of Gladiator's hoofs was again heard at the same distance away.

Vronsky was at the head of the race, just as he had wanted to be and as Cord had advised, and now he felt sure of being the winner. His excitement, his delight, and his tenderness for Frou-Frou grew keener and keener. He longed to look round again, but he did not dare do this, and tried to be cool and not to urge on his mare, so to keep the same reserve of force in her as he felt that Gladiator still kept. There remained only one obstacle, the most difficult; if he could cross it ahead of the others, he would come in first. He was flying towards the Irish barricade, Frou-Frou and he both together saw the barricade in the distance, and both the man and the mare had a moment's hesitation. He saw the uncertainty in the mare's ears and lifted the whip, but at the same time felt that his fears were groundless; the mare knew what was wanted. She quickened her pace and rose smoothly, just as he had fancied she would, and as she left the ground gave herself up to the force of her rush, which carried her far beyond the ditch; and with the same rhythm, without effort, with the same leg forward, Frou-Frou fell back into her pace again.

'Bravo, Vronsky!' he heard shouts from a knot of men—he knew they were his friends in the regiment—who were standing at the obstacle. He could not fail to recognise Yashvin's voice though he did not see him.

'O my sweet!' he said inwardly to Frou-Frou, as he listened for what was happening behind. 'He's cleared it!' he thought, catching the thud of Gladiator's hoofs behind him. There remained only the last ditch, filled with water and five feet wide. Vronsky did not even look at it, but anxious to get in a long way first began sawing away at the reins, lifting the mare's head and letting it go in time with her paces. He felt that the mare was at her very last reserve of strength; not her neck and shoulders merely were wet, but the sweat was standing in drops on her mane, her head, her sharp ears, and her breath came in short, sharp gasps. But he knew that she had strength left more than enough for the remaining five hundred yards. It was only from feeling himself nearer the ground and from the peculiar smoothness of his motion that Vronsky knew how greatly the mare had quickened her pace. She flew over the ditch as though not noticing it. She flew over it like a bird; but at the same instant Vronsky, to his horror, felt that he had failed to keep up with the mare's pace, that he had, he did not know how, made a fearful, unpardonable mistake, in recovering his seat in the saddle. All at once his position had shifted and he knew that something awful had happened. He could not yet make out what had happened, when the white legs of a chestnut horse flashed by close to him, and Mahotin passed at a swift gallop. Vronsky was touching the ground with one foot, and his mare was sinking on that foot. He just had time to free his leg when she fell on one side, gasping painfully, and, making vain efforts to rise with her delicate, soaking neck, she fluttered on the ground at his feet like a shot bird. The clumsy movement made by Vronsky had broken her back. But that he only knew much later. At that moment he knew only that Mahotin had flown swiftly by, while he stood staggering alone on the muddy, motionless ground, and Frou-Frou lay gasping before him, bending her head back and gazing at him with her exquisite eye. Still unable to realise what had happened, Vronsky tugged at his mare's reins. Again she struggled all over like a fish, and her shoulders setting the saddle heaving, she rose on her front legs, but unable to lift her back, she quivered all over and again fell on her side. With a face hideous with passion, his lower jaw trembling, and his cheeks white, Vronsky kicked her with his heel in the stomach and again fell to tugging at the rein. She did not stir, but thrusting her nose into the ground, she simply gazed at her master with her speaking eyes.

'A—a—a!' groaned Vronsky, clutching at his head. 'Ah! what have I done!' he cried. 'The race lost! And my fault! shameful, unpardonable! And the poor darling, ruined mare! Ah! what have I done!'

A crowd of men, a doctor and his assistant, the officers of his regiment, ran up to him. To his misery he felt that he was whole and unhurt. The mare had broken her back, and it was decided to shoot her. Vronsky could not answer questions, could not speak to anyone. He turned, and without picking up his cap that had fallen off walked away from the racecourse, not knowing where he was going. He felt utterly wretched. For the first time in his life he knew the bitterest sort of misfortune, misfortune beyond remedy, and caused by his own fault.

Yashvin overtook him with his cap, and led him home, and half an hour later Vronsky had regained his self-possession. But the memory of that race remained for long in his heart, the cruellest and bitterest memory of his life.

XXVI

THE external relations of Alexey Alexandrovitch and his wife had remained unchanged. The sole difference lay in the fact that he was more busily occupied than ever. As in former years, at the beginning of the spring he had gone to a foreign watering-place for the sake of his health, deranged by the winter's work that every year grew heavier. And just as always he returned in July and at once fell to work as usual with increased energy. As usual, too, his wife had moved for the summer to a villa out of town, while he remained in Petersburg. From the date of their conversation after the party at Princess Tverskoy's he had never spoken again to Anna of his suspicions and his jealousies, and that habitual tone of his of bantering mimicry was the most convenient tone possible for his present attitude to his wife. He was a little colder to his wife. He simply seemed to be slightly displeased with her for that first midnight conversation, which she had repelled. In his attitude to her there was a shade of vexation, but nothing more. 'You would not be open with me,' he seemed to say, mentally addressing her; 'so much the worse for you. Now you may beg as you please, but I won't be open with you. So much the worse for you!' he said mentally, like a man who, after vainly attempting to extinguish a fire, should fly in a rage with his vain efforts and say, 'Oh, very well then! you shall burn for this!' This man, so subtle and astute in official life, did not realise all the senselessness of such an attitude to his wife. He did not realise it, because it was too terrible to him to realise his actual position, and he shut down and locked and sealed up in his heart that secret place where lay hid his feelings towards his family, that is, his wife and son. He who had been such a careful father, had from the end of that winter become peculiarly frigid to his son, and adopted to him just the same bantering tone he used with his wife. 'Aha, young man!' was the greeting with which he met him.

Alexey Alexandrovitch asserted and believed that he had never in any previous year had so much official business as that year. But he was not aware that he sought work for himself that year, that this was one of the means for keeping shut that secret place where lay hid his feelings towards his wife and son and his thoughts about them, which became more terrible the longer they lay there. If anyone had had the right to ask Alexey Alexandrovitch what he thought of his wife's behaviour, the mild and peaceable Alexey Alexandrovitch would have made no answer, but he would have been greatly angered with any man who should question him on that subject. For this reason there positively came into

Alexey Alexandrovitch's face a look of haughtiness and severity whenever anyone inquired after his wife's health. Alexey Alexandrovitch did not want to think at all about his wife's behaviour, and he actually succeeded in not thinking about it at all.

Alexey Alexandrovitch's permanent summer villa was in Peterhof, and the Countess Lidia Ivanovna used as a rule to spend the summer there, close to Anna, and constantly seeing her. That year Countess Lidia Ivanovna declined to settle in Peterhof, was not once at Anna Arkadyevna's, and in conversation with Alexey Alexandrovitch hinted at the unsuitability of Anna's close intimacy with Betsy and Vronsky. Alexey Alexandrovitch sternly cut her short, roundly declaring his wife to be above suspicion, and from that time began to avoid Countess Lidia Ivanovna. He did not want to see, and did not see, that many people in society cast dubious glances on his wife; he did not want to understand, and did not understand, why his wife had so particularly insisted on staying at Tsarskoe, where Betsy was staying, and not far from the camp of Vronsky's regiment. He did not allow himself to think about it, and he did not think about it; but all the same, though he never admitted it to himself, and had no proofs, nor even suspicious evidence, in the bottom of his heart he knew beyond all doubt that he was a deceived husband, and he was profoundly miserable about it.

How often during those eight years of happy life with his wife Alexey Alexandrovitch had looked at other men's faithless wives and other deceived husbands and asked himself: 'How can people descend to that? how is it they don't put an end to such a hideous position?' But now, when the misfortune had come upon himself, he was so far from thinking of putting an end to the position that he would not recognise it at all, would not recognise it just because it was too awful, too unnatural.

Since his return from abroad Alexey Alexandrovitch had twice been at their country villa. Once he dined there, another time he spent the evening there with a party of friends, but he had not once stayed the night there, as it had been his habit to do in previous years.

The day of the races had been a very busy day for Alexey Alexandrovitch; but when mentally sketching out the day in the morning he made up his mind to go to their country house to see his wife immediately after dinner, and from there to the races, which all the Court were to witness, and at which he was bound to be present. He was going to see his wife, because he had determined to see her once a week to keep up appearances. And besides, on that day, as it was the fifteenth, he had to give his wife some money for her expenses, according to their usual arrangement.

With his habitual control over his thoughts, though he thought all this about his wife, he did not let his thoughts stray further in regard to her.

That morning was a very full one for Alexey Alexandrovitch. The evening before, Countess Lidia Ivanovna had sent him a pamphlet by a celebrated traveller in China, who was staying in Petersburg, and with it she enclosed a note begging him to see the traveller himself, as he was an extremely interesting person from various points of view, and likely to be useful. Alexey Alexandrovitch had not had time to read the pamphlet through in the evening, and finished it in the morning. Then people began arriving with petitions, and there came the reports, interviews, appointments, dismissals, apportionment of rewards, pensions, grants, notes, the work-a-day round, as Alexey Alexandrovitch called it, that always took up so much time. Then there was private business of his own, a visit from the doctor and the steward who managed his property. The steward did not take up much time. He simply gave Alexey Alexandrovitch the money he needed together with a brief statement of the position of his affairs, which was not altogether satisfactory, as it had happened that during that year, owing to increased expenses, more had been paid out than usual, and there was a deficit. But the doctor, a celebrated Petersburg doctor, who was an intimate acquaintance of Alexey Alexandrovitch, took up a great deal of time. Alexey Alexandrovitch had not expected him that day, and was surprised at his visit, and still more so when the doctor questioned him very carefully about his health, listened to his breathing, and tapped at his liver. Alexey Alexandrovitch did not know that his friend Lidia Ivanovna, noticing that he was not as well as usual that year, had begged the doctor to go and examine him. 'Do this for my sake,' the Countess Lidia Ivanovna had said to him.

'I will do it for the sake of Russia, countess,' replied the doctor.

'A priceless man!' said the Countess Lidia Ivanovna.

The doctor was extremely dissatisfied with Alexey Alexandrovitch. He found the liver considerably enlarged, and the digestive powers weakened, while the course of mineral waters had been quite without effect. He prescribed more physical exercise as far as possible, and as far as possible less mental strain, and above all no worry—in other words, just what was as much out of Alexey Alexandrovitch's power as abstaining from breathing. Then he withdrew, leaving in Alexey Alexandrovitch an unpleasant sense that something was wrong with him, and that there was no chance of curing it.

As he was coming away, the doctor chanced to meet on the staircase an acquaintance of his, Sludin, who was secretary of Alexey Alexandrovitch's department. They had been comrades at the university, and though they rarely met, they thought highly of each other and were excellent friends, and so there was no one to whom the doctor would have given his opinion of a patient so freely as to Sludin.

'How glad I am you've been seeing him!' said Sludin. 'He's not well, and I fancy . . . Well, what do you think of him?'

'I'll tell you,' said the doctor, beckoning over Sludin's head to his coachman to bring the carriage round. 'It's just this,' said the doctor, taking a finger of his kid glove in his white hands and pulling it, 'if you don't strain the strings, and then try to break them, you'll find it a difficult job; but strain a string to its very utmost, and the mere weight of one finger on the strained string will snap it. And with his close assiduity, his conscientious devotion to his work, he's strained to the utmost; and there's some outside burden weighing on him, and not a light one,' concluded the doctor, raising his eyebrows significantly. 'Will you be at the races?' he added, as he sank into his seat in the carriage.

'Yes, yes to be sure; it does waste a lot of time,' the doctor responded vaguely to some reply of Sludin's he had not caught.

Directly after the doctor, who had taken up so much time, came the celebrated traveller, and Alexey Alexandrovitch, by means of the pamphlet he had only just finished reading and his previous acquaintance with the subject, impressed the traveller by the depth of his knowledge of the subject and the breadth and enlightenment of his view of it.

At the same time as the traveller there was announced a provincial marshal of nobility on a visit to Petersburg, with whom Alexey Alexandrovitch had to have some conversation. After his departure, he had to finish the daily routine of business with his secretary, and then he still had to drive round to call on a certain great personage on a matter of grave and serious import. Alexey Alexandrovitch only just managed to be back by five o'clock, his dinner-hour, and after dining with his secretary, he invited him to drive with him to his country villa and to the races.

Though he did not acknowledge it to himself, Alexey Alexandrovitch always tried nowadays to secure the presence of a third person in his interviews with his wife.

XXVII

ANNA was upstairs, standing before the looking-glass, and, with Annushka's assistance, pinning the last ribbon on her gown when she heard carriage wheels crunching the gravel at the entrance.

'It's too early for Betsy,' she thought, and glancing out of window she caught sight of the carriage and the black hat of Alexey Alexandrovitch, and the ears that she knew so well sticking up each side of it. 'How unlucky! Can he be going to stay the night?' she wondered, and the thought of all that might come of such a chance struck her as so awful and terrible, that without dwelling on it for a moment, she went down to meet him with a bright and radiant face; and conscious of the presence of that spirit of falsehood and deceit in herself that she had come to know of late, she abandoned herself to that spirit and began talking, hardly knowing what she was saying.

'Ah, how nice of you!' she said, giving her husband her hand, and greeting Sludin, who was like one of the family, with a smile. 'You're staying the night, I hope?' was the first word the spirit of falsehood prompted her to utter; 'and now we'll go together. Only it's a pity I've promised Betsy. She's coming for me.'

Alexey Alexandrovitch knit his brows at Betsy's name.

'Oh, I'm not going to separate the inseparables,' he said in his usual bantering tone. 'I'm going with Mihail Vassilievitch. I'm ordered exercise by the doctors too. I'll walk, and fancy myself at the springs again.'

'There's no hurry,' said Anna. 'Would you like tea?'

She rang.

'Bring in tea, and tell Seryozha that Alexey Alexandrovitch is here. Well, tell me, how have you been? Mihail Vassilievitch, you've not been to see me before. Look how lovely it is out on the terrace,' she said, turning first to one and then to the other.

She spoke very simply and naturally, but too much and too fast. She was the more aware of this from noticing in the inquisitive look Mihail Vassilievitch turned on her that he was, as it were, keeping watch on her.

Mihail Vassilievitch promptly went out on the terrace.

She sat down beside her husband.

'You don't look quite well,' she said.

'Yes,' he said; 'the doctor's been with me today and wasted an hour of my time. I feel that someone of our friends must have sent him: my health's so precious, it seems.'

'No; what did he say?'

She questioned him about his health and what he had been doing, and tried to persuade him to take a rest and come out to her.

All this she said brightly, rapidly, and with a peculiar brilliance in her eyes. But Alexey Alexandrovitch did not now attach any special significance to this tone of hers. He heard only her words and gave them only the direct sense they bore. And he answered simply, though jestingly. There was nothing remarkable in all this conversation, but never after could Anna recall this brief scene without an agonising pang of shame.

Seryozha came in preceded by his governess. If Alexey Alexandrovitch had allowed himself to observe he would have noticed the timid and bewildered eyes with which Seryozha glanced first at his father and then at his mother. But he would not see anything, and he did not see it.

'Ah, the young man! He's grown. Really, he's getting quite a man. How are you, young man?'

And he gave his hand to the scared child. Seryozha had been shy of his father before, and now, ever since Alexey Alexandrovitch had taken to calling him young man, and since that insoluble question had occurred to him whether Vronsky were a friend or a foe, he avoided his father. He looked round towards his mother as though seeking shelter. It was only with his mother that he was at ease. Meanwhile, Alexey Alexandrovitch was holding his son by the shoulder while he was speaking to the governess, and Seryozha was so miserably uncomfortable that Anna saw he was on the point of tears.

Anna, who had flushed a little the instant her son came in, noticing that Seryozha was uncomfortable, got up hurriedly, took Alexey Alexandrovitch's hand from her son's shoulder, and kissing the boy, led him out on to the terrace, and quickly came back.

'It's time to start, though,' said she, glancing at her watch. 'How is it Betsy doesn't come? . . .'

'Yes,' said Alexey Alexandrovitch, and getting up, he folded his hands and cracked his fingers. 'I've come to bring you some money too, for nightingales, we know, can't live on fairy tales,' he said. 'You want it, I expect?'

'No, I don't . . . yes, I do,' she said, not looking at him, and crimsoning to the roots of her hair. 'But you'll come back here after the races, I suppose?'

'Oh yes!' answered Alexey Alexandrovitch. 'And here's the glory of Peterhof, Princess Tverskoy,' he added, looking out of window at the elegant English carriage with the tiny seats placed extremely high. 'What elegance! Charming! Well, let us be starting too, then.'

Princess Tverskoy did not get out of her carriage, but her groom, in high boots, a cape, and black hat, darted out at the entrance.

'I'm going; good-bye!' said Anna, and kissing her son, she went up to Alexey Alexandrovitch and held out her hand to him. 'It was ever so nice of you to come.'

Alexey Alexandrovitch kissed her hand.

'Well, *au revoir*, then! You'll come back for some tea; that's delightful!' she said, and went out, gay and radiant. But as soon as she no longer saw him, she was aware of the spot on her hand that his lips had touched, and she shuddered with repulsion.

XXVIII

WHEN Alexey Alexandrovitch reached the racecourse, Anna was already sitting in the pavilion beside Betsy, in that pavilion where all the highest society had gathered. She caught sight of her husband in the distance. Two men, her husband and her lover, were the two centres of her existence, and unaided by her external senses she was aware of their nearness. She was aware of her husband approaching a long way off, and she could not help following him in the surging crowd in the midst of which he was moving. She watched his progress towards the pavilion, saw him now responding condescendingly to an ingratiating bow, now exchanging friendly, nonchalant greetings with his equals, now assiduously trying to catch the eye of some great one of this world, and taking off his big round hat that squeezed the tips of his ears. All these ways of his she knew, and all were hateful to her. 'Nothing but ambition, nothing but the desire to get on, that's all there is in his soul,' she thought; 'as for these lofty ideals, love of culture, religion, they are only so many tools for getting on.'

From his glances towards the ladies' pavilion (he was staring straight at her, but did not distinguish his wife in the sea of muslin, ribbons, feathers, parasols and flowers) she saw that he was looking for her, but she purposely avoided noticing him.

'Alexey Alexandrovitch!' Princess Betsy called to him; 'I'm sure you don't see your wife: here she is.'

He smiled his chilly smile.

'There's so much splendour here that one's eyes are dazzled,' he said, and he went into the pavilion. He smiled to his wife as a man should smile on meeting his wife after only just parting from her, and greeted the princess and other acquaintances, giving to each what was due—that is to say, jesting with the ladies and dealing out friendly greetings among the men. Below, near the pavilion, was standing an adjutant-general of whom Alexey Alexandrovitch had a high opinion, noted for his intelligence and culture. Alexey Alexandrovitch entered into conversation with him.

There was an interval between the races, and so nothing hindered conversation. The adjutant-general expressed his disapproval of races. Alexey Alexandrovitch replied defending them. Anna heard his high, measured tones, not losing one word, and every word struck her as false, and stabbed her ears with pain.

When the three-mile steeplechase was beginning, she bent forward and gazed with fixed eyes at Vronsky as he went up to his horse and mounted, and at the same time she heard that loathsome, never-ceasing voice of her husband. She was in an agony of terror for Vronsky, but a still greater agony was the never-ceasing, as it seemed to her, stream of her husband's shrill voice with its familiar intonations.

'I'm a wicked woman, a lost woman,' she thought; 'but I don't like lying, I can't endure falsehood, while as for *him* (her husband) it's the breath of his life—falsehood. He knows all about it, he sees it all; what does he care if he can talk so calmly? If he were to kill me, if he were to kill Vronsky, I might respect him. No, all he wants is falsehood and propriety,' Anna said to herself, not considering exactly what it was she wanted of her husband, and how she would have liked to see him behave. She did not understand either that Alexey Alexandrovitch's peculiar loquacity that day, so exasperating to her, was merely the expression of his inward distress and uneasiness. As a child that has been hurt skips about, putting all his muscles into movement to drown the pain, in the same way Alexey Alexandrovitch needed mental exercise to drown the thoughts of his wife that in her presence and in Vronsky's, and with the continual iteration of his name, would force themselves on his attention. And it was as natural for him to talk well and cleverly, as it is natural for a child to skip about. He was saying—

'Danger in the races of officers, of cavalry men, is an essential element in the race. If England can point to the most brilliant feats of cavalry in military history, it is simply owing to the fact that she has historically developed this force both in beasts and in men. Sport has, in my opinion, a great value, and as is always the case, we see nothing but what is most superficial.'

'It's not superficial,' said Princess Tverskoy. 'One of the officers, they say, has broken two ribs.'

Alexey Alexandrovitch smiled his smile, which uncovered his teeth, but revealed nothing more.

'We'll admit, princess, that that's not superficial,' he said, 'but internal. But that's not the point,' and he turned again to the general with whom he was talking seriously; 'we mustn't forget that those who are taking part in the race are military men, who have chosen that career, and one must allow that every calling has its disagreeable side. It forms an integral part of the duties of an officer. Low sports, such as prize-fighting or Spanish bull-fights, are a sign of barbarity. But specialised trials of skill are a sign of development.'

'No, I shan't come another time; it's too upsetting,' said Princess Betsy. 'Isn't it, Anna?'

'It is upsetting, but one can't tear oneself away,' said another lady. 'If I'd been a Roman woman I should never have missed a single circus.'

Anna said nothing, and keeping her opera-glass up, gazed always at the same spot.

At that moment a tall general walked through the pavilion. Breaking off what he was saying, Alexey Alexandrovitch got up hurriedly, though with dignity, and bowed low to the general.

'You're not racing?' the officer asked, chaffing him.

'My race is a harder one,' Alexey Alexandrovitch responded deferentially.

And though the answer meant nothing, the general looked as though he had heard a witty remark from a witty man, and fully relished *la pointe de la sauce*.

'There are two aspects,' Alexey Alexandrovitch resumed: 'those who take part and those who look on; and love for such spectacles is an unmistakable proof of a low degree of development in the spectator, I admit, but . . .'

'Princess, bets!' sounded Stepan Arkadyevitch's voice from below, addressing Betsy. 'Who's your favourite?'

'Anna and I are for Kuzovlev,' replied Betsy.

'I'm for Vronsky. A pair of gloves?'

'Done!'

'But it is a pretty sight, isn't it?'

Alexey Alexandrovitch paused while there was talking about him, but he began again directly.

'I admit that manly sports do not . . .' he was continuing.

But at that moment the racers started, and all conversation ceased. Alexey Alexandrovitch too was silent, and everyone stood up and turned towards the stream. Alexey Alexandrovitch took no interest in the race, and so he did not watch the racers, but fell to listlessly scanning the spectators with his weary eyes. His eyes rested upon Anna.

Her face was white and set. She was obviously seeing nothing and no one but one man. Her hand had convulsively clutched her fan, and she held her breath. He looked at her and hastily turned away, scrutinising other faces.

'But here's this lady too, and others very much moved as well; it's very natural,' Alexey Alexandrovitch told himself. He tried not to look at her, but unconsciously his eyes were drawn to her. He examined that face again, trying not to read what was so plainly written on it, and against his own will, with horror read on it what he did not want to know.

The first fall—Kuzovlev's, at the stream—agitated everyone, but Alexey Alexandrovitch saw distinctly on Anna's pale, triumphant face that the man she was watching had not fallen. When, after Mahotin and Vronsky had cleared the worst barrier, the next officer had been thrown straight on his head at it and fatally injured, and a shudder of horror passed over the whole public, Alexey Alexandrovitch saw that Anna did not even notice it, and had some difficulty in realising what they were talking of about her. But more and more often, and with greater persistence, he watched her. Anna, wholly engrossed as she was with the race, became aware of her husband's cold eyes fixed upon her from one side.

She glanced round for an instant, looked inquiringly at him, and with a slight frown turned away again.

'Ah, I don't care!' she seemed to say to him, and she did not once glance at him again.

The race was an unlucky one, and of the seventeen officers who rode in it more than half were thrown and hurt. Towards the end of the race everyone was in a state of agitation, which was intensified by the fact that the Tsar was displeased.

XXIX

EVERYONE was loudly expressing disapprobation, everyone was repeating a phrase someone had uttered—'The lions and gladiators will be the next thing,' and everyone was feeling horrified; so that when Vronsky fell to the ground, and Anna moaned aloud, there was nothing very out of the way in it. But afterwards a change came over Anna's face which really was beyond decorum. She utterly lost her head. She began fluttering like a caged bird, at one moment would have got up and moved away, at the next turned to Betsy.

'Let us go, let us go!' she said.

But Betsy did not hear her. She was bending down, talking to a general who had come up to her.

Alexey Alexandrovitch went up to Anna and courteously offered her his arm.

'Let us go, if you like,' he said in French, but Anna was listening to the general and did not notice her husband.

'He's broken his leg too, so they say,' the general was saying. 'This is beyond everything.'

Without answering her husband, Anna lifted her opera-glass and gazed towards the place where Vronsky had fallen; but it was so far off, and there was such a crowd of people about it, that she could make out nothing. She laid down the opera-glass, and would have moved away, but at that moment an officer galloped up and made some announcement to the Tsar. Anna craned forward, listening.

'Stiva! Stiva!' she cried to her brother.

But her brother did not hear her. Again she would have moved away.

'Once more I offer you my arm if you want to be going,' said Alexey Alexandrovitch, reaching towards her hand.

She drew back from him with aversion, and without looking in his face answered—

'No, no, let me be, I'll stay.'

She saw now that from the place of Vronsky's accident an officer was running across the course towards the pavilion. Betsy waved her handkerchief to him. The officer brought the news that the rider was not killed, but the horse had broken its back.

On hearing this Anna sat down hurriedly, and hid her face in her fan. Alexey Alexandrovitch saw that she was weeping, and could not control her tears, nor even the sobs that were shaking her bosom. Alexey Alexandrovitch stood so as to screen her, giving her time to recover herself.

'For the third time I offer you my arm,' he said to her after a little time, turning to her. Anna gazed at him and did not know what to say. Princess Betsy came to her rescue.

'No, Alexey Alexandrovitch; I brought Anna and I promised to take her home,' put in Betsy.

'Excuse me, princess,' he said, smiling courteously, but looking her very firmly in the face, 'but I see that Anna's not very well, and I wish her to come home with me.'

Anna looked about her in a frightened way, got up submissively, and laid her hand on her husband's arm.

'I'll send to him and find out, and let you know,' Betsy whispered to her.

As they left the pavilion, Alexey Alexandrovitch, as always, talked to those he met, and Anna had, as always, to talk and answer; but she was utterly beside herself, and moved hanging on her husband's arm as though in a dream.

'Is he killed or not? Is it true? Will he come or not? Shall I see him today?' she was thinking.

She took her seat in her husband's carriage in silence, and in silence drove out of the crowd of carriages. In spite of all he had seen, Alexey Alexandrovitch still did not allow himself to consider his wife's real condition. He merely saw the outward symptoms. He saw that she was behaving unbecomingly, and considered it his duty to tell her so. But it was very difficult for him not to say more, to tell her nothing but that. He opened his mouth to tell her she had behaved unbecomingly, but he could not help saying something utterly different.

'What an inclination we all have, though, for these cruel spectacles!' he said. 'I observe . . .'

'Eh? I don't understand,' said Anna contemptuously.

He was offended, and at once began to say what he had meant to say.

'I am obliged to tell you,' he began.

'So now we are to have it out,' she thought, and she felt frightened.

'I am obliged to tell you that your behaviour has been unbecoming today,' he said to her in French.

'In what way has my behaviour been unbecoming?' she said aloud, turning her head swiftly and looking him straight in the face, not with the bright expression that seemed covering something, but with a look of determination, under which she concealed with difficulty the dismay she was feeling.

'Mind,' he said, pointing to the open window opposite the coachman.

He got up and pulled up the window.

'What did you consider unbecoming?' she repeated.

'The despair you were unable to conceal at the accident to one of the riders.'

He waited for her to answer, but she was silent, looking straight before her.

'I have already begged you so to conduct yourself in society that even malicious tongues can find nothing to say against you. There was a time when I spoke of your inward attitude, but I am not speaking of that now. Now I speak only of your external attitude. You have behaved improperly, and I would wish it not to occur again.'

She did not hear half of what he was saying; she felt panic-stricken before him, and was thinking whether it was true that Vronsky was not killed. Was it of him they were speaking when they said the rider was unhurt, but the horse had broken its back? She merely smiled with a pretence of irony when he finished, and made no reply, because she had not heard what he said. Alexey Alexandrovitch had begun to speak boldly, but as he realised plainly what he was speaking of, the dismay she was feeling infected him too. He saw the smile, and a strange misapprehension came over him.

'She is smiling at my suspicions. Yes, she will tell me directly what she told me before; that there is no foundation for my suspicions, that it's absurd.'

At that moment, when the revelation of everything was hanging over him, there was nothing he expected so much as that she would answer mockingly as before that his suspicions were absurd and utterly groundless. So terrible to him was what he knew that now he was ready to believe anything. But the expression of her face, scared and gloomy, did not now promise even deception.

'Possibly I was mistaken,' said he. 'If so, I beg your pardon.'

'No, you were not mistaken,' she said deliberately, looking desperately into his cold face. 'You were not mistaken. I was, and I could not help being in despair. I hear you, but I am thinking of him. I love him, I am his mistress; I can't bear you; I'm afraid of you, and I hate you. . . . You can do what you like to me.'

And dropping back into the corner of the carriage, she broke into sobs, hiding her face in her hands. Alexey Alexandrovitch did not stir, and kept looking straight before him. But his whole face suddenly bore the solemn rigidity of the dead, and his expression did not change during the whole time of the drive home. On reaching the house he turned his head to her, still with the same expression.

'Very well! But I expect a strict observance of the external forms of propriety till such time'—his voice shook—'as I may take measures to secure my honour and communicate them to you.'

He got out first and helped her to get out. Before the servants he pressed her hand, took his seat in the carriage, and drove back to Petersburg. Immediately afterwards a footman came from Princess Betsy and brought Anna a note.

'I sent to Alexey to find out how he is, and he writes me he is quite well and unhurt, but in despair.'

'So *he* will be here,' she thought. 'What a good thing I told him all!'

She glanced at her watch. She had still three hours to wait, and the memories of their last meeting set her blood in flame.

'My God, how light it is! It's dreadful, but I do love to see his face, and I do love this fantastic light. . . . My husband! Oh! yes . . . Well, thank God! everything's over with him.'

XXX

IN the little German watering-place to which the Shtcherbatskys had betaken themselves, as in all places indeed where people are gathered together, the usual process, as it were, of the crystallisation of society went on, assigning to each member of that society a definite and unalterable place. Just as the particle of water in frost, definitely and unalterably, takes the special form of the crystal of snow, so each new person that arrived at the springs was at once placed in his special place.

Fürst Shtcherbatsky, *sammt Gemalin, und Tochter*, by the apartments they took, and from their name and from the friends they made, were immediately crystallised into a definite place marked out for them.

There was visiting the watering-place that year a real German Fürstin, in consequence of which the crystallising process went on more vigorously than ever. Princess Shtcherbatsky wished, above everything, to present her daughter to this German princess, and the day after their arrival she duly performed this rite. Kitty made a low and graceful curtsey in the *very simple*, that is to say, very elegant frock that had been ordered her from Paris. The German princess said, 'I hope the roses will soon come back to this pretty little face,' and for the Shtcherbatskys certain definite lines of existence were at once laid down from which there was no departing. The Shtcherbatskys made the acquaintance too of the family of an English Lady Somebody, and of a German countess and her son, wounded in the last war, and of a learned Swede, and of M. Canut and his sister. But yet inevitably the Shtcherbatskys were thrown most into the society of a Moscow lady, Marya Yevgenyevna Rtishtchov and her daughter, whom Kitty disliked, because she had fallen ill, like herself, over a love affair, and a Moscow colonel, whom Kitty had known from childhood, and always seen in uniform and epaulettes, and who now, with his little eyes and his open neck and flowered cravat, was uncommonly ridiculous and tedious, because there was no getting rid of him. When all this was so firmly established, Kitty began to be very much bored, especially as the prince went away to Carlsbad and she was left alone with her mother. She took no interest in the people she knew, feeling that nothing fresh would come of them. Her chief mental interest at the watering-place consisted in watching and making theories about the people she did not know. It was characteristic of Kitty that she always imagined everything in people in the most favourable light possible, especially so in those she did not know. And now as she made surmises as to who people were, what were their relations to one another, and what they were like, Kitty endowed them with the most marvellous and noble characters, and found confirmation of her idea in her observations.

Of these people the one that attracted her most was a Russian girl who had come to the watering-place with an invalid Russian lady, Madame Stahl, as everyone called her. Madame Stahl belonged to the highest society, but she was so ill that she could not walk, and only on exceptionally fine days made her appearance at the springs in an invalid carriage. But it was not so much from ill-health as from pride—so Princess Shtcherbatsky interpreted it—that Madame Stahl had not made the acquaintance of anyone among the Russians there. The Russian girl looked after Madame Stahl, and besides that, she was, as Kitty observed, on friendly terms with all the invalids who were seriously ill, and there were many of them at the springs, and looked after them in the most natural way. This Russian girl was not, as Kitty gathered, related to Madame Stahl, nor was she a paid attendant. Madame Stahl called her Varenka, and other people called her 'Mademoiselle Varenka.' Apart from the interest Kitty took in this girl's relations with Madame Stahl and with other unknown persons, Kitty, as often happens, felt an inexplicable attraction to Mademoiselle Varenka, and was aware when their eyes met that she too liked her.

Of Mademoiselle Varenka one would not say that she had passed her first youth, but she was, as it were, a creature without youth; she might have been taken for nineteen or thirty. If her features were criticised separately, she was handsome rather than plain, in spite of the sickly hue of her face. She would have been a good figure too, if it had not been for her extreme thinness and the size of her head, which was too large for her medium height. But she was not likely to be attractive to men. She was like a fine flower, already past its bloom and without fragrance, though the petals were still unwithered. Moreover, she would have been unattractive to men also from the lack of just what Kitty had too much of—of the suppressed fire of vitality, and the consciousness of her own attractiveness.

She always seemed absorbed in work about which there could be no doubt, and so it seemed she could not take interest in anything outside it. It was just this contrast with her own position that was for Kitty the great attraction of Mademoiselle Varenka. Kitty felt that in her, in her manner of life, she would find an example of what she was now so painfully seeking: interest in life, a dignity in life—apart from the worldly relations of girls with men, which so revolted Kitty, and appeared to her now as a shameful hawking about of goods in search of a purchaser. The more attentively Kitty watched her unknown friend, the more convinced she was this girl was the perfect creature she fancied her, and the more eagerly she wished to make her acquaintance.

The two girls used to meet several times a day, and every time they met, Kitty's eyes said: 'Who are you? What are you? Are you really the exquisite creature I imagine you to be? But for goodness' sake don't suppose,' her eyes added, 'that I would force my acquaintance on you, I simply admire you and like you.' 'I like you too, and you're very,

very sweet. And I should like you better still, if I had time,' answered the eyes of the unknown girl. Kitty saw, indeed, that she was always busy. Either she was taking the children of a Russian family home from the springs, or fetching a shawl for a sick lady, and wrapping her up in it, or trying to interest an irritable invalid, or selecting and buying cakes for tea for someone.

Soon after the arrival of the Shtcherbatskys there appeared in the morning crowd at the springs two persons who attracted universal and unfavourable attention. These were a tall man with a stooping figure, and huge hands, in an old coat too short for him, with black, simple, and yet terrible, eyes, and a pock-marked, kind-looking woman, very badly and tastelessly dressed. Recognising these persons as Russians, Kitty had already in her imagination begun constructing a delightful and touching romance about them. But the princess, having ascertained from the visitors' list that this was Nikolay Levin and Marya Nikolaevna, explained to Kitty what a bad man this Levin was, and all her fancies about these two people vanished. Not so much from what her mother told her, as from the fact that it was Konstantin's brother, this pair suddenly seemed to Kitty intensely unpleasant. This Levin, with his continual twitching of his head, aroused in her now an irrepressible feeling of disgust.

It seemed to her that his big, terrible eyes, which persistently pursued her, expressed a feeling of hatred and contempt, and she tried to avoid meeting him.

XXXI

IT was a wet day; it had been raining all the morning, and the invalids, with their parasols, had flocked into the arcades.

Kitty was walking there with her mother, and the Moscow colonel, smart and jaunty in his European coat, bought ready-made at Frankfort. They were walking on one side of the arcade, trying to avoid Levin, who was walking on the other side. Varenka, in her dark dress, in a black hat with a turn-down brim, was walking up and down the whole length of the arcade with a blind Frenchwoman, and, every time she met Kitty, they exchanged friendly glances.

'Mamma, couldn't I speak to her?' said Kitty, watching her unknown friend, and noticing that she was going up to the spring, and that they might come there together.

'Oh, if you want to so much, I'll find out about her first and make her acquaintance myself,' answered her mother. 'What do you see in her out of the way? A companion, she must be. If you like, I'll make acquaintance with Madame Stahl; I used to know her *belle-sœur*,' added the princess, lifting her head haughtily.

Kitty knew that the princess was offended that Madame Stahl had seemed to avoid making her acquaintance. Kitty did not insist.

'How wonderfully sweet she is!' she said, gazing at Varenka just as she handed a glass to the Frenchwoman. 'Look how natural and sweet it all is.'

'It's so funny to see your *engouements*,' said the princess. 'No, we'd better go back,' she added, noticing Levin coming towards them with his companion and a German doctor, to whom he was talking very noisily and angrily.

They turned to go back, when suddenly they heard, not noisy talk, but shouting. Levin, stopping short, was shouting at the doctor, and the doctor, too, was excited. A crowd gathered about them. The princess and Kitty beat a hasty retreat, while the colonel joined the crowd to find out what was the matter.

A few minutes later the colonel overtook them.

'What was it?' inquired the princess.

'Scandalous and disgraceful!' answered the colonel. 'The one thing to be dreaded is meeting Russians abroad. That tall gentleman was abusing the doctor, flinging all sorts of insults at him because he wasn't treating him quite as he liked, and he began waving his stick at him. It's simply a scandal!'

'Oh, how unpleasant!' said the princess. 'Well, and how did it end?'

'Luckily at that point that . . . the one in the mushroom hat . . . intervened. A Russian lady, I think she is,' said the colonel.

'Mademoiselle Varenka?' asked Kitty.

'Yes, yes. She came to the rescue before anyone; she took the man by the arm and led him away.'

'There, mamma,' said Kitty; 'you wonder that I'm enthusiastic about her.'

The next day, as she watched her unknown friend, Kitty noticed that Mademoiselle Varenka was already on the same terms with Levin and his companion as with her other protégés. She went up to them, entered into conversation with them, and served as interpreter for the woman, who could not speak any foreign language.

Kitty began to entreat her mother still more urgently to let her make friends with Varenka. And, disagreeable as it was to the princess to seem to take the first step in wishing to make the acquaintance of Madame Stahl, who thought fit to give herself airs, she made inquiries about Varenka, and, having ascertained particulars about her tending to prove that there could be no harm though little good in the acquaintance, she herself approached Varenka and made acquaintance with her.

Choosing a time when her daughter had gone to the spring, while Varenka had stopped outside the baker's, the princess went up to her.

'Allow me to make your acquaintance,' she said, with her dignified smile. 'My daughter has lost her heart to you,' she said. 'Possibly you do not know me. I am . . .'

'That feeling is more than reciprocal, princess,' Varenka answered hurriedly.

'What a good deed you did yesterday to our poor compatriot!' said the princess.

Varenka flushed a little. 'I don't remember. I don't think I did anything,' she said.

'Why, you saved that Levin from disagreeable consequences.'

'Yes, *sa compagne* called me, and I tried to pacify him; he's very ill, and was dissatisfied with the doctor. I'm used to looking after such invalids.'

'Yes; I've heard you live at Mentone with your aunt—I think—Madame Stahl: I used to know her *belle-sœur*.'

'No, she's not my aunt. I call her mamma, but I am not related to her; I was brought up by her,' answered Varenka, flushing a little again.

This was so simply said, and so sweet was the truthful and candid expression of her face, that the princess saw why Kitty had taken such a fancy to Varenka.

'Well, and what's this Levin going to do?' asked the princess.

'He's going away,' answered Varenka.

At that instant Kitty came up from the spring beaming with delight that her mother had become acquainted with her unknown friend.

'Well, see, Kitty, your intense desire to make friends with Mademoiselle . . .'

'Varenka,' Varenka put in smiling, 'that's what everyone calls me.'

Kitty blushed with pleasure, and slowly, without speaking, pressed her new friend's hand, which did not respond to her pressure, but lay motionless in her hand. The hand did not respond to her pressure, but the face of Mademoiselle Varenka glowed with a soft, glad, though rather mournful, smile, that showed large but handsome teeth.

'I have long wished for this too,' she said.

'But you are so busy.'

'Oh no, I'm not at all busy,' answered Varenka, but at that moment she had to leave her new friends because two little Russian girls, children of an invalid, ran up to her.

'Varenka, mamma's calling!' they cried.

And Varenka went after them.

XXXII

THE particulars which the princess had learned in regard to Varenka's past and her relations with Madame Stahl were as follows.

Madame Stahl, of whom some people said that she had worried her husband out of his life, while others said it was he who had made her wretched by his immoral behaviour, had always been a woman of weak health and enthusiastic temperament. When, after her separation from her husband, she gave birth to her only child, the child had died almost immediately, and the family of Madame Stahl, knowing her sensibility, and fearing the news would kill her, had substituted another child, a baby born the same night and in the same house in Petersburg, the daughter of the chief cook of the Imperial Household. This was Varenka. Madame Stahl learned later on that Varenka was not her own child, but she went on bringing her up, especially as very soon afterwards Varenka had not a relation of her own living. Madame Stahl had now been living more than ten years continuously abroad, in the south, never leaving her couch. And some people said that Madame Stahl had made her social position as a philanthropic, highly religious woman; other people said she really was at heart the highly ethical being, living for nothing but the good of her fellow-creatures, which she represented herself to be. No one knew what her faith was—Catholic, Protestant, or Orthodox. But one fact was indubitable—she was in amicable relations with the highest dignitaries of all the churches and sects.

Varenka lived with her all the while abroad, and everyone who knew Madame Stahl knew and liked Mademoiselle Varenka, as everyone called her.

Having learned all these facts, the princess found nothing to object to in her daughter's intimacy with Varenka, more specially as Varenka's breeding and education was of the best—she spoke French and English extremely well—and what was of the most weight, brought a message from Madame Stahl expressing her regret that she was prevented by her ill-health from making the acquaintance of the princess.

After getting to know Varenka, Kitty became more and more fascinated by her friend, and every day she discovered new virtues in her.

The princess, hearing that Varenka had a good voice, asked her to come and sing to them in the evening.

'Kitty plays, and we have a piano; not a good one, it's true, but you will give us so much pleasure,' said the princess with her affected smile, which Kitty disliked particularly just then, because she noticed that Varenka had no inclination to sing. Varenka came, however, in the evening and brought a roll of music with her. The princess had invited Marya Yevgenyevna and her daughter and the colonel.

Varenka seemed quite unaffected by there being persons present she did not know, and she went directly to the piano. She could not accompany herself, but she could sing music at sight very well. Kitty, who played well, accompanied her.

'You have an extraordinary talent,' the princess said to her after Varenka had sung the first song extremely well.

Marya Yevgenyevna and her daughter expressed their thanks and admiration.

'Look,' said the colonel, looking out of window, 'what an audience has collected to listen to you.' There actually was quite a considerable crowd under the windows.

'I am very glad it gives you pleasure,' Varenka answered simply.

Kitty looked with pride at her friend. She was enchanted by her talent, and her voice and her face, but most of all by her manner, by the way Varenka obviously thought nothing of her singing and was quite unmoved by their praises. She seemed only to be asking: 'Am I to sing again, or is that enough?'

'If it had been I,' thought Kitty, 'how proud I should have been! How delighted I should have been to see that crowd under the windows! But she's utterly unmoved by it. Her only motive is to avoid refusing and to please mamma. What is there in her? What is it gives her the power to look down on everything, to be calm independently of everything? How I should like to know it and to learn it of her!' thought Kitty, gazing into her serene face. The princess asked Varenka to sing again, and Varenka sang another song, also smoothly, distinctly, and well, standing erect at the piano and beating time on it with her thin, dark-skinned hand.

The next song in the book was an Italian one. Kitty played the opening bars, and looked round at Varenka.

'Let's skip that,' said Varenka, flushing a little. Kitty let her eyes rest on Varenka's face, with a look of dismay and inquiry.

'Very well, the next one,' she said hurriedly, turning over the pages, and at once feeling that there was something connected with the song.

'No,' answered Varenka with a smile, laying her hand on the music, 'no, let's have that one.' And she sang it just as quietly, as coolly, and as well as the others.

When she had finished, they all thanked her again, and went off to tea. Kitty and Varenka went out into the little garden that adjoined the house.

'Am I right, that you have some reminiscences connected with that song?' said Kitty. 'Don't tell me,' she added hastily, 'only say, if I'm right.'

'No, why not? I'll tell you simply,' said Varenka, and, without waiting for a reply, she went on: 'Yes, it brings up memories, once painful ones. I cared for someone once, and I used to sing him that song.'

Kitty with big, wide-open eyes gazed silently, sympathetically at Varenka.

'I cared for him, and he cared for me; but his mother did not wish it, and he married another girl. He's living now not far from us, and I see him sometimes. You didn't think I had a love-story too,' she said, and there was a faint gleam in her handsome face of that fire which Kitty felt must once have glowed all over her.

'I didn't think so? Why, if I were a man, I could never care for anyone else after knowing you. Only I can't understand how he could, to please his mother, forget you and make you unhappy; he had no heart.'

'Oh no, he's a very good man, and I'm not unhappy; quite the contrary, I'm very happy. Well, so we shan't be singing any more now,' she added, turning towards the house.

'How good you are! how good you are!' cried Kitty, and stopping her, she kissed her. 'If I could only be even a little like you!'

'Why should you be like anyone? You're nice as you are,' said Varenka, smiling her gentle, weary smile.

'No, I'm not nice at all. Come, tell me . . . Stop a minute, let's sit down,' said Kitty, making her sit down again beside her. 'Tell me, isn't it humiliating to think that a man has disdained your love, that he hasn't cared for it? . . .'

'But he didn't disdain it; I believe he cared for me, but he was a dutiful son . . .'

'Yes, but if it hadn't been on account of his mother, if it had been his own doing? . . .' said Kitty, feeling she was giving away her secret, and that her face, burning with the flush of shame, had betrayed her already.

'In that case he would have done wrong, and I should not have regretted him,' answered Varenka, evidently realising that they were now talking not of her, but of Kitty.

'But the humiliation,' said Kitty, 'the humiliation one can never forget, can never forget,' she said, remembering her look at the last ball during the pause in the music.

'Where is the humiliation? Why, you did nothing wrong?'

'Worse than wrong—shameful.'

Varenka shook her head and laid her hand on Kitty's hand.

'Why, what is there shameful?' she said. 'You didn't tell a man, who didn't care for you, that you loved him, did you?'

'Of course not; I never said a word, but he knew it. No, no; there are looks, there are ways. I can't forget it, if I live a hundred years.'

'Why so? I don't understand. The whole point is whether you love him now or not,' said Varenka, who called everything by its name.

'I hate him; I can't forgive myself.'

'Why, what for?'

'The shame, the humiliation!'

'Oh! if everyone were as sensitive as you are!' said Varenka. 'There isn't a girl who hasn't been through the same. And it's all so unimportant.'

'Why, what is important?' said Kitty, looking into her face with inquisitive wonder.

'Oh, there's so much that's important,' said Varenka, smiling.

'Why, what?'

'Oh, so much that's more important,' answered Varenka, not knowing what to say. But at that instant they heard the princess's voice from the window. 'Kitty, it's cold! Either get a shawl, or come indoors.'

'It really is time to go in!' said Varenka, getting up. 'I have to go on to Madame Berthe's; she asked me to.'

Kitty held her by the hand, and with passionate curiosity and entreaty her eyes asked her: 'What is it, what is this of such importance that gives you such tranquillity? You know, tell me!' But Varenka did not even know what Kitty's eyes were asking her. She merely thought that she had to go to see Madame Berthe too that evening, and to make haste home in time for *maman's* tea at twelve o'clock. She went indoors, collected her music, and saying good-bye to everyone, was about to go.

'Allow me to see you home,' said the colonel.

'Yes; how can you go alone at night like this?' chimed in the princess. 'Anyway, I'll send Parasha.'

Kitty saw that Varenka could hardly restrain a smile at the idea that she needed an escort.

'No, I always go about alone and nothing ever happens to me,' she said, taking her hat. And kissing Kitty once more, without saying what was important, she stepped out courageously with the music under her arm and vanished into the twilight of the summer night, bearing away with her her secret of what was important and what gave her the calm and dignity so much to be envied.

XXXIII

KITTY made the acquaintance of Madame Stahl too, and this acquaintance, together with her friendship with Varenka, did not merely exercise a great influence on her, it also comforted her in her mental distress. She found this comfort through a completely new world being opened to her by means of this acquaintance, a world having nothing in common with her past, an exalted, noble world, from the height of which she could contemplate her past calmly. It was revealed to her that besides the instinctive life to which Kitty had given herself up hitherto there was a spiritual life. This life was disclosed in religion, but a religion having nothing in common with that one which Kitty had known from childhood, and which found expression in litanies and all-night services at the Widows' Home, where one might meet one's friends, and in learning by heart Slavonic texts with the priest. This was a lofty, mysterious religion connected with a whole series of noble thoughts and feelings, which one could do more than merely believe because one was told to, which one could love.

Kitty found all this out not from words. Madame Stahl talked to Kitty as to a charming child that one looks on with pleasure as on the memory of one's youth, and only once she said in passing that in all human sorrows nothing gives comfort but love and faith, and that in the sight of Christ's compassion for us no sorrow is trifling—and immediately talked of other things. But in every gesture of Madame Stahl, in every word, in every heavenly—as Kitty called it—look, and above all in the whole story of her life, which she heard from Varenka, Kitty recognised that something 'that was important,' of which, till then, she had known nothing.

Yet, elevated as Madame Stahl's character was, touching as was her story, and exalted and moving as was her speech, Kitty could not help detecting in her some traits which perplexed her. She noticed that when questioning her about her family, Madame Stahl had smiled contemptuously, which was not in accord with Christian meekness. She noticed, too, that when she had found a Catholic priest with her, Madame Stahl had studiously kept her face in the shadow of the lamp-shade and had smiled in a peculiar way. Trivial as these two observations were, they perplexed her, and she had her doubts as to Madame Stahl. But on the other hand Varenka, alone in the world, without friends or relations, with a melancholy disappointment in the past, desiring nothing, regretting nothing, was just that perfection of which Kitty dared hardly dream. In Varenka she realised that one has but to forget oneself and love others, and one will be calm, happy, and noble. And that was what Kitty longed to be. Seeing now clearly what was the *most important*, Kitty was not satisfied with being enthusiastic over it; she at once gave herself up with her whole soul to the new life that was opening to her. From Varenka's accounts of the doings of Madame Stahl and other people whom she mentioned, Kitty had already constructed the plan of her own future life. She would, like Madame Stahl's niece, Aline, of whom Varenka had talked to her a great deal, seek out those who were in trouble, wherever she might be living, help them as far as she could, give them the Gospel, read the Gospel to the sick, to criminals, to the dying. The idea of reading the Gospel to criminals, as Aline did, particularly fascinated Kitty. But all these were secret dreams, of which Kitty did not talk either to her mother or to Varenka.

While awaiting the time for carrying out her plans on a large scale, however, Kitty, even then at the springs, where there were so many people ill and unhappy, readily found a chance for practising her new principles in imitation of Varenka.

At first the princess noticed nothing but that Kitty was much under the influence of her *engouement*, as she called it, for Madame Stahl, and still more for Varenka. She saw that Kitty did not merely imitate Varenka in her conduct, but unconsciously imitated her in her manner of walking, of talking, of blinking her eyes. But later on the princess noticed that, apart from this adoration, some kind of serious spiritual change was taking place in her daughter.

The princess saw that in the evenings Kitty read a French testament that Madame Stahl had given her—a thing she had never done before; that she avoided society acquaintances and associated with the sick people who were under Varenka's protection, and especially one poor family, that of a sick painter, Petrov. Kitty was unmistakably proud of playing the part of a sister of mercy in that family. All this was well enough, and the princess had nothing to say against it, especially as Petrov's wife was a perfectly nice sort of woman, and that the German princess, noticing Kitty's devotion, praised her, calling her an angel of consolation. All this would have been very well, if there had been no exaggeration. But the princess saw that her daughter was rushing into extremes, and so indeed she told her.

'*Il ne faut jamais rien outrer*,' she said to her.

Her daughter made her no reply, only in her heart she thought that one could not talk about exaggeration where Christianity was concerned. What exaggeration could there be in the practice of a doctrine wherein one was bidden to turn the other cheek when one was smitten, and give one's cloak if one's coat were taken? But the princess disliked this exaggeration, and disliked even more the fact that she felt her daughter did not care to show her all her heart. Kitty did in fact conceal her new views and feelings from her mother. She concealed them not because she did not respect or did not love her mother, but simply because she was her mother. She would have revealed them to anyone sooner than to her mother.

'How is it Anna Pavlovna's not been to see us for so long?' the princess said one day of Madame Petrov. 'I've asked her, but she seems put out about something.'

'No, I've not noticed it, maman,' said Kitty, flushing hotly.

'Is it long since you went to see them?'

'We're meaning to make an expedition to the mountains tomorrow,' answered Kitty.

'Well, you can go,' answered the princess, gazing at her daughter's embarrassed face and trying to guess the cause of her embarrassment.

That day Varenka came to dinner and told them that Anna Pavlovna had changed her mind and given up the expedition for the morrow. And the princess noticed again that Kitty reddened.

'Kitty, haven't you had some misunderstanding with the Petrovs?' said the princess, when they were left alone. 'Why has she given up sending the children and coming to see us?'

Kitty answered that nothing had happened between them, and that she could not tell why Anna Pavlovna seemed displeased with her. Kitty answered perfectly truly. She did not know the reason Anna Pavlovna had changed to her, but she guessed it. She guessed at something which she could not tell her mother, which she did not put into words to herself. It was one of those things which one knows but which one can never speak of even to oneself, so terrible and shameful would it be to be mistaken.

Again and again she went over in her memory all her relations with the family. She remembered the simple delight expressed on the round, good-humoured face of Anna Pavlovna at their meetings; she remembered their secret confabulations about the invalid, their plots to draw him away from the work which was forbidden him, and to get him out of doors; the devotion of the youngest boy, who used to call her 'my Kitty', and would not go to bed without her. How nice it all was! Then she recalled the thin, terribly thin figure of Petrov, with his long neck, in his brown coat, his scant, curly hair, his questioning blue eyes that were so terrible to Kitty at first, and his painful attempts to seem hearty and lively in her presence. She recalled the efforts she had made at first to overcome the repugnance she felt for him, as for all consumptive people, and the pains it had cost her to think of things to say to him. She recalled the timid, softened look with which he gazed at her, and the strange feeling of compassion and awkwardness, and later of a sense of her own goodness, which she had felt at it. How nice it all was! But all that was at first. Now, a few days ago, everything was suddenly spoiled. Anna Pavlovna had met Kitty with affected cordiality, and had kept continual watch on her and on her husband.

Could that touching pleasure he showed when she came near be the cause of Anna Pavlovna's coolness?

'Yes,' she mused, 'there was something unnatural about Anna Pavlovna, and utterly unlike her good nature, when she said angrily the day before yesterday: "There, he will keep waiting for you; he wouldn't drink his coffee without you, though he's grown so dreadfully weak."'

'Yes, perhaps too she didn't like it when I gave him the rug. It was all so simple, but he took it so awkwardly, and was so long thanking me, that I felt awkward too. And then that portrait of me he did so well. And most of all that look of confusion and tenderness! Yes, yes, that's it!' Kitty repeated to herself with horror. 'No, it can't be, it oughtn't to be! He's so much to be pitied!' she said to herself directly after.

This doubt poisoned the charm of her new life.

XXXIV

BEFORE the end of the course of drinking the waters, Prince Shtcherbatsky, who had gone on from Carlsbad to Baden and Kissingen to Russian friends—to get a breath of Russian air, as he said—came back to his wife and daughter.

The views of the prince and of the princess on life abroad were completely opposed. The princess thought everything delightful, and in spite of her established position in Russian society, she tried abroad to be like a European fashionable lady, which she was not—for the simple reason that she was a typical Russian gentlewoman; and so she was affected, which did not altogether suit her. The prince, on the contrary, thought everything foreign detestable, got sick of European life, kept to his Russian habits, and purposely tried to show himself abroad less European than he was in reality.

The prince returned thinner, with the skin hanging in loose bags on his cheeks, but in the most cheerful frame of mind. His good-humour was even greater when he saw Kitty completely recovered. The news of Kitty's friendship with Madame Stahl and Varenka, and the reports the princess gave him of some kind of change she had noticed in Kitty, troubled the prince and aroused his habitual feeling of jealousy of everything that drew his daughter away from him, and a dread that his daughter might have got out of the reach of his influence into regions inaccessible to him. But these unpleasant matters were all drowned in the sea of kindliness and good-humour which was always within him, and more so than ever since his course of Carlsbad waters.

The day after his arrival the prince, in his long overcoat, with his Russian wrinkles and baggy cheeks propped up by a starched collar, set off with his daughter to the spring in the greatest good-humour.

It was a lovely morning: the bright, cheerful houses with their little gardens, the sight of the red-faced, red-armed beer-drinking German waitresses, working away merrily, did the heart good. But the nearer they got to the springs the oftener they met sick people; and their appearance seemed more pitiable than ever among the everyday conditions of prosperous German life. Kitty was no longer struck by this contrast. The bright sun, the brilliant green of the foliage, the strains of the music were for her the natural setting of all these familiar faces, with their changes to greater emaciation or to convalescence, for which she watched. But to the prince the brightness and gaiety of the June morning, and the sound of the orchestra playing a gay waltz then in fashion, and above all, the appearance of the healthy attendants, seemed something unseemly and monstrous, in conjunction with these slowly moving, dying figures gathered together from all parts of Europe. In spite of his feeling of pride and, as it were, of the return of youth, with his favourite daughter on his arm, he felt awkward, and almost ashamed of his vigorous step and his sturdy, stout limbs. He felt almost like a man not dressed in a crowd.

'Present me to your new friends,' he said to his daughter, squeezing her hand with his elbow. 'I like even your horrid Soden for making you so well again. Only it's melancholy, very melancholy here. Who's that?'

Kitty mentioned the names of all the people they met, with some of whom she was acquainted and some not. At the entrance of the garden they met the blind lady, Madame Berthe, with her guide, and the prince was delighted to see the old Frenchwoman's face light up when she heard Kitty's voice. She at once began talking to him with French exaggerated politeness, applauding him for having such a delightful daughter, extolling Kitty to the skies before her face, and calling her a treasure, a pearl, and a consoling angel.

'Well, she's the second angel, then,' said the prince, smiling. 'She calls Mademoiselle Varenka angel number one.'

'Oh! Mademoiselle Varenka, she's a real angel, allez,' Madame Berthe assented.

In the arcade they met Varenka herself. She was walking rapidly towards them carrying an elegant red bag.

'Here is papa come,' Kitty said to her.

Varenka made—simply and naturally as she did everything—a movement between a bow and a curtsey, and immediately began talking to the prince, without shyness, naturally, as she talked to everyone.

'Of course I know you; I know you very well,' the prince said to her with a smile, in which Kitty detected with joy that her father liked her friend. 'Where are you off to in such haste?'

'Maman's here,' she said, turning to Kitty. 'She has not slept all night, and the doctor advised her to go out. I'm taking her her work.'

'So that's angel number one?' said the prince when Varenka had gone on.

Kitty saw that her father had meant to make fun of Varenka, but that he could not do it because he liked her.

'Come, so we shall see all your friends,' he went on, 'even Madame Stahl, if she deigns to recognise me.'

'Why, did you know her, papa?' Kitty asked apprehensively, catching the gleam of irony that kindled in the prince's eyes at the mention of Madame Stahl.

'I used to know her husband, and her too a little, before she'd joined the Pietists.'

'What is a Pietist, papa?' asked Kitty, dismayed to find that what she prized so highly in Madame Stahl had a name.

'I don't quite know myself. I only know that she thanks God for everything, for every misfortune, and thanks God too that her husband died. And that's rather droll, as they didn't get on together.'

'Who's that? What a piteous face!' he asked, noticing a sick man of medium height sitting on a bench, wearing a brown overcoat and white trousers that fell in strange folds about his long, fleshless legs. This man lifted his straw hat, showed his scanty curly hair and high forehead, painfully reddened by the pressure of the hat.

'That's Petrov, an artist,' answered Kitty, blushing. 'And that's his wife,' she added, indicating Anna Pavlovna, who, as though on purpose, at the very instant they approached walked away after a child that had run off along a path.

'Poor fellow! and what a nice face he has!' said the prince. 'Why don't you go up to him? He wanted to speak to you.'

'Well, let us go, then,' said Kitty, turning round resolutely. 'How are you feeling today?' she asked Petrov.

Petrov got up, leaning on his stick, and looked shyly at the prince.

'This is my daughter,' said the prince. 'Let me introduce myself.'

The painter bowed and smiled, showing his strangely dazzling white teeth.

'We expected you yesterday, princess,' he said to Kitty. He staggered as he said this, and then repeated the motion, trying to make it seem as if it had been intentional.

'I meant to come, but Varenka said that Anna Pavlovna sent word you were not going.'

'Not going!' said Petrov, blushing, and immediately beginning to cough, and his eyes sought his wife. 'Anita! Anita!' he said loudly, and the swollen veins stood out like cords on his thin white neck.

Anna Pavlovna came up.

'So you sent word to the princess that we weren't going!' he whispered to her angrily, losing his voice.

'Good morning, princess,' said Anna Pavlovna, with an assumed smile utterly unlike her former manner. 'Very glad to make your acquaintance,' she said to the prince. 'You've long been expected, prince.'

'What did you send word to the princess that we weren't going for?' the artist whispered hoarsely once more, still more angrily, obviously exasperated, that his voice failed him so that he could not give his words the expression he would have liked to.

'Oh, mercy on us! I thought we weren't going,' his wife answered crossly.

'What, when . . .' He coughed and waved his hand. The prince took off his hat and moved away with his daughter.

'Ah! ah!' he sighed deeply. 'Oh, poor things!'

'Yes, papa,' answered Kitty. 'And you must know they've three children, no servant, and scarcely any means. He gets something from the Academy,' she went on briskly, trying to drown the distress that the queer change in Anna Pavlovna's manner to her had aroused in her.

'Oh, here's Madame Stahl,' said Kitty, indicating an invalid carriage, where, propped on pillows, something in grey and blue was lying under a sunshade. This was Madame Stahl. Behind her stood the gloomy, healthy-looking German workman who pushed the carriage. Close by was standing a flaxen-headed Swedish count, whom Kitty knew by name. Several invalids were lingering near the low carriage, staring at the lady as though she were some curiosity.

The prince went up to her, and Kitty detected that disconcerting gleam of irony in his eyes. He went up to Madame Stahl, and addressed her with extreme courtesy and affability in that excellent French that so few speak nowadays.

'I don't know if you remember me, but I must recall myself to thank you for your kindness to my daughter,' he said, taking off his hat and not putting it on again.

'Prince Alexander Shtcherbatsky,' said Madame Stahl, lifting upon him her heavenly eyes, in which Kitty discerned a look of annoyance. 'Delighted! I have taken a great fancy to your daughter.'

'You are still in weak health?'

'Yes; I'm used to it,' said Madame Stahl, and she introduced the prince to the Swedish count.

'You are scarcely changed at all,' the prince said to her. 'It's ten or eleven years since I had the honour of seeing you.'

'Yes; God sends the cross and sends the strength to bear it. Often one wonders what is the goal of this life? . . . The other side!' she said angrily to Varenka, who had rearranged the rug over her feet not to her satisfaction.

'To do good, probably,' said the prince with a twinkle in his eyes.

'That is not for us to judge,' said Madame Stahl, perceiving the shade of expression on the prince's face. 'So you will send me that book, dear count? I'm very grateful to you,' she said to the young Swede.

'Ah!' cried the prince, catching sight of the Moscow colonel standing near, and with a bow to Madame Stahl he walked away with his daughter and the Moscow colonel, who joined them.

'That's our aristocracy, prince!' the Moscow colonel said with ironical intention. He cherished a grudge against Madame Stahl for not making his acquaintance.

'She's just the same,' replied the prince.

'Did you know her before her illness, prince—that's to say before she took to her bed?'

'Yes. She took to her bed before my eyes,' said the prince.

'They say it's ten years since she has stood on her feet.'

'She doesn't stand up because her legs are too short. She's a very bad figure.'

'Papa, it's not possible!' cried Kitty.

'That's what wicked tongues say, my darling. And your Varenka catches it too,' he added. 'Oh, these invalid ladies!'

'Oh no, papa!' Kitty objected warmly. 'Varenka worships her. And then she does so much good! Ask anyone! Everyone knows her and Aline Stahl.'

'Perhaps so,' said the prince, squeezing her hand with his elbow; 'but it's better when one does good so that you may ask everyone and no one knows.'

Kitty did not answer, not because she had nothing to say, but because she did not care to reveal her secret thoughts even to her father. But, strange to say, although she had so made up her mind not to be influenced by her father's views, not to let him into her inmost sanctuary, she felt that the heavenly image of Madame Stahl, which she had carried for a whole month in her heart, had vanished, never to return, just as the fantastic figure made up of some clothes thrown down at random vanishes when one sees that it is only some garment lying there. All that was left was a woman with short legs, who lay down because she was a bad figure, and worried patient Varenka for not arranging her rug to her liking. And by no effort of the imagination could Kitty bring back the former Madame Stahl.

XXXV

THE prince communicated his good-humour to his own family and his friends, and even to the German landlord in whose rooms the Shtcherbatskys were staying.

On coming back with Kitty from the springs, the prince, who had asked the colonel, and Marya Yevgenyevna, and Varenka all to come and have coffee with them, gave orders for a table and chairs to be taken into the garden under the chestnut-tree, and lunch to be laid there. The landlord and the servants, too, grew brisker under the influence of his good spirits. They knew his open-handedness; and half an hour later the invalid doctor from Hamburg, who lived on the top floor, looked enviously out of window at the merry party of healthy Russians assembled under the chestnut-tree. In the trembling circles of shadow cast by the leaves, at a table covered with a white cloth, and set with coffee-pot, bread-and-butter, cheese, and cold game, sat the princess in a high cap with lilac ribbons, distributing cups and bread-and-butter. At the other end sat the prince, eating heartily, and talking loudly and merrily. The prince had spread out near him his purchases, carved boxes, and knick-knacks, paperknives of all sorts, of which he bought a heap at every watering-place, and bestowed them upon everyone, including Lieschen, the servant-girl, and the landlord, with whom he jested in his comically bad German, assuring him that it was not the water had cured Kitty, but his splendid cookery, especially his plum-soup. The princess laughed at her husband for his Russian ways, but she was more lively and good-humoured than she had been all the while she had been at the waters. The colonel smiled, as he always did, at the prince's jokes, but as far as regards Europe, of which he believed himself to be making a careful study, he took the princess's side. The simple-hearted Marya Yevgenyevna simply roared with laughter at everything absurd the prince said, and his jokes made Varenka helpless with feeble but infectious laughter, which was something Kitty had never seen before.

Kitty was glad of all this, but she could not be light-hearted. She could not solve the problem her father had unconsciously set her by his good-humoured view of her friends, and of the life that had so attracted her. To this doubt there was joined the change in her relations with the Petrovs, which had been so conspicuously and unpleasantly marked that morning. Everyone was good-humoured, but Kitty could not feel good-humoured, and this increased her distress. She felt a feeling such as she had known in childhood, when she had been shut in her room as a punishment, and had heard her sisters' merry laughter outside.

'Well, but what did you buy this mass of things for?' said the princess, smiling, and handing her husband a cup of coffee.

'One goes for a walk, one looks in a shop, and they ask you to buy. "*Ehrlaucht, Durchlaucht?*" Directly they say "*Durchlaucht,*" I can't hold out. I lose ten thalers.'

'It's simply from boredom,' said the princess.

'Of course it is. Such boredom, my dear, that one doesn't know what to do with oneself.'

'How can you be bored, prince? There's so much that's interesting now in Germany,' said Marya Yevgenyevna.

'But I know everything that's interesting: the plum-soup I know, and the pea-sausages I know. I know everything.'

'No, you may say what you like, prince, there's the interest of their institutions,' said the colonel.

'But what is there interesting about it? They're all as pleased as brass halfpence. They've conquered everybody, and why am I to be pleased at that? I haven't conquered anyone; and I'm obliged to take off my own boots, yes, and put them away too; in the morning, get up and dress at once, and go to the dining-room to drink bad tea! How different it is at home! You get up in no haste, you get cross, grumble a little, and come round again. You've time to think things over, and no hurry.'

'But time's money, you forget that,' said the colonel.

'Time, indeed, that depends! Why, there's time one would give a month of for sixpence, and time you wouldn't give half an hour of for any money. Isn't that so, Katinka? What is it? why are you so depressed?'

'I'm not depressed.'

'Where are you off to? Stay a little longer,' he said to Varenka.

'I must be going home,' said Varenka, getting up, and again she went off into a giggle. When she had recovered, she said good-bye, and went into the house to get her hat.

Kitty followed her. Even Varenka struck her as different. She was not worse, but different from what she had fancied her before.

'Oh dear! it's a long while since I've laughed so much!' said Varenka, gathering up her parasol and her bag. 'How nice he is, your father!'

Kitty did not speak.

'When shall I see you again?' asked Varenka.

'Mamma meant to go and see the Petrovs. Won't you be there?' said Kitty, to try Varenka.

'Yes,' answered Varenka. 'They're getting ready to go away, so I promised to help them pack.'

'Well, I'll come too, then.'

'No, why should you?'

'Why not? why not? why not?' said Kitty, opening her eyes wide, and clutching at Varenka's parasol, so as not to let her go. 'No, wait a minute; why not?'

'Oh, nothing; your father has come, and besides, they will feel awkward at your helping.'

'No, tell me why you don't want me to be often at the Petrovs. You don't want me to—why not?'

'I didn't say that,' said Varenka quietly.

'No, please tell me!'

'Tell you everything?' said Varenka.

'Everything, everything!' Kitty assented.

'Well, there's really nothing of any consequence; only that Mihail Alexeyevitch (that was the artist's name) had meant to leave earlier, and now he doesn't want to go away,' said Varenka, smiling.

'Well, well!' Kitty urged impatiently, looking darkly at Varenka.

'Well, and for some reason Anna Pavlovna told him that he didn't want to go because you are here. Of course, that was nonsense; but there was a dispute over it—over you. You know how irritable these sick people are.'

Kitty, scowling more than ever, kept silent, and Varenka went on speaking alone, trying to soften or soothe her, and seeing a storm coming—she did not know whether of tears or of words.

'So you'd better not go. . . . You understand; you won't be offended? . . .'

'And it serves me right! And it serves me right!' Kitty cried quickly, snatching the parasol out of Varenka's hand, and looking past her friend's face.

Varenka felt inclined to smile, looking at her childish fury, but she was afraid of wounding her.

'How does it serve you right? I don't understand,' she said.

'It serves me right, because it was all sham; because it was all done on purpose, and not from the heart. What business had I to interfere with outsiders? And so it's come about that I'm cause of a quarrel, and that I've done what nobody asked me to do. Because it was all a sham! a sham! a sham! ...'

'A sham! with what object?' said Varenka gently.

'Oh, it's so idiotic! so hateful! There was no need whatever for me. . . . Nothing but sham!' she said, opening and shutting the parasol.

'But with what object?'

'To seem better to people, to myself, to God; to deceive everyone. No! now I won't descend to that. I'll be bad; but anyway not a liar, a cheat.'

'But who is a cheat?' said Varenka reproachfully. 'You speak as if ...'

But Kitty was in one of her gusts of fury, and she would not let her finish.

'I don't talk about you, not about you at all. You're perfection. Yes, yes, I know you're all perfection; but what am I to do if I'm bad? This would never have been if I weren't bad. So let me be what I am, I won't be a sham. What have I to do with Anna Pavlovna? Let them go their way, and me go mine. I can't be different. . . . And yet it's not that, it's not that.'

'What is not that?' asked Varenka in bewilderment.

'Everything. I can't act except from the heart, and you act from principle. I liked you simply, but you most likely only wanted to save me, to improve me.'

'You are unjust,' said Varenka.

'But I'm not speaking of other people, I'm speaking of myself.'

'Kitty,' they heard her mother's voice, 'come here, show papa your necklace.'

Kitty, with a haughty air, without making peace with her friend, took the necklace in a little box from the table and went to her mother.

'What's the matter? Why are you so red?' her mother and father said to her with one voice.

'Nothing,' she answered. 'I'll be back directly,' and she ran back.

'She's still here,' she thought. 'What am I to say to her? Oh dear! what have I done, what have I said? Why was I rude to her? What am I to do? What am I to say to her?' thought Kitty, and she stopped in the doorway.

Varenka in her hat and with the parasol in her hands was sitting at the table, examining the spring which Kitty had broken. She lifted her head.

'Varenka, forgive me, do forgive me,' whispered Kitty, going up to her. 'I don't remember what I said. I . . .'

'I really didn't mean to hurt you,' said Varenka smiling.

Peace was made. But with her father's coming all the world in which she had been living was transformed for Kitty. She did not give up everything she had learned, but she became aware that she had deceived herself in supposing she could be what she wanted to be. Her eyes were, it seemed, opened; she felt all the difficulty of maintaining herself without hypocrisy and self-conceit on the pinnacle to which she had wished to mount. Moreover she became aware of all the dreariness of the world of sorrow, of sick and dying people, in which she had been living. The efforts she had made to like it seemed to her intolerable, and she felt a longing to get back quickly into the fresh air, to Russia, to Ergushovo, where, as she knew from letters, her sister Dolly had already gone with her children.

But her affection for Varenka did not wane. As she said good-bye, Kitty begged her to come to them in Russia.

'I'll come when you get married,' said Varenka.

'I shall never marry.'

'Well, then, I shall never come.'

'Well, then, I shall be married simply for that. Mind now, remember your promise,' said Kitty.

The doctor's prediction was fulfilled. Kitty returned home to Russia cured. She was not so gay and thoughtless as before, but she was serene. Her Moscow troubles had become a memory to her.

PART III

I

SERGEY IVANOVITCH KOZNISHEV wanted a rest from mental work, and instead of going abroad as he usually did, he came towards the end of May to stay in the country with his brother. In his judgment the best sort of life was a country life. He had come now to enjoy such a life at his brother's. Konstantin Levin was very glad to have him, especially as he did not expect his brother Nikolay that summer. But in spite of his affection and respect for Sergey Ivanovitch, Konstantin Levin was uncomfortable with his brother in the country. It made him uncomfortable, and it positively annoyed him to see his brother's attitude to the country. To Konstantin Levin the country was the background of life, that is of pleasures, endeavours, labour. To Sergey Ivanovitch the country meant on one hand rest from work, on the other a valuable antidote to the corrupt influences of town, which he took with satisfaction and a sense of its utility. To Konstantin Levin the country was good first because it afforded a field for labour, of the usefulness of which there could be no doubt. To Sergey Ivanovitch the country was particularly good, because there it was possible and fitting to do nothing. Moreover, Sergey Ivanovitch's attitude to the peasants rather piqued Konstantin. Sergey Ivanovitch used to say that he knew and liked the peasantry, and he often talked to the peasants, which he knew how to do without affectation or condescension, and from every such conversation he would deduce general conclusions in favour of the peasantry and in confirmation of his knowing them. Konstantin Levin did not like such an attitude to the peasants. To Konstantin the peasant was simply the chief partner in their common labour, and in spite of all the respect and the love, almost like that of kinship, he had for the peasant—sucked in probably, as he said himself, with the milk of his peasant nurse—still as a fellow-worker with him, while sometimes enthusiastic over the vigour, gentleness, and justice of these men, he was very often, when their common labours called for other qualities, exasperated with the peasant for his carelessness, lack of method, drunkenness, and lying. If he had been asked whether he liked or didn't like the peasants, Konstantin Levin would have been absolutely at a loss what to reply.

He liked and did not like the peasants, just as he liked and did not like men in general. Of course, being a good-hearted man, he liked men rather than he disliked them, and so too with the peasants. But like or dislike 'the people' as something apart he could not, not only because he lived with 'the people', and all his interests were bound up with theirs, but also because he regarded himself as a part of 'the people', did not see any special qualities or failings distinguishing himself and 'the people', and could not contrast himself with them. Moreover, although he had lived so long in the closest relations with the peasants, as farmer and arbitrator, and what was more, as adviser (the peasants trusted him, and for thirty miles round they would come to ask his advice), he had not definite views of 'the people', and would have been as much at a loss to answer the question whether he knew 'the people' as the question whether he liked them. For him to say he knew the peasantry would have been the same as to say he knew men. He was continually watching and getting to know people of all sorts, and among them peasants, whom he regarded as good and interesting people, and he was continually observing new points in them, altering his former views of them and forming new ones. With Sergey Ivanovitch it was quite the contrary. Just as he liked and praised a country life in comparison with the life he did not like, so too he liked the peasantry in contradistinction to the class of men he did not like, and so too he knew the peasantry as something distinct from and opposed to men generally. In his methodical brain there were distinctly formulated certain aspects of peasant life, deduced partly from that life itself, but chiefly from contrast with other modes of life. He never changed his opinion of the peasantry and his sympathetic attitude towards them.

In the discussions that arose between the brothers on their views of the peasantry, Sergey Ivanovitch always got the better of his brother, precisely because Sergey Ivanovitch had definite ideas about the peasant—his character, his qualities, and his tastes. Konstantin Levin had no definite and unalterable idea on the subject, and so in their arguments Konstantin was readily convicted of contradicting himself.

In Sergey Ivanovitch's eyes his younger brother was a capital fellow, *with his heart in the right place* (as he expressed it in French), but with a mind which, though fairly quick, was too much influenced by the impressions of the moment, and consequently filled with contradictions. With all the condescension of an elder brother he sometimes explained to him the true import of things, but he derived little satisfaction from arguing with him because he got the better of him too easily.

Konstantin Levin regarded his brother as a man of immense intellect and culture, as generous in the highest sense of the word, and possessed of a special faculty for working for the public good. But in the depths of his heart, the older he became, and the more intimately he knew his brother, the more and more frequently the thought struck him that this faculty of working for the public good, of which he felt himself utterly devoid, was possibly not so much a quality as a lack of something—not a lack of good, honest, noble desires and tastes, but a lack of vital force, of what is called heart, of that impulse which drives a man to choose someone out of the innumerable paths of life, and to care only for that one. The better he knew his brother, the more he noticed that Sergey Ivanovitch, and many other people who worked for the public welfare, were not led by an impulse of the heart to care for the public good, but reasoned from intellectual considerations that it was a right thing to take interest in public affairs, and consequently took interest in them. Levin was confirmed in this generalisation by observing that his brother did not take questions affecting the public welfare or the question of the immortality of the soul a bit more to heart than he did chess problems, or the ingenious construction of a new machine.

Besides this, Konstantin Levin was not at his ease with his brother, because in summer in the country Levin was continually busy with work on the land, and the long summer day was not long enough for him to get through all he had to do, while Sergey Ivanovitch was taking a holiday. But though he was taking a holiday now, that is to say, he was doing no writing, he was so used to intellectual activity that he liked to put into concise and eloquent shape the ideas that occurred to him, and liked to have someone to listen to him. His most usual and natural listener was his brother. And so in spite of the friendliness and directness of their relations, Konstantin felt an awkwardness in leaving him alone. Sergey Ivanovitch liked to stretch himself on the grass in the sun, and to lie so, basking and chatting lazily.

You wouldn't believe,' he would say to his brother, 'what a pleasaure this rural laziness is to me. Not an idea in one's brain, as empty as a drum!'

But Konstantin Levin found it dull sitting and listening to him, especially when he knew that while he was away they would be carting dung on to the fields not ploughed ready for it, and heaping it all up anyhow; and would not screw the shares in the ploughs, but would let them come off, and then say that the new ploughs were a silly invention, and there was nothing like the old Andreevna plough, and so on.

'Come, you've done enough trudging about in the heat,' Sergey Ivanovitch would say to him.

'No, I must just run round to the counting-house for a minute,' Levin would answer, and he would run off to the fields.

II

EARLY in June it happened that Agafea Mihalovna, the old nurse and housekeeper, in carrying to the cellar a jar of mushrooms she had just pickled, slipped, fell, and sprained her wrist. The district doctor, a talkative young medical student, who had just finished his studies, came to see her. He examined the wrist, said it was not broken, was delighted at a chance of talking to the celebrated Sergey Ivanovitch Koznishev, and to show his advanced views of things told him all the scandal of the district, complaining of the poor state into which the district council had fallen. Sergey Ivanovitch listened attentively, asked him questions, and, roused by a new listener, he talked fluently, uttered a few keen and weighty observations, respectfully appreciated by the young doctor, and was soon in that eager frame of mind his brother knew so well, which always, with him, followed a brilliant and eager conversation. After the departure of the doctor, he wanted to go with a fishing-rod to the river. Sergey Ivanovitch was fond of angling, and was, it seemed, proud of being able to care for such a stupid occupation.

Konstantin Levin, whose presence was needed in the ploughland and the meadows, had come to take his brother in the trap.

It was that time of the year, the turning-point of summer, when the crops of the present year are a certainty, when one begins to think of the sowing for next year, and the mowing is at hand; when the rye is all in ear, though its ears are still light, not yet full, and it waves in grey-green billows in the wind; when the green oats, with tufts of yellow grass scattered here and there among it, droop irregularly over the late-sown fields; when the early buckwheat is already out and hiding the ground; when the fallow-lands, trodden hard as stone by the cattle, are half-ploughed over, with paths left untouched by the plough; when from the dry dung-heaps carted on to the fields there comes at sunset a smell of manure mixed with meadow-sweet, and on the low-lying lands the riverside meadows are a thick sea of grass waiting for the mowing, with blackened heaps of the stalks of sorrel among it.

It was the time when there comes a brief pause in the toil of the fields before the beginning of the labours of harvest—every year recurring, every year straining every nerve of the peasants. The crop was a splendid one, and bright, hot summer days had set in with short, dewy nights.

The brothers had to drive through the woods to reach the meadows. Sergey Ivanovitch was all the while admiring the beauty of the woods, which were a tangled mass of leaves, pointing out to his brother now an old lime-tree on the point of flowering, dark on the shady side, and brightly spotted with yellow stipules, now the young shoots of this year's saplings brilliant with emerald. Konstantin Levin did not like talking and hearing about the beauty of nature. Words for him took away the beauty of what he saw. He assented to what his brother said, but he could not help beginning to think of other things. When they came out of the woods, all his attention was engrossed by the view of the fallow-land on the upland, in parts yellow with grass, in parts trampled and chequered with furrows, in parts dotted with ridges of dung, and in parts even ploughed. A string of carts was moving across it. Levin counted the carts, and was pleased that all that were wanted had been brought, and at the sight of the meadows his thoughts passed to the mowing. He always felt something special moving him to the quick at the hay-making. On reaching the meadow Levin stopped the horse.

The morning dew was still lying on the thick undergrowth of the grass, and that he might not get his feet wet, Sergey Ivanovitch asked his brother to drive him in the trap up to the willow-tree from which the carp was caught. Sorry as Konstantin Levin was to crush down his mowing-grass, he drove him into the meadow. The high grass softly turned about the wheels and the horse's legs, leaving its seeds clinging to the wet axles and spokes of the wheels. His brother seated himself under a bush, arranging his tackle, while Levin led the horse away, fastened him up, and walked into the vast grey-green sea of grass unstirred by the wind. The silky grass with its ripe seeds came almost to his waist in the dampest spots.

Crossing the meadow, Konstantin Levin came out on to the road, and met an old man with a swollen eye, carrying a skep on his shoulder.

'What? Taken a stray swarm, Fomitch?' he asked.

'No, indeed, Konstantin Mitritch! All we can do to keep our own! This is the second swarm that has flown away. . . . Luckily the lads caught them. They were ploughing your field. They unyoked the horses and galloped after them.'

'Well, what do you say, Fomitch—start mowing or wait a bit?'

'Eh, well! Our way's to wait till St. Peter's Day. But you always mow sooner. Well, to be sure, please God, the hay's good. There'll be plenty for the beasts.'

'What do you think about the weather?'

'That's in God's hands. Maybe it will be fine.'

Levin went up to his brother.

Sergey Ivanovitch had caught nothing, but he was not bored, and seemed in the most cheerful frame of mind. Levin saw that, stimulated by his conversation with the doctor, he wanted to talk. Levin, on the other hand, would have liked to get home as soon as possible to give orders about getting together the mowers for next day, and to set at rest his doubts about the mowing, which greatly absorbed him.

'Well, let's be going,' he said.

'Why be in such a hurry? Let's stay a little. But how wet you are! Even though one catches nothing, it's nice. That's the best thing about every part of sport, that one has to do with nature. How exquisite this steely water is!' said Sergey Ivanovitch. 'These riverside banks always remind me of the riddle—do you know it? "The grass says to the water: we quiver and we quiver."'

'I don't know the riddle,' answered Levin wearily.

III

'Do you know, I've been thinking about you,' said Sergey Ivanovitch. 'It's beyond everything what's being done in the district, according to what this doctor tells me. He's a very intelligent fellow. And as I've told you before, I tell you again: it's not right for you not to go to the meetings, and altogether to keep out of the district business. If decent people won't go into it, of course it's bound to go all wrong. We pay the money, and it all goes in salaries, and there are no schools, nor district nurses, nor midwives, nor drug-stores—nothing.'

'Well, I did try, you know,' Levin said slowly and unwillingly. 'I can't! and so there's no help for it.'

'But why can't you? I must own I can't make it out. Indifference, incapacity—I won't admit; surely it's not simply laziness?'

'None of those things. I've tried, and I see I can do nothing,' said Levin.

He had hardly grasped what his brother was saying. Looking towards the plough-land across the river, he made out something black, but he could not distinguish whether it was a horse or the bailiff on horseback.

'Why is it you can do nothing? You made an attempt and didn't succeed, as you think, and you give in. How can you have so little self-respect?'

'Self-respect!' said Levin, stung to the quick by his brother's words; 'I don't understand. If they'd told me at college that other people understood the integral calculus, and I didn't, then pride would have come in. But in this case one wants first to be convinced that one has certain qualifications for this sort of business, and especially that all this business is of great importance.'

'What! do you mean to say it's not of importance?' said Sergey

Ivanovitch, stung to the quick too at his brother's considering anything of no importance that interested him, and still more at his obviously paying little attention to what he was saying.

'I don't think it important; it does not take hold of me, I can't help it,' answered Levin, making out that what he saw was the bailiff, and that the bailiff seemed to be letting the peasants go off the ploughed land. They were turning the plough over. 'Can they have finished ploughing?' he wondered.

'Come, really though,' said the elder brother, with a frown on his handsome, clever face, 'there's a limit to everything. It's very well to be original and genuine, and to dislike everything conventional—I know all about that; but really, what you're saying either has no meaning, or it has a very wrong meaning. How can you think it a matter of no importance whether the peasant, whom you love as you assert, . . .'

'I never did assert it,' thought Konstantin Levin.

—'dies without help? The ignorant peasant-women starve the children, and the people stagnate in darkness, and are helpless in the hands of every village clerk, while you have at your disposal a means of helping them, and don't help them because to your mind it's of no importance.'

And Sergey Ivanovitch put before him the alternative: either you are so undeveloped that you can't see all that you can do, or you won't sacrifice your ease, your vanity, or whatever it is, to do it.

Konstantin Levin felt that there was no course open to him but to submit, or to confess to a lack of zeal for the public good. And this mortified him and hurt his feelings.

'It's both,' he said resolutely; 'I don't see that it was possible . . .'

'What! was it impossible, if the money were properly laid out, to provide medical aid?'

'Impossible, as it seems to me. . . . For the three thousand square miles of our district, what with our thaws, and the storms, and the work in the fields, I don't see how it is possible to provide medical aid all over. And besides, I don't believe in medicine.'

'Oh, well, that's unfair. . . . I can quote to you thousands of instances. . . . But the schools, anyway.'

'Why have schools?'

'What do you mean? Can there be two opinions of the advantage of education? If it's a good thing for you, it's a good thing for everyone.'

Konstantin Levin felt himself morally pinned against a wall, and so he got hot, and unconsciously blurted out the chief cause of his indifference to public business.

'Perhaps it may all be very good; but why should I worry myself about establishing dispensaries which I shall never make use of, and schools to which I shall never send my children, to which even the peasants don't want to send their children, and to which I've no very firm faith that they ought to send them?' said he.

Sergey Ivanovitch was for a minute surprised at this unexpected view of the subject; but he promptly made a new plan of attack. He was silent for a little, drew out a hook, threw it in again, and turned to his brother smiling.

'Come, now. . . . In the first place, the dispensary is needed. We ourselves sent for the district doctor for Agafea Mihalovna.'

'Oh, well, but I fancy her wrist will never be straight again.'

'That remains to be proved. . . . Next, the peasant who can read and write is as a workman of more use and value to you.'

'No; you can ask anyone you like,' Konstantin Levin answered with decision, 'the man that can read and write is much inferior as a workman. And mending the high-roads is an impossibility; and as soon as they put up bridges they're stolen.'

'Still, that's not the point,' said Sergey Ivanovitch, frowning. He disliked contradiction, and still more, arguments that were continually skipping from one thing to another, introducing new and disconnected points, so that there was no knowing to which to reply. 'Do you admit that education is a benefit for the people?'

'Yes, I admit it,' said Levin without thinking, and he was conscious immediately that he had said what he did not think. He felt that if he admitted that it would be proved that he had been talking meaningless rubbish. How it would be proved he could not tell, but he knew that this would inevitably be logically proved to him, and he awaited the proofs.

The argument turned out to be far simpler than he had expected.

'If you admit that it is a benefit,' said Sergey Ivanovitch, 'then, as an honest man, you cannot help caring about it and sympathising with the movement, and so wishing to work for it.'

'But I still do not admit this movement to be just,' said Konstantin Levin, reddening a little.

'What! But you said just now . . .'

'That's to say, I don't admit it's being either good or possible.'

'That you can't tell without making the trial.'

'Well, supposing that's so,' said Levin, though he did not suppose so at all, 'supposing that is so, still I don't see, all the same, what I'm to worry myself about it for.'

'How so?'

'No; since we are talking, explain it to me from the philosophical point of view,' said Levin.

'I can't see where philosophy comes in,' said Sergey Ivanovitch, in a tone, Levin fancied, as though he did not admit his brother's right to talk about philosophy. And that irritated Levin.

'I'll tell you, then,' he said with heat, 'I imagine the mainspring of all our actions is, after all, self-interest. Now in the local institutions I, as a nobleman, see nothing that could conduce to my prosperity, and the roads are not better and could not be better; my horses carry me well enough over bad ones. Doctors and dispensaries are no use to me. An arbitrator of disputes is no use to me. I never appeal to him, and never shall appeal to him. The schools are no good to me, but positively harmful, as I told you. For me the district institutions simply mean the liability to pay fourpence halfpenny for every three acres, to drive into the town, sleep with bugs, and listen to all sorts of idiocy and loathsomeness, and self-interest offers me no inducement.'

'Excuse me,' Sergey Ivanovitch interposed with a smile, 'self-interest did not induce us to work for the emancipation of the serfs, but we did work for it.'

'No!' Konstantin Levin broke in with still greater heat; 'the emancipation of the serfs was a different matter. There self-interest did come in. One longed to throw off that yoke that crushed us, all decent people among us. But to be a town-councillor and discuss how many dustmen are needed, and how chimneys shall be constructed in the town in which I don't live—to serve on a jury and try a peasant who's stolen a flitch of bacon, and listen for six hours at a stretch to all sorts of jabber from the counsel for the defence and the prosecution, and the president cross-examining my old half-witted Alioshka, "Do you admit, prisoner in the dock, the fact of the removal of the bacon?" "Eh?"'

Konstantin Levin had warmed to his subject, and began mimicking the president and the half-witted Alioshka: it seemed to him that it was all to the point.

But Sergey Ivanovitch shrugged his shoulders.

'Well, what do you mean to say, then?'

'I simply mean to say that those rights that touch me . . . my interest, I shall always defend to the best of my ability; that when they made raids on us students, and the police read our letters, I was ready to defend those rights to the utmost, to defend my rights to education and freedom. I can understand compulsory military service, which affects my children, my brothers, and myself, I am ready to deliberate on what concerns me; but deliberating on how to spend forty thousand roubles of district council money, or judging the half-witted Alioshka—I don't understand, and I can't do it.'

Konstantin Levin spoke as though the floodgates of his speech had burst open. Sergey Ivanovitch smiled.

'But tomorrow it'll be your turn to be tried; would it have suited your tastes better to be tried in the old criminal tribunal?'

'I'm not going to be tried. I shan't murder anybody, and I've no need of it. Well, I tell you what,' he went on, flying off again to a subject quite beside the point, 'our district self-government and all the rest of it—it's just like the birch-branches we stick in the ground on Trinity Day, for instance, to look like a copse which has grown up of itself in Europe, and I can't gush over these birch-branches and believe in them.'

Sergey Ivanovitch merely shrugged his shoulders, as though to express his wonder how the birch branches had come into their argument at that point, though he did really understand at once what his brother meant.

'Excuse me, but you know one really can't argue in that way,' he observed.

But Konstantin Levin wanted to justify himself for the failing, of which he was conscious, of lack of zeal for the public welfare, and he went on.

'I imagine,' he said, 'that no sort of activity is likely to be lasting if it is not founded on self-interest, that's a universal principle, a philosophical principle,' he said, repeating the word 'philosophical' with determination, as though wishing to show that he had as much right as anyone else to talk of philosophy.

Sergey Ivanovitch smiled. 'He too has a philosophy of his own at the service of his natural tendencies,' he thought.

'Come, you'd better let philosophy alone,' he said. 'The chief problem of the philosophy of all ages consists just in finding the indispensable connection which exists between individual and social interests. But that's not to the point; what is to the point is a correction I must make in your comparison. The birches are not simply stuck in, but some are sown and some are planted, and one must deal carefully with them. It's only those peoples that have an intuitive sense of what's of importance and significance in their institutions, and know how to value them, that have a future before them—it's only those peoples that one can truly call historical.'

And Sergey Ivanovitch carried the subject into the regions of philosophical history where Konstantin Levin could not follow him, and showed him all the incorrectness of his view.

'As for your dislike of it, excuse my saying so, that's simply our Russian sloth and old serf-owner's ways, and I'm convinced that in you it's a temporary error and will pass.'

Konstantin was silent. He felt himself vanquished on all sides, but he felt at the same time that what he wanted to say was unintelligible to his brother. Only he could not make up his mind whether it was unintelligible because he was not capable of expressing his meaning clearly, or because his brother would not or could not understand him. But he did not pursue the speculation, and without replying, he fell to musing on a quite different and personal matter.

Sergey Ivanovitch wound up the last line, untied the horse, and they drove off.

IV

THE personal matter that absorbed Levin during his conversation with his brother was this. Once in a previous year he had gone to look at the mowing, and being made very angry by the bailiff he had recourse to his favourite means for regaining his temper,—he took a scythe from a peasant and began mowing.

He liked the work so much that he had several times tried his hand at mowing since. He had cut the whole of the meadow in front of his house, and this year ever since the early spring he had cherished a plan for mowing for whole days together with the peasants. Ever since his brother's arrival, he had been in doubt whether to mow or not. He was loth to leave his brother alone all day long, and he was afraid his brother would laugh at him about it. But as he drove into the meadow, and recalled the sensations of mowing, he came near deciding that he would go mowing. After the irritating discussion with his brother, he pondered over this intention again.

'I must have physical exercise, or my temper'll certainly be ruined,' he thought, and he determined he would go mowing, however awkward he might feel about it with his brother or the peasants.

Towards evening Konstantin Levin went to his counting-house, gave directions as to the work to be done, and sent about the village to summon the mowers for the morrow, to cut the hay in Kalinov meadow, the largest and best of his grass lands.

'And send my scythe, please, to Tit, for him to set it, and bring it round tomorrow. I shall maybe do some mowing myself too,' he said, trying not to be embarrassed.

The bailiff smiled and said: 'Yes, sir.'

At tea the same evening Levin said to his brother—

'I fancy the fine weather will last,' said he. 'Tomorrow I shall start mowing.'

'I'm so fond of that form of field labour,' said Sergey Ivanovitch.

'I'm awfully fond of it. I sometimes mow myself with the peasants, and tomorrow I want to try mowing the whole day.'

Sergey Ivanovitch lifted his head, and looked with interest at his brother.

'How do you mean? Just like one of the peasants, all day long?'

'Yes, it's very pleasant,' said Levin.

'It's splendid as exercise, only you'll hardly be able to stand it,' said Sergey Ivanovitch, without a shade of irony.

'I've tried it. It's hard work at first, but you get into it. I dare say I shall manage to keep it up. . . .'

'Really! what an idea! But tell me, how do the peasants look at it? I suppose they laugh in their sleeves at their master's being such a queer fish?'

'No, I don't think so; but it's so delightful, and at the same time such hard work, that one has no time to think about it.'

'But how will you do about dining with them? To send you a bottle of Lafitte and roast turkey out there would be a little awkward.'

'No, I'll simply come home at the time of their noonday rest.'

Next morning Konstantin Levin got up earlier than usual, but he was detained giving directions on the farm, and when he reached the mowing-grass the mowers were already at their second row.

From the uplands he could get a view of the shaded cut part of the meadow below, with its greyish ridges of cut grass, and the black heaps of coats, taken off by the mowers at the place from which they had started cutting.

Gradually, as he rode towards the meadow, the peasants came into sight, some in coats, some in their shirts, mowing, one behind another in a long string, swinging their scythes differently. He counted forty-two of them.

They were mowing slowly over the uneven, low-lying parts of the meadow, where there had been an old dam. Levin recognised some of his own men. Here was old Yermil in a very long white smock, bending forward to swing his scythe; there was a young fellow, Vaska, who had been a coachman of Levin's, taking every row with a wide sweep. Here, too, was Tit, Levin's preceptor in the art of mowing, a thin little peasant. He was in front of all, and cut his wide row without bending, as though playing with the scythe.

Levin got off his mare, and fastening her up by the roadside went to meet Tit, who took a second scythe out of a bush and gave it him.

'It's ready, sir; it's like a razor, cuts of itself,' said Tit, taking off his cap with a smile and giving him the scythe.

Levin took the scythe, and began trying it. As they finished their rows, the mowers, hot and good-humoured, came out into the road one after another, and, laughing a little, greeted the master. They all stared at him, but no one made any remark, till a tall old man, with a wrinkled, beardless face, wearing a short sheepskin jacket, came out into the road and accosted him.

'Look 'ee now, master, once take hold of the rope there's no letting it go!' he said, and Levin heard smothered laughter among the mowers.

'I'll try not to let it go,' he said, taking his stand behind Tit, and waiting for the time to begin.

'Mind 'ee,' repeated the old man.

Tit made room, and Levin started behind him. The grass was short close to the road, and Levin, who had not done any mowing for a long while, and was disconcerted by the eyes fastened upon him, cut badly for the first moments, though he swung his scythe vigorously. Behind him he heard voices—

'It's not set right; handle's too high; see how he has to stoop to it,' said one.

'Press more on the heel,' said another.

'Never mind, he'll get on all right,' the old man resumed.

'He's made a start. . . . You swing it too wide, you'll tire yourself out. . . . The master, sure, does his best for himself! But see the grass missed out! For such work us fellows would catch it!'

The grass became softer, and Levin, listening without answering, followed Tit, trying to do the best he could. They moved a hundred paces. Tit kept moving on, without stopping, not showing the slightest weariness, but Levin was already beginning to be afraid he would not be able to keep it up: hc was so tired.

He felt as he swung his scythe that he was at the very end of his strength, and was making up his mind to ask Tit to stop. But at that very moment Tit stopped of his own accord, and stooping down picked up some grass, rubbed his scythe, and began whetting it. Levin straightened himself, and drawing a deep breath looked round. Behind him came a peasant, and he too was evidently tired, for he stopped at once without waiting to mow up to Levin, and began whetting his scythe. Tit sharpened his scythe and Levin's, and they went on. The next time it was just the same. Tit moved on with sweep after sweep of his scythe, not stopping nor showing signs of weariness. Levin followed him, trying not to get left behind, and he found it harder and harder: the moment came when he felt he had no strength left, but at that very moment Tit stopped and whetted the scythes.

So they mowed the first row. And this long row seemed particularly hard work to Levin; but when the end was reached, and Tit, shouldering his scythe, began with deliberate stride returning on the tracks left by his heels in the cut grass, and Levin walked back in the same way over the space he had cut, in spite of the sweat that ran in streams over his face and fell in drops down his nose, and drenched his back as though he had been soaked in water, he felt very happy. What delighted him particularly was that now he knew he would be able to hold out.

His pleasure was only disturbed by his row not being well cut. 'I will swing less with my arm and more with my whole body,' he thought, comparing Tit's row, which looked as if it had been cut with a line, with his own unevenly and irregularly lying grass.

The first row, as Levin noticed, Tit had mown specially quickly, probably wishing to put his master to the test, and the row happened to be a long one. The next rows were easier, but still Levin had to strain every nerve not to drop behind the peasants.

He thought of nothing, wished for nothing, but not to be left behind the peasants, and to do his work as well as possible. He heard nothing but the swish of the scythes, and saw before him Tit's upright figure mowing away, the crescent-shaped curve of the cut grass, the grass and flower heads slowly and rhythmically falling before the blade of his scythe, and ahead of him the end of the row, where would come the rest.

Suddenly, in the midst of his toil, without understanding what it was or whence it came, he felt a pleasant sensation of chill on his hot, moist shoulders. He glanced at the sky in the interval for whetting the scythes. A heavy, lowering storm-cloud had blown up, and big raindrops were falling. Some of the peasants went to their coats and put them on; others—just like Levin himself—merely shrugged their shoulders, enjoying the pleasant coolness of it.

Another row, and yet another row, followed—long rows and short rows, with good grass and with poor grass. Levin lost all sense of time, and could not have told whether it was late or early now. A change began to come over his work, which gave him immense satisfaction. In the midst of his toil there were moments during which he forgot what he was doing, and it came all easy to him, and at those same moments his row was almost as smooth and well cut as Tit's. But so soon as he recollected what he was doing, and began trying to do better, he was at once conscious of all the difficulty of his task, and the row was badly mown.

On finishing yet another row he would have gone back to the top of the meadow again to begin the next, but Tit stopped, and going up to the old man said something in a low voice to him. They both looked at the sun. 'What are they talking about, and why doesn't he go back?'

thought Levin, not guessing that the peasants had been mowing no less than four hours without stopping, and it was time for their lunch.

'Lunch, sir,' said the old man.

'Is it really time? That's right; lunch, then.'

Levin gave his scythe to Tit, and together with the peasants, who were crossing the long stretch of mown grass, slightly sprinkled with rain, to get their bread from the heap of coats, he went towards his house. Only then he suddenly awoke to the fact that he had been wrong about the weather and the rain was drenching his hay.

'The hay will be spoiled,' he said.

'Not a bit of it, sir; mow in the rain, and you'll rake in fine weather!' said the old man.

Levin untied his horse and rode home to his coffee. Sergey Ivanovitch was only just getting up. When he had drunk his coffee, Levin rode back again to the mowing before Sergey Ivanovitch had had time to dress and come down to the dining-room.

V

AFTER lunch Levin was not in the same place in the string of mowers as before, but stood between the old man who had accosted him jocosely, and now invited him to be his neighbour, and a young peasant, who had only been married in the autumn, and who was mowing this summer for the first time.

The old man, holding himself erect, moved in front, with his feet turned out, taking long, regular strides, and with a precise and regular action which seemed to cost him no more effort than swinging one's arms in walking, as though it were in play, he laid down the high, even row of grass. It was as though it were not he but the sharp scythe of itself swishing through the juicy grass.

Behind Levin came the lad Mishka. His pretty, boyish face, with a twist of fresh grass bound round his hair, was all working with effort; but whenever anyone looked at him he smiled. He would clearly have died sooner than own it was hard work for him.

Levin kept between them. In the very heat of the day the mowing did not seem such hard work to him. The perspiration with which he was drenched cooled him, while the sun, that burned his back, his head, and his arms, bare to the elbow, gave a vigour and dogged energy to his labour; and more and more often now came those moments of unconsciousness, when it was possible not to think what one was doing. The scythe cut of itself. These were happy moments. Still more delightful were the moments when they reached the stream where the rows ended, and the old man rubbed his scythe with the wet, thick grass, rinsed its blade in the fresh water of the stream, ladled out a little in a tin dipper, and offered Levin a drink.

'What do you say to my home-brew, eh? Good, eh?' said he, winking.

And truly Levin had never drunk any liqueur so good as this warm water with green bits floating in it, and a taste of rust from the tin dipper. And immediately after this came the delicious, slow saunter, with his hand on the scythe, during which he could wipe away the streaming sweat, take deep breaths of air, and look about at the long string of mowers and at what was happening around in the forest and the country.

The longer Levin mowed, the oftener he felt the moments of unconsciousness in which it seemed not his hands that swung the scythe, but the scythe mowing of itself, a body full of life and consciousness of its own, and as though by magic, without thinking of it, the work turned out regular and well-finished of itself. These were the most blissful moments.

It was only hard work when he had to break off the motion, which had become unconscious, and to think; when he had to mow round a hillock or a tuft of sorrel. The old man did this easily. When a hillock came he changed his action, and at one time with the heel, and at another with the tip of his scythe, clipped the hillock round both sides with short strokes. And while he did this he kept looking about and watching what came into his view: at one moment he picked a wild berry and ate it or offered it to Levin, then he flung away a twig with the blade of the scythe, then he looked at a quail's nest, from which the bird flew just under the scythe, or caught a snake that crossed his path, and lifting it on the scythe as though on a fork showed it to Levin and threw it away.

For both Levin and the young peasant behind him, such changes of position were difficult. Both of them, repeating over and over again the same strained movement, were in a perfect frenzy of toil, and were incapable of shifting their position and at the same time watching what was before them.

Levin did not notice how time was passing. If he had been asked how long he had been working he would have said half an hour—and it was getting on for dinner-time. As they were walking back over the cut grass, the old man called Levin's attention to the little girls and boys who were coming from different directions, hardly visible through the long grass, and along the road towards the mowers, carrying sacks of bread dragging at their little hands and pitchers of the sour rye-beer, with cloths wrapped round them.

'Look 'ee, the little emmets crawling!' he said, pointing to them, and he shaded his eyes with his hand to look at the sun. They mowed two more rows; the old man stopped.

'Come, master, dinner-time!' he said briskly. And on reaching the stream the mowers moved off across the lines of cut grass towards their pile of coats, where the children who had brought their dinners were sitting waiting for them. The peasants gathered into groups—those further away under a cart, those nearer under a willow bush.

Levin sat down by them; he felt disinclined to go away.

All constraint with the master had disappeared long ago. The peasants got ready for dinner. Some washed, the young lads bathed in the stream, others made a place comfortable for a rest, untied their sacks of bread, and uncovered the pitchers of rye-beer. The old man crumbled up some bread in a cup, stirred it with the handle of a spoon, poured water on it from the dipper, broke up some more bread, and having seasoned it with salt, he turned to the east to say his prayer.

'Come, master, taste my sop,' said he, kneeling down before the cup.

The sop was so good that Levin gave up the idea of going home. He dined with the old man, and talked to him about his family affairs, taking the keenest interest in them, and told him about his own affairs and all the circumstances that could be of interest to the old man. He felt much nearer to him than to his brother, and could not help smiling at the affection he felt for this man. When the old man got up again, said his prayer, and lay down under a bush, putting some grass under his head for a pillow, Levin did the same, and in spite of the clinging flies that were so persistent in the sunshine, and the midges that tickled his hot face and body, he fell asleep at once and only waked when the sun had passed to the other side of the bush and reached him. The old man had been awake a long while, and was sitting up whetting the scythes of the younger lads.

Levin looked about him and hardly recognised the place, everything was so changed. The immense stretch of meadow had been mown and was sparkling with a peculiar fresh brilliance, with its lines of already sweet-smelling grass in the slanting rays of the evening sun. And the bushes about the river had been cut down, and the river itself, not visible before, now gleaming like steel in its bends, and the moving, ascending, peasants, and the sharp wall of grass of the unmown part of the meadow, and the hawks hovering over the stripped meadow—all was perfectly new. Raising himself, Levin began considering how much had been cut and how much more could still be done that day.

The work done was exceptionally much for forty-two men. They had cut the whole of the big meadow, which had, in the years of serf labour, taken thirty scythes two days to mow. Only the corners remained to do, where the rows were short. But Levin felt a longing to get as much mowing done that day as possible, and was vexed with the sun sinking so quickly in the sky. He felt no weariness; all he wanted was to get his work done more and more quickly and as much done as possible.

'Could you cut Mashkin Upland too?—what do you think?' he said to the old man.

'As God wills, the sun's not high. A little vodka for the lads?'

At the afternoon rest, when they were sitting down again, and those who smoked had lighted their pipes, the old man told the men that 'Mashkin Upland's to be cut—there'll be some vodka.'

'Why not cut it? Come on, Tit! We'll look sharp! We can eat at night. Come on!' cried voices, and eating up their bread, the mowers went back to work.

'Come, lads, keep it up!' said Tit, and ran on ahead almost at a trot.

'Get along, get along!' said the old man, hurrying after him and easily overtaking him, 'I'll mow you down, look out!'

And young and old mowed away, as though they were racing with one another. But however fast they worked, they did not spoil the grass, and the rows were laid just as neatly and exactly. The little piece left uncut in the corner was mown in five minutes. The last of the mowers were just ending their rows while the foremost snatched up their coats on to their shoulders, and crossed the road towards Mashkin Upland.

The sun was already sinking into the trees when they went with their jingling dippers into the wooded ravine of Mashkin Upland. The grass was up to their waists in the middle of the hollow, soft, tender, and feathery, spotted here and there among the trees with wild heart's-ease.

After a brief consultation—whether to take the rows lengthwise or diagonally—Prohor Yermilin, also a renowned mower, a huge, black-haired peasant, went on ahead. He went up to the top, turned back again and started mowing, and they all proceeded to form in line behind him, going downhill through the hollow and uphill right up to the edge of the forest. The sun sank behind the forest. The dew was falling by now; the mowers were in the sun only on the hillside, but below, where a mist was rising, and on the opposite side, they mowed into the fresh, dewy shade. The work went rapidly. The grass cut with a juicy sound, and was at once laid in high, fragrant rows. The mowers from all sides, brought closer together in the short row, kept urging one another on to the sound of jingling dippers and clanging scythes, and the hiss of the whetstones sharpening them, and good-humoured shouts.

Levin still kept between the young peasant and the old man. The old man, who had put on his short sheepskin jacket, was just as good-humoured, jocose, and free in his movements. Among the trees they were continually cutting with their scythes the so-called 'birch mushrooms,' swollen fat in the succulent grass. But the old man bent down every time he came across a mushroom, picked it up and put it in his bosom. 'Another present for my old woman,' he said as he did so.

Easy as it was to mow the wet, soft grass, it was hard work going up and down the steep sides of the ravine. But this did not trouble the old man. Swinging his scythe just as ever, and moving his feet in their big, plaited shoes with firm, little steps, he climbed slowly up the steep place, and though his breeches hanging out below his smock, and his whole frame trembled with effort, he did not miss one blade of grass or one mushroom on his way, and kept making jokes with the peasants and Levin. Levin walked after him and often thought he must fall, as he climbed with a scythe up a steep cliff where it would have been hard work to clamber without anything. But he climbed up and did what he had to do. He felt as though some external force were moving him.

VI

MASHKIN UPLAND was mown, the last row finished, the peasants had put on their coats and were gaily trudging home. Levin got on his horse, and parting regretfully from the peasants, rode homewards. On the hillside he looked back; he could not see them in the mist that had risen from the valley; he could only hear rough, good-humoured voices, laughter, and the sound of clanking scythes.

Sergey Ivanovitch had long ago finished dinner, and was drinking iced lemon and water in his own room, looking through the reviews and papers which he had only just received by post, when Levin rushed into the room, talking merrily, with his wet and matted hair sticking to his forehead, and his back and chest grimed and moist.

'We mowed the whole meadow! Oh, it is nice, delicious! And how have you been getting on?' said Levin, completely forgetting the disagreeable conversation of the previous day.

'Mercy! what do you look like!' said Sergey Ivanovitch, for the first moment looking round with some dissatisfaction. 'And the door, do shut the door!' he cried. 'You must have let in a dozen at least.'

Sergey Ivanovitch could not endure flies, and in his own room he never opened the window except at night, and carefully kept the door shut.

'Not one, on my honour. But if I have, I'll catch them. You wouldn't believe what a pleasure it is! How have you spent the day?'

'Very well. But have you really been mowing the whole day? I expect you're as hungry as a wolf. Kouzma has got everything ready for you.'

'No, I don't feel hungry even. I had something to eat there. But I'll go and wash.'

'Yes, go along, go along, and I'll come to you directly,' said Sergey Ivanovitch, shaking his head as he looked at his brother. 'Go along, make haste,' he added smiling, and gathering up his books, he prepared to go too. He, too, felt suddenly good-humoured and disinclined to leave his brother's side. 'But what did you do while it was raining?'

'Rain? Why, there was scarcely a drop. I'll come directly. So you had a nice day too? That's first-rate.' And Levin went off to change his clothes.

Five minutes later the brothers met in the dining-room. Although it seemed to Levin that he was not hungry, and he sat down to dinner simply so as not to hurt Kouzma's feelings, yet when he began to eat the dinner struck him as extraordinarily good. Sergey Ivanovitch watched him with a smile.

'Oh, by the way, there's a letter for you,' said he. 'Kouzma, bring it down, please. And mind you shut the doors.'

The letter was from Oblonsky. Levin read it aloud. Oblonsky wrote to him from Petersburg: 'I have had a letter from Dolly; she's at Ergushovo, and everything seems going wrong there. Do ride over and see her, please; help her with advice; you know all about it. She will be so glad to see you. She's quite alone, poor thing. My mother-in-law and all of them are still abroad.'

'That's capital! I will certainly ride over to her,' said Levin. 'Or we'll go together. She's such a splendid woman, isn't she?'

'They're not far from here, then?'

'Twenty-five miles. Or perhaps it is thirty. But a capital road. Capital, we'll drive over.'

'I shall be delighted,' said Sergey Ivanovitch, still smiling. The sight of his younger brother's appearance had immediately put him in a good humour.

'Well, you have an appetite!' he said, looking at his dark-red, sunburnt face and neck bent over the plate.

'Splendid! You can't imagine what an effectual remedy it is for every sort of foolishness. I want to enrich medicine with a new word: *Arbeitskur*.'

'Well, but you don't need it, I should fancy.'

'No, but for all sorts of nervous invalids.'

'Yes, it ought to be tried. I had meant to come to the mowing to look at you, but it was so unbearably hot that I got no further than the forest. I sat there a little, and went on by the forest to the village, met your old nurse, and sounded her as to the peasants' view of you. As far as I can make out, they don't approve of this. She said: "It's not a gentleman's work." Altogether, I fancy that in the people's ideas there are very clear and definite notions of certain, as they call it, "gentlemanly" lines of action. And they don't sanction the gentry's moving outside bounds clearly laid down in their ideas.'

'Maybe so; but anyway it's a pleasure such as I have never known in my life. And there's no harm in it, you know. Is there?' answered Levin. 'I can't help it if they don't like it. Though I do believe it's all right. Eh?'

'Altogether,' pursued Sergey Ivanovitch, 'you're satisfied with your day?'

'Quite satisfied. We cut the whole meadow. And such a splendid old man I made friends with there! You can't fancy how delightful he was!'

'Well, so you're content with your day. And so am I. First, I solved two chess problems, and one a very pretty one—a pawn opening. I'll show it you. And then—I thought over our conversation yesterday.'

'Eh! our conversation yesterday?' said Levin, blissfully dropping his eyelids and drawing deep breaths after finishing his dinner, and absolutely incapable of recalling what their conversation yesterday was about.

'I think you are partly right. Our difference of opinion amounts to this, that you make the mainspring self-interest, while I suppose that interest in the common weal is bound to exist in every man of a certain degree of advancement. Possibly you are right too, that action founded on material interest would be more desirable. You are altogether, as the French say, too *primesautière* a nature; you must have intense, energetic action, or nothing.'

Levin listened to his brother and did not understand a single word, and did not want to understand. He was only afraid his brother might ask him some question which would make it evident he had not heard.

'So that's what I think it is, my dear boy,' said Sergey Ivanovitch, touching him on the shoulder.

'Yes, of course. But, do you know? I won't stand up for my view,' answered Levin, with a guilty, childlike smile. 'Whatever was it I was disputing about?' he wondered. 'Of course, I'm right, and he's right, and it's all first-rate. Only I must go round to the counting-house and see to things.' He got up, stretching and smiling. Sergey Ivanovitch smiled too.

'If you want to go out, let's go together,' he said, disinclined to be parted from his brother, who seemed positively breathing out freshness and energy. 'Come, we'll go to the counting-house, if you have to go there.'

'Oh, heavens!' shouted Levin, so loudly that Sergey Ivanovitch was quite frightened.

'What, what is the matter?'

'How's Agafea Mihalovna's hand?' said Levin, slapping himself on the head. 'I'd positively forgotten her even.'

'It's much better.'

'Well, anyway I'll run down to her. Before you've time to get your hat on, I'll be back.'

And he ran downstairs, clattering with his heels like a spring-rattle.

VII

STEPAN ARKADYEVITCH had gone to Petersburg to perform the most natural and essential official duty—so familiar to everyone in the government service, though incomprehensible to outsiders—that duty, but for which one could hardly be in government service, of reminding the ministry of his existence—and having, for the due performance of this rite, taken all the available cash from home, was gaily and agreeably spending his days at the races and in the summer villas. Meanwhile Dolly and the children had moved into the country, to cut down expenses as much as possible. She had gone to Ergushovo, the estate that had been her dowry, and the one where in spring the forest had been sold. It was nearly forty miles from Levin's Pokrovskoe. The big, old house at Ergushovo had been pulled down long ago, and the old prince had had the lodge done up and built on to. Twenty years before, when Dolly was a child, the lodge had been roomy and comfortable, though, like all lodges, it stood sideways to the entrance avenue, and faced the south. But by now this lodge was old and dilapidated. When Stepan Arkadyevitch had gone down in the spring to sell the forest, Dolly had begged him to look over the house and order what repairs might be needed. Stepan Arkadyevitch, like all unfaithful husbands indeed, was very solicitous for his wife's comfort, and he had himself looked over the house, and given instructions about everything that he considered necessary. What he considered necessary was to cover all the furniture with cretonne, to put up curtains, to weed the garden, to make a little bridge on the pond, and to plant flowers. But he forgot many other essential matters, the want of which greatly distressed Darya Alexandrovna later on.

In spite of Stepan Arkadyevitch's efforts to be an attentive father and husband, he never could keep in his mind that he had a wife and children. He had bachelor tastes, and it was in accordance with them that he shaped his life. On his return to Moscow he informed his wife with pride that everything was ready, that the house would be a little paradise, and that he advised her most certainly to go. His wife's staying away in the country was very agreeable to Stepan Arkadyevitch from every point of view: it did the children good, it decreased expenses, and it left him more at liberty. Darya Alexandrovna regarded staying in the country for the summer as essential for the children, especially for the little girl, who had not succeeded in regaining her strength after the scarlatina, and also as a means of escaping the petty humiliations, the little bills owing to the wood-merchant, the fishmonger, the shoemaker, which made her miserable. Besides this, she was pleased to go away to the country because she was dreaming of getting her sister Kitty to stay with her there. Kitty was to be back from abroad in the middle of the summer, and bathing had been prescribed for her. Kitty wrote that no prospect was so alluring as to spend the summer with Dolly at Ergushovo, full of childish associations for both of them.

The first days of her existence in the country were very hard for Dolly. She used to stay in the country as a child, and the impression she had retained of it was that the country was a refuge from all the unpleasantness of the town, that life there, though not luxurious—Dolly could easily make up her mind to that—was cheap and comfortable; that there was plenty of everything, everything was cheap, everything could be got, and children were happy. But now coming to the country as the head of a family, she perceived that it was all utterly unlike what she had fancied.

The day after their arrival there was a heavy fall of rain, and in the night the water came through in the corridor and in the nursery, so that the beds had to be carried into the drawing-room. There was no kitchenmaid to be found; of the nine cows, it appeared from the words of the cowherd-woman that some were about to calve, others had just calved, others were old, and others again hard-uddered; there was not butter nor milk enough even for the children. There were no eggs. They could get no fowls; old, purplish, stringy cocks were all they had for roasting and boiling. Impossible to get women to scrub the floors—all were potato-hoeing. Driving was out of the question, because one of the horses was restive, and bolted in the shafts. There was no place where they could bathe; the whole of the river-bank was trampled by the cattle and open to the road; even walks were impossible, for the cattle strayed into the garden through a gap in the hedge, and there was one terrible bull, who bellowed, and therefore might be expected to gore somebody. There were no proper cupboards for their clothes; what cupboards there were either would not close at all, or burst open whenever anyone passed by them. There were no pots and pans; there was no copper in the washhouse, nor even an ironing-board in the maids' room.

Finding instead of peace and rest all these, from her point of view, fearful calamities, Darya Alexandrovna was at first in despair. She exerted herself to the utmost, felt the hopelessness of the position, and was every instant suppressing the tears that started into her eyes. The bailiff, a retired quartermaster, whom Stepan Arkadyevitch had taken a fancy to and had appointed bailiff on account of his handsome and respectful appearance as a hall-porter, showed no sympathy for Darya Alexandrovna's woes. He said respectfully, 'nothing can be done, the peasants are such a wretched lot,' and did nothing to help her.

The position seemed hopeless. But in the Oblonskys' household, as in all families indeed, there was one inconspicuous but most valuable and useful person, Marya Filimonovna. She soothed her mistress, assured her that everything would *come round* (it was her expression, and Matvey had borrowed it from her), and without fuss or hurry proceeded to set to work herself. She had immediately made friends with the bailiff's wife, and on the very first day she drank tea with her and the bailiff under the acacias, and reviewed all the circumstances of the position. Very soon Marya Filimonovna had established her club, so to say, under the acacias, and there it was, in this club, consisting of the bailiff's wife, the village elder, and the counting-house clerk, that the difficulties of existence were gradually smoothed away, and in a week's time everything actually had come round. The roof was mended, a kitchenmaid was found—a crony of the village elder's—hens were bought, the cows began giving milk, the garden hedge was stopped up with stakes, the carpenter made a mangle, hooks were put in the cupboards, and they ceased to burst open spontaneously, and an ironing-board covered with army cloth was placed across from the arm of a chair to the chest of drawers, and there was a smell of flat-irons in the maids' room.

'Just see, now, and you were quite in despair,' said Marya Filimonovna, pointing to the ironing-board. They even rigged up a bathing-shed of straw hurdles. Lily began to bathe, and Darya Alexandrovna began to realise, if only in part, her expectations, if not of a peaceful, at least of a comfortable, life in the country. Peaceful with six children Darya Alexandrovna could not be. One would fall ill, another might easily become so, a third would be without something necessary, a fourth would show symptoms of a bad disposition, and so on. Rare indeed were the brief periods of peace. But these cares and anxieties were for Darya Alexandrovna the sole happiness possible. Had it not been for them, she would have been left alone to brood over her husband who did not love her. And besides, hard though it was for the mother to bear the dread of illness, the illnesses themselves, and the grief of seeing signs of evil propensities in her children—the children themselves were even now repaying her in small joys for her sufferings. Those joys were so small that they passed unnoticed, like gold in sand, and at bad moments she could see nothing but the pain, nothing but sand; but there were good moments too when she saw nothing but the joy, nothing but gold.

Now in the solitude of the country, she began to be more and more frequently aware of those joys. Often, looking at them, she would make every possible effort to persuade herself that she was mistaken, that she as a mother was partial to her children. All the same, she could not help saying to herself that she had charming children, all six of them in different ways, but a set of children such as is not often to be met with, and she was happy in them, and proud of them.

VIII

TOWARDS the end of May, when everything had been more or less satisfactorily arranged, she received her husband's answer to her complaints of the disorganised state of things in the country. He wrote begging her forgiveness for not having thought of everything before, and promised to come down at the first chance. This chance did not present itself, and till the beginning of June Darya Alexandrovna stayed alone in the country.

On the Sunday in St. Peter's week Darya Alexandrovna drove to mass for all her children to take the sacrament. Darya Alexandrovna in her intimate, philosophical talks with her sister, her mother, and her friends very often astonished them by the freedom of her views in regard to religion. She had a strange religion of transmigration of souls all her own, in which she had firm faith, troubling herself little about the dogmas of the Church. But in her family she was strict in carrying out all that was required by the Church—and not merely in order to set an example, but with all her heart in it. The fact that the children had not been at the sacrament for nearly a year worried her extremely, and with the full approval and sympathy of Marya Filimonovna she decided that this should take place now in the summer.

For several days before, Darya Alexandrovna was busily deliberating on how to dress all the children. Frocks were made or altered and washed, seams and flounces were let out, buttons were sewn on, and ribbons got ready. One dress, Tanya's, which the English governess had undertaken, cost Darya Alexandrovna much loss of temper. The English governess in altering it had made the seams in the wrong place, had taken up the sleeves too much, and altogether spoilt the dress. It was so narrow on Tanya's shoulders that it was quite painful to look at her. But Marya Filimonovna had the happy thought of putting in gussets, and adding a little shoulder-cape. The dress was set right, but there was nearly a quarrel with the English governess. On the morning, however, all was happily arranged, and towards ten o'clock—the time at which they had asked the priest to wait for them for the mass—the children in their new dresses, with beaming faces, stood on the step before the carriage waiting for their mother.

In the carriage, instead of the restive Raven, they had harnessed, thanks to the representations of Marya Filimonovna, the bailiff's horse, Brownie, and Darya Alexandrovna, delayed by anxiety over her own attire, came out and got in, dressed in a white muslin gown.

Darya Alexandrovna had done her hair, and dressed with care and excitement. In old days she had dressed for her own sake to look pretty and be admired. Later on, as she got older, dress became more and more distasteful to her. She saw that she was losing her good looks. But now she began to feel pleasure and interest in dress again. Now she did not dress for her own sake, not for the sake of her own beauty, but simply that as the mother of those exquisite creatures she might not spoil the general effect. And looking at herself for the last time in the looking-glass she was satisfied with herself. She looked nice. Not nice as she would have wished to look nice in old days at a ball, but nice for the object which she now had in view.

In the church there was no one but the peasants, the servants and their women-folk. But Darya Alexandrovna saw, or fancied she saw, the sensation produced by her children and her. The children were not only beautiful to look at in their smart little dresses, but they were charming in the way they behaved. Aliosha, it is true, did not stand quite correctly; he kept turning round, trying to look at his little jacket from behind; but all the same he was wonderfully sweet. Tanya behaved like a grown-up person, and looked after the little ones. And the smallest, Lily, was bewitching in her naïve astonishment at everything, and it was difficult not to smile when, after taking the sacrament, she said in English, 'Please, some more.'

On the way home the children felt that something solemn had happened, and were very sedate.

Everything went happily at home too; but at lunch Grisha began whistling, and, what was worse, was disobedient to the English governess, and was forbidden to have any tart. Darya Alexandrovna would not have let things go so far on such a day had she been present; but she had to support the English governess's authority, and she upheld her decision that Grisha should have no tart. This rather spoiled the general good-humour. Grisha cried, declaring that Nikolinka had whistled too, and he was not punished, and that he wasn't crying for the tart—he didn't care—but at being unjustly treated. This was really too tragic, and Darya Alexandrovna made up her mind to persuade the English governess to forgive Grisha, and she went to speak to her. But on her way, as she passed the drawing-room, she beheld a scene, filling her heart with such pleasure that the tears came into her eyes, and she forgave the delinquent herself.

The culprit was sitting at the window in the corner of the drawing-room; beside him was standing Tanya with a plate. On the pretext of wanting to give some dinner to her dolls, she had asked the governess's permission to take her share of tart to the nursery, and had taken it instead to her brother. While still weeping over the injustice of his punishment, he was eating the tart, and kept saying through his sobs, 'Eat yourself; let's eat it together . . . together.'

Tanya had at first been under the influence of her pity for Grisha, then of a sense of her noble action, and tears were standing in her eyes too; but she did not refuse, and ate her share.

On catching sight of their mother they were dismayed, but, looking into her face, they saw they were not doing wrong. They burst out laughing, and, with their mouths full of tart, they began wiping their smiling lips with their hands, and smearing their radiant faces all over with tears and jam.

'Mercy! Your new white frock! Tanya! Grisha!' said their mother, trying to save the frock, but, with tears in her eyes, smiling a blissful, rapturous smile.

The new frocks were taken off, and orders were given for the little girls to have their blouses put on, and the boys their old jackets, and the wagonette to be harnessed, with Brownie, to the bailiff's annoyance, again in the shafts; to drive out for mushroom-picking and bathing. A roar of delighted shrieks arose in the nursery, and never ceased till they had set off for the bathing-place.

They gathered a whole basketful of mushrooms; even Lily found a birch-bushroom. It had always happened before that Miss Hoole found them and pointed them out to her; but this time she found a big one quite of herself, and there was a general scream of delight, 'Lily has found a mushroom!'

Then they reached the river, put the horses under the birch-trees, and went to the bathing-place. The coachman, Terenty, fastened the horses, who kept whisking away the flies, to a tree, and, treading down the grass, lay down in the shade of a birch and smoked his shag, while the never-ceasing shrieks of delight of the children floated across to him from the bathing-place.

Though it was hard work to look after all the children and restrain their wild pranks, though it was difficult too to keep in one's head and not mix up all the stockings, little breeches, and shoes for the different legs, and to undo and to do up again all the tapes and buttons, Darya Alexandrovna, who had always liked bathing herself, and believed it to be very good for the children, enjoyed nothing so much as bathing with all the children. To go over all those fat little legs, pulling on their stockings, to take in her arms and dip those little naked bodies, and to hear their screams of delight and alarm, to see the breathless faces with wide-open, scared, and happy eyes of all her splashing cherubs, was a great pleasure to her.

When half the children had been dressed, some peasant women in holiday dress, out picking herbs, came up to the bathing-shed and stopped shyly. Marya Filimonovna called one of them and handed her a sheet and a shirt that had dropped into the water for her to dry them, and Darya Alexandrovna began to talk to the women. At first they laughed behind their hands and did not understand her questions, but soon they grew bolder and began to talk, winning Darya Alexandrovna's heart at once by the genuine admiration of the children that they showed.

'My, what a beauty! as white as sugar,' said one, admiring Tanitchka, and shaking her head; 'but thin . . .'

'Yes, she has been ill.'

'And so they've been bathing you too,' said another to the baby.

'No; he's only three months old,' answered Darya Alexandrovna with pride.

'You don't say so!'

'And have you any children?'

'I've had four; I've two living—a boy and a girl. I weaned her last carnival.'

'How old is she?'

'Why, two years old.'

'Why did you nurse her so long?'

'It's our custom: for three fasts. . . .'

And the conversation became more interesting to Darya Alexandrovna. What sort of time did she have? What was the matter with the boy? Where was her husband? Did it often happen?

Darya Alexandrovna felt disinclined to leave the peasant women, so interesting to her was their conversation, so completely identical were all their interests. What pleased her most of all was that she saw clearly what all the women admired more than anything was her having so many children, and such fine ones. The peasant women even made Darya Alexandrovna laugh, and offended the English governess, because she was the cause of the laughter she did not understand. One of the younger women kept staring at the Englishwoman, who was dressing after all the rest and when she put on her third petticoat she could not refrain from the remark, 'My, she keeps putting on and putting on, and she'll never have done!' she said, and they all went off into roars.

IX

ON the drive home, as Darya Alexandrovna, with all her children round her, their heads still wet from their bathe, and a kerchief tied over her own head, was getting near the house, the coachman said, 'There's some gentleman coming: the master of Pokrovskoe, I do believe.'

Darya Alexandrovna peeped out in front, and was delighted when she recognised in the grey hat and grey coat the familiar figure of Levin walking to meet them. She was glad to see him at any time, but at this moment she was specially glad he should see her in all her glory. No one was better able to appreciate her grandeur than Levin.

Seeing her, he found himself face to face with one of the pictures of his day-dream of family life.

'You're like a hen with your chickens, Darya Alexandrovna.'

'Ah, how glad I am to see you!' she said, holding out her hand to him.

'Glad to see me, but you didn't let me know. My brother's staying with me. I got a note from Stiva that you were here.'

'From Stiva?' Darya Alexandrovna asked with surprise.

'Yes; he writes that you are here, and that he thinks you might allow me to be of use to you,' said Levin, and as he said it he became suddenly embarrassed, and, stopping abruptly, he walked on in silence by the wagonette, snapping off the buds of the lime-trees and nibbling them. He was embarrassed through a sense that Darya Alexandrovna would be annoyed by receiving from an outsider help that should by rights have come from her own husband. Darya Alexandrovna certainly did not like this little way of Stepan Arkadyevitch's of foisting his domestic duties on others. And she was at once aware that Levin was aware of this. It was just for this fineness of perception, for this delicacy, that Darya Alexandrovna liked Levin.

'I know, of course,' said Levin, 'that that simply means that you would like to see me, and I'm exceedingly glad. Though I can fancy that, used to town housekeeping as you are, you must feel in the wilds here, and if there's anything wanted, I'm altogether at your disposal.'

'Oh no!' said Dolly. 'At first things were rather uncomfortable, but now we've settled everything capitally—thanks to my old nurse,' she said, indicating Marya Filimonovna, who, seeing that they were speaking of her, smiled brightly and cordially to Levin. She knew him, and knew that he would be a good match for her young lady, and was very keen to see the matter settled.

'Won't you get in, sir, we'll make room this side!' she said to him.

'No, I'll walk. Children, who'd like to race the horses with me?'

The children knew Levin very little, and could not remember when they had seen him, but they experienced in regard to him none of that strange feeling of shyness and hostility which children so often experience towards hypocritical, grown-up people, and for which they are so often and miserably punished. Hypocrisy in anything whatever may deceive the cleverest and most penetrating man, but the least wide-awake of children recognises it, and is revolted by it, however ingeniously it may be disguised. Whatever faults Levin had, there was not a trace of hypocrisy in him, and so the children showed him the same friendliness that they saw in their mother's face. On his invitation, the two elder ones at once jumped out to him and ran with him as simply as they would have done with their nurse or Miss Hoole or their mother. Lily, too, began begging to go to him, and her mother handed her to him; he sat her on his shoulder and ran along with her.

'Don't be afraid, don't be afraid, Darya Alexandrovna!' he said, smiling good-humouredly to the mother; 'there's no chance of my hurting or dropping her.'

And, looking at his strong, agile, assiduously careful and needlessly wary movements, the mother felt her mind at rest, and smiled gaily and approvingly as she watched him.

Here, in the country, with children, and with Darya Alexandrovna, with whom he was in sympathy, Levin was in a mood, not infrequent with him, of childlike light-heartedness that she particularly liked in him. As he ran with the children, he taught them gymnastic feats, set Miss Hoole laughing with his queer English accent, and talked to Darya Alexandrovna of his pursuits in the country.

After dinner, Darya Alexandrovna, sitting alone with him on the balcony, began to speak of Kitty.

'You know, Kitty's coming here, and is going to spend the summer with me.'

'Really,' he said, flushing, and at once, to change the conversation, he said: 'Then I'll send you two cows, shall I? If you insist on a bill you shall pay me five roubles a month; but it's really too bad of you.'

'No, thank you. We can manage very well now.'

'Oh, well then, I'll have a look at your cows, and if you'll allow me, I'll give directions about their food. Everything depends on their food.'

And Levin, to turn the conversation, explained to Darya Alexandrovna the theory of cow-keeping, based on the principle that the cow is simply a machine for the transformation of food into milk, and so on.

He talked of this, and passionately longed to hear more of Kitty, and, at the same time, was afraid of hearing it. He dreaded the breaking up of the inward peace he had gained with such effort.

'Yes, but still all this has to be looked after, and who is there to look after it?' Darya Alexandrovna responded, without interest.

She had by now got her household matters so satisfactorily arranged, thanks to Marya Filimonovna, that she was disinclined to make any change in them; besides, she had no faith in Levin's knowledge of farming. General principles, as to the cow being a machine for the production of milk, she looked on with suspicion. It seemed to her that such principles could only be a hindrance in farm management. It all seemed to her a far simpler matter: all that was needed, as Marya Filimonovna had explained, was to give Brindle and Whitebreast more food and drink, and not to let the cook carry all the kitchen slops to the laundry-maid's cow. That was clear. But general propositions as to feeding on meal and on grass were doubtful and obscure. And, what was most important, she wanted to talk about Kitty.

X

'KITTY writes to me that there's nothing she longs for so much as quiet and solitude,' Dolly said after the silence that had followed.

'And how is she—better?' Levin asked in agitation.

'Thank God, she's quite well again. I never believed her lungs were affected.'

'Oh, I'm very glad!' said Levin, and Dolly fancied she saw something touching, helpless, in his face as he said this and looked silently into her face.

'Let me ask you, Konstantin Dmitritch,' said Darya Alexandrovna, smiling her kindly and rather mocking smile, 'why is it you are angry with Kitty?'

'I? I'm not angry with her,' said Levin.

'Yes, you are angry. Why was it you did not come to see us nor them when you were in Moscow?'

'Darya Alexandrovna,' he said, blushing up to the roots of his hair, 'I wonder really that with your kind heart you don't feel this. How it is you feel no pity for me, if nothing else, when you know . . .'

'What do I know?'

'You know I made an offer and that I was refused,' said Levin, and all the tenderness he had been feeling for Kitty a minute before was replaced by a feeling of anger for the slight he had suffered.

'What makes you suppose I know?'

'Because everybody knows it . . .'

'That's just where you are mistaken; I did not know it, though I had guessed it was so.'

'Well, now you know it.'

'All I knew was that something had happened that made her dreadfully miserable, and that she begged me never to speak of it. And if she would not tell me, she would certainly not speak of it to anyone else. But what did pass between you? Tell me.'

'I have told you.'

'When was it?'

'When I was at their house the last time.'

'Do you know that,' said Darya Alexandrovna, 'I am awfully, awfully sorry for her. You suffer only from pride. . . .'

'Perhaps so,' said Levin, 'but . . .'

She interrupted him.

'But she, poor girl . . . I am awfully, awfully sorry for her. Now I see it all.'

'Well, Darya Alexandrovna, you must excuse me,' he said, getting up. 'Good-bye, Darya Alexandrovna, till we meet again.'

'No, wait a minute,' she said, clutching him by the sleeve. 'Wait a minute, sit down.'

'Please, please, don't let us talk of this,' he said, sitting down, and at the same time feeling rise up and stir within his heart a hope he had believed to be buried.

'If I did not like you,' she said, and tears came into her eyes; 'if I did not know you, as I do know you . . .'

The feeling that had seemed dead revived more and more, rose up and took possession of Levin's heart.

'Yes, I understand it all now,' said Darya Alexandrovna. 'You can't understand it; for you men, who are free and make your own choice, it's always clear whom you love. But a girl's in a position of suspense, with all a woman's or maiden's modesty, a girl who sees you men from afar, who takes everything on trust,—a girl may have, and often has, such a feeling that she cannot tell what to say.'

'Yes, if the heart does not speak . . .'

'No, the heart does speak; but just consider: you men have views about a girl, you come to the house, you make friends, you criticise, you wait to see if you have found what you love, and then, when you are sure you love her, you make an offer . . .'

'Well, that's not quite it.'

'Anyway you make an offer, when your love is ripe or when the balance has completely turned between the two you are choosing from. But a girl is not asked. She is expected to make her choice, and yet she cannot choose, she can only answer "yes" or "no".'

'Yes, to choose between me and Vronsky,' thought Levin, and the dead thing that had come to life within him died again, and only weighed on his heart and set it aching.

'Darya Alexandrovna,' he said, 'that's how one chooses a new dress, or some purchase or other, not love. The choice has been made, and so much the better . . . And there can be no repeating it.'

'Ah, pride, pride!' said Darya Alexandrovna, as though despising him for the baseness of this feeling in comparison with that other feeling which only women know. 'At the time when you made Kitty an offer she was just in a position in which she could not answer. She was in doubt. Doubt between you and Vronsky. Him she was seeing every day, and you she had not seen for a long while. Supposing she had been older, . . . I, for instance, in her place could have felt no doubt. I always disliked him, and so it has turned out.'

Levin recalled Kitty's answer. She had said: *'No, that cannot be . . .'*

'Darya Alexandrovna,' he said dryly, 'I appreciate your confidence in me; I believe you are making a mistake. But whether I am right or wrong, that pride you so despise makes any thought of Katerina Alexandrovna out of the question for me,—you understand, utterly out of the question.'

'I will only say one thing more: you know that I am speaking of my sister, whom I love as I love my own children. I don't say she cared for you, all I meant to say is that her refusal at that moment proves nothing.'

'I don't know!' said Levin, jumping up. 'If you only knew how you are hurting me. It's just as if a child of yours were dead, and they were to say to you, He would have been like this and like that, and he might have lived, and how happy you would have been in him. But he's dead, dead, dead! . . .'

'How absurd you are!' said Darya Alexandrovna, looking with mournful tenderness at Levin's excitement. 'Yes, I see it all more and more clearly,' she went on musingly. 'So you won't come to see us, then, when Kitty's here?'

'No, I shan't come. Of course I won't avoid meeting Katerina Alexandrovna, but as far as I can, I will try to save her the annoyance of my presence.'

'You are very, very absurd,' repeated Darya Alexandrovna, looking with tenderness into his face. 'Very well then, let it be as though we had not spoken of this. What have you come for, Tanya?' she said in French to the little girl who had come in.

'Where's my spade, mamma?'

'I speak French, and you must too.'

The little girl tried to say it in French, but could not remember the French for spade; the mother prompted her, and then told her in French where to look for the spade. And this made a disagreeable impression on Levin.

Everything in Darya Alexandrovna's house and children struck him now as by no means so charming as a little while before. 'And what does she talk French with the children for?' he thought; 'how unnatural and false it is! And the children feel it so. Learning French and unlearning sincerity,' he thought to himself, unaware that Darya Alexandrovna had thought all that over twenty times already, and yet, even at the cost of some loss of sincerity, believed it necessary to teach her children French in that way.

'But why are you going? Do stay a little.'

Levin stayed to tea; but his good-humour had vanished, and he felt ill at ease.

After tea he went out into the hall to order his horses to be put in, and, when he came back, he found Darya Alexandrovna greatly disturbed, with a troubled face, and tears in her eyes. While Levin had been outside, an incident had occurred which had utterly shattered all the happiness she had been feeling that day, and her pride in her children. Grisha and Tanya had been fighting over a ball. Darya Alexandrovna, hearing a scream in the nursery, ran in and saw a terrible sight. Tanya was pulling Grisha's hair, while he, with a face hideous with rage, was beating her with his fists wherever he could get at her. Something snapped in Darya Alexandrovna's heart when she saw this. It was as if darkness had swooped down upon her life; she felt that these children of hers, that she was so proud of, were not merely most ordinary, but positively bad, ill-bred children, with coarse, brutal propensities—wicked children.

She could not talk or think of anything else, and she could not speak to Levin of her misery.

Levin saw she was unhappy and tried to comfort her, saying that it showed nothing bad, that all children fight; but, even as he said it, he was thinking in his heart: 'No, I won't be artificial and talk French with my children; but my children won't be like that. All one has to do is not to spoil children, not to distort their nature, and they'll be delightful. No, my children won't be like that.'

He said good-bye and drove away, and she did not try to keep him.

XI

IN the middle of July the elder of the village on Levin's sister's estate, about fifteen miles from Pokrovskoe, came to Levin to report on how things were going there and on the hay. The chief source of income on his sister's estate was from the riverside meadows. In former years the hay had been bought by the peasants for twenty roubles the three acres. When Levin took over the management of the estate, he thought on examining the grass-lands that they were worth more, and he fixed the price at twenty-five roubles the three acres. The peasants would not give that price, and, as Levin suspected, kept off other purchasers. Then Levin had driven over himself, and arranged to have the grass cut, partly by hired labour, partly at a payment of a certain proportion of the crop. His own peasants put every hindrance they could in the way of this new arrangement, but it was carried out, and the first year the meadows had yielded a profit almost double. The previous year—which was the third year—the peasants had maintained the same opposition to the arrangement, and the hay had been cut on the same system. This year the peasants were doing all the mowing for a third of the hay crop, and the village elder had come now to announce that the hay had been cut, and that, fearing rain, they had invited the counting-house clerk over, had divided the crop in his presence, and had raked together eleven stacks as the owner's share. From the vague answers to his question how much hay had been cut on the principal meadow, from the hurry of the village elder who had made the division, not asking leave, from the whole tone of the peasant, Levin perceived that there was something wrong in the division of the hay, and made up his mind to drive over himself to look into the matter.

Arriving to dinner at the village, and leaving his horse at the cottage of an old friend of his, the husband of his brother's wet-nurse, Levin went to see the old man in his bee-house, wanting to find out from him the truth about the hay. Parmenitch, a talkative, comely old man, gave Levin a very warm welcome, showed him all he was doing, told him everything about his bees and the swarms of that year; but gave vague and unwilling answers to Levin's inquiries about the mowing. This confirmed Levin still more in his suspicions. He went to the hay-fields and examined the stacks. The haystacks could not possibly contain fifty wagon-loads each, and to convict the peasants Levin ordered the wagons that had carried the hay to be brought up directly, to lift one stack, and carry it into the barn. There turned out to be only thirty-two loads in the stack. In spite of the village elder's assertions about the compressibility of hay, and its having settled down in the stacks, and his swearing that everything had been done in the fear of God, Levin stuck to his point that the hay had been divided without his orders, and that, therefore, he would not accept that hay as fifty loads to a stack. After a prolonged dispute the matter was decided by the peasants taking these eleven stacks, reckoning them as fifty loads each. The arguments and the division of the haycocks lasted the whole afternoon. When the last of the hay had been divided, Levin, intrusting the superintendence of the rest to the counting-house clerk, sat down on a haycock marked off by a stake of willow, and looked admiringly at the meadow swarming with peasants.

In front of him, in the bend of the river beyond the marsh, moved a bright-coloured line of peasant women, and the scattered hay was being rapidly formed into grey winding rows over the pale green stubble. After the women came the men with pitchforks, and from the grey rows there were growing up broad, high, soft haycocks. To the left carts were rumbling over the meadow that had been already cleared, and one after another the haycocks vanished, flung up in huge forkfuls, and in their place there were rising heavy cartloads of fragrant hay hanging over the horses' hind-quarters.

'What weather for haying! What hay it'll be!' said an old man, squatting down beside Levin. 'It's tea, not hay! It's like scattering grain to the ducks, the way they pick it up!' he added, pointing to the growing haycocks. 'Since dinner-time they've carried a good half of it.'

'The last load, eh?' he shouted to a young peasant, who drove by, standing in the front of an empty cart, shaking the cord reins.

'The last, dad!' the lad shouted back, pulling in the horse, and, smiling, he looked round at a bright, rosy-cheeked peasant girl who sat in the cart smiling too, and drove on.

'Who's that? Your son?' asked Levin.

'My baby,' said the old man with a tender smile.

'What a fine fellow!'

'The lad's all right.'

'Married already?'

'Yes, it's two years last St. Philip's day.'

'Any children?'

'Children indeed! Why, for over a year he was innocent as a babe himself, and bashful too,' answered the old man. 'Well, the hay! It's as fragrant as tea!' he repeated, wishing to change the subject.

Levin looked more attentively at Ivan Parmenov and his wife. They were loading a haycock on to the cart not far from him. Ivan Parmenov was standing on the cart, taking, laying in place, and stamping down the huge bundles of hay, which his pretty young wife deftly handed up to him, at first in armfuls, and then on the pitchfork. The young wife worked easily, merrily, and dexterously. The close-packed hay did not once break away off her fork. First she gathered it together, stuck the fork into it, then with a rapid, supple movement leant the whole weight of her body on it, and at once with a bend of her back under the red belt she drew herself up, and arching her full bosom under the white smock, with a smart turn swung the fork in her arms, and flung the bundle of hay high on to the cart. Ivan, obviously doing his best to save her every minute of unnecessary labour, made haste, opening wide his arms to clutch the bundle and lay it in the cart. As she raked together what was left of the hay, the young wife shook off the bits of hay that had fallen on her neck, and straightening the red kerchief that had dropped forward over her white brow, not browned like her face by the sun, she crept under the cart to tie up the load. Ivan directed her how to fasten the cord to the cross-piece, and at something she said he laughed aloud. In the expressions of both faces was to be seen vigorous, young, freshly awakened love.

XII

THE load was tied on. Ivan jumped down and took the quiet, sleek horse by the bridle. The young wife flung the rake up on the load, and with a bold step, swinging her arms, she went to join the women, who were forming a ring for the haymakers' dance. Ivan drove off to the road and fell into line with the other loaded carts. The peasant women, with their rakes on their shoulders, gay with bright flowers, and chattering with ringing, merry voices, walked behind the hay-cart. One wild untrained female voice broke into a song, and sang it alone through a verse, and then the same verse was taken up and repeated by half a hundred strong healthy voices, of all sorts, coarse and fine, singing in unison.

The women, all singing, began to come close to Levin, and he felt as though a storm were swooping down upon him with a thunder of merriment. The storm swooped down, enveloped him and the haycock on which he was lying, and the other haycocks, and the wagon-loads, and the whole meadow and distant fields all seemed to be shaking and singing to the measures of this wild merry song with its shouts and whistles and clapping. Levin felt envious of this health and mirthfulness; he longed to take part in the expression of this joy of life. But he could do nothing, and had to lie and look on and listen. When the peasants, with their singing, had vanished out of sight and hearing, a weary feeling of despondency at his own isolation, his physical inactivity, his alienation from this world, came over Levin.

Some of the very peasants who had been most active in wrangling with him over the hay, some whom he had treated with contumely, and who had tried to cheat him, those very peasants had greeted him good-humouredly, and evidently had not, were incapable of having any feeling of rancour against him, any regret, any recollection even of having tried to deceive him. All that was drowned in a sea of merry common labour. God gave the day, God gave the strength. And the day and the strength were consecrated to labour, and that labour was its own reward. For whom the labour? What would be its fruits? These were idle considerations—beside the point.

Often Levin had admired this life, often he had a sense of envy of the men who led this life; but today for the first time, especially under the influence of what he had seen in the attitude of Ivan Parmenov to his young wife, the idea presented itself definitely to his mind that it was in his power to exchange the dreary, artificial, idle, and individualistic life he was leading for this laborious, pure, and social delightful life.

The old man who had been sitting beside him had long ago gone home; the people had all separated. Those who lived near had gone home, while those who came from far were gathered into a group for supper, and to spend the night in the meadow. Levin, unobserved by the peasants, still lay on the haycock, and still looked on and listened and mused. The peasants who remained for the night in the meadow scarcely slept all the short summer night. At first there was the sound of merry talk and laughing all together over the supper, then singing again and laughter.

All the long day of toil had left no trace in them but lightness of heart. Before the early dawn all was hushed. Nothing was to be heard but the night sounds of the frogs that never ceased in the marsh, and the horses snorting in the mist that rose over the meadow before the morning. Rousing himself, Levin got up from the haycock, and looking at the stars, he saw that the night was over.

'Well, what am I going to do? How am I to set about it?' he said to himself, trying to express to himself all the thoughts and feelings he had passed through in that brief night. All the thoughts and feelings he had passed through fell into three separate trains of thought. One was the renunciation of his old life, of his utterly useless education. This renunciation gave him satisfaction, and was easy and simple. Another series of thoughts and mental images related to the life he longed to live now. The simplicity, the purity, the sanity of this life he felt clearly, and he was convinced he would find in it the content, the peace, and the dignity, of the lack of which he was so miserably conscious. But a third series of ideas turned upon the question how to effect this transition from the old life to the new. And there nothing took clear shape for him. 'Have a wife? Have work and the necessity of work? Leave Pokrovskoe? Buy land? Become a member of a peasant community? Marry a peasant girl? How am I to set about it?' he asked himself again, and could not find an answer. 'I haven't slept all night, though, and I can't think it out clearly,' he said to himself. 'I'll work it out later. One thing's certain, this night has decided my fate. All my old dreams of home-life were absurd, not the real thing,' he told himself. 'It's all ever so much simpler and better. . . .'

'How beautiful!' he thought, looking at the strange, as it were, mother-of-pearl shell of white fleecy cloudlets resting right over his head in the middle of the sky. 'How exquisite it all is in this exquisite night! And when was there time for that cloud-shell to form? Just now I looked at the sky, and there was nothing in it—only two white streaks. Yes, and so imperceptibly too my views of life changed!'

He went out of the meadow and walked along the high-road towards the village. A slight wind arose, and the sky looked grey and sullen. The gloomy moment had come that usually precedes the dawn, the full triumph of light over darkness.

Shrinking from the cold, Levin walked rapidly, looking at the ground. 'What's that? Someone coming,' he thought, catching the tinkle of bells, and lifting his head. Forty paces from him a carriage with four horses harnessed abreast was driving towards him along the grassy high-road on which he was walking. The shaft-horses were tilted against the shafts by the ruts, but the dexterous driver sitting on the box held the shaft over the ruts, so that the wheels ran on the smooth part of the road.

This was all Levin noticed, and without wondering who it could be, he gazed absently at the coach.

In the coach was on old lady dozing in one corner, and at the window, evidently only just awake, sat a young girl holding in both hands the ribbons of a white cap. With a face full of light and thought, full of a subtle, complex inner life, that was remote from Levin, she was gazing beyond him at the glow of the sunrise.

At the very instant when this apparition was vanishing, the truthful eyes glanced at him. She recognised him, and her face lighted up with wondering delight.

He could not be mistaken. There were no other eyes like those in the world. There was only one creature in the world that could concentrate for him all the brightness and meaning of life. It was she. It was Kitty. He understood that she was driving to Ergushovo from the railway station. And everything that had been stirring Levin during that sleepless night, all the resolutions he had made, all vanished at once. He recalled with horror his dreams of marrying a peasant girl. There only, in the carriage that had crossed over to the other side of the road, and was rapidly disappearing, there only could he find the solution of the riddle of his life, which had weighed so agonisingly upon him of late.

She did not look out again. The sound of the carriage-springs was no longer audible, the bells could scarcely be heard. The barking of dogs showed the carriage had reached the village, and all that was left was the empty fields all round, the village in front, and he himself isolated and apart from it all, wandering lonely along the deserted high-road.

He glanced at the sky, expecting to find there the cloud-shell he had been admiring and taking as the symbol of the ideas and feelings of that night. There was nothing in the sky in the least like a shell. There, in the remote heights above, a mysterious change had been accomplished. There was no trace of shell, and there was stretched over fully half the sky an even cover of tiny and ever tinier cloudlets. The sky had grown blue and bright; and with the same softness, but with the same remoteness, it met his questioning gaze.

'No,' he said to himself, 'however good that life of simplicity and toil may be, I cannot go back to it. I love *her*.'

XIII

NONE but those who were most intimate with Alexey Alexandrovitch knew that, while on the surface the coldest and most reasonable of men, he had one weakness quite opposed to the general trend of his character. Alexey Alexandrovitch could not hear or see a child or woman crying without being moved. The sight of tears threw him into a state of nervous agitation, and he utterly lost all power of reflection. The chief secretary of his department and his private secretary were aware of this, and used to warn women who came with petitions on no account to give way to tears, if they did not want to ruin their chances. 'He will get angry, and will not listen to you,' they used to say. And as a fact, in such cases the emotional disturbance set up in Alexey Alexandrovitch by the sight of tears found expression in hasty anger. 'I can do nothing. Kindly leave the room!' he would commonly cry in such cases.

When returning from the races Anna had informed him of her relations with Vronsky, and immediately afterwards had burst into tears, hiding her face in her hands, Alexey Alexandrovitch, for all the fury aroused in him against her, was aware at the same time of a rush of that emotional disturbance always produced in him by tears. Conscious of it, and conscious that any expression of his feelings at that minute would be out of keeping with the position, he tried to suppress every manifestation of life in himself, and so neither stirred nor looked at her. This was what had caused that strange expression of deathlike rigidity in his face which had so impressed Anna.

When they reached the house he helped her to get out of the carriage, and making an effort to master himself, took leave of her with his usual urbanity, and uttered that phrase that bound him to nothing; he said that tomorrow he would let her know his decision.

His wife's words, confirming his worst suspicions, had sent a cruel pang to the heart of Alexey Alexandrovitch. That pang was intensified by the strange feeling of physical pity for her set up by her tears. But when he was all alone in the carriage Alexey Alexandrovitch, to his surprise and delight, felt complete relief both from this pity and from the doubts and agonies of jealousy.

He experienced the sensations of a man who has had a tooth out after suffering long from toothache. After a fearful agony and a sense of something huge, bigger than the head itself, being torn out of his jaw, the sufferer, hardly able to believe in his own good luck, feels all at once that what has so long poisoned his existence and enchained his attention, exists no longer, and that he can live and think again, and take interest in other things besides his tooth. This feeling Alexey Alexandrovitch was experiencing. The agony had been strange and terrible, but now it was over; he felt that he could live again and think of something other than his wife.

'No honour, no heart, no religion; a corrupt woman. I always knew it and always saw it, though I tried to deceive myself to spare her,' he said to himself. And it actually seemed to him that he always had seen it: he recalled incidents of their past life, in which he had never seen anything wrong before—now these incidents proved clearly that she had always been a corrupt woman. 'I made a mistake in linking my life to hers; but there was nothing wrong in my mistake, and so I cannot be unhappy. It's not I that am to blame,' he told himself, 'but she. But I have nothing to do with her. She does not exist for me. . . .'

Everything relating to her and her son, towards whom his sentiments were as much changed as towards her, ceased to interest him. The only thing that interested him now was the question in what way he could best, with most propriety and comfort for himself, and so with most justice, extricate himself from the mud with which she had spattered him in her fall, and then proceed along his path of active, honourable, and useful existence.

'I cannot be made unhappy by the fact that a contemptible woman has committed a crime. I have only to find the best way out of the difficult position in which she has placed me. And I shall find it,' he said to himself, frowning more and more; 'I'm not the first nor the last.' And to say nothing of historical instances dating from the 'Fair Helen' of Menelaus, recently revived in the memory of all, a whole list of contemporary examples of husbands with unfaithful wives in the highest society rose before Alexey Alexendrovitch's imagination. 'Daryalov, Poltavsky, Prince Karibanov, Count Paskudin, Dram . . . Yes, even Dram, such an honest, capable fellow. . . . Semyonov, Tchagin, Sigonin,' Alexey Alexandrovitch remembered. 'Admitting that a certain irrational ridicule falls to the lot of these men, yet I never saw anything but a misfortune in it, and always felt sympathy for it,' Alexey Alexandrovitch said to himself, though indeed this was not the fact, and he had never felt sympathy for misfortunes of that kind, but the more frequently he had heard of instances of unfaithful wives betraying their husbands, the more highly he had thought of himself. 'It is a misfortune which may befall anyone. And this misfortune has befallen me. The only thing to be done is to make the best of the position.' And he began passing in review the methods of proceeding of men who had been in the same position that he was in.

'Daryalov fought a duel. . . .'

The duel had particularly fascinated the thoughts of Alexey Alexandrovitch in his youth, just because he was physically a coward, and was himself well aware of the fact. Alexey Alexandrovitch could not without horror contemplate the idea of a pistol aimed at himself, and had never made use of any weapon in his life. This horror had in his youth set him pondering on duelling, and picturing himself in a position in which he would have to expose his life to danger. Having attained success and an established position in the world, he had long ago forgotten this feeling; but the habitual bent of feeling reasserted itself, and dread of his own cowardice proved even now so strong, that Alexey Alexandrovitch spent a long while thinking over the question of duelling in all its aspects, and hugging the idea of a duel, though he was fully aware beforehand that he would never under any circumstances fight one.

'There's no doubt our society is still so barbarous (it's not the same in England) that very many'—and among these were those whose opinion Alexey Alexandrovitch particularly valued—'look favourably on the duel; but what result is attained by it? Suppose I call him out,' Alexey Alexandrovitch went on to himself, and vividly picturing the night he would spend after the challenge, and the pistol aimed at him, he shuddered, and knew that he never would do it—'suppose I call him out. Suppose I am taught,' he went on musing, 'to shoot; I press the trigger,' he said to himself, closing his eyes, 'and it turns out I have killed him,' Alexey Alexandrovitch said to himself, and he shook his head as though to dispel such silly ideas. 'What sense is there in murdering a man in order to define one's relation to a guilty wife and son? I should still just as much have to decide what I ought to do with her. But what is more probable and what would doubtless occur—I should be killed or wounded. I, the innocent person, should be the victim—killed or wounded. It's even more senseless. But apart from that, a challenge to fight would be an act hardly honest on my side. Don't I know perfectly well that my friends would never allow me to fight a duel—would never allow the life of a statesman, needed by Russia, to be exposed to danger? Knowing perfectly well beforehand that the matter would never come to real danger, it would amount to my simply trying to gain a certain sham reputation by such a challenge. That would be dishonest, that would be false, that would be deceiving myself and others. A duel is quite irrational, and no one expects it of me. My aim is simply to safeguard my reputation, which is essential for the uninterrupted pursuit of my public duties.' Official duties, which had always been of great consequence in Alexey Alexandrovitch's eyes, seemed of special importance to his mind at this moment. Considering and rejecting the duel, Alexey Alexandrovitch turned to divorce—another solution selected by several of the husbands he remembered. Passing in mental review all the instances he knew of divorces (there were plenty of them in the very highest society with which he was very familiar), Alexey Alexandrovitch could not find a single example in which the object of divorce was that which he had in view. In all these instances the husband had practically ceded or sold his unfaithful wife, and the very party which, being in fault, had not the right to contract a fresh marriage, had formed counterfeit, pseudo-matrimonial ties with a self-styled husband. In his own case, Alexey Alexandrovitch saw that a legal divorce, that is to say, one in which only the guilty wife would be repudiated, was impossible of attainment. He saw that the complex conditions of the life they led made the coarse proofs of his wife's guilt, required by the law, out of the question; he saw that a certain refinement in that life would not admit of such proofs being brought forward, even if he had them, and that to bring forward such proofs would damage him in the public estimation more than it would her.

An attempt at divorce could lead to nothing but a public scandal, which would be a perfect godsend to his enemies for calumny and attacks on his high position in society. His chief object, to define the position with the least amount of disturbance possible, would not be attained by divorce either. Moreover, in the event of divorce, or even of an attempt to obtain a divorce, it was obvious that the wife broke off all relations with the husband and threw in her lot with the lover. And in spite of the complete, as he supposed, contempt and indifference he now felt for his wife, at the bottom of his heart Alexey Alexandrovitch still had one feeling left in regard to her—a disinclination to see her free to throw in her lot with Vronsky, so that her crime would be to her advantage. The mere notion of this so exasperated Alexey Alexandrovitch, that directly it rose to his mind he groaned with inward agony, and got up and changed his place in the carriage, and for a long while after he sat with scowling brows, wrapping his numbed and bony legs in the fleecy rug.

'Apart from formal divorce, one might still do like Karibanov, Paskudin, and that good fellow Dram—that is, separate from one's wife,' he went on thinking, when he had regained his composure. But this step too presented the same drawback of public scandal as a divorce, and what was more, a separation, quite as much as a regular divorce, flung his wife into the arms of Vronsky. 'No, it's out of the question, out of the question!' he said again, twisting his rug about him again. 'I cannot be unhappy, but neither she nor he ought to be happy.'

The feeling of jealousy, which had tortured him during the period of uncertainty, had passed away at the instant when the tooth had been with agony extracted by his wife's words. But that feeling had been replaced by another, the desire, not merely that she should not be triumphant, but that she should get due punishment for her crime. He did not acknowledge this feeling, but at the bottom of his heart he longed for her to suffer for having destroyed his peace of mind—his honour. And going once again over the conditions inseparable from a duel, a divorce, a separation, and once again rejecting them, Alexey Alexandrovitch felt convinced that there was only one solution,—to keep her with him, concealing what had happened from the world, and using every measure in his power to break off the intrigue, and still more—though this he did not admit to himself—to punish her. 'I must inform her of my conclusion, that thinking over the terrible position in which she has placed her family, all other solutions will be worse for both sides than an external *status quo*, and that such I agree to retain, on the strict condition of obedience on her part to my wishes, that is to say, cessation of all intercourse with her lover.' When this decision had been finally adopted, another weighty consideration occurred to Alexey Alexandrovitch in support of it. 'By such a course only shall I be acting in accordance with the dictates of religion,' he told himself. 'In adopting this course, I am not casting off a guilty wife, but giving her a chance of amendment; and, indeed, difficult as the task will be to me, I shall devote part of my energies to her reformation and salvation.'

Though Alexey Alexandrovitch was perfectly aware that he could not exert any moral influence over his wife, that such an attempt at reformation could lead to nothing but falsity; though in passing through these difficult moments he had not once thought of seeking guidance in religion, yet now, when his conclusion corresponded, as it seemed to him, with the requirements of religion, this religious sanction to his decision gave him complete satisfaction, and to some extent restored his peace of mind. He was pleased to think that, even in such an important crisis in life, no one would be able to say that he had not acted in accordance with the principles of that religion whose banner he had always held aloft amid the general coolness and indifference. As he pondered over subsequent developments, Alexey Alexandrovitch did not see, indeed, why his relations with his wife should not remain practically the same as before. No doubt, she could never regain his esteem, but there was not, and there could not be, any sort of reason that his existence should be troubled, and that he should suffer because she was a bad and faithless wife. 'Yes, time will pass, time, which arranges all things, and the old relations will be re-established,' Alexey Alexandrovitch told himself; 'so far re-established, that is, that I shall not be sensible of a break in the continuity of my life. She is bound to be unhappy, but I am not to blame, and so I cannot be unhappy.'

XIV

As he neared Petersburg, Alexey Alexandrovitch not only adhered entirely to his decision, but was even composing in his head the letter he would write to his wife. Going into the porter's room, Alexey Alexandrovitch glanced at the letters and papers brought from his office, and directed that they should be brought to him in his study.

'The horses can be taken out and I will see no one,' he said in answer to the porter, with a certain pleasure, indicative of his agreeable frame of mind, emphasising the words, 'see no one.'

In his study Alexey Alexandrovitch walked up and down twice, and stopped at an immense writing-table, on which six candles had already been lighted by the valet who had preceded him. He cracked his knuckles, and sat down, sorting out his writing appurtenances. Putting his elbows on the table, he bent his head on one side, thought a minute, and began to write, without pausing for a second. He wrote without using any form of address to her, and wrote in French, making use of the plural '*vous*', which has not the same note of coldness as the corresponding Russian form.

'At our last conversation, I notified you of my intention to communicate to you my decision in regard to the subject of that conversation. Having carefully considered everything, I am writing now with the object of fulfilling that promise. My decision is as follows. Whatever your conduct may have been, I do not consider myself justified in breaking the ties in which we are bound by a Higher Power. The family cannot be broken up by a whim, a caprice, or even by the sin of one of the partners in the marriage, and our life must go on as it has done in the past. This is essential for me, for you, and for our son. I am fully persuaded that you have repented and do repent of what has called forth the present letter, and that you will co-operate with me in eradicating the cause of our estrangement, and forgetting the past. In the contrary event, you can conjecture what awaits you and your son. All this I hope to discuss more in detail in a personal interview. As the season is drawing to a close, I would beg you to return to Petersburg as quickly as possible, not later than Tuesday. All necessary preparations shall be made for your arrival here. I beg you to note that I attach particular significance to compliance with this request. A. KARENIN.

'*P.S.*—I enclose the money which may be needed for your expenses.'

He read the letter through and felt pleased with it, and especially that he had remembered to enclose money; there was not a harsh word, not a reproach in it, nor was there undue indulgence. Most of all, it was a golden bridge for return. Folding the letter and smoothing it with a massive ivory knife, and putting it in an envelope with the money, he rang the bell with the gratification it always afforded him to use the well-arranged appointments of his writing-table.

'Give this to the courier to be delivered to Anna Arkadyevna tomorrow at the summer villa,' he said, getting up.

'Certainly, your excellency; tea to be served in the study?'

Alexey Alexandrovitch ordered tea to be brought to the study, and playing with the massive paper-knife, he moved to his easy-chair, near which there had been placed ready for him a lamp and the French work on Egyptian hieroglyphics that he had begun. Over the easy-chair there hung in a gold frame an oval portrait of Anna, a fine painting by a celebrated artist. Alexey Alexandrovitch glanced at it. The unfathomable eyes gazed ironically and insolently at him. Insufferably insolent and challenging was the effect in Alexey Alexandrovitch's eyes of the black lace about the head, admirably touched in by the painter, the black hair and handsome white hand with one finger lifted, covered with rings. After looking at the portrait for a minute, Alexey Alexandrovitch shuddered so that his lips quivered and he uttered the sound 'brrr', and turned away. He made haste to sit down in his easy-chair and opened the book. He tried to read, but he could not revive the very vivid interest he had felt before in Egyptian hieroglyphics. He looked at the book and thought of something else. He thought not of his wife, but of a complication that had arisen in his official life, which at the time constituted the chief interest of it. He felt that he had penetrated more deeply than ever before into this intricate affair, and that he had originated a leading idea—he could say it without self-flattery—calculated to clear up the whole business, to strengthen him in his official career, to discomfit his enemies, and thereby to be of the greatest benefit to the government. Directly the servant had set the tea and left the room, Alexey Alexandrovitch got up and went to the writing-table. Moving into the middle of the table a portfolio of papers, with a scarcely perceptible smile of self-satisfaction, he took a pencil from a rack and plunged into the perusal of a complex report relating to the present complication. The complication was of this nature: Alexey Alexandrovitch's characteristic quality as a politician, that special individual qualification that every rising functionary possesses, the qualification that with his unflagging ambition, his reserve, his honesty, and his self-confidence had made his career, was his contempt for red tape, his cutting down of correspondence, his direct contact, wherever possible, with the living fact, and his economy. It happened that the famous Commission of the 2nd of June had set on foot an inquiry into the irrigation of lands in the Zaraisky province, which fell under Alexey Alexandrovitch's department, and was a glaring example of fruitless expenditure and paper reforms. Alexey Alexandrovitch was aware of the truth of this. The irrigation of these lands in the Zaraisky province had been initiated by the predecessor of Alexey Alexandrovitch's predecessor. And vast sums of money had actually been spent and were still being spent on this business, and utterly unproductively, and the whole business could obviously lead to nothing whatever. Alexey Alexandrovitch had perceived this at once on entering office, and would have liked to lay hands on the Board of Irrigation. But at first, when he did not yet feel secure in his position, he knew it would affect too many interests, and would be injudicious. Later on he had been engrossed in other questions, and had simply forgotten the Board of Irrigation. It went of itself, like all such boards, by the mere force of inertia. (Many people gained their livelihood by the Board of Irrigation, especially one highly conscientious and musical family: all the daughters played on stringed instruments, and Alexey Alexandrovitch knew the family and had stood godfather to one of the elder daughters.) The raising of this question by a hostile department was in Alexey Alexandrovitch's opinion a dishonourable proceeding, seeing that in every department there were things similar and worse, which no one inquired into, for well-known reasons of official etiquette. However, now that the glove had been thrown down to him, he had boldly picked it up and demanded the appointment of a special commission to investigate and verify the workings of the Board of Irrigation of the lands in the Zaraisky province. But in compensation he gave no quarter to the enemy either. He demanded the appointment of another special commission to inquire into the question of the Native Tribes Organisation Committee. The question of the Native Tribes had been brought up incidentally in the Commission of the 2nd of June, and had been pressed forward actively by Alexey Alexandrovitch as one admitting of no delay on account of the deplorable condition of the native tribes. In the commission this question had been a ground of contention between several departments. The department hostile to Alexey Alexandrovitch proved that the condition of the native tribes was exceedingly flourishing, that the proposed reconstruction might be the ruin of their prosperity, and that if there were anything wrong, it arose mainly from the failure on the part of Alexey Alexandrovitch's department to carry out the measures prescribed by law. Now Alexey Alexandrovitch intended to demand: First, that a new commission should be formed which should be empowered to investigate the condition of the native tribes on the spot; secondly, if it should appear that the condition of the native tribes actually was such as it appeared to be from the official documents in the hands of the committee, that another new scientific commission should be appointed to investigate the deplorable condition of the native tribes from the—(1) political, (2) administrative, (3) economic, (4) ethnographical, (5) material, and (6) religious points of view; thirdly, that evidence should be required from the rival department of the measures that had been taken during the last ten years by that department for averting the disastrous conditions in which the native tribes were now placed; and fourthly and finally, that that department be asked to explain why it had, as appeared from the evidence before the committee, from No. 17,015 and 18,308, from December 5, 1863 and June 7, 1864, acted in direct contravention of the intention of the law T . . . Act 18, and the note to Act 36. A flash of eagerness suffused the face of Alexey Alexandrovitch as he rapidly wrote out a synopsis of these ideas for his own benefit. Having filled a sheet of paper, he got up, rang, and sent a note to the chief secretary of his department to look up certain necessary facts for him. Getting up and walking about the room, he glanced again at the portrait, frowned and smiled contemptuously. After reading a little more of the book on Egyptian hieroglyphics, and renewing his interest in it, Alexey Alexandrovitch went to bed at eleven o'clock, and recollecting as he lay in bed the incident with his wife, he saw it now in by no means such a gloomy light.

XV

THOUGH Anna had obstinately and with exasperation contradicted Vronsky when he told her their position was impossible, at the bottom of her heart she regarded her own position as false and dishonourable, and she longed with her whole soul to change it. On the way home from the races she had told her husband the truth in a moment of excitement, and in spite of the agony she had suffered in doing so, she was glad of it. After her husband had left her, she told herself that she was glad, that now everything was made clear, and at least there would be no more lying and deception. It seemed to her beyond doubt that her position was now made clear for ever. It might be bad, this new position, but it would be clear; there would be no indefiniteness or falsehood about it. The pain she had caused herself and her husband in uttering those words would be rewarded now by everything being made clear, she thought. That evening she saw Vronsky, but she did not tell him of what had passed between her and her husband, though, to make the position definite, it was necessary to tell him.

When she woke up next morning the first thing that rose to her mind was what she had said to her husband, and those words seemed to her so awful that she could not conceive now how she could have brought herself to utter those strange, coarse words, and could not imagine what would come of it. But the words were spoken, and Alexey Alexandrovitch had gone away without saying anything. 'I saw Vronsky and did not tell him. At the very instant he was going away I would have turned him back and told him, but I changed my mind, because it was strange that I had not told him the first minute. Why was it I wanted to tell him and did not tell him?' And in answer to this question a burning blush of shame spread over her face. She knew what had kept her from it; she knew that she had been ashamed. Her position, which had seemed to her simplified the night before, suddenly struck her now as not only not simple, but as absolutely hopeless. She felt terrified at the disgrace, of which she had not even thought before. Directly she thought of what her husband would do, the most terrible ideas came to her mind. She had a vision of being turned out of the house, of her shame being proclaimed to all the world. She asked herself where she should go when she was turned out of the house, and she could not find an answer.

When she thought of Vronsky, it seemed to her that he did not love her, that he was already beginning to be tired of her, that she could not offer herself to him, and she felt bitter against him for it. It seemed to her that the words that she had spoken to her husband, and had continually repeated in her imagination, she had said to everyone, and everyone had heard them. She could not bring herself to look those of her own household in the face. She could not bring herself to call her maid, and still less to go downstairs and see her son and his governess.

The maid, who had been listening at her door for a long while, came into her room of her own accord. Anna glanced inquiringly into her face, and blushed with a scared look. The maid begged her pardon for coming in, saying that she had fancied the bell rang. She brought her clothes and a note. The note was from Betsy. Betsy reminded her that Liza Merkalov and Baroness Shtolz were coming to play croquet with her that morning with their adorers, Kaluzhsky and old Stremov. 'Come, if only as a study in morals. I shall expect you,' she finished.

Anna read the note and heaved a deep sigh.

'Nothing, I need nothing,' she said to Annushka, who was rearranging the bottles and brushes on the dressing-table. 'You can go. I'll dress at once and come down. I need nothing.'

Annushka went out, but Anna did not begin dressing, and sat in the same position, her head and hands hanging listlessly, and every now and then she shivered all over, seemed as though she would make some gesture, utter some word, and sank back into lifelessness again. She repeated continually, 'My God! my God!' But neither 'God' nor 'my' had any meaning to her. The idea of seeking help in her difficulty in religion was as remote from her as seeking help from Alexey Alexandrovitch himself, although she had never had doubts of the faith in which she had been brought up. She knew that the support of religion was possible only upon condition of renouncing what made up for her the whole meaning of life. She was not simply miserable, she began to feel alarm at the new spiritual condition, never experienced before, in which she found herself. She felt as though everything were beginning to be double in her soul, just as objects sometimes appear double to over-tired eyes. She hardly knew at times what it was she feared, and what she hoped for. Whether she feared or desired what had happened, or what was going to happen, and exactly what she longed for, she could not have said.

'Ah, what am I doing!' she said to herself, feeling a sudden thrill of pain in both sides of her head. When she came to herself, she saw that she was holding her hair in both hands, each side of her temples, and pulling it. She jumped up, and began walking about.

'The coffee is ready, and mademoiselle and Seryozha are waiting.' said Annushka, coming back again and finding Anna in the same position.

'Seryozha? What about Seryozha?' Anna asked, with sudden eagerness, recollecting her son's existence for the first time that morning.

'He's been naughty, I think,' answered Annushka with a smile.

'In what way?'

'Some peaches were lying on the table in the corner room. I think he slipped in and ate one of them on the sly.'

The recollection of her son suddenly roused Anna from the helpless condition in which she found herself. She recalled the partly sincere, though greatly exaggerated, rôle of the mother living for her child, which she had taken up of late years, and she felt with joy that in the plight in which she found herself she had a support, quite apart from her relation to her husband or to Vronsky. This support was her son. In whatever position she might be placed, she could not lose her son. Her husband might put her to shame and turn her out, Vronsky might grow cold to her and go on living his own life apart (she thought of him again with bitterness and reproach); she could not leave her son. She had an aim in life. And she must act; act to secure this relation to her son, so that he might not be taken from her. Quickly indeed, as quickly as possible, she must take action before he was taken from her. She must take her son and go away. Here was the one thing she had to do now. She needed consolation. She must be calm, and get out of this insufferable position. The thought of immediate action binding her to her son, of going away somewhere with him, gave her this consolation.

She dressed quickly, went downstairs, and with resolute steps walked into the drawing-room, where she found, as usual, waiting for her, the coffee, Seryozha, and his governess. Seryozha, all in white, with his back and head bent, was standing at a table under a looking-glass, and with an expression of intense concentration which she knew well, and in which he resembled his father, he was doing something to the flowers he carried.

The governess had a particularly severe expression. Seryozha screamed shrilly, as he often did, 'Ah, mamma!' and stopped, hesitating whether to go to greet his mother and put down the flowers, or to finish making the wreath and go with the flowers.

The governess, after saying good-morning, began a long and detailed account of Seryozha's naughtiness, but Anna did not hear her; she was considering whether she would take her with her or not. 'No, I won't take her,' she decided. 'I'll go alone with my child.'

'Yes, it's very wrong,' said Anna, and taking her son by the shoulder she looked at him, not severely, but with a timid glance that bewildered and delighted the boy, and she kissed him. 'Leave him to me,' she said to the astonished governess, and not letting go of her son, she sat down at the table, where coffee was set ready for her.

'Mamma! I . . . I . . . didn't . . .' he said, trying to make out from her expression what was in store for him in regard to the peaches.

'Seryozha,' she said, as soon as the governess had left the room, 'that was wrong, but you'll never do it again, will you? . . . You love me?'

She felt that the tears were coming into her eyes. 'Can I help loving him?' she said to herself, looking deeply into his scared and at the same time delighted eyes. 'And can he ever join his father in punishing me? Is it possible he will not feel for me?' Tears were already flowing down her face, and to hide them she got up abruptly and almost ran out on to the terrace.

After the thunder-showers of the last few days, cold, bright weather had set in. The air was cold in the bright sun that filtered through the freshly washed leaves.

She shivered, both from the cold and from the inward horror which had clutched her with fresh force in the open air.

'Run along, run along to Mariette,' she said to Seryozha, who had followed her out, and she began walking up and down on the straw matting of the terrace. 'Can it be that they won't forgive me, won't understand how it all couldn't be helped?' she said to herself.

Standing still, and looking at the tops of the aspen-trees waving in the wind, with their freshly washed, brightly shining leaves in the cold sunshine, she knew that they would not forgive her, that everyone and everything would be merciless to her now as was that sky, that green. And again she felt that everything was split in two in her soul. 'I mustn't, mustn't think,' she said to herself. 'I must get ready. To go where? When? Whom to take with me? Yes, to Moscow by the evening train. Annushka and Seryozha, and only the most necessary things. But first I must write to them both.' She went quickly indoors into her boudoir, sat down at the table, and wrote to her husband:—'After what has happened, I cannot remain any longer in your house. I am going away, and taking my son with me. I don't know the law, and so I don't know with which of the parents the son should remain; but I take him with me because I cannot live without him. Be generous, leave him me.'

Up to this point she wrote rapidly and naturally, but the appeal to his generosity, a quality she did not recognise in him, and the necessity of winding up the letter with something touching, pulled her up. 'Of my fault and my remorse I cannot speak, because . . .'

She stopped again, finding no connection in her ideas. 'No,' she said to herself, 'there's no need of anything,' and tearing up the letter she wrote it again, leaving out the allusion to generosity, and sealed it up.

Another letter had to be written to Vronsky. 'I have told my husband,' she wrote, and she sat a long while unable to write more. It was so coarse, so unfeminine. 'And what more am I to write to him?' she said to herself. Again a flush of shame spread over her face; she recalled his composure, and a feeling of anger against him impelled her to tear the sheet with the phrase she had written into tiny bits. 'No need of anything,' she said to herself, and closing her blotting-case she went upstairs, told the governess and the servants that she was going that day to Moscow, and at once set to work to pack up her things.

XVI

ALL the rooms of the summer villa were full of porters, gardeners, and footmen going to and fro carrying out things. Cupboards and chests were open; twice they had sent to the shop for cord, pieces of newspaper were tossing about on the floor. Two trunks, some bags and strapped-up rugs, had been carried down into the hall. The carriage and two hired cabs were waiting at the steps. Anna, forgetting her inward agitation in the work of packing, was standing at a table in her boudoir, packing her travelling-bag, when Annushka called her attention to the rattle of some carriage driving up. Anna looked out of window and saw Alexey Alexandrovitch's courier on the steps, ringing at the front door bell.

'Run and find out what it is,' she said, and with a calm sense of being prepared for anything, she sat down in a low chair, folding her hands on her knees. A footman brought in a thick packet directed in Alexey Alexandrovitch's hand.

'The courier has orders to wait for an answer,' he said.

'Very well,' she said, and as soon as he had left the room she tore open the letter with trembling fingers. A roll of unfolded notes done up in a wrapper fell out of it. She disengaged the letter and began reading it at the end. 'Preparations shall be made for your arrival here. . . . I attach particular significance to compliance . . .' she read. She ran on, then back, read it all through, and once more read the letter all though again from the beginning. When she had finished she felt that she was cold all over, and that a fearful calamity, such as she had not expected, had burst upon her.

In the morning she had regretted that she had spoken to her husband, and wished for nothing so much as that those words could be unspoken. And here this letter regarded them as unspoken, and gave her what she had wanted. But now this letter seemed to her more awful than anything she had been able to conceive.

'He's right!' she said; 'of course, he's always right; he's a Christian, he's generous! Yes, vile, base creature! And no one understands it except me, and no one ever will; and I can't explain it. They say he's so religious, so high-principled, so upright, so clever; but they don't see what I've seen. They don't know how he has crushed my life for eight years, crushed everything that was living in me—he has not once even thought that I'm a live woman who must have love. They don't know how at every step he's humiliated me, and been just as pleased with himself. Haven't I striven, striven with all my strength, to find something to give meaning to my life? Haven't I struggled to love him, to love my son when I could not love my husband? But the time came when I knew that I couldn't cheat myself any longer, that I was alive, that I was not to blame, that God has made me so that I must love and live. And now what does he do? If he'd killed me, if he'd killed him, I could have borne anything, I could have forgiven anything; but no, he . . . How was it I didn't guess what he would do? He's doing just what's characteristic of his mean character. He'll keep himself in the right, while me, in my ruin, he'll drive still lower to worse ruin yet. . . .'

She recalled the words from the letter. 'You can conjecture what awaits you and your son. . . .' 'That's a threat to take away my child, and most likely by their stupid law he can. But I know very well why he says it. He doesn't believe even in my love for my child, or he despises it (just as he always used to ridicule it). He despises that feeling in me, but he knows that I won't abandon my child, that I can't abandon my child, that there could be no life for me without my child, even with him whom I love; but that if I abandoned my child and ran away from him, I should be acting like the most infamous, basest of women. He knows that, and knows that I am incapable of doing that.'

She recalled another sentence in the letter. 'Our life must go on as it has done in the past. . . .' 'That life was miserable enough in old days; it has been awful of late. What will it be now? And he knows all that; he knows that I can't repent that I breathe, that I love; he knows that it can lead to nothing but lying and deceit; but he wants to go on torturing me. I know him; I know that he's at home and is happy in deceit, like a fish swimming in the water. No, I won't give him that happiness. I'll break through the spider-web of lies in which he wants to catch me, come what may. Anything's better than lying and deceit.'

'But how? My God! my God! Was ever a woman so miserable as I am? . . .'

'No; I will break through it, I will break through it!' she cried, jumping up and keeping back her tears. And she went to the writing-table to write him another letter. But at the bottom of her heart she felt that she was not strong enough to break through anything, that she was not strong enough to get out of her old position, however false and dishonourable it might be.

She sat down at the writing-table, but instead of writing she clasped her hands on the table, and, laying her head on them, burst into tears, with sobs and heaving breast like a child crying. She was weeping that her dream of her position being made clear and definite had been annihilated for ever. She knew beforehand that everything would go on in the old way, and far worse indeed than in the old way. She felt that the position in the world that she enjoyed, and that had seemed to her of so little consequence in the morning, that this position was precious to her, that she would not have the strength to exchange it for the shameful position of a woman who has abandoned husband and child to join her lover; that however much she might struggle, she could not be stronger than herself. She would never know freedom in love, but would remain for ever a guilty wife, with the menace of detection hanging over her at every instant; deceiving her husband for the sake of a shameful connection with a man living apart and away from her, whose life she could never share. She knew that this was how it would be, and at the same time it was so awful that she could not even conceive what it would end in. And she cried without restraint, as children cry when they are punished.

The sound of the footman's steps forced her to rouse herself, and, hiding her face from him, she pretended to be writing.

'The courier asks if there's an answer,' the footman announced.

'An answer? Yes,' said Anna. 'Let him wait. I'll ring.'

'What can I write?' she thought. 'What can I decide upon alone? What do I know? What do I want? What is there I care for?' Again she felt that her soul was beginning to be split in two. She was terrified again at this feeling, and clutched at the first pretext for doing something which might divert her thoughts from herself. 'I ought to see Alexey' (so she called Vronsky in her thoughts); 'no one but he can tell me what I ought to do. I'll go to Betsy's, perhaps I shall see him there,' she said to herself, completely forgetting that when she had told him the day before that she was not going to Princess Tverskoy's, he had said that in that case he should not go either. She went up to the table, wrote to her husband, 'I have received your letter.—A.'; and, ringing the bell, gave it to the footman.

'We are not going,' she said to Annushka, as she came in.

'Not going at all?'

'No; don't unpack till tomorrow, and let the carriage wait. I'm going to the princess's.'

'Which dress am I to get ready?'

XVII

THE croquet party to which the Princess Tverskoy had invited Anna was to consist of two ladies and their adorers. These two ladies were the chief representatives of a select new Petersburg circle, nicknamed, in imitation of some imitation, *les sept merveilles du monde*. These ladies belonged to a circle which, though of the highest society, was utterly hostile to that in which Anna moved. Moreover, Stremov, one of the most influential people in Petersburg, and the elderly admirer of Liza Merkalov, was Alexey Alexandrovitch's enemy in the political world. From all these considerations Anna had not meant to go, and the hints in Princess Tverskoy's note referred to her refusal. But now Anna was eager to go, in the hope of seeing Vronsky.

Anna arrived at Princess Tverskoy's earlier than the other guests.

At the same moment as she entered, Vronsky's footman, with side-whiskers combed out like a *kammer-yunker*, went in too. He stopped at the door, and, taking off his cap, let her pass. Anna recognised him, and only then recalled that Vronsky had told her the day before that he would not come. Most likely he was sending a note to say so.

As she took off her outer garment in the hall she heard the footman, pronouncing his '*r*'s' even like a *kammer-yunker*, say, 'From the count for the princess,' and hand the note.

She longed to question him as to where his master was. She longed to turn back and send him a letter to come and see her, or to go herself to see him. But neither the first nor the second nor the third course was possible. Already she heard bells ringing to announce her arrival ahead of her, and Princess Tverskoy's footman was standing at the open door waiting for her to go forward into the inner rooms.

'The princess is in the garden; they will inform her immediately. Would you be pleased to walk into the garden?' announced another footman in another room.

The position of uncertainty, of indecision, was still the same as at home—worse, in fact, since it was impossible to take any step, impossible to see Vronsky, and she had to remain here among outsiders, in company so uncongenial to her present mood. But she was wearing a dress that she knew suited her. She was not alone; all around was that luxurious setting of idleness that she was used to, and she felt less wretched than at home. She was not forced to think what she was to do. Everything would be done of itself. On meeting Betsy coming towards her in a white gown that struck her by its elegance, Anna smiled to her just as she always did. Princess Tverskoy was walking with Tushkevitch and a young lady, a relation, who, to the great joy of her parents in the provinces, was spending the summer with the fashionable princess.

There was probably something unusual about Anna, for Betsy noticed it at once.

'I slept badly,' answered Anna, looking intently at the footman who came to meet them, and, as she supposed, brought Vronsky's note.

'How glad I am you've come!' said Betsy. 'I'm tired, and was just longing to have some tea before they come. You might go'—she turned to Tushkevitch—'with Masha, and try the croquet-ground over there where they've been cutting it. We shall have time to talk a little over tea; we'll have a cosy chat, eh?' she said in English to Anna, with a smile, pressing the hand with which she held a parasol.

'Yes, especially as I can't stay very long with you. I'm forced to go on to old Madame Vrede. I've been promising to go for a century,' said Anna, to whom lying, alien as it was to her nature, had become not merely simple and natural in society, but a positive source of satisfaction. Why she said this, which she had not thought of a second before, she could not have explained. She had said it simply from the reflection that as Vronsky would not be here, she had better secure her own freedom, and try to see him somehow. But why she had spoken of old Madame Vrede, whom she had to go and see, as she had to see many other people, she could not have explained; and yet, as it afterwards turned out, had she contrived the most cunning devices to meet Vronsky, she could have thought of nothing better.

'No, I'm not going to let you go for anything,' answered Betsy, looking intently into Anna's face. 'Really, if I were not fond of you, I should feel offended. One would think you were afraid my society would compromise you. Tea in the little dining-room, please,' she said, half closing her eyes, as she always did when addressing the footman.

Taking the note from him, she read it.

'Alexey's playing us false,' she said in French; 'he writes that he can't come,' she added in a tone as simple and natural as though it could never enter her head that Vronsky could mean anything more to Anna than a game of croquet. Anna knew that Betsy knew everything, but, hearing how she spoke of Vronsky before her, she almost felt persuaded for a minute that she knew nothing.

'Ah!' said Anna indifferently, as though not greatly interested in the matter, and she went on smiling: 'How can you or your friends compromise any one?'

This playing with words, this hiding of a secret, had a great fascination for Anna, as, indeed, it has for all women. And it was not the necessity of concealment, not the aim with which the concealment was contrived, but the process of concealment itself attracted her.

'I can't be more Catholic than the Pope,' she said. 'Stremov and Liza Merkalov, why, they're the cream of the cream of society. Besides, they're received everywhere, and *I*'—she laid special stress on the I—'have never been strict and intolerant. It's simply that I haven't the time.'

'No; you don't care, perhaps, to meet Stremov? Let him and Alexey Alexandrovitch tilt at each other in the committee—that's no affair of ours. But in the world, he's the most amiable man I know, and a devoted croquet-player. You shall see. And, in spite of his absurd position as Liza's lovesick swain at his age, you ought to see how he carries off the absurd position. He's very nice. Sappho Shtoltz you don't know? Oh, that's a new type, quite new.'

Betsy said all this, and, at the same time, from her good-humoured, shrewd glance, Anna felt that she partly guessed her plight, and was hatching something for her benefit. They were in the little boudoir.

'I must write to Alexey though,' and Betsy sat down to the table, scribbled a few lines, and put the note in an envelope.

'I'm telling him to come to dinner. I've one lady extra to dinner with me, and no man to take her in. Look what I've said, will that persuade him? Excuse me, I must leave you for a minute. Would you seal it up, please, and send it off?' she said from the door; 'I have to give some directions.'

Without a moment's thought, Anna sat down to the table with Betsy's letter, and, without reading it, wrote below: 'It's essential for me to see you. Come to the Vrede garden. I shall be there at six o'clock.' She sealed it up, and, Betsy coming back, in her presence handed the note to be taken.

At tea, which was brought them on a little tea-table in the cool little drawing-room, the cosy chat promised by Princess Tverskoy before the arrival of her visitors really did come off between the two women. They criticised the people they were expecting, and the conversation fell upon Liza Merkalov.

'She's very sweet, and I always liked her,' said Anna.

'You ought to like her. She raves about you. Yesterday she came up to me after the races and was in despair at not finding you. She says you're a real heroine of romance, and that if she were a man she would do all sorts of mad things for your sake. Stremov says she does that as it is.'

'But do tell me, please, I never could make it out,' said Anna, after being silent for some time, speaking in a tone that showed she was not asking an idle question, but what she was asking was of more importance to her than it should have been: 'do tell me, please, what are her relations with Prince Kaluzhsky, Mishka, as he's called? I've met them so little. What does it mean?'

Betsy smiled with her eyes, and looked intently at Anna.

'It's a new manner,' she said. 'They've all adopted that manner. They've flung their caps over the windmills. But there are ways and ways of flinging them.'

'Yes, but what are her relations precisely with Kaluzhsky?'

Betsy broke into unexpectedly mirthful and irrepressible laughter, a thing which rarely happened with her.

'You're encroaching on Princess Myaky's special domain now. That's the question of an *enfant terrible*,' and Betsy obviously tried to restrain herself, but could not, and went off into peals of that infectious laughter that people laugh who do not laugh often. 'You'd better ask them,' she brought out, between tears of laughter.

'No; you laugh,' said Anna, laughing too in spite of herself, 'but I never could understand it. I can't understand the husband's rôle in it.'

'The husband? Liza Merkalov's husband carries her shawl, and is always ready to be of use. But anything more than that in reality, no one cares to inquire. You know in decent society one doesn't talk or think even of certain details of the toilet. That's how it is with this.'

'Will you be at Madame Rolandak's fête?' asked Anna, to change the conversation.

'I don't think so,' answered Betsy, and, without looking at her friend, she began filling the little transparent cups with fragrant tea. Putting a cup before Anna, she took out a cigarette, and, fitting it into a silver holder, she lighted it.

'It's like this, you see: I'm in a fortunate position,' she began, quite serious now, as she took up her cup, 'I understand you, and I understand Liza. Liza now is one of those naïve natures that, like children, don't know what's good and what's bad. Anyway, she didn't comprehend it when she was very young. And now she's aware that the lack of comprehension suits her. Now, perhaps, she doesn't know on purpose,' said Betsy, with a subtle smile. 'But, anyway, it suits her. The very same thing, don't you see, may be looked at tragically, and turned into a misery, or it may be looked at simply and even humorously. Possibly you are inclined to look at things too tragically.'

'How I should like to know other people just as I know myself!' said Anna, seriously and dreamily. 'Am I worse than other people, or better? I think I'm worse.'

'*Enfant terrible, enfant terrible!*' repeated Betsy. 'But here they are.'

XVIII

THEY heard the sound of steps and a man's voice, then a woman's voice and laughter, and immediately thereafter there walked in the expected guests: Sappho Shtoltz, and a young man beaming with excess of health, the so-called Vaska. It was evident that ample supplies of beefsteak, truffles, and Burgundy never failed to reach him at the fitting hour. Vaska bowed to the two ladies, and glanced at them, but only for one second. He walked after Sappho into the drawing-room, and followed her about as though he were chained to her, keeping his sparkling eyes fixed on her as though he wanted to eat her. Sappho Shtoltz was a blonde beauty with black eyes. She walked with smart little steps in high-heeled shoes, and shook hands with the ladies vigorously like a man.

Anna had never met this new star of fashion, and was struck by her beauty, the exaggerated extreme to which her dress was carried, and the boldness of her manners. On her head there was such a superstructure of soft, golden hair—her own and false mixed—that her head was equal in size to the elegantly rounded bust, of which so much was exposed in front. The impulsive abruptness of her movements was such that at every step the lines of her knees and the upper part of her legs were distinctly marked under her dress, and the question involuntarily rose to the mind where in the undulating, piled-up mountain of material at the back the real body of the woman, so small and slender, so naked in front, and so hidden behind and below, really came to an end.

Betsy made haste to introduce her to Anna.

'Only fancy, we all but ran over two soldiers,' she began telling them at once, using her eyes, smiling and twitching away her tail, which she flung back at one stroke all on one side. 'I drove here with Vaska. . . . Ah, to be sure, you don't know each other.' And mentioning his surname she introduced the young man, and reddening a little, broke into a ringing laugh at her mistake—that is, at her having called him Vaska to a stranger. Vaska bowed once more to Anna, but he said nothing to her. He addressed Sappho: 'You've lost your bet. We got here first. Pay up,' said he, smiling.

Sappho laughed still more festively.

'Not just now,' said she.

'Oh, all right, I'll have it later.'

'Very well, very well. Oh yes.' She turned suddenly to Princess Betsy: 'I am a nice person . . . I positively forgot it . . . I've brought you a visitor. And here he comes.' The unexpected young visitor, whom Sappho had invited, and whom she had forgotten, was, however, a personage of such consequence that, in spite of his youth, both the ladies rose on his entrance.

He was a new admirer of Sappho's. He now dogged her footsteps, like Vaska.

Soon after Prince Kaluzhsky arrived, and Liza Merkalov with Stremov. Liza Merkalov was a thin brunette, with an Oriental, languid type of face, and—as everyone used to say—exquisite enigmatic eyes. The tone of her dark dress (Anna immediately observed and appreciated the fact) was in perfect harmony with her style of beauty. Liza was as soft and enervated as Sappho was smart and abrupt.

But to Anna's taste Liza was far more attractive. Betsy had said to Anna that she had adopted the pose of an innocent child, but when Anna saw her, she felt that this was not the truth. She really was both innocent and corrupt, but a sweet and passive woman. It is true that her tone was the same as Sappho's; that like Sappho she had two men, one young and one old, tacked on to her, and devouring her with their eyes. But there was something in her higher than what surrounded her. There was in her the glow of the real diamond among glass imitations. This glow shone out in her exquisite, truly enigmatic eyes. The weary, and at the same time passionate, glance of those eyes, encircled by dark rings, impressed one by its perfect sincerity. Everyone looking into those eyes fancied he knew her wholly, and knowing her, could not but love her. At the sight of Anna her whole face lighted up at once with a smile of delight.

'Ah, how glad I am to see you!' she said, going up to her. 'Yesterday at the races all I wanted was to get to you, but you'd gone away. I did so want to see you, yesterday especially. Wasn't it awful?' she said, looking at Anna with eyes that seemed to lay bare all her soul.

'Yes; I had no idea it would be so thrilling,' said Anna, blushing.

The company got up at this moment to go into the garden.

'I'm not going,' said Liza, smiling and settling herself close to Anna. 'You won't go either, will you? Who wants to play croquet?'

'Oh, I like it,' said Anna.

'There, how do you manage never to be bored by things? It's delightful to look at you. You're alive, but I'm bored.'

'How can you be bored? Why, you live in the liveliest set in Petersburg,' said Anna.

'Possibly the people who are not of our set are even more bored; but we—I certainly—are not happy, but awfully, awfully bored.'

Sappho smoking a cigarette went off into the garden with the two young men. Betsy and Stremov remained at the tea-table.

'What, bored!' said Betsy. 'Sappho says they did enjoy themselves tremendously at your house last night.'

'Ah, how dreary it all was!' said Liza Merkalov. 'We all drove back to my place after the races. And always the same people, always all the same. Always the same thing. We lounged about on sofas all the evening. What is there to enjoy in that? No: do tell me how you manage never to be bored?' she said, addressing Anna again. 'One has but to look at you and one sees, here's a woman who may be happy or unhappy, but isn't bored. Tell me how you do it?'

'I do nothing,' answered Anna, blushing at these searching questions.

'That's the best way,' Stremov put in. Stremov was a man of fifty, partly grey, but still vigorous-looking, very ugly, but with a characteristic and intelligent face. Liza Merkalov was his wife's niece, and he spent all his leisure hours with her. On meeting Anna Karenin, as he was Alexey Alexandrovitch's enemy in the government, he tried, like a shrewd man and a man of the world, to be particularly cordial with her, the wife of his enemy.

'"Nothing,"' he put in with a subtle smile, 'that's the very best way. I told you long ago,' he said, turning to Liza Merkalov, 'that if you don't want to be bored, you mustn't think you're going to be bored. It's just as you mustn't be afraid of not being able to fall asleep, if you're afraid of sleeplessness. That's just what Anna Arkadyevna has just said.'

'I should be very glad if I had said it, for it's not only clever but true,' said Anna, smiling.

'No, do tell me why is it one can't go to sleep, and one can't help being bored?'

'To sleep well one ought to work, and to enjoy oneself one ought to work too.'

'What am I to work for when my work is no use to anybody? And I can't and won't knowingly make a pretence about it.'

'You're incorrigible,' said Stremov, not looking at her, and he spoke again to Anna. As he rarely met Anna, he could say nothing but commonplaces to her, but he said those commonplaces as to when she was returning to Petersburg, and how fond Countess Lidia Ivanovna was of her, with an expression which suggested that he longed with his whole soul to please her and show his regard for her and even more than that.

Tushkevitch came in, announcing that the party were awaiting the other players to begin croquet.

'No, don't go away, please don't,' pleaded Liza Merkalov, hearing that Anna was going. Stremov joined in her entreaties.

'It's too violent a transition,' he said, 'to go from such company to old Madame Vrede. And besides, you will only give her a chance for talking scandal, while here you arouse none but such different feelings of the highest and most opposite kind,' he said to her.

Anna pondered for an instant in uncertainty. This shrewd man's flattering words, the naïve, child-like affection shown her by Liza Merkalov, and all the social atmosphere she was used to,—it was all so easy, and what was in store for her was so difficult, that she was for a minute in uncertainty whether to remain, whether to put off a little longer the painful moment of explanation. But remembering what was in store for her alone at home, if she did not come to some decision, remembering that gesture—terrible even in memory—when she had clutched her hair in both hands—she said good-bye and went away.

XIX

In spite of Vronsky's apparently frivolous life in society, he was a man who hated irregularity. In early youth in the Corps of Pages, he had experienced the humiliation of a refusal, when he had tried, being in difficulties, to borrow money, and since then he had never once put himself in the same position again.

In order to keep his affairs in some sort of order, he used about five times a year (more or less frequently, according to circumstances) to shut himself up alone and put all his affairs into definite shape. This he used to call his day of reckoning or *faire la lessive*.

On waking up the day after the races, Vronsky put on a white linen coat, and without shaving or taking his bath, he distributed about the table moneys, bills, and letters, and set to work. Petritsky, who knew he was ill-tempered on such occasions, on waking up and seeing his comrade at the writing-table, quietly dressed and went out without getting in his way.

Every man, who knows to the minutest details all the complexity of the conditions surrounding him, cannot help imagining that the complexity of these conditions, and the difficulty of making them clear, is something exceptional and personal, peculiar to himself, and never supposes that others are surrounded by just as complicated an array of personal affairs as he is. So indeed it seemed to Vronsky. And not without inward pride, and not without reason, he thought that any other man would long ago have been in difficulties, and would have been forced to some dishonourable course, if he had found himself in such a difficult position. But Vronsky felt that now especially it was essential for him to clear up and define his position if he were to avoid getting into difficulties.

What Vronsky attacked first as being the easiest was his pecuniary position. Writing out on notepaper in his minute hand all that he owed, he added up the amount and found that his debts amounted to seventeen thousand and some odd hundreds, which he left out for the sake of clearness. Reckoning up his money and his bank-book, he found that he had left one thousand eight hundred roubles, and nothing coming in before the New Year. Reckoning over again his list of debts, Vronsky copied it, dividing it into three classes. In the first class he put the debts which he would have to pay at once, or for which he must in any case have the money ready so that on demand for payment there could not be a moment's delay in paying. Such debts amounted to about four thousand: one thousand five hundred for a horse, and two thousand five hundred as surety for a young comrade, Venovsky, who had lost that sum to a cardsharper in Vronsky's presence. Vronsky had wanted to pay the money at the time (he had that amount then), but Venovsky and Yashvin had insisted that they would pay and not Vronsky, who had not played. That was so far well, but Vronsky knew that in this dirty business, though his only share in it was undertaking by word of mouth to be surety for Venovsky, it was absolutely necessary for him to have the two thousand five hundred roubles so as to be able to fling it at the swindler, and have no more words with him. And so for this first and most important division he must have four thousand roubles. The second class—eight thousand roubles—consisted of less important debts.

These were principally accounts owing in connection with his race-horses, to the purveyor of oats and hay, the English saddler, and so on. He would have to pay some two thousand roubles on these debts too, in order to be quite free from anxiety. The last class of debts—to shops, to hotels, to his tailor—were such as need not be considered. So that he needed at least six thousand roubles for current expenses, and he only had one thousand eight hundred. For a man with one hundred thousand roubles of revenue, which was what everyone fixed as Vronsky's income, such debts, one would suppose, could hardly be embarrassing; but the fact was that he was far from having one hundred thousand. His father's immense property, which alone yielded a yearly income of two hundred thousand, was left undivided between the brothers. At the time when the elder brother, with a mass of debts, married Princess Varya Tchirkov, the daughter of a Decembrist without any fortune whatever, Alexey had given up his elder brother almost the whole income from his father's estate, reserving for himself only twenty-five thousand a year from it. Alexey had said at the time to his brother that that sum would be sufficient for him till he married, which he probably never would do. And his brother, who was in command of one of the most expensive regiments, and was only just married, could not decline the gift. His mother, who had her own separate property, had allowed Alexey every year twenty thousand in addition to the twenty-five thousand he had reserved, and Alexey had spent it all. Of late his mother, incensed with him on account of his love-affair and his leaving Moscow, had given up sending him the money. And in consequence of this, Vronsky, who had been in the habit of living on the scale of forty-five thousand a year, having only received twenty thousand that year, found himself now in difficulties. To get out of these difficulties, he could not apply to his mother for money. Her last letter, which he had received the day before, had particularly exasperated him by the hints in it that she was quite ready to help him to succeed in the world and in the army, but not to lead a life which was a scandal to all good society. His mother's attempt to buy him stung him to the quick, and made him feel colder than ever to her. But he could not draw back from a generous word when it was once uttered, even though he felt now, vaguely foreseeing certain eventualities in his intrigue with Madame Karenin, that this generous word had been spoken thoughtlessly, and that even though he were not married he might need all the hundred thousand of income. But it was impossible to draw back. He had only to recall his brother's wife, to remember how that sweet, delightful Varya sought, at every convenient opportunity, to remind him that she remembered his generosity and appreciated it, to grasp the impossibility of taking back his gift. It was as impossible as beating a woman, stealing, or lying. One thing only could and ought to be done, and Vronsky determined upon it without an instant's hesitation: to borrow money from a money-lender, ten thousand roubles, a proceeding which presented no difficulty, to cut down his expenses generally, and to sell his race-horses. Resolving on this, he promptly wrote a note to Rolandak, who had more than once sent to him with offers to buy horses from him. Then he sent for the Englishman and the money-lender, and divided what money he had according to the accounts he intended to pay. Having finished this business, he wrote a cold and cutting answer to his mother. Then he took out of his notebook three notes of Anna's, read them again, burned them, and remembering their conversation on the previous day, he sank into meditation.

XX

VRONSKY'S life was particularly happy in that he had a code of principles, which defined with unfailing certitude what he ought and what he ought not to do. This code of principles covered only a very small circle of contingencies, but then the principles were never doubtful, and Vronsky, as he never went outside that circle, had never had a moment's hesitation about doing what he ought to do. These principles laid down as invariable rules: that one must pay a cardsharper, but need not pay a tailor; that one must never tell a lie to a man, but one may to a woman; that one must never cheat anyone, but one may a husband; that one must never pardon an insult, but one may give one and so on. These principles were possibly not reasonable and not good, but they were of unfailing certainty, and as long as he adhered to them, Vronsky felt that his heart was at peace and he could hold his head up. Only quite lately in regard to his relations with Anna, Vronsky had begun to feel that his code of principles did not fully cover all possible contingencies, and to foresee in the future difficulties and perplexities for which he could find no guiding clue.

His present relation to Anna and to her husband was to his mind clear and simple. It was clearly and precisely defined in the code of principles by which he was guided.

She was an honourable woman who had bestowed her love upon him, and he loved her, and therefore she was in his eyes a woman who had a right to the same, or even more, respect than a lawful wife. He would have had his hand chopped off before he would have allowed himself by a word, by a hint, to humiliate her, or even to fall short of the fullest respect a woman could look for.

His attitude to society, too, was clear. Everyone might know, might suspect it, but no one might dare to speak of it. If any did so, he was ready to force all who might speak to be silent and to respect the non-existent honour of the woman he loved.

His attitude to the husband was the clearest of all. From the moment that Anna loved Vronsky, he had regarded his own right over her as the one thing unassailable. Her husband was simply a superfluous and tiresome person. No doubt he was in a pitiable position, but how could that be helped? The one thing the husband had a right to was to demand satisfaction with a weapon in his hand, and Vronsky was prepared for this at any minute.

But of late new inner relations had arisen between him and her, which frightened Vronsky by their indefiniteness. Only the day before she had told him that she was with child. And he felt that this fact and what she expected of him called for something not fully defined in that code of principles by which he had hitherto steered his course of life. And he had been indeed caught unawares, and at the first moment when she spoke to him of her position, his heart had prompted him to beg her to leave her husband. He had said that, but now thinking things over he saw clearly that it would be better to manage to avoid that; and at the same time, as he told himself so, he was afraid whether it was not wrong.

'If I told her to leave her husband, that must mean uniting her life with mine: am I prepared for that? How can I take her away now, when I have no money? Supposing I could arrange . . . But how can I take her away while I'm in the service? If I say that—I ought to be prepared to do it, that is, I ought to have the money and to retire from the army.'

And he grew thoughtful. The question whether to retire from the service or not brought him to the other and perhaps the chief though hidden interest of his life, of which none knew but he.

Ambition was the old dream of his youth and childhood, a dream which he did not confess even to himself, though it was so strong that now this passion was even doing battle with his love. His first steps in the world and in the service had been successful, but two years before he had made a great mistake. Anxious to show his independence and to advance, he had refused a post that had been offered him, hoping that this refusal would heighten his value; but it turned out that he had been too bold, and he was passed over. And having, whether he liked or not, taken up for himself the position of an independent man, he carried it off with great tact and good sense, behaving as though he bore no grudge against anyone, did not regard himself as injured in any way, and cared for nothing but to be left alone since he was enjoying himself. In reality he had ceased to enjoy himself as long ago as the year before, when he went away to Moscow. He felt that this independent attitude of a man who might have done anything, but cared to do nothing, was already beginning to pall, that many people were beginning to fancy that he was not really capable of anything but being a straightforward, good-natured fellow. His connection with Madame Karenin, by creating so much sensation and attracting general attention, had given him a fresh distinction which soothed his gnawing worm of ambition for a while, but a week before that worm had been roused up again with fresh force. The friend of his childhood, a man of the same set, of the same coterie, his comrade in the Corps of Pages, Serpuhovskoy, who had left school with him and had been his rival in class, in gymnastics, in their scrapes and their dreams of glory, had come back a few days before from Central Asia, where he had gained two steps up in rank, and an order rarely bestowed upon generals so young.

As soon as he arrived in Petersburg, people began to talk about him as a newly risen star of the first magnitude. A schoolfellow of Vronsky's and of the same age, he was a general and was expecting a command, which might have influence on the course of political events; while Vronsky, independent and brilliant and beloved by a charming woman though he was, was simply a cavalry captain who was readily allowed to be as independent as ever he liked. 'Of course I don't envy Serpuhovskoy and never could envy him; but his advancement shows me that one has only to watch one's opportunity, and the career of a man like me may be very rapidly made. Three years ago he was in just the same position as I am. If I retire, I burn my ships. If I remain in the army, I lose nothing. She said herself she did not wish to change her position. And with her love I cannot feel envious of Serpuhovskoy.' And slowly twirling his moustaches, he got up from the table and walked about the room. His eyes shone particularly brightly, and he felt in that confident, calm, and happy frame of mind which always came after he had thoroughly faced his position. Everything was straight and clear, just as after former days of reckoning. He shaved, took a cold bath, dressed and went out.

XXI

'I'VE come to fetch you. Your *lessive* lasted a good time today,' said Petritsky. 'Well, is it over?'

'It is over,' answered Vronsky, smiling with his eyes only, and twirling the tips of his moustaches as circumspectly as though after the perfect order into which his affairs had been brought any over-bold or rapid movement might disturb it.

'You're always just as if you'd come out of a bath after it,' said Petritsky. 'I've come from Gritsky's' (that was what they called the colonel); 'they're expecting you.'

Vronsky, without answering, looked at his comrade, thinking of something else.

'Yes; is that music at his place?' he said, listening to the familiar sounds of polkas and waltzes floating across to him. 'What's the fête?'

'Serpuhovskoy's come.'

'Aha!' said Vronsky, 'why, I didn't know.'

The smile in his eyes gleamed more brightly than ever.

Having once made up his mind that he was happy in his love, that he sacrificed his ambition to it—having anyway taken up this position, Vronsky was incapable of feeling either envious of Serpuhovskoy or hurt with him for not coming first to him when he came to the regiment. Serpuhovskoy was a good friend, and he was delighted he had come.

'Ah, I'm very glad!'

The colonel, Demin, had taken a large country house. The whole party were in the wide lower balcony. In the courtyard the first objects that met Vronsky's eyes were a band of singers in white linen coats, standing near a barrel of vodka, and the robust, good-humoured figure of the colonel surrounded by officers. He had gone out as far as the first step of the balcony and was loudly shouting across the band that played Offenbach's quadrille, waving his arms and giving some orders to a few soldiers standing on one side. A group of soldiers, a quartermaster, and several subalterns came up to the balcony with Vronsky. The colonel returned to the table, went out again on to the steps with a tumbler in his hand, and proposed the toast, 'To the health of our former comrade, the gallant general, Prince Serpuhovskoy. Hurrah!'

The colonel was followed by Serpuhovskoy, who came out on to the steps smiling, with a glass in his hand.

'You always get younger, Bondarenko,' he said to the rosy-cheeked, smart-looking quartermaster standing just before him, still youngish-looking though doing his second term of service.

It was three years since Vronsky had seen Serpuhovskoy. He looked more robust, had let his whiskers grow, but was still the same graceful creature, whose face and figure were even more striking from their softness and nobility than their beauty. The only change Vronsky detected in him was that subdued, continual radiance of beaming content which settles on the faces of men who are successful and are sure of the recognition of their success by everyone. Vronsky knew that radiant air, and immediately observed it in Serpuhovskoy.

As Serpuhovskoy came down the steps he saw Vronsky. A smile of pleasure lighted up his face. He tossed his head upwards and waved the glass in his hand, greeting Vronsky, and showing him by the gesture that he could not come to him before the quartermaster, who stood craning forward his lips ready to be kissed.

'Here he is!' shouted the colonel. 'Yashvin told me you were in one of your gloomy tempers.'

Serpuhovskoy kissed the moist, fresh lips of the gallant-looking quartermaster, and wiping his mouth with his handkerchief, went up to Vronsky.

'How glad I am!' he said, squeezing his hand and drawing him on one side.

'You look after him,' the colonel shouted to Yashvin, pointing to Vronsky; and he went down below to the soldiers.

'Why weren't you at the races yesterday? I expected to see you there,' said Vronsky, scrutinising Serpuhovskoy.

'I did go, but late. I beg your pardon,' he added, and he turned to the adjutant: 'Please have this divided from me, each man as much as it runs to.' And he hurriedly took notes for three hundred roubles from his pocket-book, blushing a little.

'Vronsky! Have anything to eat or drink?' asked Yashvin. 'Hi, something for the count to eat! Ah, here it is: have a glass!'

The fête at the colonel's lasted a long while. There was a great deal of drinking. They tossed Serpuhovskoy in the air and caught him again several times. Then they did the same to the colonel. Then, to the accompaniment of the band, the colonel himself danced with Petritsky. Then the colonel, who began to show signs of feebleness, sat down on a bench in the courtyard and began demonstrating to Yashvin the superiority of Russia over Prussia, especially in cavalry attack, and there was a lull in the revelry for the moment. Serpuhovskoy went into the house to the bathroom to wash his hands, and found Vronsky there: Vronsky was drenching his head with water. He had taken off his coat and put his sunburnt, hairy neck under the tap, and was rubbing it and his head with his hands. When he had finished, Vronsky sat down by Serpuhovskoy. They both sat down in the bathroom on a lounge, and a conversation began which was very interesting to both of them.

'I've always been hearing about you through my wife,' said Serpuhovskoy. 'I'm glad you've been seeing her pretty often.'

'She's friendly with Varya, and they're the only women in Petersburg I care about seeing,' answered Vronsky, smiling. He smiled because he foresaw the topic the conversation would turn on, and he was glad of it.

'The only ones?' Serpuhovskoy queried, smiling.

'Yes; and I heard news of you, but not only through your wife,' said Vronsky, checking his hint by a stern expression of face. 'I was greatly delighted to hear of your success, but not a bit surprised. I expected even more.'

Serpuhovskoy smiled. Such an opinion of him was obviously agreeable to him, and he did not think it necessary to conceal it.

'Well, I on the contrary expected less—I'll own frankly. But I'm glad, very glad. I'm ambitious; that's my weakness, and I confess to it.'

'Perhaps you wouldn't confess to it if you hadn't been successful,' said Vronsky.

'I don't suppose so,' said Serpuhovskoy, smiling again. 'I won't say life wouldn't be worth living without it, but it would be dull. Of course I may be mistaken, but I fancy I have a certain capacity for the line I've chosen, and that power of any sort in my hands, if it is to be, will be better than in the hands of a good many people I know,' said Serpuhovskoy, with beaming consciousness of success; 'and so the nearer I get to it, the better pleased I am.'

'Perhaps that is true for you, but not for everyone. I used to think so too, but here I live and think life worth living not only for that.'

'There it's out! here it comes!' said Serpuhovskoy laughing. 'Ever since I heard about you, about your refusal, I began . . . Of course, I approved of what you did. But there are ways of doing everything. And I think your action was good in itself, but you didn't do it quite in the way you ought to have done.'

'What's done can't be undone, and you know I never go back on what I've done. And besides, I'm very well off.'

'Very well off—for the time. But you're not satisfied with that. I wouldn't say this to your brother. He's a nice child, like our host here. There he goes!' he added, listening to the roar of 'hurrah!'—'and he's happy, that does not satisfy you.'

'I didn't say it did satisfy me.'

'Yes, but that's not the only thing. Such men as you are wanted.'

'By whom?'

'By whom? By society, by Russia. Russia needs men; she needs a party, or else everything goes and will go to the dogs.'

'How do you mean? Bertenev's party against the Russian communists?'

'No,' said Serpuhovskoy, frowning with vexation at being suspected of such an absurdity. '*Tout ça est une blague*. That's always been and always will be. There are no communists. But intriguing people have to invent a noxious, dangerous party. It's an old trick. No, what's wanted is a powerful party of independent men like you and me.'

'But why so?' Vronsky mentioned a few men who were in power. 'Why aren't they independent men?'

'Simply because they have not, or have not had from birth, an independent fortune; they've not had a name, they've not been close to the sun and centre as we have. They can be bought either by money or by favour. And they have to find a support for themselves in inventing a policy. And they bring forward some notion, some policy that they don't believe in, that does harm; and the whole policy is really only a means to a government house and so much income. *Cela n'est pas plus fin que ça*, when you get a peep at their cards. I may be inferior to them, stupider perhaps, though I don't see why I should be inferior to them. But you and I have one important advantage over them for certain, in being more difficult to buy. And such men are more needed than ever.'

Vronsky listened attentively, but he was not so much interested by the meaning of the words as by the attitude of Serpuhovskoy, who was already contemplating a struggle with the existing powers, and already had his likes and dislikes in that higher world, while his own interest in the governing world did not go beyond the interests of his regiment. Vronsky felt, too, how powerful Serpuhovskoy might become through his unmistakable faculty for thinking things out and for taking things in, through his intelligence and gift of words, so rarely met with in the world in which he moved. And, ashamed as he was of the feeling, he felt envious.

'Still I haven't the one thing of most importance for that,' he answered; 'I haven't the desire for power. I had it once, but it's gone.'

'Excuse me, that's not true,' said Serpuhovskoy smiling.

'Yes, it is true, it is true . . . now!' Vronsky added, to be truthful.

'Yes, it's true now, that's another thing; but that *now* won't last for ever.'

'Perhaps,' answered Vronsky.

'You say *perhaps*,' Serpuhovskoy went on, as though guessing his thoughts, 'but I say *for certain*. And that's what I wanted to see you for. Your action was just what it should have been. I see that, but you ought not to keep it up. I only ask you to give me *carte blanche*. I'm not going to offer you my protection . . . though, indeed, why shouldn't I protect you?—you've protected me often enough! I should hope our friendship rises above all that sort of thing. Yes,' he said, smiling to him as tenderly as a woman, 'give me *carte blanche*, retire from the regiment, and I'll draw you upwards imperceptibly.'

'But you must understand that I want nothing,' said Vronsky, 'except that all should be as it is.'

Serpuhovskoy got up and stood facing him.

'You say that all should be as it is. I understand what that means. But listen: we're the same age, you've known a greater number of women perhaps than I have.' Serpuhovskoy's smile and gestures told Vronsky that he mustn't be afraid, that he would be tender and careful in touching the sore place. 'But I'm married, and believe me, in getting to know thoroughly one's wife, if one loves her, as some one has said, one gets to know all women better than if one knew thousands of them.'

'We're coming directly!' Vronsky shouted to an officer, who looked into the room and called them to the colonel.

Vronsky was longing now to hear to the end and know what Serpuhovskoy would say to him.

'And here's my opinion for you. Women are the chief stumbling-block in a man's career. It's hard to love a woman and do anything. There's only one way of having love conveniently without its being a hindrance—that's marriage. How, how am I to tell you what I mean?' said Serpuhovskoy, who liked similes. 'Wait a minute, wait a minute! Yes, just as you can only carry a *fardeau* and do something with your hands, when the *fardeau* is tied on your back, and that's marriage. And that's what I felt when I was married. My hands were suddenly set free. But to drag that *fardeau* about with you without marriage, your hands will always be so full that you can do nothing. Look at Mazankov, at Krupov. They've ruined their careers for the sake of women.'

'What women!' said Vronsky, recalling the Frenchwoman and the actress with whom the two men he had mentioned were connected.

'The firmer the woman's footing in society, the worse it is. That's much the same as—not merely carrying the *fardeau* in your arms—but tearing it away from someone else.'

'You have never loved,' Vronsky said softly, looking straight before him and thinking of Anna.

'Perhaps. But you remember what I've said to you. And another thing, women are all more materialistic than men. We make something immense out of love, but they are always *terre-à-terre*.'

'Directly, directly!' he cried to a footman who came in. But the footman had not come to call them again, as he supposed. The footman brought Vronsky a note.

'A man brought it from Princess Tverskoy.'

Vronsky opened the letter, and flushed crimson.

'My head's begun to ache; I'm going home,' he said to Serpuhovskoy.

'Oh, good-bye then. You give me *carte blanche*!'

'We'll talk about it later on; I'll look you up in Petersburg.'

XXII

IT was six o'clock already, and so, in order to be there quickly, and at the same time not to drive with his own horse, known to everyone, Vronsky got into Yashvin's hired fly, and told the driver to drive as quickly as possible. It was a roomy, old-fashioned fly, with seats for four. He sat in one corner, stretched his legs out on the front seat, and sank into meditation.

A vague sense of the order into which his affairs had been brought, a vague recollection of the friendliness and flattery of Serpuhovskoy, who had considered him a man that was needed, and most of all, the anticipation of the interview before him—all blended into a general, joyous sense of life. This feeling was so strong that he could not help smiling. He dropped his legs, crossed one leg over the other knee, and taking it in his hand, felt the springy muscle of the calf, where it had been grazed the day before by his fall, and leaning back, he drew several deep breaths.

'I'm happy, very happy!' he said to himself. He had often before had this sense of physical joy in his own body, but he had never felt so fond of himself, of his own body, as at that moment. He enjoyed the slight ache in his strong leg, he enjoyed the muscular sensation of movement in his chest as he breathed. The bright, cold August day, which had made Anna feel so hopeless, seemed to him keenly stimulating, and refreshed his face and neck that still tingled from the cold water. The scent of brilliantine on his whiskers struck him as particularly pleasant in the fresh air. Everything he saw from the carriage-window, everything in that cold pure air, in the pale light of the sunset, was as fresh, and gay, and strong as he was himself: the roofs of the houses shining in the rays of the setting sun, the sharp outlines of fences and angles of buildings, the figures of passers-by, the carriages that met him now and then, the motionless green of the trees and grass, the fields with evenly drawn furrows of potatoes, and the slanting shadows that fell from the houses, and trees, and bushes, and even from the rows of potatoes—everything was bright like a pretty landscape just finished and freshly varnished.

'Get on, get on!' he said to the driver, putting his head out of the window, and pulling a three-rouble note out of his pocket he handed it to the man as he looked round. The driver's hand fumbled with something at the lamp, the whip cracked, and the carriage rolled rapidly along the smooth high-road.

'I want nothing, nothing but this happiness,' he thought, staring at the bone button of the bell in the space between the windows, and picturing to himself Anna just as he had seen her last time. 'And so I go on, I love her more and more. Here's the garden of the Vrede Villa. Whereabouts will she be? Where? How? Why did she fix on this place to meet me, and why does she write in Betsy's letter?' he thought, wondering now for the first time at it. But there was now no time for wonder. He called to the driver to stop before reaching the avenue, and opening the door, jumped out of the carriage as it was moving, and went into the avenue that led up to the house. There was no one in the avenue; but looking round to the right he caught sight of her. Her face was hidden by a veil, but he drank in with glad eyes the special movement in walking, peculiar to her alone, the slope of the shoulders, and the setting of the head, and at once a sort of electric shock ran all over him. With fresh force, he felt conscious of himself from the springy motions of his legs to the movement of his lungs as he breathed, and something set his lips twitching.

Joining him, she pressed his hand tightly.

'You're not angry that I sent for you? I absolutely had to see you,' she said; and the serious and set line of her lips, which he saw under the veil, transformed his mood at once.

'I angry! But how have you come, where from?'

'Never mind,' she said, laying her hand on his, 'come along, I must talk to you.'

He saw that something had happened, and that the interview would not be a joyous one. In her presence he had no will of his own: without knowing the grounds of her distress, he already felt the same distress unconsciously passing over him.

'What is it? what?' he asked her, squeezing her hand with his elbow, and trying to read her thoughts in her face.

She walked on a few steps in silence, gathering up her courage; then suddenly she stopped.

'I did not tell you yesterday,' she began, breathing quickly and painfully, 'that coming home with Alexey Alexandrovitch I told him everything . . . told him I could not be his wife, that . . . and told him everything.'

He heard her, unconsciously bending his whole figure down to her as though hoping in this way to soften the hardness of her position for her. But directly she had said this he suddenly drew himself up, and a proud and hard expression came over his face.

'Yes, yes, that's better, a thousand times better! I know how painful it was,' he said. But she was not listening to his words, she was reading his thoughts from the expression of his face. She could not guess that that expression arose from the first idea that presented itself to Vronsky—that a duel was now inevitable. The idea of a duel had never crossed her mind, and so she put a different interpretation on this passing expression of hardness.

When she got her husband's letter, she knew then at the bottom of her heart that everything would go on in the old way, that she would not have the strength of will to forego her position, to abandon her son, and to join her lover. The morning spent at Princess Tverskoy's had confirmed her still more in this. But this interview was still of the utmost gravity for her. She hoped that this interview would transform her position, and save her. If on hearing this news he were to say to her resolutely, passionately, without an instant's wavering: 'Throw up everything and come with me!' she would give up her son and go away with him. But this news had not produced what she had expected in him; he simply seemed as though he were resenting some affront.

'It was not in the least painful for me. It happened of itself,' she said irritably; 'and see . . .' She pulled her husband's letter out of her glove.

'I understand, I understand,' he interrupted her, taking the letter, but not reading it, and trying to soothe her. 'The one thing I longed for, the one thing I prayed for, was to cut short this position, so as to devote my life to your happiness.'

'Why do you tell me that?' she said. 'Do you suppose I can doubt it? If I doubted . . .'

'Who's that coming?' said Vronsky suddenly pointing to two ladies walking towards them. 'Perhaps they know us!' and he hurriedly turned off, drawing her after him into a side path.

'Oh, I don't care!' she said. Her lips were quivering. And he fancied that her eyes looked with strange fury at him from under the veil. 'I tell you that's not the point—I can't doubt that; but see what he writes to me. Read it.' She stood still again.

Again, just as at the first moment of hearing of her rupture with her husband, Vronsky, on reading the letter, was unconsciously carried away by the natural sensation aroused in him by his own relation to the betrayed husband. Now while he held his letter in his hands, he could not help picturing the challenge, which he would not likely find at home today or tomorrow, and the duel itself, in which, with the same cold and haughty expression that his face was assuming at this moment, he would await the injured husband's shot, after having himself fired into the air. And at that instant there flashed across his mind the thought of what Serpuhovskoy had just said to him, and what he had himself been thinking in the morning—that it was better not to bind himself—and he knew that this thought he could not tell her.

Having read the letter, he raised his eyes to her, and there was no determination in them. She saw at once that he had been thinking about it before by himself. She knew that whatever he might say to her, he would not say all he thought. And she knew that her last hope had failed her. This was not what she had been reckoning on.

'You see the sort of man he is,' she said, with a shaking voice; 'he . . .'

'Forgive me, but I rejoice at it,' Vronsky interrupted. 'For God's sake, let me finish!' he added, his eyes imploring her to give him time to explain his words. 'I rejoice, because things cannot, cannot possibly remain as he supposes.'

'Why can't they?' Anna said, restraining her tears, and obviously attaching no sort of consequence to what he said. She felt that her fate was sealed.

Vronsky meant that after the duel—inevitable, he thought—things could not go on as before, but he said something different.

'It can't go on. I hope that now you will leave him. I hope'—he was confused, and reddened—'that you will let me arrange and plan our life. Tomorrow . . .' he was beginning.

She did not let him go on.

'But my child!' she shrieked. 'You see what he writes! I should have to leave him, and I can't and won't do that.'

'But, for God's sake, which is better?—leave your child, or keep up this degrading position?'

'To whom is it degrading?'

'To all, and most of all to you.'

'You say degrading . . . don't say that. Those words have no meaning for me,' she said in a shaking voice. She did not want him now to say what was untrue. She had nothing left her but his love, and she wanted to love him. 'Don't you understand that from the day I loved you everything has changed for me? For me there is one thing, and one thing only—your love. If that's mine, I feel so exalted, so strong, that nothing can be humiliating to me. I am proud of my position, because . . . proud of being . . . proud . . .' She could not say what she was proud of. Tears of shame and despair choked her utterance. She stood still and sobbed.

He felt, too, something swelling in his throat and twitching in his nose, and for the first time in his life he felt on the point of weeping. He could not have said exactly what it was touched him so. He felt sorry for her, and he felt he could not help her, and with that he knew that he was to blame for her wretchedness, that he had done something wrong.

'Is not a divorce possible?' he said feebly. She shook her head, not answering. 'Couldn't you take your son, and still leave him?'

'Yes; but it all depends on him. Now I must go to him,' she said shortly. Her presentiment that all would again go on in the old way had not deceived her.

'On Tuesday I shall be in Petersburg, and everything can be settled.'

'Yes,' she said. 'But don't let us talk any more of it.'

Anna's carriage, which she had sent away, and ordered to come back to the little gate of the Vrede garden, drove up. Anna said good-bye to Vronsky, and drove home.

XXIII

ON Monday there was the usual sitting of the Commission of the 2nd of June. Alexey Alexandrovitch walked into the hall where the sitting was held, greeted the members and the president, as usual, and sat down in his place, putting his hand on the papers laid ready before him. Among these papers lay the necessary evidence and a rough outline of the speech he intended to make. But he did not really need these documents. He remembered every point, and did not think it necessary to go over in his memory what he would say. He knew that when the time came, and when he saw his enemy facing him, and studiously endeavouring to assume an expression of indifference, his speech would flow of itself better than he could prepare it now. He felt that the import of his speech was of such magnitude that every word of it would have weight. Meantime, as he listened to the usual report, he had the most innocent and inoffensive air. No one, looking at his white hands, with their swollen veins and long fingers, so softly stroking the edges of the white paper that lay before him, and at the air of weariness with which his head dropped on one side, would have suspected that in a few minutes a torrent of words would flow from his lips that would arouse a fearful storm, set the members shouting and attacking one another, and force the president to call for order. When the report was over, Alexey Alexandrovitch announced in his subdued, delicate voice that he had several points to bring before the meeting in regard to the Commission for the Reorganisation of the Native Tribes. All attention was turned upon him. Alexey Alexandrovitch cleared his throat, and not looking at his opponent, but selecting, as he always did while he was delivering his speeches, the first person sitting opposite him, an inoffensive little old man, who never had an opinion of any sort in the Commission, began to expound his views. When he reached the point about the fundamental and radical law, his opponent jumped up and began to protest. Stremov, who was also a member of the Commission, and also stung to the quick, began defending himself, and altogether a stormy sitting followed; but Alexey Alexandrovitch triumphed, and his motion was carried, three new commissions were appointed, and the next day in a certain Petersburg circle nothing else was talked of but this sitting. Alexey Alexandrovitch's success had been even greater than he had anticipated.

Next morning, Tuesday, Alexey Alexandrovitch, on waking up, recollected with pleasure his triumph of the previous day, and he could not help smiling, though he tried to appear indifferent, when the chief secretary of his department, anxious to flatter him, informed him of the rumours that had reached him concerning what had happened in the Commission.

Absorbed in business with the chief secretary, Alexey Alexandrovitch had completely forgotten that it was Tuesday, the day fixed by him for the return of Anna Arkadyevna, and he was surprised and received a shock of annoyance when a servant came in to inform him of her arrival.

Anna had arrived in Petersburg early in the morning; the carriage had been sent to meet her in accordance with her telegram, and so Alexey Alexandrovitch might have known of her arrival. But when she arrived, he did not meet her. She was told that he had not yet gone out, but was busy with his secretary. She sent word to her husband that she had come, went to her own room, and occupied herself in sorting out her things, expecting he would come to her. But an hour passed; he did not come. She went into the dining-room on the pretext of giving some directions, and spoke loudly on purpose, expecting him to come out there; but he did not come, though she heard him go to the door of his study as he parted from the chief secretary. She knew he usually went out quickly to his office, and she wanted to see him before that, so that their attitude to one another might be defined.

She walked across the drawing-room and went resolutely to him. When she went into his study he was in official uniform, obviously ready to go out, sitting at a little table on which he rested his elbows, looking dejectedly before him. She saw him before he saw her, and she saw that he was thinking of her.

On seeing her, he would have risen, but changed his mind, then his face flushed hotly—a thing Anna had never seen before, and he got up quickly and went to meet her, looking not at her eyes, but above them at her forehead and hair. He went up to her, took her by the hand, and asked her to sit down.

'I am very glad you have come,' he said, sitting down beside her, and obviously wishing to say something, he stuttered. Several times he tried to begin to speak, but stopped. In spite of the fact that, preparing herself for meeting him, she had schooled herself to despise and reproach him, she did not know what to say to him, and she felt sorry for him. And so the silence lasted for some time. 'Is Seryozha quite well?' he said, and not waiting for an answer, he added: 'I shan't be dining at home today, and I have got to go out directly.'

'I had thought of going to Moscow,' she said.

'No, you did quite, quite right to come here,' he said, and was silent again.

Seeing that he was powerless to begin the conversation, she began herself.

'Alexey Alexandrovitch,' she said, looking at him and not dropping her eyes under his persistent gaze at her hair, 'I'm a guilty woman, I'm a bad woman, but I am the same as I was, as I told you then, and I have come to tell you that I can change nothing.'

'I have asked you no question about that,' he said, all at once, resolutely and with hatred looking her straight in the face; 'that was as I had supposed.' Under the influence of anger he apparently regained complete possession of all his faculties. 'But as I told you then, and have written to you,' he said in a thin, shrill voice, 'I repeat now, that I am not bound to know this. I ignore it. Not all wives are so kind as you, to be in such a hurry to communicate such agreeable news to their husbands.' He laid special emphasis on the word 'agreeable.' 'I shall ignore it so long as the world knows nothing of it, so long as my name is not disgraced. And so I simply inform you that our relations must be just as they have always been, and that only in the event of your compromising me I shall be obliged to take steps to secure my honour.'

'But our relations cannot be the same as always,' Anna began in a timid voice, looking at him with dismay.

When she saw once more those composed gestures, heard that shrill, childish, and sarcastic voice, her aversion for him extinguished her pity for him, and she felt only afraid, but at all costs she wanted to make clear her position.

'I cannot be your wife while I . . .' she began.

He laughed a cold and malignant laugh.

'The manner of life you have chosen is reflected, I suppose, in your ideas. I have too much respect or contempt, or both . . . I respect your past and despise your present . . . that I was far from the interpretation you put on my words.'

Anna sighed and bowed her head.

'Though indeed I fail to comprehend how, with the independence you show,' he went on, getting hot, '—announcing your infidelity to your husband and seeing nothing reprehensible in it, apparently—you can see anything reprehensible in performing a wife's duties in relation to your husband.'

'Alexey Alexandrovitch! What is it you want of me?'

'I want you not to meet that man here, and to conduct yourself so that neither the world nor the servants can reproach you . . . not to see him. That's not much, I think. And in return you will enjoy all the privileges of a faithful wife without fulfilling her duties. That's all I have to say to you. Now it's time for me to go. I'm not dining at home.' He got up and moved towards the door.

Anna got up too. Bowing in silence, he let her pass before him.

XXIV

THE night spent by Levin on the haycock did not pass without result for him. The way in which he had been managing his land revolted him and had lost all attraction for him. In spite of the magnificent harvest, never had there been, or, at least, never it seemed to him, had there been so many hindrances and so many quarrels between him and the peasants as that year, and the origin of these failures and this hostility was now perfectly comprehensible to him. The delight he had experienced in the work itself, and the consequent greater intimacy with the peasants, the envy he felt of them, of their life, the desire to adopt that life, which had been to him that night not a dream but an intention, the execution of which he had thought out in detail—all this had so transformed his view of the farming of the land as he had managed it, that he could not take his former interest in it, and could not help seeing that unpleasant relation between him and the workpeople which was the foundation of it all. The herd of improved cows such as Pava, the whole land ploughed over and enriched, the nine level fields surrounded with hedges, the two hundred and forty acres heavily manured, the seed sown in drills, and all the rest of it—it was all splendid if only the work had been done for themselves, or for themselves and comrades—people in sympathy with them. But he saw clearly now (his work on a book on agriculture, in which the chief element in husbandry was to have been the labourer, greatly assisted him in this) that the sort of farming he was carrying on was nothing but a cruel and stubborn struggle between him and the labourers, in which there was on one side—his side—a continual intense effort to change everything to a pattern he considered better; on the other side, the natural order of things. And in this struggle he saw that with immense expenditure of force on his side, and with no effort or even intention on the other side, all that was attained was that the work did not go to the liking of either side, and that splendid tools, splendid cattle and land were spoiled with no good to anyone. Worst of all, the energy expended on this work was not simply wasted. He could not help feeling now, since the meaning of his system had become clear to him, that the aim of his energy was a most unworthy one. In reality, what was the struggle about? He was struggling for every farthing of his share (and he could not help it, for he had only to relax his efforts, and he would not have had the money to pay his labourers' wages), while they were only struggling to be able to do their work easily and agreeably, that is to say, as they were used to doing it. It was for his interests that every labourer should work as hard as possible, and that while doing so he should keep his wits about him, so as to try not to break the winnowing-machines, the horse-rakes, the thrashing-machines, that he should attend to what he was doing. What the labourer wanted was to work as pleasantly as possible, with rests, and above all, carelessly and heedlessly, without thinking. That summer Levin saw this at every step. He sent the men to mow some clover for hay, picking out the worst patches where the clover was overgrown with grass and weeds and of no use for seed; again and again they mowed the best acres of clover, justifying themselves by the pretence that the bailiff had told them to, and trying to pacify him with the assurance that it would be splendid hay; but he knew that it was owing to those acres being so much easier to mow. He sent out a hay machine for pitching the hay—it was broken at the first row because it was dull work for a peasant to sit on the seat in front with the great wings waving above him. And he was told, 'Don't trouble, your honour, sure, the women-folks will pitch it quick enough.' The ploughs were practically useless, because it never occurred to the labourer to raise the share when he turned the plough, and forcing it round, he strained the horses and tore up the ground, and Levin was begged not to mind about it. The horses were allowed to stray into the wheat because not a single labourer would consent to be night-watchman, and in spite of orders to the contrary, the labourers insisted on taking turns for night duty, and Ivan, after working all day long, fell asleep, and was very penitent for his fault, saying, 'Do what you will to me, your honour.'

They killed three of the best calves by letting them into the clover aftermath without care as to their drinking, and nothing would make the men believe that they had been blown out by the clover, but they told him, by way of consolation, that one of his neighbours had lost a hundred and twelve head of cattle in three days. All this happened, not because anyone felt ill-will to Levin or his farm; on the contrary, he knew that they liked him, thought him a simple gentleman (their highest praise); but it happened simply because all they wanted was to work merrily and carelessly, and his interests were not only remote and incomprehensible to them, but fatally opposed to their most just claims. Long before, Levin had felt dissatisfaction with his own position in regard to the land. He saw where his boat leaked, but he did not look for the leak, perhaps purposely deceiving himself. (Nothing would be left him if he lost faith in it.) But now he could deceive himself no longer. The farming of the land, as he was managing it, had become not merely unattractive but revolting to him, and he could take no further interest in it.

To this now was joined the presence, only twenty-five miles off, of Kitty Shtcherbatsky, whom he longed to see and could not see. Darya Alexandrovna Oblonsky had invited him, when he was over there, to come; to come with the object of renewing his offer to his sister, who would, so she gave him to understand, accept him now. Levin himself had felt on seeing Kitty Shtcherbatsky that he had never ceased to love her; but he could not go over to the Oblonskys', knowing she was there. The fact that he had made her an offer, and she had refused him, had placed an insuperable barrier between her and him. 'I can't ask her to be my wife merely because she can't be the wife of the man she wanted to marry,' he said to himself. The thought of this made him cold and hostile to her. 'I should not be able to speak to her without a feeling of reproach; I could not look at her without resentment; and she will only hate me all the more, as she's bound to. And besides, how can I now, after what Darya Alexandrovna told me, go to see them? Can I help showing that I know what she told me? And me to go magnanimously to forgive her, and have pity on her! Me go through a performance before her of forgiving, and deigning to bestow my love on her! . . . What induced Darya Alexandrovna to tell me that? By chance I might have seen her, then everything would have happened of itself; but, as it is, it's out of the question, out of the question!'

Darya Alexandrovna sent him a letter, asking him for a side-saddle for Kitty's use. 'I'm told you have a side-saddle,' she wrote to him; 'I hope you will bring it over yourself.'

This was more than he could stand. How could a woman of any intelligence, of any delicacy, put her sister in such a humiliating position! He wrote ten notes, and tore them all up, and sent the saddle without any reply. To write that he would go was impossible, because he could not go; to write that he could not come because something prevented him, or that he would be away, that was still worse. He sent the saddle without an answer, and with a sense of having done something shameful; he handed over all the now revolting business of the estate to his bailiff, and set off next day to a remote district to see his friend Sviazhsky, who had splendid marshes for grouse in his neighbourhood, and had lately written to ask him to keep a long-standing promise to stay with him. The grouse marsh, in the Surovsky district, had long tempted Levin, but he had continually put off this visit on account of his work on the estate. Now he was glad to get away from the neighbourhood of the Shtcherbatskys, and still more from his farm-work, especially on a shooting expedition, which always in trouble served as the best consolation.

XXV

IN the Surovsky district there was no railway nor service of post-horses, and Levin drove there with his own horses in his big, old-fashioned carriage.

He stopped half-way at a well-to-do peasant's to feed his horses. A bald, well-preserved old man, with a broad, red beard, grey on his cheeks, opened the gate, squeezing against the gate-post to let the three horses pass. Directing the coachman to a place under the shed in the big, clean, tidy yard, with charred, old-fashioned ploughs in it, the old man asked Levin to come into the parlour. A cleanly dressed young woman, with clogs on her bare feet, was scrubbing the floor in the new outer room. She was frightened of the dog, that ran in after Levin, and uttered a shriek, but began laughing at her own fright at once when she was told the dog would not hurt her. Pointing Levin with her bare arm to the door into the parlour, she bent down again, hiding her handsome face, and went on scrubbing.

'Would you like the samovar?' she asked.

'Yes, please.'

The parlour was a big room, with a Dutch stove, and a screen dividing it into two. Under the holy picture stood a table painted in patterns, a bench, and two chairs. Near the entrance was a dresser full of crockery. The shutters were closed, there were few flies, and it was so clean that Levin was anxious that Laska, who had been running along the road and bathing in the puddles, should not muddy the floor, and ordered her to a place in the corner by the door. After looking round the parlour, Levin went out in the backyard. The good-looking young woman in clogs, swinging the empty pails on the yoke, ran on before him to the well for water.

'Look sharp, my girl!' the old man shouted after her, good-humouredly, and he went up to Levin. 'Well, sir, are you going to Nikolay Ivanovitch Sviazhsky? His honour comes to us too,' he began chatting, leaning his elbows on the railing of the steps. In the middle of the old man's account of his acquaintance with Sviazhsky, the gates creaked again, and labourers came into the yard from the fields, with wooden ploughs and harrows. The horses harnessed to the ploughs and harrows were sleek and fat. The labourers were obviously of the household: two were young men in cotton shirts and caps, the two others were hired labourers in homespun shirts, one an old man, the other a young fellow. Moving off from the steps, the old man went up to the horses and began unharnessing them.

'What have they been ploughing?' asked Levin.

'Ploughing up the potatoes. We rent a bit of land too. Fedot, don't let out the gelding, but take it to the trough, and we'll put the other in harness.'

'Oh, father, the ploughshares I ordered, has he brought them along?' asked a big, healthy-looking fellow, obviously the old man's son.

'There . . . in the outer room,' answered the old man, bundling together the harness he had taken off, and flinging it on the ground. 'You can put them on, while they have dinner.'

The good-looking young woman came into the outer room with the full pails dragging at her shoulders. More women came on the scene from somewhere, young and handsome, middle-aged, old and ugly, with children and without children.

The samovar was beginning to sing; the labourers and the family, having disposed of the horses, came in to dinner. Levin, getting his provisions out of his carriage, invited the old man to take tea with him.

'Well, I have had some today already,' said the old man, obviously accepting the invitation with pleasure. 'But just a glass for company.'

Over their tea Levin heard all about the old man's farming. Ten years before, the old man had rented three hundred acres from the lady who owned them, and a year ago he had bought them and rented another three hundred from a neighbouring landowner. A small part of the land—the worst part—he let out for rent, while a hundred acres of arable land he cultivated himself with his family and two hired labourers. The old man complained that things were doing badly. But Levin saw that he simply did so from a feeling of propriety, and that his farm was in a flourishing condition. If it had been unsuccessful he would not have bought land at thirty-five roubles the acre, he would not have married his three sons and a nephew, he would not have rebuilt twice after fires, and each time on a larger scale. In spite of the old man's complaints, it was evident that he was proud, and justly proud, of his prosperity, proud of his sons, his nephew, his sons' wives, his horses and his cows, and especially of the fact that he was keeping all this farming going. From his conversation with the old man, Levin thought he was not averse to new methods either. He had planted a great many potatoes, and his potatoes, as Levin had seen driving past, were already past flowering and beginning to die down, while Levin's were only just coming into flower. He earthed up his potatoes with a modern plough borrowed from a neighbouring landowner. He sowed wheat. The trifling fact that, thinning out his rye, the old man used the rye he thinned out for his horses, specially struck Levin. How many times had Levin seen this splendid fodder wasted, and tried to get it saved; but always it had turned out to be impossible. The peasant got this done, and he could not say enough in praise of it as food for the beasts.

'What have the wenches to do? They carry it out in bundles to the roadside, and the cart brings it away.'

'Well, we landowners can't manage well with our labourers,' said Levin, handing him a glass of tea.

'Thank you,' said the old man, and he took the glass, but refused sugar, pointing to a lump he had left. 'They're simple destruction,' said he. 'Look at Sviazhsky's, for instance. We know what the land's like—first-rate, yet there's not much of a crop to boast of. It's not looked after enough—that's all it is!'

'But you work your land with hired labourers?'

'We're all peasants together. We go into everything ourselves. If a man's no use, he can go, and we can manage by ourselves.'

'Father, Finogen wants some tar,' said the young woman in the clogs, coming in.

'Yes, yes, that's how it is, sir!' said the old man, getting up and, crossing himself deliberately, he thanked Levin and went out.

When Levin went into the kitchen to call his coachman he saw the whole family at dinner. The women were standing up waiting on them. The young, sturdy-looking son was telling something funny with his mouth full of pudding, and they were all laughing, the woman in the clogs, who was pouring cabbage-soup into a bowl, laughing most merrily of all.

Very probably the good-looking face of the young woman in the clogs had a good deal to do with the impression of well-being this peasant household made upon Levin, but the impression was so strong that Levin could never get rid of it. And all the way from the old peasant's to Sviazhsky's he kept recalling this peasant farm as though there were something in this impression that demanded his special attention.

XXVI

SVIAZHSKY was the marshal of his district. He was five years older than Levin, and had long been married. His sister-in-law, a young girl Levin liked very much, lived in his house; and Levin knew that Sviazhsky and his wife would have greatly liked to marry the girl to him. He knew this with certainty, as so-called eligible young men always know it, though he could never have brought himself to speak of it to anyone; and he knew too that, although he wanted to get married, and although by every token this very attractive girl would make an excellent wife, he could no more have married her, even if he had not been in love with Kitty Shtcherbatsky, than he could have flown up to the sky. And this knowledge poisoned the pleasure he had hoped to find in the visit to Sviazhsky.

On getting Sviazhsky's letter with the invitation for shooting, Levin had immediately thought of this; but in spite of it he had made up his mind that Sviazhsky's having such views for him was simply his own groundless supposition, and so he would go, all the same. Besides, at the bottom of his heart he had a desire to try himself, put himself to the test in regard to this girl. The Sviazhskys' home life was exceedingly pleasant, and Sviazhsky himself, the best type of man taking part in local affairs that Levin knew, was very interesting to him.

Sviazhsky was one of those people, always a source of wonder to Levin, whose convictions, very logical though never original, go one way by themselves, while their life, exceedingly definite and firm in its direction, goes its way quite apart and almost always in direct contradiction to their convictions. Sviazhsky was an extremely advanced man. He despised the nobility, and believed the mass of the nobility to be secretly in favour of serfdom, and only concealing their views from cowardice. He regarded Russia as a ruined country, rather after the style of Turkey, and the government of Russia as so bad that he never permitted himself to criticise its doings seriously, and yet he was a functionary of that government and a model marshal of nobility, and when he drove about he always wore the cockade of office and the cap with the red band. He considered human life only tolerable abroad, and went abroad to stay at every opportunity, and at the same time he carried on a complex and improved system of agriculture in Russia, and with extreme interest followed everything and knew everything that was being done in Russia. He considered the Russian peasant as occupying a stage of development intermediate between the ape and the man, and at the same time in the local assemblies no one was readier to shake hands with the peasants and listen to their opinion. He believed neither in God nor the devil, but was much concerned about the question of the improvement of the clergy and the maintenance of their revenues, and took special trouble to keep up the church in his village.

On the woman question he was on the side of the extreme advocates of complete liberty for women, and especially their right to labour. But he lived with his wife on such terms that their affectionate childless home-life was the admiration of everyone, and arranged his wife's life so that she did nothing and could do nothing but share her husband's efforts that her time should pass as happily and as agreeably as possible.

If it had not been a characteristic of Levin's to put the most favourable interpretation on people, Sviazhsky's character would have presented no doubt or difficulty to him: he would have said to himself, 'a fool or a knave', and everything would have seemed clear. But he could not say 'a fool', because Sviazhsky was unmistakably clever, and moreover, a highly cultivated man, who was exceptionally modest over his culture. There was not a subject he knew nothing of. But he did not display his knowledge except when he was compelled to do so. Still less could Levin say that he was a knave, as Sviazhsky was unmistakably an honest, good-hearted, sensible man, who worked good-humouredly, keenly, and perseveringly at his work; he was held in high honour by everyone about him, and certainly had never consciously done, and was indeed incapable of doing, anything base.

Levin tried to understand him, and could not understand him, and looked at him and his life as at a living enigma.

Levin and he were very friendly, and so Levin used to venture to sound Sviazhsky, to try to get at the very foundation of his view of life; but it was always in vain. Every time Levin tried to penetrate beyond the outer chambers of Sviazhsky's mind, which were hospitably open to all, he noticed that Sviazhsky was slightly disconcerted; faint signs of alarm were visible in his eyes, as though he were afraid Levin would understand him, and he would give him a kindly, good-humoured repulse.

Just now, since his disenchantment with farming, Levin was particularly glad to stay with Sviazhsky. Apart from the fact that the sight of this happy and affectionate couple, so pleased with themselves and everyone else, and their well-ordered home always had a cheering effect on Levin, he felt a longing, now that he was so dissatisfied with his own life, to get at that secret in Sviazhsky that gave him such clearness, definiteness, and good courage in life. Moreover, Levin knew that at Sviazhsky's he should meet the landowners of the neighbourhood, and it was particularly interesting for him just now to hear and take part in those rural conversations concerning crops, labourers' wages, and so on, which, he was aware, are conventionally regarded as something very low, but which seemed to him just now to constitute the one subject of importance. 'It was not, perhaps, of importance in the days of serfdom, and it may not be of importance in England. In both cases the conditions of agriculture are firmly established; but among us now, when everything has been turned upside down and is only just taking shape, the question what form these conditions will take is the one question of importance in Russia,' thought Levin.

The shooting turned out to be worse than Levin had expected. The marsh was dry and there were no grouse at all. He walked about the whole day and only brought back three birds, but to make up for that—he brought back, as he always did from shooting, an excellent appetite, excellent spirits, and that keen, intellectual mood which with him always accompanied violent physical exertion. And while out shooting, when he seemed to be thinking of nothing at all, suddenly the old man and his family kept coming back to his mind, and the impression of them seemed to claim not merely his attention, but the solution of some question connected with them.

In the evening at tea, two landowners who had come about some business connected with a wardship were of the party, and the interesting conversation Levin had been looking forward to sprang up.

Levin was sitting beside his hostess at the tea-table, and was obliged to keep up a conversation with her and her sister, who was sitting opposite him. Madame Sviazhsky was a round-faced, fair-haired, rather short woman, all smiles and dimples. Levin tried through her to get at a solution of the weighty enigma her husband presented to his mind; but he had not complete freedom of ideas, because he was in an agony of embarrassment. This agony of embarrassment was due to the fact that the sister-in-law was sitting opposite to him, in a dress, specially put on, as he fancied, for his benefit, cut particularly open, in the shape of a trapeze, on her white bosom. This quadrangular opening, in spite of the bosom's being very white, or just because it was very white, deprived Levin of the full use of his faculties. He imagined, probably mistakenly, that this low-necked bodice had been made on his account, and felt that he had no right to look at it, and tried not to look at it; but he felt that he was to blame for the very fact of the low-necked bodice having been made. It seemed to Levin that he had deceived someone, that he ought to explain something, but that to explain it was impossible, and for that reason he was continually blushing, was ill at ease and awkward. His awkwardness infected the pretty sister-in-law too. But their hostess appeared not to observe this, and kept purposely drawing her into the conversation.

'You say,' she said, pursuing the subject that had been started, 'that my husband cannot be interested in what's Russian. It's quite the contrary; he is always in cheerful spirits abroad, but not as he is here. Here, he feels in his proper place. He has so much to do, and he has the faculty of interesting himself in everything. Oh, you've not been to see our school, have you?'

'I've seen it. . . . The little house covered with ivy, isn't it?'

'Yes; that's Nastia's work,' she said, indicating her sister.

'You teach in it yourself?' asked Levin, trying to look above the open neck, but feeling that wherever he looked in that direction he should see it.

'Yes; I used to teach in it myself, and do teach still, but we have a first-rate schoolmistress now. And we've started gymnastic exercises.'

'No, thank you, I won't have any more tea,' said Levin, and conscious of doing a rude thing, but incapable of continuing the conversation, he got up, blushing. 'I hear a very interesting conversation,' he added, and walked to the other end of the table, where Sviazhsky was sitting with the two gentlemen of the neighbourhood. Sviazhsky was sitting sideways, with one elbow on the table, and a cup in one hand, while with the other hand he gathered up his beard, held it to his nose and let it drop again, as though he were smelling it. His brilliant black eyes were looking straight at the excited country gentleman with grey whiskers, and apparently he derived amusement from his remarks. The gentleman was complaining of the peasants. It was evident to Levin that Sviazhsky knew an answer to this gentleman's complaints, which would at once demolish his whole contention, but that in his position he could not give utterance to this answer, and listened, not without pleasure, to the landowner's comic speeches.

The gentleman with the grey whiskers was obviously an inveterate adherent of serfdom and a devoted agriculturist, who had lived all his life in the country. Levin saw proofs of this in his dress, in the old-fashioned threadbare coat, obviously not his everyday attire, in his shrewd, deep-set eyes, in his idiomatic, fluent Russian, in the imperious tone that had become habitual from long use, and in the resolute gestures of his large, red, sunburnt hands, with an old betrothal-ring on the little finger.

XXVII

'IF I'd only the heart to throw up what's been set going . . . such a lot of trouble wasted . . . I'd turn my back on the whole business, sell up, go off like Nikolay Ivanovitch . . . to hear *La Belle Hélène*,' said the landowner, a pleasant smile lighting up his shrewd old face.

'But you see you don't throw it up,' said Nikolay Ivanovitch Sviazhsky; 'so there must be something gained.'

'The only gain is that I live in my own house, neither bought nor hired. Besides, one keeps hoping the people will learn sense. Though, instead of that, you'd never believe it—the drunkenness, the immorality! They keep chopping and changing their bits of land. Not a sight of a horse or a cow. The peasant's dying of hunger, but just go and take him on as a labourer, he'll do his best to do you a mischief, and then bring you up before the justice of the peace.'

'But then you make complaints to the justice too,' said Sviazhsky.

'I lodge complaints? Not for anything in the world! Such a talking, and such a to-do, that one would have cause to regret it. At the works, for instance, they pocketed the advance-money and made off. What did the justice do? Why, acquitted them. Nothing keeps them in order but their own communal court and their village elder. He'll flog them in the good old style! But for that there'd be nothing for it but to give it all up and run away.'

Obviously the landowner was chaffing Sviazhsky, who, far from resenting it, was apparently amused by it.

'But you see we manage our land without such extreme measures,' said he, smiling: 'Levin and I and this gentleman.'

He indicated the other landowner.

'Yes, the thing's done at Mihail Petrovitch's, but ask him how it's done. Do you call that a rational system?' said the landowner, obviously rather proud of the word 'rational'.

'My system's very simple,' said Mihail Petrovitch, 'thank God. All my management rests on getting the money ready for the autumn taxes, and the peasants come to me, "Father, master, help us!" Well, the peasants are all one's neighbours; one feels for them. So one advances them a third, but one says: "Remember, lads, I have helped you, and you must help me when I need it—whether it's the sowing of the oats, or the hay-cutting, or the harvest"; and well, one agrees, so much for each taxpayer—though there are dishonest ones among them too, it's true.'

Levin, who had long been familiar with these patriarchal methods, exchanged glances with Sviazhsky and interrupted Mihail Petrovitch, turning again to the gentleman with the grey whiskers.

'Then what do you think?' he asked; 'what system is one to adopt nowadays?'

'Why, manage like Mihail Petrovitch, or let the land for half the crop or for rent to the peasants; that one can do—only that's just how the general prosperity of the country is being ruined. Where the land with serf-labour and good management gave a yield of nine to one, on the half-crop system it yields three to one. Russia has been ruined by the emancipation!'

Sviazhsky looked with smiling eyes at Levin, and even made a faint gesture of irony to him; but Levin did not think the landowner's words absurd, he understood them better than he did Sviazhsky. A great deal more of what the gentleman with the grey whiskers said to show in what way Russia was ruined by the emancipation struck him indeed as very true, new to him, and quite incontestable. The landowner unmistakably spoke his own individual thought—a thing that rarely happens—and a thought to which he had been brought not by a desire of finding some exercise for an idle brain, but a thought which had grown up out of the conditions of his life, which he had brooded over in the solitude of his village, and had considered in every aspect.

'The point is, don't you see, that progress of every sort is only made by the use of authority,' he said, evidently wishing to show he was not without culture. 'Take the reforms of Peter, of Catherine, of Alexander. Take European history. And progress in agriculture more than anything else—the potato, for instance, that was introduced among us by force. The wooden plough too wasn't always used. It was introduced maybe in the days before the Empire, but it was probably brought in by force. Now, in our own day, we landowners in the serf times used improvements in our husbandry: drying-machines and thrashing-machines, and carting manure and all the modern implements—all that we brought into use by our authority, and the peasants opposed it at first, and ended by imitating us. Now, by the abolition of serfdom we have been deprived of our authority; and so our husbandry, where it had been raised to a high level, is bound to sink to the most savage primitive condition. That's how I see it.'

'But why so? If it's rational, you'll be able to keep up the same system with hired labour,' said Sviazhsky.

'We've no power over them. With whom am I going to work the system, allow me to ask?'

'There it is—the labour force—the chief element in agriculture,' thought Levin.

'With labourers.'

'The labourers won't work well, and won't work with good implements. Our labourer can do nothing but get drunk like a pig, and when he's drunk he ruins everything you give him. He makes the horses ill with too much water, cuts good harness, barters the tyres of the wheels for drink, drops bits of iron into the thrashing-machine, so as to break it. He loathes the sight of anything that's not after his fashion. And that's how it is the whole level of husbandry has fallen. Lands gone out of cultivation, overgrown with weeds, or divided among the peasants, and where millions of bushels were raised you get a hundred thousand; the wealth of the country has decreased. If the same thing had been done, but with care that . . .'

And he proceeded to unfold his own scheme of emancipation by means of which these drawbacks might have been avoided.

This did not interest Levin, but when he had finished, Levin went back to his first position, and, addressing Sviazhsky, and trying to draw him into expressing his serious opinion: —

'That the standard of culture is falling, and that with our present relations to the peasants there is no possibility of farming on a rational system to yield a profit—that's perfectly true,' said he.

'I don't believe it,' Sviazhsky replied quite seriously; 'all I see is that we don't know how to cultivate the land, and that our system of agriculture in the serf-days was by no means too high, but too low. We have no machines, no good stock, no efficient supervision; we don't even know how to keep accounts. Ask any landowner; he won't be able to tell you what crop's profitable, and what's not.'

'Italian book-keeping,' said the gentleman of the grey whiskers ironically. 'You may keep your books as you like, but if they spoil everything for you, there won't be any profit.'

'Why do they spoil things? A poor thrashing-machine, or your Russian presser, they will break, but my steam-press they don't break. A wretched Russian nag they'll ruin, but keep good dray-horses or cart-horses—they won't ruin them. And so it is all round. We must raise our farming to a higher level.'

'Oh, if one only had the means to do it, Nikolay Ivanovitch! It's all very well for you; but for me, with a son to keep at the university, lads to be educated at the high school—how am I going to buy these dray-horses?'

'Well, that's what the land banks are for.'

'To get what's left me sold by auction? No, thank you.'

'I don't agree that it's necessary or possible to raise the level of agriculture still higher,' said Levin. 'I devote myself to it, and I have means, but I can do nothing. As to the banks, I don't know to whom they're any good. For my part, anyway, whatever I've spent money on in the way of husbandry, it has been a loss: stock—a loss, machinery—a loss.'

'That's true enough,' the gentleman with the grey whiskers chimed in, positively laughing with satisfaction.

'And I'm not the only one,' pursued Levin. 'I mix with all the neighbouring landowners, who are cultivating their land on a rational system; they all, with rare exceptions, are doing so at a loss. Come, tell us how does your land do—does it pay?' said Levin, and at once in Sviazhsky's eyes he detected that fleeting expression of alarm which he had noticed whenever he had tried to penetrate beyond the outer chambers of Sviazhsky's mind.

Moreover, this question on Levin's part was not quite in good faith. Madame Sviazhsky had just told him at tea that they had that summer invited a German expert in book-keeping from Moscow, who for a consideration of five hundred roubles had investigated the management of their property, and found that it was costing them a loss of three thousand odd roubles. She did not remember the precise sum, but it appeared that the German had worked it out to the fraction of a farthing.

The grey-whiskered landowner smiled at the mention of the profits of Sviazhsky's farming, obviously aware how much gain his neighbour and marshal was likely to be making.

'Possibly it does not pay,' answered Sviazhsky. 'That merely proves either that I'm a bad manager, or that I've sunk my capital for the increase of my rents.'

'Oh, rent!' Levin cried with horror. 'Rent there may be in Europe, where land has been improved by the labour put into it; but with us all the land is deteriorating from the labour put into it—in other words, they're working it out; so there's no question of rent.'

'How no rent? It's a law.'

'Then we're outside the law; rent explains nothing for us, but simply muddles us. No, tell me how there can be a theory of rent? . . .'

'Will you have some junket? Masha, pass us some junket or raspberries.' He turned to his wife. 'Extraordinarily late the raspberries are lasting this year.'

And in the happiest frame of mind Sviazhsky got up and walked off, apparently supposing the conversation to have ended at the very point when to Levin it seemed that it was only just beginning.

Having lost his antagonist, Levin continued the conversation with the grey-whiskered landowner, trying to prove to him that all the difficulty arises from the fact that we don't find out the peculiarities and habits of our labourer; but the landowner, like all men who think independently and in isolation, was slow in taking in any other person's idea, and particularly partial to his own. He stuck to it that the Russian peasant is a swine and likes swinishness, and that to get him out of his swinishness one must have authority, and there is none; one must have the stick, and we have become so liberal that we have all of a sudden replaced the stick that served us for a thousand years by lawyers and model prisons, where the worthless, stinking peasant is fed on good soup and has a fixed allowance of cubic feet of air.

'What makes you think,' said Levin, trying to get back to the question, 'that it's impossible to find some relation to the labourer in which the labour would become productive?'

'That never could be so with the Russian peasantry; we've no power over them,' answered the landowner.

'How can new conditions be found?' said Sviazhsky. Having eaten some junket and lighted a cigarette, he came back to the discussion. 'All possible relations to the labour force have been defined and studied,' he said. 'The relic of barbarism, the primitive commune with each guarantee for all, will disappear of itself; serfdom has been abolished—there remains nothing but free labour, and its forms are fixed and ready made, and must be adopted. Permanent hands, day-labourers, farmers—you can't get out of those forms.'

'But Europe is dissatisfied with these forms.'

'Dissatisfied, and seeking new ones. And will find them, in all probability.'

'That's just what I was meaning,' answered Levin. 'Why shouldn't we seek them for ourselves?'

'Because it would be just like inventing afresh the means for constructing railways. They are ready, invented.'

'But if they don't do for us, if they're stupid?' said Levin.

And again he detected the expression of alarm in the eyes of Sviazhsky.

'Oh yes; we'll bury the world under our caps! We've found the secret Europe was seeking for! I've heard all that; but, excuse me, do you know all that's been done in Europe on the question of the organisation of labour?'

'No, very little.'

'That question is now absorbing the best minds in Europe. The Schulze-Delitsch movement. . . . And then all this enormous literature of the labour question, the most liberal Lassalle movement . . . the

Mulhausen experiment? That's a fact by now, as you're probably aware.'

'I have some idea of it, but very vague.'

'No, you only say that; no doubt you know all about it as well as I do. I'm not a professor of sociology, of course, but it interested me, and really, if it interests you, you ought to study it.'

'But what conclusion have they come to?'

'Excuse me . . .'

The two neighbours had risen, and Sviazhsky, once more checking Levin in his inconvenient habit of peeping into what was beyond the outer chambers of his mind, went to see his guests out.

XXVIII

LEVIN was insufferably bored that evening with the ladies; he was stirred as he had never been before by the idea that the dissatisfaction he was feeling with his system of managing his land was not an exceptional case, but the general condition of things in Russia; that the organisation of some relation of the labourers to the soil in which they would work, as with the peasant he had met half-way to the Sviazhskys' was not a dream, but a problem which must be solved. And it seemed to him that the problem could be solved, and that he ought to try and solve it.

After saying good-night to the ladies, and promising to stay the whole of the next day, so as to make an expedition on horseback with them to see an interesting ruin in the crown forest, Levin went, before going to bed, into his host's study to get the books on the labour question that Sviazhsky had offered him. Sviazhsky's study was a huge room, surrounded by bookcases and with two tables in it—one a massive writing-table, standing in the middle of the room, and the other a round table, covered with recent numbers of reviews and journals in different languages, ranged like the rays of a star round the lamp. On the writing-table was a stand of drawers marked with gold lettering, and full of papers of various sorts.

Sviazhsky took out the books, and sat down in a rocking-chair.

'What are you looking at there?' he said to Levin, who was standing at the round table looking through the reviews.

'Oh yes, there's a very interesting article here,' said Sviazhsky of the review Levin was holding in his hand. 'It appears,' he went on, with eager interest, 'that Friedrich was not, after all, the person chiefly responsible for the partition of Poland. It is proved . . .'

And, with his characteristic clearness, he summed up those new, very important, and interesting revelations. Although Levin was engrossed at the moment by his ideas about the problem of the land, he wondered, as he heard Sviazhsky: 'What is there inside him? And why, why is he interested in the partition of Poland?' When Sviazhsky had finished, Levin could not help asking: 'Well, and what then?' But there was nothing to follow. It was simply interesting that it had been proved to be so and so. But Sviazhsky did not explain, and saw no need to explain why it was interesting to him.

'Yes, but I was very much interested by your irritable neighbour,' said Levin, sighing. 'He's a clever fellow, and said a lot that was true.'

'Oh, get along with you! An inveterate supporter of serfdom at heart, like all of them!' said Sviazhsky.

'Whose marshal you are.'

'Yes, only I marshal them in the other direction,' said Sviazhsky, laughing.

'I'll tell you what interests me very much,' said Levin. 'He's right that our system, that's to say of rational farming, doesn't answer, that the only thing that answers is the money-lender system, like that meek-looking gentleman's, or else the very simplest . . . Whose fault is it?'

'Our own, of course. Besides, it's not true that it doesn't answer. It answers with Vassiltchikov.'

'A factory . . .'

'But I really don't know what it is you are surprised at. The people are at such a low stage of rational and moral development, that it's obvious they're bound to oppose everything that's strange to them. In Europe, a rational system answers because the people are educated: it follows that we must educate the people—that's all.'

'But how are we to educate the people?'

'To educate the people three things are needed; schools, and schools, and schools.'

'But you said yourself the people are at such a low stage of material development: what help are schools for that?'

'Do you know, you remind me of the story of the advice given to the sick man—You should try purgative medicine. Taken: worse. Try leeches. Tried them: worse. Well, then, there's nothing left but to pray to God. Tried it: worse. That's just how it is with us. I say political economy; you say—worse. I say socialism: worse. Education: worse.'

'But how do schools help matters?'

'They give the peasant fresh wants.'

'Well, that's a thing I've never understood,' Levin replied with heat. 'In what way are schools going to help the people to improve their material position? You say schools, education, will give them fresh wants. So much the worse, since they won't be capable of satisfying them. And in what way a knowledge of addition and subtraction and the catechism is going to improve their material condition, I never could make out. The day before yesterday, I met a peasant woman in the evening with a little baby, and asked her where she was going. She said "she was going to the wise woman; her boy had screaming fits, so she was taking him to be doctored." I asked, "Why, how does the wise woman cure screaming fits?" "She puts the child on the hen-roost and repeats some charm . . ."'

'Well, you're saying it yourself! What's wanted to prevent her taking her child to the hen-roost to cure it of screaming fits is just . . .' Sviazhsky said, smiling good-humouredly.

'Oh no!' said Levin with annoyance; 'that method of doctoring I merely meant as a simile for doctoring the people with schools. The people are poor and ignorant—that we see as surely as the peasant woman sees the baby is ill because it screams. But in what way this trouble of poverty and ignorance is to be cured by schools is as incomprehensible as how the hen-roost affects the screaming. What has to be cured is what makes him poor.'

'Well, in that, at least, you're in agreement with Spencer, whom you dislike so much. He says, too, that education may be the consequence of greater prosperity and comfort, of more frequent washing, as he says, but not of being able to read and write . . .'

'Well, then, I'm very glad—or the contrary, very sorry, that I'm in agreement with Spencer; only I've known it a long while. Schools can do no good; what will do good is an economic organisation in which the people will become richer, will have more leisure—and then there will be schools.'

'Still, all over Europe now schools are obligatory.'

'And how far do you agree with Spencer yourself about it?' asked Levin.

But there was a gleam of alarm in Sviazhsky's eyes, and he said smiling—

'No; that screaming story is positively capital! Did you really hear it yourself?'

Levin saw that he was not to discover the connection between this man's life and his thoughts. Obviously he did not care in the least what his reasoning led him to; all he wanted was the process of reasoning. And he did not like it when the process of reasoning brought him into a blind alley. That was the only thing he disliked, and avoided by changing the conversation to something agreeable and amusing.

All the impressions of the day, beginning with the impression made by the old peasant, which served, as it were, as the fundamental basis of all the conceptions and ideas of the day, threw Levin into violent excitement. This dear good Sviazhsky, keeping a stock of ideas simply for social purposes, and obviously having some other principles hidden from Levin, while with the crowd, whose name is legion, he guided public opinion by ideas he did not share; that irascible country gentleman, perfectly correct in the conclusions that he had been worried into by life, but wrong in his exasperation against a whole class, and that the best class in Russia; his own dissatisfaction with the work he had been doing, and the vague hope of finding a remedy for all this—all was blended in a sense of inward turmoil and anticipation of some solution near at hand.

Left alone in the room assigned him, lying on a spring mattress that yielded unexpectedly at every movement of his arm or his leg, Levin did not fall asleep for a long while. Not one conversation with Sviazhsky, though he had said a great deal that was clever, had interested Levin; but the conclusions of the irascible landowner required consideration. Levin could not help recalling every word he had said, and in imagination amending his own replies.

'Yes, I ought to have said to him: You say that our husbandry does not answer because the peasant hates improvements, and that they must be forced on him by authority. If no system of husbandry answered at all without these improvements, you would be quite right. But the only system that does answer is when the labourer is working in accordance with his habits, just as on the old peasant's land half-way here. Your and our general dissatisfaction with the system shows that either we are to blame or the labourers. We have gone our way—the European way—a long while, without asking ourselves about the qualities of our labour force. Let us try to look upon the labour force not as an abstract force, but as the *Russian peasant* with his instincts, and we shall arrange our system of culture in accordance with that. Imagine, I ought to have said to him, that you have the same system as the old peasant has, that you have found means of making your labourers take an interest in the success of the work, and have found the happy mean in the way of improvements which they will admit, and you will, without exhausting the soil, get twice or three times the yield you got before. Divide it in halves, give half as the share of labour, the surplus left you will be greater, and the share of labour will be greater too. And to do this one must lower the standard of husbandry and interest the labourers in its success. How to do this?—that's a matter of detail; but undoubtedly it can be done.'

This idea threw Levin into great excitement. He did not sleep half the night, thinking over in detail the putting of his idea into practice. He had not intended to go away next day, but he now determined to go home early in the morning. Besides, the sister-in-law with her low-necked bodice aroused in him a feeling akin to shame and remorse for some utterly base action. Most important of all—he must get back without delay: he would have to make haste to put his new project to the peasants before the sowing of the winter wheat, so that the sowing might be undertaken on a new basis. He had made up his mind to revolutionise his whole system.

XXIX

THE carrying out of Levin's plan presented many difficulties; but he struggled on, doing his utmost, and attained a result which, though not what he desired, was enough to enable him, without self-deception, to believe that the attempt was worth the trouble. One of the chief difficulties was that the process of cultivating the land was in full swing, that it was impossible to stop everything and begin it all again from the beginning, and the machine had to be mended while in motion.

When on the evening that he arrived home he informed the bailiff of his plans, the latter with visible pleasure agreed with what he said so long as he was pointing out that all that had been done up to that time was stupid and useless. The bailiff said that he had said so a long while ago, but no heed had been paid him. But as for the proposal made by Levin—to take a part as shareholder with his labourers in each agricultural undertaking—at this the bailiff simply expressed a profound despondency, and offered no definite opinion, but began immediately talking of the urgent necessity of carrying the remaining sheaves of rye the next day, and of sending the men out for the second ploughing, so that Levin felt that this was not the time for discussing it.

On beginning to talk to the peasants about it, and making a proposition to cede them the land on new terms, he came into collision with the same great difficulty that they were so much absorbed by the current work of the day, that they had not time to consider the advantages and disadvantages of the proposed scheme.

The simple-hearted Ivan, the cowherd, seemed completely to grasp Levin's proposal—that he should with his family take a share of the profits of the cattle-yard—and he was in complete sympathy with the plan. But when Levin hinted at the future advantages, Ivan's face expressed alarm and regret that he could not hear all he had to say, and he made haste to find himself some task that would admit of no delay:

he either snatched up the fork to pitch the hay out of the pens, or ran to get water or to clear out the dung.

Another difficulty lay in the invincible disbelief of the peasant that a landowner's object could be anything else than a desire to squeeze all he could out of them. They were firmly convinced that his real aim (whatever he might say to them) would always be in what he did not say to them. And they themselves, in giving their opinion, said a great deal but never said what was their real object. Moreover (Levin felt that the irascible landowner had been right) the peasants made their first and unalterable condition of any agreement whatever that they should not be forced to any new methods of tillage of any kind, nor to use new implements. They agreed that the modern plough ploughed better, that the scarifier did the work more quickly, but they found thousands of reasons that made it out of the question for them to use either of them; and though he had accepted the conviction that he would have to lower the standard of cultivation, he felt sorry to give up improved methods, the advantages of which were so obvious. But in spite of all these difficulties he got his way, and by autumn the system was working, or at least so it seemed to him.

At first Levin had thought of giving up the whole farming of the land just as it was to the peasants, the labourers, and the bailiff on new conditions of partnership; but he was very soon convinced that this was impossible, and determined to divide it up. The cattle-yard, the garden, hay-fields, and arable land, divided into several parts, had to be made into separate lots. The simple-hearted cowherd, Ivan, who, Levin fancied, understood the matter better than any of them, collecting together a gang of workers to help him, principally of his own family, became a partner in the cattle-yard. A distant part of the estate, a tract of waste land that had lain fallow for eight years, was with the help of the clever carpenter, Fyodor Ryezunov, taken by six families of peasants on new conditions of partnership, and the peasant Shuraev took the management of all the vegetable gardens on the same terms. The remainder of the land was still worked on the old system, but these three associated partnerships were the first step to a new organisation of the whole, and they completely took up Levin's time.

It is true that in the cattle-yard things went no better than before, and Ivan strenuously opposed warm housing for the cows and butter made of fresh cream, affirming that cows require less food if kept cold, and that butter is more profitable made from sour cream, and he asked for wages just as under the old system, and took not the slightest interest in the fact that the money he received was not wages but an advance out of his future share in the profits.

It is true that Fyodor Ryezunov's company did not plough over the ground twice before sowing, as had been agreed, justifying themselves on the plea that the time was too short. It is true that the peasants of the same company, though they had agreed to work the land on new conditions, always spoke of the land, not as held in partnership, but as rented for half the crop, and more than once the peasants and Ryezunov himself said to Levin, 'If you would take a rent for the land, it would save you trouble, and we should be more free.' Moreover the same peasants kept putting off, on various excuses, the building of a cattle-yard and barn on the land as agreed upon, and delayed doing it till the winter.

It is true that Shuraev would have liked to let out the kitchen gardens he had undertaken in small lots to the peasants. He evidently quite misunderstood, and apparently intentionally misunderstood, the conditions upon which the land had been given to him.

Often, too, talking to the peasants and explaining to them all the advantages of the plan, Levin felt that the peasants heard nothing but the sound of his voice, and were firmly resolved, whatever he might say, not to let themselves be taken in. He felt this especially when he talked to the cleverest of the peasants, Ryezunov, and detected the gleam in Ryezunov's eyes which showed so plainly both ironical amusement at Levin, and the firm conviction that, if anyone were to be taken in, it would not be he, Ryezunov. But in spite of all this Levin thought the system worked, and that by keeping accounts strictly and insisting on his own way, he would prove to them in the future the advantages of the arrangement, and then the system would go of itself.

These matters, together with the management of the land still left on his hands, and the indoor work over his book, so engrossed Levin the whole summer that he scarcely ever went out shooting. At the end of August he heard that the Oblonskys had gone away to Moscow, from their servant who brought back the side-saddle. He felt that in not answering Darya Alexandrovna's letter he had by his rudeness, of which he could not think without a flush of shame, burned his ships, and that he would never go and see them again. He had been just as rude with the Sviazhskys, leaving them without saying good-bye. But he would never go to see them again either. He did not care about that now. The business of reorganising the farming of his land absorbed him as completely as though there would never be anything else in his life. He read the books lent him by Sviazhsky, and copying out what he had not got, he read both the economic and socialistic books on the subject, but, as he had anticipated, found nothing bearing on the scheme he had undertaken. In the books on political economy—in Mill, for instance—

whom he studied first with great ardour, hoping every minute to find an answer to the questions that were engrossing him, he found laws deduced from the condition of land culture in Europe; but he did not see why these laws, which did not apply in Russia, must be general. He saw just the same thing in the socialistic books: either they were the beautiful but impracticable fantasies which had fascinated him when he was a student, or they were attempts at improving, rectifying the economic position in which Europe was placed, with which the system of land tenure in Russia had nothing in common. Political economy told him that the laws by which the wealth of Europe had been developed, and was developing, were universal and unvarying. Socialism told him that development along these lines leads to ruin. And neither of them gave an answer, or even a hint, in reply to the question what he, Levin and all the Russian peasants and landowners, were to do with their millions of hands and millions of acres, to make them as productive as posible for the common weal.

Having once taken the subject up, he read conscientiously everything bearing on it, and intended in the autumn to go abroad to study land systems on the spot, in order that he might not on this question be confronted with what so often met him on various subjects. Often, just as he was beginning to understand the idea in the mind of anyone he was talking to, and was beginning to explain his own, he would suddenly be told: 'But Kauffmann, but Jones, but Dubois, but Michelli? You haven't read them: they've thrashed that question out thoroughly.'

He saw now distinctly that Kauffmann and Michelli had nothing to tell him. He knew what he wanted. He saw that Russia has splendid land, splendid labourers, and that in certain cases, as at the peasant's on the way to Sviazhsky's, the produce raised by the labourers and the land is great—in the majority of cases when capital is applied in the European way the produce is small, and that this simply arises from the fact that the labourers want to work and work well only in their own peculiar way, and that this antagonism is not incidental but invariable, and has its roots in the national spirit. He thought that the Russian people whose task it was to colonise and cultivate vast tracts of unoccupied land, consciously adhered, till all their land was occupied, to the methods suitable to their purpose, and that their methods were by no means so bad as was generally supposed. And he wanted to prove this theoretically in his book and practically on his land.

XXX

AT the end of September the timber had been carted for building the cattle-yard on the land that had been allotted to the association of peasants, and the butter from the cows was sold and the profits divided. In practice the system worked capitally, or, at least, so it seemed to Levin. In order to work out the whole subject theoretically and to complete his book, which, in Levin's day-dreams, was not merely to effect a revolution in political economy, but to annihilate that science entirely and to lay the foundation of a new science of the relation of the people to the soil, all that was left to do was to make a tour abroad, and to study on the spot all that had been done in the same direction, and to collect conclusive evidence that all that had been done there was not what was wanted. Levin was only waiting for the delivery of his wheat to receive the money for it and go abroad. But the rains began, preventing the harvesting of the corn and potatoes left in the fields, and putting a stop to all work, even to the delivery of the wheat. The mud was impassable along the roads; two mills were carried away, and the weather got worse and worse.

On the 30th of September the sun came out in the morning, and hoping for fine weather, Levin began making final preparations for his journey. He gave orders for the wheat to be delivered, sent the bailiff to the merchant to get the money owing him, and went out himself to give some final directions on the estate before setting off.

Having finished all his business, soaked through with the streams of water which kept running down the leather behind his neck and his gaiters, but in the keenest and most confident temper, Levin returned homewards in the evening. The weather had become worse than ever towards evening; the hail lashed the drenched mare so cruelly that she went along sideways, shaking her head and ears; but Levin was all right under his hood, and he looked cheerfully about him at the muddy streams running under the wheels, at the drops hanging on every bare twig, at the whiteness of the patch of unmelted hailstones on the planks of the bridge, at the thick layer of still juicy, fleshy leaves that lay heaped up about the stripped elm-tree. In spite of the gloominess of nature around him, he felt peculiarly eager. The talks he had been having with the peasants in the further village had shown that they were beginning to get used to their new position. The old servant to whose hut he had gone to get dry evidently approved of Levin's plan, and of his own accord proposed to enter the partnership by the purchase of cattle.

'I have only to go stubbornly on towards my aim, and I shall attain my end,' thought Levin; 'and it's something to work and take trouble for. This is not a matter of myself individually, the question of the public welfare comes into it. The whole system of culture, the chief element in the condition of the people, must be completely transformed. Instead of poverty, general prosperity and content; instead of hostility, harmony and unity of interests. In short, a bloodless revolution, but a revolution of the greatest magnitude, beginning in the little circle of our district, then the province, then Russia, the whole world. Because a just idea cannot but be fruitful. Yes, it's an aim worth working for. And it's being me, Kostya Levin, who went to a ball in a black tie, and was refused by the Shtcherbatsky girl, and who was intrinsically such a pitiful, worthless creature—that proves nothing; I feel sure Franklin felt just as worthless, and he too had no faith in himself, thinking of himself as a whole. That means nothing. And he too, most likely, had an Agafea Mihalovna to whom he confided his secrets.'

Musing on such thoughts Levin reached home in the darkness.

The bailiff, who had been to the merchant, had come back and brought part of the money for the wheat. An agreement had been made with the old servant, and on the road the bailiff had learned that everywhere the corn was still standing in the fields, so that his one hundred and sixty shocks that had not been carried were nothing in comparison with the losses of others.

After dinner Levin was sitting, as he usually did, in an easy-chair with a book, and as he read he went on thinking of the journey before him in connection with his book. Today all the significance of his book rose before him with special distinctness, and whole periods ranged themselves in his mind in illustration of his theories. 'I must write that down,' he thought. 'That ought to form a brief introduction, which I thought unnecessary before.' He got up to go to his writing-table, and Laska, lying at his feet, got up too, stretching and looking at him as though to inquire where to go. But he had not time to write it down, for the head peasants had come round, and Levin went out into the hall to them.

After his levee, that is to say, giving directions about the labours of the next day, and seeing all the peasants who had business with him, Levin went back to his study and sat down to work.

Laska lay under the table; Agafea Mihalovna settled herself in her place with her stocking.

After writing for a little while, Levin suddenly thought with exceptional vividness of Kitty, her refusal, and their last meeting. He got up and began walking about the room.

'What's the use of being dreary?' said Agafea Mihalovna. 'Come, why do you stay on at home? You ought to go to some warm springs, especially now you're ready for the journey.'

'Well, I am going away the day after tomorrow, Agafea Mihalovna; I must finish my work.'

'There, there, your work, you say! As if you hadn't done enough for the peasants! Why, as 'tis, they're saying, "Your master will be getting some honour from the Tsar for it." Indeed and it is a strange thing; why need you worry about the peasants?'

'I'm not worrying about them; I'm doing it for my own good.'

Agafea Mihalovna knew every detail of Levin's plans for his land. Levin often put his views before her in all their complexity, and not uncommonly he argued with her and did not agree with her comments. But on this occasion she entirely misinterpreted what he had said.

'Of one's soul's salvation we all know and must think before all else,' she said with a sigh. 'Parfen Denisitch now, for all he was no scholar, he died a death that God grant everyone of us the like,' she said, referring to a servant who had died recently. 'Took the sacrament and all.'

'That's not what I mean,' said he. 'I mean that I'm acting for my own advantage. It's all the better for me if the peasants do their work better.'

'Well, whatever you do, if he's a lazy good-for-nought, everything'll be at sixes and sevens. If he has a conscience, he'll work, and if not, there's no doing anything.'

'Oh, come, you say yourself Ivan has begun looking after the cattle better.'

'All I say is,' answered Agafea Mihalovna, evidently not speaking at random, but in strict sequence of ideas, 'that you ought to get married, that's what I say.'

Agafea Mihalovna's allusion to the very subject he had only just been thinking about, hurt and stung him. Levin scowled, and without answering her, he sat down again to his work, repeating to himself all that he had been thinking of the real significance of that work. Only at intervals he listened in the stillness to the click of Agafea Mihalovna's needles, and recollecting what he did not want to remember, he frowned again.

At nine o'clock they heard the bell and the faint vibration of a carriage over the mud.

'Well, here's visitors come to us, and you won't be dull,' said Agafea Mihalovna, getting up and going to the door. But Levin overtook her. His work was not going well now, and he was glad of a visitor, whoever it might be.

XXXI

RUNNING half-way down the staircase, Levin caught a sound he knew, a familiar cough in the hall. But he heard it indistinctly through the sound of his own footsteps, and hoped he was mistaken. Then he caught sight of a long, bony, familiar figure, and now it seemed there was no possibility of mistake; and yet he still went on hoping that this tall man taking off his fur cloak and coughing was not his brother Nikolay.

Levin loved his brother, but being with him was always a torture. Just now, when Levin, under the influence of the thoughts that had come to him, and Agafea Mihalovna's hint, was in a troubled and uncertain humour, the meeting with his brother that he had to face seemed particularly difficult. Instead of a lively, healthy visitor, some outsider who would, he hoped, cheer him up in his uncertain humour, he had to see his brother, who knew him through and through, who would call forth all the thoughts nearest his heart, would force him to show himself fully. And that he was not disposed to do.

Angry with himself for so base a feeling, Levin ran into the hall; as soon as he had seen his brother close, this feeling of selfish disappointment vanished instantly and was replaced by pity. Terrible as his brother Nikolay had been before in his emaciation and sickliness, now he looked still more emaciated, still more wasted. He was a skeleton covered by skin.

He stood in the hall, jerking his long thin neck, and pulling the scarf off it, and smiled a strange and pitiful smile. When he saw that smile, submissive and humble, Levin felt something clutching at his throat.

'You see I've come to you,' said Nikolay in a thick voice, never for one second taking his eyes off his brother's face. 'I've been meaning to a long while, but I've been unwell all the time. Now I'm ever so much better,' he said, rubbing his beard with his big thin hands.

'Yes, yes!' answered Levin. And he felt still more frightened when, kissing him, he felt with his lips the dryness of his brother's skin and saw close to him his big eyes, full of a strange light.

A few weeks before, Konstantin Levin had written to his brother that through the sale of the small part of the property, that had remained undivided, there was a sum of about two thousand roubles to come to him as his share.

Nikolay said that he had come now to take his money and, what was more important, to stay a while in the old nest, to get in touch with the earth, so as to renew his strength like the heroes of old for the work that lay before him. In spite of his exaggerated stoop, and the emaciation that was so striking from his height, his movements were as rapid and abrupt as ever. Levin led him into his study.

His brother dressed with particular care—a thing he never used to do—combed his scanty, lank hair, and, smiling, went upstairs.

He was in the most affectionate and good-humoured mood, just as Levin often remembered him in childhood. He even referred to Sergey Ivanovitch without rancour. When he saw Agafea Mihalovna, he made jokes with her and asked after the old servants. The news of the death of Parfen Denisitch made a painful impression on him. A look of fear crossed his face, but he regained his serenity immediately.

'Oh course he was quite old,' he said, and changed the subject. 'Well, I'll spend a month or two with you, and then I'm off to Moscow. Do you know, Myakov has promised me a place there, and I'm going into the service. Now I'm going to arrange my life quite differently,' he went on. 'You know I got rid of that woman.'

'Marya Nikolaevna? Why, what for?'

'Oh, she was a horrid woman! She caused me all sorts of worries.' But he did not say what the annoyances were. He could not say that he had cast off Marya Nikolaevna because the tea was weak, and, above all, because she would look after him, as though he were an invalid.

'Besides, I want to turn over a new leaf completely now. I've done silly things, of course, like everyone else, but money's the last consideration; I don't regret it. So long as there's health, and my health, thank God, is quite restored.'

Levin listened and racked his brains, but could think of nothing to say. Nikolay probably felt the same; he began questioning his brother about his affairs; and Levin was glad to talk about himself, because then he could speak without hypocrisy. He told his brother of his plans and his doings.

His brother listened, but evidently he was not interested by it.

These two men were so akin, so near each other, that the slightest gesture, the tone of voice, told both more than could be said in words.

Both of them now had only one thought—the illness of Nikolay and the nearness of his death—which stifled all else. But neither of them dared to speak of it, and so whatever they said—not uttering the one thought that filled their minds—was all falsehood. Never had Levin been so glad when the evening was over and it was time to go to bed. Never with any outside person, never on any official visit had he been so unnatural and false as he was that evening. And the consciousness of this unnaturalness, and the remorse he felt at it, made him even more unnatural. He wanted to weep over his dying, dearly loved brother, and he had to listen and keep on talking of how he meant to live.

As the house was damp, and only one bedroom had been kept heated, Levin put his brother to sleep in his own bedroom behind a screen.

His brother got into bed, and whether he slept or did not sleep, tossed about like a sick man, coughed, and when he could not get his throat clear, mumbled something. Sometimes when his breathing was painful, he said, 'Oh, my God!' Sometimes when he was choking he muttered angrily, 'Ah, the devil!' Levin could not sleep for a long while, hearing him. His thoughts were of the most various, but the end of all his thoughts was the same—death. Death, the inevitable end of all, for the first time presented itself to him with irresistible force. And death, which was here in this loved brother, groaning half asleep and from habit calling without distinction on God and the devil, was not so remote as it had hitherto seemed to him. It was in himself too he felt that. If not today, tomorrow, if not tomorrow, in thirty years, wasn't it all the same! And what was this inevitable death—he did not know, had never thought about it, and what was more, had not the power, had not the courage to think about it.

'I work, I want to do something, but I had forgotten it must all end; I had forgotten—death.'

He sat on his bed in the darkness, crouched up, hugging his knees, and holding his breath from the strain of thought, he pondered. But the more intensely he thought, the clearer it became to him that it was indubitably so, that in reality, looking upon life, he had forgotten one little fact—that death will come, and all ends; that nothing was even worth beginning, and that there was no helping it any way. Yes, it was awful, but it was so.

'But I am alive still. Now what's to be done? what's to be done?' he said in despair. He lighted a candle, got up cautiously and went to the looking-glass, and began looking at his face and hair. Yes, there were grey hairs about his temples. He opened his mouth. His back teeth were beginning to decay. He bared his muscular arms. Yes, there was strength in them. But Nikolay, who lay there breathing with what was left of lungs, had had a strong, healthy body too. And suddenly he recalled how they used to go to bed together as children, and how they only waited till Fyodor Bogdanitch was out of the room to fling pillows at each other and laugh, laugh irrepressibly, so that even their awe of Fyodor Bogdanitch could not check the effervescing, over-brimming sense of life and happiness. 'And now that bent, hollow chest

. . . and I, not knowing what will become of me, or wherefore . . .'

'K . . . ha! K . . . ha! Damnation! Why do you keep fidgeting, why don't you go to sleep?' his brother's voice called to him.

'Oh, I don't know; I'm not sleepy.'

'I have had a good sleep, I'm not in a sweat now. Just see, feel my shirt; it's not wet, is it?'

Levin felt, withdrew behind the screen, and put out the candle, but for a long while he could not sleep. The question how to live had hardly begun to grow a little clearer to him, when a new, insoluble question presented itself—death.

'Why, he's dying—yes, he'll die in the spring, and how help him? What can I say to him? What do I know about it? I'd even forgotten that it was at all.'

XXXII

LEVIN had long before made the observation that when one is uncomfortable with people from their being excessively amenable and meek, one is apt very soon after to find things intolerable from their touchiness and irritability. He felt that this was how it would be with his brother. And his brother Nikolay's gentleness did in fact not last out for long. The very next morning he began to be irritable, and seemed doing his best to find fault with his brother, attacking him on his tenderest points.

Levin felt himself to blame, and could not set things right. He felt that if they had both not kept up appearances, but had spoken, as it is called, from the heart—that is to say, had said only just what they were thinking and feeling—they would simply have looked into each other's faces, and Konstantin could only have said, 'You're dying, you're dying!' and Nikolay could only have answered, 'I know I'm dying, but I'm afraid, I'm afraid, I'm afraid!' And they could have said nothing more, if they had said only what was in their hearts. But life like that was impossible, and so Konstantin tried to do what he had been trying to do all his life, and never could learn to do, though, as far as he could observe, many people knew so well how to do it, and without it there was no living at all. He tried to say what he was not thinking, but he felt continually that it had a ring of falsehood, that his brother detected him in it, and was exasperated at it.

The third day Nikolay induced his brother to explain his plan to him again, and began not merely attacking it, but intentionally confounding it with communism.

'You've simply borrowed an idea that's not your own, but you've distorted it, and are trying to apply it where it's not applicable.'

'But I tell you it's nothing to do with it. They deny the justice of property, of capital, of inheritance, while I do not deny this chief stimulus.' (Levin felt disgusted himself at using such expressions, but ever since he had been engrossed by his work, he had unconsciously come more and more frequently to use words not Russian.) 'All I want is to regulate labour.'

'Which means, you've borrowed an idea, stripped it of all that gave it its force, and want to make believe that it's something new,' said Nikolay, angrily tugging at his necktie.

'But my idea has nothing in common . . .'

'That, anyway,' said Nikolay Levin, with an ironical smile, his eyes flashing malignantly, 'has the charm of—what's one to call it?—geometrical symmetry, of clearness, of definiteness. It may be a Utopia. But if once one allows the possibility of making of all the past a *tabula rasa*—no property, no family—then labour would organise itself. But you gain nothing . . .'

'Why do you mix things up? I've never been a communist.'

'But I have, and I consider it's premature, but rational, and it has a future, just like Christianity in its first ages.'

'All that I maintain is that the labour force ought to be investigated from the point of view of natural science; that is to say, it ought to be studied, its qualities ascertained . . .'

'But that's utter waste of time. That force finds a certain form of activity of itself, according to the stage of its development. There have been slaves first everywhere, then metayers; and we have the half-crop system, rent, and day-labourers. What are you trying to find?'

Levin suddenly lost his temper at these words, because at the bottom of his heart he was afraid that it was true—true that he was trying to hold the balance even between communism and the familiar forms, and that this was hardly possible.

'I am trying to find means of working productively for myself and for the labourers. I want to organise . . .' he answered hotly.

'You don't want to organise anything; it's simply just as you've been all your life, that you want to be original, to pose as not exploiting the peasants simply, but with some idea in view.'

'Oh, all right, that's what you think—and let me alone!' answered Levin, feeling the muscles of his left cheek twitching uncontrollably.

'You've never had, and never have, convictions; all you want is to please your vanity.'

'Oh, very well; then let me alone!'

'And I will let you alone! and it's high time I did, and go to the devil with you! and I'm very sorry I ever came!'

In spite of all Levin's efforts to soothe his brother afterwards, Nikolay would listen to nothing he said, declaring that it was better to part, and Konstantin saw that it simply was that life was unbearable to him.

Nikolay was just getting ready to go, when Konstantin went in to him again and begged him, rather unnaturally, to forgive him if he had hurt his feelings in any way.

'Ah, generosity!' said Nikolay, and he smiled. 'If you want to be right, I can give you that satisfaction. You're in the right; but I'm going all the same.'

It was only just at parting that Nikolay kissed him, and said, looking with sudden strangeness and seriousness at his brother—

'Anyway, don't remember evil against me, Kostya!' and his voice quivered. These were the only words that had been spoken sincerely between them. Levin knew that those words meant, 'You see, and you know, that I'm in a bad way, and maybe we shall not see each other again.' Levin knew this, and the tears gushed from his eyes. He kissed his brother once more, but he could not speak, and knew not what to say.

Three days after his brother's departure, Levin too set off for his foreign tour. Happening to meet Shtcherbatsky, Kitty's cousin, in the railway train, Levin greatly astonished him by his depression.

'What's the matter with you?' Shtcherbatsky asked him.

'Oh, nothing; there's not much happiness in life.'

'Not much? You come with me to Paris instead of to Mulhausen. You shall see how to be happy.'

'No, I've done with it all. It's time I was dead.'

'Well, that's a good one!' said Shtcherbatsky, laughing, 'why, I'm only just getting ready to begin.'

'Yes, I thought the same not long ago, but now I know I shall soon be dead.'

Levin said what he had genuinely been thinking of late. He saw nothing but death or the advance towards death in everything. But his cherished scheme only engrossed him the more. Life had to be got through somehow till death did come. Darkness had fallen upon everything for him; but just because of this darkness he felt that the one guiding clue in the darkness was his work, and he clutched it and clung to it with all his strength.

PART IV

I

THE Karenins, husband and wife, continued living in the same house, met every day, but were complete strangers to one another. Alexey Alexandrovitch made it a rule to see his wife every day, so that the servants might have no grounds for suppositions, but avoided dining at home. Vronsky was never at Alexey Alexandrovitch's house, but Anna saw him away from home, and her husband was aware of it.

The position was one of misery for all three; and not one of them would have been equal to enduring this position for a single day, if it had not been for the expectation that it would change, that it was merely a temporary, painful ordeal which would pass over. Alexey Alexandrovitch hoped that this passion would pass, as everything does pass, that everyone would forget about it, and his name would remain unsullied. Anna, on whom the position depended, and for whom it was more miserable than for anyone, endured it because she not merely hoped, but firmly believed, that it would all very soon be settled and come right. She had not the least idea what would settle the position, but she firmly believed that something would very soon turn up now. Vronsky, against his own will or wishes, following her lead, hoped too that something, apart from his own action, would be sure to solve all difficulties.

In the middle of the winter Vronsky spent a very tiresome week. A foreign prince, who had come on a visit to Petersburg, was put under his charge, and he had to show him the sights worth seeing. Vronsky was of distinguished appearance; he possessed, moreover, the art of behaving with respectful dignity, and was used to having to do with such grand personages—that was how he came to be put in charge of the prince. But he felt his duties very irksome. The prince was anxious to miss nothing of which he would be asked at home, had he seen that in Russia? And on his own account he was anxious to enjoy to the utmost all Russian forms of amusement. Vronsky was obliged to be his guide in satisfying both these inclinations. The mornings they spent driving to look at places of interest; the evenings they passed enjoying the national entertainments. The prince rejoiced in health exceptional even among princes. By gymnastics and careful attention to his health he had brought himself to such a point that in spite of his excesses in pleasure he looked as fresh as a big glossy green Dutch cucumber. The prince had travelled a great deal, and considered one of the chief advantages of modern facilities of communication was the accessibility of the pleasures of all nations.

He had been in Spain, and there had indulged in serenades and had made friends with a Spanish girl who played the mandoline. In Switzerland he had killed chamois. In England he had galloped in a red coat over hedges and killed two hundred pheasants for a bet. In Turkey he had got into a harem; in India he had hunted on an elephant, and now in Russia he wished to taste all the specially Russian forms of pleasure.

Vronsky, who was, as it were, chief master of the ceremonies to him, was at great pains to arrange all the Russian amusements suggested by various persons to the prince. They had race-horses, and Russian pancakes and bear-hunts and three-horse sledges, and gypsies and drinking feasts, with the Russian accompaniment of broken crockery. And the prince with surprising ease fell in with the Russian spirit, smashed trays full of crockery, sat with a gypsy girl on his knee, and seemed to be asking—what more, and does the whole Russian spirit consist in just this?

In reality, of all the Russian entertainments the prince liked best French actresses and ballet-dancers and white-seal champagne. Vronsky was used to princes, but, either because he had himself changed of late, or that he was in too close proximity to the prince, that week seemed fearfully wearisome to him. The whole of that week he experienced a sensation such as a man might have set in charge of a dangerous madman, afraid of the madman, and at the same time, from being with him, fearing for his own reason. Vronsky was continually conscious of the necessity of never for a second relaxing the tone of stern official respectfulness, that he might not himself be insulted. The prince's manner of treating the very people who, to Vronsky's surprise, were ready to descend to any depths to provide him with Russian amusements, was contemptuous. His criticisms of Russian women, whom he wished to study, more than once made Vronsky crimson with indignation. The chief reason why the prince was so particularly disagreeable to Vronsky was that he could not help seeing himself in him. And what he saw in this mirror did not gratify his self-esteem. He was a very stupid and very self-satisfied and very healthy and very well-washed man, and nothing else. He was a gentleman—that was true, and Vronsky could not deny it. He was equable and not cringing with his superiors, was free and ingratiating in his behaviour with his equals, and was contemptuously indulgent with his inferiors. Vronsky was himself the same, and regarded it as a great merit to be so. But for this prince he was an inferior, and his contemptuous and indulgent attitude to him revolted him.

'Brainless beef! can I be like that?' he thought.

Be that as it might, when, on the seventh day, he parted from the prince, who was starting for Moscow, and received his thanks, he was happy to be rid of his uncomfortable position and the unpleasant reflection of himself. He said goodbye to him at the station on their return from a bear-hunt, at which they had had a display of Russian prowess kept up all night.

II

WHEN he got home, Vronsky found there a note from Anna. She wrote, 'I am ill and unhappy. I cannot come out, but I cannot go on longer without seeing you. Come in this evening. Alexey Alexandrovitch goes to the council at seven and will be there till ten.' Thinking for an instant of the strangeness of her bidding him come straight to her, in spite of her husband's insisting on her not receiving him, he decided to go.

Vronsky had that winter got his promotion, was now a colonel, had left the regimental quarters, and was living alone. After having some lunch, he lay down on the sofa immediately, and in five minutes memories of the hideous scenes he had witnessed during the last few days were confused together and joined on to a mental image of Anna and of the peasant who had played an important part in the bear-hunt, and Vronsky fell asleep. He waked up in the dark, trembling with horror, and made haste to light a candle. 'What was it? What? what was the dreadful thing I dreamed? Yes, yes; I think a little dirty man with a dishevelled beard was stooping down doing something, and all of a sudden he began saying some strange words in French. Yes, there was nothing else in the dream,' he said to himself. 'But why was it so awful?' He vividly recalled the peasant again and those incomprehensible French words the peasant had uttered, and a chill of horror ran down his spine.

'What nonsense!' thought Vronsky, and glanced at his watch.

It was half-past eight already. He rang up his servant, dressed in haste, and went out on to the steps, completely forgetting the dream and only worried at being late. As he drove up to the Karenins' entrance he looked at his watch and saw it was ten minutes to nine. A high, narrow carriage with a pair of greys was standing at the entrance. He recognised Anna's carriage. 'She is coming to me,' thought Vronsky, 'and better she should. I don't like going into that house. But no matter; I can't hide myself,' he thought, and with that manner peculiar to him from childhood, as of a man who has nothing to be ashamed of, Vronsky got out of his sledge and went to the door. The door opened, and the hall-porter with a rug on his arm called the carriage. Vronsky, though he did not usually notice details, noticed at this moment the amazed expression with which the porter glanced at him. In the very doorway Vronsky almost ran up against Alexey Alexandrovitch. The gas jet threw its full light on the bloodless, sunken face under the black hat and on the white cravat, brilliant against the beaver of the coat. Karenin's fixed, dull eyes were fastened upon Vronsky's face. Vronsky bowed, and Alexey Alexandrovitch, chewing his lips, lifted his hand to his hat and went on. Vronsky saw him without looking round get into the carriage, pick up the rug and the opera-glass at the window and disappear. Vronsky went into the hall. His brows were scowling, and his eyes gleamed with a proud and angry light in them.

'What a position!' he thought. 'If he would fight, would stand up for his honour, I could act, could express my feelings; but this weakness or baseness . . . He puts me in the position of playing false, which I never meant and never mean to do.'

Vronsky's ideas had changed since the day of his conversation with Anna in the Vrede garden. Unconsciously yielding to the weakness of Anna—who had surrendered herself up to him utterly, and simply looked to him to decide her fate, ready to submit to anything—he had long ceased to think that their tie might end as he had thought then. His ambitious plans had retreated into the background again, and feeling that he had got out of that circle of activity in which everything was definite, he had given himself entirely to his passion, and that passion was binding him more and more closely to her.

He was still in the hall when he caught the sound of her retreating footsteps. He knew she had been expecting him, had listened for him, and was now going back to the drawing-room.

'No,' she cried, on seeing him, and at the first sound of her voice the tears came into her eyes. 'No; if things are to go on like this, the end will come much, much too soon.'

'What is it, dear one?'

'What? I've been waiting in agony for an hour, two hours. . . . No, I won't . . . I can't quarrel with you. Of course you couldn't come. No, I won't.' She laid her two hands on his shoulders, and looked a long while at him with a profound, passionate, and at the same time searching look. She was studying his face to make up for the time she had not seen him. She was, every time she saw him, making the picture of him in her imagination (incomparably superior, impossible in reality) fit with him as he really was.

III

'You met him?' she asked, when they sat down at the table in the lamp-light. 'You're punished, you see, for being late.'

'Yes; but how was it? Wasn't he to be at the council?'

'He had been and come back, and was going out somewhere again. But that's no matter. Don't talk about it. Where have you been? With the prince still?'

She knew every detail of his existence. He was going to say that he had been up all night and had dropped asleep, but looking at her thrilled and rapturous face, he was ashamed. And he said he had had to go to report on the prince's departure.

'But it's over now? He is gone?'

'Thank God it's over! You wouldn't believe how insufferable it's been for me.'

'Why so? Isn't it the life all of you, all young men, always lead?' she said, knitting her brows; and taking up the crochet-work that was lying on the table, she began drawing the hook out of it, without looking at Vronsky.

'I gave that life up long ago,' said he, wondering at the change in her face, and trying to divine its meaning. 'And I confess,' he said, with a smile, showing his thick, white teeth, 'this week I've been, as it were, looking at myself in a glass, seeing that life, and I didn't like it.'

She held the work in her hands, but did not crochet, and looked at him with strange, shining, and hostile eyes.

'This morning Liza came to see me—they're not afraid to call on me, in spite of the Countess Lidia Ivanovna,' she put in—'and she told me about your Athenian evening. How loathsome!'

'I was just going to say . . .'

She interrupted him.

'It was that Thérèse you used to know?'

'I was just saying . . .'

'How disgusting you are, you men! How is it you can't understand that a woman can never forget that,' she said, getting more and more angry, and so letting him see the cause of her irritation, 'especially a woman who cannot know your life? What do I know? What have I ever known?' she said, 'what you tell me. And how do I know whether you tell me the truth? . . .'

'Anna, you hurt me. Don't you trust me? Haven't I told you that I haven't a thought I wouldn't lay bare to you?'

'Yes, yes,' she said, evidently trying to suppress her jealous thoughts. 'But if only you knew how wretched I am! I believe you, I believe you. . . . What were you saying?'

But he could not at once recall what he had been going to say. These fits of jealousy, which of late had been more and more frequent with her, horrified him, and however much he tried to disguise the fact, made him feel cold to her, although he knew the cause of her jealousy was her love for him. How often he had told himself that her love was happiness; and now she loved him as a woman can love when love has outweighed for her all the good things of life—and he was much further from happiness than when he had followed her from Moscow. Then he had thought himself unhappy, but happiness was before him; now he felt that the best happiness was already left behind. She was utterly unlike what she had been when he first saw her. Both morally and physically she had changed for the worse. She had broadened out all over, and in her face at the time when she was speaking of the actress there was an evil expression of hatred that distorted it. He looked at her as a man looks at a faded flower he has gathered, with difficulty recognising in it the beauty for which he picked and ruined it. And in spite of this he felt that then, when his love was stronger, he could, if he had greatly wished it, have torn that love out of his heart; but now, when as at that moment it seemed to him he felt no love for her, he knew that what bound him to her could not be broken.

'Well, well, what was it you were going to say about the prince? I have driven away the fiend,' she added. The fiend was the name they had given her jealousy. 'What did you begin to tell me about the prince? Why did you find it so tiresome?'

'Oh, it was intolerable!' he said, trying to pick up the thread of his interrupted thought. 'He does not improve on closer acquaintance. If you want him defined, here he is: a prime, well-fed beast such as takes medals at the cattle-shows, and, nothing more,' he said, with a tone of vexation that interested her.

'No; how so?' she replied. 'He's seen a great deal, any way; he's cultured?'

'It's an utterly different culture—their culture. He's cultivated, one sees, simply to be able to despise culture, as they despise everything but animal pleasures.'

'But don't you all care for these animal pleasures?' she said, and again he noticed a dark look in her eyes that avoided him.

'How is it you're defending him?' he said, smiling.

'I'm not defending him, it's nothing to me; but I imagine, if you had not cared for those pleasures yourself, you might have got out of them. But if it affords you satisfaction to gaze at Thérèse in the attire of Eve . . .'

'Again, the devil again,' Vronsky said, taking the hand she had laid on the table, and kissing it.

'Yes; but I can't help it. You don't know what I have suffered waiting for you. I believe I'm not jealous. I'm not jealous: I believe you when you're here; but when you're away somewhere leading your life, so incomprehensible to me . . .'

She turned away from him, pulled the hook at last out of the crochet-work, and rapidly, with the help of her forefinger, began working loop after loop of the wool that was dazzling white in the lamplight, while the slender wrist moved swiftly, nervously in the embroidered cuff.

'How was it, then? Where did you meet Alexey Alexandrovitch?' Her voice sounded in an unnatural and jarring tone.

'We ran up against each other in the doorway.'

'And he bowed to you like this?'

She drew a long face, and half-closing her eyes, quickly transformed her expression, folded her hands, and Vronsky suddenly saw in her beautiful face the very expression with which Alexey Alexandrovitch had bowed to him. He smiled, while she laughed gaily, with that sweet, deep laugh, which was one of her greatest charms.

'I don't understand him in the least,' said Vronsky. 'If after your avowal to him at your country house he had broken with you, if he had called me out—but this I can't understand. How can he put up with such a position? He feels it, that's evident.'

'He?' she said sneeringly. 'He's perfectly satisfied.'

'What are we all miserable for, when everything might be so happy?'

'Only not he. Don't I know him, the falsity in which he's utterly steeped? . . . Could one, with any feeling, live as he is living with me? He understands nothing, and feels nothing. Could a man of any feeling live in the same house with his unfaithful wife? Could he talk to her, call her " my dear"?'

And again she could not help mimicking him: "Anna, *ma chère*; Anna, dear!" '

'He's not a man, not a human being—he's a doll! No one knows him; but I know him. Oh, if I'd been in his place, I'd long ago have killed, have torn to pieces a wife like me. I wouldn't have said, "Anna, *ma chère*"! He's not a man, he's an official machine. He doesn't understand that I'm your wife, that he's outside, that he's superfluous. . . . Don't let's talk of him! . . .'

'You're unfair, very unfair, dearest,' said Vronsky, trying to soothe her. 'But never mind, don't let's talk of him. Tell me what you've been doing? What is the matter? What has been wrong with you, and what did the doctor say?'

She looked at him with mocking amusement. Evidently she had hit on other absurd and grotesque aspects in her husband, and was awaiting the moment to give expression to them.

But he went on—

'I imagine that it's no illness, but your condition. When will it be?'

The ironical light died away in her eyes, but a different smile, a consciousness of something, he did not know what, and of quiet melancholy, came over her face.

'Soon, soon. You say that our position is miserable, that we must put an end to it. If you knew how terrible it is to me, what I would give to be able to love you freely and boldly! I should not torture myself and torture you with my jealousy. . . . And it will come soon, but not as we expect.'

And at the thought of how it would come, she seemed so pitiable to herself that tears came into her eyes, and she could not go on. She laid her hand on his sleeve, dazzling and white with its rings in the lamplight.

'It won't come as we suppose. I didn't mean to say this to you, but you've made me. Soon, soon, all will be over, and we shall all, all be at peace, and suffer no more.'

'I don't understand,' he said, understanding her.

'You asked when? Soon. And I shan't live through it. Don't interrupt me!' and she made haste to speak. 'I know it; I know it for certain. I shall die; and I'm very glad I shall die, and release myself and you.'

Tears dropped from her eyes; he bent down over her hand and began kissing it, trying to hide his emotion, which, he knew, had no sort of grounds, though he could not control it.

'Yes, it's better so,' she said, tightly gripping his hand. 'That's the only way, the only way left us.'

He had recovered himself, and lifted his head.

'How absurd! What absurd nonsense you are talking!'

'No, it's the truth.'

'What, what's the truth?'

'That I shall die. I have had a dream.'

'A dream?' repeated Vronsky, and instantly he recalled the peasant of his dream.

'Yes, a dream,' she said. 'It's a long while since I dreamed it. I dreamed that I ran into my bedroom, that I had to get something there, to find out something; you know how it is in dreams,' she said, her eyes wide with horror; 'and in the bedroom, in the corner, stood something.'

'Oh, what nonsense! How can you believe . . .'

But she would not let him interrupt her. What she was saying was too important to her.

'And the something turned round, and I saw it was a peasant with a dishevelled beard, little, and dreadful-looking. I wanted to run away, but he bent down over a sack, and was fumbling there with his hands . . .'

She showed how he had moved his hands. There was terror in her face. And Vronsky, remembering his dream, felt the same terror filling his soul.

'He was fumbling and kept talking quickly, quickly in French, you know: *Il faut le battre, le fer, le broyer, le pétrir. . . .* And in my horror I tried to wake up, and woke up . . . but woke up in the dream. And I began asking myself what it meant. And Korney said to me: "In childbirth you'll die, ma'am, you'll die. . . ." And I woke up.'

'What nonsense, what nonsense!' said Vronsky; but he felt himself that there was no conviction in his voice.

'But don't let's talk of it. Ring the bell, I'll have tea. And stay a little, now; it's not long I shall . . .'

But all at once she stopped. The expression of her face instantaneously changed. Horror and excitement were suddenly replaced by a look of soft, solemn, blissful attention. He could not comprehend the meaning of the change. She was listening to the stirring of the new life within her.

IV

ALEXEY ALEXANDROVITCH, after meeting Vronsky on his own steps, drove, as he had intended, to the Italian opera. He sat through two acts there, and saw everyone he had wanted to see. On returning home, he carefully scrutinised the hat-stand, and noticing that there was not a military overcoat there, he went, as usual, to his own room. But, contrary to his usual habit, he did not go to bed, he walked up and down his study till three o'clock in the morning. The feeling of furious anger with his wife, who would not observe the proprieties and keep to the one stipulation he had laid on her, not to receive her lover in her own house, gave him no peace. She had not complied with his request, and he was bound to punish her and carry out his threat—obtain a divorce and take away his son. He knew all the difficulties connected with this course, but he had said he would do it, and now he must carry out his threat. Countess Lidia Ivanovna had hinted that this was the best way out of his position, and of late the obtaining of divorces had been brought to such perfection, that Alexey Alexandrovitch saw a possibility of overcoming the formal difficulties. Misfortunes never come singly, and the affairs of the reorganisation of the native tribes, and of the irrigation of the lands of the Zaraisky province, had brought such official worries upon Alexey Alexandrovitch, that he had been of late in a continual condition of extreme irritability.

He did not sleep the whole night, and his fury growing in a sort of vast, arithmetical progression, reached its highest limits in the morning. He dressed in haste, and as though carrying his cup full of wrath, and fearing to spill any over, fearing to lose with his wrath the energy necessary for the interview with his wife, he went into her room directly he heard she was up.

Anna, who thought she knew her husband so well was amazed at his appearance when he went in to her. His brow was lowering, and his eyes stared darkly before him, avoiding her eyes; his mouth was tightly and contemptuously shut. In his walk, in his gestures, in the sound of his voice there was a determination and firmness such as his wife had never seen in him. He went into her room, and without greeting her, walked straight up to her writing-table, and taking her keys, opened a drawer.

'What do you want?' she cried.

'Your lover's letters,' he said.

'They're not here,' she said, shutting the drawer; but from that action he saw he had guessed right, and roughly pushing away her hand, he quickly snatched a portfolio in which he knew she used to put her most important papers. She tried to pull the portfolio away, but he pushed her back.

'Sit down! I have to speak to you,' he said, putting the portfolio under his arm, and squeezing it so tightly with his elbow that his shoulder stood up. Amazed and intimidated, she gazed at him in silence.

'I told you that I would not allow you to receive your lover in this house.'

'I had to see him to . . .'

She stopped, not finding a reason.

'I do not enter into the details of why a woman wants to see her lover.'

'I meant, I only . . .' she said, flushing hotly. This coarseness of his angered her, and gave her courage. 'Surely you must feel how easy it is for you to insult me?' she said.

'An honest man and an honest woman may be insulted, but to tell a thief he's a thief is simply *la constatation d'un fait.*'

'This cruelty is something new I did not know in you.'

'You call it cruelty for a husband to give his wife liberty, giving her the honourable protection of his name, simply on the condition of observing the proprieties: is that cruelty?'

'It's worse than cruel—it's base, if you want to know!' Anna cried, in a rush of hatred, and getting up, she was going away.

'No!' he shrieked, in his shrill voice, which pitched a note higher than usual even, and his big hands clutching her by the arm so violently that red marks were left from the bracelet he was squeezing, he forcibly sat her down in her place.

'Base! If you care to use that word, what is base is to forsake husband and child for a lover, while you eat your husband's bread!'

She bowed her head. She did not say what she had said the evening before to her lover, that *he* was her husband, and her husband was superfluous; she did not even think that. She felt all the justice of his words, and only said softly—

'You cannot describe my position as worse than I feel it to be myself; but what are you saying all this for?'

'What am I saying it for? what for?' he went on, as angrily. 'That you may know that since you have not carried out my wishes in regard to observing outward decorum, I will take measures to put an end to this state of things.'

'Soon, very soon, it will end, anyway,' she said; and again, at the thought of death near at hand and now desired, tears came into her eyes.

'It will end sooner than you and your lover have planned! If you must have the satisfaction of animal passion . . .'

'Alexey Alexandrovitch! I won't say it's not generous, but it's not like a gentleman to strike anyone who's down.'

'Yes, you only think of yourself! But the sufferings of a man who was your husband have no interest for you. You don't care that his whole life is ruined, that he is thuff . . . thuff . . .'

Alexey Alexandrovitch was speaking so quickly that he stammered, and was utterly unable to articulate the word 'suffering.' In the end he pronounced it 'thuffering.' She wanted to laugh, and was immediately ashamed that anything could amuse her at such a moment. And for the first time, for an instant, she felt for him, put herself in his place, and was sorry for him. But what could she say or do? Her head sank, and she sat silent. He too was silent for some time, and then began speaking in a frigid, less shrill voice, emphasising random words that had no special significance.

'I came to tell you . . .' he said.

She glanced at him. 'No, it was my fancy,' she thought, recalling the expression of his face when he stumbled over the word 'suffering.' 'No; can a man with those dull eyes, with that self-satisfied complacency, feel anything?'

'I cannot change anything,' she whispered.

'I have come to tell you that I am going tomorrow to Moscow, and shall not return again to this house, and you will receive notice of what I decide through the lawyer into whose hands I shall intrust the task of getting a divorce. My son is going to my sister's,' said Alexey Alexandrovitch, with an effort recalling what he had meant to say about his son.

'You take Seryozha to hurt me,' she said, looking at him from under her brows. 'You do not love him. . . . Leave me Seryozha!'

'Yes, I have lost even my affection for my son, because he is associated with the repulsion I feel for you. But still I shall take him. Goodbye!'

And he was going away, but now she detained him.

'Alexey Alexandrovitch, leave me Seryozha!' she whispered once more. 'I have nothing else to say. Leave Seryozha till my . . . I shall soon be confined; leave him!'

Alexey Alexandrovitch flew into a rage, and, snatching his hand from her, he went out of the room without a word.

V

THE waiting-room of the celebrated Petersburg lawyer was full when Alexey Alexandrovitch entered it. Three ladies—an old lady, a young lady, and a merchant's wife—and three gentlemen—one a German banker with a ring on his finger, the second a merchant with a beard, and the third a wrathful-looking government clerk in official uniform, with a cross on his neck—had obviously been waiting a long while already. Two clerks were writing at tables with scratching pens. The appurtenances of the writing-tables, about which Alexey Alexandrovitch was himself very fastidious, were exceptionally good. He could not help observing this. One of the clerks, without getting up, turned wrathfully to Alexey Alexandrovitch, half closing his eyes.

'What are you wanting?'

He replied that he wanted to see the lawyer on some business.

'He is engaged,' the clerk responded severely, and he pointed with his pen at the persons waiting, and went on writing.

'Can't he spare time to see me?' said Alexey Alexandrovitch.

'He has no time free; he is always busy. Kindly wait your turn.'

'Then I must trouble you to give him my card,' Alexey Alexandrovitch said with dignity, seeing the impossibility of preserving his incognito.

The clerk took the card and, obviously not approving of what he read on it, went to the door.

Alexey Alexandrovitch was in principle in favour of the publicity of legal proceedings, though for some higher official considerations he disliked the application of the principle in Russia, and disapproved of it, as far as he could disapprove of anything instituted by authority of the Emperor. His whole life had been spent in administrative work, and consequently, when he did not approve of anything, his disapproval was softened by the recognition of the inevitability of mistakes and the possibility of reform in every department. In the new public law-courts he disliked the restrictions laid on the lawyers conducting cases. But till then he had had nothing to do with the law-courts, and so had disapproved of their publicity simply in theory; now his disapprobation was strengthened by the unpleasant impression made on him in the lawyer's waiting-room.

'Coming immediately,' said the clerk; and two minutes later there did actually appear in the doorway the large figure of an old solicitor who had been consulting with the lawyer himself.

The lawyer was a little, squat, bald man, with a dark, reddish beard, light-coloured long eyebrows, and an overhanging brow. He was attired as though for a wedding, from his cravat to his double watch-chain, and varnished boots. His face was clever and manly, but his dress was dandified and in bad taste.

'Pray walk in,' said the lawyer, addressing Alexey Alexandrovitch; and, gloomily ushering Karenin in before him, he closed the door.

'Won't you sit down?' He indicated an arm-chair at a writing-table covered with papers. He sat down himself, and, rubbing his little hands with short fingers covered with white hairs, he bent his head on one side. But as soon as he was settled in this position a moth flew over the table. The lawyer, with a swiftness that could never have been expected of him, opened his hands, caught the moth, and resumed his former attitude.

'Before beginning to speak of my business,' said Alexey Alexandrovitch, following the lawyer's movements with wondering eyes, 'I ought to observe that the business about which I have to speak to you is to be strictly private.'

The lawyer's overhanging reddish moustaches were parted in a scarcely perceptible smile.

'I should not be a lawyer if I could not keep the secrets confided to me. But if you would like proof . . .'

Alexey Alexandrovitch glanced at his face, and saw that the shrewd, grey eyes were laughing, and seemed to know all about it already.

'You know my name?' Alexey Alexandrovitch resumed.

'I know you and the good'—again he caught a moth—'work you are doing, like every Russian,' said the lawyer, bowing.

Alexey Alexandrovitch sighed, plucking up his courage. But having once made up his mind he went on in his shrill voice, without timidity or hesitation, accentuating here and there a word.

'I have the misfortune,' Alexey Alexandrovitch began, 'to have been deceived in my married life, and I desire to break off all relations with my wife by legal means—that is, to be divorced, but to do this so that my son may not remain with his mother.'

The lawyer's grey eyes tried not to laugh, but they were dancing with irrepressible glee, and Alexey Alexandrovitch saw that it was not simply the delight of a man who has just got a profitable job: there was triumph and joy, there was a gleam like the malignant gleam he saw in his wife's eyes.

'You desire my assistance in securing a divorce?'

'Yes, precisely so; but I ought to warn you that I may be wasting your time and attention. I have come simply to consult you as a preliminary step. I want a divorce, but the form in which it is possible is of great consequence to me. It is very possible that if that form does not correspond with my requirements I may give up a legal divorce.'

'Oh, that's always the case,' said the lawyer, 'and that's always for you to decide.'

He let his eyes rest on Alexey Alexandrovitch's feet, feeling that he might offend his client by the sight of his irrepressible amusement. He looked at a moth that flew before his nose, and moved his hand, but did not catch it from regard for Alexey Alexandrovitch's position.

'Though in their general features our laws on this subject are known to me,' pursued Alexey Alexandrovitch, 'I should be glad to have an idea of the forms in which such things are done in practice.'

'You would be glad,' the lawyer, without lifting his eyes, responded, adopting, with a certain satisfaction, the tone of his client's remarks, 'for me to lay before you all the methods by which you could secure what you desire?'

And on receiving an assenting nod from Alexey Alexandrovitch, he went on, stealing a glance now and then at Alexey Alexandrovitch's face, which was growing red in patches.

'Divorce by our laws,' he said, with a slight shade of disapprobation of our laws, 'is possible, as you are aware, in the following cases . . . Wait a little!' he called to a clerk who put his head in at the door, but he got up all the same, said a few words to him, and sat down again. '. . . In the following cases: physical defect in the married parties, desertion without communication for five years,' he said, crooking a short finger covered with hair, 'adultery' (this word he pronounced with obvious satisfaction), 'subdivided as follows' (he continued to crook his fat fingers, though the three cases and their sub-divisions could obviously not be classified together): 'physical defect of the husband or of the wife, adultery of the husband or of the wife.' As by now all his fingers were used up, he uncrooked all his fingers and went on: 'This is the theoretical view; but I imagine you have done me the honour to apply to me in order to learn its application in practice. And therefore, guided by precedents, I must inform you that in practice cases of divorce may all be reduced to the following—there's no physical defect, I may assume, nor desertion? . . .'

Alexey Alexandrovitch bowed his head in assent.

'—May be reduced to the following: adultery of one of the married parties and the detection in the fact of the guilty party by mutual agreement, and failing such agreement, accidental detection. It must be admitted that the latter case is rarely met with in practice,' said the lawyer, and stealing a glance at Alexey Alexandrovitch he paused, as a man selling pistols, after enlarging on the advantages of each weapon, might await his customer's choice. But Alexey Alexandrovitch said nothing, and therefore the lawyer went on: 'The most usual and simple, the sensible course, I consider, is adultery by mutual consent. I should not permit myself to express it so, speaking with a man of no education,' he said, 'but I imagine that to you this is comprehensible.'

Alexey Alexandrovitch was, however, so perturbed that he did not immediately comprehend all the good sense of adultery by mutual consent, and his eyes expressed this uncertainty; but the lawyer promptly came to his assistance.

'People cannot go on living together—here you have a fact. And if both are agreed about it, the details and formalities become a matter of no importance. And at the same time this is the simplest and most certain method.'

Alexey Alexandrovitch fully understood now. But he had religious scruples, which hindered the execution of such a plan.

'That is out of the question in the present case,' he said. 'Only one alternative is possible: undesigned detection, supported by letters which I have.'

At the mention of letters the lawyer pursed up his lips, and gave utterance to a thin little compassionate and contemptuous sound.

'Kindly consider,' he began, 'cases of that kind are, as you are aware, under ecclesiastical jurisdiction; the reverend fathers are fond of going into the minutest details in cases of the kind,' he said with a smile, which betrayed his sympathy with the reverend fathers' taste. 'Letters may, of course, be a partial confirmation; but detection in the fact there must be of the most direct kind, that is, by eye-witnesses. In fact, if you do me the honour to intrust your confidence to me, you will do well to leave me the choice of the measures to be employed. If one wants the result, one must admit the means.'

'If it is so . . .' Alexey Alexandrovitch began, suddenly turning white; but at that moment the lawyer rose and again went to the door to speak to the intruding clerk.

'Tell her we don't haggle over fees!' he said, and returned to Alexey Alexandrovitch.

On his way back he caught unobserved another moth. 'Nice state my rep curtains will be in by the summer!' he thought, frowning.

'And so you were saying? . . .' he said.

'I will communicate my decision to you by letter,' said Alexey Alexandrovitch, getting up, and he clutched at the table. After standing a moment in silence, he said: 'From your words I may consequently conclude that a divorce may be obtained? I would ask you to let me know what are your terms.'

'It may be obtained if you give me complete liberty of action,' said the lawyer, not answering his question. 'When can I reckon on receiving information from you?' he asked, moving towards the door, his eyes and his varnished boots shining.

'In a week's time. Your answer as to whether you will undertake to conduct the case, and on what terms, you will be so good as to communicate to me.'

'Very good.'

The lawyer bowed respectfully, let his client out of the door, and, left alone, gave himself up to his sense of amusement. He felt so mirthful that, contrary to his rules, he made a reduction in his terms to the haggling lady, and gave up catching moths, finally deciding that next winter he must have the furniture covered with velvet, like Sigonin's.

VI

ALEXEY ALEXANDROVITCH had gained a brilliant victory at the sitting of the Commission of the 17th of August, but in the sequel this victory cut the ground from under his feet. The new commission for the inquiry into the condition of the native tribes in all its branches had been formed and despatched to its destination with an unusual speed and energy inspired by Alexey Alexandrovitch. Within three months a report was presented. The conditions of the native tribes was investigated in its political, administrative, economic, ethnographic, material, and religious aspects. To all these questions there were answers admirably stated, and answers admitting no shade of doubt, since they were not a product of human thought, always liable to error, but were all the product of official activity. The answers were all based on official data furnished by governors and heads of churches, and founded on the reports of district magistrates and ecclesiastical superintendents, founded in their turn on the reports of parochial overseers and parish priests; and so all of these answers were unhesitating and certain. All such questions as, for instance, of the cause of failure of crops, of the adherence of certain tribes to their ancient beliefs, etc.—questions which, but for the convenient intervention of the official machine, are not, and cannot be solved for ages— received full, unhesitating solution. And this solution was in favour of Alexey Alexandrovitch's contention. But Stremov, who had felt stung to the quick at the last sitting, had, on the reception of the commission's report, resorted to tactics which Alexey Alexandrovitch had not anticipated. Stremov, carrying with him several other members, went over to Alexey Alexandrovitch's side, and not contenting himself with warmly defending the measure proposed by Karenin, proposed other more extreme measures in the same direction. These measures, still further exaggerated in opposition to what was Alexey Alexandrovitch's fundamental idea, were passed by the commission, and then the aim of Stremov's tactics became apparent. Carried to an extreme, the measures seemed at once to be so absurd that the highest authorities, and public opinion, and intellectual ladies, and the newspapers, all at the same time fell foul of them, expressing their indignation both with the measures and their nominal father, Alexey Alexandrovitch. Stremov drew back, affecting to have blindly followed Karenin, and to be astounded and distressed at what had been done. This meant the defeat of Alexey Alexandrovitch. But in spite of failing health, in spite of his domestic griefs, he did not give in. There was a split in the commission. Some members, with Stremov at their head, justified their mistake on the ground that they had put faith in the commission of revision, instituted by Alexey Alexandrovitch, and maintained that the report of the commission was rubbish, and simply so much waste paper. Alexey Alexandrovitch, with a following of those who saw the danger of so revolutionary an attitude to official documents, persisted in upholding the statements obtained by the revising commission. In consequence of this, in the higher spheres, and even in society, all was chaos, and although everyone was interested, no one could tell whether the native tribes really were becoming impoverished and ruined, or whether they were in a flourishing condition. The position of Alevey Alexandrovitch, owing to this, and partly owing to the contempt lavished on him for his wife's infidelity, became very precarious. And in this position he took an important resolution. To the astonishment of the commission, he announced that he should ask permission to go himself to investigate the question on the spot. And having obtained permission, Alexey Alexandrovitch prepared to set off to these remote provinces.

Alexey Alexandrovitch's departure made a great sensation, the more so as just before he started he officially returned the posting-fares allowed him for twelve horses, to drive to his destination.

'I think it very noble,' Betsy said about this to the Princess Myaky. 'Why take money for posting-horses when everyone knows that there are railways everywhere now?'

But Princess Myaky did not agree, and the Princess Tverskoy's opinion annoyed her indeed.

'It's all very well for you to talk,' said she, 'when you have I don't know how many millions; but I am very glad when my husband goes on a revising tour in the summer. It's very good for him and pleasant travelling about, and it's a settled arrangement for me to keep a carriage and coachman on the money.'

On his way to the remote provinces Alexey Alexandrovitch stopped for three days at Moscow.

The day after his arrival he was driving back from calling on the governor-general. At the cross-roads by Gazetny Place, where there are always crowds of carriages and sledges, Alexey Alexandrovitch suddenly heard his name called out in such a loud and cheerful voice that he could not help looking round. At the corner of the pavement, in a short, stylish overcoat and a low-crowned fashionable hat, jauntily askew, with a smile that showed a gleam of white teeth and red lips, stood Stepan Arkadyevitch, radiant, young, and beaming. He called him vigorously and urgently, and insisted on his stopping. He had one arm on the window of a carriage that was stopping at the corner, and out of the window were thrust the heads of a lady in a velvet hat, and two children. Stepan Arkadyevitch was smiling and beckoning to his brother-in-law. The lady smiled a kindly smile too, and she too waved her hand to Alexey Alexandrovitch. It was Dolly with her children.

Alexey Alexandrovitch did not want to see anyone in Moscow, and least of all his wife's brother. He raised his hat and would have driven on, but Stepan Arkadyevitch told his coachman to stop, and ran across the snow to him.

'Well, what a shame not to have let us know! Been here long? I was at Dussot's yesterday and saw "Karenin" on the visitors' list, but it never entered my head that it was you,' said Stepan Arkadyevitch, sticking his head in at the window of the carriage, 'or I should have looked you up. I am glad to see you!' he said, knocking one foot against the other to shake the snow off. 'What a shame of you not to let us know!' he repeated.

'I had no time; I am very busy,' Alexey Alexandrovitch responded dryly.

'Come to my wife, she does so want to see you.'

Alexey Alexandrovitch unfolded the rug in which his frozen feet were wrapped, and getting out of his carriage made his way over the snow to Darya Alexandrovna.

'Why, Alexey Alexandrovitch, what are you cutting us like this for?' said Dolly, smiling.

'I was very busy. Delighted to see you!' he said in a tone clearly indicating that he was annoyed by it. 'How are you?'

'Tell me, how is my darling Anna?'

Alexey Alexandrovitch mumbled something and would have gone on. But Stepan Arkadyevitch stopped him.

'I tell you what we'll do tomorrow. Dolly, ask him to dinner. We'll ask Koznishev and Pestsov, so as to entertain him with our Moscow celebrities.'

'Yes, please, do come,' said Dolly; 'we will expect you at five, or six o'clock, if you like. How is my darling Anna? How long . . .'

'She is quite well,' Alexey Alexandrovitch mumbled, frowning. 'Delighted!' and he moved away towards his carriage.

'You will come?' Dolly called after him.

Alexey Alexandrovitch said something which Dolly could not catch in the noise of the moving carriages.

'I shall come round tomorrow!' Stepan Arkadyevitch shouted to him.

Alexey Alexandrovitch got into his carriage, and buried himself in it so as neither to see nor be seen.

'Queer fish!' said Stepan Arkadyevitch to his wife, and glancing at his watch, he made a motion of his hand before his face, indicating a caress to his wife and children, and walked jauntily along the pavement.

'Stiva! Stiva!' Dolly called, reddening.

He turned round.

'I must get coats, you know, for Grisha and Tanya. Give me the money.'

'Never mind; you tell them I'll pay the bill!' and he vanished, nodding genially to an acquaintance who drove by.

VII

THE next day was Sunday. Stepan Arkadyevitch went to the Grand Theatre to a rehearsal of the ballet, and gave Masha Tchibisov, a pretty dancing-girl whom he had just taken under his protection, the coral necklace he had promised her the evening before, and behind the scenes in the dim daylight of the theatre, managed to kiss her pretty little face, radiant over her present. Besides the gift of the necklace, he wanted to arrange with her about meeting after the ballet. After explaining that he could not come at the beginning of the ballet, he promised he would come for the last act and take her to supper. From the theatre Stepan Arkadyevitch drove to Ohotny Row, selected himself the fish and asparagus for dinner, and by twelve o'clock was at Dussot's, where he had to see three people, luckily all staying at the same hotel: Levin, who had recently come back from abroad and was staying there; the new head of his department, who had just been promoted to that position, and had come on a tour of revision to Moscow; and his brother-in-law, Karenin, whom he must see, so as to be sure of bringing him to dinner.

Stepan Arkadyevitch liked dining, but still better he liked to give a dinner, small, but very choice, both as regards the food and drink and as regards the selection of guests. He particularly liked the programme of that day's dinner. There would be fresh perch, asparagus, and *la pièce de résistance*—first-rate, but quite plain, roast-beef, and wines to suit; so much for the eating and drinking. Kitty and Levin would be of the party, and that this might not be obtrusively evident, there would be a girl cousin too, and young Shtcherbatsky, and *la pièce de résistance* among the guests—Sergey Koznishev and Alexey Alexandrovitch. Sergey Ivanovitch was a Moscow man, and a philosopher; Alexey Alexandrovitch a Petersburger, and a practical politician. He was asking, too, the well-known eccentric enthusiast, Pestsov, a liberal, a great talker, a musician, an historian, and the most delightfully youthful person of fifty, who would be a sauce or garnish for Koznishev and Karenin. He would provoke them and set them off.

The second instalment for the forest had been received from the merchant and was not yet exhausted; Dolly had been very amiable and good-humoured of late, and the idea of the dinner pleased Stepan Arkadyevitch from every point of view. He was in the most light-hearted mood. There were two circumstances a little unpleasant, but these two circumstances were drowned in the sea of good-humoured gaiety which flooded the soul of Stepan Arkadyevitch. These two circumstances were: first, that on meeting Alexey Alexandrovitch the day before in the street he had noticed that he was cold and reserved with him, and putting the expression of Alexey Alexandrovitch's face and the fact that he had not come to see them or let them know of his arrival with the rumours he had heard about Anna and Vronsky, Stepan Arkadyevitch guessed that something was wrong between the husband and wife.

That was one disagreeable thing. The other slightly disagreeable fact was that the new head of his department, like all new heads, had the reputation already of a terrible person, who got up at six o'clock in the morning, worked like a horse, and insisted on his subordinates working in the same way. Moreover, this new head had the further reputation of being a bear in his manners, and was, according to all reports, a man of a class in all respects the opposite of that to which his predecessor had belonged, and to which Stepan Arkadyevitch had hitherto belonged himself. On the previous day Stepan Arkadyevitch had appeared at the office in a uniform, and the new chief had been very affable and had talked to him as to an acquaintance. Consequently Stepan Arkadyevitch deemed it his duty to call upon him in his non-official dress. The thought that the new chief might not give him a warm reception was the other unpleasant thing. But Stepan Arkadyevitch instinctively felt that everything would *come round* all right. 'They're all people, all men, like us poor sinners; why be nasty and quarrelsome?' he thought as he went into the hotel.

'Good day, Vassily,' he said, walking into the corridor with his hat cocked on one side, and addressing a footman he knew; 'why, you've let your whiskers grow! Levin, number seven eh? Take me up, please. And find out whether Count Anitchkin' (this was the new head) 'is receiving.'

'Yes, sir,' Vassily responded, smiling. 'You've not been to see us for a long while.'

'I was here yesterday, but at the other entrance. Is this number seven?'

Levin was standing with a peasant from Tver in the middle of the room, measuring a fresh bearskin, when Stepan Arkadyevitch went in.

'What! you killed him?' cried Stepan Arkadyevitch. 'Well done! A she-bear? How are you, Arhip!'

He shook hands with the peasant and sat down on the edge of a chair, without taking off his coat and hat.

'Come, take off your coat and stay a little,' said Levin, taking his hat.

'No, I haven't time; I've only looked in for a tiny second,' answered

Stepan Arkadyevitch. He threw open his coat, but afterwards did take it off, and sat on for a whole hour, talking to Levin about hunting and the most intimate subjects.

'Come, tell me, please, what you did abroad? Where have you been?' said Stepan Arkadyevitch, when the peasant had gone.

'Oh, I stayed in Germany, in Prussia, in France, and in England—not in the capitals, but in the manufacturing towns, and saw a great deal that was new to me. And I'm glad I went.'

'Yes, I knew your idea of the solution of the labour question.'

'Not a bit: in Russia there can be no labour question. In Russia the question is that of the relation of the working people to the land; though the question exists there too—but there it's a matter of repairing what's been ruined, while with us . . .'

Stepan Arkadyevitch listened attentively to Levin.

'Yes, yes!' he said, 'it's very possible you're right. But I'm glad you're in good spirits, and are hunting bears, and working, and interested. Shtcherbatsky told me another story—he met you—that you were in such a depressed state, talking of nothing but death. . . .'

'Well, what of it? I've not given up thinking of death,' said Levin. 'It's true that it's high time I was dead; and that all this is nonsense. It's the truth I'm telling you. I do value my idea and my work awfully; but in reality only consider this: all this world of ours is nothing but a speck of mildew, which has grown up on a tiny planet. And for us to suppose we can have something great—ideas, work—it's all dust and ashes.'

'But all that's as old as the hills, my boy!'

'It is old; but do you know, when you grasp this fully, then somehow everything becomes of no consequence. When you understand that you will die tomorrow, if not today, and nothing will be left, then everything is so unimportant! And I consider my idea very important, but it turns out really to be as unimportant too, even if it were carried out, as doing for that bear. So one goes on living, amusing oneself with hunting, with work—anything so as not to think of death!'

Stepan Arkadyevitch smiled a subtle and affectionate smile as he listened to Levin.

'Well, of course! Here you've come round to my point. Do you remember you attacked me for seeking enjoyment in life? Don't be so severe, O moralist!'

'No; all the same, what's fine in life is . . .' Levin hesitated—'oh, I don't know. All I know is that we shall soon be dead.'

'Why so soon?'

'And do you know, there's less charm in life, when one thinks of death, but there's more peace.'

'On the contrary, the finish is always the best. But I must be going,' said Stepan Arkadyevitch, getting up for the tenth time.

'Oh no, stay a bit!' said Levin, keeping him. 'Now, when shall we see each other again? I'm going tomorrow.'

'I'm a nice person! Why, that's just what I came for! You simply must come to dinner with us today. Your brother's coming and Karenin, my brother-in-law.'

'You don't mean to say he's here?' said Levin, and he wanted to inquire about Kitty. He had heard at the beginning of the winter that she was at Petersburg with her sister, the wife of the diplomat, and he did not know whether she had come back or not; but he changed his mind and did not ask. 'Whether she's coming or not, I don't care,' he said to himself.

'So you'll come?'

'Of course.'

'At five o'clock, then, and not evening dress.'

And Stepan Arkadyevitch got up and went down below to the new head of his department. Instinct had not misled Stepan Arkadyevitch. The terrible new head turned out to be an extremely amenable person, and Stepan Arkadyevitch lunched with him and stayed on, so that it was four o'clock before he got to Alexey Alexandrovitch.

VIII

ALEXEY ALEXANDROVITCH, on coming back from church service, had spent the whole morning indoors. He had two pieces of business before him that morning: first, to receive and send on a deputation from the native tribes which was on its way to Petersburg, and now at Moscow; secondly, to write the promised letter to the lawyer. The deputation, though it had been summoned at Alexey Alexandrovitch's instigation, was not without its discomforting and even dangerous aspect, and he was very glad he had found it in Moscow. The members of this deputation had not the slightest conception of their duty and the part they were to play. They naïvely believed that it was their business to lay before the commission their needs and the actual condition of things, and to ask assistance of the government, and utterly failed to grasp that some of their statements and requests supported the contention of the enemy's side, and so spoiled the whole business. Alexey Alexandrovitch was busily engaged with them for a long while, drew up a programme for them from which they were not to depart, and on dismissing them wrote a letter to Petersburg for the guidance of the deputation. He had his chief support in this affair in the Countess Lidia Ivanovna. She was a specialist in the matter of deputations, and no one knew better than she how to manage them, and put them in the way they should go. Having completed this task, Alexey Alexandrovitch wrote the letter to the lawyer. Without the slightest hesitation he gave him permission to act as he might judge best. In the letter he enclosed three of Vronsky's notes to Anna, which were in the portfolio he had taken away.

Since Alexey Alexandrovitch had left home with the intention of not returning to his family again, and since he had been at the lawyer's and had spoken, though only to one man, of his intention, since especially he had translated the matter from the world of real life to the world of ink and paper, he had grown more and more used to his own intention, and by now distinctly perceived the feasibility of its execution.

He was sealing the envelope to the lawyer, when he heard the loud tones of Stepan Arkadyevitch's voice. Stepan Arkadyevitch was disputing with Alexey Alexandrovitch's servant, and insisting on being announced.

'No matter,' thought Alexey Alexandrovitch, 'so much the better. I will inform him at once of my position in regard to his sister, and explain why it is I can't dine with him.'

'Come in!' he said aloud, collecting his papers, and putting them in the blotting-paper.

'There, you see, you're talking nonsense, and he's at home!' responded Stepan Arkadyevitch's voice, addressing the servant, who had refused to let him in, and taking off his coat as he went, Oblonsky walked into the room. 'Well, I'm awfully glad I've found you! So I hope . . .' Stepan Arkadyevitch began cheerfully.

'I cannot come,' Alexey Alexandrovitch said coldly, standing and not asking his visitor to sit down.

Alexey Alexandrovitch had thought to pass at once into those frigid relations in which he ought to stand with the brother of a wife against whom he was beginning a suit for divorce. But he had not taken into account the ocean of kindliness brimming over in the heart of Stepan Arkadyevitch.

Stepan Arkadyevitch opened wide his clear, shining eyes.

'Why can't you? What do you mean?' he asked in perplexity, speaking in French. 'Oh, but it's a promise. And we're all counting on you.'

'I want to tell you that I can't dine at your house, because the terms of relationship which have existed between us must cease.'

'How? How do you mean? What for?' said Stepan Arkadyevitch with a smile.

'Because I am beginning an action for divorce against your sister, my wife. I ought to have . . .'

But, before Alexey Alexandrovitch had time to finish his sentence, Stepan Arkadyevitch was behaving not at all as he had expected. He groaned and sank into an arm-chair.

'No, Alexey Alexandrovitch! What are you saying?' cried Oblonsky, and his suffering was apparent in his face.

'It is so.'

'Excuse me, I can't, I can't believe it!'

Alexey Alexandrovitch sat down, feeling that his words had not had the effect he anticipated, and that it would be unavoidable for him to explain his position, and that, whatever explanations he might make, his relations with his brother-in-law would remain unchanged.

'Yes, I am brought to the painful necessity of seeking a divorce,' he said.

'I will say one thing, Alexey Alexandrovitch. I know you for an excellent, upright man; I know Anna—excuse me, I can't change my opinion of her—for a good, an excellent woman; and so, excuse me, I cannot believe it. There is some misunderstanding,' said he.

'Oh, if it were merely a misunderstanding! . . .'

'Pardon, I understand,' interposed Stepan Arkadyevitch. 'But of course . . . One thing: you must not act in haste. You must not, you must not act in haste!'

'I am not acting in haste,' Alexey Alexandrovitch said coldly, 'but one cannot ask advice of anyone in such a matter. I have quite made up my mind.'

'This is awful!' said Stepan Arkadyevitch. 'I would do one thing, Alexey Alexandrovitch. I beseech you, do it!' he said. 'No action has yet been taken, if I understand rightly. Before you take advice, see my wife, talk to her. She loves Anna like a sister, she loves you, and she's a wonderful woman. For God's sake, talk to her! Do me that favour, I beseech you!'

Alexey Alexandrovitch pondered, and Stepan Arkadyevitch looked at him sympathetically, without interrupting his silence.

'You will go to see her?'

'I don't know. That was just why I have not been to see you. I imagine our relations must change.'

'Why so? I don't see that. Allow me to believe that apart from our connection you have for me, at least in part, the same friendly feeling I have always had for you . . . and sincere esteem,' said Stepan Arkadyevitch, pressing his hand. 'Even if your worst suppositions were correct, I don't—and never would—take on myself to judge either side, and I see no reason why our relations should be affected. But now, do this, come and see my wife.'

'Well, we look at the matter differently,' said Alexey Alexandrovitch coldly. 'However, we won't discuss it.'

'No; why shouldn't you come today to dine, anyway? My wife's expecting you. Please, do come. And, above all, talk it over with her. She's a wonderful woman. For God's sake, on my knees, I implore you!'

'If you so much wish it, I will come,' said Alexey Alexandrovitch, sighing.

And, anxious to change the conversation, he inquired about what interested them both—the new head of Stepan Arkadyevitch's department, a man not yet old, who had suddenly been promoted to so high a position.

Alexey Alexandrovitch had previously felt no liking for Count Anitchkin, and had always differed from him in his opinions. But now, from a feeling readily comprehensible to officials—that hatred felt by one who has suffered a defeat in the service for one who has received a promotion, he could not endure him.

'Well, have you seen him?' said Alexey Alexandrovitch with a malignant smile.

'Of course; he was at our sitting yesterday. He seems to know his work capitally, and to be very energetic.'

'Yes, but what is his energy directed to?' said Alexey Alexandrovitch. 'Is he aiming at doing anything, or simply undoing what's been done? It's the great misfortune of our government—this paper administration, of which he's a worthy representative.'

'Really, I don't know what fault one could find with him. His policy I don't know, but one thing—he's a very nice fellow,' answered Stepan Arkadyevitch. 'I've just been seeing him, and he's really a capital fellow. We lunched together, and I taught him how to make, you know that drink, wine and oranges. It's so cooling. And it's a wonder he didn't know it. He liked it awfully. No, really, he's a capital fellow.'

Stepan Arkadyevitch glanced at his watch.

'Why, good heavens, it's four already, and I've still to go to Dolgovushin's! So please come round to dinner. You can't imagine how you will grieve my wife and me.'

The way in which Alexey Alexandrovitch saw his brother-in-law out was very different from the manner in which he had met him.

'I've promised, and I'll come,' he answered wearily.

'Believe me, I appreciate it, and I hope you won't regret it,' answered Stepan Arkadyevitch, smiling.

And, putting on his coat as he went, he patted the footman on the head, chuckled, and went out.

'At five o'clock, and not evening dress, please,' he shouted once more, turning at the door.

IX

IT was past five, and several guests had already arrived, before the host himself got home. He went in together with Sergey Ivanovitch Koznishev and Pestsov, who had reached the street door at the same moment. These were the two leading representatives of the Moscow intellectuals, as Oblonsky had called them. Both were men respected for their character and their intelligence. They respected each other, but were in complete and hopeless disagreement upon almost every subject, not because they belonged to opposite parties, but precisely because they were of the same party (their enemies refused to see any distinction between their views); but, in that party, each had his own special shade of opinion. And since no difference is less easily overcome than difference of opinion about semi-abstract questions, they never agreed in any opinion, and had long, indeed, been accustomed to jeer without anger, each at the other's incorrigible aberrations.

They were just going in at the door, talking of the weather, when Stepan Arkadyevitch overtook them. In the drawing-room there were already sitting Prince Alexander Dmitrievitch Shtcherbatsky, young Shtcherbatsky, Turovtsin, Kitty, and Karenin.

Stepan Arkadyevitch saw immediately that things were not going well in the drawing-room without him. Darya Alexandrovna, in her best grey silk gown, obviously worried about the children, who were to have their dinner by themselves in the nursery, and by her husband's absence, was not equal to the task of making the party mix without him. All were sitting like so many priests' wives on a visit (so the old prince expressed it), obviously wondering why they were there, and pumping up remarks simply to avoid being silent. Turovtsin—good, simple man—felt unmistakably a fish out of water, and the smile with which his thick lips greeted Stepan Arkadyevitch said, as plainly as words: 'Well, old boy, you have popped me down in a learned set! A drinking-party now, or the Château des Fleurs, would be more in my line!' The old prince sat in silence, his bright little eyes watching Karenin from one side, and Stepan Arkadyevitch saw that he had already formed a phrase to sum up that politician of whom guests were invited to partake as though he were a sturgeon. Kitty was looking at the door, calling up all her energies to keep her from blushing at the entrance of Konstantin Levin. Young Shtcherbatsky, who had not been introduced to Karenin, was trying to look as though he were not in the least conscious of it. Karenin himself had followed the Petersburg fashion for a dinner with ladies and was wearing evening dress and a white tie. Stepan Arkadyevitch saw by his face that he had come simply to keep his promise, and was performing a disagreeable duty in being present at this gathering. He was indeed the person chiefly responsible for the chill benumbing all the guests before Stepan Arkadyevitch came in.

On entering the drawing-room Stepan Arkadyevitch apologised, explaining that he had been detained by that prince, who was always the scapegoat for all his absences and unpunctualities, and in one moment he had made all the guests acquainted with each other, and, bringing together Alexey Alexandrovitch and Sergey Koznishev, started them on a discussion of the Russification of Poland, into which they immediately plunged with Pestsov. Slapping Turovtsin on the shoulder, he whispered something comic in his ear, and set him down by his wife and the old prince. Then he told Kitty she was looking very pretty that evening, and presented Shtcherbatsky to Karenin. In a moment he had so kneaded together the social dough that the drawing-room became very lively, and there was a merry buzz of voices. Konstantin Levin was the only person who had not arrived. But this was so much the better, as on going into the dining-room, Stepan Arkadyevitch found to his horror that the port and sherry had been procured from Depré, and not from Levy, and, directing that the coachman should be sent off as speedily as possible to Levy's, he was going back to the drawing-room.

In the dining-room he was met by Konstantin Levin.

'I'm not late?'

'You can never help being late!' said Stephan Arkadyevitch, taking his arm.

'Have you a lot of people? Who's here?' asked Levin, unable to help blushing, as he knocked the snow off his cap with his glove.

'All our own set. Kitty's here. Come along, I'll introduce you to Karenin.'

Stepan Arkadyevitch, for all his liberal views, was well aware that to meet Karenin was sure to be felt a flattering distinction, and so treated his best friends to this honour. But at that instant Konstantin Levin was not in a condition to feel all the gratification of making such an acquaintance. He had not seen Kitty since that memorable evening when he met Vronsky, not counting, that is, the moment when he had had a glimpse of her on the high-road. He had known at the bottom of his heart that he would see her here today. But to keep his thoughts free, he had tried to persuade himself that he did not know it. Now when he heard that she was here, he was suddenly conscious of such delight, and at the same time of such dread, that his breath failed him and he could not utter what he wanted to say.

'What is she like, what is she like? Like what she used to be, or like what she was in the carriage? What if Darya Alexandrovna told the truth? Why shouldn't it be the truth?' he thought.

'Oh, please, introduce me to Karenin,' he brought out with an effort, and with a desperately determined step he walked into the drawing-room and beheld her.

She was not the same as she used to be, nor was she as she had been in the carriage; she was quite different.

She was scared, shy, shame-faced, and still more charming from it. She saw him the very instant he walked into the room. She had been expecting him. She was delighted, and so confused at her own delight that there was a moment, the moment when he went up to her sister and glanced again at her, when she, and he, and Dolly, who saw it all, thought she would break down and would begin to cry. She crimsoned, turned white, crimsoned again, and grew faint, waiting with quivering lips for him to come to her. He went up to her, bowed, and held out his hand without speaking. Except for the slight quiver of her lips and the moisture in her eyes that made them brighter, her smile was almost calm as she said—

'How long it is since we've seen each other!' and with desperate determination she pressed his hand with her cold hand.

'You've not seen me, but I've seen you,' said Levin, with a radiant smile of happiness. 'I saw you when you were driving from the railway station to Ergushovo.'

'When?' she asked, wondering.

'You were driving to Ergushovo,' said Levin, feeling as if he would sob with the rapture that was flooding his heart. 'And how dared I associate a thought of anything not innocent with this touching creature? And, yes, I do believe it's true what Darya Alexandrovna told me,' he thought.

Stepan Arkadyevitch took him by the arm and led him away to Karenin.

'Let me introduce you.' He mentioned their names.

'Very glad to meet you again,' said Alexey Alexandrovitch coldly, shaking hands with Levin.

'You are acquainted?' Stepan Arkadyevitch asked in surprise.

'We spent three hours together in the train,' said Levin smiling, 'but got out, just as in a masquerade, quite mystified—at least I was.'

'Nonsense! Come along, please,' said Stepan Arkadyevitch, pointing in the direction of the dining-room.

The men went into the dining-room and went up to a table, laid with six sorts of spirits and as many kinds of cheese, some with little silver spades and some without, caviare herrings, preserves of various kinds, and plates with slices of French bread.

The men stood round the strong-smelling spirits and salt delicacies, and the discussion of the Russification of Poland between Koznishev, Karenin, and Pestsov died down in anticipation of dinner.

Sergey Ivanovitch was unequalled in his skill in winding up the most heated and serious argument by some unexpected pinch of Attic salt that changed the disposition of his opponent. He did this now.

Alexey Alexandrovitch had been maintaining that the Russification of Poland could only be accomplished as a result of larger measures which ought to be introduced by the Russian government.

Pestsov insisted that one country can only absorb another when it is the more densely populated.

Koznishev admitted both points, but with limitations. As they were going out of the drawing-room to conclude the argument, Koznishev said smiling—

'So, then, for the Russification of our foreign populations there is but one method—to bring up as many children as one can. My brother and I are terribly in fault, I see. You married men, especially you, Stepan Arkadyevitch, are the real patriots: what number have you reached?' he said, smiling genially at their host and holding out a tiny wine-glass to him.

Everyone laughed, and Stepan Arkadyevitch with particular good-humour.

'Oh yes, that's the best method!' he said, munching cheese and filling the wine-glass with a special sort of spirit. The conversation dropped at the jest.

'This cheese is not bad. Shall I give you some?' said the master of the house. 'Why, have you been going in for gymnastics again?' he asked Levin, pinching his muscle with his left hand. Levin smiled, bent his arm, and under Stepan Arkadyevitch's fingers the muscles swelled up like a sound cheese, hard as a knob of iron, through the fine cloth of the coat.

'What biceps! A perfect Samson!'

'I imagine great strength is needed for hunting bears,' observed Alexey Alexandrovitch, who had the mistiest notions about the chase.

He cut off and spread with cheese a wafer of bread fine as a spider-web.

Levin smiled.

'Not at all. Quite the contrary; a child can kill a bear,' he said, with a slight bow moving aside for the ladies, who were approaching the table.

'You have killed a bear, I've been told?' said Kitty, trying assiduously to catch with her fork a perverse mushroom that would slip away, and setting the lace quivering over her white arm. 'Are there bears on your place?' she added, turning her charming little head to him and smiling.

There was apparently nothing extraordinary in what she said, but what unutterable meaning there was for him in every sound, in every turn of her lips, her eyes, her hand as she said it! There was entreaty for forgiveness, and trust in him and tenderness—soft, timid tenderness—and promise and hope and love for him, which he could not but believe in and which choked him with happiness.

'No, we've been hunting in the Tver province. It was coming back from there that I met your *beaufrère* in the train, or your *beaufrère's* brother-in-law,' he said with a smile. 'It was an amusing meeting.'

And he began telling with droll good-humour how, after not sleeping all night, he had, wearing an old fur-lined, full-skirted coat, got into Alexey Alexandrovitch's compartment.

'The conductor, forgetting the proverb, would have chucked me out on account of my attire; but thereupon I began expressing my feelings in elevated language, and . . . you, too,' he said, addressing Karenin and forgetting his name, 'at first would have ejected me on the ground of the old coat, but afterwards you took my part, for which I am extremely grateful.'

'The rights of passengers generally to choose their seats are too ill-defined,' said Alexey Alexandrovitch, rubbing the tips of his fingers on his handkerchief.

'I saw you were in uncertainty about me,' said Levin, smiling good-naturedly, 'but I made haste to plunge into intellectual conversation to smooth over the defects of my attire.'

Sergey Ivanovitch, while he kept up a conversation with their hostess, had one ear for his brother, and he glanced askance at him. 'What is the matter with him today? Why such a conquering hero?' he thought. He did not know that Levin was feeling as though he had grown wings. Levin knew she was listening to his words and that she was glad to listen to him. And this was the only thing that interested him. Not in that room only, but in the whole world, there existed for him only himself, with enormously increased importance and dignity in his own eyes, and she. He felt himself on a pinnacle that made him giddy, and far away down below were all those nice excellent Karenins, Oblonskys, and all the world.

Quite without attracting notice, without glancing at them, as though there were no other places left, Stepan Arkadyevitch put Levin and Kitty side by side.

'Oh, you may as well sit there,' he said to Levin.

The dinner was as choice as the china, in which Stepan Arkadyevitch was a connoisseur. The *soupe Marie-Louise* was a splendid success; the tiny pies eaten with it melted in the mouth and were irreproachable. The two footmen and Matvey, in white cravats, did their duty with the dishes and wines unobtrusively, quietly, and swiftly. On the material side the dinner was a success; it was no less so on the immaterial. The conversation, at times general and at times between individuals, never paused, and towards the end the company was so lively that the men rose from table, without stopping speaking, and even Alexey Alexandrovitch thawed.

X

PESTSOV liked thrashing an argument out to the end, and was not satisfied with Sergey Ivanovitch's words, especially as he felt the injustice of his view.

'I did not mean,' he said over the soup, addressing Alexey Alexandrovitch, 'mere density of population alone, but in conjunction with fundamental ideas, and not by means of principles.'

'It seems to me,' Alexey Alexandrovitch said languidly, and with no haste, 'that that's the same thing. In my opinion, influence over another people is only possible to the people which has the higher development, which . . .'

'But that's just the question,' Pestsov broke in in his bass. He was always in a hurry to speak, and seemed always to put his whole soul into what he was saying: 'In what are we to make higher development consist? The English, the French, the Germans, which is at the highest stage of development? Which of them will nationalise the other? We see the Rhine provinces have been turned French, but the Germans are not at a lower stage!' he shouted. 'There is another law at work there.'

'I fancy that the greater influence is always on the side of true civilisation,' said Alexey Alexandrovitch, slightly lifting his eyebrows.

'But what are we to lay down as the outward signs of true civilisation?' said Pestsov.

'I imagine such signs are generally very well known,' said Alexey Alexandrovitch.

'But are they fully known?' Sergey Ivanovitch put in with a subtle smile. 'It is the accepted view now that real culture must be purely classical; but we see most intense disputes on each side of the question, and there is no denying that the opposite camp has strong points in its favour.'

'You are for classics, Sergey Ivanovitch. Will you take red wine?' said Stepan Arkadyevitch.

'I am not expressing my own opinion of either form of culture,' Sergey Ivanovitch said, holding out his glass with a smile of condescension, as to a child. 'I only say that both sides have strong arguments to support them,' he went on, addressing Alexey Alexandrovitch. 'My sympathies are classical from education, but in this discussion I am personally unable to arrive at a conclusion. I see no distinct grounds for classical studies being given a pre-eminence over scientific studies.'

'The natural sciences have just as great an educational value,' put in Pestsov. 'Take astronomy, take botany, or zoology with its system of general principles.'

'I cannot quite agree with that,' responded Alexey Alexandrovitch. 'It seems to me that one must admit that the very process of studying the forms of language has a peculiarly favourable influence on intellectual development. Moreover, it cannot be denied that the influence of the classical authors is in the highest degree moral, while, unfortunately, with the study of the natural sciences are associated the false and noxious doctrines which are the curse of our day.'

Sergey Ivanovitch would have said something, but Pestsov interrupted him in his rich bass. He began warmly contesting the justice of this view. Sergey Ivanovitch waited serenely to speak, obviously with a convincing reply ready.

'But,' said Sergey Ivanovitch, smiling subtly, and addressing Karenin, 'one must allow that to weigh all the advantages and disadvantages of classical and scientific studies is a difficult task, and the question which form of education was to be preferred would not have been so quickly and conclusively decided if there had not been in favour of classical education, as you expressed it just now, its moral—*disons le mot*—anti-nihilist influence.'

'Undoubtedly.'

'If it had not been for the distinctive property of anti-nihilistic influence on the side of classical studies, we should have considered the subject more, have weighed the arguments on both sides,' said Sergey Ivanovitch with a subtle smile, 'we should have given elbow-room to both tendencies. But now we know that these little pills of classical learning possess the medicinal property of anti-nihilism, and we boldly prescribe them to our patients. . . . But what if they had no such medicinal property?' he wound up humorously.

At Sergey Ivanovitch's little pills, everyone laughed; Turovtsin in especial roared loudly and jovially, glad at last to have found something to laugh at, all he ever looked for in listening to conversation.

Stepan Arkadyevitch had not made a mistake in inviting Pestsov. With Pestsov intellectual conversation never flagged for an instant. Directly Sergey Ivanovitch had concluded the conversation with his jest, Pestsov promptly started a new one.

'I can't agree even,' said he, 'that the government had that aim. The government obviously is guided by abstract considerations, and remains indifferent to the influence its measures may exercise. The education of women, for instance, would naturally be regarded as likely to be harmful, but the government opens schools and universities for women.'

And the conversation at once passed to the new subject of the education of women.

Alexey Alexandrovitch expressed the idea that the education of women is apt to be confounded with the emancipation of women, and that it is only so that it can be considered dangerous.

'I consider, on the contrary, that the two questions are inseparably connected together,' said Pestsov; 'it is a vicious circle. Woman is deprived of rights from lack of education, and the lack of education results from the absence of rights. We must not forget that the subjection of women is so complete, and dates from such ages back that we are often unwilling to recognise the gulf that separates them from us,' said he.

'You said rights,' said Sergey Ivanovitch, waiting till Pestsov had finished, 'meaning the right of sitting on juries, of voting, of presiding at official meetings, the right of entering the civil service, of sitting in parliament . . .'

'Undoubtedly.'

'But if women, as a rare exception, can occupy such positions, it seems to me you are wrong in using the expression "rights". It would be more correct to say duties. Every man will agree that in doing the duty of a juryman, a witness, a telegraph clerk, we feel we are performing duties. And therefore it would be correct to say that women are seeking duties, and quite legitimately. And one can but sympathise with this desire to assist in the general labour of man.'

'Quite so,' Alexey Alexandrovitch assented. 'The question, I imagine, is simply whether they are fitted for such duties.'

'They will most likely be perfectly fitted,' said Stepan Arkadyevitch, 'when education has become general among them. We see this . . .'

'How about the proverb?' said the prince, who had a long while been intent on the conversation, his little comical eyes twinkling. 'I can say it before my daughters: her hair is long, because her wit is . . .'

'Just what they thought of the negroes before their emancipation!' said Pestsov angrily.

'What seems strange to me is that women should seek fresh duties,' said Sergey Ivanovitch, 'while we see, unhappily, that men usually try to avoid them.'

'Duties are bound up with rights—power, money, honour; those are what women are seeking,' said Pestsov.

'Just as though I should seek the right to be a wet-nurse, and feel injured because women are paid for the work, while no one will take me,' said the old prince.

Turovtsin exploded in a loud roar of laughter, and Sergey Ivanovitch regretted that he had not made this comparison. Even Alexey Alexandrovitch smiled.

'Yes, but a man can't nurse a baby,' said Pestsov, 'while a woman . . .'

'No, there was an Englishman who did suckle his baby on board ship,' said the old prince, feeling this freedom in conversation permissible before his own daughters.

'There are as many such Englishmen as there would be women officials,' said Sergey Ivanovitch.

'Yes, but what is a girl to do who has no family?' put in Stepan Arkadyevitch, thinking of Masha Tchibisov, whom he had had in his mind all along, in sympathising with Pestsov and supporting him.

'If the story of such a girl were thoroughly sifted, you would find she had abandoned a family—her own or a sister's, where she might have found a woman's duties,' Darya Alexandrovna broke in unexpectedly in a tone of exasperation, probably suspecting what sort of girl Stepan Arkadyevitch was thinking of.

'But we take our stand on principle as the ideal,' replied Pestsov in his mellow bass. 'Woman desires to have rights, to be independent, educated. She is oppressed, humiliated by the consciousness of her disabilities.'

'And I'm oppressed and humiliated that they won't engage me at the Foundling,' the old prince said again, to the huge delight of Turovtsin, who in his mirth dropped his asparagus with the thick end in the sauce.

XI

EVERYONE took part in the conversation except Kitty and Levin. At first, when they were talking of the influence that one people has on another, there rose to Levin's mind what he had to say on the subject. But these ideas, once of such importance in his eyes, seemed to come into his brain as in a dream, and had now not the slightest interest for him. It even struck him as strange that they should be so eager to talk of what was of no use to anyone. Kitty, too, should, one would have supposed, have been interested in what they were saying of the rights and education of women. How often she had mused on the subject, thinking of her friend abroad, Varenka, of her painful state of dependence, how often she had wondered about herself what would become of her if she did not marry, and how often she had argued with her sister about it! But it did not interest her at all. She and Levin had a conversation of their own, yet not a conversation, but a sort of mysterious communication, which brought them every moment nearer, and stirred in both a sense of glad terror before the unknown into which they were entering.

At first Levin, in answer to Kitty's question how he could have seen her last year in the carriage, told her how he had been coming home from the mowing along the high-road and had met her.

'It was very, very early in the morning. You were probably only just awake. Your mother was asleep in the corner. It was an exquisite morning. I was walking along wondering who it could be in a four-in-hand? It was a splendid set of four horses with bells, and in a second you flashed by, and I saw at the window—you were sitting like this, holding the strings of your cap in both hands, and thinking awfully deeply about something,' he said, smiling. 'How I should like to know what you were thinking about then! Something important?'

'Wasn't I dreadfully untidy?' she wondered, but seeing the smile of ecstasy these reminiscences called up, she felt that the impression she had made had been very good. She blushed and laughed with delight: 'Really I don't remember.'

'How nicely Turovtsin laughs!' said Levin, admiring his moist eyes and shaking chest.

'Have you known him long?' asked Kitty.

'Oh, everyone knows him!'

'And I see you think he's a horrid man?'

'Not horrid, but nothing in him.'

'Oh, you're wrong! And you must give up thinking so directly!' said

Kitty. 'I used to have a very poor opinion of him too, but he, he's an awfully nice and wonderfully good-hearted man. He has a heart of gold.'

'How could you find out what sort of heart he has?'

'We are great friends. I know him very well. Last winter, soon after . . . you came to see us,' she said, with a guilty and at the same time confiding smile, 'all Dolly's children had scarlet fever, and he happened to come and see her. And only fancy,' she said in a whisper, 'he felt so sorry for her that he stayed and began to help her look after the children. Yes, and for three weeks he stopped with them, and looked after the children like a nurse.'

'I am telling Konstantin Dmitritch about Turovtsin in the scarlet fever,' she said, bending over to her sister.

'Yes, it was wonderful, noble!' said Dolly, glancing towards Turovtsin, who had become aware they were talking of him, and smiling gently to him. Levin glanced once more at Turovtsin, and wondered how it was he had not realised all this man's goodness before.

'I'm sorry, I'm sorry, and I'll never think ill of people again!' he said gaily, genuinely expressing what he felt at the moment.

XII

CONNECTED with the conversation that had sprung up on the rights of women there were certain questions as to the inequality of rights in marriage improper to discuss before the ladies. Pestsov had several times during dinner touched upon these questions, but Sergey Ivanovitch and Stepan Arkadyevitch carefully drew him off them.

When they rose from the table and the ladies had gone out, Pestsov did not follow them, but addressing Alexey Alexandrovitch, began to expound the chief ground of inequality. The inequality in marriage, in his opinion, lay in the fact that the infidelity of the wife and the infidelity of the husband are punished unequally, both by the law and by public opinion. Stepan Arkadyevitch went hurriedly up to Alexey Alexandrovitch and offered him a cigar.

'No, I don't smoke,' Alexey Alexandrovitch answered calmly, and as though purposely wishing to show that he was not afraid of the subject, he turned to Pestsov with a chilly smile.

'I imagine that such a view has a foundation in the very nature of things,' he said, and would have gone on to the drawing-room. But at this point Turovtsin broke suddenly and unexpectedly into the conversation, addressing Alexey Alexandrovitch.

'You heard, perhaps, about Pryatchnikov?' said Turovtsin, warmed up by the champagne he had drunk, and long waiting for an opportunity to break the silence that had weighed on him. 'Vasya Pryatchnikov,' he said, with a good-natured smile on his damp, red lips, addressing himself principally to the most important guest, Alexey Alexandrovitch, 'they told me today he fought a duel with Kvitsky at Tver, and has killed him.'

Just as it always seems that one bruises oneself on a sore place, so Stepan Arkadyevitch felt now that the conversation would by ill luck fall every moment on Alexey Alexandrovitch's sore spot. He would again have got his brother-in-law away, but Alexey Alexandrovitch himself inquired, with curiosity—

'What did Pryatchnikov fight about?'

'His wife. Acted like a man, he did! Called him out and shot him!'

'Ah!' said Alexey Alexandrovitch indifferently, and lifting his eyebrows, he went into the drawing-room.

'How glad I am you have come,' Dolly said with a frightened smile, meeting him in the outer drawing-room. 'I must talk to you. Let's sit here.'

Alexey Alexandrovitch, with the same expression of indifference, given him by his lifted eyebrows, sat down beside Darya Alexandrovna, and smiled affectedly.

'It's fortunate,' said he, 'especially as I was meaning to ask you to excuse me, and to be taking leave. I have to start tomorrow.'

Darya Alexandrovna was firmly convinced of Anna's innocence, and she felt herself growing pale and her lips quivering with anger at this frigid, unfeeling man, who was so calmly intending to ruin her innocent friend.

'Alexey Alexandrovitch,' she said, with desperate resolution looking him in the face, 'I asked you about Anna; you made me no answer. How is she?'

'She is, I believe, quite well, Darya Alexandrovna,' replied Alexey Alexandrovitch, not looking at her.

'Alexey Alexandrovitch, forgive me, I have no right . . . but I love Anna as a sister, and esteem her; I beg, I beseech you to tell me what is wrong between you? what fault do you find with her?'

Alexey Alexandrovitch frowned, and almost closing his eyes, dropped his head.

'I presume that your husband has told you the grounds on which I consider it necessary to change my attitude to Anna Arkadyevna?' he said, not looking her in the face, but eyeing with displeasure Shtcherbatsky, who was walking across the drawing-room.

'I don't believe it, I don't believe it, I can't believe it!' Dolly said, clasping her bony hands before her with a vigorous gesture. She rose quickly, and laid her hand on Alexey Alexandrovitch's sleeve. 'We shall be disturbed here. Come this way, please.'

Dolly's agitation had an effect on Alexey Alexandrovitch. He got up and submissively followed her to the schoolroom. They sat down to a table covered with an oilcloth cut in slits by penknives.

'I don't, I don't believe it!' Dolly said, trying to catch his glance that avoided her.

'One cannot disbelieve facts, Darya Alexandrovna,' said he, with an emphasis on the word 'facts'.

'But what has she done?' said Darya Alexandrovna. 'What precisely has she done?'

'She has forsaken her duty, and deceived her husband. That's what she has done,' said he.

'No, no, it can't be! No, for God's sake, you are mistaken,' said Dolly, putting her hands to her temples and closing her eyes.

Alexey Alexandrovitch smiled coldly, with his lips alone, meaning to signify to her and to himself the firmness of his conviction; but this warm defence, though it could not shake him, reopened his wound. He began to speak with greater heat.

'It is extremely difficult to be mistaken when a wife herself informs her husband of the fact—informs him that eight years of her life, and a son, all that's a mistake, and that she wants to begin life again,' he said angrily, with a snort.

'Anna and sin—I cannot connect them, I cannot believe it!'

'Darya Alexandrovna,' he said, now looking straight into Dolly's kindly, troubled face, and feeling that his tongue was being loosened in spite of himself, 'I would give a great deal for doubt to be still possible. When I doubted, I was miserable, but it was better than now. When I doubted, I had hope; but now there is no hope, and still I doubt of everything. I am in such doubt of everything that I even hate my son, and sometimes do not believe he is my son. I am very unhappy.'

He had no need to say that. Darya Alexandrovna had seen that as soon as he glanced into her face; and she felt sorry for him, and her faith in the innocence of her friend began to totter.

'Oh, this is awful, awful! But can it be true that you are resolved on a divorce?'

'I am resolved on extreme measures. There is nothing else for me to do.'

'Nothing else to do, nothing else to do. . .' she replied with tears in her eyes. 'Oh no, don't say nothing else to do!' she said.

'What is horrible in a trouble of this kind is that one cannot, as in any other—in loss, in death—bear one's trouble in peace, but that one must act,' said he, as though guessing her thought. 'One must get out of the humiliating position in which one is placed; one can't live *à trois*.'

'I understand, I quite understand that,' said Dolly, and her head sank. She was silent for a little, thinking of herself, of her own grief in her family, and all at once, with an impulsive movement, she raised her head and clasped her hands with an imploring gesture. 'But wait a little! You are a Christian. Think of her! What will become of her, if you cast her off?'

'I have thought, Darya Alexandrovna, I have thought a great deal,' said Alexey Alexandrovitch. His face turned red in patches, and his dim eyes looked straight before him. Darya Alexandrovna at that moment pitied him with all her heart. 'That was what I did indeed when she herself made known to me my humiliation; I left everything as of old. I gave her a chance to reform, I tried to save her. And with what result? She would not regard the slightest request—that she should observe decorum,' he said, getting heated. 'One may save anyone who does not want to be ruined; but if the whole nature is so corrupt, so depraved, that ruin itself seems to her salvation, what's to be done?'

'Anything, only not divorce!' answered Darya Alexandrovna.

'But what is anything?'

'No, it is awful! She will be no one's wife; she will be lost!'

'What can I do?' said Alexey Alexandrovitch, raising his shoulders and his eyebrows. The recollection of his wife's last act had so incensed him that he had become frigid, as at the beginning of the conversation. 'I am very grateful for your sympathy, but I must be going,' he said, getting up.

'No, wait a minute. You must not ruin her. Wait a little; I will tell you about myself. I was married, and my husband deceived me; in anger and jealousy, I would have thrown up everything, I would myself . . . But I came to myself again; and who did it? Anna saved me. And here I am living on. The children are growing up, my husband has come back to his family, and feels his fault, is growing purer, better, and I live on. . . . I have forgiven it, and you ought to forgive!'

Alexey Alexandrovitch heard her, but her words had no effect on him now. All the hatred of that day when he had resolved on a divorce had sprung up again in his soul. He shook himself, and said in a shrill, loud voice—

'Forgive I cannot, and do not wish to, and I regard it as wrong. I have done everything for this woman, and she has trodden it all in the mud to which she is akin. I am not a spiteful man, I have never hated anyone, but I hate her with my whole soul, and I cannot even forgive her, because I hate her too much for all the wrong she has done me!' he said, with tones of hatred in his voice.

'Love those that hate you . . .' Darya Alexandrovna whispered timorously.

Alexey Alexandrovitch smiled contemptuously. That he knew long ago, but it could not be applied to this case.

'Love those that hate you, but to love those one hates is impossible. Forgive me for having troubled you. Everyone has enough to bear in his own grief!' And regaining his self-possession, Alexey Alexandrovitch quietly took leave and went away.

XIII

WHEN they rose from table, Levin would have liked to follow Kitty into the drawing-room; but he was afraid she might dislike this, as too obviously paying her attention. He remained in the little ring of men, taking part in the general conversation, and without looking at Kitty, he was aware of her movements, her looks, and the place where she was in the drawing-room.

He did at once, and without the smallest effort, keep the promise he had made her—always to think well of all men, and to like everyone always. The conversation fell on the village commune, in which Pestsov saw a sort of special principle, called by him the 'choral' principle. Levin did not agree with Pestsov, nor with his brother, who had a special attitude of his own, both admitting and not admitting the significance of the Russian commune. But he talked to them, simply trying to reconcile and soften their differences. He was not in the least interested in what he said himself, and even less so in what they said; all he wanted was that they and everyone should be happy and contented. He knew now the one thing of importance; and that one thing was at first there, in the drawing-room, and then began moving across and came to a standstill at the door. Without turning round he felt the eyes fixed on him, and the smile, and he could not help turning round. She was standing in the doorway with Shtcherbatsky, looking at him.

'I thought you were going towards the piano,' said he, going up to her. 'That's something I miss in the country—music.'

'No; we only came to fetch you and thank you,' she said, rewarding him with a smile that was like a gift, 'for coming. What do they want to argue for? No one ever convinces anyone, you know.'

'Yes; that's true,' said Levin; 'it generally happens that one argues warmly simply because one can't make out what one's opponent wants to prove.'

Levin had often noticed in discussions between the most intelligent people that after enormous efforts, and an enormous expenditure of logical subtleties and words, the disputants finally arrived at being aware that what they had so long been struggling to prove to one another had long ago, from the beginning of the argument, been known to both, but that they liked different things, and would not define what they liked for fear of its being attacked. He had often had the experience of suddenly in a discussion grasping what it was his opponent liked and at once liking it too, and immediately he found himself agreeing, and then all arguments fell away as useless. Sometimes, too, he had experienced the opposite, expressing at last what he liked himself, which he was devising arguments to defend, and, chancing to express it well and genuinely, he had found his opponent at once agreeing and ceasing to dispute his position. He tried to say this.

She knitted her brow, trying to understand. But directly he began to illustrate his meaning, she understood at once.

'I know: one must find out what he is arguing for, what is precious to him, then one can . . .'

She had completely guessed and expressed his badly expressed idea. Levin smiled joyfully; he was struck by this transition from the confused, verbose discussion with Pestsov and his brother to this laconic, clear, almost wordless communication of the most complex ideas.

Shtcherbatsky moved away from them, and Kitty, going up to a card-table, sat down, and, taking up the chalk, began drawing diverging circles over the new green cloth.

They began again on the subject that had been started at dinner—the liberty and occupations of women. Levin was of the opinion of Darya Alexandrovna that a girl who did not marry should find a woman's duties in a family. He supported this view by the fact that no family can get on without women to help; that in every family, poor or rich, there are and must be nurses, either relations or hired.

'No,' said Kitty, blushing, but looking at him all the more boldly with her truthful eyes; 'a girl may be so circumstanced that she cannot live in the family without humiliation, while she herself . . .'

At the hint he understood her.

'Oh yes,' he said. 'Yes, yes, yes—you're right; you're right!'

And he saw all that Pestsov had been maintaining at dinner of the liberty of woman, simply from getting a glimpse of the terror of an old maid's existence and its humiliation in Kitty's heart; and loving her, he felt that terror and humiliation, and at once gave up his arguments.

A silence followed. She was still drawing with the chalk on the table. Her eyes were shining with a soft light. Under the influence of her mood he felt in all his being a continually growing tension of happiness.

'Ah! I've scribbled all over the table!' she said, and, laying down the chalk, she made a movement as though to get up.

'What! shall I be left alone—without her?' he thought with horror, and took the chalk. 'Wait a minute,' he said, sitting down to the table. 'I've long wanted to ask you one thing.'

He looked straight into her caressing, though frightened eyes.

'Please, ask it.'

'Here,' he said; and he wrote the initial letters, *w*, *y*, *t*, *m*, *i*, *c*, *n*, *b*, *d*, *t*, *m*, *n*, *o*, *t*. These letters meant, 'When you told me it could never be, did that mean never, or then?' There seemed no likelihood that she could make out this complicated sentence; but he looked at her as though his life depended on her understanding the words. She glanced at him seriously, then leaned her puckered brow on her hands and began to read. Once or twice she stole a look at him, as though asking him, 'Is it what I think?'

'I understand,' she said, flushing a little.

'What is this word?' he said, pointing to the *n* that stood for *never*.

'It means *never*,' she said; 'but that's not true!'

He quickly rubbed out what he had written, gave her the chalk, and stood up. She wrote, *t*, *i*, *c*, *n*, *a*, *d*.

Dolly was completely comforted in the depression caused by her conversation with Alexey Alexandrovitch when she caught sight of the two figures: Kitty with the chalk in her hand, with a shy and happy smile looking upwards at Levin, and his handsome figure bending over the table with glowing eyes fastened one minute on the table and the next on her. He was suddenly radiant: he had understood. It meant, 'Then I could not answer differently.'

He glanced at her questioningly, timidly.

'Only then?'

'Yes,' her smile answered.

'And n . . . and now?' he asked.

'Well, read this. I'll tell you what I should like—should like so much!' She wrote the initial letters, *i*, *y*, *c*, *f*, *a*, *f*, *w*, *h*. This meant, 'If you could forget and forgive what happened.'

He snatched the chalk with nervous, trembling fingers, and, breaking it, wrote the initial letters of the following phrase, 'I have nothing to forget and to forgive; I have never ceased to love you.'

She glanced at him with a smile that did not waver.

'I understand,' she said in a whisper.

He sat down and wrote a long phrase. She understood it all, and without asking him, 'Is it this?' took the chalk and at once answered.

For a long while he could not understand what she had written, and often looked into her eyes. He was stupefied with happiness. He could not supply the words she had meant; but in her charming eyes, beaming with happiness, he saw all he needed to know. And he wrote three letters. But he had hardly finished writing when she read them over her arm, and herself finished and wrote the answer, 'Yes.'

'You're playing secrétaire?' said the old prince. 'But we must really be getting along if you want to be in time at the theatre.'

Levin got up and escorted Kitty to the door.

In their conversation everything had been said; it had been said that she loved him, and that she would tell her father and mother that he would come tomorrow morning.

XIV

WHEN Kitty had gone and Levin was left alone, he felt such uneasiness without her, and such an impatient longing to get as quickly, as quickly as possible, to tomorrow morning, when he would see her again and be plighted to her for ever, that he felt afraid, as though of death, of those fourteen hours that he had to get through without her. It was essential for him to be with someone to talk to, so as not to be left alone, to kill time. Stepan Arkadyevitch would have been the companion most congenial to him, but he was going out, he said, to a soirée, in reality to the ballet. Levin only had time to tell him he was happy, and that he loved him, and would never, never forget what he had done for him. The eyes and the smile of Stepan Arkadyevitch showed Levin that he comprehended that feeling fittingly.

'Oh, so it's not time to die yet?' said Stepan Arkadyevitch, pressing Levin's hand with emotion.

'N-n-no!' said Levin.

Darya Alexandrovna too, as she said good-bye to him, gave him a sort of congratulation, saying, 'How glad I am you have met Kitty again! One must value old friends.' Levin did not like these words of Darya Alexandrovna's. She could not understand how lofty and beyond her it all was, and she ought not to have dared to allude to it. Levin said good-bye to them, but, not to be left alone, he attached himself to his brother.

'Where are you going?'

'I'm going to a meeting.'

'Well, I'll come with you. Can I?'

'What for? Yes, come along,' said Sergey Ivanovitch, smiling. 'What is the matter with you today?'

'With me? Happiness is the matter with me!' said Levin, letting down the window of the carriage they were driving in. 'You don't mind? —it's so stifling. It's happiness is the matter with me! Why is it you have never married?'

Sergey Ivanovitch smiled.

'I am very glad, she seems a nice gi . . .' Sergey Ivanovitch was beginning.

'Don't say it! don't say it!' shouted Levin, clutching at the collar of his fur coat with both hands, and muffling him up in it. 'She's a nice girl' were such simple, humble words, so out of harmony with his feeling.

Sergey Ivanovitch laughed outright a merry laugh, which was rare with him.

'Well, anyway, I may say that I'm very glad of it.'

'That you may do tomorrow, tomorrow and nothing more! Nothing, nothing, silence,' said Levin, and muffling him once more in his fur coat, he added: 'I do like you so! Well, is it possible for me to be present at the meeting?'

'Of course it is.'

'What is your discussion about today?' asked Levin, never ceasing smiling.

They arrived at the meeting. Levin heard the secretary hesitatingly read the minutes which he obviously did not himself understand; but Levin saw from this secretary's face what a good, nice, kind-hearted person he was. This was evident from his confusion and embarrassment in reading the minutes. Then the discussion began. They were disputing about the misappropriation of certain sums and the laying of certain pipes, and Sergey Ivanovitch was very cutting to two members, and said something at great length with an air of triumph; and another member, scribbling something on a bit of paper, began timidly at first, but afterwards answered him very viciously and delightfully. And then Sviazhsky (he was there too) said something too, very handsomely and nobly. Levin listened to them, and saw clearly that these missing sums and these pipes were not anything real, and that they were not at all angry, but were all the nicest, kindest people, and everything was as happy and charming as possible among them. They did no harm to anyone, and were all enjoying it. What struck Levin was that he could see through them all today, and from little, almost imperceptible signs knew the soul of each, and saw distinctly that they were all good at heart. And Levin himself in particular they were all extremely fond of that day. That was evident from the way they spoke to him, from the friendly, affectionate way even those he did not know looked at him.

'Well, did you like it?' Sergey Ivanovitch asked him.

'Very well. I never supposed it was so interesting! Capital! Splendid!'

Sviazhsky went up to Levin and invited him to come round to tea with him. Levin was utterly at a loss to comprehend or recall what it was he had disliked in Sviazhsky, what he had failed to find in him. He was a clever and wonderfully good-hearted man.

'Most delighted,' he said, and asked after his wife and sister-in-law. And from a queer association of ideas, because in his imagination the idea of Sviazhsky's sister-in-law was connected with marriage, it occurred to him that there was no one to whom he could more suitably speak of his happiness, and he was very glad to go and see them.

Sviazhsky questioned him about his improvements on his estate, presupposing, as he always did, that there was no possibility of doing anything not done already in Europe, and now this did not in the least annoy Levin. On the contrary, he felt that Sviazhsky was right, that the whole business was of little value, and he saw the wonderful softness and consideration with which Sviazhsky avoided fully expressing his correct view. The ladies of the Sviazhsky household were particularly delightful. It seemed to Levin that they knew all about it already and sympathised with him, saying nothing merely from delicacy. He stayed with them one hour, two, three, talking of all sorts of subjects but the one thing that filled his heart, and did not observe that he was boring them dreadfully, and that it was long past their bedtime.

Sviazhsky went with him into the hall, yawning and wondering at the strange humour his friend was in. It was past one o'clock. Levin went back to his hotel, and was dismayed at the thought that all alone now with his impatience he had ten hours still left to get through. The servant, whose turn it was to be up all night, lighted his candles, and would have gone away, but Levin stopped him. This servant, Yegor, whom Levin had noticed before, struck him as a very intelligent, excellent, and, above all, good-hearted man.

'Well, Yegor, it's hard work not sleeping, isn't it?'

'One's got to put up with it! It's part of our work, you see. In a gentleman's house it's easier; but then here one makes more.'

It appeared that Yegor had a family, three boys and a daughter, a sempstress, whom he wanted to marry to a cashier in a saddler's shop.

Levin, on hearing this, informed Yegor that, in his opinion, in marriage the great thing was love, and that with love one would always be happy, for happiness rests only on oneself.

Yegor listened attentively, and obviously quite took in Levin's idea, but by way of assent to it he enunciated, greatly to Levin's surprise, the observation that when he had lived with good masters he had always been satisfied with his masters, and now was perfectly satisfied with his employer, though he was a Frenchman.

'Wonderfully good-hearted fellow!' thought Levin.

'Well, but you yourself, Yegor, when you got married, did you love your wife?'

'Ay! and why not?' responded Yegor.

And Levin saw that Yegor too was in an excited state and intending to express all his most heartfelt emotions.

'My life, too, has been a wonderful one. From a child up . . .' he was beginning with flashing eyes, apparently catching Levin's enthusiasm, just as people catch yawning.

But at that moment a ring was heard. Yegor departed, and Levin was left alone. He had eaten scarcely anything at dinner, had refused tea and supper at Sviazhsky's, but he was incapable of thinking of supper. He had not slept the previous night, but was incapable of thinking of sleep either. His room was cool, but he was oppressed by heat. He opened both the movable panes in his window and sat down to the table opposite the open panes. Over the snow-covered roofs could be seen a decorated cross with chains, and above it the rising triangle of Charles's Wain with the yellowish light of Capella. He gazed at the cross, then at the stars, drank in the fresh freezing air that flowed evenly into the room, and followed as though in a dream the images and memories that rose in his imagination. At four o'clock he heard steps in the passage and peeped out at the door. It was the gambler Myaskin, whom he knew, coming from the club. He walked gloomily, frowning and coughing. 'Poor, unlucky fellow!' thought Levin, and tears came into his eyes from love and pity for this man. He would have talked with him, and tried to comfort him, but remembering that he had nothing but his shirt on, he changed his mind and sat down again at the open pane to bathe in the cold air and gaze at the exquisite lines of the cross, silent, but full of meaning for him, and the mounting lurid yellow star. At seven o'clock there was a noise of people polishing the floors, and bells ringing in some servants' department, and Levin felt that he was beginning to get frozen. He closed the pane, washed, dressed, and went out into the street.

XV

THE streets were still empty. Levin went to the house of the Shtcherbatskys. The visitors' doors were closed and everything was asleep. He walked back, went into his room again, and asked for coffee. The day servant, not Yegor this time, brought it him. Levin would have entered into conversation with him, but a bell rang for the servant, and he went out. Levin tried to drink coffee and put some roll in his mouth, but his mouth was quite at a loss what to do with the roll. Levin, rejecting the roll, put on his coat and went out again for a walk. It was nine o'clock when he reached the Shtcherbatskys' steps the second time. In the house they were only just up, and the cook came out to go marketing. He had to get through at least two hours more.

All that night and morning Levin lived perfectly unconsciously, and felt perfectly lifted out of the conditions of material life. He had eaten nothing for a whole day, he had not slept for two nights, had spent several hours undressed in the frozen air, and felt not simply fresher and stronger than ever, but felt utterly independent of his body; he moved without muscular effort, and felt as if he could do anything. He was convinced he could fly upwards or lift the corner of the house, if need be. He spent the remainder of the time in the street, incessantly looking at his watch and gazing about him.

And what he saw then, he never saw again after. The children especially going to school, the bluish doves flying down from the roofs to the pavement, and the little loaves covered with flour, thrust out by an unseen hand, touched him. Those loaves, those doves, and those two boys were not earthly creatures. It all happened at the same time: a boy ran towards a dove and glanced smiling at Levin; the dove, with a whir of her wings, darted away, flashing in the sun, amid grains of snow that quivered in the air, while from a little window there came a smell of fresh-baked bread, and the loaves were put out. All of this together was so extraordinarily nice that Levin laughed and cried with delight. Going a long way round by Gazetny Place and Kislovka, he went back again to the hotel, and putting his watch before him, he sat down to wait for twelve o'clock. In the next room they were talking about some sort of machines, and swindling, and coughing their morning coughs. They did not realise that the hand was near twelve. The hand reached it. Levin went out on to the steps. The sledge-drivers clearly knew all about it. They crowded round Levin with happy faces, quarrelling among themselves, and offering their services. Trying not to offend the other sledge-drivers, and promising to drive with them too, Levin took one and told him to drive to the Shtcherbatskys'. The sledge-driver was splendid in a white shirt-collar, sticking out over his overcoat and into his strong, full-blooded red neck. The sledge was high and comfortable, and altogether such a one as Levin never drove in after, and the horse was a good one, and tried to gallop but didn't seem to move. The driver knew the Shtcherbatskys' house, and drew up at the entrance with a curve of his arm and a 'Wo!' especially indicative of respect for his fare. The Shtcherbatskys' hall-porter certainly knew all about it. This was evident from the smile in his eyes and the way he said—

'Well, it's a long while since you've been to see us, Konstantin Dmitrievitch!'

Not only he knew all about it, but he was unmistakably delighted and making efforts to conceal his joy. Looking into his kindly old eyes, Levin realised even something new in his happiness.

'Are they up?'

'Pray walk in! Leave it here,' said he, smiling, as Levin would have come back to take his hat. That meant something.

'To whom shall I announce your honour?' asked the footman.

The footman, though a young man, and one of the new school of footmen, a dandy, was a very kind-hearted, good fellow, and he too knew all about it.

'The princess . . . the prince . . . the young princess . . .' said Levin.

The first person he saw was Mademoiselle Linon. She walked across the room, and her ringlets and her face were beaming. He had only just spoken to her, when suddenly he heard the rustle of a skirt at the door, and Mademoiselle Linon vanished from Levin's eyes, and a joyful terror came over him at the nearness of his happiness. Mademoiselle Linon was in great haste, and leaving him, went out at the other door. Directly she had gone out, swift, swift light steps sounded on the parquet, and his bliss, his life, himself—what was best in himself, what he had so long sought and longed for—was quickly, so quickly approaching him. She did not walk, but seemed, by some unseen force, to float to him. He saw nothing but her clear, truthful eyes, frightened by the same bliss of love that flooded his heart. Those eyes were shining nearer and nearer, blinding him with their light of love. She stopped still close to him, touching him. Her hands rose and dropped on to his shoulders.

She had done all she could—she had run up to him and given herself up entirely, shy and happy. He put his arms round her and pressed his lips to her mouth that sought his kiss.

She too had not slept all night, and had been expecting him all the morning.

Her mother and father had consented without demur, and were happy in her happiness. She had been waiting for him. She wanted to be the first to tell him her happiness and his. She had got ready to see him alone, and had been delighted at the idea, and had been shy and ashamed, and did not know herself what she was doing. She had heard his steps and voice, and had waited at the door for Mademoiselle Linon to go. Mademoiselle Linon had gone away. Without thinking, without asking herself how and what, she had gone up to him, and did as she was doing.

'Let us go to mamma!' she said, taking him by the hand. For a long while he could say nothing, not so much because he was afraid of desecrating the loftiness of his emotion by a word, as that every time he tried to say something, instead of words he felt that tears of happiness were welling up. He took her hand and kissed it.

'Can it be true?' he said at last in a choked voice. 'I can't believe you love me, dear!'

She smiled at that 'dear,' and at the timidity with which he glanced at her.

'Yes!' she said significantly, deliberately. 'I am so happy!'

Not letting go his hands, she went into the drawing-room. The princess, seeing them, breathed quickly, and immediately began to cry and then immediately began to laugh, and with a vigorous step Levin had not expected, ran up to him, and hugging his head, kissed him, wetting his cheeks with her tears.

'So it is all settled! I am glad. Love her. I am glad . . . Kitty!'

'You've not been long settling things,' said the old prince trying to seem unmoved; but Levin noticed that his eyes were wet when he turned to him.

'I've long, always wished for this!' said the prince, taking Levin by the arm and drawing him towards himself. 'Even when this little featherhead fancied . . .'

'Papa!' shrieked Kitty, and shut his mouth with her hands.

'Well, I won't!' he said. 'I'm very, very . . . plea . . . Oh, what a fool I am . . .'

He embraced Kitty, kissed her face, her hand, her face again, and made the sign of the cross over her.

And there came over Levin a new feeling of love for this man, till then so little known to him, when he saw how slowly and tenderly Kitty kissed his muscular hand.

XVI

THE princess sat in her armchair, silent and smiling; the prince sat down beside her. Kitty stood by her father's chair, still holding his hand. All were silent.

The princess was the first to put everything into words, and to translate all thoughts and feelings into practical questions. And all equally felt this strange and painful for the first minute.

'When is it to be? We must have the benediction and announcement. And when's the wedding to be? What do you think, Alexander?'

'Here he is,' said the old prince, pointing to Levin—'he's the principal person in the matter.'

'When?' said Levin blushing. 'Tomorrow. If you ask me, I should say, the benediction today and the wedding tomorrow.'

'Come, *mon cher,* that's nonsense!'

'Well, in a week.'

'He's quite mad.'

'No, why so?'

'Well, upon my word!' said the mother, smiling, delighted at this haste. 'How about the trousseau?'

'Will there really be a trousseau and all that?' Levin thought with horror. 'But can the trousseau and the benediction and all that—can it spoil my happiness? Nothing can spoil it!' He glanced at Kitty, and noticed that she was not in the least, not in the very least, disturbed by the idea of the trousseau. 'Then it must be all right,' he thought.

'Oh, I know nothing about it; I only said what I should like,' he said apologetically.

'We'll talk it over, then. The benediction and announcement can take place now. That's very well.'

The princess went up to her husband, kissed him, and would have gone away, but he kept her, embraced her, and, tenderly as a young lover, kissed her several times, smiling. The old people were obviously muddled for a moment, and did not quite know whether it was they who were in love again or their daughter. When the prince and the princess had gone, Levin went up to his betrothed and took her hand. He was self-possessed now and could speak, and he had a great deal he wanted to tell her. But he said not at all what he had to say.

'How I knew it would be so! I never hoped for it; and yet in my heart I was always sure,' he said. 'I believe that it was ordained.'

'And I!' she said. 'Even when . . .' She stopped and went on again, looking at him resolutely with her truthful eyes, 'Even when I thrust from me my happiness. I always loved you alone, but I was carried away. I ought to tell you . . . Can you forgive it?'

'Perhaps it was for the best. You will have to forgive me so much. I ought to tell you . . .'

This was one of the things he had meant to speak about. He had resolved from the first to tell her two things— that he was not chaste as she was, and that he was not a believer. It was agonising, but he considered he ought to tell her both these facts.

'No, not now, later!' he said.

'Very well, later, but you must certainly tell me. I'm not afraid of anything. I want to know everything. Now it is settled.'

He added: 'Settled that you'll take me whatever I may be—you won't give me up? Yes?'

'Yes, yes.'

Their conversation was interrupted by Mademoiselle Linon, who with an affected but tender smile came to congratulate her favourite pupil. Before she had gone, the servants came in with their congratulations. Then relations arrived, and there began that state of blissful absurdity from which Levin did not emerge till the day after his wedding. Levin was in a continual state of awkwardness and discomfort, but the intensity of his happiness went on all the while increasing. He felt continually that a great deal was being expected of him—what, he did not know; and he did everything he was told, and it all gave him happiness. He had thought his engagement would have nothing about it like others, that the ordinary conditions of engaged couples would spoil his special happiness; but it ended in his doing exactly as other people did, and his happiness being only increased thereby and becoming more and more special, more and more unlike anything that had ever happened.

'Now we shall have sweetmeats to eat,' said Mademoiselle Linon—and Levin drove off to buy sweetmeats.

'Well, I'm very glad,' said Sviazhsky. 'I advise you to get the bouquets from Fomin's.'

'Oh, are they wanted?' And he drove to Fomin's.

His brother offered to lend him money, as he would have so many expenses, presents to give. . . .

'Oh, are presents wanted?' And he galloped to Foulde's.

And at the confectioner's, and at Fomin's, and at Foulde's he saw that he was expected; that they were pleased to see him, and prided themselves on his happiness, just as everyone whom he had to do with during those days. What was extraordinary was that everyone not only liked him, but even people previously unsympathetic, cold, and callous, were enthusiastic over him, gave way to him in everything, treated his feeling with tenderness and delicacy, and shared his conviction that he was the happiest man in the world because his betrothed was beyond perfection. Kitty too felt the same thing. When Countess Nordston ventured to hint that she had hoped for something better, Kitty was so angry and proved so conclusively that nothing in the world could be better than Levin, that Countess Nordston had to admit it, and in Kitty's presence never met Levin without a smile of ecstatic admiration.

The confession he had promised was the one painful incident of this time. He consulted the old prince, and with his sanction gave Kitty his diary, in which there was written the confession that tortured him. He had written this diary at the time with a view to his future wife. Two things caused him anguish: his lack of purity and his lack of faith. His confession of unbelief passed unnoticed. She was religious, had never doubted the truths of religion, but his external unbelief did not affect her in the least. Through love she knew all his soul, and in his soul she saw what she wanted, and that such a state of soul should be called unbelieving was to her a matter of no account. The other confession set her weeping bitterly.

Levin, not without an inner struggle, handed her his diary. He knew that between him and her there could not be, and should not be, secrets, and so he had decided that so it must be. But he had not realised what an effect it would have on her, he had not put himself in her place. It was only when the same evening he came to their house before the theatre, went into her room and saw her tear-stained, pitiful, sweet face, miserable with suffering he had caused and nothing could undo, he felt the abyss that separated his shameful past from her dovelike purity, and was appalled at what he had done.

'Take them, take these dreadful books!' she said, pushing away the notebooks lying before her on the table. 'Why did you give them me? No, it was better anyway,' she added, touched by his despairing face. 'But it's awful, awful!'

His head sank, and he was silent. He could say nothing.

'You can't forgive me,' he whispered.

'Yes, I forgive you; but it's terrible!'

But his happiness was so immense that this confession did not shatter it, it only added another shade to it. She forgave him; but from that time more than ever he considered himself unworthy of her, morally bowed down lower than ever before her, and prized more highly than ever his undeserved happiness.

XVII

UNCONSCIOUSLY going over in his memory the conversations that had taken place during and after dinner, Alexey Alexandrovitch returned to his solitary room. Darya Alexandrovna's words about forgiveness had aroused in him nothing but annoyance. The applicability or non-applicability of the Christian precept to his own case was too difficult a question to be discussed lightly, and this question had long ago been answered by Alexey Alexandrovitch in the negative. Of all that had been said, what stuck most in his memory was the phrase of stupid, good-natured Turovtsin—'*Acted like a man, he did! Called him out and shot him!*' Everyone had apparently shared this feeling, though from politeness they had not expressed it.

'But the matter is settled, it's useless thinking about it,' Alexey Alexandrovitch told himself. And thinking of nothing but the journey before him, and the revision work he had to do, he went into his room and asked the porter who escorted him where his man was. The porter said that the man had only just gone out. Alexey Alexandrovitch ordered tea to be sent him, sat down to the table, and taking the guidebook, began considering the route of his journey.

'Two telegrams,' said the manservant, coming into the room. 'I beg your pardon, your excellency; I'd only just that minute gone out.'

Alexey Alexandrovitch took the telegrams and opened them. The first telegram was the announcement of Stremov's appointment to the very post Karenin had coveted. Alexey Alexandrovitch flung the telegram down, and flushing a little, got up and began to pace up and down the room. '*Quos vult perdere dementat*,' he said, meaning by *quos* the persons responsible for this appointment. He was not so much annoyed that he had not received the post, that he had been conspicuously passed over; but it was incomprehensible, amazing to him that they did not see that the wordy phrase-monger Stremov was the last man fit for it. How could they fail to see how they were ruining themselves, lowering their *prestige* by this appointment?

'Something else in the same line,' he said to himself bitterly, opening the second telegram. The telegram was from his wife. Her name, written in blue pencil, 'Anna,' was the first thing that caught his eye. 'I am dying; I beg, I implore you to come. I shall die easier with your forgiveness,' he read. He smiled contemptuously, and flung down the telegram. That this was a trick and a fraud, of that, he thought for the first minute, there could be no doubt.

'There is no deceit she would stick at. She was near her confinement.

Perhaps it is the confinement. But what can be their aim? To legitimise the child, to compromise me, and prevent a divorce,' he thought. 'But something was said in it: I am dying . . .' He read the telegram again, and suddenly the plain meaning of what was said in it struck him.

'And if it is true?' he said to himself. 'If it is true that in the moment of agony and nearness to death she is genuinely penitent, and I, taking it for a trick, refuse to go? That would not only be cruel, and everyone would blame me, but it would be stupid on my part.'

'Piotr, call a coach; I am going to Petersburg,' he said to his servant.

Alexey Alexandrovitch decided that he would go to Petersburg and see his wife. If her illness was a trick, he would say nothing and go away again. If she were really in danger, and wished to see him before her death, he would forgive her if he found her alive, and pay her the last duties if he came too late.

All the way he thought no more of what he ought to do.

With a sense of weariness and uncleanliness from the night spent in the train, in the early fog of Petersburg Alexey Alexandrovitch drove through the deserted Nevsky and stared straight before him, not thinking of what was awaiting him. He could not think about it, because in picturing what would happen, he could not drive away the reflection that her death would at once remove all the difficulty of his position. Bakers, closed shops, night-cabmen, porters sweeping the pavements flashed past his eyes, and he watched it all, trying to smother the thought of what was awaiting him, and what he dared not hope for, and yet was hoping for. He drove up to the steps. A sledge and a carriage with the coachman asleep stood at the entrance. As he went into the entry, Alexey Alexandrovitch, as it were, got out his resolution from the remotest corner of his brain, and mastered it thoroughly. Its meaning ran: 'If it's a trick, then calm contempt and departure. If truth, do what is proper.'

The porter opened the door before Alexey Alexandrovitch rang. The porter, Kapitonitch, looked queer in an old coat, without a tie, and in slippers.

'How is your mistress?'

'A successful confinement yesterday.'

Alexey Alexandrovitch stopped short and turned white. He felt distinctly now how intensely he had longed for her death.

'And how is she?'

Korney in his morning apron ran downstairs..

'Very ill,' he answered. 'There was a consultation yesterday, and the doctor's here now.'

'Take my things,' said Alexey Alexandrovitch, and feeling some relief at the news that there was still hope of her death, he went into the hall.

On the hatstand there was a military overcoat. Alexey Alexandrovitch noticed it and asked—

'Who is here?'

'The doctor, the midwife, and Count Vronsky.'

Alexey Alexandrovitch went into the inner rooms.

In the drawing-room there was no one; at the sound of his steps there came out of her boudoir the midwife in a cap with lilac ribbons.

She went up to Alexey Alexandrovitch, and with the familiarity given by the approach of death took him by the arm and drew him towards the bedroom.

'Thank God you've come! She keeps on about you and nothing but you,' she said.

'Make haste with the ice!' the doctor's peremptory voice said from the bedroom.

Alexey Alexandrovitch went into her boudoir.

At the table, sitting sideways in a low chair, was Vronsky, his face hidden in his hands, weeping. He jumped up at the doctor's voice, took his hands from his face, and saw Alexey Alexandrovitch. Seeing the husband, he was so overwhelmed that he sat down again, drawing his head down to his shoulders, as if he wanted to disappear; but he made an effort over himself, got up and said—

'She is dying. The doctors say there is no hope. I am entirely in your power, only let me be here . . . though I am at your disposal. I . . .'

Alexey Alexandrovitch, seeing Vronsky's tears, felt a rush of that nervous emotion always produced in him by the sight of other people's sufferings, and turning away his face, he moved hurriedly to the door, without hearing the rest of his words. From the bedroom came the sound of Anna's voice saying something. Her voice was lively, eager, with exceedingly distinct intonations. Alexey Alexandrovitch went into the bedroom, and went up to the bed. She was lying turned with her face towards him. Her cheeks were flushed crimson, her eyes glittered, her little white hands thrust out from the sleeves of her dressing-gown were playing with the quilt, twisting it about. It seemed as though she were not only well and blooming, but in the happiest frame of mind. She was talking rapidly, musically, and with exceptionally correct articulation and expressive intonation.

'For Alexey— I am speaking of Alexey Alexandrovitch (what a strange and awful thing that both are Alexey, isn't it?)—Alexey would not refuse me. I should forget, he would forgive. . . . But why doesn't he come? He's so good, he doesn't know himself how good he is. Ah, my God, what agony! Give me some water, quick! Oh, that will be bad for her, my little girl! Oh, very well then, give her to a nurse. Yes, I agree, it's better in fact. He'll be coming; it will hurt him to see her. Give her to the nurse.'

'Anna Arkadyevna, he has come. Here he is!' said the midwife, trying to attract her attention to Alexey Alexandrovitch.

'Oh, what nonsense!' Anna went on, not seeing her husband. 'No, give her to me; give me my little one! He has not come yet. You say he won't forgive me, because you don't know him. No one knows him. I'm the only one, and it was hard for me even. His eyes I ought to know—Seryozha has just the same eyes—and I can't bear to see them because of it. Has Seryozha had his dinner? I know everyone will forget him. He would not forget. Seryozha must be moved into the corner room, and Mariette must be asked to sleep with him.'

All of a sudden she shrank back, was silent; and in terror, as though expecting a blow, as though to defend herself, she raised her hands to her face. She had seen her husband.

'No, no!' she began. 'I am not afraid of him; I am afraid of death. Alexey, come here. I am in a hurry, because I've no time, I've not long left to live; the fever will begin directly and I shall understand nothing more. Now I understand, I understand it all, I see it all!'

Alexey Alexandrovitch's wrinkled face wore an expression of agony; he took her by the hand and tried to say something, but he could not utter it; his lower lip quivered, but he still went on struggling with his emotion, and only now and then glanced at her. And each time he glanced at her, he saw her eyes gazing at him with such passionate and triumphant tenderness as he had never seen in them.

'Wait a minute, you don't know . . . stay a little, stay! . . .' She stopped, as though collecting her ideas. 'Yes,' she began; 'yes, yes, yes. This is what I wanted to say. Don't be surprised at me. I'm still the same . . . But there is another woman in me, I'm afraid of her, she loved that man, and I tried to hate you, and could not forget about her that used to be. I'm not that woman. Now I'm my real self, all myself. I'm dying now, I know I shall die, ask him. Even now I feel—see here, the weights on my feet, on my hands, on my fingers. My fingers—see how huge they are! But this will soon all be over . . . Only one thing I want: forgive me, forgive me quite. I'm terrible, but my nurse used to tell me; the holy martyr—what was her name? She was worse. And I'll go to Rome; there's a wilderness, and there I shall be no trouble to anyone, only I'll take Seryozha and the little one . . . No, you can't forgive me! I know, it can't be forgiven! No, no, go away, you're too good!' She held his hand in one burning hand, while she pushed him away with the other.

The nervous agitation of Alexey Alexandrovitch kept increasing, and had by now reached such a point that he ceased to struggle with it. He suddenly felt that what he had regarded as nervous agitation was on the contrary a blissful spiritual condition that gave him all at once a new happiness he had never known. He did not think that the Christian law that he had been all his life trying to follow, enjoined on him to forgive and love his enemies; but a glad feeling of love and forgiveness for his enemies filled his heart. He knelt down, and laying his head in the curve of her arm, which burned him as with fire through the sleeve, he sobbed like a little child. She put her arm round his head, moved towards him, and with defiant pride lifted up her eyes.

'That is he. I knew him! Now, forgive me, everyone, forgive me! . . . They've come again; why don't they go away? . . . Oh, take these cloaks off me!'

The doctor unloosed her hands, carefully laying her on the pillow, and covered her up to the shoulders. She lay back submissively, and looked before her with beaming eyes.

'Remember one thing, that I needed nothing but forgiveness, and I want nothing more. . . Why doesn't *he* come?' she said, turning to the door towards Vronsky. 'Do come, do come! Give him your hand.'

Vronsky came to the side of the bed, and seeing Anna, again hid his face in his hands.

'Uncover your face—look at him! He's a saint,' she said. 'Oh! uncover your face, do uncover it!' she said angrily. 'Alexey Alexandrovitch, do uncover his face! I want to see him.

Alexey Alexandrovitch took Vronsky's hands and drew them away from his face, which was awful with the expression of agony and shame upon it.

'Give him your hand. Forgive him.'

Alexey Alexandrovitch gave him his hand, not attempting to restrain the tears that streamed from his eyes.

'Thank God, thank God!' she said, 'now everything is ready. Only to stretch my legs a little. There, that's capital. How badly these flowers are done—not a bit like a violet,' she said, pointing to the hangings. 'My God, my God! when will it end? Give me some morphine. Doctor, give me some morphine. Oh, my God, my God!'

And she tossed about on the bed.

The doctors said that it was puerperal fever, and that it was ninety-nine chances in a hundred it would end in death. The whole day long there was fever, delirium, and unconsciousness. At midnight the patient lay without consciousness, and almost without pulse.

The end was expected every minute.

Vronsky had gone home, but in the morning he came to inquire, and Alexey Alexandrovitch meeting him in the hall, said: 'Better stay, she might ask for you,' and himself led him to his wife's boudoir. Towards morning there was a return again of excitement, rapid thought and talk, and again it ended in unconsciousness. On the third day it was the same thing, and the doctors said there was hope. That day Alexey Alexandrovitch went into the boudoir where Vronsky was sitting, and closing the door sat down opposite him.

'Alexey Alexandrovitch,' said Vronsky, feeling that a statement of the position was coming, 'I can't speak, I can't understand. Spare me! However hard it is for you, believe me, it is more terrible for me.'

He would have risen; but Alexey Alexandrovitch took him by the hand and said—

'I beg you to hear me out; it is necessary. I must explain my feelings, the feelings that have guided me and will guide me, so that you may not be in error regarding me. You know I had resolved on a divorce, and had even begun to take proceedings. I won't conceal from you that in beginning this I was in uncertainty, I was in misery; I will confess that I was pursued by a desire to revenge myself on you and on her. When I got the telegram, I came here with the same feelings; I will say more, I longed for her death. But . . .' He paused, pondering whether to disclose or not to disclose his feeling to him. 'But I saw her and forgave her. And the happiness of forgiveness has revealed to me my duty. I forgive completely. I would offer the other cheek, I would give my cloak if my coat be taken. I pray to God only not to take from me the bliss of forgiveness!'

Tears stood in his eyes, and the luminous, serene look in them impressed Vronsky.

'This is my position: you can trample me in the mud, make me the laughing-stock of the world, I will not abandon her, and I will never utter a word of reproach to you,' Alexey Alexandrovitch went on. 'My duty is clearly marked for me; I ought to be with her, and I will be. If she wishes to see you, I will let you know, but now I suppose it would be better for you to go away.'

He got up, and sobs cut short his words. Vronsky too was getting up, and in a stooping, not yet erect posture, looked up at him from under his brows. He did not understand Alexey Alexandrovitch's feeling, but he felt that it was something higher and even unattainable for him with his view of life.

XVIII

AFTER the conversation with Alexey Alexandrovitch, Vronsky went out on to the steps of the Karenins' house and stood still, with difficulty remembering where he was, and where he ought to walk or drive. He felt disgraced, humiliated, guilty, and deprived of all possibility of washing away his humiliation. He felt thrust out of the beaten track along which he had so proudly and lightly walked till then. All the habits and rules of his life that had seemed so firm, had turned out suddenly false and inapplicable. The betrayed husband, who had figured till that time as a pitiful creature, an incidental and somewhat ludicrous obstacle to his happiness, had suddenly been summoned by her herself, elevated to an awe-inspiring pinnacle, and on the pinnacle that husband had shown himself, not malignant, not false, not ludicrous, but kind and straightforward and large. Vronsky could not but feel this, and the parts were suddenly reversed. Vronsky felt his elevation and his own abasement, his truth and his own falsehood. He felt that the husband was magnanimous even in his sorrow, while he had been base and petty in his deceit. But this sense of his own humiliation before the man he had unjustly despised made up only a small part of his misery. He felt unutterably wretched now, for his passion for Anna, which had seemed to him of late to be growing cooler, now that he knew he had lost her for ever, was stronger than ever it had been. He had seen all of her in her illness, had come to know her very soul, and it seemed to him that he had never loved her till then. And now when he had learned to know her, to love her as she should be loved, he had been humiliated before her, and had lost her for ever, leaving with her nothing of himself but a shameful memory. Most terrible of all had been his ludicrous, shameful position when Alexey Alexandrovitch had pulled his hands away from his humiliated face. He stood on the steps of the Karenins' house like one distraught, and did not know what to do.

'A sledge, sir?' asked the porter.

'Yes, a sledge.'

On getting home, after three sleepless nights, Vronsky without undressing, lay down flat on the sofa, clasping his hands and laying his head on them. His head was heavy. Images, memories, and ideas of the strangest description followed one another with extraordinary rapidity and vividness. First it was the medicine he had poured out for the patient and spilt over the spoon, then the midwife's white hands, then the queer posture of Alexey Alexandrovitch on the floor beside the bed.

'To sleep! To forget!' he said to himself with the serene confidence of a healthy man that if he is tired and sleepy, he will go to sleep at once. And the same instant his head did begin to feel drowsy and he began to drop off into forgetfulness. The waves of the sea of unconsciousness had begun to meet over his head, when all at once—it was as though a violent shock of electricity had passed over him. He started so that he leapt up on the springs of the sofa, and leaning on his arms got in a panic on to his knees. His eyes were wide open as though he had never been asleep. The heaviness in his head and the weariness in his limbs that he had felt a minute before had suddenly gone.

'You may trample me in the mud,' he heard Alexey Alexandrovitch's words and saw him standing before him, and saw Anna's face with its burning flush and glittering eyes, gazing with love and tenderness not at him but at Alexey Alexandrovitch; he saw his own, as he fancied, foolish and ludicrous figure when Alexey Alexandrovitch took his hands away from his face. He stretched out his legs again and flung himself on the sofa in the same position and shut his eyes.

'To sleep! To forget!' he repeated to himself. But with his eyes shut he saw more distinctly than ever Anna's face as it had been on the memorable evening before the races.

'That is not and will not be, and she wants to wipe it out of her memory. But I cannot live without it. How can we be reconciled? how can we be reconciled?' he said aloud, and unconsciously began to repeat these words. This repetition checked the rising up of fresh images and memories, which he felt were thronging in his brain. But repeating words did not check his imagination for long. Again in extraordinarily rapid succession his best moments rose before his mind, and then his recent humiliation. 'Take away his hands,' Anna's voice says. He takes away his hands and feels the shame-struck and idiotic expression of his face.

He still lay down, trying to sleep, though he felt there was not the smallest hope of it, and kept repeating stray words from some chain of thought, trying by this to check the rising flood of fresh images. He listened, and heard in a strange, mad whisper words repeated: 'I did not appreciate it, did not make enough of it. I did not appreciate it, did not make enough of it.'

'What's this? Am I going out of my mind?' he said to himself. 'Perhaps. What makes men go out of their minds; what makes men shoot themselves?' he answered himself, and opening his eyes, he saw with wonder an embroidered cushion beside him, worked by Varya, his brother's wife. He touched the tassel of the cushion, and tried to think of Varya, of when he had seen her last. But to think of anything extraneous was an agonising effort. 'No, I must sleep!' He moved the cushion up, and pressed his head into it, but he had to make an effort to keep his eyes shut. He jumped up and sat down. 'That's all over for me,' he said to himself. 'I must think what to do. What is left?' His mind rapidly ran through his life apart from his love of Anna.

'Ambition? Serpuhovskoy? Society? The court?' He could not come to a pause anywhere. All of it had had meaning before, but now there was no reality in it. He got up from the sofa, took off his coat, undid his belt, and uncovering his hairy chest to breathe more freely, walked up and down the room. 'This is how people go mad,' he repeated, 'and how they shoot themselves . . . to escape humiliation,' he added slowly.

He went to the door and closed it, then with fixed eyes and clenched teeth he went up to the table, took a revolver, looked round him, turned it to a loaded barrel, and sank into thought. For two minutes, his head bent forward with an expression of an intense effort of thought, he stood with the revolver in his hand, motionless, thinking.

'Of course,' he said to himself, as though a logical, continuous, and clear chain of reasoning had brought him to an indubitable conclusion. In reality this 'of course', that seemed convincing to him, was simply the result of exactly the same circle of memories and images through which he had passed ten times already during the last hour—memories of happiness lost for ever. There was the same conception of the senselessness of everything to come in life, the same consciousness of humiliation. Even the sequence of these images and emotions was the same.

'Of course,' he repeated, when for the third time his thought passed again round the same spellbound circle of memories and images, and pulling the revolver to the left side of his chest, and clutching it vigorously with his whole hand, as it were squeezing it in his fist, he pulled the trigger. He did not hear the sound of the shot, but a violent blow on his chest sent him reeling. He tried to clutch at the edge of the table, dropped the revolver, staggered, and sat down on the ground, looking about him in astonishment. He did not recognise his room, looking up from the ground, at the bent legs of the table, at the waste-paper-basket, and the tiger-skin rug. The hurried, creaking steps of his servant coming through the drawing-room brought him to his senses. He made an effort at thought, and was aware that he was on the floor; and seeing blood on the tiger-skin rug and on his arm, he knew he had shot himself.

'Idiotic! Missed!' he said, fumbling after the revolver. The revolver was close beside him—he sought further off. Still feeling for it, he stretched out to the other side, and not being strong enough to keep his balance, fell over, streaming with blood.

The elegant, whiskered manservant, who used to be continually complaining to his acquaintances of the delicacy of his nerves, was so panic-stricken on seeing his master lying on the floor, that he left him losing blood while he ran for assistance. An hour later Varya, his brother's wife, had arrived, and with the assistance of three doctors, whom she had sent for in all directions, and who all appeared at the same moment, she got the wounded man to bed, and remained to nurse him.

XIX

THE mistake made by Alexey Alexandrovitch in that, when preparing for seeing his wife, he had overlooked the possibility that her repentance might be sincere, and he might forgive her, and she might not die—this mistake was two months after his return from Moscow brought home to him in all its significance. But the mistake made by him had arisen not simply from his having overlooked that contingency, but also from the fact that until that day of his interview with his dying wife, he had not known his own heart. At his sick wife's bedside he had for the first time in his life given way to that feeling of sympathetic suffering always aroused in him by the sufferings of others, and hitherto looked on by him with shame as a harmful weakness. And pity for her, and remorse for having desired her death, and most of all, the joy of forgiveness, made him at once conscious, not simply of the relief of his own sufferings, but of a spiritual peace he had never experienced before. He suddenly felt that the very thing that was the source of his sufferings had become the source of his spiritual joy; that what had seemed insoluble while he was judging, blaming, and hating, had become clear and simple when he forgave and loved.

He forgave his wife and pitied her for her sufferings and her remorse. He forgave Vronsky, and pitied him, especially after reports reached him of his despairing action. He felt more for his son than before. And he blamed himself now for having taken too little interest in him. But for the little new-born baby he felt a quite peculiar sentiment, not of pity only, but of tenderness. At first, from a feeling of compassion alone, he had been interested in the delicate little creature, who was not his child, and who was cast on one side during her mother's illness, and would certainly have died if he had not troubled about her, and he did not himself observe how fond he became of her. He would go into the nursery several times a day, and sit there for a long while, so that the nurses, who were at first afraid of him, got quite used to his presence. Sometimes for half an hour at a stretch he would sit silently gazing at the saffron-red, downy, wrinkled face of the sleeping baby, watching the movements of the frowning brows, and the fat little hands, with clenched fingers, that rubbed the little eyes and nose. At such moments particularly Alexey Alexandrovitch had a sense of perfect peace and inward harmony, and saw nothing extraordinary in his position, nothing that ought to be changed.

But as time went on, he saw more and more distinctly that however natural the position now seemed to him, he would not long be allowed to remain in it. He felt that besides the blessed spiritual force controlling his soul, there was another, a brutal force, as powerful, or more powerful, which controlled his life, and that this force would not allow him that humble peace he longed for. He felt that everyone was looking at him with inquiring wonder, that he was not understood, and that something was expected of him. Above all, he felt the instability and unnaturalness of his relations with his wife.

When the softening effect of the near approach of death had passed away, Alexey Alexandrovitch began to notice that Anna was afraid of him, ill at ease with him, and could not look him straight in the face. She seemed to be wanting, and not daring, to tell him something; and as though forseeing their present relations could not continue, she seemed to be expecting something from him.

Towards the end of February it happened that Anna's baby daughter, who had been named Anna too, fell ill. Alexey Alexandrovitch was in the nursery in the morning, and leaving orders for the doctor to be sent for, he went to his office. On finishing his work, he returned home at four. Going into the hall he saw a handsome groom, in a braided livery and a bear fur cape, holding a white fur cloak.

'Who is here?' asked Alexey Alexandrovitch.

'Princess Elizaveta Federovna Tverskoy,' the groom answered, and it seemed to Alexey Alexandrovitch that he grinned.

During all this difficult time Alexey Alexandrovitch had noticed that his worldly acquaintances, especially women, took a peculiar interest in him and his wife. All these acquaintances he observed with difficulty concealing their mirth at something; the same mirth that he had perceived in the lawyer's eyes, and just now in the eyes of this groom. Everyone seemed, somehow, hugely delighted, as though they had just been at a wedding. When they met him, with ill-disguised enjoyment they inquired after his wife's health. The presence of Princess Tverskoy was unpleasant to Alexey Alexandrovitch from the memories associated with her, and also because he disliked her, and he went straight to the nursery. In the day-nursery Seryozha, leaning on the table with his legs on a chair, was drawing and chatting away merrily. The English governess, who had during Anna's illness replaced the French one, was sitting near the boy knitting a shawl. She hurriedly got up, curtseyed, and pulled Seryozha.

Alexey Alexandrovitch stroked his son's hair, answered the governess's inquiries about his wife, and asked what the doctor had said of baby.

'The doctor said it was nothing serious, and he ordered a bath, sir.'

'But she is still in pain,' said Alexey Alexandrovitch, listening to the baby's screaming in the next room.

'I think it's the wet-nurse, sir,' the Englishwoman said firmly.

'What makes you think so?' he asked, stopping short.

'It's just as it was at Countess Paul's, sir. They gave the baby medicine, and it turned out that the baby was simply hungry: the nurse had no milk, sir.'

Alexey Alexandrovitch pondered, and after standing still a few seconds he went in at the other door. The baby was lying with its head thrown back, stiffening itself in the nurse's arms, and would not take the plump breast offered it; and it never ceased screaming in spite of the double hushing of the wet-nurse and the other nurse, who was bending over her.

'Still no better?' said Alexey Alexandrovitch.

'She's very restless,' answered the nurse in a whisper.

'Miss Edwarde says that perhaps the wet-nurse has no milk,' he said.

'I think so too, Alexey Alexandrovitch.'

'Then why didn't you say so?'

'Who's one to say it to? Anna Arkadyevna still ill . . .' said the nurse discontentedly.

The nurse was an old servant of the family. And in her simple words there seemed to Alexey Alexandrovitch an allusion to his position.

The baby screamed louder than ever, struggling and sobbing. The nurse, with a gesture of despair, went to it, took it from the wet-nurse's arms, and began walking up and down, rocking it.

'You must ask the doctor to examine the wet-nurse,' said Alexey Alexandrovitch. The smartly dressed and healthy-looking nurse, frightened at the idea of losing her place, muttered something to herself, and covering her bosom, smiled contemptuously at the idea of doubts being cast on her abundance of milk. In that smile, too, Alexey Alexandrovitch saw a sneer at his position.

'Luckless child!' said the nurse, hushing the baby, and still walking up and down with it.

Alexey Alexandrovitch sat down, and with a despondent and suffering face watched the nurse walking to and fro.

When the child at last was still, and had been put in a deep bed, and the nurse, after smoothing the little pillow, had left her, Alexey Alexandrovitch got up, and walking awkwardly on tiptoe, approached the baby. For a minute he was still, and with the same despondent face gazed at the baby; but all at once a smile, that moved his hair and the skin of his forehead, came out on his face, and he went as softly out of the room.

In the dining-room he rang the bell, and told the servant who came in to send again for the doctor. He felt vexed with his wife for not being anxious about this exquisite baby, and in this vexed humour he had no wish to go to her; he had no wish, either, to see Princess Betsy. But his wife might wonder why he did not go to her as usual; and so, overcoming his disinclination, he went towards the bedroom. As he walked over the soft rug towards the door, he could not help overhearing a conversation he did not want to hear.

'If he hadn't been going away, I could have understood your answer and his too. But your husband ought to be above that,' Betsy was saying.

'It's not for my husband; for myself I don't wish it. Don't say that!' answered Anna's excited voice.

'Yes, but you must care to say good-bye to a man who has shot himself on your account . . .'

'That's just why I don't want to.'

With a dismayed and guilty expression, Alexey Alexandrovitch stopped and would have gone back unobserved. But reflecting that this would be undignified, he turned back again, and clearing his throat, he went up to the bedroom. The voices were silent, and he went in.

Anna, in a grey dressing-gown, with a crop of short clustering black curls on her round head, was sitting on a settee. The eagerness died out of her face, as it always did, at the sight of her husband; she dropped her head and looked round uneasily at Betsy. Betsy, dressed in the height of a the latest fashion, in a hat that towered somewhere over her head like a shade on a lamp, in a blue dress with violet cross-way stripes slanting one way on the bodice and the other way on the skirt, was sitting beside Anna, her tall flat figure held erect. Bowing her head, she greeted Alexey Alexandrovitch with an ironical smile.

'Ah!' she said, as though surprised. 'I'm very glad you're at home. You never put in an appearance anywhere, and I haven't seen you ever since Anna has been ill. I have heard all about it—your anxiety. Yes, you're a wonderful husband!' she said, with a meaning and affable air, as though she were bestowing an order of magnanimity on him for his conduct to his wife.

Alexey Alexandrovitch bowed frigidly, and kissing his wife's hand, asked how she was.

'Better, I think,' she said, avoiding his eyes.

'But you're rather a feverish-looking colour,' he said, laying stress on the word 'feverish'.

'We've been talking too much,' said Betsy. 'I feel it's selfishness on my part, and I am going away.'

She got up, but Anna, suddenly flushing, quickly caught at her hand.

'No, wait a minute, please. I must tell you . . . no, you.' She turned to Alexey Alexandrovitch, and her neck and brow were suffused with crimson. 'I won't and can't keep anything secret from you,' she said.

Alexey Alexandrovitch cracked his fingers and bowed his head.

'Betsy's been telling me that Count Vronsky wants to come here to say good-bye before his departure for Tashkend.' She did not look at her husband, and was evidently in haste to have everything out, however hard it might be for her. 'I told her I could not receive him.'

'You said, my dear, that it would depend on Alexey Alexandrovitch,' Betsy corrected her.

'Oh no, I can't receive him; and what object would there . . .' She stopped suddenly, and glanced inquiringly at her husband (he did not look at her). 'In short, I don't wish it . . .'

Alexey Alexandrovitch advanced and would have taken her hand.

Her first impulse was to jerk back her hand from the damp hand with big swollen veins that sought hers, but with an obvious effort to control herself she pressed his hand.

'I am very grateful to you for your confidence, but . . .' he said, feeling with confusion and annoyance that what he could decide easily and clearly by himself, he could not discuss before Princess Tverskoy, who to him stood for the incarnation of that brute force which would inevitably control him in the life he led in the eyes of the world, and hinder him from giving way to his feeling of love and forgiveness. He stopped short, looking at Princess Tverskoy.

'Well, good-bye, my darling,' said Betsy, getting up. She kissed Anna, and went out. Alexey Alexandrovitch escorted her out.

'Alexey Alexandrovitch! I know you are a truly magnanimous man,' said Betsy, stopping in the little drawing-room, and with special warmth shaking hands with him once more. 'I am an outsider, but I so love her and respect you that I venture to advise. Receive him. Alexey Vronsky is the soul of honour, and he is going away to Tashkend.'

'Thank you, princess, for your sympathy and advice. But the question of whether my wife can or cannot see anyone she must decide herself.'

He said this from habit, lifting his brows with dignity, and reflected immediately that whatever his words might be, there could be no dignity in his position. And he saw this by the suppressed, malicious, and ironical smile with which Betsy glanced at him after this phrase.

XX

ALEXEY ALEXANDROVITCH took leave of Betsy in the drawing-room, and went to his wife. She was lying down, but hearing his steps she sat up hastily in her former attitude, and looked in a scared way at him. He saw she had been crying.

'I am very grateful for your confidence in me.' He repeated gently in Russian the phrase he had said in Betsy's presence in French, and sat down beside her. When he spoke to her in Russian, using the Russian 'thou' of intimacy and affection, it was insufferably irritating to Anna. 'And I am very grateful for your decision. I, too, imagine that since he is going away, there is no sort of necessity for Count Vronsky to come here. However, if . . .'

'But I've said so already, so why repeat it?' Anna suddenly interrupted him with an irritation she could not succeed in repressing. 'No sort of necessity,' she thought, 'for a man to come and say good-bye to the woman he loves, for whom he was ready to ruin himself, and has ruined himself, and who cannot live without him. No sort of necessity!' She compressed her lips, and dropped her burning eyes to his hands with their swollen veins. They were rubbing each other.

'Let us never speak of it,' she added more calmly.

'I have left this question to you to decide, and I am very glad to see . . .' Alexey Alexandrovitch was beginning.

'That my wish coincides with your own,' she finished quickly, exasperated at his talking so slowly while she knew beforehand all he would say.

'Yes,' he assented; 'and Princess Tverskoy's interference in the most difficult private affairs is utterly uncalled for. She especially . . .'

'I don't believe a word of what's said about her,' said Anna quickly. 'I know she really cares for me.'

Alexey Alexandrovitch sighed and said nothing. She played nervously with the tassel of her dressing-gown, glancing at him with that torturing sensation of physical repulsion for which she blamed herself, though she could not control it. Her only desire now was to be rid of his oppressive presence.

'I have just sent for the doctor,' said Alexey Alexandrovitch.

'I am very well; what do I want the doctor for?'

'No, the little one cries, and they say the nurse hasn't enough milk.'

'Why didn't you let me nurse her, when I begged to? Anyway' (Alexey Alexandrovitch knew what was meant by that 'anyway'), 'she's a baby, and they're killing her.' She rang the bell and ordered the baby to be brought her. 'I begged to nurse her, I wasn't allowed to, and now I'm blamed for it.'

'I don't blame . . .'

'Yes, you do blame me! My God! why didn't I die!' And she broke into sobs. 'Forgive me, I'm nervous, I'm unjust,' she said, controlling herself, 'but do go away . . .'

'No, it can't go on like this,' Alexey Alexandrovitch said to himself decidedly as he left his wife's room.

Never had the impossibility of his position in the world's eyes, and his wife's hatred of him, and altogether the might of that mysterious brutal force that guided his life against his spiritual inclinations, and exacted conformity with its decrees and change in his attitude to his wife, been presented to him with such distinctness as that day. He saw clearly that all the world and his wife expected of him something, but what exactly, he could not make out. He felt that this was rousing in his soul a feeling of anger destructive of his peace of mind and of all the good of his achievement. He believed that for Anna herself it would be better to break off all relations with Vronsky; but if they all thought this out of the question, he was even ready to allow these relations to be renewed, so long as the children were not disgraced, and he was not deprived of them nor forced to change his position. Bad as this might be, it was anyway better than a rupture, which would put her in a hopeless and shameful position, and deprive him of everything he cared for. But he felt helpless; he knew beforehand that everyone was against him, and that he would not be allowed to do what seemed to him now so natural and right, but would be forced to do what was wrong, though it seemed the proper thing to them.

XXI

BEFORE Betsy had time to walk out of the drawing-room, she was met in the doorway by Stepan Arkadyevitch, who had just come from Yeliseev's, where a consignment of fresh oysters had been received.

'Ah! princess! what a delightful meeting!' he began. 'I've been to see you.'

'A meeting for one minute, for I'm going,' said Betsy, smiling and putting on her glove.

'Don't put on your glove yet, princess; let me kiss your hand. There's nothing I'm so thankful to the revival of the old fashions for as the kissing the hand.' He kissed Betsy's hand. 'When shall we see each other?'

'You don't deserve it,' answered Betsy, smiling.

'Oh yes, I deserve a great deal, for I've become a most serious person. I don't only manage my own affairs, but other people's too,' he said, with a significant expression.

'Oh, I'm so glad!' answered Betsy, at once understanding that he was speaking of Anna. And going back into her drawing-room, they stood in a corner. 'He's killing her,' said Betsy in a whisper full of meaning. 'It's impossible, impossible . . .'

'I'm so glad you think so,' said Stepan Arkadyevitch, shaking his head with a serious and sympathetically distressed expression, 'that's what I've come to Petersburg for.'

'The whole town's talking of it,' she said. 'It's an impossible position. She pines and pines away. He doesn't understand that she's one of those women who can't trifle with their feelings. One of two things: either let him take her away, act with energy, or give her a divorce. This is stifling her.'

'Yes, yes . . . just so . . .' Oblonsky said, sighing. 'That's what I've come for. At least not solely for that . . . I've been made a *kammer-herr*; of course, one has to say thank you. But the chief thing was having to settle this.'

'Well, God help you!' said Betsy.

After accompanying Betsy to the outside hall, once more kissing her hand above the glove, at the point where the pulse beats, and murmuring to her such unseemly nonsense that she did not know whether to laugh or be angry, Stepan Arkadyevitch went to his sister. He found her in tears.

Although he happened to be bubbling over with good spirits, Stepan Arkadyevitch immediately and quite naturally fell into the sympathetic, poetically emotional tone which harmonised with her mood. He asked her how she was, and how she had spent the morning.

'Very, very miserably. Today and this morning and all past days and days to come,' she said.

'I think you're giving way to pessimism. You must rouse yourself, you must look life in the face. I know it's hard, but . . .'

'I have heard it said that women love men even for their vices,' Anna began suddenly, 'but I hate him for his virtues. I can't live with him. Do you understand? the sight of him has a physical effect on me, it makes me beside myself. I can't, I can't live with him. What am I to do? I have been unhappy, and used to think one couldn't be more unhappy, but the awful state of things I am going through now, I could never have conceived. Would you believe it, that knowing he's a good man, a splendid man, that I'm not worth his little finger, still I hate him. I hate him for his generosity. And there's nothing left for me but . . .'

She would have said death, but Stepan Arkadyevitch would not let her finish.

'You are ill and overwrought,' he said; 'believe me, you're exaggerating dreadfully. There's nothing so terrible in it.'

And Stepan Arkadyevitch smiled. No one else in Stepan Arkadyevitch's place, having to do with such despair, would have ventured to smile (the smile would have seemed brutal); but in his smile there was so much of sweetness and almost feminine tenderness that his smile did not wound, but softened and soothed. His gentle, soothing words and smiles were as soothing and softening as almond oil. And Anna soon felt this.

'No, Stiva,' she said, 'I'm lost, lost! worse than lost! I can't say yet that all is over; on the contrary, I feel that it's not over. I'm an overstrained string that must snap. But it's not ended yet . . . and it will have a fearful end.'

'No matter, we must let the string be loosened, little by little. There's no position from which there is no way of escape.'

'I have thought, and thought. Only one . . .'

Again he knew from her terrified eyes that this one way of escape in her thought was death, and he would not let her say it.

'Not at all,' he said. 'Listen to me. You can't see your own position as I can. Let me tell you candidly my opinion.' Again he smiled discreetly his almond-oil smile. 'I'll begin from the beginning. You married a man twenty years older than yourself. You married him without love and not knowing what love was. It was a mistake, let's admit.'

'A fearful mistake!' said Anna.

'But I repeat, it's an accomplished fact. Then you had, let us say, the misfortune to love a man not your husband. That was a misfortune; but that, too, is an accomplished fact. And your husband knew it and forgave it.' He stopped at each sentence, waiting for her to object, but she made no answer. 'That's so. Now the question is: can you go on living with your husband? Do you wish it? Does he wish it?'

'I know nothing, nothing.'

'But you said yourself that you can't endure him.'

'No, I didn't say so. I deny it. I can't tell, I don't know anything about it.'

'Yes, but let . . .'

'You can't understand. I feel I'm lying head downwards in a sort of pit, but I ought not to save myself. And I can't . . .'

'Never mind, we'll slip something under and pull you out. I understand you; I understand that you can't take it on yourself to express your wishes, your feelings.'

'There's nothing, nothing I wish . . . except for it to be all over.'

'But he sees this and knows it. And do you suppose it weighs on him any less than on you? You're wretched, he's wretched, and what good can come of it? while divorce would solve the whole difficulty.' With some effort Stepan Arkadyevitch brought out his central idea, and looked significantly at her.

She said nothing, and shook her cropped head in dissent. But from the look in her face, that suddenly brightened into its old beauty, he saw that if she did not desire this, it was simply because it seemed to her unattainable happiness.

'I'm awfully sorry for you! And how happy I should be if I could arrange things!' said Stepan Arkadyevitch, smiling more boldly. 'Don't speak, don't say a word! God grant only that I may speak as I feel. I'm going to him.'

Anna looked at him with dreamy, shining eyes, and said nothing.

XXII

STEPAN ARKADYEVITCH, with the same somewhat solemn expression with which he used to take his presidential chair at his board, walked into Alexey Alexandrovitch's room. Alexey Alexandrovitch was walking about his room with his hands behind his back, thinking of just what Stepan Arkadyevitch had been discussing with his wife.

'I'm not interrupting you?' said Stepan Arkadyevitch, on the sight of his brother-in-law becoming suddenly aware of a sense of embarrassment unusual with him. To conceal this embarrassment he took out a cigarette-case he had just bought that opened in a new way, and sniffing the leather, took a cigarette out of it.

'No. Do you want anything?' Alexey Alexandrovitch asked without eagerness.

'Yes, I wished . . . I wanted . . . yes, I wanted to talk to you,' said Stepan Arkadyevitch, with surprise aware of an unaccustomed timidity.

This feeling was so unexpected and so strange that he did not believe it was the voice of conscience telling him that what he was meaning to do was wrong.

Stepan Arkadyevitch made an effort and struggled with the timidity that had come over him.

'I hope you believe in my love for my sister and my sincere affection and respect for you,' he said, reddening.

Alexey Alexandrovitch stood still and said nothing, but his face struck Stepan Arkadyevitch by its expression of an unresisting sacrifice.

'I intended . . . I wanted to have a little talk with you about my sister and your mutual position,' he said, still struggling with an unaccustomed constraint.

Alexey Alexandrovitch smiled mournfully, looked at his brother-in-law, and without answering went up to the table, took from it an unfinished letter, and handed it to his brother-in-law.

'I think unceasingly of the same thing. And here is what I had begun writing, thinking I could say it better by letter, and that my presence irritates her,' he said, as he gave him the letter.

Stepan Arkadyevitch took the letter, looked with incredulous surprise at the lustreless eyes fixed so immovably on him, and began to read.

'I see that my presence is irksome to you. Painful as it is to me to believe it, I see that it is so, and cannot be otherwise. I don't blame you, and God is my witness that on seeing you at the time of your illness I resolved with my whole heart to forget all that had passed between us and to begin a new life. I do not regret, and shall never regret, what I have done; but I have desired one thing—your good, the good of your soul—and now I see I have not attained that. Tell me yourself what will give you true happiness and peace to your soul. I put myself entirely in your hands, and trust to your feeling of what's right.'

Stepan Arkadyevitch handed back the letter, and with the same surprise continued looking at his brother-in-law, not knowing what to say. This silence was so awkward for both of them that Stepan Arkadyevitch's lips began twitching nervously, while he still gazed without speaking at Karenin's face.

'That's what I wanted to say to her,' said Alexey Alexandrovitch, turning away.

'Yes, yes . . .' said Stepan Arkadyevitch, not able to answer for the tears that were choking him.

'Yes, yes, I understand you,' he brought out at last.

'I want to know what she would like,' said Alexey Alexandrovitch.

'I am afraid she does not understand her own position. She is not a judge,' said Stepan Arkadyevitch, recovering himself. 'She is crushed, simply crushed by your generosity. If she were to read this letter, she would be incapable of saying anything, she would only hang her head lower than ever.'

'Yes, but what's to be done in that case? how explain, how find out her wishes?'

'If you will allow me to give my opinion, I think that it lies with you to point out directly the steps you consider necessary to end the position.'

'So you consider it must be ended?' Alexey Alexandrovitch interrupted him. 'But how?' he added, with a gesture of his hands before his eyes not usual with him. 'I see no possible way out of it.'

'There is some way of getting out of every position,' said Stepan Arkadyevitch, standing up and becoming more cheerful. 'There was a time when you thought of breaking off . . . If you are convinced now that you cannot make each other happy . . .'

'Happiness may be variously understood. But suppose that I agree to everything, that I want nothing: what way is there of getting out of our position?'

'If you care to know my opinion,' said Stepan Arkadyevitch with the same smile of softening, almond-oil tenderness with which he had been talking to Anna. His kindly smile was so winning that Alexey Alexandrovitch, feeling his own weakness and unconsciously swayed by it, was ready to believe what Stepan Arkadyevitch was saying.

'She will never speak out about it. But one thing is possible, one thing she might desire,' he went on, 'that is the cessation of your relations and all memories associated with them. To my thinking, in your position what's essential is the formation of a new attitude to one another. And that can only rest on a basis of freedom on both sides.'

'Divorce,' Alexey Alexandrovitch interrupted, in a tone of aversion.

'Yes, I imagine that divorce—yes, divorce,' Stepan Arkadyevitch repeated, reddening. 'That is from every point of view the most rational course for married people who find themselves in the position you are in. What can be done if married people find that life is impossible for them together? That may always happen.'

Alexey Alexandrovitch sighed heavily and closed his eyes.

'There's only one point to be considered: is either of the parties desirous of forming new ties? If not, it is very simple,' said Stepan Arkadyevitch, feeling more and more free from constraint.

Alexey Alexandrovitch, scowling with emotion, muttered something to himself, and made no answer. All that seemed so simple to Stepan Arkadyevitch, Alexey Alexandrovitch had thought over thousands of times. And, so far from being simple, it all seemed to him utterly impossible. Divorce, the details of which he knew by this time, seemed to him now out of the question, because the sense of his own dignity and respect for religion forbade his taking upon himself a fictitious charge of adultery, and still more suffering his wife, pardoned and beloved by him, to be caught in the fact and put to public shame. Divorce appeared to him impossible also on other still more weighty grounds.

What would become of his son in case of a divorce? To leave him with his mother was out of the question. The divorced mother would have her own illegitimate family, in which his position as a stepson and his education would not be good. Keep him with him? He knew that would be an act of vengeance on his part, and that he did not want. But apart from this, what more than all made divorce seem impossible to Alexey Alexandrovitch was, that by consenting to a divorce he would be completely ruining Anna. The saying of Darya Alexandrovna at Moscow, that in deciding on a divorce he was thinking of himself, and not considering that by this he would be ruining her irrevocably, had sunk into his heart. And connecting this saying with his forgiveness of her, with his devotion to the children, he understood it now in his own way. To consent to a divorce, to give her her freedom, meant in his thoughts to take from himself the last tie that bound him to life—the children whom he loved; and to take from her the last prop that stayed her on the path of right, to thrust her down to her ruin. If she were divorced, he knew she would join her life to Vronsky's, and their tie would be an illegitimate and criminal one, since a wife, by the interpretation of the ecclesiastical law, could not marry while her husband was living. 'She will join him, and in a year or two he will throw her over, or she will form a new tie,' thought Alexey Alexandrovitch. 'And I, by agreeing to an unlawful divorce, shall be to blame for her ruin.' He had thought it all over hundreds of times, and was convinced that a divorce was not at all simple, as Stepan Arkadyevitch had said, but was utterly impossible. He did not believe a single word Stepan Arkadyevitch said to him; to every word he had a thousand objections to make, but he listened to him, feeling that his words were the expression of that mighty brutal force which controlled his life and to which he would have to submit.

'The only question is on what terms you agree to give her a divorce. She does not want anything, does not dare ask you for anything, she leaves it all to your generosity.'

'My God, my God! what for?' thought Alexey Alexandrovitch, remembering the details of divorce proceedings in which the husband took the blame on himself, and with just the same gesture with which Vronsky had done the same, he hid his face for shame in his hands.

'You are distressed, I understand that. But if you think it over . . .'

'Whosoever shall smite thee on thy right cheek, turn to him the other also; and if any man take away thy coat, let him have thy cloak also,' thought Alexey Alexandrovitch.

'Yes, yes!' he cried in a shrill voice. 'I will take the disgrace on myself, I will give up even my son, but . . . but wouldn't it be better to let it alone? Still you may do as you like . . .'

And turning away so that his brother-in-law could not see him, he sat down on a chair at the window. There was bitterness, there was shame in his heart, but with this bitterness and shame he felt joy and emotion at the height of his own meekness.

Stepan Arkadyevitch was touched. He was silent for a space.

'Alexey Alexandrovitch, believe me, she appreciates your generosity,' he said. 'But it seems it was the will of God,' he added, and as he said it felt how foolish a remark it was, and with difficulty repressed a smile at his own foolishness.

Alexey Alexandrovitch would have made some reply, but tears stopped him.

'This is an unhappy fatality, and one must accept it as such. I accept the calamity as an accomplished fact, and am doing my best to help both her and you,' said Stepan Arkadyevitch.

When he went out of his brother-in-law's room he was touched, but that did not prevent him from being glad he had successfully brought the matter to a conclusion, for he felt certain Alexey Alexandrovitch would not go back on his words. To this satisfaction was added the fact that an idea had just struck him for a riddle turning on his successful achievement, that when the affair was over he would ask his wife and most intimate friends. He put this riddle into two or three different ways. 'But I'll work it out better than that,' he said to himself with a smile.

XXIII

VRONSKY'S wound had been a dangerous one, though it did not touch the heart, and for several days he had lain between life and death. The first time he was able to speak, Varya, his brother's wife, was alone in the room.

'Varya,' he said, looking sternly at her, 'I shot myself by accident. And please never speak of it, and tell everyone so. Or else it's too ridiculous.'

Without answering his words, Varya bent over him, and with a delighted smile gazed into his face. His eyes were clear, not feverish; but their expression was stern.

'Thank God!' she said: 'You're not in pain?'

'A little here.' He pointed to his breast.

'Then let me change your bandages.'

In silence, stiffening his broad jaws, he looked at her while she bandaged him up. When she had finished he said—

'I'm not delirious. Please manage that there may be no talk of my having shot myself on purpose.'

'No one does say so. Only I hope you won't shoot yourself by accident any more,' she said, with a questioning smile.

'Of course I won't, but it would have been better . . .'

And she smiled gloomily.

In spite of these words and this smile, which so frightened Varya, when the inflammation was over and he began to recover, he felt that he was completely free from one part of his misery. By his action he had, as it were, washed away the shame and humiliation he had felt before. He could now think calmly of Alexey Alexandrovitch. He recognised all his magnanimity, but he did not now feel himself humiliated by it. Besides, he got back again into the beaten track of his life. He saw the possibility of looking men in the face again without shame, and he could live in accordance with his own habits. One thing he could not pluck out of his heart, though he never ceased struggling with it, was the regret, amounting to despair, that he had lost her for ever. That now, having expiated his sin against the husband, he was bound to renounce her, and never in future to stand between her with her repentance and her husband, he had firmly decided in his heart; but he could not tear out of his heart his regret at the loss of her love, he could not erase from his memory those moments of happiness that he had so little prized at the time, and that haunted him in all their charm.

Serpuhovskoy had planned his appointment at Tashkend, and Vronsky agreed to the proposition without the slightest hesitation. But the nearer the time of departure came, the bitterer was the sacrifice he was making to what he thought his duty.

His wound had healed, and he was driving about making preparations for his departure for Tashkend.

'To see her once and then to bury myself, to die,' he thought, and as he was paying farewell visits, he uttered this thought to Betsy. Charged with this commission, Betsy had gone to Anna, and brought him back a negative reply.

'So much the better,' thought Vronsky, when he received the news. 'It was a weakness, which would have shattered what strength I have left.'

Next day Betsy herself came to him in the morning, and announced that she had heard through Oblonsky as a positive fact that Alexey Alexandrovitch had agreed to a divorce, and that therefore Vronsky could see Anna.

Without even troubling himself to see Betsy out of his flat, forgetting all his resolutions, without asking when he could see her, where her husband was, Vronsky drove straight to the Karenins'. He ran up the stairs seeing no one and nothing, and with a rapid step, almost breaking into a run, he went into her room. And without considering, without noticing whether there was anyone in the room or not, he flung his arms round her, and began to cover her face, her hands, her neck with kisses.

Anna had been preparing herself for this meeting, had thought what she would say to him, but she did not succeed in saying anything of it; his passion mastered her. She tried to calm him, to calm herself, but it was too late. His feeling infected her. Her lips trembled so that for a long while she could say nothing.

'Yes, you have conquered me, and I am yours,' she said at last, pressing his hands to her bosom.

'So it had to be,' he said. 'So long as we live, it must be so. I know it now.'

'That's true,' she said, getting whiter and whiter, and embracing his head. 'Still there is something terrible in it after all that has happened.'

'It will all pass, it will all pass; we shall be so happy. Our love, if it could be stronger, will be strengthened by there being something terrible in it,' he said, lifting his head and parting his strong teeth in a smile.

And she could not but respond with a smile—not to his words, but to the love in his eyes. She took his hand and stroked her chilled cheeks and cropped head with it.

'I don't know you with this short hair. You've grown so pretty. A boy. But how pale you are!'

'Yes, I'm very weak,' she said, smiling. And her lips began trembling again.

'We'll go to Italy; you will get strong,' he said.

'Can it be possible we could be like husband and wife, alone, your family with you?' she said, looking close into his eyes.

'It only seems strange to me that it can ever have been otherwise.'

'Stiva says that *he* has agreed to everything, but I can't accept *his* generosity,' she said, looking dreamily past Vronsky's face. 'I don't want a divorce; it's all the same to me now. Only I don't know what he will decide about Seryozha.'

He could not conceive how at this moment of their meeting she could remember and think of her son, of divorce. What did it all matter?

'Don't speak of that, don't think of it,' he said, turning her hand in his, and trying to draw her attention to him; but still she did not look at him.

'Oh, why didn't I die! it would have been better,' she said, and silent tears flowed down both her cheeks; but she tried to smile, so as not to wound him.

To decline the flattering and dangerous appointment at Tashkend would have been, Vronsky had till then considered, disgraceful and impossible. But now, without an instant's consideration, he declined it, and observing dissatisfaction in the most exalted quarters at this step, he immediately retired from the army.

A month later Alexey Alexandrovitch was left alone with his son in his house at Petersburg, while Anna and Vronsky had gone abroad, not having obtained a divorce, but having absolutely declined all idea of one.

PART V

I

PRINCESS SHTCHERBATSKY considered that it was out of the question for the wedding to take place before Lent, just five weeks off, since not half the trousseau could possibly be ready by that time. But she could not but agree with Levin that to fix it for after Lent would be putting it off too late, as an old aunt of Prince Shtcherbatsky's was seriously ill and might die, and then the mourning would delay the wedding still longer. And therefore, deciding to divide the trousseau into two parts—a larger and a smaller trousseau—the princess consented to have the wedding before Lent. She determined that she would get the smaller part of the trousseau all ready now, and the larger part should be made later, and she was much vexed with Levin because he was incapable of giving her a serious answer to the question whether he agreed to this arrangement or not. The arrangement was the more suitable as, immediately after the wedding, the young people were to go to the country, where the more important part of the trousseau would not be wanted.

Levin still continued in the same delirious condition in which it seemed to him that he and his happiness constituted the chief and sole aim of all existence, and that he need not now think or care about anything, that everything was being done and would be done for him by others. He had not even plans and aims for the future, he left its arrangements to others, knowing that everything would be delightful. His brother Sergey Ivanovitch, Stepan Arkadyevitch, and the princess guided him in doing what he had to do. All he did was to agree entirely with everything suggested to him. His brother raised money for him, the princess advised him to leave Moscow after the wedding. Stepan Arkadyevitch advised him to go abroad. He agreed to everything. 'Do what you choose, if it amuses you. I'm happy, and my happiness can be no greater and no less for anything you do,' he thought. When he told Kitty of Stepan Arkadyevitch's advice that they should go abroad, he was much surprised that she did not agree to this, and had some definite requirement of her own in regard to their future. She knew Levin had work he loved in the country. She did not, as he saw, understand this work, she did not even care to understand it. But that did not prevent her from regarding it as a matter of great importance. And then she knew their home would be in the country, and she wanted to go, not abroad where she was not going to live, but to the place where their home would be. This definitely expressed purpose astonished Levin. But since he did not care either way, he immediately asked Stepan Arkadyevitch, as though it were his duty, to go down to the country and to arrange everything there to the best of his ability with the taste of which he had so much.

'But I say,' Stepan Arkadyevitch said to him one day after he had come back from the country, where he had got everything ready for the young people's arrival, 'have you a certificate of having been at confession?'

'No. But what of it?'

'You can't be married without it.'

'*Aïe, aïe, aïe!*' cried Levin. 'Why, I believe it's nine years since I've taken the sacrament! I never thought of it.'

'You're a pretty fellow!' said Stepan Arkadyevitch laughing, 'and you call me a Nihilist! But this won't do, you know. You must take the sacrament.'

'When? There are four days left now.'

Stepan Arkadyevitch arranged this also, and Levin had to go to confession. To Levin, as to any unbeliever who respects the beliefs of others, it was exceedingly disagreeable to be present at and take part in church ceremonies. At this moment, in his present softened state of feeling, sensitive to everything, this inevitable act of hypocrisy was not merely painful to Levin, it seemed to him utterly impossible. Now, in the hey-day of his highest glory, his fullest flower, he would have to be a liar or a scoffer. He felt incapable of being either. But though he repeatedly plied Stepan Arkadyevitch with questions as to the possibility of obtaining a certificate without actually communicating, Stepan Arkadyevitch maintained that it was out of the question.

'Besides, what is it to you—two days? And he's an awfully nice clever old fellow. He'll pull the tooth out for you so gently, you won't notice it.'

Standing at the first litany, Levin attempted to revive in himself his youthful recollections of the intense religious emotion he had passed through between the ages of sixteen and seventeen.

But he was at once convinced that it was utterly impossible to him. He attempted to look at it all as an empty custom, having no sort of meaning, like the custom of paying calls. But he felt that he could not do that either. Levin found himself, like the majority of his contemporaries, in the vaguest position in regard to religion. Believe he could not, and at the same time he had no firm conviction that it was all wrong. And consequently, not being able to believe in the significance of what he was doing nor to regard it with indifference as an empty formality, during the whole period of preparing for the sacrament he was conscious of a feeling of discomfort and shame at doing what he did not himself understand, and what, as an inner voice told him, was therefore false and wrong.

During the service he would first listen to the prayers, trying to attach some meaning to them not discordant with his own views; then feeling that he could not understand and must condemn them, he tried not to listen to them, but to attend to the thoughts, observations, and memories which floated through his brain with extreme vividness during this idle time of standing in church.

He had stood through the litany, the evening service and the midnight service, and the next day he got up earlier than usual, and without having tea he went at eight o'clock in the morning to the church for the morning service and the confession.

There was no one in the church but a beggar soldier, two old women, and the church officials. A young deacon, whose long back showed in two distinct halves through his thin undercassock, met him, and at once going to a little table at the wall read the exhortation. During the reading, especially at the frequent and rapid repetition of the same words, 'Lord, have mercy on us!' which resounded with an echo, Levin felt that thought was shut and sealed up, and that it must not be touched or stirred now or confusion would be the result; and so standing behind the deacon he went on thinking of his own affairs, neither listening nor examining what was said. 'It's wonderful what expression there is in her hand,' he thought, remembering how they had been sitting the day before at a corner table. They had nothing to talk about, as was almost always the case at this time, and laying her hand on the table she kept opening and shutting it, and laughed herself as she watched her action. He remembered how he had kissed it and then had examined the lines on the pink palm. 'Have mercy on us again!' thought Levin, crossing himself, bowing, and looking at the supple spring of the deacon's back bowing before him. 'She took my hand then and examined the lines. "You've got a splendid hand,"' she said. And he looked at his own hand and the short hand of the deacon. 'Yes, now it will soon be over,' he thought. 'No, it seems to be beginning again,' he thought, listening to the prayers. 'No, it's just ending: there he is bowing down to the ground. That's always at the end.'

The deacon's hand in a plush cuff unobtrusively accepted a three-rouble note, and the deacon said he would put it down in the register, and his new boots creaking jauntily over the flagstones of the empty church, he went to the altar. A moment later he peeped out thence and beckoned to Levin. Thought, till then locked up, began to stir in Levin's head, but he made haste to drive it away. 'It will come right somehow,' he thought, and went towards the altar-rails. He went up to the steps, and turning to the right saw the priest. The priest, a little old man with a scanty grizzled beard and weary, good-natured eyes, was standing at the altar-rails, turning over the pages of a missal. With a slight bow to Levin he began immediately reading prayers in the official voice. When he had finished them he bowed down to the ground and turned, facing Levin.

'Christ is present here unseen, receiving your confession,' he said, pointing to the crucifix. 'Do you believe in all the doctrines of the Holy Apostolic Church?' the priest went on, turning his eyes away from Levin's face and folding his hands under his stole.

'I have doubted, I doubt everything,' said Levin in a voice that jarred on himself, and he ceased speaking.

The priest waited a few seconds to see if he would not say more, and closing his eyes he said quickly, with a broad, Vladimirsky accent—

'Doubt is natural to the weakness of mankind, but we must pray that God in His mercy will strengthen us. What are your special sins?' he added, without the slightest interval, as though anxious not to waste time.

'My chief sin is doubt. I have doubts of everything, and for the most part I am in doubt.'

'Doubt is natural to the weakness of mankind,' the priest repeated the same words. 'What do you doubt about principally?'

'I doubt of everything. I sometimes even have doubts of the existence of God,' Levin could not help saying, and he was horrified at the impropriety of what he was saying. But Levin's words did not, it seemed, make much impression on the priest.

'What sort of doubt can there be of the existence of God?' he said hurriedly, with a just perceptible smile.

Levin did not speak.

'What doubt can you have of the Creator when you behold His creation?' the priest went on in the rapid customary jargon. 'Who has decked the heavenly firmament with its lights? Who has clothed the earth in its beauty? How explain it without the Creator?' he said, looking inquiringly at Levin.

Levin felt that it would be improper to enter upon a metaphysical discussion with the priest, and so he said in reply merely what was a direct answer to the question.

'I don't know,' he said.

'You don't know! Then how can you doubt that God created all?' the priest said, with good-humoured perplexity.

'I don't understand it at all,' said Levin, blushing; and feeling that his words were stupid, and that they could not be anything but stupid in such a position.

'Pray to God and beseech Him. Even the holy fathers had doubts, and prayed to God to strengthen their faith. The devil has great power, and we must resist him. Pray to God, beseech Him. Pray to God,' he repeated hurriedly.

The priest paused for some time, as though meditating.

'You're about, I hear, to marry the daughter of my parishioner and son in the spirit, Prince Shtcherbatsky?' he resumed, with a smile. 'An excellent young lady.'

'Yes,' answered Levin, blushing for the priest. 'What does he want to ask me about this at confession for?' he thought.

And, as though answering his thought, the priest said to him—

'You are about to enter into holy matrimony, and God may bless you with offspring. Well, what sort of bringing-up can you give your babes if you do not overcome the temptation of the devil, enticing you to infidelity?' he said, with gentle reproachfulness. 'If you love your child as a good father, you will not desire only wealth, luxury, honour for your infant; you will be anxious for his salvation, his spiritual enlightenment with the light of truth. Eh? What answer will you make him when the innocent babe asks you: "Papa! who made all that enchants me in this world—the earth, the waters, the sun, the flowers, the grass?" Can you say to him: "I don't know"? You cannot but know, since the Lord God in His infinite mercy has revealed it to us. Or your child will ask you: "What awaits me in the life beyond the tomb?" What will you say to him when you know nothing? How will you answer him? Will you leave him to the allurements of the world and the devil? That's not right,' he said, and he stopped, putting his head on one side and looking at Levin with his kindly, gentle eyes.

Levin made no answer this time, not because he did not want to enter upon a discussion with the priest, but because, so far, no one had ever asked him such questions, and when his babes did ask him those questions, it would be time enough to think about answering them.

'You are entering upon a time of life,' pursued the priest, 'when you must choose your path and keep to it. Pray to God that He may in His mercy aid you and have mercy on you!' he concluded. 'Our Lord and God, Jesus Christ, in the abundance and riches of His loving-kindness, forgives this child . . .' and, finishing the prayer of absolution, the priest blessed him and dismissed him.

On getting home that day, Levin had a delightful sense of relief at the awkward position being over and having been got through without his having to tell a lie. Apart from this, there remained a vague memory that what the kind, nice old fellow had said had not been at all so stupid as he had fancied at first, and that there was something in it that must be cleared up.

'Of course, not now,' thought Levin, 'but some day later on.' Levin felt more than ever now that there was something not clear and not clean in his soul, and that, in regard to religion, he was in the same position which he perceived so clearly and disliked in others, and for which he blamed his friend Sviazhsky.

Levin spent that evening with his betrothed at Dolly's, and was in very high spirits. To explain to Stepan Arkadyevitch the state of excitement in which he found himself, he said that he was happy like a dog being trained to jump through a hoop, who, having at last caught the idea, and done what was required of him, whines and wags its tail, and jumps up to the table and the windows in its delight.

II

ON the day of the wedding, according to the Russian custom (the princess and Darya Alexandrovna insisted on strictly keeping all the customs), Levin did not see his betrothed, and dined at his hotel with three bachelor friends, casually brought together at his rooms. These were Sergey Ivanovitch, Katavasov, a university friend, now professor of natural science, whom Levin had met in the street and insisted on taking home with him, and Tchirikov, his best man, a Moscow conciliation-board judge, Levin's companion in his bear-hunts. The dinner was a very merry one: Sergey Ivanovitch was in his happiest mood, and was much amused by Katavasov's originality. Katavasov, feeling his originality was appreciated and understood, made the most of it. Tchirikov always gave a lively and good-humoured support to conversation of any sort.

'See, now,' said Katavasov, drawling his words from a habit acquired in the lecture-room, 'what a capable fellow was our friend Konstantin Dmitritch. I'm not speaking of present company, for he's absent. At the time he left the university he was fond of science, took an interest in humanity; now one-half of his abilities is devoted to deceiving himself, and the other to justifying the deceit.'

'A more determined enemy of matrimony than you I never saw,' said Sergey Ivanovitch.

'Oh no, I'm not an enemy of matrimony. I'm in favour of division of labour. People who can do nothing else ought to rear people while the rest work for their happiness and enlightenment. That's how I look at it. To muddle up two trades is the error of the amateur; I'm not one of their number.'

'How happy I shall be when I hear that you're in love!' said Levin. 'Please invite me to the wedding.'

'I'm in love now.'

'Yes, with a cuttlefish! You know,' Levin turned to his brother, 'Mihail Semyonovitch is writing a work on the digestive organs of the . . .'

'Now, make a muddle of it! It doesn't matter what about. And the fact is, I certainly do love cuttlefish.'

'But that's no hindrance to your loving your wife.'

'The cuttlefish is no hindrance. The wife is the hindrance.'

'Why so?'

'Oh, you'll see! You care about farming, hunting,—well, you'd better look out!'

'Arhip was here today; he said there were a lot of elks in Prudno, and two bears,' said Tchirikov.

'Well, you must go and get them without me.'

'Ah, that's the truth,' said Sergey Ivanovitch. 'And you may say good-bye to bear-hunting for the future—your wife won't allow it!'

Levin smiled. The picture of his wife not letting him go was so pleasant that he was ready to renounce the delights of looking upon bears for ever.

'Still, it's a pity they should get those two bears without you. Do you remember last time at Hapilovo? That was a delightful hunt!' said Tchirikov.

Levin had not the heart to disillusion him of the notion that there could be something delightful apart from her, and so said nothing.

'There's some sense in this custom of saying good-bye to bachelor life,' said Sergey Ivanovitch. 'However happy you may be, you must regret your freedom.'

'And confess there is a feeling that you want to jump out of window, like Gogol's bridegroom?'

'Of course there is, but it isn't confessed,' said Katavasov, and he broke into loud laughter.

'Oh, well, the window's open. Let's start off this instant to Tver! There's a big she-bear: one can go right up to the lair. Seriously, let's go by the five o'clock! And here let them do what they like,' said Tchirikov smiling.

'Well now, on my honour,' said Levin smiling, 'I can't find in my heart that feeling of regret for my freedom.'

'Yes, there's such a chaos in your heart just now that you can't find anything there,' said Katavasov. 'Wait a bit, when you set it to rights a little, you'll find it!'

'No; if so, I should have felt a little, apart from my feeling' (he could not say love before them) 'and happiness, a certain regret at losing my freedom. . . . On the contrary, I am glad at the very loss of my freedom.'

'Awful! It's a hopeless case!' said Katavasov. 'Well, let's drink to his recovery, or wish that a hundredth part of his dreams may be realised—and that would be happiness such as never has been seen on earth!'

Soon after dinner the guests went away to be in time to be dressed for the wedding.

When he was left alone, and recalled the conversation of these bachelor friends, Levin asked himself: had he in his heart that regret for his freedom of which they had spoken? He smiled at the question. 'Freedom! What is freedom for? Happiness is only in loving and wishing her wishes, thinking her thoughts, that is to say, not freedom at all—that's happiness!'

'But do I know her ideas, her wishes, her feelings?' some voice suddenly whispered to him. The smile died away from his face, and he grew thoughtful. And suddenly a strange feeling came upon him. There came over him a dread and doubt—doubt of everything.

'What if she does not love me? What if she's marrying me simply to be married? What if she doesn't see herself what she's doing?' he asked himself. 'She may come to her senses, and only when she is being married realise that she does not and cannot love me.' And strange, most evil thoughts of her began to come to him. He was jealous of Vronsky, as he had been a year ago, as though the evening he had seen her with Vronsky had been yesterday. He suspected she had not told him everything.

He jumped up quickly. 'No, this can't go on!' he said to himself in despair. 'I'll go to her; I'll ask her; I'll say for the last time: we are free, and hadn't we better stay so? Anything's better than endless misery, disgrace, unfaithfulness!' With despair in his heart and bitter anger against all men, against himself, against her, he went out of the hotel and drove to her house.

He found her in one of the back-rooms. She was sitting on a chest and making some arrangements with her maid, sorting over heaps of dresses of different colours, spread on the backs of chairs and on the floor.

'Ah!' she cried, seeing him, and beaming with delight. 'Kostya! Konstantin Dmitritch!' (These latter days she used these names almost alternately.) 'I didn't expect you! I'm going through my wardrobe to see what's for whom . . .'

'Oh! that's very nice!' he said gloomily, looking at the maid.

'You can go, Dunyasha, I'll call you presently,' said Kitty. 'Kostya, what's the matter?' she asked, definitely, adopting this familiar name as soon as the maid had gone out. She noticed his strange face, agitated and gloomy, and a panic came over her.

'Kitty, I'm in torture. I can't suffer alone,' he said with despair in his voice, standing before her and looking imploringly into her eyes. He saw already from her loving, truthful face, that nothing could come of what he had meant to say, but yet he wanted her to reassure him herself. 'I've come to say that there's still time. This can all be stopped and set right.'

'What? I don't understand. What is the matter?'

'What I have said a thousand times over, and can't help thinking . . . that I'm not worthy of you. You couldn't consent to marry me. Think a little. You've made a mistake. Think it over thoroughly. You can't love me. . . . If . . . better say so,' he said, not looking at her. 'I shall be wretched. Let people say what they like; anything's better than misery. . . . Far better now while there's still time. . . .'

'I don't understand,' she answered, panic-stricken; 'you mean you want to give it up . . . don't want it?'

'Yes, if you don't love me.'

'You're out of your mind!' she cried, turning crimson with vexation. But his face was so piteous, that she restrained her vexation, and flinging some clothes off an armchair, she sat down beside him. 'What are you thinking? tell me all.'

'I am thinking you can't love me. What can you love me for?'

'My God! what can I do? . . .' she said, and burst into tears.

'Oh! what have I done?' he cried, and kneeling before her, he fell to kissing her hands.

When the princess came into the room five minutes later, she found them completely reconciled. Kitty had not simply assured him that she loved him, but had gone so far—in answer to his question, what she loved him for—as to explain what for. She told him that she loved him because she understood him completely, because she knew what he would like, and because everything he liked was good. And this seemed to him perfectly clear. When the princess came to them, they were sitting side by side on the chest, sorting the dresses and disputing over Kitty's wanting to give Dunyasha the brown dress she had been wearing when Levin proposed to her, while he insisted that that dress must never be given away, but Dunyasha must have the blue one.

'How is it you don't see? She's a brunette, and it won't suit her. . . . I've worked it all out.'

Hearing why he had come, the princess was half humorously, half seriously angry with him, and sent him home to dress and not to hinder Kitty's hairdressing, as Charles the hairdresser was just coming.

'As it is, she's been eating nothing lately and is losing her looks, and then you must come and upset her with your nonsense,' she said to him. 'Get along with you, my dear!'

Levin, guilty and shamefaced, but pacified, went back to his hotel. His brother, Darya Alexandrovna, and Stepan Arkadyevitch, all in full dress, were waiting for him to bless him with the holy picture. There was no time to lose. Darya Alexandrovna had to drive home again to fetch her curled and pomaded son, who was to carry the holy pictures after the bride. Then a carriage had to be sent for the best man, and another that would take Sergey Ivanovitch away would have to be sent back. . . . Altogether there was a great many most complicated matters to be considered and arranged. One thing was unmistakable, that there must be no delay, as it was already half-past six.

Nothing special happened at the ceremony of benediction with the holy picture. Stepan Arkadyevitch stood in a comically solemn pose beside his wife, took the holy picture, and telling Levin to bow down to the ground, he blessed him with his kindly, ironical smile, and kissed him three times! Darya Alexandrovna did the same, and immediately was in a hurry to get off, and again plunged into the intricate question of the destinations of the various carriages.

'Come, I'll tell you how we'll manage: you drive in our carriage to fetch him, and Sergey Ivanovitch, if he'll be so good, will drive there and then send his carriage.'

'Of course; I shall be delighted.'

'We'll come on directly with him. Are your things sent off?' said Stepan Arkadyevitch.

'Yes,' answered Levin, and he told Kouzma to put out his clothes for him to dress.

III

A CROWD of people, principally women, was thronging round the church lighted up for the wedding. Those who had not succeeded in getting into the main entrance were crowding about the windows, pushing, wrangling, and peeping through the gratings.

More than twenty carriages had already been drawn up in ranks along the street by the police. A police officer, regardless of the frost, stood at the entrance, gorgeous in his uniform. More carriages were continually driving up, and ladies wearing flowers and carrying their trains, and men taking off their helmets or black hats kept walking into the church. Inside the church both lustres were already lighted, and all the candles before the holy pictures. The gilt on the red ground of the holy picture-stand, and the gilt relief on the pictures, and the silver of the lustres and candlesticks, and the stones of the floor, and the rugs, and the banners above in the choir, and the steps of the altar, and the old blackened books, and the cassocks and surplices—all were flooded with light. On the right side of the warm church, in the crowd of frock-coats and white ties, uniforms and broadcloth, velvet, satin, hair and flowers, bare shoulders and arms and long gloves, there was discreet but lively conversation that echoed strangely in the high cupola. Every time there was heard the creak of the opened door the conversation in the crowd died away, and everybody looked round expecting to see the bride and bridegroom come in. But the door had opened more than ten times, and each time it was either a belated guest or guests, who joined the circle of the invited on the right, or a spectator, who had eluded or softened the police officer, and went to join the crowd of outsiders on the left. Both the guests and the outside public had by now passed through all the phases of anticipation.

At first they imagined that the bride and bridegroom would arrive immediately, and attached no importance at all to their being late. Then they began to look more and more often towards the door, and to talk of whether anything could have happened. Then the long delay began to be positively discomforting, and relations and guests tried to look as if they were not thinking of the bridegroom but were engaged in conversation.

The head deacon, as though to remind them of the value of his time, coughed impatiently, making the window-panes quiver in their frames. In the choir the bored choristers could be heard trying their voices and blowing their noses. The priest was continually sending first the beadle and then the deacon to find out whether the bridegroom had not come, more and more often he went himself, in a lilac vestment and an embroidered sash, to the side-door, expecting to see the bridegroom. At last one of the ladies, glancing at her watch, said, 'It really is strange, though!' and all the guests became uneasy and began loudly expressing their wonder and dissatisfaction. One of the bridegroom's best men went to find out what had happened. Kitty meanwhile had long ago been quite ready, and in her white dress and long veil and wreath of orange blossoms she was standing in the drawing-room of the Shtcherbatskys' house with her sister, Madame Lvov, who was her bridal-mother. She was looking out of the window, and had been for over half an hour anxiously expecting to hear from her best man that the bridegroom was at the church.

Levin meanwhile, in his trousers, but without his coat and waistcoat, was walking to and fro in his room at the hotel, continually putting his head out of the door and looking up and down the corridor. But in the corridor there was no sign of the person he was looking for and he came back in despair, and frantically waving his hands addressed Stepan Arkadyevitch, who was smoking serenely.

'Was ever man in such a fearful fool's position?' he said.

'Yes, it is stupid,' Stepan Arkadyevitch assented, smiling soothingly. 'But don't worry, it'll be brought directly.'

'No, what is to be done!' said Levin, with smothered fury. 'And these fools of open waistcoats! Out of the question!' he said, looking at the crumpled front of his shirt. 'And what if the things have been taken on to the railway station!' he roared in desperation.

'Then you must put on mine.'

'I ought to have done so long ago, if at all.'

'It's not nice to look ridiculous . . . Wait a bit! it will *come round*.'

The point was that when Levin asked for his evening suit, Kouzma, his old servant, had brought him the coat, waistcoat, and everything that was wanted.

'But the shirt!' cried Levin.

'You've got a shirt on,' Kouzma answered, with a placid smile.

Kouzma had not thought of leaving out a clean shirt, and on receiving instructions to pack up everything and send it round to the Shtcherbatskys' house, from which the young people were to set out the same evening, he had done so, packing everything but the dress suit. The shirt worn since the morning was crumpled and out of the question with the fashionable open waistcoat. It was a long way to send to the Shtcherbatskys'. They sent out to buy a shirt. The servant came back; everything was shut up—it was Sunday. They sent to Stepan Arkadyevitch's and brought a shirt—it was impossibly wide and short. They sent finally to the Shtcherbatskys' to unpack the things. The bridegroom was expected at the church while he was pacing up and down his room like a wild beast in a cage, peeping out into the corridor, and with horror and despair recalling what absurd things he had said to Kitty and what she might be thinking now.

At last the guilty Kouzma flew panting into the room with the shirt.

'Only just in time. They were just lifting it into the van,' said Kouzma.

Three minutes later Levin ran full speed into the corridor, not looking at his watch for fear of aggravating his sufferings.

'You won't help matters like this,' said Stepan Arkadyevitch with a smile, hurrying with more deliberation after him. '*It will come round, it will come round* . . . I tell you.'

IV

'THEY'VE come!' 'Here he is!' 'Which one?' 'Rather young, eh?' 'Why, my dear soul, she looks more dead than alive!' were the comments in the crowd when Levin, meeting his bride in the entrance, walked with her into the church.

Stepan Arkadyevitch told his wife the cause of the delay, and the guests were whispering it with smiles to one another. Levin saw nothing and no one; he did not take his eyes off his bride.

Everyone said she had lost her looks dreadfully of late, and was not nearly so pretty on her wedding-day as usual; but Levin did not think so. He looked at her hair done up high, with the long white veil and white flowers and the high, stand-up, scolloped collar, that in such a maidenly fashion hid her long neck at the sides and only showed it in front, her strikingly slender figure, and it seemed to him that she looked better than ever—not because these flowers, this veil, this gown from Paris added anything to her beauty; but because, in spite of the elaborate sumptuousness of her attire, the expression of her sweet face, of her eyes, of her lips was still her own characteristic expression of guileless truthfulness.

'I was beginning to think you meant to run away,' she said, and smiled at him.

'It's so stupid, what happened to me, I'm ashamed to speak of it!' he said, reddening, and he was obliged to turn to Sergey Ivanovitch, who came up to him.

'This is a pretty story of yours about the shirt!' said Sergey Ivanovitch, shaking his head and smiling.

'Yes, yes!' answered Levin, without an idea of what they were talking about.

'Now, Kostya, you have to decide,' said Stepan Arkadyevitch with an air of mock dismay, 'a weighty question. You are at this moment just in the humour to appreciate all its gravity. They ask me, are they to light candles that have been lighted before or candles that have never been lighted? It's a matter of ten roubles,' he added, relaxing his lips into a smile. 'I have decided, but I was afraid you might not agree.'

Levin saw it was a joke, but he could not smile.

'Well, how's it to be then?—unlighted or lighted candles? that's the question.'

'Yes, yes, unlighted.'

'Oh, I'm very glad. The question's decided!' said Stepan Arkadyevitch, smiling. 'How silly men are, though, in this position,' he said to Tchirikov, when Levin, after looking absently at him, had moved back to his bride.

'Kitty, mind you're the first to step on the carpet,' said Countess Nordston, coming up. 'You're a nice person!' she said to Levin.

'Aren't you frightened, eh?' said Marya Dmitrievna, an old aunt.

'Are you cold? You're pale. Stop a minute, stoop down,' said Kitty's sister, Madame Lvov, and with her plump, handsome arms she smilingly set straight the flowers on her head.

Dolly came up, tried to say something, but could not speak, cried, and then laughed unnaturally.

Kitty looked at all of them with the same absent eyes as Levin.

Meanwhile the officiating clergy had got into their vestments, and the priest and deacon came out to the lectern, which stood in the forepart of the church. The priest turned to Levin saying something. Levin did not hear what the priest said.

'Take the bride's hand and lead her up,' the best man said to Levin.

It was a long while before Levin could make out what was expected of him. For a long time they tried to set him right and made him begin again—because he kept taking Kitty by the wrong arm or with the wrong arm—till he understood at last that what he had to do was, without changing his position, to take her right hand in his right hand. When at last he had taken the bride's hand in the correct way, the priest walked a few paces in front of them and stopped at the lectern. The crowd of friends and relations moved after them, with a buzz of talk and a rustle of skirts. Some one stooped down and pulled out the bride's train. The church became so still that the drops of wax could be heard falling from the candles.

The little old priest in his ecclesiastical cap, with his long silvery-grey locks of hair parted behind his ears, was fumbling with something at the lectern, putting out his little old hands from under the heavy silver vestment with the gold cross on the back of it.

Stepan Arkadyevitch approached him cautiously, whispered something, and making a sign to Levin, walked back again.

The priest lighted two candles, wreathed with flowers, and holding them sideways so that the wax dropped slowly from them he turned, facing the bridal pair. The priest was the same old man that had confessed Levin. He looked with weary and melancholy eyes at the bride and bridegroom, sighed, and putting his right hand out from his vestment, blessed the bridegroom with it, and also with a shade of solicitous tenderness laid the crossed fingers on the bowed head of Kitty. Then he gave them the candles, and taking the censer, moved slowly away from them.

'Can it be true?' thought Levin, and he looked round at his bride. Looking down at her he saw her face in profile, and from the scarcely perceptible quiver of her lips and eyelashes he knew she was aware of his eyes upon her. She did not look round, but the high scolloped collar, that reached her little pink ear, trembled faintly. He saw that a sigh was held back in her throat, and the little hand in the long glove shook as it held the candle.

All the fuss of the shirt, of being late, all the talk of friends and relations, their annoyance, his ludicrous position—all suddenly passed away and he was filled with joy and dread.

The handsome, stately head-deacon wearing a silver robe, and his curly locks standing out at each side of his head, stepped smartly forward, and lifting his stole on two fingers, stood opposite the priest.

'Blessed be the name of the Lord,' the solemn syllables rang out slowly one after another, setting the air quivering with waves of sound.

'Blessed is the name of our God, from the beginning, is now, and ever shall be,' the little old priest answered in a submissive, piping voice, still fingering something at the lectern. And the full chorus of the unseen choir rose up, filling the whole church, from the windows to the vaulted roof, with broad waves of melody. It grew stronger, rested for an instant, and slowly died away.

They prayed, as they always do, for peace from on high and for salvation, for the Holy Synod, and for the Tsar; they prayed, too, for the servants of God, Konstantin and Ekaterina, now plighting their troth.

'Vouchsafe to them love made perfect, peace and help, O Lord, we beseech Thee,' the whole church seemed to breathe with the voice of the head-deacon.

Levin heard the words, and they impressed him. 'How did they guess that it is help, just help that one wants?' he thought, recalling all his fears and doubts of late. 'What do I know? what can I do in this fearful business,' he thought, 'without help? Yes, it is help I want now.'

When the deacon had finished the prayer for the Imperial family, the priest turned to the bridal pair with a book: 'Eternal God, that joinest together in love them that were separate,' he read in a gentle, piping voice: 'who hath ordained the union of holy wedlock that cannot be set asunder. Thou who didst bless Isaac and Rebecca and their descendants, according to Thy Holy Covenant; bless Thy servants, Konstantin and Ekaterina, leading them in the path of all good works. For gracious and merciful art Thou, our Lord, and glory be to Thee, the Father, the Son, and the Holy Ghost, now and ever shall be.'

'Amen!' the unseen choir sent rolling again upon the air.

'"Joinest together in love them that were separate." What deep meaning in those words, and how they correspond with what one feels at this moment,' thought Levin. 'Is she feeling the same as I?'

And looking round, he met her eyes, and from their expression he concluded that she was understanding it just as he was. But this was a mistake; she almost completely missed the meaning of the words of the service; she had not heard them, in fact. She could not listen to them and take them in, so strong was the one feeling that filled her breast and grew stronger and stronger. That feeling was joy at the completion of the process that for the last month and a half had been going on in her soul, and had during those six weeks been a joy and a torture to her. On the day when in the drawing-room of the house in Arbaty Street she had gone up to him in her brown dress, and given herself to him without a word—on that day, at that hour, there took place in her heart a complete severance from all her old life, and a quite different, new, utterly strange life had begun for her, while the old life was actually going on as before. Those six weeks had for her been a time of the utmost bliss and the utmost misery. All her life, all her desires and hopes were concentrated on this one man, still uncomprehended by her, to whom she was bound by a feeling of alternate attraction and repulsion, even less comprehended than the man himself, and all the while she was going on living in the outward conditions of her old life. Living the old life, she was horrified at herself, at her utter insurmountable callousness to all her own past, to things, to habits, to the people she had loved, who loved her—to her mother, who was wounded by her indifference, to her kind, tender father, till then dearer than all the world. At one moment she was horrified at this indifference, at another she rejoiced at what had brought her to this indifference. She could not frame a thought, not a wish apart from life with this man; but this new life was not yet, and she could not even picture it clearly to herself. There was only anticipation, the dread and joy of the new and the unknown. And now behold—anticipation and uncertainty and remorse at the abandonment of the old life—all was ending, and the new was beginning. This new life could not but have terrors for her inexperience; but, terrible or not, the change had been wrought six weeks before in her soul, and this was merely the final sanction of what had long been completed in her heart.

Turning again to the lectern, the priest with some difficulty took Kitty's little ring, and asking Levin for his hand, put it on the first joint of his finger. 'The servant of God, Konstantin, plights his troth to the servant of God, Ekaterina.' And putting his big ring on Kitty's touchingly weak, pink little finger, the priest said the same thing.

And the bridal pair tried several times to understand what they had to do, and each time made some mistake and were corrected by the priest in a whisper. At last, having duly performed the ceremony, having signed the rings with the cross, the priest handed Kitty the big ring, and Levin the little one. Again they were puzzled, and passed the rings from hand to hand, still without doing what was expected.

Dolly, Tchirikov, and Stepan Arkadyevitch stepped forward to set them right. There was an interval of hesitation, whispering, and smiles; but the expression of solemn emotion on the faces of the betrothed pair did not change: on the contrary, in their perplexity over their hands they looked more grave and deeply moved than before, and the smile with which Stepan Arkadyevitch whispered to them that now they would each put on their own ring died away on his lips. He had a feeling that any smile would jar on them.

'Thou who didst from the beginning create male and female,' the priest read after the exchange of rings, 'from Thee woman was given to man to be a helpmeet to him, and for the procreation of children. O Lord our God, who hast poured down the blessings of Thy Truth according to Thy Holy Covenant upon Thy chosen servants, our fathers, from generation to generation, bless Thy servants Konstantin and Ekaterina, and make their troth fast in faith, and union of hearts, and truth, and love. . . .'

Levin felt more and more that all his ideas of marriage, all his dreams of how he would order his life, were mere childishness, and that it was something he had not understood hitherto, and now understood less than ever, though it was being performed upon him. The lump in his throat rose higher and higher, tears that would not be checked came into his eyes.

V

IN the church there was all Moscow, all the friends and relations; and during the ceremony of plighting troth, in the brilliantly lighted church, there was an incessant flow of discreetly subdued talk in the circle of gaily dressed women and girls, and men in white ties, frock-coats, and uniforms. The talk was principally kept up by the men, while the women were absorbed in watching every detail of the ceremony, which always means so much to them.

In the little group nearest to the bride were her two sisters: Dolly and the elder one, the self-possessed beauty, Madame Lvov, who had just arrived from abroad.

'Why is it Marie's in lilac, as bad as black, at a wedding?' said Madame Korsunsky.

'With her complexion, it's the one salvation,' responded Madame Trubetsky. 'I wonder why they had the wedding in the evening? It's like shop-people . . .'

'So much prettier. I was married in the evening too . . .' answered Madame Korsunsky, and she sighed, remembering how charming she had been that day, and how absurdly in love her husband was, and how different it all was now.

'They say if any one's best man more than ten times, he'll never be married. I wanted to be for the tenth time, but the post was taken,' said Count Siniavin to the pretty Princess Tcharsky, who had designs on him.

Princess Tcharsky only answered with a smile. She looked at Kitty, thinking how and when she would stand with Count Siniavin in Kitty's place, and how she would remind him then of his joke today.

Shtcherbatsky told the old maid of honour, Madame Nikolaev, that he meant to put the crown on Kitty's chignon for luck.

'She ought not to have worn a chignon,' answered Madame Nikolaev, who had long ago made up her mind that if the elderly widower she was angling for married her, the wedding should be of the simplest. 'I don't like such grandeur.'

Sergey Ivanovitch was talking to Darya Dmitrievna, jestingly assuring her that the custom of going away after the wedding was becoming common because newly married people always felt a little ashamed of themselves.

'Your brother may feel proud of himself. She's a marvel of sweetness. I believe you're envious.'

'Oh, I've got over that, Darya Dmitrievna,' he answered, and a melancholy and serious expression suddenly came over his face.

Stepan Arkadyevitch was telling his sister-in-law his joke about divorce.

'The wreath wants setting straight,' she answered, not hearing him.

'What a pity she's lost her looks so,' Countess Nordston said to Madame Lvov. 'Still he's not worth her little finger, is he?'

'Oh, I like him so—not because he's my future *beau-frère*,' answered Madame Lvov. 'And how well he's behaving! It's so difficult, too, to look well in such a position, not to be ridiculous. And he's not ridiculous, and not affected; one can see he's moved.'

'You expected it, I suppose?'

'Almost. She always cared for him.'

'Well, we shall see which of them will step on the rug first. I warned Kitty.'

'It will make no difference,' said Madame Lvov; 'we're all obedient wives; it's in our family.'

'Oh, I stepped on the rug before Vassily on purpose. And you, Dolly?'

Dolly stood beside them; she heard them, but she did not answer. She was deeply moved. The tears stood in her eyes, and she could not have spoken without crying. She was rejoicing over Kitty and Levin; going back in thought to her own wedding, she glanced at the radiant figure of Stepan Arkadyevitch, forgot all the present, and remembered only her own innocent love. She recalled not herself only, but all her women-friends, and acquaintances. She thought of them on the one day of their triumph, when they had stood like Kitty under the wedding crown, with love and hope and dread in their hearts, renouncing the past, and stepping forward into the mysterious future. Among the brides that came back to her memory, she thought too of her darling Anna, of whose proposed divorce she had just been hearing. And she had stood just as innocent in orange flowers and bridal veil. And now? 'It's terribly strange,' she said to herself. It was not merely the sisters, the women-friends and female relations of the bride who were following every detail of the ceremony. Women who were quite strangers, mere spectators, were watching it excitedly, holding their breath, in fear of losing a single movement or expression of the bride and bridegroom, and angrily not answering, often not hearing, the remarks of the callous men, who kept making joking or irrelevant observations.

'Why has she been crying? Is she being married against her will?'

'Against her will to a fine fellow like that? A prince, isn't he?'

'Is that her sister in the white satin? Just listen how the deacon booms out, "and fearing her husband."'

'Are the choristers from Tchudovo?'

'No, from the Synod.'

'I asked the footman. He says he's going to take her home to his country place at once. Awfully rich, they say. That's why she's being married to him.'

'No, they're a well-matched pair.'

'I say, Marya Vassilievna, you were making out those fly-away crinolines were not being worn. Just look at her in the puce dress—an ambassador's wife they say she is—how her skirt bounces out from side to side!'

'What a pretty dear the bride is—like a lamb decked with flowers! Well, say what you will, we women feel for our sister.'

Such were the comments in the crowd of gazing women who had succeeded in slipping in at the church doors.

VI

WHEN the ceremony of plighting troth was over, the beadle spread before the lectern in the middle of the church a piece of pink silken stuff, the choir sang a complicated and elaborate psalm, in which the bass and tenor sang responses to one another, and the priest turning round pointed the bridal pair to the pink silk rug. Though both had often heard a great deal about the saying that the one who steps first on the rug will be the head of the house, neither Levin nor Kitty were capable of recollecting it, as they took the few steps towards it. They did not hear the loud remarks and disputes that followed, some maintaining he had stepped on first, and others that both had stepped on together.

After the customary questions, whether they desired to enter upon matrimony, and whether they were pledged to anyone else, and their answers, which sounded strange to themselves, a new ceremony began. Kitty listened to the words of the prayer, trying to make out their meaning, but she could not. The feeling of triumph and radiant happiness flooded her soul more and more as the ceremony went on, and deprived her of all power of attention.

They prayed: 'Endow them with continence and fruitfulness, and vouchsafe that their hearts may rejoice looking upon their sons and daughters.' They alluded to God's creation of a wife from Adam's rib, 'and for this cause a man shall leave father and mother, and cleave unto his wife, and they two shall be one flesh,' and that 'this is a great mystery'; they prayed that God would make them fruitful and bless them, like Isaac and Rebecca, Joseph, Moses and Zipporah, and that they might look upon their children's children. 'That's all splendid,' thought Kitty, catching the words, 'all that's just as it should be,' and a smile of happiness, unconsciously reflected in every one who looked at her, beamed on her radiant face.

'Put it on quite,' voices were heard urging when the priest had put on the wedding crowns, and Shtcherbatsky, his hand shaking in its three-buttoned glove, held the crown high above her head.

'Put it on!' she whispered smiling.

Levin looked round at her, and was struck by the joyful radiance on her face, and unconsciously her feeling infected him. He too, like her, felt glad and happy.

They enjoyed hearing the epistle read, and the roll of the head-deacon's voice at the last verse, awaited with such impatience by the outside public. They enjoyed drinking out of the shallow cup of warm red wine and water, and they were still more pleased when the priest, flinging back his stole and taking both their hands in his, led them round the lectern to the accompaniment of bass voices chanting 'Glory to God.'

Shtcherbatsky and Tchirikov, supporting the crowns and stumbling over the bride's train, smiling too and seeming delighted at something, were at one moment left behind, at the next treading on the bridal pair as the priest came to a halt. The spark of joy kindled in Kitty seemed to have infected every one in the church. It seemed to Levin that the priest and the deacon too wanted to smile just as he did.

Taking the crowns off their heads the priest read the last prayer and congratulated the young people. Levin looked at Kitty, and he had never before seen her look as she did. She was charming with the new radiance of happiness in her face. Levin longed to say something to her, but he did not know whether it was all over. The priest got him out of his difficulty. He smiled his kindly smile and said gently, 'Kiss your wife, and you kiss your husband,' and took the candles out of their hands.

Levin kissed her smiling lips with timid care, gave her his arm, and with a new strange sense of closeness, walked out of the church. He did not believe, he could not believe, that it was true. It was only when their wondering and timid eyes met that he believed in it, because he felt that they were one.

After supper, the same night, the young people left for the country.

VII

VRONSKY and Anna had been travelling for three months together in Europe. They had visited Venice, Rome, and Naples, and had just arrived at a small Italian town where they meant to stay some time. A handsome head waiter, with thick pomaded hair parted from the neck upwards, an evening coat, a broad white cambric shirt-front, and a bunch of trinkets hanging above his rounded stomach, stood with his hands in the full curve of his pockets, looking contemptuously from under his eyelids while he gave some frigid reply to a gentleman who had stopped him. Catching the sound of footsteps coming from the other side of the entry towards the staircase, the head waiter turned round, and seeing the Russian count, who had taken their best rooms, he took his hands out of his pockets deferentially, and with a bow informed him that a courier had been, and that the business about the palazzo had been arranged. The steward was prepared to sign the agreement.

'Ah! I'm glad to hear it,' said Vronsky. 'Is madame at home or not?'

'Madame has been out for a walk but has returned now,' answered the waiter.

Vronsky took off his soft wide-brimmed hat and passed his handkerchief over his heated brow and hair, which had grown half over his ears, and was brushed back covering the bald patch on his head. And glancing casually at the gentleman, who still stood there gazing intently at him, he would have gone on.

'This gentleman is a Russian, and was inquiring after you,' said the head waiter.

With mingled feelings of annoyance at never being able to get away from acquaintances anywhere, and longing to find some sort of diversion from the monotony of his life, Vronsky looked once more at the gentleman, who had retreated and stood still again, and at the same moment a light came into the eyes of both.

'Golenishtchev!'

'Vronsky!'

It really was Golenishtchev, a comrade of Vronsky's in the Corps of Pages. In the corps Golenishtchev had belonged to the liberal party; he left the corps without entering the army, and had never taken office under the government. Vronsky and he had gone completely different ways on leaving the corps, and had only met once since.

At that meeting Vronsky perceived that Golenishtchev had taken up a sort of lofty intellectually liberal line, and was consequently disposed to look down upon Vronsky's interests and calling in life. Hence Vronsky had met him with the chilling and haughty manner he so well knew how to assume, the meaning of which was: 'You may like or dislike my way of life, that's a matter of the most perfect indifference to me; you will have to treat me with respect, if you want to know me.' Golenishtchev had been contemptuously indifferent to the tone taken by Vronsky. This second meeting might have been expected, one would have supposed, to estrange them still more. But now they beamed and exclaimed with delight on recognising one another. Vronsky would never have expected to be so pleased to see Golenishtchev, but probably he was not himself aware how bored he was. He forgot the disagreeable impression of their last meeting, and with a face of frank delight held out his hand to his old comrade. The same expression of delight replaced the look of uneasiness on Golenishtchev's face.

'How glad I am to meet you!' said Vronsky, showing his strong white teeth in a friendly smile.

'I heard the name Vronsky, but I didn't know which one. I'm very, very glad!'

'Let's go in. Come, tell me what you're doing.'

'I've been living here for two years. I'm working.'

'Ah!' said Vronsky with sympathy; 'let's go in.' And with the habit common with Russians, instead of saying in Russian what he wanted to keep from the servants, he began to speak in French.

'Do you know Madame Karenin? We are travelling together. I am going to see her now,' he said in French, carefully scrutinising Golenishtchev's face.

'Ah! I did not know' (though he did know), Golenishtchev answered carelessly. 'Have you been here long?' he added.

'Four days,' Vronsky answered once more, scrutinising his friend's face intently.

'Yes, he's a decent fellow, and will look at the thing properly,' Vronsky said to himself, catching the significance of Golenishtchev's face and the change of subject. 'I can introduce him to Anna, he looks at it properly.'

During those three months that Vronsky had spent abroad with Anna, he had always on meeting new people asked himself how the new person would look at his relations with Anna, and for the most part, in men, he had met with the 'proper' way of looking at it. But if he had been asked, and those who looked at it 'properly' had been asked, exactly how they did look at it, both he and they would have been greatly puzzled to answer.

In reality, those who in Vronsky's opinion had the 'proper' view had no sort of view at all, but behaved in general as well-bred persons do behave in regard to all the complex and insoluble problems with which life is encompassed on all sides; they behaved with propriety, avoiding allusions and unpleasant questions. They assumed an air of fully comprehending the import and force of the situation, of accepting and even approving of it, but of considering it superfluous and uncalled for to put all this into words.

Vronsky at once divined that Golenishtchev was of this class, and therefore was doubly pleased to see him. And in fact, Golenishtchev's manner to Madame Karenin, when he was taken to call on her, was all that Vronsky could have desired. Obviously without the slightest effort he steered clear of all subjects which might lead to embarrassment.

He had never met Anna before, and was struck by her beauty, and still more by the frankness with which she accepted her position. She blushed when Vronsky brought in Golenishtchev, and he was extremely charmed by this childish blush overspreading her candid and handsome face. But what he liked particularly was the way in which at once, as though on purpose that there might be no misunderstanding with an outsider, she called Vronsky simply Alexey, and said they were moving into a house they had just taken, what was here called a palazzo. Golenishtchev liked this direct and simple attitude to her own position. Lookink at Anna's manner of simple-hearted, spirited gaiety, and knowing Alexey Alexandrovitch and Vronsky, Golenishtchev fancied that he understood her perfectly. He fancied that he understood what she was utterly unable to understand: how it was that, having made her husband wretched, having abandoned him and her son and lost her good name, she yet felt full of spirits, gaiety, and happiness.

'It's in the guide-book,' said Golenishtchev, referring to the palazzo Vronsky had taken. 'There's a first-rate Tintoretto there. One of his latest period.'

'I tell you what: it's a lovely day, let's go and have another look at it,' said Vronsky, addressing Anna.

'I shall be very glad to; I'll go and put on my hat. Would you say it's hot?' she said, stopping short in the doorway and looking inquiringly at Vronsky. And again a vivid flush overspread her face.

Vronsky saw from her eyes that she did not know on what terms he cared to be with Golenishtchev, and so was afraid of not behaving as he would wish.

He looked a long, tender look at her.

'No, not very,' he said.

And it seemed to her that she understood everything, most of all, that he was pleased with her; and smiling to him, she walked with her rapid step out at the door.

The friends glanced at one another, and a look of hesitation came into both faces, as though Golenishtchev, unmistakably admiring her, would have liked to say something about her, and could not find the right thing to say, while Vronsky desired and dreaded his doing so.

'Well then,' Vronsky began to start a conversation of some sort; 'so you're settled here? You're still at the same work, then?' he went on, recalling that he had been told Golenishtchev was writing something.

'Yes, I'm writing the second part of the *Two Elements*,' said Golenishtchev, colouring with pleasure at the question—'that is, to be exact, I am not writing it yet; I am preparing, collecting materials. It will be of far wider scope, and will touch on almost all questions. We in Russia refuse to see that we are the heirs of Byzantium,' and he launched into a long and heated explanation of his views.

Vronsky at the first moment felt embarrassed at not even knowing of the first part of the *Two Elements*, of which the author spoke as something well known. But as Golenishtchev began to lay down his opinions and Vronsky was able to follow them even without knowing the *Two Elements*, he listened to him with some interest, for Golenishtchev spoke well. But Vronsky was startled and annoyed by the nervous irascibility with which Golenishtchev talked of the subject that engrossed him. As he went on talking, his eyes glittered more and more angrily; he was more and more hurried in his replies to imaginary opponents, and his face grew more and more excited and worried. Remembering Golenishtchev, a thin, lively, good-natured and well-bred boy, always at the head of the class, Vronsky could not make out the reason of his irritability, and he did not like it. What he particularly disliked was that Golenishtchev, a man belonging to a good set, should put himself on a level with some scribbling fellows, with whom he was irritated and angry. Was it worth it? Vronsky disliked it, yet he felt that Golenishtchev was unhappy, and was sorry for him. Unhappiness, almost mental derangement, was visible on his mobile, rather handsome face, while without even noticing Anna's coming in, he went on hurriedly and hotly expressing his views.

When Anna came in in her hat and cape, and her lovely hand rapidly swinging her parasol, and stood beside him, it was with a feeling of relief that Vronsky broke away from the plaintive eyes of Golenishtchev which fastened persistently upon him, and with a fresh rush of love looked at his charming companion, full of life and happiness. Golenishtchev recovered himself with an effort, and at first was dejected and gloomy, but Anna, disposed to feel friendly with every one as she was at that time, soon revived his spirits by her direct and lively manner. After trying various subjects of conversation, she got him upon painting, of which he talked very well, and she listened to him attentively. They walked to the house they had taken, and looked over it.

'I am very glad of one thing,' said Anna to Golenishtchev when they were on their way back, 'Alexey will have a capital *atelier*. You must certainly take that room,' she said to Vronsky in Russian, using the affectionately familiar form as though she saw that Golenishtchev would become intimate with them in their isolation, and that there was no need of reserve before him.

'Do you paint?' said Golenishtchev, turning round quickly to Vronsky.

'Yes, I used to study long ago, and now I have begun to do a little,' said Vronsky, reddening.

'He has great talent,' said Anna with a delighted smile. 'I'm no judge, of course. But good judges have said the same.'

VIII

ANNA, in that first period of her emancipation and rapid return to health, felt herself unpardonably happy, and full of the joy of life. The thought of her husband's unhappiness did not poison her happiness. On one side that memory was too awful to be thought of. On the other side her husband's unhappiness had given her too much happiness to be regretted. The memory of all that had happened after her illness: her reconciliation with her husband, its breakdown, the news of Vronsky's wound, his visit, the preparations for divorce, the departure from her husband's house, the parting from her son—all that seemed to her like a delirious dream, from which she had waked up alone with Vronsky abroad. The thought of the harm caused to her husband aroused in her a feeling like repulsion, and akin to what a drowning man might feel who has shaken off another man clinging to him. That man did drown. It was an evil action, of course, but it was the sole means of escape, and better not to brood over these fearful facts.

One consolatory reflection upon her conduct had occurred to her at the first moment of the final rupture, and when now she recalled all the past, she remembered that one reflection. 'I have inevitably made that man wretched,' she thought; 'but I don't want to profit by his misery. I too am suffering, and shall suffer; I am losing what I prized above everything—I am losing my good name and my son. I have done wrong, and so I don't want happiness, I don't want a divorce, and shall suffer from my shame and the separation from my child.' But, however sincerely Anna had meant to suffer, she was not suffering. Shame there was not. With the tact of which both had such a large share, they had succeeded in avoiding Russian ladies abroad, and so had never placed themselves in a false position, and everywhere they had met people who pretended that they perfectly understood their position, far better indeed than they did themselves. Separation from the son she loved—even that did not cause her anguish in these early days. The baby-girl —*his* child—was so sweet, and had so won Anna's heart, since she was all that was left her, that Anna rarely thought of her son.

The desire for life, waxing stronger with recovered health, was so intense, and the conditions of life were so new and pleasant, that Anna felt unpardonably happy. The more she got to know Vronsky, the more she loved him. She loved him for himself, and for his love for her. Her complete ownership of him was a continual joy to her. His presence was always sweet to her. All the traits of his character, which she learned to know better and better, were unutterably dear to her. His appearance, changed by his civilian dress, was as fascinating to her as though she were some young girl in love. In everything he said, thought, and did, she saw something particularly noble and elevated. Her adoration of him alarmed her indeed; she sought and could not find in him anything not fine. She dared not show him her sense of her own insignificance beside him. It seemed to her that, knowing this, he might sooner cease to love her; and she dreaded nothing now so much as losing his love, though she had no grounds for fearing it. But she could not help being grateful to him for his attitude to her, and showing that she appreciated it. He, who had in her opinion such a marked aptitude for a political career, in which he would have been certain to play a leading part—he had sacrificed his ambition for her sake, and never betrayed the slightest regret. He was more lovingly respectful to her than ever, and the constant care that she should not feel the awkwardness of her position never deserted him for a single instant. He, so manly a man, never opposed her, had indeed, with her, no will of his own, and was anxious, it seemed, for nothing but to anticipate her wishes. And she could not but appreciate this, even though the very intensity of his solicitude for her, the atmosphere of care with which he surrounded her, sometimes weighed upon her.

Vronsky, meanwhile, in spite of the complete realisation of what he had so long desired, was not perfectly happy. He soon felt that the realisation of his desires gave him no more than a grain of sand out of the mountain of happiness he had expected. It showed him the mistake men make in picturing to themselves happiness as the realisation of their desires. For a time after joining his life to hers, and putting on civilian dress, he had felt all the delight of freedom in general, of which he had known nothing before, and of freedom in his love,—and he was content, but not for long. He was soon aware that there was springing up in his heart a desire for desires—*ennui*. Without conscious intention he began to clutch at every passing caprice, taking it for a desire and an object. Sixteen hours of the day must be occupied in some way, since they were living abroad in complete freedom, outside the conditions of social life which filled up time in Petersburg. As for the amusements of bachelor existence, which had provided Vronsky with entertainment on previous tours abroad, they could not be thought of, since the sole attempt of the sort had led to a sudden attack of depression in Anna, quite out of proportion with the cause—a late supper with bachelor friends. Relations with the society of the place—foreign and Russian—were equally out of the question owing to the irregularity of their position. The inspection of objects of interest, apart from the fact that everything had been seen already, had not for Vronsky, a Russian and a sensible man, the immense significance Englishmen are able to attach to that pursuit.

And just as the hungry stomach eagerly accepts every object it can get, hoping to find nourishment in it, Vronsky quite unconsciously clutched first at politics, then at new books, and then at pictures.

As he had from a child a taste for painting, and as, not knowing what to spend his money on, he had begun collecting engravings, he came to a stop at painting, began to take interest in it, and concentrated upon it the unoccupied mass of desires which demanded satisfaction.

He had a ready appreciation of art, and probably, with a taste for imitating art, he supposed himself to have the real thing essential for an artist, and after hesitating for some time which style of painting to select—religious, historical, realistic, or genre painting—he set to work to paint. He appreciated all kinds, and could have felt inspired by any one of them; but he had no conception of the possibility of knowing nothing at all of any school of painting, and of being inspired directly by what is within the soul, without caring whether what is painted will belong to any recognised school. Since he knew nothing of this, and drew his inspiration, not directly from life, but indirectly from life embodied in art, his inspiration came very quickly and easily, and as quickly and easily came his success in painting something very similar to the sort of painting he was trying to imitate.

More than any other style he liked the French—graceful and effective—and in that style he began to paint Anna's portrait in Italian costume, and the portrait seemed to him, and to every one who saw it, extremely successful.

IX

THE old neglected palazzo, with its lofty carved ceilings and frescoes on the walls, with its floors of mosaic, with its heavy yellow stuff curtains on the windows, with its vases on pedestals, and its open fireplaces, its carved doors and gloomy reception-rooms, hung with pictures—this palazzo did much, by its very appearance after they had moved into it, to confirm in Vronsky the agreeable illusion that he was not so much a Russian country gentleman, a retired army officer, as an enlightened amateur and patron of the arts, himself a modest artist who had renounced the world, his connections, and his ambition for the sake of the woman he loved.

The pose chosen by Vronsky with their removal into the palazzo was completely successful, and having, through Golenishtchev, made acquaintance with a few interesting people, for a time he was satisfied. He painted studies from nature under the guidance of an Italian professor of painting, and studied mediæval Italian life. Mediæval Italian life so fascinated Vronsky that he even wore a hat and flung a cloak over his shoulder in the mediæval style, which, indeed, was extremely becoming to him.

'Here we live, and know nothing of what's going on,' Vronsky said to Golenishtchev as he came to see him one morning. 'Have you seen Mihailov's picture?' he said, handing him a Russian gazette he had received that morning, and pointing to an article on a Russian artist, living in the very same town, and just finishing a picture which had long been talked about, and had been bought beforehand. The article reproached the government and the academy for letting so remarkable an artist be left without encouragement and support.

'I've seen it,' answered Golenishtchev. 'Of course he's not without talent, but it's all in a wrong direction. It's all the Ivanov-Strauss-Renan attitude to Christ and to religious painting.'

'What is the subject of the picture?' asked Anna.

'Christ before Pilate. Christ is represented as a Jew with all the realism of the new school.'

And the question of the subject of the picture having brought him to one of his favourite theories, Golenishtchev launched forth into a disquisition on it.

'I can't understand how they can fall into such a gross mistake. Christ always has His definite embodiment in the art of the great masters. And therefore, if they want to depict, not God, but a revolutionist or a sage, let them take from history a Socrates, a Franklin, a

Charlotte Corday, but not Christ. They take the very figure which cannot be taken for their art, and then . . .'

'And is it true that this Mihailov is in such poverty?' asked Vronsky, thinking that, as a Russian Mæcenas, it was his duty to assist the artist regardless of whether the picture were good or bad.

'I should say not. He's a remarkable portrait-painter. Have you ever seen his portrait of Madame Vassiltchikov? But I believe he doesn't care about painting any more portraits, and so very likely he is in want. I maintain that . . .'

'Couldn't we ask him to paint a portrait of Anna Arkadyevna?' said Vronsky.

'Why mine?' said Anna. 'After yours I don't want another portrait. Better have one of Annie' (so she called her baby girl). 'Here she is,' she added, looking out of the window at the handsome Italian nurse, who was carrying the child out into the garden, and immediately glancing unnoticed at Vronsky. The handsome nurse, from whom Vronsky was painting a head for his picture, was the one hidden grief in Anna's life. He painted with her as his model, admired her beauty and mediævalism, and Anna dared not confess to herself that she was afraid of becoming jealous of this nurse, and was for that reason particularly gracious and condescending both to her and her little son. Vronsky, too, glanced out of window and into Anna's eyes, and, turning at once to Golenishtchev, he said—

'Do you know this Mihailov?'

'I have met him. But he's a queer fish, and quite without breeding. You know, one of those uncouth new people one's so often coming across nowadays, one of those free-thinkers, you know, who are reared *d'emblée* in theories of atheism, scepticism, and materialism. In former days,' said Golenishtchev, not observing, or willing to observe, that both Anna and Vronsky wanted to speak, 'in former days the free-thinker was a man who had been brought up in ideas of religion, law, and morality, and only through conflict and struggle came to free-thought; but now there has sprung up a new type of born free-thinkers who grow up without even having heard of principles of morality or of religion, of the existence of authorities, who grow up directly in ideas of negation in everything, that is to say, savages. Well, he's of that class. He's the son, it appears, of some Moscow butler, and has never had any sort of bringing-up. When he got into the academy and made his reputation he tried, as he's no fool, to educate himself. And he turned to what seemed to him the very source of culture—the magazines. In old times, you see, a man who wanted to educate himself—a Frenchman, for instance—would have set to work to study all the classics and theologians and tragedians and historians and philosophers, and, you know, all the intellectual work that came in his way. But in our day he goes straight for the literature of negation, very quickly assimilates all the extracts of the science of negation, and he's ready. And that's not all—twenty years ago he would have found in that literature traces of conflict with authorities, with the creeds of the ages; he would have perceived from this conflict that there was something else; but now he comes at once upon a literature in which the old creeds do not even furnish matter for discussion, but it is stated baldly that there is nothing else—evolution, natural selection, struggle for existence—and that's all. In my article I've . . .'

'I tell you what,' said Anna, who had for a long while been exchanging wary glances with Vronsky, and knew that he was not in the least interested in the education of this artist, but was simply absorbed by the idea of assisting him and ordering a portrait of him; 'I tell you what,' she said, resolutely interrupting Golenishtchev, who was still talking away, 'let's go and see him!'

Golenishtchev recovered his self-possession and readily agreed. But as the artist lived in a remote suburb, it was decided to take the carriage.

An hour later Anna, with Golenishtchev by her side and Vronsky on the front seat of the carriage, facing them, drove up to a new ugly house in the remote suburb. On learning from the porter's wife, who came out to them, that Mihailov saw visitors at his studio, but that at that moment he was in his lodging only a couple of steps off, they sent her to him with their cards, asking permission to see his picture.

X

THE artist Mihailov was, as always, at work when the cards of Count Vronsky and Golenishtchev were brought to him. In the morning he had been working in his studio at his big picture. On getting home he flew into a rage with his wife for not having managed to put off the landlady, who had been asking for money.

'I've said it to you twenty times, don't enter into details. You're fool enough at all times, and when you start explaining things in Italian you're a fool three times as foolish,' he said, after a long dispute.

'Don't let it run so long; it's not my fault. If I had the money . . .'

'Leave me in peace, for God's sake!' Mihailov shrieked, with tears in his voice, and, stopping his ears, he went off into his working room, the other side of a partition wall, and closed the door after him. 'Idiotic woman!' he said to himself, sat down to the table, and, opening a portfolio, he set to work at once with peculiar fervour at a sketch he had begun.

Never did he work with such fervour and success as when things went ill with him, and especially when he quarrelled with his wife. 'Oh! damn them all!' he thought as he went on working. He was making a sketch for the figure of a man in a violent rage. A sketch had been made before, but he was dissatisfied with it. 'No, that one was better . . . where is it?' He went back to his wife, and scowling, and not looking at her, asked his eldest little girl, where was that piece of paper he had given them? The paper with the discarded sketch on it was found, but it was dirty, and spotted with candle-grease. Still, he took the sketch, laid it on his table, and, moving a little away, screwing up his eyes, he fell to gazing at it. All at once he smiled and gesticulated gleefully.

'That's it! that's it!' he said, and, at once picking up the pencil, he began rapidly drawing. The spot of tallow had given the man a new pose.

He had sketched this new pose, when all at once he recalled the face of a shopkeeper of whom he had bought cigars, a vigorous face with a prominent chin, and he sketched this very face, this chin on to the figure of the man. He laughed aloud with delight. The figure from a lifeless imagined thing had become living, and such that it could never be changed. That figure lived, and was clearly and unmistakably defined. The sketch might be corrected in accordance with the requirements of the figure, the legs, indeed, could and must be put differently, and the position of the left hand must be quite altered; the hair too might be thrown back. But in making these corrections he was not altering the figure but simply getting rid of what concealed the figure. He was, as it were, stripping off the wrappings which hindered it from being distinctly seen. Each new feature only brought out the whole figure in all its force and vigour, as it had suddenly come to him from the spot of tallow. He was carefully finishing the figure when the cards were brought him.

'Coming, coming!'

He went in to his wife.

'Come, Sasha, don't be cross!' he said, smiling timidly and affectionately at her. 'You were to blame. I was to blame. I'll make it all right.' And having made peace with his wife he put on an olive-green overcoat with a velvet collar and a hat, and went towards his studio. The successful figure he had already forgotten. Now he was delighted and excited at the visit of these people of consequence, Russians, who had come in their carriage.

Of his picture, the one that stood now on his easel, he had at the bottom of his heart one conviction—that no one had ever painted a picture like it. He did not believe that his picture was better than all the pictures of Raphael, but he knew that what he tried to convey in that picture, no one ever had conveyed. This he knew positively, and had known a long while, ever since he had begun to paint it. But other people's criticisms, whatever they might be, had yet immense consequence in his eyes, and they agitated him to the depths of his soul. Any remark, the most insignificant, that showed that the critic saw even the tiniest part of what he saw in the picture, agitated him to the depths of his soul. He always attributed to his critics a more profound comprehension than he had himself, and always expected from them something he did not himself see in the picture. And often in their criticisms he fancied that he had found this.

He walked rapidly to the door of his studio, and in spite of his excitement he was struck by the soft light on Anna's figure as she stood in the shade of the entrance listening to Golenishtchev, who was eagerly telling her something, while she evidently wanted to look round at the artist. He was himself unconscious how, as he approached them, he seized on this impression and absorbed it, as he had the chin of the shopkeeper who had sold him the cigars, and put it away somewhere to be brought out when he wanted it. The visitors, not agreeably impressed beforehand by Golenishtchev's account of the artist, were still less so by his personal appearance. Thick-set and of middle height, with nimble movements, with his brown hat, olive-green coat and narrow trousers—though wide trousers had been a long while in fashion,—most of all, with the ordinariness of his broad face, and the combined expression of timidity and anxiety to keep up his dignity, Mihailov made an unpleasant impression.

'Please step in,' he said, trying to look indifferent, and going into the passage he took a key out of his pocket and opened the door.

XI

ON entering the studio, Mihailov once more scanned his visitors and noted down in his imagination Vronsky's expression too, and especially his jaws. Although his artistic sense was unceasingly at work collecting materials, although he felt a continually increasing excitement as the moment of criticising his work drew nearer, he rapidly and subtly formed, from imperceptible signs, a mental image of these three persons.

That fellow (Golenishtchev) was a Russian living here. Mihailov did not remember his surname nor where he had met him, nor what he had said to him. He only remembered his face as he remembered all the faces he had ever seen; but he remembered, too, that it was one of the faces laid by in his memory in the immense class of the falsely consequential and poor in expression. The abundant hair and very open forehead gave an appearance of consequence to the face, which had only one expression—a petty, childish, peevish expression, concentrated just above the bridge of the narrow nose. Vronsky and Madame Karenin must be, Mihailov supposed, distinguished and wealthy Russians, knowing nothing about art, like all those wealthy Russians, but posing as amateurs and connoisseurs. 'Most likely they've already looked at all the antiques, and now they're making the round of the studios of the new people, the German humbug, and the cracked Pre-Raphaelite English fellow, and have only come to me to make the point of view complete,' he thought. He was well acquainted with the way dilettanti have (the cleverer they were the worse he found them) of looking at the works of contemporary artists with the sole object of being in a position to say that art is a thing of the past, and that the more one sees of the new men the more one sees how inimitable the works of the great old masters have remained. He expected all this; he saw it all in their faces, he saw it in the careless indifference with which they talked among themselves, stared at the lay figures and busts, and walked about in leisurely fashion, waiting for him to uncover his picture. But in spite of this, while he was turning over his studies, pulling up the blinds and taking off the sheet, he was in intense excitement, especially as, in spite of his conviction that all distinguished and wealthy Russians were certain to be beasts and fools, he liked Vronsky, and still more Anna.

'Here, if you please,' he said, moving on one side with his nimble gait and pointing to his picture, 'it's the exhortation to Pilate. Matthew, chapter xxvii,' he said, feeling his lips were beginning to tremble with emotion. He moved away and stood behind them.

For the few seconds during which the visitors were gazing at the picture in silence Mihailov too gazed at it with the indifferent eye of an outsider. For those few seconds he was sure in anticipation that a higher, juster criticism would be uttered by them, by those very visitors whom he had been so despising a moment before. He forgot all he had thought about his picture before during the three years he had been painting it; he forgot all its qualities which had been absolutely certain to him—he saw the picture with their indifferent, new, outside eyes, and saw nothing good in it. He saw in the foreground Pilate's irritated face and the serene face of Christ, and in the background the figures of Pilate's retinue and the face of John watching what was happening. Every face that, with such agony, such blunders and corrections had grown up within him with its special character, every face that had given him such torments and such raptures, and all these faces so many times transposed for the sake of the harmony of the whole, all the shades of colour and tones that he had attained with such labour—all of this together seemed to him now, looking at it with their eyes, the merest vulgarity, something that had been done a thousand times over. The face dearest to him, the face of Christ, the centre of the picture, which had given him such ecstasy as it unfolded itself to him, was utterly lost to him when he glanced at the picture with their eyes. He saw a well-painted (no, not even that—he distinctly saw now a mass of defects) repetition of those endless Christs of Titian, Raphael, Rubens, and the same soldiers and Pilate. It was all common, poor, and stale, and positively badly painted—weak and unequal. They would be justified in repeating hypocritically civil speeches in the presence of the painter, and pitying him and laughing at him when they were alone again.

The silence (though it lasted no more than a minute) became too intolerable to him. To break it, and to show he was not agitated, he made an effort and addressed Golenishtchev.

'I think I've had the pleasure of meeting you,' he said, looking uneasily first at Anna, then at Vronsky, in fear of losing any shade of their expression.

'To be sure! We met at Rossi's, do you remember, at that soirée when that Italian lady recited—the new Rachel?' Golenishtchev answered easily, removing his eyes without the slightest regret from the picture and turning to the artist.

Noticing, however, that Mihailov was expecting a criticism of the picture, he said—

'Your picture has got on a great deal since I saw it last time; and what strikes me particularly now, as it did then, is the figure of Pilate. One so knows the man: a good-natured, capital fellow, but an official through and through, who does not know what it is he's doing. But I fancy . . .'

All Mihailov's mobile face beamed at once; his eyes sparkled. He tried to say something, but he could not speak for excitement, and pretended to be coughing. Low as was his opinion of Golenishtchev's capacity for understanding art, trifling as was the true remark upon the fidelity of the expression of Pilate as an official, and offensive as might have seemed the utterance of so unimportant an observation while nothing was said of more serious points, Mihailov was in an ecstasy of delight at this observation. He had himself thought about Pilate's figure just what Golenishtchev said. The fact that this reflection was but one of millions of reflections, which as Mihailov knew for certain would be true, did not diminish for him the significance of Golenishtchev's remark. His heart warmed to Golenishtchev for this remark, and from a state of depression he suddenly passed to ecstasy. At once the whole of his picture lived before him in all the indescribable complexity of everything living. Mihailov again tried to say that that was how he understood Pilate, but his lips quivered intractably, and he could not pronounce the words. Vronsky and Anna too said something in that subdued voice in which, partly to avoid hurting the artist's feelings and partly to avoid saying out loud something silly—so easily said when talking of art—people usually speak at exhibitions of pictures. Mihailov fancied that the picture had made an impression on them too. He went up to them.

'How marvellous Christ's expression is!' said Anna. Of all she saw she liked that expression most of all, and she felt that it was the centre of the picture, and so praise of it would be pleasant to the artist. 'One can see that He is pitying Pilate.'

This again was one of the million true reflections that could be found in his picture and in the figure of Christ. She said that He was pitying Pilate. In Christ's expression there ought to be indeed an expression of pity, since there is an expression of love, of heavenly peace, of readiness for death, and of a sense of the vanity of words. Of course there is the expression of an official in Pilate and of pity in Christ, seeing that one is the incarnation of the fleshly and the other of the spiritual life. All this and much more flashed into Mihailov's thoughts.

'Yes, and how that figure is done—what atmosphere! One can walk round it,' said Golenishtchev, unmistakably betraying by his remark that he did not approve of the meaning and idea of the figure.

'Yes, there's a wonderful mastery!' said Vronsky. 'How those figures in the background stand out. There you have technique,' he said, addressing Golenishtchev, alluding to a conversation between them about Vronsky's despair of attaining this technique.

'Yes, yes, marvellous!' Golenishtchev and Anna assented. In spite of the excited condition in which he was, the sentence about technique had sent a pang to Mihailov's heart, and looking angrily at Vronsky he suddenly scowled. He had often heard this word technique, and was utterly unable to understand what was understood by it. He knew that by this term was understood a mechanical facility for painting or drawing, entirely apart from its subject. He had noticed often that even in actual praise technique was opposed to essential quality, as though one could paint well something that was bad. He knew that a great deal of attention and care was necessary in taking off the coverings, to avoid injuring the creation itself, and to take off all the coverings; but there was no art of painting—no technique of any sort—about it. If to a little child or to his cook were revealed what he saw, it or she would have been able to peel the wrappings off what was seen. And the most experienced and adroit painter could not by mere mechanical facility paint anything if the lines of the subject were not revealed to him first. Besides, he saw that if it came to talking about technique, it was impossible to praise him for it. In all he had painted and repainted he saw faults that hurt his eyes, coming from want of care in taking off the wrappings—faults he could not correct now without spoiling the whole. And in almost all the figures and faces he saw, too, remnants of the wrappings not perfectly removed that spoiled the picture.

'One thing might be said, if you will allow me to make the remark . . .' observed Golenishtchev.

'Oh, I shall be delighted, I beg you,' said Mihailov with a forced smile.

'That is, that you make Him the man-god, and not the God-man. But I know that was what you meant to do.'

'I cannot paint a Christ that is not in my heart,' said Mihailov gloomily.

'Yes; but in that case, if you will allow me to say what I think . . . Your picture is so fine that my observation cannot detract from it, and, besides, it is only my personal opinion. With you it is different. Your very motive is different. But let us take Ivanov. I imagine that if Christ is brought down to the level of an historical character, it would have been better for Ivanov to select some other historical subject, fresh, untouched.'

'But if this is the greatest subject presented to art?'

'If one looked one would find others. But the point is that art cannot suffer doubt and discussion. And before the picture of Ivanov the question arises for the believer and the unbeliever alike, "Is it God, or is it not God?" and the unity of the impression is destroyed.'

'Why so? I think that for educated people,' said Mihailov, 'the question cannot exist.'

Golenishtchev did not agree with this, and confounded Mihailov by his support of his first idea of the unity of the impression being essential to art.

Mihailov was greatly perturbed, but he could say nothing in defence of his own idea.

XII

ANNA and Vronsky had long been exchanging glances, regretting their friend's flow of cleverness. At last Vronsky, without waiting for the artist, walked away to another small picture.

'Oh, how exquisite! What a lovely thing! A gem! How exquisite!' they cried with one voice.

'What is it they're so pleased with?' thought Mihailov. He had positively forgotten that picture he had painted three years ago. He had forgotten all the agonies and the ecstasies he had lived through with that picture when for several months it had been the one thought haunting him day and night. He had forgotten, as he always forgot, the pictures he had finished. He did not even like to look at it, and had only brought it out because he was expecting an Englishman who wanted to buy it.

'Oh, that's only an old study,' he said.

'How fine!' said Golenishtchev, he too, with unmistakable sincerity, falling under the spell of the picture.

Two boys were angling in the shade of a willow-tree. The elder had just dropped in the hook, and was carefully pulling the float from behind a bush, entirely absorbed in what he was doing. The other, a little younger, was lying in the grass leaning on his elbows, with his tangled, flaxen head in his hands, staring at the water with his dreamy blue eyes. What was he thinking of?

The enthusiasm over this picture stirred some of the old feeling for it in Mihailov, but he feared and disliked this waste of feeling for things past, and so, even though this praise was grateful to him, he tried to draw his visitors away to a third picture.

But Vronsky asked whether the picture was for sale? To Mihailov at that moment, excited by visitors, it was extremely distasteful to speak of money matters.

'It is put up there to be sold,' he answered, scowling gloomily.

When the visitors had gone, Mihailov sat down opposite the picture of Pilate and Christ, and in his mind went over what had been said, and what, though not said, had been implied by those visitors. And, strange to say, what had had such weight with him, while they were there and while he mentally put himself at their point of view, suddenly lost all importance for him. He began to look at his picture with all his own full artist vision, and was soon in that mood of conviction of the perfectibility, and so of the significance, of his picture—a conviction essential to the intensest fervour, excluding all other interests—in which alone he could work.

Christ's foreshortened leg was not right, though. He took his palette and began to work. As he corrected the leg he looked continually at the figure of John in the background, which his visitors had not even noticed, but which he knew was beyond perfection. When he had finished the leg he wanted to touch that figure, but he felt too much excited for it. He was equally unable to work when he was cold and when he was too much affected and saw everything too much. There was only one stage in the transition from coldness to inspiration, at which work was possible. Today he was too much agitated. He would have covered the picture, but he stopped, holding the cloth in his hand, and, smiling blissfully, gazed a long while at the figure of John. At last, as it were regretfully tearing himself away, he dropped the cloth, and, exhausted but happy, went home.

Vronsky, Anna, and Golenishtchev, on their way home, were particularly lively and cheerful. They talked of Mihailov and his pictures. The word *talent*, by which they meant an inborn, almost physical, aptitude apart from brain and heart, and in which they tried to find an expression for all the artist had gained from life, recurred particularly often in their talk, as though it were necessary for them to sum up what they had no conception of, though they wanted to talk of it. They said that there was no denying his talent, but that his talent could not develop for want of education—the common defect of our Russian artists. But the picture of the boys had imprinted itself on their memories, and they were continually coming back to it. 'What an exquisite thing! How he has succeeded in it, and how simply! He doesn't even comprehend how good it is. Yes, I mustn't let it slip; I must buy it,' said Vronsky.

XIII

MIHAILOV sold Vronsky his picture, and agreed to paint a portrait of Anna. On the day fixed he came and began the work.

From the fifth sitting the portrait impressed everyone, especially Vronsky, not only by its resemblance, but by its characteristic beauty. It was strange how Mihailov could have discovered just her characteristic beauty. 'One needs to know and love her as I have loved her to discover the very sweetest expression of her soul,' Vronsky thought, though it was only from this portrait that he had himself learned this sweetest expression of her soul. But the expression was so true that he, and others too, fancied they had long known it.

'I have been struggling on for ever so long without doing anything,' he said of his own portrait of her, 'and he just looked and painted it. That's where technique comes in.'

'That will come,' was the consoling reassurance given him by Golenishtchev, in whose view Vronsky had both talent, and what was most important, culture, giving him a wider outlook on art. Golenishtchev's faith in Vronsky's talent was propped up by his own need of

Vronsky's sympathy and approval for his own articles and ideas, and he felt that the praise and support must be mutual.

In another man's house, and especially in Vronsky's palazzo, Mihailov was quite a different man from what he was in his studio. He behaved with hostile courtesy, as though he were afraid of coming closer to people he did not respect. He called Vronsky 'your excellency,' and notwithstanding Anna's and Vronsky's invitations, he would never stay to dinner, nor come except for the sittings. Anna was even more friendly to him than to other people, and was very grateful for her portrait. Vronsky was more than cordial with him, and was obviously interested to know the artist's opinion of his picture. Golenishtchev never let slip an opportunity of instilling sound ideas about art into Mihailov. But Mihailov remained equally chilly to all of them. Anna was aware from his eyes that he liked looking at her, but he avoided conversation with her. Vronsky's talk about his painting he met with stubborn silence, and he was as stubbornly silent when he was shown Vronsky's picture. He was unmistakably bored by Golenishtchev's conversation, and he did not attempt to oppose him.

Altogether Mihailov, with his reserved and disagreeable, as it were hostile attitude, was quite disliked by them as they got to know him better; and they were glad when the sittings were over, and they were left with a magnificent portrait in their possession, and he gave up coming. Golenishtchev was the first to give expression to an idea that had occurred to all of them, which was that Mihailov was simply jealous of Vronsky.

'Not envious, let us say, since he has *talent*; but it annoys him that a wealthy man of the highest society, and a count, too (you know they all detest a title), can, without any particular trouble, do as well, if not better, than he who has devoted all his life to it. And more than all, it's a question of culture, which he is without.'

Vronsky defended Mihailov, but at the bottom of his heart he believed it, because in his view a man of a different, lower world would be sure to be envious.

Anna's portrait—the same subject painted from nature both by him and by Mihailov—ought to have shown Vronsky the difference between him and Mihailov; but he did not see it. Only after Mihailov's portrait was painted he left off painting his portrait of Anna, deciding that it was now not needed. His picture of mediæval life he went on with. And he himself, and Golenishtchev, and still more Anna, thought it very good, because it was far more like the celebrated pictures they knew than Mihailov's picture.

Mihailov meanwhile, although Anna's portrait greatly fascinated him, was even more glad than they were when the sittings were over, and he had no longer to listen to Golenishtchev's disquisitions upon art, and could forget about Vronsky's painting. He knew that Vronsky could not be prevented from amusing himself with painting: he knew that he and all dilettanti had a perfect right to paint what they liked, but it was distasteful to him. A man could not be prevented from making himself a big wax doll, and kissing it. But if the man were to come with the doll and sit before a man in love, and began caressing his doll as the lover caressed the woman he loved, it would be distasteful to the lover. Just such a distasteful sensation was what Mihailov felt at the sight of Vronsky's painting: he felt it both ludicrous and irritating, both pitiable and offensive.

Vronsky's interest in painting and the Middle Ages did not last long. He had enough taste for painting to be unable to finish his picture. The picture came to a standstill. He was vaguely aware that its defects, inconspicuous at first, would be glaring if he were to go on with it. The same experience befell him as Golenishtchev, who felt that he had nothing to say, and continually deceived himself with the theory that his idea was not yet mature, that he was working it out and collecting materials. This exasperated and tortured Golenishtchev, but Vronsky was incapable of deceiving and torturing himself, and even more incapable of exasperation. With his characteristic decision, without explanation or apology, he simply ceased working at painting.

But without this occupation, the life of Vronsky and of Anna, who wondered at his loss of interest in it, struck them as intolerably tedious in an Italian town. The palazzo suddenly seemed so obtrusively old and dirty, the spots on the curtains, the cracks in the floors, the broken plaster on the cornices became so disagreeably obvious, and the everlasting sameness of Golenishtchev, and the Italian professor and the German traveller became so wearisome, that they had to make some change. They resolved to go to Russia, to the country. In Petersburg Vronsky intended to arrange a partition of the land with his brother, while Anna meant to see her son. The summer they intended to spend on Vronsky's great family estate.

XIV

LEVIN had been married three months. He was happy, but not at all in the way he had expected to be. At every step he found his former dreams disappointed, and new, unexpected surprises of happiness. He was happy; but on entering upon family life he saw at every step that it was utterly different from what he had imagined. At every step he experienced what a man would experience who, after admiring the smooth, happy course of a little boat on a lake, should get himself into that little boat. He saw that it was not all sitting still, floating smoothly; that one had to think too, not for an instant to forget where one was floating; and that there was water under one, and that one must row; and that his unaccustomed hands would be sore; and that it was only to look at it that was easy; but that doing it, though very delightful, was very difficult.

As a bachelor, when he had watched other people's married life, seen the petty cares, the squabbles, the jealousy, he had only smiled contemptuously in his heart. In his future married life there could be, he was convinced, nothing of that sort; even the external forms, indeed, he fancied, must be utterly unlike the life of others in everything. And all of a sudden, instead of his life with his wife being made on an individual pattern, it was, on the contrary, entirely made up of the pettiest details, which he had so despised before, but which now, by no will of his own, had gained an extraordinary importance that it was useless to contend against. And Levin saw that the organisation of all these details was by no means so easy as he had fancied before. Although Levin believed himself to have the most exact conceptions of domestic life, unconsciously, like all men, he pictured domestic life as the happy enjoyment of love, with nothing to hinder and no petty cares to distract. He ought, as he conceived the position, to do his work, and to find repose from it in the happiness of love. She ought to be beloved, and nothing more. But, like all men, he forgot that she too would want work. And he was surprised that she, his poetic, exquisite Kitty, could not merely in the first weeks, but even in the first days of their married life, think, remember, and busy herself about tablecloths, and furniture, about mattresses for visitors, about a tray, about the cook, and the dinner, and so on. While they were still engaged, he had been struck by the definiteness with which she had declined the tour abroad and decided to go into the country, as though she knew of something she wanted, and could still think of something outside her love. This had jarred upon him then, and now her trivial cares and anxieties jarred upon him several times. But he saw that this was essential for her. And, loving her as he did, though he did not understand the reason of them, and jeered at these domestic pursuits, he could not help admiring them. He jeered at the way in which she arranged the furniture they had brought from Moscow; rearranged their room; hung up curtains; prepared rooms for visitors; a room for Dolly; saw after an abode for her new maid; ordered dinner of the old cook; came into collision with Agafea Mihalovna, taking from her the charge of the stores. He saw how the old cook smiled, admiring her, and listening to her inexperienced, impossible orders, how mournfully and tenderly Agafea Mihalovna shook her head over the young mistress's new arrangements. He saw that Kitty was extraordinarily sweet when, laughing and crying, she came to tell him that her maid, Masha, was used to looking upon her as her young lady, and so no one obeyed her. It seemed to him sweet, but strange, and he thought it would have been better without this.

He did not know how great a sense of change she was experiencing: she, who at home had sometimes wanted some favourite dish, or sweets, without the possibility of getting either, now could order what she liked, buy pounds of sweets, spend as much money as she liked, and order any puddings she pleased.

She was dreaming with delight now of Dolly's coming to them with her children, especially because she would order for the children their favourite puddings, and Dolly would appreciate all her new housekeeping. She did not know herself why and wherefore, but the arranging of her house had an irresistible attraction for her. Instinctively feeling the approach of spring, and knowing that there would be days of rough weather too, she built her nest as best she could, and was in haste at the same time to build it and to learn how to do it.

This care for domestic details in Kitty, so opposed to Levin's ideal of exalted happiness, was at first one of the disappointments; and this sweet care of her household, the aim of which he did not understand, but could not help loving, was one of the new happy surprises.

Another disappointment and happy surprise came in their quarrels. Levin could never have conceived that between him and his wife any relations could arise other than tender, respectful, and loving, and all at once in the very early days they quarrelled, so that she said he did not care for her, that he cared for no one but himself, burst into tears, and wrung her hands.

This first quarrel arose from Levin's having gone out to a new farmhouse and having been away half an hour too long, because he had tried to get home by a short cut and had lost his way. He drove home thinking of nothing but her, of her love, of his own happiness, and the nearer he drew to home, the warmer was his tenderness for her. He ran into the room with the same feeling, with an even stronger feeling, than he had had when he reached the Shtcherbatskys' house to make his offer. And suddenly he was met by a lowering expression he had never seen in her. He would have kissed her; she pushed him away.

'What is it?'

'You've been enjoying yourself,' she began, trying to be calm and spiteful. But as soon as she opened her mouth, a stream of reproach, of senseless jealousy, of all that had been torturing her during that half-hour which she had spent sitting motionless at the window, burst from her. It was only then, for the first time, that he clearly understood what he had not understood when he led her out of the church after the wedding. He felt now that he was not simply close to her, but that he did not know where he ended and she began. He felt this from the agonising sensation of division that he experienced at that instant. He was offended for the first instant, but the very same second he felt that he could not be offended by her, that she was himself. He felt for the first moment as a man feels when, having suddenly received a violent blow from behind, turns round, angry and eager to avenge himself, to look for his antagonist, and finds that it is he himself who has accidentally struck himself, that there is no one to be angry with, and that he must put up with and try to soothe the pain.

Never afterwards did he feel it with such intensity, but this first time he could not for a long while get over it. His natural feeling urged him to defend himself, to prove to her she was wrong; but to prove her wrong would mean irritating her still more and making the rupture greater that was the cause of all his suffering. One habitual feeling impelled him to get rid of the blame and to pass it on to her. Another feeling, even stronger, impelled him as quickly as possible to smooth over the rupture without letting it grow greater. To remain under such undeserved reproach was wretched, but to make her suffer by justifying himself was worse still. Like a man half-awake in an agony of pain, he wanted to tear out, to fling away the aching place, and coming to his senses, he felt that the aching place was himself. He could do nothing but try to help the aching place to bear it, and this he tried to do.

They made peace. She, recognising that she was wrong, though she did not say so, became tenderer to him, and they experienced new, redoubled happiness in their love. But that did not prevent such quarrels from happening again, and exceedingly often too, on the most unexpected and trivial grounds. These quarrels frequently arose from the fact that they did not yet know what was of importance to each other, and that all this early period they were both often in a bad temper. When one was in a good temper, and the other in a bad temper, the peace was not broken; but when both happened to be in an ill-humour, quarrels sprang up from such incomprehensibly trifling causes, that they could never remember afterwards what they had quarrelled about. It is true that when they were both in a good temper their enjoyment of life was redoubled. But still this first period of their married life was a difficult time for them.

During all this early time they had a peculiarly vivid sense of tension, as it were a tugging in opposite directions of the chain by which they were bound. Altogether their honeymoon—that is to say, the month after their wedding—from which from tradition Levin expected so much, was not merely not a time of sweetness, but remained in the memories of both as the bitterest and most humiliating period in their lives. They both alike tried in later life to blot out from their memories all the monstrous, shameful incidents of that morbid period, when both were rarely in a normal frame of mind, both were rarely quite themselves.

It was only in the third month of their married life, after their return from Moscow, where they had been staying for a month, that their life began to go more smoothly.

XV

THEY had just come back from Moscow, and were glad to be alone. He was sitting at the writing-table in his study, writing. She, wearing the dark lilac dress she had worn during the first days of their married life, and put on again today, a dress particularly remembered and loved by him, was sitting on the sofa, the same old-fashioned leather sofa which had always stood in the study in Levin's father's and grandfather's days. She was sewing at *broderie anglaise*. He thought and wrote, never losing the happy consciousness of her presence. His work, both on the land and on the book, in which the principles of the new land system were to be laid down, had not been abandoned; but just as formerly these pursuits and ideas had seemed to him petty and trivial in comparison with the darkness that overspread all life, now they seemed as unimportant and petty in comparison with the life that lay before him suffused with the brilliant light of happiness. He went on with his work, but he felt now that the centre of gravity of his attention had passed to something else, and that consequently he looked at his work quite differently and more clearly. Formerly this work had been for him an escape from life. Formerly he had felt that without this work his life would be too gloomy. Now these pursuits were necessary for him that life might not be too uniformly bright. Taking up his manuscript, reading through what he had written, he found with pleasure that the work was worth his working at. Many of his old ideas seemed to him superfluous and extreme, but many blanks became distinct to him when he reviewed the whole thing in his memory. He was writing now a new chapter on the causes of the present disastrous condition of agriculture in Russia. He maintained that the poverty of

Russia arises not merely from the anomalous distribution of landed property and misdirected reforms, but that what had contributed of late years to this result was the civilisation from without abnormally grafted upon Russia, especially facilities of communication, as railways, leading to centralisation in towns, the development of luxury, and the consequent development of manufactures, credit and its accompaniment of speculation—all to the detriment of agriculture. It seemed to him that in a normal development of wealth in a state all these phenomena would arise only when a considerable amount of labour had been put into agriculture, when it had come under regular, or at least definite, conditions; that the wealth of a country ought to increase proportionally, and especially in such a way that other sources of wealth should not outstrip agriculture; that in harmony with a certain stage of agriculture there should be means of communication corresponding to it, and that in our unsettled condition of the land, railways, called into being by political and not by economic needs, were premature, and instead of promoting agriculture, as was expected of them, they were competing with agriculture and promoting the development of manufactures and credit, and so arresting its progress; and that just as the one-sided and premature development of one organ in an animal would hinder its general development, so in the general development of wealth in Russia, credit, facilities of communication, manufacturing activity, indubitably necessary in Europe, where they had arisen in their proper time, had with us only done harm, by throwing into the background the chief question calling for settlement—the question of the organisation of agriculture.

While he was writing his ideas she was thinking how unnaturally cordial her husband had been to young Prince Tcharsky, who had, with great want of tact, flirted with her the day before they left Moscow. 'He's jealous,' she thought. 'Goodness! How sweet and silly he is! He's jealous of me! If he knew that I think no more of them than of Piotr the cook,' she thought, looking at his head and red neck with a feeling of possession strange to herself. 'Though it's a pity to take him from his work (but he has plenty of time!), I must look at his face; will he feel I'm looking at him? I wish he'd turn round . . . I'll *will* him to!' and she opened her eyes wide, as though to intensify the influence of her gaze.

'Yes, they draw away all the sap and give a false appearance of prosperity,' he muttered, stopping to write, and, feeling that she was looking at him and smiling, he looked round.

'Well?' he queried, smiling, and getting up.

'He looked round,' she thought.

'It's nothing; I wanted you to look round,' she said, watching him, and trying to guess whether he was vexed at being interrupted or not.

'How happy we are alone together!—I am, that is,' he said, going up to her with a radiant smile of happiness.

'I'm just as happy. I'll never go anywhere, especially not to Moscow.'

'And what were you thinking about?'

'I? I was thinking . . . No, no, go along, go on writing; don't break off,' she said, pursing up her lips, 'and I must cut out these little holes now, do you see?'

She took up her scissors and began cutting them out.

'No; tell me, what was it?' he said, sitting down beside her and watching the tiny scissors moving round.

'Oh! what was I thinking about? I was thinking about Moscow, about the back of your head.'

'Why should I, of all people, have such happiness! It's unnatural, too good,' he said, kissing her hand.

'I feel quite the opposite; the better things are, the more natural it seems to me.'

'And you've got a little curl loose,' he said, carefully turning her head round.

'A little curl, oh yes. No, no, we are busy at our work!'

Work did not progress further, and they darted apart from one another like culprits when Kouzma came in to announce that tea was ready.

'Have they come from the town?' Levin asked Kouzma.

'They've just come; they're unpacking the things.'

'Come quickly,' she said to him as she went out of the study, 'or else I shall read your letters without you.'

Left alone, after putting his manuscripts together in the new portfolio bought by her, he washed his hands at the new washstand with the elegant fittings, that had all made their appearance with her. Levin smiled at his own thoughts, and shook his head disapprovingly at those thoughts; a feeling akin to remorse fretted him. There was something shameful, effeminate, Capuan, as he called it to himself, in his present mode of life. 'It's not right to go on like this,' he thought. 'It'll soon be three months, and I'm doing next to nothing. Today, almost for the first time, I set to work seriously, and what happened? I did nothing but begin and throw it aside. Even my ordinary pursuits I have almost given up. On the land I scarcely walk or drive about at all to look after things. Either I am loath to leave her, or I see she's dull alone. And I used to think that, before marriage, life was nothing much, somehow didn't count, but that after marriage, life began in earnest. And here almost three months have passed, and I have spent my time so idly and unprofitably. No, this won't do; I must begin. Of course, it's not her fault. She's not to blame in any way. I ought myself to be firmer, to maintain my masculine independence of action; or else I shall get into such ways, and she'll get used to them too. . . . Of course she's not to blame,' he told himself.

But it is hard for anyone who is dissatisfied not to blame someone else, and especially the person nearest of all to them, for the ground of his dissatisfaction. And it vaguely came into Levin's mind that she herself was not to blame (she could not be to blame for anything), but what was to blame was her education, too superficial and frivolous. ('That fool Tcharsky: she wanted, I know, to stop him, but didn't know how to.') 'Yes, apart from her interest in the house (that she has), apart from dress and *broderie anglaise*, she has no serious interests. No interest in her work, in the estate, in the peasants, nor in music, though she's rather good at it, nor in reading. She does nothing, and is perfectly satisfied.' Levin, in his heart, censured this, and did not as yet understand that she was preparing for that period of activity which was to come for her when she would at once be the wife of her husband and mistress of the house, and would bear, and nurse, and bring up children. He knew not that she was instinctively aware of this, and, preparing herself for this time of terrible toil, did not reproach herself for the moments of carelessness and happiness in her love that she enjoyed now while gaily building her nest for the future.

XVI

WHEN Levin went upstairs, his wife was sitting near the new silver samovar behind the new tea service, and, having settled old Agafea Mihalovna at a little table with a full cup of tea, was reading a letter from Dolly, with whom they were in continual and frequent correspondence.

'You see, your good lady's settled me here, told me to sit a bit with her,' said Agafea Mihalovna, smiling affectionately at Kitty.

In these words of Agafea Mihalovna, Levin read the final act of the drama which had been enacted of late between her and Kitty. He saw that, in spite of Agafea Mihalovna's feelings being hurt by a new mistress taking the reins of government out of her hands, Kitty had yet conquered her and made her love her.

'Here, I opened your letter too,' said Kitty, handing him an illiterate letter. 'It's from that woman, I think, your brother's . . .' she said. 'I did not read it through. This is from my people and from Dolly.

Fancy! Dolly took Tanya and Grisha to a children's ball at the Sarmatskys': Tanya was a French marquise.'

But Levin did not hear her. Flushing, he took the letter from Marya Nikolaevna, his brother's former mistress, and began to read it. This was the second letter he had received from Marya Nikolaevna. In the first letter, Marya Nikolaevna wrote that his brother had sent her away for no fault of hers, and, with touching simplicity, added that though she was in want again, she asked for nothing, and wished for nothing, but was only tormented by the thought that Nikolay Dmitrievitch would come to grief without her, owing to the weak state of his health, and begged his brother to look after him. Now she wrote quite differently. She had found Nikolay Dmitrievitch, had again made it up with him in Moscow, and had moved with him to a provincial town, where he had received a post in the government service. But that he had quarrelled with the head official, and was on his way back to Moscow, only he had been taken so ill on the road that it was doubtful if he would ever leave his bed again, she wrote. 'It's always of you he has talked, and, besides, he has no more money left.'

'Read this; Dolly writes about you,' Kitty was beginning, with a smile; but she stopped suddenly, noticing the changed expression on her husband's face.

'What is it? What's the matter?'

'She writes to me that Nikolay, my brother, is at death's door. I shall go to him.'

Kitty's face changed at once. Thoughts of Tanya as a marquise, of Dolly, all had vanished.

'When are you going?' she said.

'Tomorrow.'

'And I will go with you, can I?' she said.

'Kitty! What are you thinking of?' he said reproachfully.

'How do you mean?' offended that he should seem to take her suggestion unwillingly and with vexation. 'Why shouldn't I go? I shan't be in your way. I . . .'

'I'm going because my brother is dying,' said Levin. 'Why should you . . .'

'Why? For the same reason as you.'

'And, at a moment of such gravity for me, she only thinks of her being dull by herself,' thought Levin. And this lack of candour in a matter of such gravity infuriated him.

'It's out of the question,' he said sternly.

Agafea Mihalovna, seeing that it was coming to a quarrel, gently put down her cup and withdrew. Kitty did not even notice her. The tone in which her husband had said the last words wounded her, especially because he evidently did not believe what she had said.

'I tell you, that if you go, I shall come with you; I shall certainly come,' she said hastily and wrathfully. 'Why out of the question? Why do you say it's out of the question?'

'Because it'll be going God knows where, by all sorts of roads and to all sorts of hotels. You would be a hindrance to me,' said Levin, trying to be cool.

'Not at all. I don't want anything. Where you can go, I can. . . .'

'Well, for one thing then, because this woman's there whom you can't meet.'

'I don't know and don't care to know who's there and what. I know that my husband's brother is dying and my husband is going to him, and I go with my husband too. . . .'

'Kitty! Don't get angry. But just think a little: this is a matter of such importance that I can't bear to think that you should bring in a feeling of weakness, of dislike to being left alone. Come, you'll be dull alone, so go and stay at Moscow a little.'

'There, you always ascribe base, vile motives to me,' she said with tears of wounded pride and fury. 'I didn't mean, it wasn't weakness, it wasn't. . . . I feel that it's my duty to be with my husband when he's in trouble, but you try on purpose to hurt me, you try on purpose not to understand. . . .'

'No; this is awful! To be such a slave!' cried Levin, getting up, and unable to restrain his anger any longer. But at the same second he felt that he was beating himself.

'Then why did you marry? You could have been free. Why did you, if you regret it?' she said, getting up and running away into the drawing-room.

When he went to her, she was sobbing.

He began to speak, trying to find words not to dissuade but simply to soothe her. But she did not heed him, and would not agree to anything. He bent down to her and took her hand, which resisted him. He kissed her hand, kissed her hair, kissed her hand again—still she was silent. But when he took her face in both his hands and said, 'Kitty!' she suddenly recovered herself, and began to cry, and they were reconciled.

It was decided that they should go together the next day. Levin told his wife that he believed she wanted to go simply in order to be of use, agreed that Marya Nikolaevna's being with his brother did not make her going improper, but he set off at the bottom of his heart dissatisfied both with her and with himself. He was dissatisfied with her for being unable to make up her mind to let him go when it was necessary (and how strange it was for him to think that he, so lately hardly daring to believe in such happiness as that she could love him—now was unhappy because she loved him too much!), and he was dissatisfied with himself for not showing more strength of will. Even greater was the feeling of disagreement at the bottom of his heart as to her not needing to consider the woman who was with his brother, and he thought with horror of all the contingencies they might meet with. The mere idea of his wife, his Kitty, being in the same room with a common wench, set him shuddering with horror and loathing.

XVII

THE hotel of the provincial town where Nikolay Levin was lying ill was one of those provincial hotels which are constructed on the newest model of modern improvements, with the best intentions of cleanliness, comfort, and even elegance, but owing to the public that patronises them, are with astounding rapidity transformed into filthy taverns with a pretension of modern improvement that only makes them worse than the old-fashioned, honestly filthy hotels. This hotel had already reached that stage, and the soldier in a filthy uniform smoking in the entry, supposed to stand for a hall-porter, and the cast-iron, slippery, dark, and disagreeable staircase, and the free and easy waiter in a filthy frock-coat, and the common dining-room with a dusty bouquet of wax flowers adorning the table, and filth, dust, and disorder everywhere, and at the same time the sort of modern up-to-date self-complacent railway uneasiness of this hotel, aroused a most painful feeling in Levin after their fresh young life, especially because the impression of falsity made by the hotel was so out of keeping with what awaited them.

As is invariably the case, after they had been asked at what price they wanted rooms, it appeared that there was not one decent room for them; one decent room had been taken by the inspector of railroads, another by a lawyer from Moscow, a third by Princess Astafiev from the country. There remained only one filthy room, next to which they promised that another should be empty by the evening. Feeling angry with his wife because what he had expected had come to pass, which was that at the moment of arrival, when his heart throbbed with emotion and anxiety to know how his brother was getting on, he should have to be seeing after her, instead of rushing straight to his brother, Levin conducted her to the room assigned them.

'Go, do go!' she said, looking at him with timid and guilty eyes.

He went out of the door without a word, and at once stumbled over Marya Nikolaevna, who had heard of his arrival and had not dared to go in to see him. She was just the same as when he saw her in Moscow; the same woollen gown, and bare arms and neck, and the same good-naturedly stupid, pock-marked face, only a little plumper.

'Well, how is he? how is he?'

'Very bad. He can't get up. He has kept expecting you. He . . . Are you . . . with your wife?'

Levin did not for the first moment understand what it was confused her, but she immediately enlightened him.

'I'll go away. I'll go down to the kitchen,' she brought out. 'Nikolay Dmitrievitch will be delighted. He heard about it, and knows your lady, and remembers her abroad.'

Levin realised that she meant his wife, and did not know what answer to make.

'Come along, come along to him!' he said.

But as soon as he moved, the door of his room opened and Kitty peeped out. Levin crimsoned both from shame and anger with his wife, who had put herself and him in such a difficult position; but Marya Nikolaevna crimsoned still more. She positively shrank together and flushed to the point of tears, and clutching the ends of her apron in both hands, twisted them in her red fingers without knowing what to say and what to do.

For the first instant Levin saw an expression of eager curiosity in the eyes with which Kitty looked at this awful woman, so incomprehensible to her; but it lasted only a single instant.

'Well! how is he?' she turned to her husband and then to her.

'But one can't go on talking in the passage like this!' Levin said, looking angrily at a gentleman who walked jauntily at that instant across the corridor, as though about his affairs.

'Well then, come in,' said Kitty, turning to Marya Nikolaevna, who had recovered herself, but noticing her husband's face of dismay; 'or go on; go, and then come for me,' she said, and went back into the room.

Levin went to his brother's room. He had not in the least expected what he saw and felt in his brother's room. He had expected to find him in the same state of self-deception which he had heard was so frequent with the consumptive, and which had struck him so much during his brother's visit in the autumn. He had expected to find the physical signs of the approach of death more marked—greater weakness, greater emaciation, but still almost the same condition of things. He had expected himself to feel the same distress at the loss of the brother he loved and the same horror in face of death as he had felt then, only in a greater degree. And he had prepared himself for this; but he found something utterly different.

In a little dirty room with the painted panels of its walls filthy with spittle, and conversation audible through the thin partition from the next room, in a stifling atmosphere saturated with impurities, on a bedstead moved away from the wall, there lay covered with a quilt, a body. One arm of this body was above the quilt, and the wrist, huge as a rake-handle, was attached, inconceivably it seemed, to the thin, long bone of the arm smooth from the beginning to the middle. The head lay sideways on the pillow. Levin could see the scanty locks wet with sweat on the temples and tense, transparent-looking forehead.

'It cannot be that that fearful body was my brother Nikolay?' thought Levin. But he went closer, saw the face, and doubt became impossible. In spite of the terrible change in the face, Levin had only to glance at those eager eyes raised at his approach, only to catch the faint movement of the mouth under the sticky moustache, to realise the terrible truth that this death-like body was his living brother.

The glittering eyes looked sternly and reproachfully at his brother as he drew near. And immediately this glance established a living relationship between living men. Levin immediately felt the reproach in the eyes fixed on him, and felt remorse at his own happiness.

When Konstantin took him by the hand, Nikolay smiled. The smile was faint, scarcely perceptible, and in spite of the smile the stern expression of the eyes was unchanged.

'You did not expect to find me like this,' he articulated with effort.

'Yes . . . no,' said Levin, hesitating over his words. 'How was it you didn't let me know before, that is, at the time of my wedding? I made inquirics in all directions.'

He had to talk so as not to be silent, and he did not know what to say, especially as his brother made no reply, and simply stared without dropping his eyes, and evidently penetrated to the inner meaning of each word. Levin told his brother that his wife had come with him. Nikolay expressed pleasure, but said he was afraid of frightening her by his condition. A silence followed. Suddenly Nikolay stirred, and began to say something. Levin expected something of peculiar gravity and importance from the expression of his face, but Nikolay began speaking of his health. He found fault with the doctor, regretting he had not a celebrated Moscow doctor. Levin saw that he still hoped.

Seizing the first moment of silence, Levin got up, anxious to escape, if only for an instant, from his agonising emotion, and said that he would go and fetch his wife.

'Very well, and I'll tell her to tidy up here. It's dirty and stinking here, I expect. Marya! clear up the room,' the sick man said with effort. 'Oh, and when you've cleared up, go away yourself,' he added, looking inquiringly at his brother.

Levin made no answer. Going out into the corridor, he stopped short. He had said he would fetch his wife, but now, taking stock of the emotion he was feeling, he decided that he would try on the contrary to persuade her not to go in to the sick man. 'Why should she suffer as I am suffering?' he thought.

'Well, how is he?' Kitty asked with a frightened face.

'Oh, it's awful, it's awful! What did you come for?' said Levin.

Kitty was silent for a few seconds, looking timidly and ruefully at her husband; then she went up and took him by the elbow with both hands.

'Kostya! take me to him; it will be easier for us to bear it together. You only take me, take me to him, please, and go away,' she said. 'You must understand that for me to see you, and not to see him, is far more painful. There I might be a help to you and to him. Please, let me!' she besought her husband, as though the happiness of her life depended on it.

Levin was obliged to agree, and regaining his composure, and completely forgetting about Marya Nikolaevna by now, he went again in to his brother with Kitty.

Stepping lightly, and continually glancing at her husband, showing him a valorous and sympathetic face, Kitty went into the sick-room, and, turning without haste, noiselessly closed the door. With inaudible steps she went quickly to the sick man's bedside, and going up so that he had not to turn his head, she immediately clasped in her fresh young hand the skeleton of his huge hand, pressed it, and began speaking with that soft eagerness, sympathetic and not jarring, which is peculiar to women.

'We have met, though we were not acquainted, at Soden,' she said. 'You never thought I was to be your sister?'

'You would not have recognised me?' he said, with a radiant smile at her entrance.

'Yes, I should. What a good thing you let us know! Not a day has passed that Kostya has not mentioned you, and been anxious.'

But the sick man's interest did not last long.

Before she had finished speaking, there had come back into his face the stern, reproachful expression of the dying man's envy of the living.

'I am afraid you are not quite comfortable here,' she said, turning away from his fixed stare, and looking about the room. 'We must ask about another room,' she said to her husband, 'so that we might be nearer.'

XVIII

LEVIN could not look calmly at his brother; he could not himself be natural and calm in his presence. When he went in to the sick man, his eyes and his attention were unconsciously dimmed, and he did not see and did not distinguish the details of his brother's position. He smelt the awful odour, saw the dirt, disorder, and miserable condition, and heard the groans, and felt that nothing could be done to help. It never entered his head to analyse the details of the sick man's situation, to consider how that body was lying under the quilt, how those emaciated legs and thighs and spine were lying huddled up, and whether they could not be made more comfortable, whether anything could not be done to make things, if not better, at least less bad. It made his blood run cold when he began to think of all these details. He was absolutely convinced that nothing could be done to prolong his brother's life or to relieve his suffering. But a sense of his regarding all aid as out of the question was felt by the sick man, and exasperated him. And this made it still more painful for Levin. To be in the sick-room was agony to him, not to be there still worse. And he was continually, on various pretexts, going out of the room, and coming in again, because he was unable to remain alone.

But Kitty thought, and felt, and acted quite differently. On seeing the sick man, she pitied him. And pity in her womanly heart did not arouse at all that feeling of horror and loathing that it aroused in her husband, but a desire to act, to find out all the details of his state, and to remedy them. And since she had not the slightest doubt that it was her duty to help him, she had no doubt either that it was possible, and immediately set to work. The very details, the mere thought of which reduced her husband to terror, immediately engaged her attention. She sent for the doctor, sent to the chemist's, set the maid who had come with her and Marya Nikolaevna to sweep and dust and scrub; she herself washed up something, washed out something else, laid something under the quilt. Something was by her directions brought into the sick-room, something else was carried out. She herself went several times to her room, regardless of the men she met in the corridor, got out and brought in sheets, pillow-cases, towels, and shirts.

The waiter, who was busy with a party of engineers dining in the dining-hall, came several times with an irate countenance in answer to her summons, and could not avoid carrying out her orders, as she gave them with such gracious insistence that there was no evading her. Levin did not approve of all this; he did not believe it would be any good to the patient. Above all he was afraid the patient would be angry at it. But the sick man, though he seemed and was indifferent about it, was not angry, but only abashed, and on the whole as it were interested in what she was doing with him. Coming back from the doctor to whom Kitty had sent him, Levin, on opening the door, came upon the sick man at the instant when, by Kitty's directions, they were changing his linen. The long white ridge of his spine, with the huge, prominent, shoulder-blades and jutting ribs and vertebrae, was bare, and Marya Nikolaevna and the waiter were struggling with the sleeve of the night-shirt, and could not get the long, limp arm into it. Kitty, hurriedly closing the door after Levin, was not looking that way; but the sick man groaned, and she moved rapidly towards him.

'Make haste,' she said.

'Oh, don't you come,' said the sick man angrily. 'I'll do it myself....'

'What say?' queried Marya Nikolaevna. But Kitty heard and saw he was ashamed and uncomfortable at being naked before her.

'I'm not looking, I'm not looking!' she said, putting the arm in. 'Marya Nikolaevna, you come this side, you do it,' she added.

'Please go for me, there's a little bottle in my small bag,' she said, turning to her husband, 'you know, in the side pocket; bring it, please, and meanwhile they'll finish clearing up here.'

Returning with the bottle, Levin found the sick man settled comfortably and everything about him completely changed. The heavy smell was replaced by the smell of aromatic vinegar, which Kitty with pouting lips and puffed-out, rosy cheeks was squirting through a little pipe. There was no dust visible anywhere, a rug was laid by the bedside. On the table stood medicine bottles and decanters tidily arranged, and the linen needed was folded up there, and Kitty's *broderie anglaise*. On the other table by the patient's bed there were candles and drink and powders. The sick man himself, washed and combed, lay in clean sheets on high raised pillows, in a clean night-shirt with a white collar about his astoundingly thin neck, and with a new expression of hope looked fixedly at Kitty.

The doctor brought by Levin, and found by him at the club, was not the one who had been attending Nikolay Levin, as the patient was dissatisfied with him. The new doctor took up a stethoscope and sounded the patient, shook his head, prescribed medicine, and with extreme minuteness explained first how to take the medicine and then what diet was to be kept to. He advised eggs, raw or hardly cooked, and seltzer water, with warm milk at a certain temperature. When the doctor had gone away the sick man said something to his brother, of which Levin could distinguish only the last words: 'Your Katya.' By the expression with which he gazed at her, Levin saw that he was praising her. He called indeed to Katya, as he called her.

'I'm much better already,' he said. 'Why, with you I should have got well long ago. How nice it is!' he took her hand and drew it towards his lips, but as though afraid she would dislike it he changed his mind, let it go, and only stroked it. Kitty took his hand in both hers and pressed it.

'Now turn me over on the left side and go to bed,' he said.

No one could make out what he said but Kitty; she alone understood. She understood because she was all the while mentally keeping watch on what he needed.

'On the other side,' she said to her husband, 'he always sleeps on that side. Turn him over, it's so disagreeable calling the servants. I'm not strong enough. Can you?' she said to Marya Nikolaevna.

'I'm afraid not,' answered Marya Nikolaevna.

Terrible as it was to Levin to put his arms round that terrible body, to take hold of that under the quilt, of which he preferred to know nothing, under his wife's influence he made his resolute face that she knew so well, and putting his arms into the bed took hold of the body, but in spite of his own strength he was struck by the strange heaviness of those powerless limbs. While he was turning him over, conscious of the huge, emaciated arm about his neck, Kitty swiftly and noiselessly turned the pillow, beat it up and settled in it the sick man's head, smoothing back his hair, which was sticking again to his moist brow.

The sick man kept his brother's hand in his own. Levin felt that he meant to do something with his hand and was pulling it somewhere. Levin yielded with a sinking heart: yes, he drew it to his mouth and kissed it. Levin, shaking with sobs and unable to articulate a word, went out of the room.

XIX

'THOU hast hid these things from the wise and prudent, and hast revealed them unto babes.' So Levin thought about his wife as he talked to her that evening.

Levin thought of the text, not because he considered himself 'wise and prudent.' He did not so consider himself, but he could not help knowing that he had more intellect than his wife and Agafea Mihalovna, and he could not help knowing that when he thought of death, he thought with all the force of his intellect. He knew too that the brains of many great men, whose thoughts he had read, had brooded over death and yet knew not a hundredth part of what his wife and Agafea

Mihalovna knew about it. Different as those two women were, Agafea Mihalovna and Katya, as his brother Nikolay had called her, and as Levin particularly liked to call her now, they were quite alike in this. Both knew, without a shade of doubt, what sort of thing life was and what was death, and though neither of them could have answered, and would even not have understood the questions that presented themselves to Levin, both had no doubt of the significance of this event, and were precisely alike in their way of looking at it, which they shared with millions of people. The proof that they knew for a certainty the nature of death lay in the fact that they knew without a second of hesitation how to deal with the dying, and were not frightened of them. Levin and other men like him, though they could have said a great deal about death, obviously did not know this since they were afraid of death, and were absolutely at a loss what to do when people were dying. If Levin had been alone now with his brother Nikolay, he would have looked at him with terror, and with still greater terror waited, and would not have known what else to do.

More than that, he did not know what to say, how to look, how to move. To talk of outside things seemed to him shocking, impossible, to talk of death and depressing subjects—also impossible. To be silent, also impossible. 'If I look at him he will think I am studying him, I am afraid; if I don't look at him, he'll think I'm thinking of other things. If I walk on tiptoe, he will be vexed; to tread firmly, I'm ashamed.' Kitty evidently did not think of herself, and had no time to think about herself: she was thinking about him because she knew something, and all went well. She told him about herself even and about her wedding, and smiled and sympathised with him and petted him, and talked of cases of recovery and all went well; so then she must know. The proof that her behaviour and Agafea Mihalovna's was not instinctive, animal, irrational, was that apart from the physical treatment, the relief of suffering, both Agafea Mihalovna and Kitty required for the dying man something else more important than the physical treatment, and something which had nothing in common with physical conditions. Agafea Mihalovna, speaking of the man just dead, had said: 'Well, thank God, he took the sacrament and received absolution; God grant each one of us such a death.' Katya in just the same way, besides all her care about linen, bedsores, drink, found time the very first day to persuade the sick man of the necessity of taking the sacrament and receiving absolution.

On getting back from the sickroom to their own two rooms for the night, Levin sat with hanging head not knowing what to do. Not to speak of supper, of preparing for bed, of considering what they were going to do, he could not even talk to his wife; he was ashamed to. Kitty, on the contrary, was more active than usual. She was even livelier than usual. She ordered supper to be brought, herself unpacked their things, and herself helped to make the beds, and did not even forget to sprinkle them with Persian powder. She showed that alertness, that swiftness of reflection which comes out in men before a battle, in conflict, in the dangerous and decisive moments of life—those moments when a man shows once and for all his value, and that all his past has not been wasted but has been a preparation for these moments.

Everything went rapidly in her hands, and before it was twelve o'clock all their things were arranged cleanly and tidily in her rooms, in such a way that the hotel rooms seemed like home: the beds were made, brushes, combs, looking-glasses were put out, table-napkins were spread.

Levin felt that it was unpardonable to eat, to sleep, to talk even now, and it seemed to him that every movement he made was unseemly. She arranged the brushes, but she did it all so that there was nothing shocking in it.

They could neither of them eat, however, and for a long while they could not sleep, and did not even go to bed.

'I am very glad I persuaded him to receive extreme unction to-morrow,' she said, sitting in her dressing-jacket before her folding looking-glass, combing her soft, fragrant hair with a fine comb. 'I have never seen it, but I know, mamma has told me, there are prayers said for recovery.'

'Do you suppose he can possibly recover?' said Levin, watching a slender tress at the back of her round little head that was continually hidden when she passed the comb through the front.

'I asked the doctor; he said he couldn't live more than three days. But can they be sure? I'm very glad, anyway, that I persuaded him,' she said, looking askance at her husband through her hair. 'Anything is possible,' she added with that peculiar, rather sly expression that was always in her face when she spoke of religion.

Since their conversation about religion when they were engaged neither of them had ever started a discussion of the subject, but she performed all the ceremonies of going to church, saying her prayers, and so on, always with the unvarying conviction that this ought to be so. In spite of his assertion to the contrary, she was firmly persuaded that he was as much a Christian as she, and indeed a far better one; and all that he said about it was simply one of his absurd masculine freaks, just as he would say about her *broderie anglaise*, that good people patch holes but that she cut them on purpose, and so on.

'Yes, you see this woman, Marya Nikolaevna, did not know how to manage all this,' said Levin. 'And . . . I must own I'm very, very glad you came. You are such purity that . . .' He took her hand and did not kiss it (to kiss her hand in such closeness to death seemed to him improper); he merely squeezed it with a penitent air, looking at her brightening eyes.

'It would have been miserable for you to be alone,' she said, and, lifting her hands, which hid her cheeks flushing with pleasure, twisted her coil of hair on the nape of her neck and pinned it there. 'No,' she went on, 'she did not know how. . . . Luckily I learned a lot at Soden.'

'Surely there are not people there so ill?'

'Worse.'

'What's so awful to me is that I can't see him as he was when he was young. You would not believe how charming he was as a youth, but I did not understand him then.'

'I can quite, quite believe it. How I feel that we might have been friends!' she said; and, distressed at what she had said, she looked round at her husband, and tears came into her eyes.

'Yes, *might have been,*' he said mournfully. 'He's just one of those people of whom they say they're not for this world.'

'But we have many days before us; we must go to bed,' said Kitty, glancing at her tiny watch.

XX

THE next day the sick man received the sacrament and extreme unction. During the ceremony Nikolay Levin prayed fervently. His great eyes, fastened on the holy image that was set out on a card-table covered with a coloured napkin, expressed such passionate prayer and hope that it was awful to Levin to see it. Levin knew that this passionate prayer and hope would only make him feel more bitterly parting from the life he so loved. Levin knew his brother and the workings of his intellect: he knew that his unbelief came not from life being easier for him without faith, but had grown up because step by step the contemporary scientific interpretation of natural phenomena crushed out the possibility of faith; and so he knew that his present return was not a legitimate one, brought about by way of the same working of his intellect, but simply a temporary, interested return to faith in a desperate hope of recovery. Levin knew too that Kitty had strengthened this hope by accounts of the marvellous recoveries she had heard of. Levin knew all this; and it was agonisingly painful to him to behold the supplicating, hopeful eyes and the emaciated wrist, lifted with difficulty, making the sign of the cross on the tense brow, and the prominent shoulders and hollow, gasping chest, which one could not feel consistent with the life the sick man was praying for. During the sacrament Levin did what he, an unbeliever, had done a thousand times. He said, addressing God, 'If Thou dost exist, make this man to recover' (of course this same thing has been repeated many times), 'and Thou wilt save him and me.'

After extreme unction the sick man became suddenly much better. He did not cough once in the course of an hour, smiled, kissed Kitty's hand, thanking her with tears, and said he was comfortable, free from pain, and that he felt strong and had an appetite. He even raised himself when his soup was brought, and asked for a cutlet as well. Hopelessly ill as he was, obvious as it was at the first glance that he could not recover, Levin and Kitty were for that hour both in the same state of excitement, happy, though fearful of being mistaken.

'Is he better?'

'Yes, much.'

'It's wonderful.'

'There's nothing wonderful in it.'

'Anyway he's better,' they said in a whisper, smiling to one another.

This self-deception was not of long duration. The sick man fell into a quiet sleep, but he was waked up half an hour later by his cough. And all at once every hope vanished in those about him and in himself. The reality of his suffering crushed all hopes in Levin and Kitty and in the sick man himself, leaving no doubt, no memory even of past hopes.

Without referring to what he had believed in half an hour before, as though ashamed even to recall it, he asked for iodine to inhale in a bottle covered with perforated paper. Levin gave him the bottle, and the same look of passionate hope with which he had taken the sacrament was now fastened on his brother, demanding from him the confirmation of the doctor's words that inhaling iodine worked wonders.

'Is Katya not here?' he gasped, looking round while Levin reluctantly assented to the doctor's words. 'No; so I can say it. . . . It was for her sake I went through that farce. She's so sweet; but you and I can't deceive ourselves. This is what I believe in,' he said, and, squeezing the bottle in his bony hand, he began breathing over it.

At eight o'clock in the evening Levin and his wife were drinking tea in their room, when Marya Nikolaevna ran in to them breathlessly. She was pale, and her lips were quivering. 'He is dying!' she whispered. 'I'm afraid he will die this minute.'

Both of them ran to him. He was sitting raised up with one elbow on the bed, his long back bent, and his head hanging low.

'How do you feel?' Levin asked in a whisper, after a silence.

'I feel I'm setting off,' Nikolay said with difficulty, but with extreme distinctness, screwing the words out of himself. He did not raise his head, but simply turned his eyes upwards, without their reaching his brother's face. 'Katya, go away!' he added.

Levin jumped up, and with a peremptory whisper made her go out.

'I'm setting off,' he said again.

'Why do you think so?' said Levin, so as to say something.

'Because I'm setting off,' he repeated, as though he had a liking for the phrase. 'It's the end.'

Marya Nikolaevna went up to him.

'You had better lie down; you'd be easier,' she said.

'I shall lie down soon enough,' he pronounced slowly, 'when I'm dead,' he said sarcastically, wrathfully. 'Well, you can lay me down if you like.'

Levin laid his brother on his back, sat down beside him, and gazed at his face, holding his breath. The dying man lay with closed eyes, but the muscles twitched from time to time on his forehead, as with one thinking deeply and intensely. Levin involuntarily thought with him of what it was that was happening to him now, but in spite of all his mental efforts to go along with him he saw by the expression of that calm, stern face that for the dying man all was growing clearer and clearer that was still as dark as ever for Levin.

'Yes, yes, so,' the dying man articulated slowly at intervals. 'Wait a little.' He was silent. 'Right!' he pronounced all at once reassuringly, as though all were solved for him. 'O Lord!' he murmured, and sighed deeply.

Marya Nikolaevna felt his feet. 'They're getting cold,' she whispered.

For a long while, a very long while it seemed to Levin, the sick man lay motionless. But he was still alive, and from time to time he sighed. Levin by now was exhausted from mental strain. He felt that, with no mental effort, could he understand what it was that was *right*. He could not even think of the problem of death itself, but with no will of his own thoughts kept coming to him of what he had to do next; closing the dead man's eyes, dressing him, ordering the coffin. And, strange to say, he felt utterly cold, and was not conscious of sorrow nor of loss, less still of pity for his brother. If he had any feeling for his brother at that moment, it was envy for the knowledge the dying man had now that he could not have.

A long time more he sat over him so, continually expecting the end. But the end did not come. The door opened and Kitty appeared. Levin got up to stop her. But at the moment he was getting up, he caught the sound of the dying man stirring.

'Don't go away,' said Nikolay, and held out his hand. Levin gave him his, and angrily waved to his wife to go away.

With the dying man's hand in his hand, he sat for half an hour, an hour, another hour. He did not think of death at all now. He wondered what Kitty was doing; who lived in the next room; whether the doctor lived in a house of his own. He longed for food and for sleep. He cautiously drew away his hand and felt the feet. The feet were cold, but the sick man was still breathing. Levin tried again to move away on tiptoe, but the sick man stirred again and said: 'Don't go.'

. . . . . .

The dawn came; the sick man's condition was unchanged. Levin stealthily withdrew his hand, and without looking at the dying man, went off to his own room and went to sleep. When he woke up, instead of news of his brother's death which he expected, he learned that the sick man had returned to his earlier condition. He had begun sitting up again, coughing, had begun eating again, talking again, and again had ceased to talk of death, again had begun to express hope of his recovery, and had become more irritable and gloomier than ever. No one, neither his brother nor Kitty, could soothe him. He was angry with everyone, and said nasty things to everyone, reproached everyone for his sufferings, and insisted that they should get him a celebrated doctor from Moscow. To all inquiries made him as to how he felt, he made the same answer with an expression of vindictive reproachfulness: 'I'm suffering horribly, intolerably!'

The sick man was suffering more and more, especially from bedsores, which it was impossible now to remedy, and grew more and more angry with every one about him, blaming them for everything, and especially for not having brought him a doctor from Moscow. Kitty tried in every possible way to relieve him, to soothe him; but it was all in vain, and Levin saw that she herself was exhausted both physically and morally, though she would not admit it. The sense of death, which had been evoked in all by his taking leave of life on the night when he had sent for his brother, was broken up. Every one knew that he must inevitably die soon, that he was half dead already. Everyone wished for nothing but that he should die as soon as possible, and every one, concealing this, gave him medicines, tried to find remedies and doctors, and deceived him and themselves and each other. All this was falsehood, disgusting, irreverent deceit. And owing to the bent of his character, and because he loved the dying man more than anyone else did, Levin was most painfully conscious of this deceit.

Levin, who had long been possessed by the idea of reconciling his brothers, at least in face of death, had written to his brother Sergey Ivanovitch, and having received an answer from him, he read this letter to the sick man. Sergey Ivanovitch wrote that he could not come himself, and in touching terms he begged his brother's forgiveness.

The sick man said nothing.

'What am I to write to him?' said Levin. 'I hope you are not angry with him?'

'No, not the least!' Nikolay answered, vexed at the question. 'Tell him to send me a doctor.'

Three more days of agony followed; the sick man was still in the same condition. The sense of longing for his death was felt by everyone now at the mere sight of him, by the waiters and the hotel-keeper and all the people staying in the hotel, and the doctor and Marya Nikolaevna and Levin and Kitty. The sick man alone did not express this feeling, but on the contrary was furious at their not getting him doctors, and went on taking medicine and talking of life. Only at rare moments, when the opium gave him an instant's relief from the never-ceasing pain, he would sometimes, half asleep, utter what was even more intense in his heart than in all the others: 'Oh, if it were only the end!' or 'When will it be over?'

His sufferings, steadily growing more intense, did their work and prepared him for death. There was no position in which he was not in pain, there was not a minute in which he was unconscious of it, not a limb, not a part of his body that did not ache and cause him agony. Even the memories, the impressions, the thought of this body awakened in him now the same aversions as the body itself. The sight of other people, their remarks, his own reminiscenses, everything was for him a source of agony. Those about him felt this, and instinctively did not allow themselves to move freely, to talk, to express their wishes before him. All his life was merged in the one feeling of suffering and desire to be rid of it.

There was evidently coming over him that revulsion that would make him look upon death as the goal of his desires, as happiness. Hitherto each individual desire, aroused by suffering or privation, such as hunger, fatigue, thirst, had been satisfied by some bodily function giving pleasure. But now no physical craving or suffering received relief, and the effort to relieve them only caused fresh suffering. And so all desires were merged in one—the desire to be rid of all his sufferings and their source, the body. But he had no words to express this desire of deliverance, and so he did not speak of it, and from habit asked for the satisfaction of desires which could not now be satisfied. 'Turn me over on the other side,' he would say, and immediately after he would ask to be turned back again as before. 'Give me some broth. Take away the broth. Talk of something: why are you silent?' And directly they began to talk he would close his eyes, and would show weariness, indifference, and loathing.

On the tenth day from their arrival at the town, Kitty was unwell. She suffered from headache and sickness, and she could not get up all the morning.

The doctor opined that the indisposition arose from fatigue and excitement, and prescribed rest.

After dinner, however, Kitty got up and went as usual with her work to the sick man. He looked at her sternly when she came in, and smiled contemptuously when she said she had been unwell. That day he was continually blowing his nose, and groaning piteously.

'How do you feel?' she asked him.

'Worse,' he articulated with difficulty. 'In pain!'

'In pain, where?'

'Everywhere.'

'It will be over today, you will see,' said Marya Nikolaevna. Though it was said in a whisper, the sick man, whose hearing Levin had noticed was very keen, must have heard. Levin said hush to her, and looked round at the sick man. Nikolay had heard; but these words produced no effect on him. His eyes had still the same intense, reproachful look.

'Why do you think so?' Levin asked her, when she had followed him into the corridor.

'He has begun picking at himself,' said Marya Nikolaevna.

'How do you mean?'

'Like this,' she said, tugging at the folds of her woollen skirt. Levin noticed, indeed, that all that day the patient pulled at himself, as it were, trying to snatch something away.

Marya Nikolaevna's prediction came true. Towards night the sick man was not able to lift his hands, and could only gaze before him with the same intensely concentrated expression in his eyes. Even when his brother or Kitty bent over him, so that he could see them, he looked just the same. Kitty sent for the priest to read the prayer for the dying.

While the priest was reading it, the dying man did not show any sign of life; his eyes were closed. Levin, Kitty, and Marya Nikolaevna stood at the bedside. The priest had not quite finished reading the prayer when the dying man stretched, sighed, and opened his eyes. The priest, on finishing the prayer, put the cross to the cold forehead, then slowly returned it to the stand, and after standing for two minutes more in silence, he touched the huge, bloodless hand that was turning cold.

'He is gone,' said the priest, and would have moved away; but suddenly there was a faint stir in the moustaches of the dead man that seemed glued together, and quite distinctly in the hush they heard from the bottom of the chest the sharply defined sounds—

'Not quite . . . soon.'

And a minute later the face brightened, a smile came out under the moustaches, and the women who had gathered round began carefully laying out the corpse.

The sight of his brother, and the nearness of death, revived in Levin that sense of horror in face of the insoluble enigma, together with the nearness and inevitability of death, that had come upon him that autumn evening when his brother had come to him. This feeling was now even stronger than before; even less than before did he feel capable of apprehending the meaning of death, and its inevitability rose up before him more terrible than ever. But now, thanks to his wife's presence, that feeling did not reduce him to despair. In spite of death, he felt the need of life and love. He felt that love saved him from despair, and that this love, under the menace of despair, had become still stronger and purer. The one mystery of death, still unsolved, had scarcely passed before his eyes, when another mystery had arisen, as insoluble, urging him to love and to life.

The doctor confirmed his suppositions in regard to Kitty. Her indisposition was a symptom that she was with child.

XXI

FROM the moment when Alexey Alexandrovitch understood from his interviews with Betsy and with Stepan Arkadyevitch that all that was expected of him was to leave his wife in peace, without burdening her with his presence, and that his wife herself desired this, he felt so distraught that he could come to no decision of himself; he did not know himself what he wanted now, and putting himself in the hands of those who were so pleased to interest themselves in his affairs, he met everything with unqualified assent. It was only when Anna had left his house, and the English governess sent to ask him whether she should dine with him or separately, that for the first time he clearly comprehended his position, and was appalled by it. Most difficult of all in this position was the fact that he could not in any way connect and reconcile his past with what was now. It was not the past when he had lived happily with his wife that troubled him. The transition from that past to a knowledge of his wife's unfaithfulness he had lived through miserably already; that state was painful, but he could understand it. If his wife had then, on declaring to him her unfaithfulness, left him, he would have been wounded, unhappy, but he would not have been in the hopeless position—incomprehensible to himself—in which he felt himself now. He could not now reconcile his immediate past, his tenderness, his love for his sick wife, and for the other man's child with what was now the case, that is with the fact that, as it were, in return for all this he now found himself alone, put to shame, a laughing-stock, needed by no one, and despised by everyone.

For the first two days after his wife's departure Alexey Alexandrovitch received applicants for assistance and his chief secretary drove to the committee, and went down to dinner in the dining-room as usual. Without giving himself a reason what he was doing, he strained every nerve of his being for those two days, simply to preserve an appearance of composure, and even of indifference. Answering inquiries about the disposition of Anna Arkadyevna's rooms and belongings, he had exercised immense self-control to appear like a man in whose eyes what had occurred was not unforeseen nor out of the ordinary course of events, and he attained his aim; no one could have detected in him signs of despair. But on the second day after her departure, when Korney gave him a bill from a fashionable draper's shop, which Anna had forgotten to pay, and announced that the clerk from the shop was waiting, Alexey Alexandrovitch told him to show the clerk up.

'Excuse me, your excellency, for venturing to trouble you. But if you direct us to apply to her excellency, would you graciously oblige us with her address?'

Alexey Alexandrovitch pondered, as it seemed to the clerk, and all at once, turning round, he sat down to the table. Letting his head sink into his hands, he sat for a long while in that position, several times attempted to speak and stopped short. Korney, perceiving his master's emotion, asked the clerk to call another time. Left alone, Alexey Alexandrovitch recognised that he had not the strength to keep up the line of firmness and composure any longer. He gave orders for the carriage that was awaiting him to be taken back, and for no one to be admitted, and he did not go down to dinner.

He felt that he could not endure the weight of universal contempt and exasperation, which he had distinctly seen in the face of the clerk and of Korney, and of every one, without exception, whom he had met during those two days. He felt that he could not turn aside from himself the hatred of men, because that hatred did not come from his being bad (in that case he could have tried to be better), but from his being shamefully and repulsively unhappy. He knew that for this, for the very fact that his heart was torn with grief, they would be merciless to him. He felt that men would crush him as dogs strangle a torn dog yelping with pain. He knew that his sole means of security against people was to hide his wounds from them, and instinctively he tried to do this for two days, but now he felt incapable of keeping up the unequal struggle.

His despair was even intensified by the consciousness that he was utterly alone in his sorrow. In all Petersburg there was not a human being to whom he could express what he was feeling, who would feel for him, not as a high official, not as a member of society, but simply as a suffering man; indeed he had not such a one in the whole world.

Alexey Alexandrovitch grew up an orphan. There were two brothers. They did not remember their father, and their mother died when Alexey Alexandrovitch was ten years old. The property was a small one. Their uncle, Karenin, a government official of high standing, at one time a favourite of the late Tsar, had brought them up.

On completing high school and university courses with medals, Alexey Alexandrovitch had, with his uncle's aid, immediately started in a prominent position in the service, and from that time forward he had devoted himself exclusively to political ambition. In the high school and the university, and afterwards in the service, Alexey Alexandrovitch had never formed a close friendship with anyone. His brother had been the person nearest to his heart, but he had a post in the Ministry of Foreign Affairs, and was always abroad, where he had died shortly after Alexey Alexandrovitch's marriage.

While he was governor of a province, Anna's aunt, a wealthy provincial lady, had thrown him—middle-aged as he was, though young for a governor—with her niece, and had succeeded in putting him in such a position that he had either to declare himself or to leave the town. Alexey Alexandrovitch was not long in hesitation. There were at the time as many reasons for the step as against it, and there was no overbalancing consideration to outweigh his invariable rule of abstaining when in doubt. But Anna's aunt had through a common acquaintance insinuated that he had already compromised the girl, and that he was in honour bound to make her an offer. He made the offer, and concentrated on his betrothed and wife all the feeling of which he was capable.

The attachment he felt to Anna precluded in his heart every need of intimate relations with others. And now among all his acquaintances he had not one friend. He had plenty of so-called connections, but no friendships. Alexey Alexandrovitch had plenty of people whom he could invite to dinner, to whose sympathy he could appeal in any public affair he was concerned about, whose interest he could reckon upon for anyone he wished to help, with whom he could candidly discuss other people's business and affairs of state. But his relations with these people were confined to one clearly defined channel, and had a certain routine from which it was impossible to depart. There was one man, a comrade of his at the university, with whom he had made friends later, and with whom he could have spoken of a personal sorrow; but this friend had a post in the Department of Education in a remote part of Russia. Of the people in Petersburg the most intimate and most possible were his chief secretary and his doctor.

Mihail Vassilievitch Sludin, the chief secretary, was a straightforward, intelligent, good-hearted, and conscientious man, and Alexey Alexandrovitch was aware of his personal goodwill. But their five years of official work together seemed to have put a barrier between them that cut off warmer relations.

After signing the papers brought him, Alexey Alexandrovitch had sat for a long while in silence, glancing at Mihail Vassilievitch, and several times he attempted to speak, but could not. He had already prepared the phrase: 'You have heard of my trouble?' But he ended by saying, as usual: 'So you'll get this ready for me?' and with that dismissed him.

The other person was the doctor, who had also a kindly feeling for him; but there had long existed a taciturn understanding between them that both were weighed down by work, and always in a hurry.

Of his women-friends, foremost among them Countess Lidia Ivanovna, Alexey Alexandrovitch never thought. All women, simply as women, were terrible and distasteful to him.

XXII

ALEXEY ALEXANDROVITCH had forgotten the Countess Lidia Ivanovna, but she had not forgotten him. At the bitterest moment of his lonely despair she came to him, and without waiting to be announced, walked straight into his study. She found him as he was sitting with his head in both hands.

'*J'ai forcé la consigne,*' she said, walking in with rapid steps and breathing hard with excitement and rapid exercise. 'I have heard all! Alexey Alexandrovitch! Dear friend!' she went on, warmly squeezing his hand in both of hers and gazing with her fine pensive eyes into his.

Alexey Alexandrovitch, frowning, got up, and disengaging his hand, moved her a chair.

'Won't you sit down, countess? I'm seeing no one because I'm unwell, countess,' he said, and his lips twitched.

'Dear friend!' repeated Countess Lidia Ivanovna, never taking her eyes off his, and suddenly her eyebrows rose at the inner corners, describing a triangle on her forehead, her ugly yellow face became still uglier, but Alexey Alexandrovitch felt that she was sorry for him and was preparing to cry. And he too was softened; he snatched her plump hand and proceeded to kiss it.

'Dear friend!' she said in a voice breaking with emotion. 'You ought not to give way to grief. Your sorrow is a great one, but you ought to find consolation.'

'I am crushed, I am annihilated, I am no longer a man!' said Alexey Alexandrovitch, letting go her hand, but still gazing into her brimming eyes. 'My position is so awful because I can find nowhere, I cannot find within me strength to support me.'

'You will find support; seek it—not in me, though I beseech you to believe in my friendship,' she said, with a sigh. 'Our support is love, that love that He has vouchsafed us. His burden is light,' she said, with the look of ecstasy Alexey Alexandrovitch knew so well. 'He will be your support and your succour.'

Although there was in these words a flavour of that sentimental emotion at her own lofty feelings, and that new mystical fervour which had lately gained ground in Petersburg, and which seemed to Alexey Alexandrovitch disproportionate, still it was pleasant to him to hear this now.

'I am weak. I am crushed. I foresaw nothing, and now I understand nothing.'

'Dear friend,' repeated Lidia Ivanovna.

'It's not the loss of what I have not now, it's not that!' pursued Alexey Alexandrovitch. 'I do not grieve for that. But I cannot help feeling humiliated before other people for the position I am placed in. It is wrong, but I can't help it, I can't help it.'

'Not you it was performed that noble act of forgiveness, at which I was moved to ecstacy, and every one else too, but He, working within your heart,' said Countess Lidia Ivanovna, raising her eyes rapturously, 'and so you cannot be ashamed of your act.'

Alexey Alexandrovitch knitted his brows, and crooking his hands, he cracked his fingers.

'One must know all the facts,' he said in his thin voice. 'A man's strength has its limits, countess, and I have reached my limits. The whole day I have had to be making arrangements, arrangements about household matters arising (he emphasised the word *arising*) from my new, solitary position. The servants, the governess, the accounts. . . . These pin-pricks have stabbed me to the heart, and I have not the strength to bear it. At dinner . . . yesterday, I was almost getting up from the dinner-table. I could not bear the way my son looked at me. He did not ask me the meaning of it all, but he wanted to ask, and I could not bear the look in his eyes. He was afraid to look at me, but that is not all . . .' Alexey Alexandrovitch would have referred to the bill that had been brought to him, but his voice shook, and he stopped. That bill on blue paper, for a hat and ribbons, he could not recall without a rush of self-pity.

'I understand, dear friend,' said Lidia Ivanovna. 'I understand it all. Succour and comfort you will find not in me, though I have come only to aid you if I can. If I could take from off you all these petty, humiliating cares . . . I understand that a woman's word, a woman's superintendence is needed. You will intrust it to me?'

Silently and gratefully Alexey Alexandrovitch pressed her hand.

'Together we will take care of Seryozha. Practical affairs are not my strong point. But I will set to work. I will be your housekeeper. Don't thank me. I do it not from myself . . .'

'I cannot help thanking you.'

'But, dear friend, do not give way to the feeling of which you spoke—being ashamed of what is the Christian's highest glory: *he who humbles himself shall be exalted*. And you cannot thank me. You must thank Him, and pray to Him for succour. In Him alone we find peace, consolation, salvation, and love,' she said, and turning her eyes heavenwards, she began praying, as Alexey Alexandrovitch gathered from her silence.

Alexey Alexandrovitch listened to her now, and those expressions which had seemed to him, if not distasteful, at least exaggerated, now seemed to him natural and consolatory. Alexey Alexandrovitch had disliked this new enthusiastic fervour. He was a believer, who was interested in religion primarily in its political aspect, and the new doctrine which ventured upon several new interpretations, just because it paved the way to discussion and analysis, was in principle disagreeable to him. He had hitherto taken up a cold and even antagonistic attitude to this new doctrine, and with Countess Lidia Ivanovna, who had been carried away by it, he had never argued, but by silence had assiduously parried her attempts to provoke him into argument. Now for the first time he heard her words with pleasure, and did not inwardly oppose them.

'I am very, very grateful to you both, for your deeds and for your words,' he said, when she had finished praying.

Countess Lidia Ivanovna once more pressed both her friend's hands.

'Now I will enter upon my duties,' she said with a smile after a pause, as she wiped away the trace of tears. 'I am going to Seryozha. Only in the last extremity I shall apply to you.' And she got up and went out.

Countess Lidia Ivanovna went into Seryozha's part of the house, and dropping tears on the scared child's cheeks, she told him that his father was a saint and his mother was dead.

Countess Lidia Ivanovna kept her promise. She did actually take upon herself the care of the organisation and management of Alexey Alexandrovitch's household. But she had not overstated the case when saying that practical affairs were not her strong point. All her arrangements had to be modified because they could not be carried out, and they were modified by Korney, Alexey Alevandrovitch's valet, who, though no one was aware of the fact, now managed Karenin's household, and quietly and discreetly reported to his master while he was dressing all it was necessary for him to know. But Lidia Ivanovna's help was none the less real; she gave Alexey Alexandrovitch moral support in the consciousness of her love and respect for him, and still more, as it was soothing to her to believe, in that she almost turned him to Christianity—that is, from an indifferent and apathetic believer she turned him into an ardent and steadfast adherent of the new interpretation of Christian doctrine, which had been gaining ground of late in Petersburg. It was easy for Alexey Alexandrovitch to believe in this teaching. Alexey Alexandrovitch, like Lidia Ivanovna indeed, and others who shared their views, was completely devoid of vividness of imagination, that spiritual faculty in virtue of which the conceptions evoked by the imagination become so vivid that they must needs be in harmony with other conceptions, and with actual fact. He saw nothing impossible and inconceivable in the idea that death, though existing for unbelievers, did not exist for him, and that, as he was possessed of the most perfect faith, of the measure of which he was himself the judge, therefore there was no sin in his soul, and he was experiencing complete salvation here on earth.

It is true that the erroneousness and shallowness of this conception of his faith was dimly perceptible to Alexey Alexandrovitch, and he knew that when, without the slightest idea that his forgiveness was the action of a higher power, he had surrendered directly to the feeling of forgiveness, he had felt more happiness than now when he was thinking every instant that Christ was in his heart, and that in signing official papers he was doing His will. But for Alexey Alexandrovitch it was a necessity to think in that way; it was such a necessity for him in his humiliation to have some elevated standpoint, however imaginary, from which, looked down upon by all, he could look down on others, that he clung, as to his one salvation, to his delusion of salvation.

XXIII

THE Countess Lidia Ivanovna had, as a very young and sentimental girl, been married to a wealthy man of high rank, a very good-natured, jovial, and extremely dissipated rake. Two months after marriage her husband abandoned her, and her impassioned protestations of affection he met with a sarcasm and even hostility that people knowing the count's good heart, and seeing no defects in the sentimental Lidia, were at a loss to explain. Though they were divorced and lived apart, yet whenever the husband met the wife, he invariably behaved to her with the same malignant irony, the cause of which was incomprehensible.

Countess Lidia Ivanovna had long given up being in love with her husband, but from that time she had never given up being in love with someone. She was in love with several people at once, both men and women; she had been in love with almost everyone who had been particularly distinguished in any way. She was in love with all the new princes and princesses who married into the Imperial family; she had been in love with a high dignitary of the Church, a vicar, and a parish priest; she had been in love with a journalist, three Slavophils, the Komissarov, with a minister, a doctor, an English missionary, and Karenin. All these passions, constantly waning or growing more ardent, did not prevent her from keeping up the most extended and complicated relations with the court and fashionable society. But from the time that after Karenin's trouble she took him under her special protection, from the time that she set to work in Karenin's household looking after his welfare, she felt that all her other attachments were not the real thing, and that she was now genuinely in love, and with no one but Karenin. The feeling she now experienced for him seemed to her stronger than any of her former feelings. Analysing her feeling, and comparing it with former passions, she distinctly perceived that she would not have been in love with Komissarov if he had not saved the life of the Tsar, that she would not have been in love with Ristitch-Kudzhitsky if there had been no Slavonic question, but that she loved Karenin for himself, for his lofty, uncomprehended soul, for the sweet —to her—high notes of his voice, for his drawling intonation, his weary eyes, his character, and his soft white hands with their swollen veins. She was not simply overjoyed at meeting him, but she sought in his face signs of the impression she was making on him. She tried to please him, not by her words only, but in her whole person. For his sake it was that she now lavished more care on her dress than before. She caught herself in reveries on what might have been, if she had not been married and he had been free. She blushed with emotion when he came into the room, she could not repress a smile of rapture when he said anything amiable to her.

For several days now Countess Lidia Ivanovna had been in a state of intense excitement. She had learned that Anna and Vronsky were in Petersburg. Alexey Alexandrovitch must be saved from seeing her, he must be saved even from the torturing knowledge that that awful woman was in the same town with him, and that he might meet her any minute.

Lidia Ivanovna made inquiries through her friends as to what those *infamous people*, as she called Anna and Vronsky, intended doing, and she endeavoured so to guide every movement of her friend during those days that he could not come across them. The young adjutant, an acquaintance of Vronsky, through whom she obtained her information, and who hoped through Countess Lidia Ivanovna to obtain a concession, told her that they had finished their business and were going away next day. Lidia Ivanovna had already begun to calm down, when the next morning a note was brought her, the handwriting of which she recognised with horror. It was the handwriting of Anna Karenin. The envelope was of paper as thick as bark; on the oblong yellow paper there was a huge monogram, and the letter smelt of agreeable scent.

'Who brought it?'

'A commissionaire from the hotel.'

It was some time before Countess Lidia Ivanovna could sit down to read the letter. Her excitement brought on an attack of asthma, to which she was subject. When she had recovered her composure, she read the following letter in French:—

'MADAME LA COMTESSE,—The Christian feelings with which your heart is filled give me the, I feel, unpardonable boldness to write to you. I am miserable at being separated from my son. I entreat permission to see him once before my departure. Forgive me for recalling myself to your memory. I apply to you and not to Alexey Alexandrovitch, simply because I do not wish to cause that generous man to suffer in remembering me. Knowing your friendship for him, I know you will understand me. Could you send Seryozha to me, or should I come to the house at some fixed hour, or will you let me know when and where I could see him away from home? I do not anticipate a refusal, knowing the magnanimity of him with whom it rests. You cannot conceive the craving I have to see him, and so cannot conceive the gratitude your help will arouse in me.

ANNA.'

Everything in this letter exasperated Countess Lidia Ivanovna; its contents and the allusion to magnanimity, and especially its free and easy—as she considered—tone.

'Say that there is no answer,' said Countess Lidia Ivanovna, and immediately opening her blotting-book, she wrote to Alexey Alexandrovitch that she hoped to see him at one o'clock at the levee.

'I must talk with you of a grave and painful subject. There we will arrange where to meet. Best of all at my house, where I will order tea *as you like it*. Urgent. He lays the cross, but He gives the strength to bear it,' she added, so as to give him some slight preparation. Countess Lidia Ivanovna usually wrote some two or three letters a day to Alexey Alexandrovitch. She enjoyed that form of communication, which gave opportunity for a refinement and air of mystery not afforded by their personal interviews.

XXIV

THE levee was drawing to a close. People met as they were going away, and gossiped of the latest news, of the newly bestowed honours and the changes in the positions of the higher functionaries.

'If only Countess Marya Borissovna were Minister of War, and Princess Vatkovsky were Commander-in-Chief,' said a grey-headed, little old man in a gold-embroidered uniform, addressing a tall, handsome maid of honour who had questioned him about the new appointments.

'And me among the adjutants,' said the maid of honour, smiling.

'You have an appointment already. You're over the ecclesiastical department. And your assistant's Madame Karenin.'

'Good day, prince!' said the little old man to a man who came up to him.

'What were you saying of Karenin?' said the prince.

'He and Putyatov have received the Alexander Nevsky.'

'I thought he had it already.'

'No. Just look at him,' said the little old man, pointing with his embroidered hat to Karenin in a court uniform with the new red ribbon across his shoulders, standing in the doorway of the hall with an influential member of the Imperial Council. 'Pleased and happy as a brass farthing,' he added, stopping to shake hands with a handsome gentleman of the bedchamber of colossal proportions.

'No; he's looking older,' said the gentleman of the bedchamber.

'From overwork. He's always drawing up projects nowadays. He won't let a poor devil go nowadays till he's explained it all to him under heads.'

'Looking older, did you say? *Il fait des passions*. I believe Countess Lidia Ivanovna's now jealous of his wife.'

'Oh, come now, please don't say any harm of Countess Lidia Ivanovna.'

'Why, is there any harm in her being in love with Karenin?'

'But is it true Madame Karenin's here?'

'Well, not here in the palace, but in Petersburg. I met her yesterday with Alexey Vronsky, *bras dessus, bras dessous*, in the Morsky.'

'C'est un homme qui n'a pas, . . .' the gentleman of the bedchamber was beginning, but he stopped to make room, bowing, for a member of the Imperial family to pass.

Thus people talked incessantly of Alexey Alexandrovitch, finding fault with him and laughing at him, while he, blocking up the way of the member of the Imperial Council he had captured, was explaining to him point by point his new financial project, never interrupting his discourse for an instant for fear he should escape.

Almost at the same time that his wife left Alexey Alexandrovitch there had come to him that bitterest moment in the life of an official—the moment when his upward career comes to a full stop. This full stop had arrived and everyone perceived it, but Alexey Alexandrovitch himself was not yet aware that his career was over. Whether it was due to his feud with Stremov, or his misfortune with his wife, or simply that Alexey Alexandrovitch had reached his destined limits, it had become evident to everyone in the course of that year that his career was at an end. He still filled a position of consequence, he sat on many commissions and committees, but he was a man whose day was over, and from whom nothing was expected. Whatever he said, whatever he proposed, was heard as though it were something long familiar, and the very thing that was not needed. But Alexey Alexandrovitch was not aware of this, and, on the contrary, being cut off from direct participation in governmental activity, he saw more clearly than ever the errors and defects in the action of others, and thought it his duty to point out means for their correction. Shortly after his separation from his wife, he began writing his first note on the new judicial procedure, the first of the endless series of notes he was destined to write in the future.

Alexey Alexandrovitch did not merely fail to observe his hopeless position in the official world, he was not merely free from anxiety on this head, he was positively more satisfied than ever with his own activity.

'He that is unmarried careth for the things that belong to the Lord, how he may please the Lord: but he that is married careth for the things of the world, how he may please his wife,' says the Apostle Paul, and Alexey Alexandrovitch, who was now guided in every action by Scripture, often recalled this text. It seemed to him that ever since he had been left without a wife, he had in these very projects of reform been serving the Lord more zealously than before.

The unmistakable impatience of the member of the Council trying to get away from him did not trouble Alexey Alexandrovitch; he gave up his exposition only when the member of the Council, seizing his chance when one of the Imperial family was passing, slipped away from him.

Left alone, Alexey Alexandrovitch looked down, collecting his thoughts, then looked casually about him and walked towards the door, where he hoped to meet Countess Lidia Ivanovna.

'And how strong they all are, how sound physically,' thought Alexey Alexandrovitch, looking at the powerfully built gentleman of the bed-chamber with his well-combed, perfumed whiskers, and at the red neck of the prince, pinched by his tight uniform. He had to pass them on his way. 'Truly is it said that all in the world is evil,' he thought, with another sidelong glance at the calves of the gentleman of the bed-chamber.

Moving forward deliberately, Alexey Alexandrovitch bowed with his customary air of weariness and dignity to the gentleman who had been talking about him, and looking towards the door, his eyes sought Countess Lidia Ivanovna.

'Ah! Alexey Alexandrovitch!' said the little old man, with a malicious light in his eyes, at the moment when Karenin was on a level with them, and was nodding with a frigid gesture, 'I haven't congratulated you yet,' said the old man, pointing to his newly received ribbon.

'Thank you,' answered Alexey Alexandrovitch. 'What an *exquisite* day today,' he added, laying emphasis in his peculiar way on the word *exquisite*.

That they laughed at him he was well aware, but he did not expect anything but hostility from them; he was used to that by now.

Catching sight of the yellow shoulders of Lidia Ivanovna jutting out above her corset, and her fine pensive eyes bidding him to her, Alexey Alexandrovitch smiled, revealing untarnished white teeth, and went towards her.

Lidia Ivanovna's dress had cost her great pains, as indeed all her dresses had done of late. Her aim in dress was now quite the reverse of that she had pursued thirty years before. Then her desire had been to adorn herself with something, and the more adorned the better. Now, on the contrary, she was perforce decked out in a way so inconsistent with her age and her figure, that her one anxiety was to contrive that the contrast between these adornments and her own exterior should not be too appalling. And as far as Alexey Alexandrovitch was concerned she succeeded, and was in his eyes attractive. For him she was the one island not only of goodwill to him, but of love in the midst of the sea of hostility and jeering that surrounded him.

Passing through rows of ironical eyes, he was drawn as naturally to her loving glance as a plant to the sun.

'I congratulate you,' she said to him, her eyes on his ribbon.

Suppressing a smile of pleasure, he shrugged his shoulders, closing his eyes, as though to say that that could not be a source of joy to him. Countess Lidia Ivanovna was very well aware that it was one of his chief sources of satisfaction, though he never admitted it.

'How is our angel!' said Countess Lidia Ivanovna, meaning Seryozha.

'I can't say I was quite pleased with him,' said Alexey Alexandrovitch, raising his eyebrows and opening his eyes. 'And Sitnikov is not satisfied with him.' (Sitnikov was the tutor to whom Seryozha's secular education had been intrusted.) 'As I have mentioned to you, there's a sort of coldness in him towards the most important questions which ought to touch the heart of every man and every child.'. . . Alexey Alexandrovitch began expounding his views on the sole question that interested him besides the service—the education of his son.

When Alexey Alexandrovitch with Lidia Ivanovna's help had been brought back anew to life and activity, he felt it his duty to undertake the education of the son left on his hands. Having never before taken any interest in educational questions, Alexey Alexandrovitch devoted some time to the theoretical study of the subject. After reading several books on anthropology, education, and didactics, Alexey Alexandrovitch drew up a plan of education, and engaging the best tutor in Petersburg to superintend it, he set to work, and the subject continually absorbed him.

'Yes, but the heart. I see in him his father's heart, and with such a heart a child cannot go far wrong,' said Lidia Ivanovna with enthusiasm.

'Yes, perhaps . . . As for me, I do my duty. It's all I can do.'

'You're coming to me,' said Countess Lidia Ivanovna, after a pause; 'we have to speak of a subject painful for you. I would give anything to have spared you certain memories, but others are not of the same mind. I have received a letter from *her*. *She* is here in Petersburg.'

Alexey Alexandrovitch shuddered at the allusion to his wife, but immediately his face assumed the deathlike rigidity which expressed utter helplessness in the matter.

'I was expecting it,' he said.

Countess Lidia Ivanovna looked at him ecstatically, and tears of rapture at the greatness of his soul came into her eyes.

XXV

WHEN Alexey Alexandrovitch came into the Countess Lidia Ivanovna's snug little boudoir, decorated with old china and hung with portraits, the lady herself had not yet made her appearance.

She was changing her dress.

A cloth was laid on a round table, and on it stood a china tea-service and a silver spirit-lamp and tea-kettle. Alexey Alexandrovitch looked idly about at the endless familiar portraits which adorned the room, and sitting down to the table, he opened a New Testament lying upon it. The rustle of the countess's silk skirt drew his attention off.

'Well now, we can sit quietly,' said Countess Lidia Ivanovna, slipping hurriedly with an agitated smile between the table and the sofa, 'and talk over our tea.'

After some words of preparation, Countess Lidia Ivanovna, breathing hard and flushing crimson, gave into Alexey Alexandrovitch's hands the letter she had received.

After reading the letter, he sat a long while in silence.

'I don't think I have the right to refuse her,' he said, timidly lifting his eyes.

'Dear friend, you never see evil in anyone!'

'On the contrary, I see that all is evil. But whether it is just . . .'

His face showed irresolution, and a seeking for counsel, support, and guidance in a matter he did not understand.

'No,' Countess Lidia Ivanovna interrupted him, 'there are limits to everything. I can understand immorality,' she said, not quite truthfully, since she never could understand that which leads women to immorality; 'but I don't understand cruelty: to whom? to you! How can she stay in the town where you are? No, the longer one lives the more one learns. And I'm learning to understand your loftiness and her baseness.'

'Who is to throw a stone?' said Alexey Alexandrovitch, unmistakably pleased with the part he had to play. 'I have forgiven all, and so I cannot deprive her of what is exacted by love in her—by her love for her son . . .'

'But is that love, my friend? Is it sincere? Admitting that you have forgiven—that you forgive—have we the right to work on the feelings of that angel? He looks on her as dead. He prays for her, and beseeches God to have mercy on her sins. And it is better so. But now what will he think?'

'I had not thought of that,' said Alexey Alexandrovitch, evidently agreeing.

Countess Lidia Ivanovna hid her face in her hands and was silent. She was praying.

'If you ask my advice,' she said, having finished her prayer and uncovered her face, 'I do not advise you to do this. Do you suppose I don't see how you are suffering, how this has torn open your wounds? But supposing that, as always, you don't think of yourself, what can it lead to?—to fresh suffering for you, to torture for the child. If there were a trace of humanity left in her, she ought not to wish for it herself. No, I have no hesitation in saying I advise not, and if you will intrust it to me, I will write to her.'

And Alexey Alexandrovitch consented, and Countess Lidia Ivanovna sent the following letter in French:—

'DEAR MADAME,—To be reminded of you might have results for your son in leading to questions on his part which could not be answered without implanting in the child's soul a spirit of censure towards what should be for him sacred, and therefore I beg you to interpret your husband's refusal in the spirit of Christian love. I pray to Almighty God to have mercy on you. COUNTESS LIDIA.'

This letter attained the secret object which Countess Lidia Ivanovna had concealed from herself. It wounded Anna to the quick.

For his part, Alexey Alexandrovitch, on returning home from Lidia Ivanovna's, could not all that day concentrate himself on his usual pursuits, and find that spiritual peace of one saved and believing which he had felt of late.

The thought of his wife, who had so greatly sinned against him, and towards whom he had been so saintly, as Countess Lidia Ivanovna had so justly told him, ought not to have troubled him; but he was not easy; he could not understand the book he was reading; he could not drive away harassing recollections of his relations with her, of the mistake which, as it now seemed, he had made in regard to her. The memory of how he had received her confession of infidelity on their way home from the races (especially that he had insisted only on the observance of external decorum, and had not sent a challenge) tortured him like a remorse. He was tortured too by the thought of the letter he had written her; and most of all, his forgiveness, which nobody wanted, and his care of the other man's child made his heart burn with shame and remorse.

And just the same feeling of shame and regret he felt now, as he reviewed all his past with her, recalling the awkward words in which, after long wavering, he had made her an offer.

'But how have I been to blame?' he said to himself. And this question always excited another question in him—whether they felt differently, did their loving and marrying differently, these Vronskys and Oblonskys . . . these gentlemen of the bedchamber, with their fine calves. And there passed before his mind a whole series of these mettlesome, vigorous, self-confident men, who always and everywhere drew his inquisitive attention in spite of himself. He tried to dispel these thoughts, he tried to persuade himself that he was not living for this transient life, but for the life of eternity, and that there was peace and love in his heart. But the fact that he had in this transient, trivial life made, as it seemed to him, a few trivial mistakes tortured him as though the eternal salvation in which he believed had no existence. But this temptation did not last long, and soon there was re-established once more in Alexey Alexandrovitch's soul the peace and the elevation by virtue of which he could forget what he did not want to remember.

XXVI

'WELL, Kapitonitch?' said Seryozha, coming back rosy and good-humoured from his walk the day before his birthday, and giving his overcoat to the tall old hall-porter, who smiled down at the little person from the height of his long figure. 'Well, has the bandaged clerk been today? Did papa see him?'

'He saw him. The minute the chief secretary came out, I announced him,' said the hall-porter with a good-humoured wink. 'Here, I'll take it off.'

'Seryozha!' said the tutor, stopping in the doorway leading to the inner rooms. 'Take it off yourself.' But Seryozha, though he heard his tutor's feeble voice, did not pay attention to it. He stood keeping hold of the hall-porter's belt, and gazing into his face.

'Well, and did papa do what he wanted for him?'

The hall-porter nodded his head affirmatively. The clerk with his face tied up, who had already been seven times to ask some favour of Alexey Alexandrovitch, interested both Seryozha and the hall-porter. Seryozha had come upon him in the hall, and had heard him plaintively beg the hall-porter to announce him, saying that he and his children had death staring them in the face.

Since then Seryozha, having met him a second time in the hall, took great interest in him.

'Well, was he very glad?' he asked.

'Glad? I should think so! Almost dancing as he walked away.'

'And has anything been left?' asked Seryozha, after a pause.

'Come, sir,' said the hall-porter; then with a shake of his head he whispered, 'Something from the countess.'

Seryozha understood at once that what the hall-porter was speaking of was a present from Countess Lidia Ivanovna for his birthday.

'What do you say? Where?'

'Korney took it to your papa. A fine plaything it must be too!'

'How big? Like this?'

'Rather smaller, but a fine thing.'

'A book.'

'No, a thing. Run along, run along, Vassily Lukitch is calling you,' said the porter, hearing the tutor's steps approaching, and carefully taking away from his belt the little hand in the glove half pulled off, he signed with his head towards the tutor.

'Vassily Lukitch, in a tiny minute!' answered Seryozha with that gay and loving smile which always won over the conscientious Vassily Lukitch.

Seryozha was too happy, everything was too delightful for him to be able to help sharing with his friend the porter the family good fortune of which he had heard during his walk in the public gardens from Lidia Ivanovna's niece. This piece of good news seemed to him particularly important from its coming at the same time with the gladness of the bandaged clerk and his own gladness at toys having come for him. It seemed to Seryozha that this was a day on which everyone ought to be glad and happy.

'You know papa's received the Alexander Nevsky today?'

'To be sure I do! People have been already to congratulate him.'

'And is he glad?'

'Glad at the Tsar's gracious favour! I should think so! It's a proof he's deserved it,' said the porter severely and seriously.

Seryozha fell to dreaming, gazing up at the face of the porter, which he had thoroughly studied in every detail, especially the chin that hung down between the grey whiskers, never seen by anyone but Seryozha, who saw him only from below.

'Well, and has your daughter been to see you lately?'

The porter's daughter was a ballet-dancer.

'When is she to come on weekdays? They've their lessons to learn too. And you've your lesson, sir; run along.'

On coming into the room, Seryozha, instead of sitting down to his lessons, told his tutor of his supposition that what had been brought him must be a machine. 'What do you think?' he inquired.

But Vassily Lukitch was thinking of nothing but the necessity of learning the grammar lesson for the teacher, who was coming at two.

'No, do just tell me, Vassily Lukitch,' he asked suddenly, when he was seated at their work-table with the book in his hands, 'what is greater than the Alexander Nevsky? You know papa's received the Alexander Nevsky?'

Vassily Lukitch replied that the Vladimir was greater than the Alexander Nevsky.

'And higher still?'

'Well, highest of all is the Andrey Pervozvanny.'

'And higher than the Andrey?'

'I don't know.'

'What, you don't know?' and Seryozha, leaning on his elbows sank into deep meditation.

His meditations were of the most complex and diverse character. He imagined his father's having suddenly been presented with both the Vladimir and the Andrey today, and in consequence being much better tempered at his lesson, and dreamed how, when he was grown up, he would himself receive all the orders, and what they might invent higher than the Andrey. Directly any higher order were invented, he would win it. They would make a higher one still, and he would immediately win that too.

The time passed in such meditations, and when the teacher came, the lesson about the adverbs of place and time and manner of action was not ready, and the teacher was not only displeased, but hurt. This touched Seryozha. He felt he was not to blame for not having learned the lesson; however much he tried, he was utterably unable to do that. As long as the teacher was explaining to him, he believed him and seemed to comprehend, but as soon as he was left alone, he was positively unable to recollect and to understand that the short and familiar word 'suddenly' is an adverb of manner of action. Still he was sorry that he had disappointed the teacher.

He chose a moment when the teacher was looking in silence at the book.

'Mihail Ivanitch, when is your birthday?' he asked, all of a sudden.

'You'd much better be thinking about your work. Birthdays are of no importance to a rational being. It's a day like any other on which one has to do one's work.'

Seryozha looked intently at the teacher, at his scanty beard, at his spectacles, which had slipped down below the ridge on his nose, and fell into so deep a reverie that he heard nothing of what the teacher was explaining to him. He knew that the teacher did not think what he said, he felt it from the tone in which it was said. 'But why have they all agreed to speak just in the same manner always the dreariest and most useless stuff? Why does he keep me off; why doesn't he love me?' he asked himself mournfully, and could not think of an answer.

XXVII

AFTER the lesson with the grammar teacher came his father's lesson. While waiting for his father, Seryozha sat at the table playing with a penknife, and fell to dreaming. Among Seryozha's favourite occupations was searching for his mother during his walks. He did not believe in death generally, and in her death in particular, in spite of what Lidia Ivanovna had told him and his father had confirmed, and it was just because of that, and after he had been told she was dead, that he had begun looking for her when out for a walk. Every woman of full, graceful figure with dark hair was his mother. At the sight of such a woman such a feeling of tenderness was stirred within him that his breath failed him, and tears came into his eyes. And he was on the tiptoe of expectation that she would come up to him, would lift her veil. All her face would be visible, she would smile, she would hug him, he would sniff her fragrance, feel the softness of her arms, and cry with happiness, just as he had one evening lain on her lap while she tickled him, and he laughed and bit her white, ring-covered fingers. Later, when he accidentally learned from his old nurse that his mother was not dead, and his father and Lidia Ivanovna had explained to him that she was dead to him because she was wicked (which he could not possibly believe, because he loved her), he went on seeking her and expecting her in the same way. That day in the public gardens there had been a lady in a lilac veil, whom he had watched with a throbbing heart, believing it to be her as she came towards them along the path. The lady had not come up to them, but had disappeared somewhere. That day, more intensely than ever, Seryozha felt a rush of love for her, and now, waiting for his father, he forgot everything, and cut all round the edge of the table with his penknife, staring straight before him with sparkling eyes and dreaming of her.

'Here is your papa!' said Vassily Lukitch, rousing him.

Seryozha jumped up and went up to his father, and kissing his hand, looked at him intently, trying to discover signs of his joy at receiving the Alexander Nevsky.

'Did you have a nice walk?' said Alexey Alexandrovitch, sitting down in his easy-chair, pulling the volume of the Old Testament to him and opening it. Although Alexey Alexandrovitch had more than once told Seryozha that every Christian ought to know Scripture history thoroughly, he often referred to the Bible himself during the lesson, and Seryozha observed this.

'Yes, it was very nice indeed, papa,' said Seryozha, sitting sideways on his chair and rocking it, which was forbidden. 'I saw Nadinka' (Nadinka was a niece of Lidia Ivanovna's who was being brought up in her house). 'She told me you'd been given a new star. Are you glad, papa?'

'First of all, don't rock your chair, please,' said Alexey Alexandrovitch. 'And secondly, it's not the reward that's precious, but the work itself. And I could have wished you to understand that. If you now are going to work, to study in order to win a reward, then the work will seem hard to you; but when you work' (Alexey Alexandrovitch, as he spoke, thought of how he had been sustained by a sense of duty through the wearisome labour of the morning, consisting of signing one hundred and eighty papers), 'loving your work, you will find your reward in it.'

Seryozha's eyes, that had been shining with gaiety and tenderness, grew dull and dropped before his father's gaze. This was the same long-familiar tone his father always took with him, and Seryozha had learned by now to fall in with it. His father always talked to him—so Seryozha felt—as though he were addressing some boy of his own imagination, one of those boys that exist in books, utterly unlike himself. And Seryozha always tried with his father to act being this story-book boy.

'You understand that, I hope?' said his father.

'Yes, papa,' answered Seryozha, acting the part of the imaginary boy.

The lesson consisted of learning by heart several verses out of the Gospel and the repetition of the beginning of the Old Testament. The verses from the Gospel Seryozha knew fairly well, but at the moment when he was saying them he became so absorbed in watching the sharply protruding, bony knobbiness of his father's forehead, that he lost the thread, and he transposed the end of one verse and the beginning of another. So it was evident to Alexey Alexandrovitch that he did not understand what he was saying, and that irritated him.

He frowned, and began explaining what Seryozha had heard many times before and never could remember, because he understood it too well, just as that 'suddenly' is an adverb of manner of action. Seryozha looked with scared eyes at his father, and could think of nothing but whether his father would make him repeat what he had said, as he sometimes did. And this thought so alarmed Seryozha that he now understood nothing. But his father did not make him repeat it, and passed on to the lesson out of the Old Testament. Seryozha recounted the events themselves well enough, but when he had to answer questions as to what certain events prefigured, he knew nothing, though he had already been punished over this lesson. The passage at which he was utterably unable to say anything, and began fidgeting and cutting the table and swinging his chair, was where he had to repeat the patriarchs before the Flood. He did not know one of them, except Enoch, who had been taken up alive to heaven. Last time he had remembered their names, but now he had forgotten them utterly, chiefly because Enoch was the personage he liked best in the whole of the Old Testament, and Enoch's translation to heaven was connected in his mind with a whole long train of thought, in which he became absorbed now while he gazed with fascinated eyes at his father's watch-chain and a half-unbuttoned button on his waistcoat.

In death, of which they talked to him so often, Seryozha disbelieved entirely. He did not believe that those he loved could die, above all that he himself would die. That was to him something utterly inconceivable and impossible. But he had been told that all men die; he had asked people, indeed, whom he trusted, and they, too, had confirmed it; his old nurse, too, said the same, though reluctantly. But Enoch had not died, and so it followed that everyone did not die. 'And why cannot anyone else so serve God and be taken alive to heaven?' thought Seryozha. Bad people, that is those Seryozha did not like, they might die, but the good might all be like Enoch.

'Well, what are the names of the patriarchs?'

'Enoch, Enos——'

'But you have said that already. This is bad, Seryozha, very bad. If you don't try to learn what is more necessary than anything for a Christian,' said his father, getting up, 'whatever can interest you? I am displeased with you, and Piotr Ignatitch' (this was the most important of his teachers) 'is displeased with you. . . . I shall have to punish you.'

His father and his teacher were both displeased with Seryozha, and he certainly did learn his lessons very badly. But still it could not be said he was a stupid boy. On the contrary, he was far cleverer than the boys his teacher held up as examples to Seryozha. In his father's opinion, he did not want to learn what he was taught. In reality he could not learn that. He could not, because the claims of his own soul were more binding on him than those claims his father and his teacher made upon him. Those claims were in opposition, and he was in direct conflict with his education. He was nine years old; he was a child; but he knew his own soul, it was precious to him, he guarded it as the eyelid guards the eye, and without the key of love he let no one into his soul. His teachers complained that he would not learn, while his soul was brimming over with thirst for knowledge. And he learned from Kapitonitch, from his nurse, from Nadinka, from Vassily Lukitch, but not from his teachers. The spring his father and teachers reckoned upon to turn their mill-wheels had long dried up at the source, but its waters did their work in another channel.

His father punished Seryozha by not letting him go to see Nadinka, Lidia Ivanovna's niece; but this punishment turned out happily for Seryozha. Vassily Lukitch was in a good humour, and showed him how to make windmills. The whole evening passed over this work and in dreaming how to make a windmill on which he could turn himself—clutching at the sails or tying himself on and whirling round. Of his mother Seryozha did not think all the evening, but when he had gone to bed, he suddenly remembered her, and prayed in his own words that his mother tomorrow for his birthday might leave off hiding herself and come to him.

'Vassily Lukitch, do you know what I prayed for tonight extra besides the regular things?'

'That you might learn your lessons better?'

'No.'

'Toys?'

'No. You'll never guess. A splendid thing; but it's a secret! When it comes to pass I'll tell you. Can't you guess?'

'No, I can't guess. You tell me,' said Vassily Lukitch with a smile, which was rare with him. 'Come, lie down, I'm putting out the candle.'

'Without the candle I can see better what I see and what I prayed for. There! I was almost telling the secret!' said Seryozha, laughing gaily.

When the candle was taken away, Seryozha heard and felt his mother. She stood over him, and with loving eyes caressed him. But then came windmills, a knife, everything began to be mixed up, and he fell asleep.

XXVIII

ON arriving in Petersburg, Vronsky and Anna stayed at one of the best hotels; Vronsky apart in a lower storey, Anna above with her child, its nurse, and her maid, in a large suite of four rooms.

On the day of his arrival Vronsky went to his brother's. There he found his mother, who had come from Moscow on business. His mother and sister-in-law greeted him as usual: they asked him about his stay abroad, and talked of their common acquaintances, but did not let drop a single word in allusion to his connection with Anna. His brother came the next morning to see Vronsky, and of his own accord asked him about her, and Alexey Vronsky told him directly that he looked upon his connection with Madame Karenin as marriage; that he hoped to arrange a divorce, and then to marry her, and until then he considered her as much a wife as any other wife, and he begged him to tell their mother and his wife so.

'If the world disapproves, I don't care,' said Vronsky; 'but if my relations want to be on terms of relationship with me, they will have to be on the same terms with my wife.'

The elder brother, who had always a respect for his younger brother's judgment, could not well tell whether he was right or not till the world had decided the question; for his part he had nothing against it, and with Alexey he went up to see Anna.

Before his brother, as before every one, Vronsky addressed Anna with a certain formality, treating her as he might a very intimate friend, but it was understood that his brother knew their real relations, and they talked about Anna's going to Vronsky's estate.

In spite of all his social experience Vronsky was, in consequence of the new position in which he was placed, labouring under a strange misapprehension. One would have thought he must have understood that society was closed for him and Anna; but now some vague ideas had sprung up in his brain that this was only the case in old-fashioned days, and that now with the rapidity of modern progress (he had unconsciously become by now a partisan of every sort of progress) the views of society had changed, and that the question whether they would be received in society was not a foregone conclusion. 'Of course,' he thought, 'she would not be received at court, but intimate friends can and must look at it in the proper light.' One may sit for several hours at a stretch with one's legs crossed in the same position, if one knows that there's nothing to prevent one's changing one's position; but if a man knows that he must remain sitting so with crossed legs, then cramps come on, the legs begin to twitch and to strain towards the spot to which one would like to draw them. This was what Vronsky was experiencing in regard to the world. Though at the bottom of his heart he knew that the world was shut on them, he put it to the test whether the world had not changed by now and would not receive them. But he very quickly perceived that though the world was open for him personally, it was closed for Anna. Just as in the game of cat and mouse, the hands raised for him were dropped to bar the way for Anna.

One of the first ladies of Petersburg society whom Vronsky saw was his cousin Betsy.

'At last!' she greeted him joyfully. 'And Anna? How glad I am! Where are you stopping? I can fancy after your delightful travels you must find our poor Petersburg horrid. I can fancy your honeymoon in Rome. How about the divorce? Is that all over?'

Vronsky noticed that Betsy's enthusiasm waned when she learned that no divorce had as yet taken place.

'People will throw stones at me, I know,' she said, 'but I shall come and see Anna; yes, I shall certainly come. You won't be here long, I suppose?'

And she did certainly come to see Anna the same day, but her tone was not at all the same as in former days. She unmistakably prided herself on her courage, and wished Anna to appreciate the fidelity of her friendship. She only stayed ten minutes, talking of society gossip, and on leaving she said—

'You've never told me when the divorce is to be? Supposing I'm ready to fling my cap over the mill, other starchy people will give you the cold shoulder until you're married. And that's so simple nowadays. *Ça se fait.* So you're going on Friday? Sorry we shan't see each other again.'

From Betsy's tone Vronsky might have grasped what he had to expect from the world; but he made another effort in his own family. His mother he did not reckon upon. He knew that his mother, who had been so enthusiastic over Anna at their first acquaintance, would have no mercy on her now for having ruined her son's career. But he had more hope of Varya, his brother's wife. He fancied she would not throw stones, and would go simply and directly to see Anna, and would receive her in her own house.

The day after his arrival Vronsky went to her, and finding her alone, expressed his wishes directly.

'You know, Alexey,' she said after hearing him, 'how fond I am of you, and how ready I am to do anything for you; but I have not spoken, because I knew I could be of no use to you and to Anna Arkadyevna,' she said, articulating the name 'Anna Arkadyevna' with particular care.

'Don't suppose, please, that I judge her. Never; perhaps in her place I should have done the same. I don't and can't enter into that,' she said, glacing timidly at his gloomy face. 'But one must call things by their names. You want me to go and see her, to ask her here, and to rehabilitate her in society; but do understand that *I cannot* do so. I have daughters growing up, and I must live in the world for my husband's sake. Well, I'm ready to come and see Anna Arkadyevna: she will understand that I can't ask her here, or I should have to do so in such a way that she would not meet people who look at things differently; that would offend her. I can't raise her . . .'

'Oh, I don't regard her as fallen more than hundreds of women you do receive!' Vronsky interrupted her still more gloomily, and he got up in silence, understanding that his sister-in-law's decision was not to be shaken.

'Alexey! don't be angry with me. Please understand that I'm not to blame,' began Varya, looking at him with a timid smile.

'I'm not angry with you,' he said still as gloomily; 'but I'm sorry in two ways. I'm sorry, too, that this means breaking up our friendship —if not breaking up, at least weakening it. You will understand that for me, too, it cannot be otherwise.'

And with that he left her.

Vronsky knew that further efforts were useless, and that he had to spend these few days in Petersburg as though in a strange town, avoiding every sort of relation with his own old circle in order not to be exposed to the annoyances and humiliations which were so intolerable to him. One of the most unpleasant features of his position in Petersburg was that Alexey Alexandrovitch and his name seemed to meet him everywhere. He could not begin to talk of anything without the conversation turning on Alexey Alexandrovitch, he could not go anywhere without risk of meeting him. So at least it seemed to Vronsky, just as it seems to a man with a sore finger that he is continually, as though on purpose, grazing his sore finger on everything.

Their stay in Petersburg was the more painful to Vronsky that he perceived all the time a sort of new mood that he could not understand in Anna. At one time she would seem in love with him, and then she would become cold, irritable, and impenetrable. She was worrying over something, and keeping something back from him, and did not seem to notice the humiliations which poisoned his existence, and for her, with her delicate intuition, must have been still more unbearable.

XXIX

ONE of Anna's objects in coming back to Russia had been to see her son. From the day she left Italy the thought of it had never ceased to agitate her. And as she got nearer to Petersburg, the delight and importance of this meeting grew ever greater in her imagination. She did not even put to herself the question how to arrange it. It seemed to her natural and simple to see her son when she should be in the same town with him. But on her arrival in Petersburg, she was suddenly made distinctly aware of her present position in society, and she grasped the fact that to arrange this meeting was no easy matter.

She had now been two days in Petersburg. The thought of her son never left her for a single instant, but she had not yet seen him. To go straight to the house, where she might meet Alexey Alexandrovitch, that she felt she had no right to do. She might be refused admittance and insulted. To write and so enter into relations with her husband—

that it made her miserable to think of doing; she could only be at peace when she did not think of her husband. To get a glimpse of her son out walking, finding out where and when he went out, was not enough for her; she had so looked forward to this meeting, she had so much she must say to him, she so longed to embrace him, to kiss him. Seryozha's old nurse might be a help to her and show her what to do. But the nurse was not now living in Alexey Alexandrovitch's house. In this uncertainty, and in efforts to find the nurse, two days had slipped by.

Hearing of the close intimacy between Alexey Alexandrovitch and Countess Lidia Ivanovna, Anna decided on the third day to write to her a letter, which cost her great pains, and in which she intentionally said that permission to see her son must depend on her husband's generosity. She knew that if the letter were shown to her husband, he would keep up his character of magnanimity, and would not refuse her request.

The commissionaire who took the letter had brought her back the most cruel and unexpected answer, that there was no answer. She had never felt so humiliated as at the moment when, sending for the commissionaire, she heard from him the exact account of how he had waited, and how afterwards he had been told there was no answer. Anna felt humiliated, insulted, but she saw that from her point of view Countess Lidia Ivanovna was right. Her suffering was the more poignant that she had to bear it in solitude. She could not and would not share it with Vronsky. She knew that to him, although he was the primary cause of her distress, the question of her seeing her son would seem a matter of very little consequence. She knew that he would never be capable of understanding all the depth of her suffering, that for his cool tone at any allusion to it she would begin to hate him. And she dreaded that more than anything in the world, and so she hid from him everything that related to her son. Spending the whole day at home she considered ways of seeing her son, and had reached a decision to write to her husband. She was just composing this letter when she was handed the letter from Lidia Ivanovna. The countess's silence had subdued and depressed her, but the letter, all that she read between the lines in it, so exasperated her, this malice was so revolting beside her passionate, legitimate tenderness for her son, that she turned against other people and left off blaming herself.

'This coldness—this pretence of feeling!' she said to herself. 'They must needs insult me and torture the child, and I am to submit to it! Not on any consideration! She is worse than I am. I don't lie, anyway.' And she decided on the spot that next day, Seryozha's birthday, she would go straight to her husband's house, bribe or deceive the servants, but at any cost see her son and overturn the hideous deception with which they were encompassing the unhappy child.

She went to a toy-shop, bought toys and thought over a plan of action. She would go early in the morning at eight o'clock, when Alexey Alexandrovitch would be certain not to be up. She would have money in her hand to give the hall-porter and the footman, so that they should let her in, and not raising her veil, she would say that she had come from Seryozha's godfather to congratulate him, and that she had been charged to leave the toys at his bedside. She had prepared everything but the words she should say to her son. Often as she had dreamed of it, she could never think of anything.

The next day, at eight o'clock in the morning, Anna got out of a hired sledge and rang at the front entrance of her former home.

'Run and see what's wanted. Some lady,' said Kapitonitch, who, not yet dressed, in his overcoat and goloshes, had peeped out of window and seen a lady in a veil standing close up to the door. His assistant, a lad Anna did not know, had no sooner opened the door to her than she came in, and pulling a three-rouble note out of her muff put it hurriedly into his hand.

'Seryozha—Sergey Alexandrovitch,' she said, and was going on. Scrutinising the note, the porter's assistant stopped her at the second glass-door.

'Whom do you want?' he asked.

She did not hear his words and made no answer.

Noticing the embarrassment of the unknown lady, Kapitonitch went out to her, opened the second door for her, and asked her what she was pleased to want.

'From Prince Skorodumov for Sergey Alexeitch,' she said.

'His honour's not up yet,' said the porter, looking at her attentively.

Anna had not anticipated that the absolutely unchanged hall of the house where she had lived for nine years would so greatly affect her. Memories sweet and painful rose one after another in her heart, and for a moment she forgot what she was here for.

'Would you kindly wait?' said Kapitonitch, taking off her fur cloak.

As he took off the cloak, Kapitonitch glanced at her face, recognised her, and made her a low bow in silence.

'Please walk in, your excellency,' he said to her.

She tried to say something, but her voice refused to utter any sound; with a guilty and imploring glance at the old man she went with light, swift steps up the stairs. Bent double, and his goloshes catching in the steps, Kapitonitch ran after her, trying to overtake her.

'The tutor's there; maybe he's not dressed. I'll let him know.'

Anna still mounted the familiar staircase, not understanding what the old man was saying.

'This way, to the left, if you please. Excuse it's not being tidy. His honour's in the old parlour now,' the hall-porter said, panting. 'Excuse me, wait a little, your excellency; I'll just see,' he said, and overtaking her, he opened the high door and disappeared behind it. Anna stood still waiting. 'He's only just awake,' said the hall-porter, coming out. And at the very instant the porter said this, Anna caught the sound of a childish yawn. From the sound of this yawn alone she knew her son and seemed to see him living before her eyes.

'Let me in; go away!' she said, and went in through the high doorway. On the right of the door stood a bed, and sitting up in the bed was the boy. His little body bent forward with his nightshirt unbuttoned, he was stretching and still yawning. The instant his lips came together they curved into a blissfully sleepy smile, and with that smile he slowly and deliciously rolled back again.

'Seryozha!' she whispered, going noiselessly up to him.

When she was parted from him, and all this latter time when she had been feeling a fresh rush of love for him, she had pictured him as he was at four years old, when she had loved him most of all. Now he was not even the same as when she had left him; he was still further from the four year old baby, more grown and thinner. How thin his face was, how short his hair was! What long hands! How he had changed since she left him! But it was he with his head, his lips, his soft neck and broad little shoulders.

'Seryozha!' she repeated just in the child's ear.

He raised himself again on his elbow, turned his tangled head from side to side as though looking for something, and opened his eyes. Slowly and inquiringly he looked for several seconds at his mother standing motionless before him, then all at once he smiled a blissful smile, and shutting his eyes, rolled not backwards but towards her into her arms.

'Seryozha! my darling boy!' she said, breathing hard and putting her arms round his plump little body. 'Mother!' he said, wriggling about in her arms so as to touch her hands with different parts of him.

Smiling sleepily still with closed eyes, he flung his fat little arms round her shoulders, rolled towards her, with the delicious sleepy warmth and fragrance that is only found in children, and began rubbing his face against her neck and shoulders.

'I know,' he said, opening his eyes; 'it's my birthday today. I knew you'd come. I'll get up directly.'

And saying that he dropped asleep.

Anna looked at him hungrily; she saw how he had grown and changed in her absence. She knew, and did not know, the bare legs so long now, that were thrust out below the quilt, those short-cropped curls on his neck in which she had so often kissed him. She touched all this and could say nothing; tears choked her.

'What are you crying for, mother?' he said, waking completely up. 'Mother, what are you crying for?' he cried in a tearful voice.

'I won't cry . . . I'm crying for joy. It's so long since I've seen you. I won't, I won't,' she said, gulping down her tears and turning away. 'Come, it's time for you to dress now,' she added, after a pause, and, never letting go his hands, she sat down by his bedside on the chair, where his clothes were put ready for him.

'How do you dress without me? How . . .' she tried to begin talking simply and cheerfully, but she could not, and again she turned away.

'I don't have a cold bath, papa didn't order it. And you've not seen Vassily Lukitch? He'll come in soon. Why, you're sitting on my clothes!'

And Seryozha went off into a peal of laughter. She looked at him and smiled.

'Mother, darling, sweet one!' he shouted, flinging himself on her again and hugging her. It was as though only now, on seeing her smile, he fully grasped what had happened.

'I don't want that on,' he said, taking off her hat. And as it were, seeing her afresh without her hat, he fell to kissing her again.

'But what did you think about me? You didn't think I was dead?'

'I never believed it.'

'You didn't believe it, my sweet?'

'I knew, I knew!' he repeated his favourite phrase, and snatching the hand that was stroking his hair, he pressed the open palm to his mouth and kissed it.

XXX

MEANWHILE Vassily Lukitch had not at first understood who this lady was, and had learned from their conversation that it was no other person than the mother who had left her husband, and whom he had not seen, as he had entered the house after her departure. He was in doubt whether to go in or not, or whether to communicate with Alexey Alexandrovitch. Reflecting finally that his duty was to get Seryozha up at the hour fixed, and that it was therefore not his business to consider who was there, the mother or anyone else, but simply to do his duty, he finished dressing, went to the door and opened it.

But the embraces of the mother and child, the sound of their voices, and what they were saying, made him change his mind.

He shook his head, and with a sigh he closed the door. 'I'll wait another ten minutes,' he said to himself, clearing his throat and wiping away tears.

Among the servants of the household there was intense excitement all this time. All had heard that their mistress had come, and that Kapitonitch had let her in, and that she was even now in the nursery, and that their master always went in person to the nursery at nine o'clock, and everyone fully comprehended that it was impossible for the husband and wife to meet, and that they must prevent it. Korney, the valet, going down to the hall-porter's room, asked who had let her in, and how it was he had done so, and ascertaining that Kapitonitch had admitted her and shown her up, he gave the old man a talking-to. The hall-porter was doggedly silent, but when Korney told him he ought to be sent away, Kapitonitch darted up to him, and waving his hands in Korney's face, began—

'Oh yes, to be sure you'd not have let her in! After ten years' service, and never a word but of kindness, and there you'd up and say, "Be off, go along, get away with you!" Oh yes, you're a shrewd one at politics, I dare say! You don't need to be taught how to swindle the master, and to filch fur-coats!'

'Soldier!' said Korney contemptuously, and he turned to the nurse who was coming in. 'Here, what do you think, Marya Efimovna: he let her in without a word to anyone,' Korney said addressing her. 'Alexey Alexandrovitch will be down immediately—and go into the nursery!'

'A pretty business, a pretty business!' said the nurse. 'You Korney Vassilievitch, you'd best keep him some way or other, the master, while I'll run and get her away somehow. A pretty business!'

When the nurse went into the nursery, Seryozha was telling his mother how he and Nadinka had had a fall in sledging downhill, and had turned over three times. She was listening to the sound of his voice, watching his face and the play of expression on it, touching his hand, but she did not follow what he was saying. She must go, she must leave him,—this was the only thing she was thinking and feeling. She heard the steps of Vassily Lukitch coming up to the door and coughing; she heard, too, the steps of the nurse as she came near; but she sat like one turned to stone, incapable of beginning to speak or to get up.

'Mistress, darling!' began the nurse, going up to Anna and kissing her hands and shoulders. 'God has brought joy indeed to our boy on his birthday. You aren't changed one bit.'

'Oh, nurse dear, I didn't know you were in the house,' said Anna, rousing herself for a moment.

'I'm not living here, I'm living with my daughter. I came for the birthday, Anna Arkadyevna, darling.'

The nurse suddenly burst into tears, and began kissing her hand again.

Seryozha, with radiant eyes and smiles, holding his mother by one hand and his nurse by the other, pattered on the rug with his fat little bare feet. The tenderness shown by his beloved nurse to his mother threw him into an ecstasy.

'Mother! She often comes to see me, and when she comes . . .' he was beginning, but he stopped, noticing that the nurse was saying something in a whisper to his mother, and that in his mother's face there was a look of dread and something like shame, which was so strangely unbecoming to her.

She went up to him.

'My sweet!' she said.

She could not say *good-bye*, but the expression on her face said it, and he understood. 'Darling, darling Kootik!' she used the name by which she had called him when he was little, 'you won't forget me? You . . .' but she could not say more.

How often afterwards she thought of words she might have said. But now she did not know how to say it, and could say nothing. But Seryozha knew all she wanted to say to him. He understood that she was unhappy and loved him. He understood even what the nurse had whispered. He had caught the words 'always at nine o'clock,' and he knew that this was said of his father, and that his father and mother could not meet. That he understood, but one thing he could not understand—why there should be a look of dread and shame in her face? . . . She was not in fault, but she was afraid of him and ashamed of something. He would have liked to put a question that would have set at rest this doubt, but he did not dare; he saw that she was miserable, and he felt for her. Silently he pressed close to her and whispered, 'Don't go yet. He won't come just yet.'

The mother held him away from her to see what he was thinking, what to say to him, and in his frightened face she read not only that he was speaking of his father, but, as it were, asking her what he ought to think about his father.

'Seryozha, my darling,' she said, 'love him; he's better and kinder than I am, and I have done him wrong. When you grow up you will judge.'

'There's no one better than you! . . .' he cried in despair through his tears, and, clutching her by the shoulders, he began squeezing her with all his force to him, his arms trembling with the strain.

'My sweet, my little one!' said Anna, and she cried as weakly and childishly as he.

At that moment the door opened. Vassily Lukitch came in.

At the other door there was the sound of steps, and the nurse in a scared whisper said, 'He's coming,' and gave Anna her hat.

Seryozha sank on to the bed and sobbed, hiding his face in his hands. Anna removed his hands, once more kissed his wet face, and with rapid steps went to the door. Alexey Alexandrovitch walked in, meeting her. Seeing her, he stopped short and bowed his head.

Although she had just said he was better and kinder than she, in the rapid glance she flung at him, taking in his whole figure in all its details, feelings of repulsion and hatred for him and jealousy over her son took possession of her. With a swift gesture she put down her veil, and, quickening her pace, almost ran out of the room.

She had not time to undo, and so carried back with her, the parcel of toys she had chosen the day before in a toy-shop with such love and sorrow.

XXXI

INTENSELY as Anna had longed to see her son, and long as she had been thinking of it and preparing herself for it, she had not in the least expected that seeing him would affect her so deeply. On getting back to her lonely rooms in the hotel she could not for a long while understand why she was there. 'Yes, it's all over, and I am again alone,' she said to herself, and without taking off her hat she sat down in a low chair by the hearth. Fixing her eyes on a bronze clock standing on a table between the windows, she tried to think.

The French maid brought from abroad came in to suggest she should dress. She gazed at her wonderingly and said, 'Presently.' A footman offered her coffee. 'Later on,' she said.

The Italian nurse, after taking the baby out in her best, came in with her, and brought her to Anna. The plump, well-fed little baby, on seeing her mother, as she always did, held out her fat little hands, and with a smile on her toothless mouth, began, like a fish with a float, bobbing her fingers up and down the starched folds of her embroidered skirt, making them rustle. It was impossible not to smile, not to kiss the baby, impossible not to hold out a finger for her to clutch, crowing and prancing all over; impossible not to offer her a lip which she sucked into her little mouth by way of a kiss. And all this Anna did, and took her in her arms and made her dance, and kissed her fresh little cheek and bare little elbows; but at the sight of this child it was plainer than ever to her that the feeling she had for her could not be called love in comparison with what she felt for Seryozha. Everything in this baby was charming, but for some reason all this did not go deep to her heart. On her first child, though the child of an unloved father, had been concentrated all the love that had never found satisfaction. Her baby girl had been born in the most painful circumstances and had not had a hundredth part of the care and thought which had been concentrated on her first child. Besides, in the little girl everything was still in the future, while Seryozha was by now almost a personality, and a personality dearly loved. In him there was a conflict of thought and feeling; he understood her, he loved her, he judged her, she thought, recalling his words and his eyes. And she was for ever—not physically only but spiritually—divided from him, and it was impossible to set this right.

She gave the baby back to the nurse, let her go, and opened the locket in which there was Seryozha's portrait when he was almost of the same age as the girl. She got up, and, taking off her hat, took up from a little table an album in which there were photographs of her son at different ages. She wanted to compare them, and began taking them out of the album. She took them all out except one, the latest and best photograph. In it he was in a white smock, sitting astride a chair, with frowning eyes and smiling lips. It was his best, most characteristic expression. With her little supple hands, her white, delicate fingers, that moved with a peculiar intensity today, she pulled at a corner of the photograph, but the photograph had caught somewhere, and she could not get it out. There was no paper-knife on the table, and so, pulling out the photograph that was next her son's (it was a photograph of Vronsky taken at Rome in a round hat and with long hair), she used it to push out her son's photograph. 'Oh, here is he!' she said, glancing at the portrait of Vronsky, and she suddenly recalled that he was the cause of her present misery. She had not once thought of him all the morning. But now, coming all at once upon that manly, noble face, so familiar and so dear to her, she felt a sudden rush of love for him.

'But where is he? How is it he leaves me alone in my misery?' she thought all at once with a feeling of reproach, forgetting she had herself kept from him everything concerning her son. She sent to ask him to come to her immediately; with a throbbing heart she awaited him, rehearsing to herself the words in which she would tell him all, and the expressions of love with which he would console her. The messenger returned with the answer that he had a visitor with him, but that he would come immediately, and that he asked whether she would let him bring with him Prince Yashvin, who had just arrived in Petersburg. 'He's not coming alone, and since dinner yesterday he has not seen me,' she thought; 'he's not coming so that I could tell him everything, but coming with Yashvin.' And all at once a strange idea came to her: what if he had ceased to love her?

And going over the events of the last few days, it seemed to her that she saw in everything a confirmation of this terrible idea. The fact that he had not dined at home yesterday, and the fact that he had insisted on their taking separate sets of rooms at Petersburg, and that even now he was not coming to her alone, as though he were trying to avoid meeting her face to face.

'But he ought to tell me so. I must know that it is so. If I knew it, then I know what I should do,' she said to herself, utterly unable to picture to herself the position she would be in if she were convinced of his not caring for her. She thought he had ceased to love her, she felt close upon despair, and consequently she felt exceptionally alert. She rang for her maid and went to her dressing-room. As she dressed, she took more care over her appearance than she had done all those days, as though he might if he had grown cold to her, fall in love with her again because she had dressed and arranged her hair in the way most becoming to her.

She heard the bell ring before she was ready. When she went into the drawing-room it was not he, but Yashvin, who met her eyes. Vronsky was looking through the photographs of her son, which she had forgotten on the table, and he made no haste to look round at her.

'We have met already,' she said, putting her little hand into the huge hand of Yashvin, whose bashfulness was so queerly out of keeping with his immense frame and coarse face. 'We met last year at the races. Give them to me,' she said, with a rapid movement snatching from Vronsky the photographs of her son, and glancing significantly at him with flashing eyes. 'Were the races good this year? Instead of them I saw the races in the Corso in Rome. But you don't care for life abroad,' she said with a cordial smile. 'I know you and all your tastes, though I have seen so little of you.'

'I'm awfully sorry for that, for my tastes are mostly bad,' said Yashvin, gnawing at his left moustache.

Having talked a little while, and noticing that Vronsky glanced at the clock, Yashvin asked her whether she would be staying much longer in Petersburg, and unbending his huge figure reached after his cap.

'Not long, I think,' she said hesitatingly, glancing at Vronsky.

'So then we shan't meet again?'

'Come and dine with me,' said Anna resolutely, angry it seemed with herself for her embarrassment, but flushing as she always did when she defined her position before a fresh person. 'The dinner here is not good, but at least you will see him. There is no one of his old friends in the regiment Alexey cares for as he does for you.'

'Delighted,' said Yashvin with a smile, from which Vronsky could see that he liked Anna very much.

Yashvin said good-bye and went away; Vronsky stayed behind.

'Are you going too?' she said to him.

'I'm late already,' he answered. 'Run along! I'll catch you up in a moment,' he called to Yashvin.

She took him by the hand, and without taking her eyes off him, gazed at him while she ransacked her mind for the words to say that would keep him.

'Wait a minute, there's something I want to say to you,' and taking his broad hand she pressed it on her neck. 'Oh, was it right my asking him to dinner?'

'You did quite right,' he said with a serene smile that showed his even teeth, and he kissed her hand.

'Alexey, you have not changed to me?' she said, pressing his hand in both of hers. 'Alexey, I am miserable here. When are we going away?'

'Soon, soon. You wouldn't believe how disagreeable our way of living here is to me too,' he said, and he drew away his hand.

'Well, go, go!' she said in a tone of offence, and she walked quickly away from him.

XXXII

WHEN Vronsky returned home, Anna was not yet home. Soon after he had left, some lady, so they told him, had come to see her, and she had gone out with her. That she had gone out without leaving word where she was going, that she had not yet come back, and that all the morning she had been going about somewhere without a word to him—all this, together with the strange look of excitement in her face in the morning, and the recollection of the hostile tone with which she had before Yashvin almost snatched her son's photographs out of his hands, made him serious. He decided he absolutely must speak openly with her. And he waited for her in her drawing-room. But Anna did not return alone, but brought with her her old unmarried aunt, Princess Oblonsky. This was the lady who had come in the morning, and with whom Anna had gone out shopping. Anna appeared not to notice Vronsky's worried and inquiring expression, and began a lively account of her morning's shopping. He saw that there was something working within her; in her flashing eyes, when they rested for a moment on him, there was an intense concentration, and in her words and movements there was that nervous rapidity and grace which, during the early period of their intimacy, had so fascinated him, but which now so disturbed and alarmed him.

The dinner was laid for four. All were gathered together and about to go into the little dining-room when Tushkevitch made his appearance with a message from Princess Betsy. Princess Betsy begged her to excuse her not having come to say good-bye; she had been indisposed, but begged Anna to come to her between half-past six and nine o'clock. Vronsky glanced at Anna at the precise limit of time, so suggestive of steps having been taken that she should meet no one; but Anna appeared not to notice it.

'Very sorry that I can't come just between half-past six and nine,' she said with a faint smile.

'The princess will be very sorry.'

'And so am I.'

'You're going, no doubt, to hear Patti?' said Tushkevitch.

'Patti? You suggest the idea to me. I would go if it were possible to get a box.'

'I can get one,' Tushkevitch offered his services.

'I should be very, very grateful to you,' said Anna. 'But won't you dine with us?'

Vronsky gave a hardly perceptible shrug. He was at a complete loss to understand what Anna was about. What had she brought the old Princess Oblonsky home for, what had she made Tushkevitch stay to dinner for, and, most amazing of all, why was she sending him for a box? Could she possibly think in her position of going to Patti's benefit, where all the circle of her acquaintances would be? He looked at her with serious eyes, but she responded with that defiant, half-mirthful, half-desperate look, the meaning of which he could not comprehend. At dinner Anna was in aggressively high spirits—she almost flirted both with Tushkevitch and with Yashvin. When they got up from dinner and Tushkevitch had gone to get a box at the opera, Yashvin went to smoke, and Vronsky went down with him to his own rooms. After sitting there for some time he ran upstairs. Anna was already dressed in a low-necked gown of light silk and velvet that she had had made in Paris, and with costly white lace on her head, framing her face, and particularly becoming, showing up her dazzling beauty.

'Are you really going to the theatre?' he said, trying not to look at her.

'Why do you ask with such alarm?' she said, wounded again at his not looking at her. 'Why shouldn't I go?'

She appeared not to understand the motive of his words.

'Oh, of course there's no reason whatever,' he said frowning.

'That's just what I say,' she said, wilfully refusing to see the irony of his tone, and quietly turning back her long, perfumed glove.

'Anna, for God's sake! what is the matter with you?' he said, appealing to her exactly as once her husband had done.

'I don't understand what you are asking.'

'You know that it's out of the question to go.'

'Why so? I'm not going alone. Princess Varvara has gone to dress, she is going with me.'

He shrugged his shoulders with an air of perplexity and despair.

'But do you mean to say you don't know? . . .' he began.

'But I don't care to know!' she almost shrieked. 'I don't care to. Do I regret what I have done? No, no, no! If it were all to do again from the beginning, it would be the same. For us, for you and for me, there is only one thing that matters, whether we love each other. Other people we need not consider. Why are we living here apart and not seeing each other? Why can't I go? I love you, and I don't care for anything,' she said in Russian, glancing at him with a peculiar gleam in her eyes that he could not understand. 'If you have not changed to me, why don't you look at me?'

He looked at her. He saw all the beauty of her face and full dress, always so becoming to her. But now her beauty and elegance were just what irritated him.

'My feeling cannot change, you know, but I beg you, I entreat you,' he said again in French, with a note of tender supplication in his voice, but with coldness in his eyes.

She did not hear his words, but she saw the coldness of his eyes, and answered with irritation—

'And I beg you to explain why I should not go.'

'Because it might cause you . . .' He hesitated.

'I don't understand. Yashvin *n'est pas compromettant*, and Princess Varvara is no worse than others. Oh, here she is!'

XXXIII

VRONSKY for the first time experienced a feeling of anger against Anna, almost a hatred for her wilfully refusing to understand her own position. This feeling was aggravated by his being unable to tell her plainly the cause of his anger. If he had told her directly what he was thinking, he would have said—

'In that dress, with a princess only too well known to everyone, to show yourself at the theatre is equivalent not merely to acknowledging your position as a fallen woman, but is flinging down a challenge to society, that is to say, cutting yourself off from it for ever.'

He could not say that to her. 'But how can she fail to see it, and what is going on in her?' he said to himself. He felt at the same time that his respect for her was diminished while his sense of her beauty was intensified.

He went back scowling to his rooms, and sitting down beside Yashvin, who, with his long legs stretched out on a chair, was drinking brandy and seltzer water, he ordered a glass of the same for himself.

'You were talking of Lankovsky's Powerful. That's a fine horse, and I would advise you to buy him,' said Yashvin, glancing at his comrade's gloomy face. 'His hind-quarters aren't quite first-rate, but the legs and head—one couldn't wish for anything better.'

'I think I will take him,' answered Vronsky.

Their conversation about horses interested him, but he did not for an instant forget Anna, and could not help listening to the sound of steps in the corridor and looking at the clock on the chimney-piece.

'Anna Arkadyevna gave orders to announce that she has gone to the theatre.'

Yashvin, tipping another glass of brandy into the bubbling water, drank it and got up, buttoning his coat.

'Well, let's go,' he said, faintly smiling under his moustaches, and showing by this smile that he knew the cause of Vronsky's gloominess, and did not attach any significance to it.

'I'm not going,' Vronsky answered gloomily.

'Well, I must, I promised to. Good-bye, then. If you do, come to the stalls; you can take Kruzin's stall,' added Yashvin as he went out.

'No, I'm busy.'

'A wife is a care, but it's worse when she's not a wife,' thought Yashvin, as he walked out of the hotel.

Vronsky, left alone, got up from his chair and began pacing up and down the room.

'And what's today? The fourth night. . . . Yegor and his wife are there, and my mother, most likely. Of course all Petersburg's there. Now she's gone in, taken off her cloak and come into the light. Tushkevitch, Yashvin, Princess Varvara,' he pictured them to himself. . . . 'What about me? Either that I'm frightened or have given up to Tushkevitch the right to protect her? From every point of view—stupid,

stupid! . . . And why is she putting me in such a position?' he said with a gesture of despair.

With that gesture he knocked against the table, on which there was standing the seltzer water and the decanter of brandy, and almost upset it. He tried to catch it, let it slip, and angrily kicked the table over and rang.

'If you care to be in my service,' he said to the valet who came in, 'you had better remember your duties. This shouldn't be here. You ought to have cleared away.'

The valet, conscious of his own innocence, would have defended himself, but glancing at his master, he saw from his face that the only thing to do was to be silent, and hurriedly threading his way in and out, dropped down on the carpet and began gathering up the whole and broken glasses and bottles.

'That's not your duty; send the waiter to clear away, and get my dress-coat out.'

Vronsky went into the theatre at half-past eight. The performance was in full swing. The little old box-keeper, recognising Vronsky as he helped him off with his fur coat, called him 'Your Excellency', and suggested he should not take a number but should simply call Fyodor. In the brightly lighted corridor there was no one but the box-opener and two attendants with fur cloaks on their arms listening at the doors. Through the closed doors came the sounds of the discreet *staccato* accompaniment of the orchestra, and a single female voice rendering distinctly a musical phrase. The door opened to let the box-opener slip through, and the phrase drawing to the end reached Vronsky's hearing clearly. But the doors were closed again at once, and Vronsky did not hear the end of the phrase and the cadence of the accompaniment, though he knew from the thunder of applause that it was over. When he entered the hall, brilliantly lighted with chandeliers and gas jets, the noise was still going on. On the stage the singer, bowing and smiling, with bare shoulders flashing with diamonds, was, with the help of the tenor who had given her his arm, gathering up the bouquets that were flying awkwardly over the footlights. Then she went up to a gentleman with glossy pomaded hair parted down the centre, who was stretching across the footlights holding out something to her, and all the public in the stalls as well as in the boxes was in excitement, craning forward, shouting and clapping. The conductor in his high chair assisted in passing the offering, and straightened his white tie. Vronsky walked into the middle of the stalls, and, standing still, began looking about him. That day less than ever was his attention turned upon the familiar, habitual surroundings, the stage, the noise, all the familiar, uninteresting, particoloured herd of spectators in the packed theatre.

There were, as always, the same ladies of some sort with officers of some sort in the back of the boxes; the same gaily dressed women—God knows who—and uniforms and black coats; the same dirty crowd in the upper gallery, and among the crowd, in the boxes and in the front rows, were some forty of the *real* people. And to those oases Vronsky at once directed his attention, and with them he entered at once into relation.

The act was over when he went in, and so he did not go straight to his brother's box, but going up to the first row of the stalls stopped at the footlights with Serpuhovskoy, who, standing with one knee raised and his heel on the footlights, caught sight of him in the distance and beckoned to him, smiling.

Vronsky had not yet seen Anna. He purposely avoided looking in her direction. But he knew by the direction of people's eyes where she was. He looked round discreetly, but he was not seeking her; expecting the worst, his eyes sought for Alexey Alexandrovitch. To his relief Alexey Alexandrovitch was not in the theatre that evening.

'How little of the military man there is left in you!' Serpuhovskoy was saying to him. 'A diplomat, an artist, something of that sort, one would say.'

'Yes, it was like going back home when I put on a black coat,' answered Vronsky, smiling and slowly taking out his opera-glass.

'Well, I'll own I envy you there. When I come back from abroad and put on this,' he touched his epaulettes, 'I regret my freedom.'

Serpuhovskoy had long given up all hope of Vronsky's career, but he liked him as before, and was now particularly cordial to him.

'What a pity you were not in time for the first act!'

Vronsky, listening with one ear, moved his opera-glass from the stalls and scanned the boxes. Near a lady in a turban and a bald old man, who seemed to wave angrily in the moving opera-glass, Vronsky suddenly caught sight of Anna's head, proud, strikingly beautiful, and smiling in the frame of lace. She was in the fifth box, twenty paces from him. She was sitting in front, and slightly turning, was saying something to Yashvin. The setting of her head on her handsome, broad shoulders, and the restrained excitement and brilliance of her eyes and her whole face reminded him of her just as he had seen her at the ball in Moscow. But he felt utterly different towards her beauty now. In his feeling for her now there was no element of mystery, and so her beauty, though it attracted him even more intensely than before, gave him now a sense of injury. She was not looking in his direction, but

Vronsky felt that she had seen him already.

When Vronsky turned the opera-glass again in that direction, he noticed that Princess Varvara was particularly red, and kept laughing unnaturally and looking round at the next box. Anna, folding her fan and tapping it on the red velvet, was gazing away and did not see, and obviously did not wish to see, what was taking place in the next box. Yashvin's face wore the expression which was common when he was losing at cards. Scowling, he sucked the left end of his moustache further and further into his mouth, and cast sidelong glances at the next box.

In that box on the left were the Kartasovs. Vronsky knew them, and knew that Anna was acquainted with them. Madame Kartasov, a thin little woman was standing up in her box, and, her back turned upon Anna, she was putting on a mantle that her husband was holding for her. Her face was pale and angry, and she was talking excitedly. Kartasov, a fat, bald man, was continually looking round at Anna, while he attempted to soothe his wife. When the wife had gone out, the husband lingered a long while, and tried to catch Anna's eye, obviously anxious to bow to her. But Anna, with unmistakable intention, avoided noticing him, and talked to Yashvin, whose cropped head was bent down to her. Kartasov went out without making his salutation, and the box was left empty.

Vronsky could not understand exactly what had passed between the Kartasovs and Anna, but he saw that something humiliating for Anna had happened. He knew this both from what he had seen, and most of all from the face of Anna, who, he could see, was taxing every nerve to carry through the part she had taken up. And in maintaining this attitude of external composure she was completely successful. Anyone who did not know her and her circle, who had not heard all the utterances of the women expressive of commiseration, indignation, and amazement, that she should show herself in society, and show herself so conspicuously with her lace and her beauty, would have admired the serenity and loveliness of this woman without a suspicion that she was undergoing the sensations of a man in the stocks.

Knowing that something had happened, but not knowing precisely what, Vronsky felt a thrill of agonising anxiety, and hoping to find out something, he went towards his brother's box. Purposely choosing the way round furthest from Anna's box, he jostled as he came out against the colonel of his old regiment, talking to two acquaintances. Vronsky heard the name of Madame Karenin, and noticed how the colonel hastened to address Vronsky loudly by name, with a meaning glance at his companions.

'Ah, Vronsky! When are you coming to the regiment? We can't let you off without a supper. You're one of the old set,' said the colonel of his regiment.

'I can't stop, awfully sorry, another time,' said Vronsky, and he ran upstairs towards his brother's box.

The old countess, Vronsky's mother, with her steel-grey curls, was in his brother's box. Varya with the young Princess Sorokin met him in the corridor.

Leaving the Princess Sorokin with her mother, Varya held out her hand to her brother-in-law, and began immediately to speak of what interested him. She was more excited than he had ever seen her.

'I think it's mean and hateful, and Madame Kartasov had no right to do it. Madame Karenin . . .' she began.

'But what is it? I don't know.'

'What? you've not heard?'

'You know I should be the last person to hear of it.'

'There isn't a more spiteful creature than that Madame Kartasov!'

'But what did she do?'

'My husband told me. . . . She has insulted Madame Karenin. Her husband began talking to her across the box, and Madame Kartasov made a scene. She said something aloud, he says, something insulting, and went away.'

'Count, your maman is asking for you,' said the young Princess Sorokin, peeping out of the door of the box.

'I've been expecting you all the while,' said his mother, smiling sarcastically. 'You were nowhere to be seen.'

Her son saw that she could not suppress a smile of delight.

'Good evening, maman. I have come to you,' he said coldly.

'Why aren't you going to *faire la cour à Madame Karenin*?' she went on, when Princess Sorokin had moved away. '*Elle fait sensation. On oublie la Patti pour elle.*'

'Maman, I have asked you not to say anything to me of that,' he answered, scowling.

'I'm only saying what everyone's saying.'

Vronsky made no reply, and saying a few words to Princess Sorokin, he went away. At the door he met his brother.

'Ah, Alexey!' said his brother. 'How disgusting! Idiot of a woman, nothing else. . . . I wanted to go straight to her. Let's go together.'

Vronsky did not hear him. With rapid steps he went downstairs; he felt that he must do something, but he did not know what. Anger with her for having put herself and him in such a false position, together with pity for her suffering, filled his heart. He went down, and made straight for Anna's box. At her box stood Stremov, talking to her.

'There are no more tenors. *Le moule en est brisé!*'

Vronsky bowed to her and stopped to greet Stremov.

'You came in late, I think, and have missed the best song,' Anna said to Vronsky, glancing ironically, he thought, at him.

'I am a poor judge of music,' he said, looking sternly at her.

'Like Prince Yashvin,' she said smiling, 'who considers that Patti sings too loud.'

'Thank you,' she said, her little hand in its long glove taking the play-bill Vronsky picked up, and suddenly at that instant her lovely face quivered. She got up and went into the interior of the box.

Noticing in the next act that her box was empty, Vronsky rousing indignant 'hushes' in the silent audience, went out in the middle of a solo and drove home.

Anna was already at home. When Vronsky went up to her, she was in the same dress as she had worn at the theatre. She was sitting in the first armchair against the wall, looking straight before her. She looked at him, and at once resumed her former position.

'Anna,' he said.

'You, you are to blame for everything!' she cried, with tears of despair and hatred in her voice, getting up.

'I begged, I implored you not to go; I knew it would be unpleasant . . .'

'Unpleasant!' she cried—'hideous! As long as I live I shall never forget it. She said it was a disgrace to sit beside me.'

'A silly woman's chatter,' he said; 'but why risk it, why provoke? . . .'

'I hate your calm. You ought not to have brought me to this. If you had loved me . . .'

'Anna! How does the question of my love come in?'

'Oh, if you loved me, as I love, if you were tortured as I am! . . .' she said, looking at him with an expression of terror.

He was sorry for her, and angry notwithstanding. He assured her of his love because he saw that this was the only means of soothing her, and he did not reproach her in words, but in his heart he reproached her.

And the asseverations of his love, which seemed to him so vulgar that he was ashamed to utter them, she drank in eagerly, and gradually became calmer. The next day, completely reconciled, they left for the country.

PART VI

I

DARYA ALEXANDROVNA spent the summer with her children at Pokrovskoe, at her sister Kitty Levin's. The house on her own estate was quite in ruins, and Levin and his wife had persuaded her to spend the summer with them. Stepan Arkadyevitch greatly approved of the arrangement. He said he was very sorry his official duties prevented him from spending the summer in the country with his family, which would have been the greatest happiness for him; and remaining in Moscow, he came down to the country from time to time for a day or two. Besides the Oblonskys, with all their children and their governess, the old princess too came to stay that summer with the Levins, as she considered it her duty to watch over her inexperienced daughter in her *interesting condition*. Moreover Varenka, Kitty's friend abroad, kept her promise to come to Kitty when she was married, and stayed with her friend. All of these were friends or relations of Levin's wife. And though he liked them all, he rather regretted his own Levin world and ways, which was smothered by this influx of the 'Shtcherbatsky element', as he called it to himself. Of his own relations there stayed with him only Sergey Ivanovitch, but he too was a man of the Koznishev and not the Levin stamp, so that the Levin spirit was utterly obliterated.

In the Levins' house, so long deserted, there were now so many people that almost all the rooms were occupied, and almost every day it happened that the old princess, sitting down to table, counted them all over, and put the thirteenth grandson or granddaughter at a separate table. And Kitty, with her careful housekeeping, had no little trouble to get all the chickens, turkeys, and geese, of which so many were needed to satisfy the summer appetites of the visitors and children.

The whole family were sitting at dinner. Dolly's children, with their governess and Varenka, were making plans for going to look for mushrooms. Sergey Ivanovitch, who was looked up to by all the party for his intellect and learning, with a respect that almost amounted to awe, surprised everyone by joining in the conversation about mushrooms.

'Take me with you. I am very fond of picking mushrooms,' he said, looking at Varenka; 'I think it's a very nice occupation.'

'Oh, we shall be delighted,' answered Varenka, colouring a little. Kitty exchanged meaning glances with Dolly. The proposal of the learned and intellectual Sergey Ivanovitch to go looking for mushrooms with Varenka confirmed certain theories of Kitty's with which her mind had been very busy of late. She made haste to address some remark to her mother, so that her look should not be noticed. After dinner Sergey Ivanovitch sat with his cup of coffee at the drawing-room window, and while he took part in a conversation he had begun with his brother, he watched the door through which the children would start on the mushroom-picking expedition. Levin was sitting in the window near his brother.

Kitty stood beside her husband, evidently awaiting the end of a conversation that had no interest for her, in order to tell him something.

'You have changed in many respects since your marriage, and for the better,' said Sergey Ivanovitch, smiling to Kitty, and obviously little interested in the conversation, 'but you have remained true to your passion for defending the most paradoxical theories.'

'Katya, it's not good for you to stand,' her husband said to her, putting a chair for her and looking significantly at her.

'Oh, and there's no time either,' added Sergey Ivanovitch, seeing the children running out.

At the head of them all Tanya galloped sideways, in her tightly-drawn stockings, and waving a basket and Sergey Ivanovitch's hat, she ran straight up to him.

Boldly running up to Sergey Ivanovitch with shining eyes, so like her father's fine eyes, she handed him his hat and made as though she would put it on for him, softening her freedom by a shy and friendly smile.

'Varenka's waiting,' she said, carefully putting his hat on, seeing from Sergey Ivanovitch's smile that she might do so.

Varenka was standing at the door, dressed in a yellow print gown, with a white kerchief on her head.

'I'm coming, I'm coming, Varvara Andreevna,' said Sergey Ivanovitch, finishing his cup of coffee, and putting into their separate pockets his handkerchief and cigar-case.

'And how sweet my Varenka is! eh?' said Kitty to her husband, as soon as Sergey Ivanovitch rose. She spoke so that Sergey Ivanovitch could hear, and it was clear that she meant him to do so. 'And how good-looking she is—such a refined beauty! Varenka!' Kitty shouted. 'Shall you be in the mill copse? We'll come out to you.'

'You certainly forget your condition, Kitty,' said the old princess, hurriedly coming out at the door. 'You mustn't shout like that.'

Varenka, hearing Kitty's voice and her mother's reprimand, went with light, rapid steps up to Kitty. The rapidity of her movement, her flushed and eager face, everything betrayed that something out of the common was going on in her. Kitty knew what this was, and had been watching her intently. She called Varenka at that moment merely in order mentally to give her a blessing for the important event which, as Kitty fancied, was bound to come to pass that day after dinner in the wood.

'Varenka, I should be very happy if a certain something were to happen,' she whispered as she kissed her.

'And are you coming with us?' Varenka said to Levin in confusion, pretending not to have heard what had been said.

'I am coming, but only as far as the threshing-floor, and there I shall stop.'

'Why, what do you want there?' said Kitty.

'I must go to have a look at the new wagons, and to check the invoice,' said Levin; 'and where will you be?'

'On the terrace.'

II

ON the terrace were assembled all the ladies of the party. They always liked sitting there after dinner, and that day they had work to do there too. Besides the sewing and knitting of baby-clothes, with which all of them were busy, that afternoon jam was being made on the terrace by a method new to Agafea Mihalovna, without the addition of water. Kitty had introduced this new method, which had been in use in her home. Agafea Mihalovna, to whom the task of jam-making had always been intrusted, considering that what had been done in the Levin household could not be amiss, had nevertheless put water with the strawberries, maintaining that the jam could not be made without it. She had been caught in the act, and was now making jam before everyone, and it was to be proved to her conclusively that jam could be very well made without water.

Agafea Mihalovna, her face heated and angry, her hair untidy, and her thin arms bare to the elbows, was turning the preserving-pan over the charcoal stove, looking darkly at the raspberries and devoutly hoping they would stick and not cook properly. The princess, conscious that Agafea Mihalovna's wrath must be chiefly directed against her, as the person responsible for the raspberry jam-making, tried to appear to be absorbed in other things and not interested in the jam, talked of other matters, but cast stealthy glances in the direction of the stove.

'I always buy my maids' dresses myself, of some cheap material,' the princess said, continuing the previous conversation. 'Isn't it time to skim it, my dear?' she added, addressing Agafea Mihalovna. 'There's not the slightest need for you to do it, and it's hot for you,' she said, stopping Kitty.

'I'll do it,' said Dolly, and getting up, she carefully passed the spoon over the frothing sugar, and from time to time shook off the clinging jam from the spoon by knocking it on a plate that was covered with yellow-red scum and blood-coloured syrup. 'How they'll enjoy this at tea-time!' she thought of her children, remembering how she herself as a child had wondered how it was the grown-up people did not eat what was best of all—the scum of the jam.

'Stiva says it's much better to give money.' Dolly took up meanwhile the weighty subject under discussion, what presents should be made to servants. 'But . . .'

'Money's out of the question!' the princess and Kitty exclaimed with one voice. 'They appreciate a present . . .'

'Well, last year, for instance, I bought our Matrona Semyenovna, not a poplin, but something of that sort,' said the princess.

'I remember she was wearing it on your nameday.'

'A charming pattern—so simple and refined,—I should have liked it myself, if she hadn't had it. Something like Varenka's. So pretty and inexpensive.'

'Well, now I think it's done,' said Dolly, dropping the syrup from the spoon.

'When it sets as it drops, it's ready. Cook it a little longer, Agafea Mihalovna.'

'The flies!' said Agafea Mihalovna angrily. 'It'll be just the same,' she added.

'Ah, how sweet it is! don't frighten it!' Kitty said suddenly, looking at a sparrow that had settled on the step and was pecking at the centre of a raspberry.

'Yes, but you keep a little further from the stove,' said her mother.

'*A propos de Varenka*,' said Kitty, speaking in French, as they had been doing all the while, so that Agafea Mihalovna should not understand them, 'you know, maman, I somehow expect things to be settled today. You know what I mean. How splendid it would be!'

'But what a famous matchmaker she is!' said Dolly. 'How carefully and cleverly she throws them together! . . .'

'No! Tell me, maman, what do you think?'

'Why, what is one to think? He' (*he* meant Sergey Ivanovitch) 'might at any time have been a match for anyone in Russia; now, of course, he's not quite a young man, still I know ever so many girls would be glad to marry him even now. . . . She's a very nice girl, but he might . . .'

'Oh no, mamma, do understand why, for him and for her too, nothing better could be imagined. In the first place, she's charming!' said Kitty, crooking one of her fingers.

'He thinks her very attractive, that's certain,' assented Dolly.

'Then he occupies such a position in society that he has no need to look for either fortune or position in his wife. All he needs is a good, sweet wife—a restful one.'

'Well, with her he would certainly be restful,' Dolly assented.

'Thirdly, that she should love him. And so it is . . . that is, it would be so splendid! . . . I look forward to seeing them coming out of the forest—and everything settled. I shall see at once by their eyes. I should be so delighted! What do you think, Dolly?'

'But don't excite yourself. It's not at all the thing for you to be excited,' said her mother.

'Oh, I'm not excited, mamma. I fancy he will make her an offer today.'

'Ah, that's so strange, how and when a man makes an offer! . . . There is a sort of barrier, and all at once it's broken down,' said Dolly, smiling pensively and recalling her past with Stepan Arkadyevitch.

'Mamma, how did papa make you an offer?' Kitty asked suddenly.

'There was nothing out of the way, it was very simple,' answered the princess, but her face beamed all over at the recollection.

'Oh, but how was it? You loved him, anyway, before you were allowed to speak?'

Kitty felt a peculiar pleasure in being able now to talk to her mother on equal terms about those questions of such paramount interest in a woman's life.

'Of course I did; he had come to stay with us in the country.'

'But how was it settled between you, mamma?'

'You imagine, I dare say, that you invented something quite new? It's always just the same: it was settled by the eyes, by smiles . . .'

'How nicely you said that, mamma! It's just by the eyes, by smiles that it's done,' Dolly assented.

'But what words did he say?'

'What did Kostya say to you?'

'He wrote it in chalk. It was wonderful . . . How long ago it seems!' she said.

And the three women all fell to musing on the same thing. Kitty was the first to break the silence. She remembered all that last winter before her marriage, and her passion for Vronsky.

'There's one thing . . . that old love-affair of Varenka's,' she said, a natural chain of ideas bringing her to this point. 'I should have liked to say something to Sergey Ivanovitch, to prepare him. They're all—all men, I mean,' she added, 'awfully jealous over our past.'

'Not all,' said Dolly. 'You judge by your own husband. It makes him miserable even now to remember Vronsky. Eh? that's true, isn't it?'

'Yes,' Kitty answered, a pensive smile in her eyes.

'But I really don't know,' the mother put in in defence of her motherly care of her daughter, 'what there was in your past that could worry him? That Vronsky paid you attentions—that happens to every girl.'

'Oh yes, but we didn't mean that,' Kitty said, flushing a little.

'No, let me speak,' her mother went on, 'why, you yourself would not let me have a talk to Vronsky. Don't you remember?'

'Oh, mamma!' said Kitty, with an expression of suffering.

'There's no keeping you young people in check nowadays. . . . Your friendship could not have gone beyond what was suitable. I should myself have called upon him to explain himself. But, my darling, it's not right for you to be agitated. Please remember that, and calm yourself.'

'I'm perfectly calm, maman.'

'How happy it was for Kitty that Anna came then,' said Dolly, 'and how unhappy for her. It turned out quite the opposite,' she said, struck by her own ideas. 'Then Anna was so happy, and Kitty thought herself unhappy. Now it is just the opposite. I often think of her.'

'A nice person to think about! Horrid, repulsive woman—no heart,' said her mother, who could not forget that Kitty had married not Vronsky, but Levin.

'What do you want to talk of it for?' Kitty said with annoyance. 'I never think about it, and I don't want to think of it . . . And I don't want to think of it,' she said, catching the sound of her husband's well-known step on the steps of the terrace.

'What's that you don't want to think about?' inquired Levin, coming on to the terrace.

But no one answered him, and he did not repeat the question.

'I'm sorry I've broken in on your feminine parliament,' he said, looking round on everyone discontentedly, and perceiving that they had been talking of something which they would not talk about before him.

For a second he felt that he was sharing the feeling of Agafea Mihalovna, vexation at their making jam without water, and altogether at the outside Shtcherbatsky element. He smiled, however, and went up to Kitty.

'Well, how are you?' he asked her, looking at her with the expression with which everyone looked at her now.

'Oh, very well,' said Kitty, smiling, 'and how have things gone with you?'

'The wagon held three times as much as the old carts did. Well, are we going for the children? I've ordered the horses to be put in.'

'What! You want to take Kitty in the wagonette?' her mother said reproachfully.

'Yes, at a walking-pace, princess.'

Levin never called the princess 'maman' as men often do call their mothers-in-law, and the princess disliked his not doing so. But though he liked and respected the princess, Levin could not call her so without a sense of profaning his feeling for his dead mother.

'Come with us, maman,' said Kitty.

'I don't like to see such imprudence.'

'Well, I'll walk then, I'm so well.' Kitty got up and went to her husband and took his hand.

'You may be well, but everything in moderation,' said the princess.

'Well, Agafea Mihalovna, is the jam done?' said Levin, smiling to Agafea Mihalovna, and trying to cheer her up. 'Is it all right in the new way?'

'I suppose it's all right. For our notions it's boiled too long.'

'It'll be all the better, Agafea Mihalovna, it won't mildew, even though our ice has begun to thaw already, so that we've no cool cellar to store it,' said Kitty, at once divining her husband's motive, and addressing the old housekeeper with the same feeling; 'but your pickle's so good that mamma says she never tasted any like it,' she added, smiling, and putting her kerchief straight.

Agafea Mihalovna looked angrily at Kitty.

'You needn't try to console me, mistress. I need only to look at you with him, and I feel happy,' she said, and something in the rough familiarity of that *with him* touched Kitty.

'Come along with us to look for mushrooms, you will show us the best places.' Agafea Mihalovna smiled and shook her head, as though to say: 'I should like to be angry with you too, but I can't.'

'Do it, please, by my receipt,' said the princess; 'put some paper over the jam, and moisten it with a little rum, and without even ice, it will never go mildewy.'

III

KITTY was particularly glad of a chance of being alone with her husband, for she had noticed the shade of mortification that had passed over his face—always so quick to reflect every feeling—at the moment when he had come on to the terrace and asked what they were talking of, and had got no answer.

When they had set off on foot ahead of the others, and had come out of sight of the house on to the beaten dusty road, marked with rusty wheels and sprinkled with grains of corn, she clung faster to his arm and pressed it closer to her. He had quite forgotten the momentary unpleasant impression, and alone with her he felt, now that the thought of her approaching motherhood was never for a moment absent from his mind, a new and delicious bliss, quite pure from all alloy of sense, in the being near to the woman he loved. There was no need of speech, yet he longed to hear the sound of her voice, which like her eyes had changed since she had been with child. In her voice, as in her eyes, there was that softness and gravity which is found in people continually concentrated on some cherished pursuit.

'So you're not tired? Lean more on me,' said he.

'No, I'm so glad of a chance of being alone with you, and I must own though I'm happy with them, I do regret our winter evenings alone.'

'That was good, but this is even better. Both are better,' he said, squeezing her hand.

'Do you know what we were talking about when you came in?'

'About jam?'

'Oh yes, about jam too; but afterwards, about how men make offers.'

'Ah!' said Levin, listening more to the sound of her voice than to the words she was saying, and all the while paying attention to the road, which passed now through the forest, and avoiding places where she might make a false step.

'And about Sergey Ivanovitch and Varenka. You've noticed? . . . I'm very anxious for it,' she went on. 'What do you think about it?' And she peeped into his face.

'I don't know what to think,' Levin answered, smiling. 'Sergey seems very strange to me in that way. I told you, you know . . .'

'Yes, that he was in love with that girl who died . . .'

'That was when I was a child; I know about it from hearsay and tradition. I remember him then. He was wonderfully sweet. But I've watched him since with women; he is friendly, some of them he likes, but one feels that to him they're simply people, not women.'

'Yes, but now with Varenka. . . . I fancy there's something . . .'

'Perhaps there is . . . But one has to know him . . . He's a peculiar, wonderful person. He lives a spiritual life only. He's too pure, too exalted a nature.'

'Why? Would this lower him, then?'

'No, but he's so used to a spiritual life that he can't reconcile himself with actual fact, and Varenka is after all fact.'

Levin had grown used by now to uttering his thought boldly, without taking the trouble of clothing it in exact language. He knew that his wife, in such moments of loving tenderness as now, would understand what he meant to say from a hint, and she did understand him.

'Yes, but there's not so much of that actual fact about her as about me. I can see that he would never have cared for me. She is altogether spiritual.'

'Oh no, he is so fond of you, and I am always so glad when my people like you. . . .'

'Yes, he's very nice to me; but . . .'

'It's not as it was with poor Nikolay . . . you really cared for each other,' Levin finished. 'Why not speak of him?' he added. 'I sometimes blame myself for not; it ends in one's forgetting. Ah, how terrible and dear he was! . . . Yes, what were we talking about?' Levin said, after a pause.

'You think he can't fall in love,' said Kitty, translating into her own language.

'It's not so much that he can't fall in love,' Levin said, smiling, 'but he has not the weakness necessary. . . . I've always envied him, and even now, when I'm so happy, I still envy him.'

'You envy him for not being able to fall in love?'

'I envy him for being better than me,' said Levin. 'He does not live for himself. His whole life is subordinated to his duty. And that's why he can be calm and contented.'

'And you?' Kitty asked, with an ironical and loving smile.

She could never have explained the chain of thought that made her smile; but the last link in it was that her husband, in exalting his brother and abasing himself, was not quite sincere. Kitty knew that this insincerity came from his love for his brother, from his sense of shame at being too happy, and above all from his unflagging craving to be better —she loved it in him, and so she smiled.

'And you? What are you dissatisfied with?' she asked, with the same smile.

Her disbelief in his self-dissatisfaction delighted him, and unconsciously he tried to draw her into giving utterance to the grounds of her disbelief.

'I am happy, but dissatisfied with myself . . .' he said.

'Why, how can you be dissatisfied with yourself if you are happy?'

'Well, how shall I say? . . . In my heart I really care for nothing whatever but that you should not stumble—see? Oh, but really you mustn't skip about like that!' he cried, breaking off to scold her for too agile a movement in stepping over a branch that lay in the path. 'But when I think about myself, and compare myself with others, especially with my brother, I feel I'm a poor creature.'

'But in what way?' Kitty pursued with the same smile. 'Don't you too work for others? What about your cooperative settlement, and your work on the estate, and your book? . . .'

'Oh, but I feel, and particularly just now—it's your fault,' he said, pressing her hand—'that all that doesn't count. I do it in a way half-heartedly. If I could care for all that as I care for you! . . . Instead of that, I do it in these days like a task that is set me.'

'Well, what would you say about papa?' asked Kitty. 'Is he a poor creature then, as he does nothing for the public good?'

'He?—no! But then one must have the simplicity, the straightforwardness, the goodness of your father: and I haven't got that. I do nothing, and I fret about it. It's all your doing. Before there was you—and *this* too,' he added with a glance towards her waist that she understood—'I put all my energies into work; now I can't, and I'm ashamed; I do it just as though it were a task set me, I'm pretending. . . .'

'Well, but would you like to change this minute with Sergey Ivanovitch?' said Kitty. 'Would you like to do this work for the general good, and to love the task set you, as he does, and nothing else?'

'Of course not,' said Levin. 'But I'm so happy that I don't understand anything. So you think he'll make her an offer today?' he added after a brief silence.

'I think so, and I don't think so. Only, I'm awfully anxious for it. Here, wait a minute.' She stooped down and picked a wild camomile at the edge of the path. 'Come, count: he does propose, he doesn't,' she said, giving him the flower.

'He does, he doesn't,' said Levin, tearing off the white petals.

'No, no!' Kitty, snatching at his hand, stopped him. She had been watching his fingers with interest. 'You picked off two.'

'Oh, but see, this little one shan't count to make up,' said Levin, tearing off a little half-grown petal. 'Here's the wagonette overtaking us.'

'Aren't you tired, Kitty?' called the princess.

'Not in the least.'

'If you are you can get in, as the horses are quiet and walking.'

But it was not worth while to get in, they were quite near the place, and all walked on together.

IV

VARENKA, with her white kerchief on her black hair, surrounded by the children, gaily and good-humouredly looking after them, and at the same time visibly excited at the possibility of receiving a declaration from the man she cared for, was very attractive. Sergey Ivanovitch walked beside her, and never left off admiring her. Looking at her, he recalled all the delightful things he had heard from her lips, all the good he knew about her, and became more and more conscious that the feeling he had for her was something special that he had felt long, long ago, and only once, in his early youth. The feeling of happiness in being near her continually grew, and at last reached such a point that, as he put a huge, slender-stalked agaric fungus in her basket, he looked straight into her face, and noticing the flush of glad and alarmed excitement that overspread her face, he was confused himself, and smiled to her in silence a smile that said too much.

'If so,' he said to himself, 'I ought to think it over and make up my mind, and not give way like a boy to the impulse of a moment.'

'I'm going to pick by myself apart from all the rest, or else my efforts will make no show,' he said, and he left the edge of the forest where they were walking on low silky grass between old birch-trees standing far apart, and went more into the heart of the wood, where between the white birch-trunks there were grey trunks of aspen and dark bushes of hazel. Walking some forty paces away, Sergey Ivanovitch, knowing he was out of sight, stood still behind a bushy spindle tree in full flower with its rosy red catkins. It was perfectly still all round him. Only overhead in the birches under which he stood, the flies, like a swarm of bees, buzzed unceasingly, and from time to time the children's voices were floated across to him. All at once he heard, not far from the edge of the wood, the sound of Varenka's contralto voice, calling Grisha, and a smile of delight passed over Sergey Ivanovitch's face. Conscious of this smile, he shook his head disapprovingly at his own condition, and taking out a cigar, he began lighting it. For a long while he could not get a match to light against the trunk of a birch-tree. The soft scales of the white bark rubbed off the phosphorus, and the light went out. At last one of the matches burned, and the fragrant cigar smoke, hovering uncertainly in flat, wide coils, stretched away forwards and upwards over a bush under the overhanging branches of a birch-tree. Watching the streak of smoke, Sergey Ivanovitch walked gently on, deliberating on his position.

'Why not?' he thought. 'If it were only a passing fancy or a passion, if it were only this attraction—this mutual attraction (I can call it a *mutual* attraction), but I felt that it was in contradiction with the whole bent of my life—if I felt that in giving way to this attraction I should be false to my vocation and my duty . . . but it's not so. The only thing I can say against it is that, when I lost Marie, I said to myself that I would remain faithful to her memory. That's the only thing I can say against my feeling. . . . That's a great thing,' Sergey Ivanovitch said to himself, feeling at the same time that this consideration had not the slightest importance for him personally, but would only perhaps detract from his romantic character in the eyes of others. 'But apart from that, however much I searched, I should never find anything to say against my feeling. If I were choosing by considerations of suitability alone, I could not have found anything better.'

However many women and girls he thought of whom he knew, he could not think of a girl who united to such a degree all, positively all, the qualities he would wish to see in his wife. She had all the charm and freshness of youth, but she was not a child; and if she loved him, she loved him consciously as a woman ought to love; that was one thing. Another point: she was not only far from being worldly, but had an unmistakable distaste for worldly society, and at the same time she knew the world, and had all the ways of a woman of the best society, which were absolutely essential to Sergey Ivanovitch's conception of the woman who was to share his life. Thirdly: she was religious, and not like a child, unconsciously religious and good, as Kitty, for example, was, but her life was founded on religious principles. Even in trifling matters, Sergey Ivanovitch found in her all that he wanted in his wife: she was poor and alone in the world, so she would not bring with her a mass of relations and their influence into her husband's house, as he saw now in Kitty's case. She would owe everything to her husband, which was what he had always desired too for his future family life. And this girl, who united all these qualities, loved him. He was a modest man, but he could not help seeing it. And he loved her. There was one consideration against it—his age. But he came of a long-lived family, he had not a single grey hair, no one would have taken him for forty, and he remembered Varenka's saying that it was only in Russia that men of fifty thought themselves old, and that in France a man of fifty considers himself *dans la force de l'age*, while a man of forty is *un jeune homme*. But what did the mere reckoning of years matter when he felt as young in heart as he had been twenty years ago? Was it not youth to feel as he felt now, when coming from the other side to the edge of the wood he saw in the glowing light of the slanting sunbeams the gracious figure of Varenka in her yellow gown with her basket, walking lightly by the trunk of an old birch-tree, and when this impression of the sight of Varenka blended so harmoniously with the beauty of the view, of the yellow oatfield lying bathed in the slanting sunshine, and beyond it the distant ancient forest flecked with yellow and melting into the blue of the distance? His heart throbbed joyously. A softened feeling came over him. He felt that he had made up his mind. Varenka, who had just crouched down to pick a mushroom, rose with a supple movement and looked round. Flinging away the cigar, Sergey Ivanovitch advanced with resolute steps towards her.

V

'VARVARA ANDREEVNA, when I was very young, I set before myself the ideal of the woman I loved and should be happy to call my wife. I have lived through a long life, and now for the first time I have met what I sought—in you. I love you, and offer you my hand.'

Sergey Ivanovitch was saying this to himself while he was ten paces from Varvara. Kneeling down, with her hands over the mushrooms to guard them from Grisha, she was calling little Masha.

'Come here, little ones! There are so many!' she was saying in her sweet, deep voice.

Seeing Sergey Ivanovitch approaching, she did not get up and did not change her position, but everything told him that she felt his presence and was glad of it.

'Well, did you find some?' she asked from under the white kerchief, turning her handsome, gently smiling face to him.

'Not one,' said Sergey Ivanovitch. 'Did you?'

She did not answer, busy with the children who thronged about her.

'That one too, near the twig,' she pointed out to little Masha a little fungus, split in half across its rosy cap by the dry grass from under which it thrust itself. Varenka got up while Masha picked the fungus, breaking it into two white halves. 'This brings back my childhood,' she added, moving apart from the children beside Sergey Ivanovitch.

They walked on for some steps in silence. Varenka saw that he wanted to speak; she guessed of what, and felt faint with joy and panic. They had walked so far away that no one could hear them now, but still he did not begin to speak. It would have been better for Varenka to be silent. After a silence it would have been easier for them to say what they wanted to say than after talking about mushrooms. But against her own will, as it were accidentally, Varenka said—

'So you found nothing? In the middle of the wood there are always fewer, though.' Sergey Ivanovitch sighed and made no answer. He was annoyed that she had spoken about the mushrooms. He wanted to bring her back to the first words she had uttered about her childhood; but after a pause of some length, as though against his own will, he made an observation in response to her last words.

'I have heard that the white edible funguses are found principally at the edge of the wood, though I can't tell them apart.'

Some minutes more passed, they moved still further away from the children, and were quite alone. Varenka's heart throbbed so that she heard it beating, and felt that she was turning red and pale and red again.

To be the wife of a man like Koznishev, after her position with Madame Stahl, was to her imagination the height of happiness. Besides, she was almost certain that she was in love with him. And this moment it would have to be decided. She felt frightened. She dreaded both his speaking and his not speaking.

Now or never it must be said—that Sergey Ivanovitch felt too. Everything in the expression, the flushed cheeks and the downcast eyes of Varenka betrayed a painful suspense. Sergey Ivanovitch saw it and felt sorry for her. He felt even that to say nothing now would be a slight to her. Rapidly in his own mind he ran over all the arguments in support of his decision. He even said over to himself the words in which he meant to put his offer, but instead of those words, some utterly unexpected reflection that occurred to him made him ask—

'What is the difference between the "birch" mushroom and the "white" mushroom?'

Varenka's lips quivered with emotion as she answered—

'In the top part there is scarcely any difference, it's in the stalk.'

And as soon as these words were uttered, both he and she felt that it was over, that what was to have been said would not be said; and their emotion, which had up to then been continually growing more intense, began to subside.

'The birch mushroom's stalk suggests a dark man's chin after two days without shaving,' said Sergey Ivanovitch, speaking quite calmly now.

'Yes, that's true,' answered Varenka smiling, and unconsciously the direction of their walk changed. They began to turn towards the children. Varenka felt both sore and ashamed; at the same time she had a sense of relief.

When he had got home again and went over the whole subject, Sergey Ivanovitch thought his previous decision had been a mistaken one. He could not be false to the memory of Marie.

'Gently, children, gently!' Levin shouted quite angrily to the children, standing before his wife to protect her when the crowd of children flew with shrieks of delight to meet them.

Behind the children Sergey Ivanovitch and Varenka walked out of the wood. Kitty had no need to ask Varenka; she saw from the calm and somewhat crestfallen faces of both that her plans had not come off.

'Well?' her husband questioned her as they were going home again.

'It doesn't bite,' said Kitty, her smile and manner of speaking recalling her father, a likeness Levin often noticed with pleasure.

'How doesn't bite?'

'I'll show you,' she said, taking her husband's hand, lifting it to her mouth, and just faintly brushing it with closed lips. 'Like a kiss on a priest's hand.'

'Which didn't it bite with?' he said, laughing.

'Both. But it should have been like this . . .'

'There are some peasants coming . . .'

'Oh, they didn't see.'

VI

DURING the time of the children's tea the grown-up people sat in the balcony and talked as though nothing had happened, though they all, especially Sergey Ivanovitch and Varenka, were very well aware that there had happened an event which, though negative, was of very great importance. They both had the same feeling, rather like that of a schoolboy after an examination, which has left him in the same class or shut him out of the school for ever. Everyone present, feeling too that something had happened, talked eagerly about extraneous subjects. Levin and Kitty were particularly happy and conscious of their love that evening. And their happiness in their love seemed to imply a disagreeable slur on those who would have liked to feel the same and could not—and they felt a prick of conscience.

'Mark my words, Alexander will not come,' said the old princess.

That evening they were expecting Stepan Arkadyevitch to come down by train, and the old prince had written that possibly he might come too.

'And I know why,' the princess went on; 'he says that young people ought to be left alone for a while at first.'

'But papa has left us alone. We've never seen him,' said Kitty. 'Besides, we're not young people!—we're old, married people by now.'

'Only if he doesn't come, I shall say good-bye to you children,' said the princess, sighing mournfully.

'What nonsense, mamma!' both the daughters fell upon her at once. 'How do you suppose he is feeling? Why, now . . .'

And suddenly there was an unexpected quiver in the princess's voice. Her daughters were silent, and looked at one another. 'Maman always finds something to be miserable about,' they said in that glance. They did not know that happy as the princess was in her daughter's house, and useful as she felt herself to be there, she had been extremely miserable, both on her own account and her husband's, ever since they had married their last and favourite daughter, and the old home had been left empty.

'What is it, Agafea Mihalovna?' Kitty asked suddenly of Agafea Mihalovna, who was standing with a mysterious air, and a face full of meaning.

'About supper.'

'Well, that's right,' said Dolly; 'you go and arrange about it, and I'll go and hear Grisha repeat his lesson, or else he will have done nothing all day.'

'That's my lesson! No, Dolly, I'm going,' said Levin, jumping up.

Grisha, who was by now at a high school, had to go over the lessons of the term in the summer holidays. Darya Alexandrovna, who had been studying Latin with her son in Moscow before, had made it a rule on coming to the Levins' to go over with him, at least once a day, the most difficult lessons of Latin and arithmetic. Levin had offered to take her place, but the mother, having once overheard Levin's lesson, and noticing that it was not given exactly as the teacher in Moscow had given it, said resolutely, though with much embarrassment and anxiety not to mortify Levin, that they must keep strictly to the book as the teacher had done, and that she had better undertake it again herself. Levin was amazed both at Stepan Arkadyevitch, who, by neglecting his duty, threw upon the mother the supervision of studies of which she had no comprehension, and at the teachers for teaching the children so badly. But he promised his sister-in-law to give the lessons exactly as she wished. And he went on teaching Grisha, not in his own way, but by the book, and so took little interest in it, and often forgot the hour of the lesson. So it had been today.

'No, I'm going, Dolly, you sit still,' he said. 'We'll do it all properly, like the book. Only when Stiva comes, and we go out shooting, then we shall have to miss it.'

And Levin went to Grisha.

Varenka was saying the same thing to Kitty. Even in the happy, well-ordered household of the Levins Varenka had succeeded in making herself useful.

'I'll see to the supper, you sit still,' she said, and got up to go to Agafea Mihalovna.

'Yes, yes, most likely they've not been able to get chickens. If so, ours . . .'

'Agafea Mihalovna and I will see about it,' and Varenka vanished with her.

'What a nice girl!' said the princess.

'Not nice, maman; she's an exquisite girl; there's no one else like her.'

'So you are expecting Stepan Arkadyevitch today?' said Sergey Ivanovitch, evidently not disposed to pursue the conversation about Varenka. 'It would be difficult to find two sons-in-law more unlike than yours,' he said with a subtle smile. 'One all movement, only living in society, like a fish in water; the other our Kostya, lively, alert, quick in everything, but as soon as he is in society, he either sinks into apathy, or struggles helplessly like a fish on land.'

'Yes, he's very heedless,' said the princess, addressing Sergey Ivanovitch. 'I've been meaning, indeed, to ask you to tell him that it's out of the question for her' (she indicated Kitty) 'to stay here; that she positively must come to Moscow. He talks of getting a doctor down . . .'

'Maman, he'll do everything; he has agreed to everything,' Kitty said, angry with her mother for appealing to Sergey Ivanovitch to judge in such a matter.

In the middle of their conversation they heard the snorting of horses and the sound of wheels on the gravel. Dolly had not time to get up to go and meet her husband, when from the window of the room below, where Grisha was having his lesson, Levin leaped out and helped Grisha out after him.

'It's Stiva!' Levin shouted from under the balcony. 'We've finished, Dolly, don't be afraid!' he added, and started running like a boy to meet the carriage.

'*Is ea id, ejus, ejus, ejus!*' shouted Grisha, skipping along the avenue.

'And someone else too! Papa, of course!' cried Levin, stopping at the entrance of the avenue. 'Kitty, don't come down the steep staircase, go round.'

But Levin had been mistaken in taking the person sitting in the carriage for the old prince. As he got nearer to the carriage he saw beside Stepan Arkadyevitch not the prince, but a handsome, stout young man in a Scotch cap, with long ends of ribbon behind. This was Vassenka Veslovsky, a distant cousin of the Shtcherbatskys, a brilliant young gentleman in Petersburg and Moscow society. 'A capital fellow, and a keen sportsman,' as Stepan Arkadyevitch said, introducing him.

Not a whit abashed by the disappointment caused by his having come in place of the old prince, Veslovsky greeted Levin gaily, claiming acquaintance with him in the past, and snatching up Grisha into the carriage, lifted him over the pointer that Stepan Arkadyevitch had brought with him.

Levin did not get into the carriage, but walked behind. He was rather vexed at the non-arrival of the old prince, whom he liked more and more the more he saw of him, and also at the arrival of this Vassenka Veslovsky, a quite uncongenial and superfluous person. He seemed to him still more uncongenial and superfluous when, on approaching the steps where the whole party, children and grown-ups, were gathered together in much excitement, Levin saw Vassenka Veslovsky, with a particularly warm and gallant air, kissing Kitty's hand.

'Your wife and I are cousins and very old friends,' said Vassenka Veslovsky, once more shaking Levin's hand with great warmth.

'Well, are there plenty of birds?' Stepan Arkadyevitch said to Levin, hardly leaving time for everyone to utter their greetings. 'We've come with the most savage intentions. Why, maman, they've not been in Moscow since! Look, Tanya, here's something for you! Get it, please, it's in the carriage, behind!' he talked in all directions. 'How pretty you've grown, Dolly,' he said to his wife, once more kissing her hand, holding it in one of his, and patting it with the other.

Levin, who a minute before had been in the happiest frame of mind, now looked darkly at everyone, and everything displeased him.

'Who was it he kissed yesterday with those lips?' he thought, looking at Stepan Arkadyevitch's tender demonstrations to his wife. He looked at Dolly, and he did not like her either.

'She doesn't believe in his love. So what is she so pleased about? Revolting!' thought Levin.

He looked at the princess, who had been so dear to him a minute before, and he did not like the manner in which she welcomed this Vassenka, with his ribbons, just as though she were in her own house.

Even Sergey Ivanovitch, who had come out too on to the steps, seemed to him unpleasant with the show of cordiality with which he met Stepan Arkadyevitch, though Levin knew that his brother neither liked nor respected Oblonsky.

And Varenka, even she seemed hateful, with her air *sainte nitouche* making the acquaintance of this gentleman, while all the while she was thinking of nothing but getting married.

And more hateful than anyone was Kitty for falling in with the tone of gaiety with which this gentleman regarded his visit in the country, as though it were a holiday for himself and everyone else. And, above all, unpleasant was that particular smile with which she responded to his smile.

Noisily talking, they all went into the house; but as soon as they were all seated, Levin turned and went out.

Kitty saw something was wrong with her husband. She tried to seize a moment to speak to him alone, but he made haste to get away from her, saying he was wanted at the counting-house. It was long since his own work on the estate had seemed to him so important as at that moment. 'It's all holiday for them,' he thought; 'but these are no holiday matters, they won't wait, and there's no living without them.'

VII

LEVIN came back to the house only when they sent to summon him to supper. On the stairs were standing Kitty and Agafea Mihalovna, consulting about wines for supper.

'But why are you making all this fuss? Have what we usually do.'

'No, Stiva doesn't drink . . . Kostya, stop, what's the matter?' Kitty began, hurrying after him, but he strode ruthlessly away to the dining-room without waiting for her, and at once joined in the lively general conversation which was being maintained there by Vassenka Veslovsky and Stepan Arkadyevitch.

'Well, what do you say, are we going shooting tomorrow?' said Stepan Arkadyevitch.

'Please, do let's go,' said Veslovsky, moving to another chair, where he sat down sideways, with one fat leg crossed under him.

'I shall be delighted, we will go. And have you had any shooting yet this year?' said Levin to Veslovsky, looking intently at his leg, but speaking with that forced amiability that Kitty knew so well in him, and that was so out of keeping with him. 'I can't answer for our finding grouse, but there are plenty of snipe. Only we ought to start early. You're not tired? Aren't you tired, Stiva?'

'Me tired? I've never been tired yet. Suppose we stay up all night. Let's go a walk!'

'Yes, really, let's not go to bed at all! Capital!' Veslovsky chimed in.

'Oh, we all know you can do without sleep, and keep other people up too,' Dolly said to her husband, with that faint note of irony in her voice which she almost always had now with her husband. 'But to my thinking, it's time for bed now. . . . I'm going, I don't want supper.'

'No, do stay a little, Dolly,' said Stepan Arkadyevitch, going round to her side behind the table where they were having supper. 'I've so much still to tell you.'

'Nothing really, I suppose.'

'Do you know Veslovsky has been at Anna's, and he's going to them again? You know they're hardly fifty miles from you, and I too must certainly go over there. Veslovsky, come here!'

Vassenka crossed over to the ladies, and sat down beside Kitty.

'Ah, do tell me, please; you have stayed with her? How was she?' Darya Alexandrovna appealed to him.

Levin was left at the other end of the table, and though never pausing in his conversation with the princess and Varenka, he saw that there was an eager and mysterious conversation going on between Stepan Arkadyevitch, Dolly, Kitty, and Veslovsky. And that was not all. He saw on his wife's face an expression of real feeling as she gazed with fixed eyes on the handsome face of Vassenka, who was telling them something with great animation.

'It's exceedingly nice at their place,' Veslovsky was telling them about Vronsky and Anna. 'I can't, of course, take it upon myself to judge, but in their house you feel the real feeling of home.'

'What do they intend doing?'

'I believe they think of going to Moscow.'

'How jolly it would be for us all to go over to them together! When are you going there?' Stepan Arkadyevitch asked Vassenka.

'I'm spending July there.'

'Will you go?' Stepan Arkadyevitch said to his wife.

'I've been wanting to a long while; I shall certainly go,' said Dolly. 'I am sorry for her, and I know her. She's a splendid woman. I will go alone, when you go back, and then I shall be in no one's way. And it will be better indeed without you.'

'To be sure,' said Stepan Arkadyevitch. 'And you, Kitty?'

'I? Why should I go?' Kitty said, flushing all over, and she glanced round at her husband.

'Do you know Anna Arkadyevna, then?' Veslovsky asked her. 'She's a very fascinating woman?'

'Yes,' she answered Veslovsky, crimsoning still more. She got up and walked across to her husband.

'Are you going shooting, then, tomorrow?' she said.

His jealousy had in these few moments, especially at the flush that had overspread her cheeks while she was talking to Veslovsky, gone far indeed. Now as he heard her words, he construed them in his own fashion. Strange as it was to him afterwards to recall it, it seemed to him at the moment clear that in asking whether he was going shooting, all she cared to know was whether he would give that pleasure to Vassenka Veslovsky, with whom, as he fancied, she was in love.

'Yes, I'm going,' he answered her in an unnatural voice, disagreeable to himself.

'No, better spend the day here tomorrow, or Dolly won't see anything of her husband, and set off the day after,' said Kitty.

The motive of Kitty's words was interpreted by Levin thus: 'Don't separate me from *him*. I don't care about *your* going, but do let me enjoy the society of this delightful young man.'

'Oh, if you wish, we'll stay here tomorrow,' Levin answered, with peculiar amiability.

Vassenka meanwhile, utterly unsuspecting the misery his presence had occasioned, got up from the table after Kitty, and watching her with smiling and admiring eyes, he followed her.

Levin saw that look. He turned white, and for a minute he could hardly breathe. 'How dare he look at my wife like that!' was the feeling that boiled within him.

'Tomorrow, then? Do, please, let us go,' said Vassenka, sitting down on a chair, and again crossing his leg as his habit was.

Levin's jealousy went further still. Already he saw himself a deceived husband, looked upon by his wife and her lover as simply necessary to provide them with the conveniences and pleasures of life. . . . But in spite of that he made polite and hospitable inquiries of Vassenka about his shooting, his gun, and his boots, and agreed to go shooting next day.

Happily for Levin, the old princess cut short his agonies by getting up herself and advising Kitty to go to bed. But even at this point Levin could not escape another agony. As he said good-night to his hostess, Vassenka would again have kissed her hand, but Kitty, reddening, drew back her hand and said with a naïve bluntness, for which the old princess scolded her afterwards—

'We don't like that fashion.'

In Levin's eyes she was to blame for having allowed such relations to arise, and still more to blame for showing so awkwardly that she did not like them.

'Why, how can one want to go to bed!' said Stepan Arkadyevitch, who, after drinking several glasses of wine at supper, was now in his most charming and sentimental humour. 'Look, Kitty,' he said, pointing to the moon, which had just risen behind the lime-trees—'how exquisite! Veslovsky, this is the time for a serenade. You know, he has a splendid voice; we practised songs together along the road. He has brought some lovely songs with him, two new ones. Varvara Andreevna and he must sing some duets.'

When the party had broken up, Stepan Arkadyevitch walked a long while about the avenue with Veslovsky; their voices could be heard singing one of the new songs.

Levin hearing these voices sat scowling in an easy-chair in his wife's bedroom, and maintained an obstinate silence when she asked him what was wrong. But when at last with a timid glance she hazarded the question: 'Was there perhaps something you disliked about Veslovsky?' —it all burst out, and he told her all. He was humiliated himself at what he was saying, and that exasperated him all the more.

He stood facing her with his eyes glittering menacingly under his scowling brows, and he squeezed his strong arms across his chest, as though he were straining every nerve to hold himself in. The expression of his face would have been grim, and even cruel, if it had not at the same time had a look of suffering which touched her. His jaws were twitching, and his voice kept breaking.

'You must understand that I'm not jealous, that's a nasty word. I can't be jealous, and believe that. . . . I can't say what I feel, but this is awful. . . . I'm not jealous, but I'm wounded, humiliated that anybody dare think, that anybody dare look at you with eyes like that.'

'Eyes like what?' said Kitty, trying as conscientiously as possible to recall every word and gesture of that evening and every shade implied in them.

At the very bottom of her heart she did think there had been something precisely at the moment when he had crossed over after her to the other end of the table; but she dared not own it even to herself, and would have been even more unable to bring herself to say so to him, and so increase his suffering.

'And what can there possibly be attractive about me as I am now? . . .'

'Ah!' he cried, clutching at his head, 'you shouldn't say that! . . . If you had been attractive then . . .'

'Oh no, Kostya, oh, wait a minute, oh, do listen!' she said, looking at him with an expression of pained commiseration. 'Why, what can you be thinking about! When for me there's no one in the world, no one, no one! . . . Would you like me never to see anyone?'

For the first minute she had been offended at his jealousy; she was angry that the slightest amusement, even the most innocent, should be forbidden her; but now she would readily have sacrificed, not merely such trifles, but everything, for his peace of mind, to save him from the agony he was suffering.

'You must understand the horror and comedy of my position,' he went on in a desperate whisper; 'that he's in my house, that he's done nothing improper positively except his free and easy airs and the way he sits on his legs. He thinks it's the best possible form, and so I'm obliged to be civil to him.'

'But, Kostya, you're exaggerating,' said Kitty, at the bottom of her heart rejoicing at the depth of his love for her, shown now in his jealousy.

'The most awful part of it all is that you're just as you always are, and especially now when to me you're something sacred, and we're so happy, so particularly happy—and all of a sudden a little wretch . . . He's not a little wretch; why should I abuse him? I have nothing to do with him. But why should my, and your, happiness . . .'

'Do you know, I understand now what it's all come from,' Kitty was beginning.

'Well, what? what?'

'I saw how you looked while we were talking at supper.'

'Well, well!' Levin said in dismay.

She told him what they had been talking about. And as she told him, she was breathless with emotion. Levin was silent for a space, then he scanned her pale and distressed face, and suddenly he clutched at his head.

'Katya, I've been worrying you! Darling, forgive me! It's madness! Katya, I'm a criminal. And how could you be so distressed at such idiocy?'

'Oh, I was sorry for you.'

'For me? for me? How mad I am! . . . But why make you miserable? It's awful to think that any outsider can shatter our happiness.'

'It's humiliating too, of course.'

'Oh, then I'll keep him here all the summer, and will overwhelm him with civility,' said Levin, kissing her hands. 'You shall see. Tomorrow . . . Oh yes, we are going tomorrow.'

VIII

NEXT day, before the ladies were up, the wagonette and a trap for the shooting-party were at the door, and Laska, aware since early morning that they were going shooting, after much whining and darting to and fro, had sat herself down in the wagonette beside the coachman, and, disapproving of the delay, was excitedly watching the door from which the sportsmen still did not come out. The first to come out was Vassenka Veslovsky, in new high boots that reached halfway up his thick thighs, in a green blouse, with a new Russian leather cartridge-belt, and in his Scotch cap with ribbons, with a brand-new English gun without a sling. Laska flew up to him, welcomed him, and jumping up, asked him in her own way whether the others were coming soon, but getting no answer from him, she returned to her post of observation and sank into repose again, her head on one side, and one ear pricked up to listen. At last the door opened with a creak, and Stepan Arkadyevitch's spot-and-tan pointer Krak flew out, running round and round and turning over in the air. Stepan Arkadyevitch himself followed with a gun in his hand and a cigar in his mouth.

'Good dog, good dog, Krak!' he cried encouragingly to the dog, who put his paws up on his chest, catching at his game-bag. Stepan Arkadyevitch was dressed in rough leggings and spats, in torn trousers and a short coat. On his head there was a wreck of a hat of indefinite form, but his gun of a new patent was a perfect gem, and his game-bag and cartridge-belt, though worn, were of the very best quality.

Vassenka Veslovsky had had no notion before that it was truly *chic* for a sportsman to be in tatters, but to have his shooting outfit of the best quality. He saw it now as he looked at Stepan Arkadyevitch, radiant in his rags, graceful, well-fed, and joyous, a typical Russian nobleman. And he made up his mind that next time he went shooting he would certainly adopt the same get-up.

'Well, and what about our host?' he asked.

'A young wife,' said Stepan Arkadyevitch, smiling.

'Yes, and such a charming one!'

'He came down dressed. No doubt he's run up to her again.'

Stepan Arkadyevitch guessed right. Levin had run up again to his wife to ask her once more if she forgave him for his idiocy yesterday, and, moreover, to beg her for Christ's sake to be more careful. The great thing was for her to keep away from the children—they might any minute push against her. Then he had once more to hear her declare that she was not angry with him for going away for two days, and to beg her to be sure to send him a note next morning by a servant on horseback, to write him, if it were but two words only, to let him know that all was well with her.

Kitty was distressed, as she always was, at parting for a couple of days from her husband, but when she saw his eager figure, looking big and strong in his shooting-boots and his white blouse, and a sort of sportsman elation and excitement incomprehensible to her, she forgot her own chagrin for the sake of his pleasure, and said good-bye to him cheerfully.

'Pardon, gentlemen!' he said, running out on to the steps. 'Have you put the lunch in? Why is the chestnut on the right? Well, it doesn't matter. Laska, down; go and lie down!'

'Put it with the herd of oxen,' he said to the herdsman, who was waiting for him at the steps with some question. 'Excuse me, here comes another villain.'

Levin jumped out of the wagonette, in which he had already taken his seat, to meet the carpenter, who came towards the steps with a rule in his hand.

'You didn't come to the counting-house yesterday, and now you're detaining me. Well, what is it?'

'Would your honour let me make another turning? It's only three steps to add. And we make it just fit at the same time. It will be much more convenient.'

'You should have listened to me,' Levin answered with annoyance. 'I said: Put the lines and then fit in the steps. Now there's no setting it right. Do as I told you, and make a new staircase.'

The point was that in the lodge that was being built the carpenter had spoilt the staircase, fitting it together without calculating the space it was to fill, so that the steps were all sloping when it was put in place. Now the carpenter wanted keeping the same staircase, to add three steps.

'It will be much better.'

'But where's your staircase coming out with its three steps?'

'Why, upon my word, sir,' the carpenter said with a contemptuous smile. 'It comes out right at the very spot. It starts, so to speak,' he said with a persuasive gesture; 'it comes down, and comes down, and comes out.'

'But three steps will add to the length too . . . where is it to come out?'

'Why, to be sure, it'll start from the bottom and go up and go up, and come out so,' the carpenter said obstinately and convincingly.

'It'll reach the ceiling and the wall.'

'Upon my word! Why, it'll go up, and up, and come out like this.'

Levin took out a ramrod and began sketching him the staircase in the dust.

'There, do you see?'

'As your honour likes,' said the carpenter, with a sudden gleam in his eyes, obviously understanding the thing at last. 'It seems it'll be best to make a new one.'

'Well, then, do it as you're told,' Levin shouted, seating himself in the wagonette. 'Down! Hold the dogs, Philip!'

Levin felt now at leaving behind all his family and household cares such an eager sense of joy in life and expectation that he was not disposed to talk. Besides that, he had that feeling of concentrated excitement that every sportsman experiences as he approaches the scene of action. If he had anything on his mind at that moment, it was only the doubt whether they would start anything in the Kolpensky marsh, whether Laska would show to advantage in comparison with Krak, and whether he would shoot well that day himself. Not to disgrace himself before a new spectator—not to be outdone by Oblonsky—that too was a thought that crossed his brain.

Oblonsky was feeling the same, and he too was not talkative. Vassenka Veslovsky kept up alone a ceaseless flow of cheerful chatter. As he listened to him now, Levin felt ashamed to think how unfair he had been to him the day before. Vassenka was really a nice fellow, simple, good-hearted, and very good-humoured. If Levin had met him before he was married, he would have made friends with him. Levin rather disliked his holiday attitude to life and a sort of free and easy assumption of elegance. It was as though he assumed a high degree of importance in himself that could not be disputed, because he had long nails and a stylish cap, and everything else to correspond; but this could be forgiven for the sake of his good nature and good breeding. Levin liked him for his good education, for speaking French and English with such an excellent accent, and for being a man of his world.

Vassenka was extremely delighted with the left horse, a horse of the Don steppes. He kept praising him enthusiastically. 'How fine it must be galloping over the steppes on a steppe horse! Eh? isn't it?' he said. He had imagined riding on a steppe horse as something wild and romantic, and it had turned out nothing of the sort. But his simplicity, particularly in conjunction with his good looks, his amiable smile, and the grace of his movements, was very attractive. Either because his nature was sympathetic to Levin, or because Levin was trying to atone for his sins of the previous evening by seeing nothing but what was good in him, anyway he liked his society.

After they had driven over two miles from home, Veslovsky all at once felt for a cigar and his pocket-book, and did not know whether he had lost them or left them on the table. In the pocket-book there were thirty-seven pounds, and so the matter could not be left in uncertainty.

'Do you know what, Levin, I'll gallop home on that left trace-horse. That will be splendid. Eh?' he said, preparing to get out.

'No, why should you?' answered Levin, calculating that Vassenka could hardly weigh less than seventeen stone. 'I'll send the coachman.'

The coachman rode back on the trace-horse, and Levin himself drove the remaining pair.

IX

'WELL, now, what's our plan of campaign? Tell us all about it,' said Stepan Arkadyevitch.

'Our plan is this. Now we're driving to Gvozdyov. In Gvozdyov there's a grouse marsh on this side, and beyond Gvozdyov come some magnificent snipe marshes where there are grouse too. It's hot now, and we'll get there—it's fifteen miles or so—towards evening and have some evening shooting; we'll spend the night there and go on tomorrow to the bigger moors.'

'And is there nothing on the way?'

'Yes; but we'll reserve ourselves;; besides it's hot. There are two nice little places, but I doubt there being anything to shoot.'

Levin would himself have liked to go into these little places, but they were near home; he could shoot over them any time, and they were only little places—there would hardly be room for three to shoot. And so, with some insincerity, he said that he doubted there being anything to shoot. When they reached a little marsh Levin would have driven by, but Stepan Arkadyevitch, with the experienced eye of a sportsman, at once detected reeds visible from the road.

'Shan't we try that?' he said, pointing to the little marsh.

'Levin, do, please! how delightful!' Vassenka Veslovsky began begging, and Levin could but consent.

Before they had time to stop, the dogs had flown one before the other into the marsh.

'Krak! Laska! . . .'

The dogs came back.

'There won't be room for three. I'll stay here,' said Levin, hoping they would find nothing but peewits, who had been startled by the dogs, and turning over in their flight, were plaintively wailing over the marsh.

'No! Come along, Levin, let's go together!' Veslovsky called.

'Really, there's not room. Laska, back, Laska! You won't want another dog, will you?'

Levin remained with the wagonette, and looked enviously at the sportsmen. They walked right across the marsh. Except little birds and peewits, of which Vassenka killed one, there was nothing in the marsh.

'Come, you see now that it was not that I grudged the marsh,' said Levin, 'only it's wasting time.'

'Oh no, it was jolly all the same. Did you see us?' said Vassenka Veslovsky, clambering awkwardly into the wagonette with his gun and his peewit in his hands. 'How splendidly I shot this bird! Didn't I? Well, shall we soon be getting to the real place?'

The horses started off suddenly, Levin knocked his head against the stock of someone's gun, and there was the report of a shot. The gun did actually go off first, but that was how it seemed to Levin. It appeared that Vassenka Veslovsky had pulled only one trigger, and had left the other hammer still cocked. The charge flew into the ground without doing harm to anyone. Stepan Arkadyevitch shook his head and laughed reprovingly at Veslovsky. But Levin had not the heart to reprove him. In the first place, any reproach would have seemed to be called forth by the danger he had incurred and the bump that had come up on Levin's forehead. And besides, Veslovsky was at first so naïvely distressed, and then laughed so good-humouredly and infectiously at their general dismay, that one could not but laugh with him.

When they reached the second marsh, which was fairly large, and would inevitably take some time to shoot over, Levin tried to persuade them to pass it by. But Veslovsky again over-persuaded him. Again, as the marsh was narrow, Levin, like a good host, remained with the carriage.

Krak made straight for some clumps of sedge. Vassenka Veslovsky was the first to run after the dog. Before Stepan Arkadyevitch had time to come up, a grouse flew out. Veslovsky missed it and it flew into an unmown meadow. This grouse was left for Veslovsky to follow up. Krak found it again and pointed, and Veslovsky shot it and went back to the carriage. 'Now you go and I'll stay with the horses,' he said.

Levin had begun to feel the pangs of a sportsman's envy. He handed the reins to Veslovsky and walked into the marsh.

Laska, who had been plaintively whining and fretting against the injustice of her treatment, flew straight ahead to a hopeful place that Levin knew well, and that Krak had not yet come upon.

'Why don't you stop her?' shouted Stepan Arkayevitch.

'She won't scare them,' answered Levin, sympathising with his bitch's pleasure and hurrying after her.

As she came nearer and nearer to the familiar breeding-places there was more and more earnestness in Laska's exploration. A little marsh bird did not divert her attention for more than an instant. She made one circuit round the clump of reeds, was beginning a second, and suddenly quivered with excitement and became motionless.

'Come, come, Stiva!' shouted Levin, feeling his heart beginning to beat more violently; and all of a sudden, as though some sort of shutter had been drawn back from his straining ears, all sounds, confused but loud, began to beat on his hearing, losing all sense of distance. He heard the steps of Stepan Arkadyevitch, mistaking them for the tramp of the horses in the distance; he heard the brittle sound of the twigs on which he had trodden, taking this sound for the flying of a grouse. He heard too, not far behind him, a splashing in the water, which he could not explain to himself.

Picking his steps, he moved up to the dog.

'Fetch it!'

Not a grouse but a snipe flew up from beside the dog. Levin had lifted his gun, but at the instant when he was taking aim, the sound of splashing grew louder, came closer, and was joined with the sound of Veslovsky's voice, shouting something with strange loudness. Levin saw he had his gun pointed behind the snipe, but still he fired.

When he had made sure he had missed, Levin looked round and saw the horses and the wagonette not on the road but in the marsh.

Veslovsky, eager to see the shooting, had driven into the marsh, and got the horses stuck in the mud.

'Damn the fellow!' Levin said to himself, as he went back to the carriage that had sunk in the mire. 'What did you drive in for?' he said to him drily, and calling the coachman, he began pulling the horses out.

Levin was vexed both at being hindered from shooting and at his horses getting stuck in the mud, and still more at the fact that neither Stepan Arkadyevitch nor Veslovsky helped him and the coachman to unharness the horses and get them out, since neither of them had the slightest notion of harnessing. Without vouchsafing a syllable in reply to Vassenka's protestations that it had been quite dry there, Levin worked in silence with the coachman at extricating the horses. But then, as he got warm at the work and saw how assiduously Veslovsky was tugging at the wagonette by one of the mud-guards, so that he broke it indeed, Levin blamed himself for having under the influence of yesterday's feelings been too cold to Veslovsky, and tried to be particularly genial so as to smooth over his chilliness. When everything had been put right, and the carriage had been brought back to the road, Levin had the lunch served.

'*Bon appétit—bonne conscience! Ce poulet va tomber jusqu'au fond de mes bottes,*' Vassenka, who had recovered his spirits, quoted the French saying as he finished his second chicken. 'Well, now our troubles are over, now everything's going to go well. Only, to atone for my sins, I'm bound to sit on the box. That's so? eh? No, no! I'll be your Automedon. You shall see how I'll get you along,' he answered, not letting go the rein, when Levin begged him to let the coachman drive. 'No, I must atone for my sins, and I'm very comfortable on the box.' And he drove.

Levin was a little afraid he would exhaust the horses, especially the chestnut, whom he did not know how to hold in; but unconsciously he fell under the influence of his gaiety and listened to the songs he sang all the way on the box, or the descriptions and representations he gave of driving in the English fashion, four-in-hand; and it was in the very best of spirits that after lunch they drove to the Gvozdyov marsh.

X

VASSENKA drove the horses so smartly that they reached the marsh too early, while it was still hot.

As they drew near this more important marsh, the chief aim of their expedition, Levin could not help considering how he could get rid of Vassenka and be free in his movements. Stepan Arkadyevitch evidently had the same desire, and on his face Levin saw the look of anxiety always present in a true sportsman when beginning shooting, together with a certain good-humoured slyness peculiar to him.

'How shall we go? It's a splendid marsh, I see, and there are hawks,' said Stepan Arkadyevitch, pointing to two great birds hovering over the reeds. 'Where there are hawks, there is sure to be game.'

'Now, gentlemen,' said Levin, pulling up his boots and examining the lock of his gun with rather a gloomy expression, 'do you see those reeds?' He pointed to an oasis of blackish green in the huge half-mown wet meadow that stretched along the right bank of the river. 'The marsh begins here, straight in front of us, do you see—where it is greener? From here it runs to the right where the horses are; there are breeding-places there, and grouse, and all round those reeds as far as that alder, and right up to the mill. Over there, do you see, where the pools are? That's the best place. There I once shot seventeen snipe. We'll separate with the dogs and go in different directions, and then meet over there at the mill.'

'Well, which shall go to left and which to right?' asked Stepan Arkadyevitch. 'It's wider to the right; you two go that way and I'll take the left,' he said with apparent carelessness.

'Capital! we'll make the bigger bag! Yes, come along, come along!' Vassenka exclaimed.

Levin could do nothing but agree, and they divided.

As soon as they entered the marsh, the two dogs began hunting about together and made towards the green, slime-covered pool. Levin knew Laska's method, wary and indefinite; he knew the place too and expected a whole covey of snipe.

'Veslovsky, beside me, walk beside me!' he said in a faint voice to his companion splashing in the water behind him. Levin could not help feeling an interest in the direction his gun was pointed, after that casual shot near the Kolpensky marsh.

'Oh, I won't get in your way, don't trouble about me.'

But Levin could not help troubling, and recalled Kitty's words at parting: 'Mind you don't shoot one another.' The dogs came nearer and nearer, passed each other, each pursuing its own scent. The expectation of snipe was so intense that to Levin the squelching sound of his own heel, as he drew it up out of the mire, seemed to be the call of a snipe, and he clutched and pressed the lock of his gun.

'Bang! bang!' sounded almost in his ear. Vassenka had fired at a flock of ducks which was hovering over the marsh and flying at that moment towards the sportsmen, far out of range. Before Levin had time to look round, there was the whir of one snipe, another, a third, and some eight more rose one after another.

Stepan Arkadyevitch hit one at the very moment when it was beginning its zigzag movements, and the snipe fell in a heap into the mud. Oblonsky aimed deliberately at another, still flying low in the reeds, and together with the report of the shot, that snipe too fell, and it could be seen fluttering out where the sedge had been cut, its unhurt wing showing white beneath.

Levin was not so lucky: he aimed at his first bird too low, and missed; he aimed at it again, just as it was rising, but at that instant another snipe flew up at his very feet, distracting him so that he missed again.

While they were loading their guns, another snipe rose, and Veslovsky, who had had time to load again, sent two charges of small-shot into the water. Stepan Arkadyevitch picked up his snipe, and with sparkling eyes looked at Levin.

'Well, now let us separate,' said Stepan Arkadyevitch, and limping on his left foot, holding his gun in readiness and whistling to his dog, he walked off in one direction. Levin and Veslovsky walked in the other.

It always happened with Levin that when his first shots were a failure he got hot and out of temper, and shot badly the whole day. So it was that day. The snipe showed themselves in numbers. They kept flying up from just under the dogs, from under the sportmen's legs, and Levin might have retrieved his ill-luck. But the more he shot, the more he felt disgraced in the eyes of Veslovsky, who kept popping away merrily and indiscriminately, killing nothing, and not in the slightest abashed by his ill-success. Levin, in feverish haste, could not restrain himself, got more and more out of temper, and ended by shooting almost without a hope of hitting. Laska, indeed, seemed to understand this. She began looking more languidly, and gazed back at the sportsmen, as it were, with perplexity or reproach in her eyes. Shots followed shots in rapid succession. The smoke of the powder hung about the sportsmen, while in the great roomy net of the game-bag there were only three light little snipe. And of these one had been killed by Veslovsky alone, and one by both of them together. Meanwhile from the other side of the marsh came the sound of Stepan Arkadyevitch's shots, not frequent, but, as Levin fancied, well-directed, for almost after each they heard 'Krak, Krak, *apporte*!'

This excited Levin still more. The snipe were floating continually in the air over the reeds. Their whirring wings close to the earth, and their harsh cries high in the air, could be heard on all sides; the snipe that had risen first and flown up into the air, settled again before the sportsmen. Instead of two hawks there were now dozens of them hovering with shrill cries over the marsh.

After walking through the larger half of the marsh, Levin and Veslovsky reached the place where the peasants' mowing-grass was divided into long strips reaching to the reeds, marked off in one place by the trampled grass, in another by a path mown through it. Half of these strips had already been mown.

Though there was not so much hope of finding birds in the uncut part as the cut part, Levin had promised Stepan Arkadyevitch to meet him, and so he walked on with his companion through the cut and uncut patches.

'Hi, sportsmen!' shouted one of a group of peasants, sitting on an unharnessed cart; 'come and have some lunch with us! Have a drop of wine!'

Levin looked round.

'Come along, it's all right!' shouted a good-humoured-looking bearded peasant with a red face, showing his white teeth in a grin, and holding up a greenish bottle that flashed in the sunlight.

'*Qu'est-ce qu'ils disent?*' asked Veslovsky.

'They invite you to have some vodka. Most likely they've been dividing the meadow into lots. I should have some,' said Levin, not without some guile, hoping Veslovsky would be tempted by the vodka, and would go away to them.

'Why do they offer it?'

'Oh, they're merry-making. Really, you should join them. You would be interested.'

'*Allons, c'est curieux.*'

'You go, you go, you'll find the way to the mill!' cried Levin, and looking round he perceived with satisfaction that Veslovsky, bent and stumbling with weariness, holding his gun out at arm's length, was making his way out of the marsh towards the peasants.

'You come too!' the peasant shouted to Levin. 'Never fear! You taste our cake!'

Levin felt a strong inclination to drink a little vodka and to eat some bread. He was exhausted, and felt it a great effort to drag his staggering legs out of the mire, and for a minute he hesitated. But Laska was setting. And immediately all his weariness vanished, and he walked lightly through the swamp towards the dog. A snipe flew up at his feet; he fired and killed it. Laska still pointed.—'Fetch it!' Another bird flew up close to the dog. Levin fired. But it was an unlucky day for him; he missed it, and when he went to look for the one he had shot, he could not find that either. He wandered all about the reeds, but Laska did not believe he had shot it, and when he sent her to find it, she pretended to hunt for it, but did not really. And in the absence of Vassenka, on whom Levin threw the blame of his failure, things went no better. There were plenty of snipe still, but Levin made one miss after another.

The slanting rays of the sun were still hot; his clothes soaked through with perspiration, stuck to his body; his left boot full of water weighed heavily on his leg and squeaked at every step; the sweat ran in drops down his powder-grimed face, his mouth was full of the bitter taste, his nose of the smell of powder and stagnant water, his ears were ringing with the incessant whir of the snipe; he could not touch the stock of his gun, it was so hot; his heart beat with short, rapid throbs; his hands shook with excitement, and his weary legs stumbled and staggered over the hillocks and in the swamp, but still he walked on and still he shot. At last, after a disgraceful miss, he flung his gun and his hat on the ground.

'No, I must control myself,' he said to himself. Picking up his gun and his hat, he called Laska, and went out of the swamp. When he got on to dry ground he sat down, pulled off his boot and emptied it, then walked to the marsh, drank some stagnant-tasting water, moistened his burning hot gun, and washed his face and hands. Feeling refreshed, he went back to the spot where a snipe had settled, firmly resolved to keep cool.

He tried to be calm, but it was the same again. His finger pressed the cock before he had taken a good aim at the bird. It got worse and worse.

He had only five birds in his game-bag when he walked out of the marsh towards the alders where he was to rejoin Stepan Arkadyevitch.

Before he caught sight of Stepan Arkadyevitch he saw his dog. Krak darted out from behind the twisted root of an alder, black all over with the stinking mire of the marsh, and with the air of a conqueror sniffed at Laska. Behind Krak there came into view in the shade of the alder-tree the shapely figure of Stepan Arkadyevitch. He came to meet him, red and perspiring, with unbuttoned neckband, still limping in the same way.

'Well? You have been popping away!' he said, smiling good-humouredly.

'How have you got on?' queried Levin. But there was no need to ask, for he had already seen the full game-bag.

'Oh, pretty fair.'

He had fourteen birds.

'A splendid marsh! I've no doubt Veslovsky got in your way. It's awkward too, shooting with one dog,' said Stepan Arkadyevitch, to soften his triumph.

XI

WHEN Levin and Stepan Arkadyevitch reached the peasant's hut where Levin always used to stay, Veslovsky was already there. He was sitting in the middle of the hut, clinging with both hands to the bench from which he was being pulled by a soldier, the brother of the peasant's wife, who was helping him off with his miry boots. Veslovsky was laughing his infectious, good-humoured laugh.

'I've only just come. *Ils ont été charmants*. Just fancy, they gave me drink, fed me! Such bread, it was exquisite! *Délicieux!* And the vodka, I never tasted any better. And they would not take a penny for anything. And they kept saying: "Excuse our homely ways."'

'What should they take anything for? They were entertaining you, to be sure. Do you suppose they keep vodka for sale?' said the soldier, succeeding at last in pulling the soaked boot off the blackened stocking.

In spite of the dirtiness of the hut, which was all muddied by their boots and the filthy dogs licking themselves clean, and the smell of marsh mud and powder that filled the room, and the absence of knives and forks, the party drank their tea and ate their supper with a relish only known to sportsmen. Washed and clean, they went into a hay-barn swept ready for them, where the coachman had been making up beds for the gentlemen.

Though it was dusk, not one of them wanted to go to sleep.

After wavering among reminiscences and anecdotes of guns, of dogs, and of former shooting-parties, the conversation rested on a topic that interested all of them. After Vassenka had several times over expressed his appreciation of this delightful sleeping-place among the fragrant hay, this delightful broken cart (he supposed it to be broken because the shafts had been taken out), of the good-nature of the peasants that had treated him to vodka, of the dogs who lay at the feet of their respective masters, Oblonsky began telling them of a delightful shooting-party at Malthus's, where he had stayed the previous summer.

Malthus was a well-known capitalist, who had made his money by speculation in railway shares. Stepan Arkadyevitch described what grouse moors this Malthus had bought in the Tver province, and how they were preserved, and of the carriages and dogcarts in which the shooting-party had been driven, and the luncheon pavilion that had been rigged up at the marsh.

'I don't understand you,' said Levin, sitting up in the hay; 'how is it such people don't disgust you? I can understand a lunch with Lafitte is all very pleasant, but don't you dislike just that very sumptuousness? All these people, just like our spirit monopolists in old days, get their money in a way that gains them the contempt of everyone. They don't care for their contempt, and then they use their dishonest gains to buy off the contempt they have deserved.'

'Perfectly true!' chimed in Vassenka Veslovsky. 'Perfectly! Oblonsky, of course, goes out of *bonhomie*, but other people say: "Well, Oblonsky stays with them." . . .'

'Not a bit of it.' Levin could hear that Oblonsky was smiling as he spoke. 'I simply don't consider him more dishonest than any other wealthy merchant or nobleman. They've all made their money alike—by their work and their intelligence.'

'Oh, by what work? Do you call it work to get hold of concessions and speculate with them?'

'Of course it's work. Work in this sense, that if it were not for him and others like him, there would have been no railways.'

'But that's not work, like the work of a peasant or a learned profession.'

'Granted, but it's work in the sense that his activity produces a result—the railways. But of course you think the railways useless.'

'No, that's another question; I am prepared to admit that they're useful. But all profit that is out of proportion to the labour expended is dishonest.'

'But who is to define what is proportionate?'

'Making profit by dishonest means, by trickery,' said Levin, conscious that he could not draw a distinct line between honesty and dishonesty. 'Such as banking, for instance,' he went on. 'It's an evil—the amassing of huge fortunes without labour, just the same thing as with the spirit monopolies, it's only the form that's changed. *Le roi est mort, vive le roi!* No sooner were the spirit monopolies abolished than the railways came up, and banking companies; that, too, is profit without work.'

'Yes, that may all be very true and clever . . . Lie down, Krak!' Stepan Arkadyevitch called to his dog, who was scratching and turning over all the hay. He was obviously convinced of the correctness of his position, and so talked serenely and without haste. 'But you have not drawn the line between honest and dishonest work. That I receive a bigger salary than my chief clerk, though he knows more about the work than I do—that's dishonest, I suppose?'

'I can't say.'

'Well, but I can tell you: your receiving some five thousand, let's say, for your work on the land, while our host, the peasant here, however hard he works, can never get more than fifty roubles, is just as dishonest as my earning more than my chief clerk, and Malthus getting more than a station-master. No, quite the contrary; I see that society takes up a sort of antagonistic attitude to these people, which is utterly baseless, and I fancy there's envy at the bottom of it. . . .'

'No, that's unfair,' said Veslovsky; 'how could envy come in? There is something not nice about that sort of business.'

'You say,' Levin went on, 'that it's unjust for me to receive five thousand, while the peasant has fifty; that's true. It is unfair, and I feel it, but . . .'

'It really is. Why is it we spend our time riding, drinking, shooting, doing nothing, while they are for ever at work?' said Vassenka Veslovsky, obviously for the first time in his life reflecting on the question, and consequently considering it with perfect sincerity.

'Yes, you feel it, but you don't give him your property,' said Stepan Arkadyevitch, intentionally, as it seemed, provoking Levin.

There had arisen of late something like a secret antagonism between the two brothers-in-law; as though, since they had married sisters, a kind of rivalry had sprung up between them as to which was ordering his life best, and now this hostility showed itself in the conversation, as it began to take a personal note.

'I don't give it away, because no one demands that from me, and if I wanted to, I could not give it away,' answered Levin, 'and have no one to give it to.'

'Give it to this peasant, he would not refuse it.'

'Yes, but how am I to give it up? Am I to go to him and make a deed of conveyance?'

'I don't know; but if you are convinced that you have no right . . .'

'I'm not at all convinced. On the contrary, I feel I have no right to give it up, that I have duties both to the land and to my family.'

'No, excuse me, but if you consider this inequality is unjust, why is it you don't act accordingly? . . .'

'Well, I do act negatively on that idea, so far as not trying to increase the difference of position existing between him and me.'

'No, excuse me, that's a paradox.'

'Yes, there's something of a sophistry about that,' Veslovsky agreed. 'Ah! our host; so you're not asleep yet?' he said to the peasant who came into the barn, opening the creaking door. 'How is it you're not asleep?'

'No, how's one to sleep! I thought our gentlemen would be asleep, but I heard them chattering. I want to get a hook from here. She won't bite?' he added, stepping cautiously with his bare feet.

'And where are you going to sleep?'

'We are going out for the night with the beasts.'

'Ah, what a night!' said Veslovsky, looking out at the edge of the hut and the unharnessed wagonette that could be seen in the faint light of the evening glow in the great frame of the open doors. 'But listen, there are women's voices singing, and, on my word, not badly too. Who's that singing, my friend?'

'That's the maids from hard by here.'

'Let's go, let's have a walk! We shan't go to sleep, you know. Oblonsky, come along!'

'If one could only do both, lie here and go,' answered Oblonsky, stretching. 'It's capital lying here.'

'Well, I shall go by myself,' said Veslovsky, getting up eagerly, and putting on his shoes and stockings. 'Good-bye, gentlemen. If it's fun, I'll fetch you. You've treated me to some good sport, and I won't forget you.'

'He really is a capital fellow, isn't he?' said Stepan Arkadyevitch, when Veslovsky had gone out and the peasant had closed the door after him.

'Yes, capital,' answered Levin, still thinking of the subject of their conversation just before. It seemed to him that he had clearly expressed his thoughts and feelings to the best of his capacity, and yet both of them, straightforward men and not fools, had said with one voice that he was comforting himself with sophistries. This disconcerted him.

'It's just this, my dear boy. One must do one of two things: either admit that the existing order of society is just, and then stick up for one's rights in it; or acknowledge that you are enjoying unjust privileges, as I do, and then enjoy them and be satisfied.'

'No, if it were unjust, you could not enjoy these advantages and be satisfied—at least I could not. The great thing for me is to feel that I'm not to blame.'

'What do you say, why not go after all?' said Stepan Arkadyevitch, evidently weary of the strain of thought. 'We shan't go to sleep, you know. Come, let's go!'

Levin did not answer. What they had said in the conversation that he acted justly only in a negative sense absorbed his thoughts. 'Can it be that it's only possible to be just negatively?' he was asking himself.

'How strong the smell of the fresh hay is, though,' said Stepan Arkadyevitch, getting up. 'There's not a chance of sleeping. Vassenka has been getting up some fun there. Do you hear the laughing and his voice? Hadn't we better go? Come along!'

'No, I'm not coming,' answered Levin.

'Surely that's not a matter of principle too,' said Stepan Arkadyevitch, smiling, as he felt about in the dark for his cap.

'It's not a matter of principle, but why should I go?'

'But do you know you are preparing trouble for yourself,' said Stepan Arkadyevitch, finding his cap and getting up.

'How so?'

'Do you suppose I don't see the line you've taken up with your wife? I heard how it's a question of the greatest consequence, whether or not you're to be away for a couple of days' shooting. That's all very well as an idyllic episode, but for your whole life that won't answer. A man must be independent; he has his masculine interests. A man has to be manly,' said Oblonsky, opening the door.

'In what way? To go running after servant-girls?' said Levin.

'Why not, if it amuses him? *Ca ne tire pas à conséquence.* It won't do my wife any harm, and it'll amuse me. The great thing is to respect the sanctity of the home. There should be nothing in the home. But don't tie your own hands.'

'Perhaps so,' said Levin drily, and he turned on his side. 'Tomorrow, early, I want to go shooting, and I won't wake anyone, and shall set off at daybreak.'

'*Messieurs, venez vite!*' they heard the voice of Veslovsky coming back. '*Charmante!* I've made such a discovery. *Charmante!* a perfect Gretchen, and I've already made friends with her. Really, exceedingly pretty,' he declared in a tone of approval, as though she had been made pretty entirely on his account, and he were expressing his satisfaction with the entertainment that had been provided for him.

Levin pretended to be asleep, while Oblonsky, putting on his slippers, and lighting a cigar, walked out of the barn, and soon their voices were lost.

For a long while Levin could not get to sleep. He heard the horses munching hay, then he heard the peasant and his elder boy getting ready for the night, and going off for the nightwatch with the beasts, then he heard the soldier arranging his bed on the other side of the barn, with his nephew, the younger son of their peasant host. He heard the boy in his shrill little voice telling his uncle what he thought about the dogs, who seemed to him huge and terrible creatures, and asking what the dogs were going to hunt next day, and the soldier in a husky, sleepy voice, telling him the sportsmen were going in the morning to the marsh, and would shoot with their guns; and then, to check the boy's questions, he said, 'Go to sleep, Vaska; go to sleep, or you'll catch it,' and soon after he began snoring himself, and everything was still. He could only hear the snort of the horses, and the guttural cry of a snipe.

'Is it really only negative?' he repeated to himself. 'Well, what of it. It's not my fault.' And he began thinking about the next day.

'Tomorrow I'll go out early, and I'll make a point of keeping cool. There are lots of snipe; and there are grouse too. When I come back there'll be the note from Kitty. Yes, Stiva may be right, I'm not manly with her, I'm tied to her apron-strings. . . . Well, it can't be helped! Negative again. . . .'

Half asleep, he heard the laughter and mirthful talk of Veslovsky and Stepan Arkadyevitch. For an instant he opened his eyes: the moon was up, and in the open doorway, brightly lighted up by the moonlight, they were standing talking. Stepan Arkadyevitch was saying something of the freshness of one girl, comparing her to a freshly peeled nut, and Veslovsky with his infectious laugh was repeating some words, probably said to him by a peasant: 'Ah, you do your best to get round her!' Levin, half asleep, said—

'Gentlemen, tomorrow before daylight!' and fell asleep.

XII

WAKING up at earliest dawn, Levin tried to wake his companions. Vassenka, lying on his stomach, with one leg in a stocking thrust out, was sleeping so soundly that he could elicit no response. Oblonsky, half asleep, declined to get up so early. Even Laska, who was asleep, curled up in the hay, got up unwillingly, and lazily stretched out and straightened her hind legs one after the other. Getting on his boots and stockings, taking his gun, and carefully opening the creaking door of the barn, Levin went out into the road. The coachmen were sleeping in their carriages, the horses were dozing. Only one was lazily eating oats, dipping its nose into the manger. It was still grey out of doors.

'Why are you up so early, my dear?' the old woman, their hostess, said, coming out of the hut and addressing him affectionately as an old friend.

'Going shooting, granny. Do I go this way to the marsh?'

'Straight out at the back; by our threshing-floor, my dear, and hemp-patches; there's a little footpath.' Stepping carefully with her sunburnt, bare feet, the old woman conducted Levin, and moved back the fence for him by the threshing-floor.

'Straight on and you'll come to the marsh. Our lads drove the cattle there yesterday evening.'

Laska ran eagerly forward along the little path. Levin followed her with a light, rapid step, continually looking at the sky. He hoped the sun would not be up before he reached the marsh. But the sun did not delay. The moon, which had been bright when he went out, by now shone only like a crescent of quicksilver. The pink flush of dawn, which one could not help seeing before, now had to be sought to be discerned at all. What were before undefined, vague blurs in the distant countryside could now be distinctly seen. They were sheaves of rye. The dew, not visible till the sun was up, wetted Levin's legs and his blouse above his belt in the high-growing, fragrant hemp-patch, from which the pollen had already fallen out. In the transparent stillness of morning the smallest sounds were audible. A bee flew by Levin's ear with the whizzing sound of a bullet. He looked carefully, and saw a second and a third. They were all flying from the bee-hives behind the hedge, and they disappeared over the hemp-patch in the direction of the marsh. The path led straight to the marsh. The marsh could be recognised by the mist which rose from it, thicker in one place and thinner in another, so that the reeds and willow-bushes swayed like islands in this mist. At the edge of the marsh and the road peasant boys and men, who had been herding for the night, were lying, and in the dawn all were asleep under their coats. Not far from them were three hobbled horses. One of them clanked a chain. Laska walked beside her master, pressing a little forward and looking round. Passing the sleeping peasants and reaching the first reeds, Levin examined his pistons and let his dog off. One of the horses, a sleek, dark-brown three-year-old, seeing the dog, started away, switched its tail and snorted. The other horses too were frightened, and splashing through the water with their hobbled legs, and drawing their hoofs out of the thick mud with a squelching sound, they bounded out of the marsh. Laska stopped, looked ironically at the horses and inquiringly at Levin. Levin patted Laska, and whistled as a sign that she might begin.

Laska ran joyfully and anxiously through the slush that swayed under her.

Running into the marsh among the familiar scents of roots, marsh plants, and slime and the extraneous smell of horse dung, Laska detected at once a smell that pervaded the whole marsh, the scent of that strong-smelling bird that always excited her more than any other. Here and there among the moss and marsh plants this scent was very strong, but it was impossible to determine in which direction it grew stronger or fainter. To find the direction, she had to go further away from the wind. Not feeling the motion of her legs, Laska bounded with a stiff gallop, so that at each bound she could stop short, to the right, away from the wind that blew from the east before sunrise, and turned facing the wind. Sniffing in the air with dilated nostrils, she felt at once that not their tracks only but they themselves were here before her, and not one, but many. Laska slackened her speed. They were here, but where precisely she could not yet determine. To find the very spot, she began to make a circle, when suddenly her master's voice drew her off. 'Laska! here?' he asked, pointing her to a different direction. She stopped, asking him if she had better not go on doing as she had begun. But he repeated his command in an angry voice, pointing to a spot covered with water, where there could not be anything. She obeyed him, pretending she was looking, so as to please him, went round it, and went back to her former position, and was at once aware of the scent again. Now when he was not hindering her, she knew what to do, and without looking at what was under her feet, and to her vexation stumbling over a high stump into the water, but righting herself with her strong, supple legs, she began making the circle which was to make all clear to her. The scent of them reached her, stronger, and more and more defined, and all at once it became perfectly clear to her that one of them was here, behind this tuft of reeds, five paces in front of her; she stopped, and her whole body was still and rigid. On her short legs she could see nothing in front of her, but by the scent she knew it was sitting not more than five paces off. She stood still, feeling more and more conscious of it, and enjoying it in anticipation. Her tail was stretched straight and tense, and only wagging at the extreme end. Her mouth was slightly open, her ears raised. One ear had been turned wrong side out as she ran up, and she breathed heavily but warily, and still more warily looked round, but more with her eyes than her head, to her master. He was coming along with the face she knew so well, though the eyes were always terrible to her. He stumbled over the stump as he came, and moved, as she thought, extraordinarily slowly. She thought he came slowly, but he was running.

Noticing Laska's special attitude as she crouched on the ground, as it were scratching big prints with her hind paws, and with her mouth slightly open, Levin knew she was pointing at grouse, and with an inward prayer for luck, especially with the first bird, he ran up to her. Coming quite close up to her, he could from his height look beyond her, and he saw with his eyes what she was seeing with her nose. In a space between two little thickets, at a couple of yards' distance, he could see a grouse. Turning its head, it was listening. Then lightly preening and folding its wings, it disappeared round a corner with a clumsy wag of its tail.

'Fetch it, fetch it!' shouted Levin, giving Laska a shove from behind.

'But I can't go,' thought Laska. 'Where am I to go? From here I feel them, but if I move forward I shall know nothing of where they are or who they are.' But then he shoved her with his knee, and in an excited whisper said, 'Fetch it, Laska.'

'Well, if that's what he wishes, I'll do it, but I can't answer for myself now,' she thought, and darted forward as fast as her legs would carry her between the thick bushes. She scented nothing now; she could only see and hear, without understanding anything.

Ten paces from her former place a grouse rose with a guttural cry and the peculiar round sound of its wings. And immediately after the shot it splashed heavily with its white breast on the wet mire. Another bird did not linger, but rose behind Levin without the dog. When Levin turned towards it, it was already some way off. But his shot caught it. Flying twenty paces further, the second grouse rose upwards, and whirling round like a ball, dropped heavily on a dry place.

'Come, this is going to be some good!' thought Levin, packing the warm and fat grouse into his game-bag. 'Eh, Laska, will it be good?'

When Levin, after loading his gun, moved on, the sun had fully risen, though unseen behind the storm-clouds. The moon had lost all its lustre, and was like a white cloud in the sky. Not a single star could be seen. The sedge, silvery with dew before, now shone like gold. The stagnant pools were all like amber. The blue of the grass had changed to yellow-green. The marsh-birds twittered and swarmed about the brook and upon the bushes that glittered with dew and cast long shadows. A hawk woke up and settled on a haycock, turning its head from side to side and looking discontentedly at the marsh. Crows were flying about the field, and a bare-legged boy was driving the horses to an old man, who had got up from under his long coat and was combing his hair. The smoke from the gun was white as milk over the green of the grass.

One of the boys ran up to Levin.

'Uncle, there were ducks here yesterday!' he shouted to him, and he walked a little way off behind him.

And Levin was doubly pleased, in sight of the boy, who expressed his approval, at killing three snipe, one after another, straight off.

XIII

THE sportsman's saying, that if the first beast or the first bird is not missed, the day will be lucky, turned out correct.

At ten o'clock Levin, weary, hungry, and happy after a tramp of twenty miles, returned to his night's lodging with nineteen head of fine game and one duck, which he tied to his belt, as it would not go into the game-bag. His companions had long been awake, and had had time to get hungry and have breakfast.

'Wait a bit, wait a bit, I know there are nineteen,' said Levin, counting a second time over the grouse and snipe, that looked so much less important now bent and dry and bloodstained, with heads crooked aside, than they did when they were flying.

The number was verified, and Stepan Arkadyevitch's envy pleased Levin. He was pleased too on returning to find the man sent by Kitty with a note was already there.

'I am perfectly well and happy. If you were uneasy about me, you can feel easier than ever. I've a new bodyguard, Marya Vlasyevna,'—this was the midwife, a new and important personage in Levin's domestic life. 'She has come to have a look at me. She found me perfectly well, and we have kept her till you are back. All are happy and well, and please, don't be in a hurry to come back, but, if the sport is good, stay another day.'

These two pleasures, his lucky shooting and the letter from his wife, were so great that two slightly disagreeable incidents passed lightly over Levin. One was that the chestnut trace-horse, who had been unmistakably overworked on the previous day, was off his feed and out of sorts. The coachman said he was 'Overdriven yesterday, Konstantin Dmitritch,' he said. 'Yes, indeed! driving ten miles with no sense!'

The other unpleasant incident, which for the first minute destroyed his good-humour, thought later he laughed at it a great deal, was to find that of all the provisions Kitty had provided in such abundance that one would have thought there was enough for a week, nothing was left. On his way back, tired and hungry, from shooting, Levin had so distinct a vision of meat-pies, that as he approached the hut he seemed to smell and taste them, as Laska had smelt the game, and he immediately told Philip to give him some. It appeared that there were no pies left, or even any chicken.

'Well, this fellow's appetite!' said Stepan Arkadyevitch, laughing and pointing at Vassenka Veslovsky. 'I never suffer from loss of appetite, but he's really marvellous! . . .'

'Well, it can't be helped,' said Levin, looking gloomily at Veslovsky. 'Well, Philip, give me some beef, then.'

'The beef's been eaten, and the bones given to the dogs,' answered Philip.

Levin was so hurt that he said, in a tone of vexation, 'You might have left me something!' and he felt ready to cry.

'Then put away the game,' he said in a shaking voice to Philip, trying not to look at Vassenka, 'and cover them with some nettles. And you might at least ask for some milk for me.'

But when he had drunk some milk, he felt ashamed immediately at having shown his annoyance to a stranger, and he began to laugh at his hungry mortification.

In the evening they went shooting again, and Veslovsky had several successful shots, and in the night they drove home.

Their homeward journey was as lively as their drive out had been. Veslovsky sang songs and related with enjoyment his adventures with the peasants, who had regaled him with vodka, and said to him, 'Excuse our homely ways,' and his night's adventures with kiss-in-the-ring and the servant-girl and the peasant, who had asked him was he married, and on learning that he was not, said to him, 'Well, mind you don't run after other men's wives—you'd better get one of your own.' These words had particularly amused Veslovsky.

'Altogther, I've enjoyed our outing awfully. And you, Levin?'

'I have, very much,' Levin said quite sincerely. It was particularly delightful to him to have got rid of the hostility he had been feeling towards Vassenka Veslovsky at home, and to feel instead the most friendly disposition to him.

XIV

NEXT day at ten o'clock Levin, who had already gone his rounds, knocked at the room where Vassenka had been put for the night.

'*Entrez!*' Veslovsky called to him. 'Excuse me, I've only just finished my ablutions,' he said, smiling, standing before him in his underclothes only.

'Don't mind me, please.' Levin sat down in the window. 'Have you slept well?'

'Like the dead. What sort of day is it for shooting?'

'What will you take, tea or coffee?'

'Neither. I'll wait till lunch. I'm really ashamed. I suppose the ladies are down? A walk now would be capital. You show me your horses.'

After walking about the garden, visiting the stable, and even doing some gymnastic exercises together on the parallel bars, Levin returned to the house with his guest, and went with him into the drawing-room.

'We had splendid shooting, and so many delightful experiences!' said Veslovsky, going up to Kitty, who was sitting at the samovar. 'What a pity ladies are cut off from these delights!'

'Well, I suppose he must say something to the lady of the house,' Levin said to himself. Again he fancied something in the smile, in the all-conquering air with which their guest addressed Kitty. . . .

The princess, sitting on the other side of the table with Marya Vlasyevna and Stepan Arkadyevitch, called Levin to her side, and began to talk to him about moving to Moscow for Kitty's confinement, and getting ready rooms for them. Just as Levin had disliked all the trivial preparations for his wedding, as derogatory to the grandeur of the event, now he felt still more offensive the preparations for the approaching birth, the date of which they reckoned, it seemed, on their fingers. He tried to turn a deaf ear to these discussions of the best patterns of long clothes for the coming baby; tried to turn away and avoid seeing the mysterious, endless strips of knitting, the triangles of linen, and so on, to which Dolly attached special importance. The birth of a son (he was certain it would be a son) which was promised him, but which he still could not believe in—so marvellous it seemed—presented itself to his mind, on one hand, as a happiness so immense, and therefore so incredible; on the other, as an event so mysterious, that this assumption of a definite knowledge of what would be, and consequent preparation for it, as for something ordinary that did happen to people, jarred on him as confusing and humiliating.

But the princess did not understand his feelings, and put down his reluctance to think and talk about it to carelessness and indifference, and so she gave him no peace. She had commissioned Stepan Arkadyevitch to look at a flat, and now she called Levin up.

'I know nothing about it, princess. Do as you think fit,' he said.

'You must decide when you will move.'

'I really don't know. I know millions of children are born away from Moscow, and doctors . . . why . . .'

'But if so . . .'

'Oh no, as Kitty wishes.'

'We can't talk to Kitty about it! Do you want me to frighten her? Why, this spring Natalia Golitzin died from having an ignorant doctor.'

'I will do just what you say,' he said gloomily.

The princess began talking to him, but he did not hear her. Though the conversation with the princess had indeed jarred upon him, he was gloomy, not on account of that conversation, but from what he saw at the samovar.

'No, it's impossible,' he thought, glancing now and then at Vassenka bending over Kitty, telling her something with his charming smile, and at her, flushed and disturbed.

There was something not nice in Vassenka's attitude, in his eyes, in his smile. Levin even saw something not nice in Kitty's attitude and look. And again the light died away in his eyes. Again, as before, all of a sudden, without the slightest transition, he felt cast down from a pinnacle of happiness, peace, and dignity, into an abyss of despair, rage, and humiliation. Again everything and everyone had become hateful to him.

'You do just as you think best, princess,' he said again, looking round.

'Heavy is the cap of Monomach,' Stepan Arkadyevitch said playfully, hinting, evidently, not simply at the princess's conversation, but at the cause of Levin's agitation, which he had noticed.

'How late you are today, Dolly!'

Every one got up to greet Darya Alexandrovna. Vassenka only rose for an instant, and with the lack of courtesy to ladies characteristic of the modern young man, he scarcely bowed, and resumed his conversation again, laughing at something.

'I've been worried about Masha. She did not sleep well, and is dreadfully tiresome today,' said Dolly.

The conversation Vassenka had started with Kitty was running on the same lines as on the previous evening, discussing Anna, and whether love is to be put higher than worldly considerations. Kitty disliked the conversation, and she was disturbed both by the subject and the tone in which it was conducted, and also by the knowledge of the effect it would have on her husband. But she was too simple and innocent to know how to cut short this conversation, or even to conceal the superficial pleasure afforded her by the young man's very obvious admiration. She wanted to stop it, but she did not know what to do. Whatever she did she knew would be observed by her husband, and the worst interpretation put on it. And, in fact, when she asked Dolly what was wrong with Masha, and Vassenka, waiting till this uninteresting conversation was over, began to gaze indifferently at Dolly, the question struck Levin as an unnatural and disgusting piece of hypocrisy.

'What do you say, shall we go and look for mushrooms today?' said Dolly.

'By all means, please, and I shall come too,' said Kitty, and she blushed. She wanted from politeness to ask Vassenka whether he would come, and she did not ask him. 'Where are you going, Kostya?' she asked her husband with a guilty face, as he passed by her with a resolute step. This guilty air confirmed all his suspicions.

'The mechanician came when I was away; I haven't seen him yet,' he said, not looking at her.

He went downstairs, but before he had time to leave his study he heard his wife's familiar footsteps running with reckless speed to him.

'What do you want?' he said to her shortly. 'We are busy.'

'I beg your pardon,' she said to the German mechanician; 'I want a few words with my husband.'

The German would have left the room, but Levin said to him—

'Don't disturb yourself.'

'The train is at three?' queried the German. 'I mustn't be late.'

Levin did not answer, but walked out himself with his wife.

'Well, what have you to say to me?' he said to her in French.

He did not look her in the face, and did not care to see that she in her condition was trembling all over, and had a piteous, crushed look.

'I . . . I want to say that we can't go on like this; that this is misery . . .' she said.

'The servants are here at the sideboard,' he said angrily; 'don't make a scene.'

'Well, let's go in here!'

They were standing in the passage. Kitty would have gone into the next room, but there the English governess was giving Tanya a lesson.

'Well, come into the garden.'

In the garden they came upon a peasant weeding the path. And no longer considering that the peasant could see her tear-stained and his agitated face, that they looked like people fleeing from some disaster, they went on with rapid steps, feeling that they must speak out and clear up misunderstandings, must be alone together, and so get rid of the misery they were both feeling.

'We can't go on like this! It's misery! I am wretched! you are wretched. What for?' she said, when they had at last reached a solitary garden-seat at a turn in the lime-tree avenue.

'But tell me one thing: was there in his tone anything unseemly, not nice, humiliatingly horrible?' he said, standing before her again in the same position with his clenched fists on his chest, as he had stood before her that night.

'Yes,' she said in a shaking voice; 'but, Kostya, surely you see I'm not to blame? All the morning I've been trying to take a tone . . . but such people . . . Why did he come? How happy we were!' she said, breathless with the sobs that shook her.

Although nothing had been pursuing them, and there was nothing to run away from, and they could not possibly have found anything very delightful on that garden-seat, the gardener saw with astonishment that they passed him on their way home with comforted and radiant faces.

XV

AFTER escorting his wife upstairs, Levin went to Dolly's part of the house. Darya Alexandrovna, for her part, was in great distress too that day. She was walking about the room, talking angrily to a little girl, who stood in the corner roaring.

'And you shall stand all day in the corner, and have your dinner all alone, and not see one of your dolls, and I won't make you a new frock,' she said, not knowing how to punish her.

'Oh, she is a disgusting child!' she turned to Levin. 'Where does she get such wicked propensities?'

'Why, what has she done?' Levin said without much interest, for he had wanted to ask her advice, and so was annoyed that he had come at an unlucky moment.

'Grisha and she went into the raspberries, and there . . . I can't tell you really what she did. It's a thousand pities Miss Elliot's not with us. This one sees to nothing—she's a machine . . . *Figurez-vous que la petite?* . . .'

And Darya Alexandrovna described Masha's crime.

'That proves nothing; it's not a question of evil propensities at all, it's simply mischief,' Levin assured her.

'But you are upset about something? What have you come for?' asked Dolly. 'What's going on there?'

And in the tone of her question Levin heard that it would be easy for him to say what he had meant to say.

'I've not been in there, I've been alone in the garden with Kitty. We've had a quarrel for the second time since . . . Stiva came.'

Dolly looked at him with her shrewd, comprehending eyes.

'Come, tell me, honour bright, has there been . . . not in Kitty, but in that gentleman's behaviour, a tone which might be unpleasant—not unpleasant, but horrible, offensive to a husband?'

'You mean, how shall I say . . . Stay, stay in the corner!' she said to Masha, who, detecting a faint smile on her mother's face, had been turning round. 'The opinion of the world would be that he is behaving as young men do behave. *Il fait la cour à une jeune et jolie femme*, and a husband who's a man of the world should only be flattered by it.'

'Yes, yes,' said Levin gloomily; 'but you noticed it?'

'Not only I, but Stiva noticed it. Just after breakfast he said to me in so many words, "*Je crois que Veslovsky fait un petit brin de cour à Kitty.*"'

'Well, that's all right then; now I'm satisfied. I'll send him away,' said Levin.

'What do you mean! Are you crazy?' Dolly cried in horror; 'nonsense, Kostya, only think!' she said, laughing. 'You can go now to Fanny,' she said to Masha. 'No, if you wish it, I'll speak to Stiva. He'll take him away. He can say you're expecting visitors. Altogether he doesn't fit into the house.'

'No, no, I'll do it myself.'

'But you'll quarrel with him?'

'Not a bit. I shall so enjoy it,' Levin said, his eyes flashing with real enjoyment. 'Come, forgive her, Dolly, she won't do it again,' he said of the little sinner, who had not gone to Fanny, but was standing irresolutely before her mother, waiting and looking up from under her brows to catch her mother's eye.

The mother glanced at her. The child broke into sobs, hid her face on her mother's lap, and Dolly laid her thin, tender hand on her head.

'And what is there in common between us and him?' thought Levin, and he went off to look for Veslovsky.

As he passed through the passage he gave orders for the carriage to be got ready to drive to the station.

'The spring was broken yesterday,' said the footman.

'Well, the covered trap then, and make haste. Where's the visitor?'

'The gentleman's gone to his room.'

Levin came upon Veslovsky at the moment when the latter, having unpacked his things from his trunk, and laid out some new songs, was putting on his gaiters to go out riding.

Whether there was something exceptional in Levin's face, or that Vassenka was himself conscious that *ce petit brin de cour* he was making was out of place in this family; but he was somewhat (as much as a young man in society can be) disconcerted at Levin's entrance.

'You ride in gaiters?'

'Yes, it's much cleaner,' said Vassenka, putting his fat leg on a chair, fastening the bottom hook, and smiling with simple-hearted good humour.

He was undoubtedly a good-natured fellow, and Levin felt sorry for him and ashamed of himself, as his host, when he saw the shy look on Vassenka's face.

On the table lay a piece of stick which they had broken together that morning, trying their strength. Levin took the fragment in his hands and began smashing it up, breaking bits off the stick, not knowing how to begin.

'I wanted . . .' He paused, but suddenly, remembering Kitty and everything that had happened, he said, looking him resolutely in the face: 'I have ordered the horses to be put-to for you.'

'How so?' Vassenka began in surprise. 'To drive where?'

'For you to drive to the station,' Levin said gloomily.

'Are you going away, or has something happened?'

'It happens that I expect visitors,' said Levin, his strong fingers more and more rapidly breaking off the ends of the split stick. 'And I'm not expecting visitors, and nothing has happened, but I beg you to go away. You can explain my rudeness as you like.'

Vassenka drew himself up.

'I beg you to explain . . .' he said with dignity, understanding at last.

'I can't explain,' Levin said softly and deliberately, trying to control the trembling of his jaw; 'and you'd better not ask.'

And as the split ends were all broken off, Levin clutched the thick ends in his finger, broke the stick in two, and carefully caught the end as it fell.

Probably the sight of those nervous fingers, of the muscles he had proved that morning at gymnastics, of the glittering eyes, the soft voice, and quivering jaws, convinced Vassenka better than any words. He bowed, shrugging his shoulders, and smiling contemptuously.

'Can I not see Oblonsky?'

The shrug and the smile did not irritate Levin.

'What else was there for him to do?' he thought.

'I'll send him to you at once.'

'What madness is this?' Stepan Arkadyevitch said when, after hearing from his friend that he was being turned out of the house, he found Levin in the garden, where he was walking about waiting for his guest's departure. '*Mais c'est ridicule!* What fly has stung you? *Mais c'est du dernier ridicule!* What did you think, if a young man . . .'

But the place where Levin had been stung was evidently still sore, for he turned pale again, when Stepan Arkadyevitch would have enlarged on the reason, and he himself cut him short.

'Please don't go into it! I can't help it. I feel ashamed of how I'm treating you and him. But it won't be, I imagine, a great grief to him to go, and his presence was distasteful to me and to my wife.'

'But it's insulting to him! *Et puis c'est ridicule.*'

'And to me it's both insulting and distressing! And I'm not in fault in any way, and there's no need for me to suffer.'

'Well, this I didn't expect of you! *On peut être jaloux, mais à ce point, c'est du dernier ridicule!*'

Levin turned quickly, and walked away from him into the depths of the avenue, and he went on walking up and down alone. Soon he heard the rumble of the trap, and saw from behind the trees how Vassenka, sitting in the hay (unluckily there was no seat in the trap) in his Scotch cap, was driven along the avenue, jolting up and down over the ruts.

'What's this?' Levin thought, when a footman ran out of the house and stopped the trap. It was the mechanician, whom Levin had totally forgotten. The mechanician, bowing low, said something to Veslovsky, then clambered into the trap, and they drove off together.

Stepan Arkadyevitch and the princess were much upset by Levin's action. And he himself felt not only in the highest degree *ridicule*, but also utterly guilty and disgraced. But remembering what sufferings he and his wife had been through, when he asked himself how he should act another time, he answered that he should do just the same again.

In spite of all this, towards the end of that day, everyone except the princess, who could not pardon Levin's action, became extraordinarily lively and good-humoured, like children after a punishment or grown-up people after a dreary, ceremonious reception, so that by the evening Vassenka's dismissal was spoken of, in the absence of the princess, as though it were some remote event. And Dolly, who had inherited her father's gift of humorous story-telling, made Varenka helpless with laughter as she related for the third and fourth time, always with fresh humorous additions, how she had only just put on her new shoes for the benefit of the visitor, and on going into the drawing-room, heard suddenly the rumble of the trap. And who should be in the trap but Vassenka himself, with his Scotch cap, and his songs and his gaiters, and all, sitting in the hay.

'If only you'd ordered out the carriage! But no! and then I hear: "Stop!" Oh, I thought, they've relented. I look out, and behold a fat German being sat down by him and driving away . . . And my new shoes all for nothing! . . .'

XVI

DARYA ALEXANDROVNA carried out her intention and went to see Anna. She was sorry to annoy her sister and to do anything Levin disliked. She quite understood how right the Levins were in not wishing to have anything to do with Vronsky. But she felt she must go and see Anna, and show her that her feelings could not be changed, in spite of the change in her position. That she might be independent of the Levins in this expedition, Darya Alexandrovitch sent to the village to hire horses for the drive; but Levin learning of it went to her to protest.

'What makes you suppose that I dislike your going? But, even if I did dislike it, I should still more dislike your not taking my horses,' he said. 'You never told me that you were going for certain. Hiring horses in the village is disagreeable to me, and, what's of more importance, they'll undertake the job and never get you there. I have horses. And if you don't want to wound me, you'll take mine.'

Darya Alexandrovna had to consent, and on the day fixed Levin had ready for his sister-in-law a set of four horses and relays, getting them together from the farm and saddle-horses—not at all a smart-looking set, but capable of taking Darya Alexandrovna the whole distance in a single day. At that moment, when horses were wanted for the princess, who was going, and for the midwife, it was a difficult matter for Levin to make up the number, but the duties of hospitality would not let him allow Darya Alexandrovna to hire horses when staying in his house. Moreover he was well aware that the twenty roubles that would be asked for the journey were a serious matter for her; Darya Alexandrovna's pecuniary affairs, which were in a very unsatisfactory state, were taken to heart by the Levins as if they were their own.

Darya Alexandrovna, by Levin's advice, started before daybreak. The road was good, the carriage comfortable, the horses trotted along merrily, and on the box, besides the coachman, sat the counting-house clerk, whom Levin was sending instead of a groom for greater security. Darya Alexandrovna dozed and waked up only on reaching the inn where the horses were to be changed.

After drinking tea at the same well-to-do peasant's with whom Levin had stayed on the way to Sviazhsky's, and chatting with the women about their children, and with the old man about Count Vronsky, whom the latter praised very highly, Darya Alexandrovna, at ten o'clock, went on again. At home, looking after her children, she had no time to think. So now, after this journey of four hours, all the thoughts she had suppressed before rushed swarming into her brain, and she thought over all her life as she never had before, and from the most different points of view. Her thoughts seemed strange even to herself. At first she thought about the children, about whom she was uneasy, although the princess and Kitty (she reckoned more upon her) had promised to look after them. 'If only Masha does not begin her naughty tricks, if Grisha isn't kicked by a horse, and Lily's stomach isn't upset again!' she thought. But these questions of the present were succeeded by questions of the immediate future. She began thinking how she had to get a new flat in Moscow for the coming winter, to renew the drawing-room furniture, and to make her elder girl a cloak. Then questions of the more remote future occurred to her; how she was to place her children in the world. 'The girls are all right,' she thought; 'but the boys?'

'It's very well that I'm teaching Grisha, but of course that's only because I am free myself now, I'm not with child. Stiva, of course, there's no counting on. And with the help of good-natured friends I can bring them up; but if there's another baby coming? . . .' And the thought struck her how untruly it was said that the curse laid on woman was that in sorrow she should bring forth children.

'The birth itself, that's nothing; but the months of carrying the child—that's what's so intolerable,' she thought, picturing to herself her last pregnancy, and the death of the last baby. And she recalled the conversation she had just had with the young woman at the inn. On being asked whether she had any children, the handsome young woman had answered cheerfully—

'I had a baby girl, but God set me free, I buried her last Lent.'

'Well, did you grieve very much for her?' asked Darya Alexandrovna.

'Why grieve? The old man has grandchildren enough as it is. It was only trouble. No working, nor nothing. Only a tie.'

This answer had struck Darya Alexandrovna as revolting in spite of the good-natured and pleasing face of the young woman; but now she could not help recalling these words. In those cynical words there was indeed a grain of truth.

'Yes, altogether,' thought Darya Alexandrovna, looking back over her whole existence during those fifteen years of her married life, 'pregnancy, sickness, mental incapacity, indifference to everything, and most of all—hideousness. Kitty, young and pretty as she is, even Kitty has lost her looks; and I when I'm with child become hideous, I know it. The birth, the agony, the hideous agonies, that last moment . . . then the nursing, the sleepless nights, the fearful pains. . . .'

Darya Alexandrovna shuddered at the mere recollection of the pain from sore breasts which she had suffered with almost every child. 'Then the children's illnesses, that everlasting apprehension; then bringing them up; evil propensities (she thought of little Masha's crime among the raspberries), education, Latin—it's all so incomprehensible and difficult. And on the top of it all, the death of these children.' And there rose again before her imagination the cruel memory, that always tore her mother's heart, of the death of her last little baby, who had died of croup; his funeral, the callous indifference of all at the little pink coffin, and her own torn heart, and her lonely anguish at the sight of the pale little brow with its projecting temples, and the open, wondering little mouth seen in the coffin at the moment when it was being covered with the little pink lid with a cross braided on it.

'And all this, what's it for? What is to come of it all? That I'm wasting my life, never having a moment's peace, either with child, or nursing a child, for ever irritable, peevish, wretched myself and worrying others, repulsive to my husband, while the children are growing up unhappy, badly educated and penniless. Even now, if it weren't for spending the summer at the Levins', I don't know how we should be managing to live. Of course Kostya and Kitty have so much tact that we don't feel it; but it can't go on. They'll have children, they won't be able to keep us; it's a drag on them as it is. How is papa, who has hardly anything left for himself, to help us? So that I can't even bring the children up by myself, and may find it hard with the help of other people, at the cost of humiliation. Why, even if we suppose the greatest good luck, that the children don't die, and I bring them up somehow. At the very best they'll simply be decent people. That's all I can hope for. And to gain simply that—what agonies, what toil! . . . One's whole life ruined!' Again she recalled what the young peasant woman had said, and again she was revolted at the thought; but she could not help admitting that there was a grain of brutal truth in the words.

'Is it far now, Mihail?' Darya Alexandrovna asked the counting-house clerk, to turn her mind from thoughts that were frightening her.

'From this village, they say, it's five miles.' The carriage drove along the village street and on to a bridge. On the bridge was a crowd of peasant women with coils of ties for the sheaves on their shoulders, gaily and noisily chattering. They stood still on the bridge, staring inquisitively at the carriage. All the faces turned to Darya Alexandrovna looked to her healthy and happy, making her envious of their enjoyment of life. 'They're all living, they're all enjoying life,' Darya Alexandrovna still mused when she had passed the peasant women and was driving uphill again at a trot, seated comfortably on the soft springs of the old carriage, 'while I, let out, as it were from prison, from the world of worries that fret me to death, am only looking about me now for an instant. They all live; those peasant women and my sister Natalia and Varenka and Anna, whom I am going to see—all, but not I.

'And they attack Anna. What for? am I any better? I have, anyway, a husband I love—not as I should like to love him, still I do love him, while Anna never loved hers. How is she to blame? She wants to live.

God has put that in our hearts. Very likely I should have done the same. Even to this day I don't feel sure I did right in listening to her at that terrible time when she came to me in Moscow. I ought then to have cast off my husband and have begun my life fresh. I might have loved and have been loved in reality. And is it any better as it is? I don't respect him. He's necessary to me,' she thought about her husband, 'and I put up with him. Is that any better? At that time I could still have been admired, I had beauty left me still,' Darya Alexandrovna pursued her thoughts, and she would have liked to look at herself in the looking-glass. She had a travelling looking-glass in her handbag, and she wanted to take it out; but looking at the backs of the coachman and the swaying counting-house clerk, she felt that she would be ashamed if either of them were to look round, and she did not take out the glass.

But without looking in the glass, she thought that even now it was not too late; and she thought of Sergey Ivanovitch, who was always particularly attentive to her, of Stiva's good-hearted friend, Turovtsin, who had helped her nurse her children through the scarlatina, and was in love with her. And there was someone else, a quite young man, who—her husband had told her it as a joke—thought her more beautiful than either of her sisters. And the most passionate and impossible romances rose before Darya Alexandrovna's imagination. 'Anna did quite right, and certainly I shall never reproach her for it. She is happy, she makes another person happy, and she's not broken down as I am, but most likely just as she always was, bright, clever, open to every impression,' thought Darya Alexandrovna,—and a sly smile curved her lips, for, as she pondered on Anna's love-affair, Darya Alexandrovna constructed on parallel lines an almost identical love-affair for herself, with an imaginary composite figure, the ideal man who was in love with her. She, like Anna, confessed the whole affair to her husband. And the amazement and perplexity of Stepan Arkadyevitch at this avowal made her smile.

In such day-dreams she reached the turning of the high-road that led to Vozdvizhenskoe.

XVII

THE coachman pulled up his four horses and looked round to the right, to a field of rye, where some peasants were sitting on a cart. The counting-house clerk was just going to jump down, but on second thoughts he shouted peremptorily to the peasants instead, and beckoned to them to come up. The wind, that seemed to blow as they drove, dropped when the carriage stood still; gadflies settled on the steaming horses that angrily shook them off. The metallic clank of a whet-stone against a scythe, that came to them from the cart, ceased. One of the peasants got up and came towards the carrige.

'Well, you are slow!' the counting-house clerk shouted angrily to the peasant who was stepping slowly with his bare feet over the ruts of the rough dry road. 'Come along, do!'

A curly-headed old man with a bit of bast tied round his hair, and his bent back dark with perspiration, came towards the carriage, quickening his steps, and took hold of the mudguard with his sunburnt hand.

'Vozdvizhenskoe, the manor-house? the count's?' he repeated; 'Go on to the end of this track. Then turn to the left. Straight along the avenue and you'll come right upon it. But whom do you want? The count himself?'

'Well, are they at home, my good man?' Darya Alexandrovna said vaguely, not knowing how to ask about Anna, even of this peasant.

'At home for sure,' said the peasant, shifting from one bare foot to the other, and leaving a distinct print of five toes and a heel in the dust. 'Sure to be at home,' he repeated, evidently eager to talk. 'Only yesterday visitors arrived. There's a sight of visitors come. What do you want?' He turned round and called to a lad, who was shouting something to him from the cart. 'Oh! They all rode by here not long since, to look at a reaping-machine. They'll be home by now. And who will you be belonging to? . . .'

'We've come a long way,' said the coachman, climbing on to the box. 'So it's not far?'

'I tell you, it's just here. As soon as you get out . . .' he said, keeping hold all the while of the carriage.

A healthy-looking, broad-shouldered young fellow came up too.

'What, is it labourers they want for the harvest?' he asked.

'I don't know, my boy.'

'So, you keep to the left, and you'll come right on it,' said the peasant, unmistakably loath to let the travellers go, and eager to converse.

The coachman started the horses, but they were only just turning off when the peasant shouted: 'Stop! Hi, friend! Stop!' called the two voices. The coachman stopped.

'They're coming! They're yonder!' shouted the peasant. 'See what a turn-out!' he said, pointing to four persons on horseback, and two in a *char-à-banc*, coming along the road.

They were Vronsky with a jockey, Veslovsky, and Anna on horseback, and Princess Varvara and Sviazhsky in the *char-à-banc*. They had gone out to look at the working of a new reaping-machine.

When the carriage stopped, the party on horseback were coming at a walking-pace. Anna was in front beside Veslovsky. Anna, quietly walking her horse, a sturdy English cob with cropped mane and short tail, her beautiful head with her black hair straying loose under her high hat, her full shoulders, her slender waist in her black riding-habit, and all the ease and grace of her deportment, impressed Dolly.

For the first minute it seemed to her unsuitable for Anna to be on horseback. The conception of riding on horseback for a lady was, in Darya Alexandrovna's mind, associated with ideas of youthful flirtation and frivolity, which, in her opinion, was unbecoming in Anna's position. But when she had scrutinised her, seeing her closer, she was at once reconciled to her riding. In spite of her elegance, everything was so simple, quiet, and dignified in the attitude, the dress and the movements of Anna, that nothing could have been more natural.

Beside Anna, on a hot-looking grey cavalry-horse, was Vassenka Veslovsky in his Scotch cap with floating ribbons, his stout legs stretched out in front, obviously pleased with his own appearance. Darya Alexandrovna could not suppress a good-humoured smile as she recognised him. Behind rode Vronsky on a dark bay mare, obviously heated from galloping. He was holding her in, pulling at the reins.

After him rode a little man in the dress of a jockey. Sviazhsky and Princess Varvara in a new *char-à-banc* with a big, raven-black trotting-horse, overtook the party on horseback.

Anna's face suddenly beamed with a joyful smile at the instant when, in the little figure huddled in a corner of the old carriage, she recognised Dolly. She uttered a cry, started in the saddle, and set her horse into a gallop. On reaching the carriage she jumped off without assistance, and holding up her riding-habit, she ran up to greet Dolly.

'I thought it was you and dared not think it. How delightful! You can't fancy how glad I am!' she said, at one moment pressing her face against Dolly and kissing her, and at the next holding her off and examining her with a smile.

'Here's a delightful surprise, Alexey!' she said, looking round at Vronsky, who had dismounted, and was walking towards them.

Vronsky, taking off his tall grey hat, went up to Dolly.

'You wouldn't believe how glad we are to see you,' he said, giving peculiar significance to the words, and showing his strong white teeth in a smile.

Vassenka Veslovsky, without getting off his horse, took off his cap and greeted the visitor by gleefully waving the ribbons over his head.

'That's Princess Varvara,' Anna said in reply to a glance of inquiry from Dolly as the *char-à-banc* drove up.

'Ah!' said Darya Alexandrovna, and unconsciously her face betrayed her dissatisfaction.

Princess Varvara was her husband's aunt, and she had long known her, and did not respect her. She knew that Princess Varvara had passed her whole life toadying on her rich relations, but that she should now be sponging on Vronsky, a man who was nothing to her, mortified Dolly on account of her kinship with her husband. Anna noticed Dolly's expression, and was disconcerted by it. She blushed, dropped her riding-habit, and stumbled over it.

Darya Alexandrovna went up to the *char-à-banc* and coldly greeted Princess Varvara. Sviazhsky too she knew. He inquired how his queer friend with the young wife was, and running his eyes over the ill-matched horses and the carriage with its patched mudguards, proposed to the ladies that they should get into the *char-à-banc*.

'And I'll get into this vehicle,' he said. 'The horse is quiet, and the princess drives capitally.'

'No, stay as you were,' said Anna, coming up, 'and we'll go in the carriage,' and taking Dolly's arm, she drew her away.

Darya Alexandrovna's eyes were fairly dazzled by the elegant carriage of a pattern she had never seen before, the splendid horses, and the elegant and gorgeous people surrounding her. But what struck her most of all was the change that had taken place in Anna, whom she knew so well and loved. Any other woman, a less close observer, not knowing Anna before, or not having thought as Darya Alexandrovna had been thinking on the road, would not have noticed anything special in Anna. But now Dolly was struck by that temporary beauty, which is only found in women during the moments of love, and which she saw now in Anna's face. Everything in her face, the clearly marked dimples in her cheeks and chin, the line of her lips, the smile which, as it were, fluttered about her face, the brilliance of her eyes, the grace and rapidity of her movements, the fullness of the notes of her voice, even the manner in which, with a sort of angry friendliness, she answered Veslovsky when he asked permission to get on her cob, so as to teach it to gallop with the right leg foremost—it was all peculiarly fascinating, and it seemed as if she were herself aware of it, and rejoicing in it.

When both the women were seated in the carriage, a sudden embarrassment came over both of them. Anna was disconcerted by the intent look of inquiry Dolly fixed upon her. Dolly was embarrassed because after Sviazhsky's phrase about 'this vehicle,' she could not help feeling ashamed of the dirty old carriage in which Anna was sitting with her. The coachman Philip and the counting-house clerk were experiencing the same sensation. The counting-house clerk, to conceal his confusion, busied himself settling the ladies, but Philip the coachman became sullen, and was bracing himself not to be over-awed in future by this external superiority. He smiled ironically, looking at the raven horse, and was already deciding in his own mind that this smart trotter in the *char-à-banc* was only good for *promenage*, and wouldn't do thirty miles straight off in the heat.

The peasants had all got up from the cart and were inquisitively and mirthfully staring at the meeting of the friends, making their comments on it.

'They're pleased, too; haven't seen each other for a long while,' said the curly-headed old man with the bast round his hair.

'I say, Uncle Gerasim, if we could take that raven horse now, to cart the corn, that 'ud be quick work!'

'Look-ee! Is that a woman in breeches?' said one of them, pointing to Vassenka Veslovsky sitting in a side-saddle.

'Nay, a man! See how smartly he's going it!'

'Eh, lads! seems we're not going to sleep, then?'

'What chance of sleep today!' said the old man, with a sidelong look at the sun. 'Midday's past, look-ee! Get your hooks, and come along!'

XVIII

ANNA looked at Dolly's thin, careworn face, with its wrinkles filled with dust from the road, and she was on the point of saying what she was thinking, that is, that Dolly had got thinner. But, conscious that she herself had grown handsomer, and that Dolly's eyes were telling her so, she sighed and began to speak about herself.

'You are looking at me,' she said, 'and wondering how I can be happy in my position? Well! it's shameful to confess, but I . . . I'm inexcusably happy. Something magical has happened to me, like a dream, when you're frightened, panic-stricken, and all of a sudden you wake up and all the horrors are no more. I have waked up. I have lived through the misery, the dread, and now for a long while past, especially since we've been here, I've been so happy! . . .' she said, with a timid smile of inquiry looking at Dolly.

'How glad I am!' said Dolly smiling, involuntarily speaking more coldly than she wanted to. 'I'm very glad for you. Why haven't you written to me?'

'Why? . . . Because I hadn't the courage. . . . You forget my position. . . .'

'To me? hadn't the courage? If you knew how I . . . I look at . . .'

Darya Alexandrovna wanted to express her thoughts of the morning, but for some reason it seemed to her now out of place to do so.

'But of that we'll talk later. What's this, what are all these buildings?' she asked, wanting to change the conversation and pointing to the red and green roofs that came into view behind the green hedges of acacia and lilac. 'Quite a little town.'

But Anna did not answer her.

'No, no! How do you look at my position, what do you think of it?' she asked.

'I consider . . .' Darya Alexandrovna was beginning, but at that instant Vassenka Veslovsky, having brought the cob to gallop with the right leg foremost, galloped past them, bumping heavily up and down in his short jacket on the chamois leather of the side-saddle. 'He's doing it, Anna Arkadyevna!' he shouted.

Anna did not even glance at him; but again it seemed to Darya Alexandrovna out of place to enter upon such a long conversation in the carriage, and so she cut short her thought.

'I don't think anything,' she said, 'but I always loved you, and if one loves anyone, one loves the whole person, just as they are and not as one would like them to be. . . .'

Anna, taking her eyes off her friend's face and dropping her eyelids (this was a new habit Dolly had not seen in her before), pondered, trying to penetrate the full significance of the words. And obviously interpreting them as she would have wished, she glanced at Dolly.

'If you had any sins,' she said, 'they would all be forgiven you for your coming to me and these words.'

And Dolly saw that the tears stood in her eyes. She pressed Anna's hand in silence.

'Well, what are these buildings? How many there are of them!' After a moment's silence she repeated her question.

'These are the servants' houses, barns and stables,' answered Anna. 'And there the park begins. It had all gone to ruin, but Alexey had everything renewed. He is very fond of this place, and, what I never expected, he has become intensely interested in looking after it. But his is such a rich nature! Whatever he takes up, he does splendidly. So far from being bored by it, he works with passionate interest. He—with his temperament as I know it—he has become careful and business-like, a first-rate manager, he positively reckons every penny in his management of the land. But only in that. When it's a question of tens of thousands, he doesn't think of money.' She spoke with that gleefully sly smile with which women often talk of the secret characteristics only known to them—of those they love. 'Do you see that big building? that's the new hospital. I believe it will cost over a hundred thousand; that's his hobby just now. And do you know how it all came about? The peasants asked him for some meadow-land, I think it was, at a cheaper rate, and he refused, and I accused him of being miserly. Of course it was not really because of that, but everything together, he began this hospital to prove, do you see, that he was not miserly about money. *C'est une petitesse*, if you like, but I love him all the more for it. And now you'll see the house in a moment. It was his grandfather's house, and he has had nothing changed outside.'

'How beautiful!' said Dolly, looking with involuntary admiration at the handsome house with columns, standing out among the different-coloured greens of the old trees in the garden.

'Isn't it fine? And from the house, from the top, the view is wonderful.'

They drove into a courtyard strewn with gravel and bright with flowers, in which two labourers were at work putting an edging of stones round the light mould of a flower-bed, and drew up in a covered entry.

'Ah, they're here already!' said Anna, looking at the saddle-horses, which were just being led away from the steps. 'It is a nice horse, isn't it? It's my cob; my favourite. Lead him here and bring me some sugar. Where is the count?' she inquired of two smart footmen who darted out. 'Ah, there he is!' she said, seeing Vronsky coming to meet her with Veslovsky.

'Where are you going to put the princess?' said Vronsky in French, addressing Anna, and without waiting for a reply, he once more greeted Darya Alexandrovna, and this time he kissed her hand. 'I think the big balcony room.'

'Oh no, that's too far off! Better in the corner room, we shall see each other more. Come, let's go up,' said Anna, as she gave her favourite horse the sugar the footman had brought her.

'*Et vous oubliez votre devoir*,' she said to Veslovsky, who came out too on the steps.

'*Pardon, j'en ai tout plein les poches*,' he answered, smiling, putting his fingers in his waistcoat pocket.

'*Mais vous venez trop tard*,' she said, rubbing her handkerchief on her hand, which the horse had made wet in taking the sugar.

Anna turned to Dolly. 'You can stay some time? For one day only? That's impossible!'

'I promised to be back, and the children . . .' said Dolly, feeling embarrassed both because she had to get her bag out of the carriage, and because she knew her face must be covered with dust.

'No, Dolly, darling! . . . Well, we'll see. Come along, come along!' and Anna led Dolly to her room.

That room was not the smart guest-chamber Vronsky had suggested, but the one of which Anna had said that Dolly would excuse it. And this room, for which excuse was needed, was more full of luxury than any in which Dolly had ever stayed, a luxury that reminded her of the best hotels abroad.

'Well, darling, how happy I am!' Anna said, sitting down in her riding-habit for a moment beside Dolly. 'Tell me about all of you. Stiva I had only a glimpse of, and he cannot tell one about the children. How is my favourite, Tanya? Quite a big girl, I expect?'

'Yes, she's very tall,' Darya Alexandrovna answered shortly, surprised herself that she should respond so coolly about her children. 'We are having a delightful stay at the Levins',' she added.

'Oh, if I had known,' said Anna, 'that you do not despise me! . . . You might have all come to us. Stiva's an old friend and a great friend of Alexey's, you know,' she added, and suddenly she blushed.

'Yes, but we are all . . .' Dolly answered in confusion.

'But in my delight I'm talking nonsense. The one thing, darling, is that I am so glad to have you!' said Anna, kissing her again. 'You haven't told me yet how and what you think about me, and I keep wanting to know. But I'm glad you will see me as I am. The chief thing I shouldn't like would be for people to imagine I want to prove anything. I don't want to prove anything; I merely want to live, to do no one harm but myself. I have the right to do that, haven't I? But it is a big subject, and we'll talk over everything properly later. Now I'll go and dress and send a maid to you.'

XIX

LEFT alone, Darya Alexandrovna, with a good housewife's eye, scanned her room. All she had seen in entering the house and walking through it, and all she saw now in her room, gave her an impression of wealth and sumptuousness and of that modern European luxury of which she had only read in English novels, but had never seen in Russia and in the country. Everything was new from the new French hangings on the walls to the carpet which covered the whole floor. The bed had a spring mattress, and a special sort of bolster and silk pillow-cases on the little pillows. The marble washstand, the dressing-table, the little sofa, the tables, the bronze clock on the chimneypiece, the window-curtains and the portières were all new and expensive.

The smart maid, who came in to offer her services, with her hair done up high, and a gown more fashionable than Dolly's, was as new and expensive as the whole room. Darya Alexandrovna liked her neatness, her deferential and obliging manners, but she felt ill at ease with her. She felt ashamed of her seeing the patched dressing-jacket that had unluckily been packed by mistake for her. She was ashamed of the very patches and darned places of which she had been so proud at home. At home it had been so clear that for six dressing-jackets there would be needed twenty-four yards of nainsook at sixteenpence the yard, which was a matter of thirty shillings besides the cutting-out and making, and these thirty shillings had been saved. But before the maid she felt, if not exactly ashamed, at least uncomfortable.

Darya Alexandrovna had a great sense of relief when Annushka, whom she had known for years, walked in. The smart maid was sent for to go to her mistress, and Annushka remained with Darya Alexandrovna.

Annushka was obviously much pleased at that lady's arrival, and began to chatter away without a pause. Dolly observed that she was longing to express her opinion in regard to her mistress's position, especially as to the love and devotion of the count to Anna Arkadyevna, but Dolly carefully interrupted her whenever she began to speak about this.

'I grew up with Anna Arkadyevna; my lady's dearer to me than anything. Well, it's not for us to judge. And, to be sure, there seems so much love . . .'

'Kindly pour out the water for me to wash now, please,' Darya Alexandrovna cut her short.

'Certainly. We've two women kept especially for washing small things, but most of the linen's done by machinery. The count goes into everything himself. Ah, what a husband! . . .'

Dolly was glad when Anna came in, and by her entrance put a stop to Annushka's gossip.

Anna had put on a very simple batiste gown. Dolly scrutinised that simple gown attentively. She knew what it meant, and the price at which such simplicity was obtained.

'An old friend,' said Anna of Annushka.

Anna was not embarrassed now. She was perfectly composed and at ease. Dolly saw that she had now completely recovered from the impression her arrival had made on her, and had assumed that superficial, careless tone which, as it were, closed the door on that compartment in which her deeper feelings and ideas were kept.

'Well, Anna, and how is your little girl?' asked Dolly.

'Annie?' (this was what she called her little daughter Anna). 'Very well. She has got on wonderfully. Would you like to see her? Come, I'll show her to you. We had a terrible bother,' she began telling her, 'over nurses. We had an Italian wet-nurse. A good creature, but so stupid! We wanted to get rid of her, but the baby is so used to her, that we've gone on keeping her still.'

'But how have you managed? . . .' Dolly was beginning a question as to what name the little girl would have; but noticing a sudden frown on Anna's face, she changed the drift of her question.

'How did you manage? have you weaned her yet?'

But Anna had understood.

'You didn't mean to ask that? You meant to ask about her surname. Yes? That worries Alexey. She has no name—that is, she's a Karenin,' said Anna, dropping her eyelids till nothing could be seen but the eyelashes meeting. 'But we'll talk about all that later,' her face suddenly brightening. 'Come, I'll show you her. *Elle est très gentille*. She crawls now.'

In the nursery the luxury which had impressed Dolly in the whole house struck her still more. There were little go-carts ordered from England, and appliances for learning to walk, and a sofa after the fashion of a billiard-table, purposely constructed for crawling, and swings and baths, all of special pattern, and modern. They were all English, solid, and of good make, and obviously very expensive. The room was large, and very light and lofty.

When they went in, the baby, with nothing on but her little smock, was sitting in a little elbow-chair at the table, having her dinner of broth, which she was spilling all over her little chest. The baby was being fed, and the Russian nursery-maid was evidently sharing her meal. Neither the wet-nurse nor the head-nurse were there; they were in the next room, from which came the sound of their conversation in the queer French, which was their only means of communication.

Hearing Anna's voice, a smart, tall English nurse with a disagreeable face and a dissolute expression walked in at the door, hurriedly shaking her fair curls, and immediately began to defend herself though Anna had not found fault with her. At every word Anna said the English nurse said hurriedly several times, 'Yes, my lady.'

The rosy baby with her black eyebrows and hair, her sturdy red little body with tight goose-flesh skin, delighted Darya Alexandrovna in spite of the cross expression with which she stared at the stranger. She positively envied the baby's healthy appearance. She was delighted, too, at the baby's crawling. Not one of her own children had crawled like that. When the baby was put on the carpet and its little dress tucked up behind, it was wonderfully charming. Looking round like some little wild animal at the grown-up big people with her bright black eyes, she smiled, unmistakably pleased at their admiring her, and holding her legs sideways, she pressed vigorously on her arms, and rapidly drew her whole back up after, and then made another step forward with her little arms.

But the whole atmosphere of the nursery, and especially the English nurse, Darya Alexandrovna did not like at all. It was only on the supposition that no good nurse would have entered so irregular a household as Anna's that Darya Alexandrovna could explain to herself how Anna with her insight into people could take such an unprepossessing, disreputable-looking woman as nurse to her child.

Besides, from a few words that were dropped, Darya Alexandrovna saw at once that Anna, the two nurses and the child had no common existence, and that the mother's visit was something exceptional. Anna wanted to get the baby her plaything, and could not find it.

Most amazing of all was the fact that on being asked how many teeth the baby had, Anna answered wrong, and knew nothing about the two last teeth.

'I sometimes feel sorry I'm so superfluous here,' said Anna, going out of the nursery and holding up her skirt so as to escape the plaything standing in the doorway. 'It was very different with my first child.'

'I expected it to be the other way,' said Darya Alexandrovna shyly.

'Oh no! By the way, do you know I saw Seryozha?' said Anna, screwing up her eyes, as though looking at something far away. 'But we'll talk about that later. You wouldn't believe it, I'm like a hungry beggar-woman when a full dinner is set before her, and she does not know what to begin on first. The dinner is you, and the talks I have before me with you, which I could never have with anyone else; and I don't know which subject to begin upon first. *Mais je ne vous ferai grâce de rien*. I must have everything out with you.'

'Oh, I ought to give you a sketch of the company you will meet with us,' she began. 'I'll begin with the ladies. Princess Varvara—you know her, and I know your opinion and Stiva's about her. Stiva says the whole aim of her existence is to prove her superiority over Auntie Katerina Pavlovna: that's all true; but she's a good-natured woman, and I am so grateful to her. In Petersburg there was a moment when a chaperon was absolutely essential for me. Then she turned up. But really she is good-natured. She did a great deal to alleviate my position. I see you don't understand all the difficulty of my position . . . there in Petersburg,' she added. 'Here I'm perfectly at ease and happy. Well, of that later on, though. Then Sviazhsky—he's the marshal of the district, and he's a very good sort of man, but he wants to get something out of Alexey. You understand, with his property, now that we are settled in the country, Alexey can exercise great influence. Then there's Tushkevitch—you have seen him, you know—Betsy's admirer. Now he's been thrown over and he's come to see us. As Alexey says, he's one of those people who are very pleasant if one accepts them for what they try to appear to be, *et puis il est comme il faut*, as Princess Varvara says. Then Veslovsky . . . you know him. A very nice boy,' she said, and a sly smile curved her lips. 'What's this wild story about him and the Levins? Veslovsky told Alexey about it, and we don't believe it. *Il est très gentil et naïf*,' she said again with the same smile. 'Men need occupation, and Alexey needs a circle, so I value all these people. We have to have the house lively and gay, so that Alexey may not long for any novelty. Then you'll see the steward—a German, a very good fellow, and he understands his work. Alexey has a very high opinion of him. Then the doctor, a young man, not quite a Nihilist perhaps, but you know, eats with his knife . . . but a very good doctor. Then the architect . . . Une *petite cour*.'

XX

'HERE'S Dolly for you, princess, you were so anxious to see her,' said Anna, coming out with Darya Alexandrovna on to the stone terrace where Princess Varvara was sitting in the shade at an embroidery frame, working at a cover for Count Alexey Kirillovitch's easy-chair. 'She says she doesn't want anything before dinner, but please order some lunch for her, and I'll go and look for Alexey and bring them all in.'

Princess Varvara gave Dolly a cordial and rather patronising reception, and began at once explaining to her that she was living with Anna because she had always cared more for her than her sister Katerina Pavlovna, the aunt that had brought Anna up, and that now, when everyone had abandoned Anna, she thought it her duty to help her in this most difficult period of transition.

'Her husband will give her a divorce, and then I shall go back to my solitude; but now I can be of use, and I am doing my duty, however difficult it may be for me—not like some other people. And how sweet it is of you, how right of you to have come! They live like the best of married couples; it's for God to judge them, not for us. And didn't Biryuzovsky and Madame Aveniev . . . and Sam Nikandrov, and Vassiliev and Madame Mamonov, and Liza Neptunov. . . . Did no one say anything about them? And it has ended by their being received by everyone. And then, *c'est un intérieur si joli, si comme il faut. Tout-à-fait à l'anglaise. On se réunit le matin au breakfast, et puis on se sépare.* Everyone does as he pleases till dinner-time. Dinner at seven o'clock. Stiva did very rightly to send you. He needs their support. You know that through his mother and brother he can do anything. And then they do so much good. He didn't tell you about his hospital? *Ce sera admirable*—everything from Paris.

Their conversation was interrupted by Anna, who had found the men of the party in the billiard-room, and returned with them to the terrace. There was still a long time before the dinner-hour, it was exquisite weather, and so several different methods of spending the next two hours were proposed. There were very many methods of passing the time at Vozdvizhenskoe, and these were all unlike those in use at Pokrovskoe.

'*Une partie de lawn-tennis*,' Veslovsky proposed, with his handsome smile. 'We'll be partners again, Anna Arkadyevna.'

'No, it's too hot; better stroll about the garden and have a row in the boat, show Darya Alexandrovna the river-banks,' Vronsky proposed.

'I agree to anything,' said Sviazhsky.

'I imagine that what Dolly would like best would be a stroll—wouldn't you? And then the boat, perhaps,' said Anna.

So it was decided. Veslovsky and Tushkevitch went off to the bathing-place, promising to get the boat ready and to wait there for them.

They walked along the path in two couples, Anna with Sviazhsky, and Dolly with Vronsky. Dolly was a little embarrassed and anxious in the new surroundings in which she found herself. Abstractly, theoretically, she did not merely justify, she positively approved of Anna's conduct. As is indeed not unfrequent with women of unimpeachable virtue, weary of the monotony of respectable existence, at a distance she not only excused illicit love, she positively envied it. Besides, she loved Anna with all her heart. But seeing Anna in actual life among these strangers, with this fashionable tone that was so new to Darya Alexandrovna, she felt ill at ease. What she disliked particularly was seeing Princess Varvara ready to overlook everything for the sake of the comforts she enjoyed.

As a general principle, abstractly, Dolly approved of Anna's action; but to see the man for whose sake her action had been taken was disagreeable to her. Moreover, she had never liked Vronsky. She thought him very proud, and saw nothing in him of which he could be proud except his wealth. But against her own will, here in his own house, he overawed her more than ever, and she could not be at ease with him. She felt with him the same feeling she had had with the maid about her dressing-jacket. Just as with the maid she had felt not exactly ashamed, but embarrassed at her darns, so she felt with him not exactly ashamed, but embarrassed at herself.

Dolly was ill at ease, and tried to find a subject of conversation. Even though she supposed that, through his pride, praise of his house and garden would be sure to be disagreeable to him, she did all the same tell him how much she liked his house.

'Yes, it's a very fine building, and in the good old-fashioned style,' he said.

'I like so much the court in front of the steps. Was that always so?'

'Oh, no!' he said, and his face beamed with pleasure. 'If you could only have seen that court last spring!'

And he began, at first rather diffidently, but more and more carried away by the subject as he went on, to draw her attention to the various details of the decoration of his house and garden. It was evident that, having devoted a great deal of trouble to improve and beautify his home, Vronsky felt a need to show off the improvements to a new person, and was genuinely delighted at Darya Alexandrovna's praise.

'If you would care to look at the hospital, and are not tired, indeed, it's not far. Shall we go?' he said, glancing into her face to convince himself that she was not bored. 'Are you coming, Anna?' he turned to her.

'We will come, won't we?' she said, addressing Sviazhsky. '*Mais il ne faut pas laisser le pauvre Veslovsky et Tushkevitch se morfondre là dans le bateau*. We must send and tell them.'

'Yes, this is a monument he is setting up here,' said Anna, turning to Dolly with that sly smile of comprehension with which she had previously talked about the hospital.

'Oh, it's a work of real importance!' said Sviazhsky. But to show he was not trying to ingratiate himself with Vronsky, he promptly added some slightly critical remarks.

'I wonder, though, count,' he said, 'that while you do so much for the health of the peasants, you take so little interest in the schools.'

'*C'est devenu tellement commun les écoles*,' said Vronsky. 'You understand it's not on that account, but it just happens so, my interest has been diverted elsewhere. This way then to the hospital,' he said to Darya Alexandrovna, pointing to a turning out of the avenue.

The ladies put up their parasols and turned into the side-path. After going down several turnings, and going through a little gate, Darya Alexandrovna saw standing on rising ground before her a large pretentious-looking red building, almost finished. The iron roof, which was not yet painted, shone with dazzling brightness in the sunshine. Beside the finished building another had been begun, surrounded by scaffolding. Workmen in aprons, standing on scaffolds, were laying bricks, pouring mortar out of vats, and smoothing it with trowels.

'How quickly work gets done with you!' said Sviazhsky. 'When I was here last time the roof was not on.'

'By the autumn it will all be ready. Inside almost everything is done,' said Anna.

'And what's this new building?'

'That's the house for the doctor and the dispensary,' answered Vronsky, seeing the architect in a short jacket coming towards him; and excusing himself to the ladies, he went to meet him.

Going round a hole where the workmen were slaking lime, he stood still with the architect and began talking rather warmly.

'The front is still too low,' he said to Anna, who had asked what was the matter.

'I said the foundation ought to be raised,' said Anna.

'Yes, of course it would have been much better, Anna Arkadyevna,' said the architect, 'but now it's too late.'

'Yes, I take a great interest in it,' Anna answered Sviazhsky, who was expressing his surprise at her knowledge of architecture. 'This new building ought to have been in harmony with the hospital. It was an afterthought, and was begun without a plan.'

Vronsky, having finished his talk with the architect, joined the ladies, and led them inside the hospital.

Although they were still at work on the cornices outside and were painting on the ground-floor, upstairs almost all the rooms were finished. Going up the broad cast-iron staircase to the landing, they walked into the first large room. The walls were stuccoed to look like marble, the huge plate-glass windows were already in, only the parquet floor was not yet finished, and the carpenters, who were planing a block of it, left their work, taking off the bands that fastened their hair, to greet the gentry.

'This is the reception-room,' said Vronsky. 'Here there will be a desk, tables, and benches, and nothing more.'

'This way; let us go in here. Don't go near the window,' said Anna, trying the paint to see if it were dry. 'Alexey, the paint's dry already,' she added.

From the reception-room they went into the corridor. Here Vronsky showed them the mechanism for ventilation on a novel system. Then he showed them marble baths, and beds with extraordinary springs. Then he showed them the wards one after another, the store-room, the linen-room, then the heating-stove of a new pattern, then the trolleys, which would make no noise as they carried everything needed along the corridors, and many other things. Sviazhsky, as a connoisseur in the latest mechanical improvements, appreciated everything fully. Dolly simply wondered at all she had not seen before, and, anxious to understand it all, made minute inquiries about everything, which gave Vronsky great satisfaction.

'Yes, I imagine that this will be the solitary example of a properly fitted hospital in Russia,' said Sviazhsky.

'And won't you have a lying-in ward?' asked Dolly. 'That's so much needed in the country. I have often . . .'

In spite of his usual courtesy, Vronsky interrupted her.

'This is not a lying-in home, but a hospital for the sick, and is intended for all diseases, except infectious complaints,' he said. 'Ah! look at this,' and he rolled up to Darya Alexandrovna an invalid-chair that had just been ordered for convalescents. 'Look.' He sat down in the chair and began moving it. 'The patient can't walk—still too weak, perhaps, or something wrong with his legs, but he must have air, and he moves, rolls himself along. . . .'

Darya Alexandrovna was interested by everything. She liked everything very much, but most of all she liked Vronsky himself with his natural, simple-hearted eagerness. 'Yes, he's a very nice, good man,' she thought several times, not hearing what he said, but looking at him and penetrating into his expression, while she mentally put herself in Anna's place. She liked him so much just now with his eager interest that she saw how Anna could be in love with him.

XXI

'No, I think the princess is tired, and horses don't interest her,' Vronsky said to Anna, who wanted to go on to the stables, where Sviazhsky wished to see the new stallion. 'You go on, while I escort the princess home, and we'll have a little talk,' he said, 'if you would like that?' he added, turning to her.

'I know nothing about horses, and I shall be delighted,' answered Darya Alexandrovna, rather astonished.

She saw by Vronsky's face that he wanted something from her. She was not mistaken. As soon as they had passed through the little gate back into the garden, he looked in the direction Anna had taken, and having made sure that she could neither hear nor see them, he began—

'You guess that I have something I want to say to you,' he said, looking at her with laughing eyes. 'I am not wrong in believing you to be a friend of Anna's.' He took off his hat, and taking out his handkerchief, wiped his head, which was growing bald.

Darya Alexandrovna made no answer, and merely stared at him with dismay. When she was left alone with him, she suddenly felt afraid; his laughing eyes and stern expression scared her.

The most diverse suppositions as to what he was about to speak of to her flashed into her brain. 'He is going to beg me to come to stay with them with the children, and I shall have to refuse; or to create a set that will receive Anna in Moscow. . . . Or isn't it Vassenka Veslovsky and his relations with Anna? Or perhaps about Kitty, that he feels he was to blame?' All her conjectures were unpleasant, but she did not guess what he really wanted to talk about to her.

'You have so much influence with Anna, she is so fond of you,' he said; 'do help me.'

Darya Alexandrovna looked with timid inquiry into his energetic face, which under the lime-trees was continually being lighted up in patches by the sunshine, and then passing into complete shadow again. She waited for him to say more, but he walked in silence beside her, scratching with his cane in the gravel.

'You have come to see us, you, the only woman of Anna's former friends—I don't count Princess Varvara—but I know that you have done this not because you regard our position as normal, but because, understanding all the difficulty of the position, you still love her and want to be a help to her. Have I understood you rightly?' he asked, looking round at her.

'Oh, yes,' answered Darya Alexandrovna, putting down her sunshade, 'but . . .'

'No,' he broke in, and unconsciously, oblivious of the awkward position in which he was putting his companion, he stopped abruptly, so that she had to stop short too. 'No one feels more deeply and intensely than I do all the difficulty of Anna's position; and that you may well understand, if you do me the honour of supposing I have any heart. I am to blame for that position, and that is why I feel it.'

'I understand,' said Darya Alexandrovna, involuntarily admiring the sincerity and firmness with which he said this. 'But just because you feel yourself responsible, you exaggerate it, I am afraid,' she said. 'Her position in the world is difficult, I can well understand.'

'In the world it is hell!' he brought out quickly, frowning darkly. 'You can't imagine moral sufferings greater than what she went through in Petersburg in that fortnight . . . and I beg you to believe it.'

'Yes, but here, so long as neither Anna . . . nor you miss society . . .'

'Society!' he said contemptuously, 'how could I miss society?'

'So far—and it may be so always—you are happy and at peace. I see in Anna that she is happy, perfectly happy, she has had time to tell me so much already,' said Darya Alexandrovna, smiling; and involuntarily, as she said this, at the same moment a doubt entered her mind whether Anna really were happy.

But Vronsky, it appeared, had no doubts on that score.

'Yes, yes,' he said, 'I know that she has revived after all her sufferings; she is happy. She is happy in the present. But I? . . . I am afraid of what is before us . . . I beg your pardon, you would like to walk on?'

'No, I don't mind.'

'Well, then, let us sit here.'

Darya Alexandrovna sat down on a garden seat in a corner of the avenue. He stood up facing her.

'I see that she is happy,' he repeated, and the doubt whether she were happy sank more deeply into Darya Alexandrovna's mind. 'But can it last? Whether we have acted rightly or wrongly is another question, but the die is cast,' he said, passing from Russian to French, 'and we are bound together for life. We are united by all the ties of love that we hold most sacred. We have a child, we may have other children. But the law and all the conditions of our position are such that thousands of complications arise which she does not see and does not want to see. And that one can well understand. But I can't help seeing them. My daughter is by law not my daughter, but Karenin's. I cannot bear this falsity!' he said, with a vigorous gesture of refusal, and he looked with gloomy inquiry towards Darya Alexandrovna.

She made no answer, but simply gazed at him. He went on—

'One day a son may be born, my son, and he will be legally a Karenin; he will not be the heir of my name nor of my property, and however happy we may be in our home life and however many children we have, there will be no real tie between us. They will be Karenins. You can understand the bitterness and horror of this position! I have tried to speak of this to Anna. It irritates her. She does not understand, and to her I cannot speak plainly of all this. Now look at another side. I am happy, happy in her love, but I must have occupation. I have found occupation, and am proud of what I am doing and consider it nobler than the pursuits of my former companions at court and in the army. And most certainly I would not change the work I am doing for theirs. I am working here, settled in my own place, and I am happy and contented, and we need nothing more to make us happy. I love my work here. *Ce n'est pas un pis-aller*, on the contrary . . .'

Darya Alexandrovna noticed that at this point in his explanation he grew confused, and she did not quite understand this digression, but she felt that having once begun to speak of matters near his heart, of which he could not speak to Anna, he was now making a clean breast of everything, and that the question of his pursuits in the country fell into the same category of matters near his heart, as the question of his relations with Anna.

'Well, I will go on,' he said, collecting himself. 'The great thing is that as I work I want to have a conviction that what I am doing will not die with me, that I shall have heirs to come after me,—and this I have not. Conceive the position of a man who knows that his children, the children of the woman he loves, will not be his, but will belong to someone who hates them and cares nothing about them! It is awful!'

He paused, evidently much moved.

'Yes, indeed, I see that. But what can Anna do?' queried Darya Alexandrovna.

'Yes, that brings me to the object of my conversation,' he said, calming himself with an effort. 'Anna can, it depends on her. . . . Even to petition the Tsar for legitimisation, a divorce is essential. And that depends on Anna. Her husband agreed to a divorce—at that time your husband had arranged it completely. And now, I know, he would not refuse it. It is only a matter of writing to him. He said plainly at that time that if she expressed the desire, he would not refuse. Of course,' he said gloomily, 'it is one of those Pharisaical cruelties of which only such heartless men are capable. He knows what agony any recollection of him must give her, and knowing her, he must have a letter from her. I can understand that it is agony to her. But the matter is of such importance, that one must *passer par-dessus toutes ces finesses de sentiment. Il y va du bonheur et de l'existence d'Anne et de ses enfants*. I won't speak of myself, though it's hard for me, very hard,' he said, with an expression as though he were threatening someone for its being hard for him. 'And so it is, princess, that I am shamelessly clutching at you as an anchor of salvation. Help me to persuade her to write to him and ask for a divorce.'

'Yes, of course,' Darya Alexandrovna said dreamily, as she vividly recalled her last interview with Alexey Alexandrovitch. 'Yes, of course,' she repeated with decision, thinking of Anna.

'Use your influence with her, make her write. I don't like—I'm almost unable to speak about this to her.'

'Very well, I will talk to her. But how is it she does not think of it herself?' said Darya Alexandrovna, and for some reason she suddenly at that point recalled Anna's strange new habit of half-closing her eyes. And she remembered that Anna drooped her eyelids just when the deeper questions of life were touched upon. 'Just as though she half-shut her eyes to her own life, so as not to see everything,' thought Dolly. 'Yes, indeed, for my own sake and for hers I will talk to her,' Dolly said in reply to his look of gratitude.

They got up and walked to the house.

XXII

WHEN Anna found Dolly at home before her, she looked intently in her eyes, as though questioning her about the talk she had had with Vronsky, but she made no inquiry in words.

'I believe it's dinner-time,' she said. 'We've not seen each other at all yet. I am reckoning on the evening. Now I want to go and dress. I expect you do too; we all got splashed at the buildings.'

Dolly went to her room and she felt amused. To change her dress was impossible, for she had already put on her best dress. But in order to signify in some way her preparation for dinner, she asked the maid to brush her dress, changed her cuffs and tie, and put some lace on her head.

'This is all I can do,' she said with a smile to Anna, who came in to her in a third dress, again of extreme simplicity.

'Yes, we are too formal here,' she said, as it were apologising for her magnificence. 'Alexey is delighted at your visit, as he rarely is at anything. He has completely lost his heart to you,' she added. 'You're not tired?'

There was no time for talking about anything before dinner. Going into the drawing-room they found Princess Varvara already there, and the gentlemen of the party in black frock-coats. The architect wore a swallow-tail coat. Vronsky presented the doctor and the steward to his guest. The architect he had already introduced to her at the hospital.

A stout butler, resplendent with a smoothly shaven round chin and a starched white cravat, announced that dinner was ready, and the ladies got up. Vronsky asked Sviazhsky to take in Anna Arkadyevna, and himself offered his arm to Dolly. Veslovsky was before Tushkevitch in offering his arm to Princess Varvara, so that Tushkevitch with the steward and the doctor walked in alone.

The dinner, the dining-room, the service, the waiting at table, the wine, and the food, were not simply in keeping with the general tone of modern luxury throughout the house, but seemed even more sumptuous and modern. Darya Alexandrovna watched this luxury which was novel to her, and as a good housekeeper used to managing a household—though she never dreamed of adapting anything she saw to her own household, as it was all in a style of luxury far above her own manner of living—she could not help scrutinising every detail, and wondering how and by whom it was all done. Vassenka Veslovsky, her husband, and even Sviazhsky, and many other people she knew, would never have considered this question, and would have readily believed what every well-bred host tries to make his guests feel, that is, that all that is well-ordered in his house has cost him, the host, no trouble whatever, but comes of itself. Darya Alexandrovna was well aware that even porridge for the children's breakfast does not come of itself, and that therefore, where so complicated and magnificent a style of luxury was maintained, someone must give earnest attention to its organisation. And from the glance with which Alexey Kirillovitch scanned the table, from the way he nodded to the butler, and offered Darya Alexandrovna her choice between cold soup and hot soup, she saw that it was all organised and maintained by the care of the master of the house himself. It was evident that it all rested no more upon Anna than upon Veslovsky. She, Sviazhsky, the princess, and Veslovsky, were equally guests, with light hearts enjoying what had been arranged for them.

Anna was the hostess only in conducting the conversation. The conversation was a difficult one for the lady of the house at a small table with persons present, like the steward and the architect, belonging to a completely different world, struggling not be over-awed by an elegance to which they were unaccustomed, and unable to sustain a large share in the general conversation. But this difficult conversation Anna directed with her usual tact and naturalness, and indeed she did so with actual enjoyment, as Darya Alevandrovna observed. The conversation began about the row Tushkevitch and Veslovsky had taken alone together in the boat, and Tushkevitch began describing the last boat-races in Petersburg at the Yacht Club. But Anna, seizing the first pause, at once turned to the architect to draw him out of his silence.

'Nikolay Ivanitch was struck,' she said, meaning Sviazhsky, 'at the progress the new building had made since he was here last; but I am there every day, and every day I wonder at the rate at which it grows.'

'It's first-rate working with his excellency,' said the architect with a smile (he was respectful and composed, though with a sense of his own dignity). 'It's a very different matter to have to do with the district authorities. Where one would have to write out sheaves of papers, here I call upon the count, and in three words we settle the business.'

'The American way of doing business,' said Sviazhsky, with a smile.

'Yes, there they build in a rational fashion . . .'

The conversation passed to the misuse of political power in the United States, but Anna quickly brought it round to another topic, so as to draw the steward into talk.

'Have you ever seen a reaping-machine,' she said, addressing Darya Alexandrovna. 'We had just ridden over to look at one when we met. It's the first time I ever saw one.'

'How do they work?' asked Dolly.

'Exactly like little scissors. A plank and a lot of little scissors. Like this.'

Anna took a knife and fork in her beautiful white hands, covered with rings, and began showing how the machine worked. It was clear that she saw nothing would be understood from her explanation; but aware that her talk was pleasant and her hands beautiful she went on explaining.

'More like little penknives,' Veslovsky said playfully, never taking his eyes off her.

Anna gave a just perceptible smile, but made no answer. 'Isn't it true, Karl Fedoritch, that it's just like little scissors?' she said to the steward.

'*Oh, ja,*' answered the German. '*Es ist ein ganz einfaches Ding,*' and he began to explain the construction of the machine.

'It's a pity it doesn't bind too. I saw one at the Vienna exhibition, which binds with a wire,' said Sviazhsky. 'They would be more profitable in use.'

'*Es kommt drauf an . . . Der Preis vom Draht muss ausgerechnet werden.*' And the German, roused from his taciturnity, turned to Vronsky. '*Das lässt sich ausrechnen, Erlaucht.*' The German was just feeling in the pocket where were his pencil and the notebook he always wrote in, but recollecting that he was at dinner, and observing Vronsky's chilly glance, he checked himself. '*Zu complicirt, macht zu viel Klopot,*' he concluded.

'*Wünscht man Dorhots, so hat man auch Klopots,*' said Vassenka Veslovsky, mimicking the German. '*J'adore l'allemand,*' he addressed Anna again with the same smile.

'*Cessez,*' she said with playful severity.

'We expected to find you in the fields, Vassily Semyonitch,' she said to the doctor, a sickly-looking man; 'have you been there?'

'I went there, but I had taken flight,' the doctor answered with gloomy jocoseness.

'Then you've taken a good constitutional?'

'Splendid!'

'Well, and how was the old woman? I hope it's not typhus?'

'Typhus it is not, but it's taking a bad turn.'

'What a pity!' said Anna, and having thus paid the dues of civility to her domestic circle, she turned to her own friends.

'It would be a hard task, though, to construct a machine from your description, Anna Arkadyevna,' Sviazhsky said jestingly.

'Oh, no, why so?' said Anna with a smile that betrayed that she knew there was something charming in her disquisitions upon the machine that had been noticed by Sviazhsky. This new trait of girlish coquettishness made an unpleasant impression on Dolly.

'But Anna Arkadyevna's knowledge of architecture is marvellous,' said Tushkevitch.

'To be sure, I heard Anna Arkadyevna talking yesterday about plinths and damp-courses,' said Veslovsky. 'Have I got it right?'

'There's nothing marvellous about it, when one sees and hears so much of it,' said Anna. 'But, I dare say, you don't even know what houses are made of?'

Darya Alexandrovna saw that Anna disliked the tone of raillery that existed between her and Veslovsky, but fell in with it against her will.

Vronsky acted in this matter quite differently from Levin. He obviously attached no significance to Veslovsky's chattering; on the contrary, he encouraged his jests.

'Come now, tell us, Veslovsky, how are the stones held together?'

'By cement, of course.'

'Bravo! And what is cement?'

'Oh, some sort of paste . . . no, putty,' said Veslovsky, raising a general laugh.

The company at dinner, with the exception of the doctor, the architect, and the steward, who remained plunged in gloomy silence, kept up a conversation that never paused, glancing off one subject, fastening on another, and at times stinging one or the other to the quick. Once Darya Alexandrovna felt wounded to the quick, and got so hot that she positively flushed and wondered afterwards whether she had said anything extreme or unpleasant. Sviazhsky began talking of Levin, describing his strange view that machinery is simply pernicious in its effects on Russian agriculture.

'I have not the pleasure of knowing this M. Levin,' Vronsky said, smiling, 'but most likely he has never seen the machines he condemns; or if he has seen and tried any, it must have been after a queer fashion, some Russian imitation, not a machine from abroad. What sort of views can anyone have on such a subject?'

'Turkish views, in general,' Veslovsky said, turning to Anna with a smile.

'I can't defend his opinions,' Darya Alexandrovna said, firing up; 'but I can say that he's a highly cultivated man, and if he were here he would know very well how to answer you, though I am not capable of doing so.'

'I like him extremely, and we are great friends,' Sviazhsky said, smiling good-naturedly. '*Mais pardon, il est un petit peu toqué*; he maintains, for instance, that district councils and arbitration boards are all of no use, and he is unwilling to take part in anything.'

'It's our Russian apathy,' said Vronsky, pouring water from an iced decanter into a delicate glass on a high stem; 'we've no sense of the duties our privileges impose upon us, and so we refuse to recognise these duties.'

'I know no man more strict in the performance of his duties,' said Darya Alexandrovna, irritated by Vronsky's tone of superiority.

'For my part,' pursued Vronsky, who was evidently for some reason or other keenly affected by this conversation, 'such as I am, I am, on the contrary, extremely grateful for the honour they have done me, thanks to Nikolay Ivanitch' (he indicated Sviazhsky), 'in electing me a justice of the peace. I consider that for me the duty of being present at the session, of judging some peasants' quarrel about a horse, is as important as anything I can do. And I shall regard it as an honour if they elect me for the district council. It's only in that way I can pay for the advantages I enjoy as a landowner. Unluckily they don't understand the weight that the big landowners ought to have in the state.'

It was strange to Darya Alexandrovna to hear how serenely confident he was of being right at his own table. She thought how Levin, who believed the opposite, was just as positive in his opinions at his own table. But she loved Levin, and so she was on his side.

'So we can reckon upon you, count, for the coming elections?' said Sviazhsky. 'But you must come a little beforehand, so as to be on the spot by the eighth. If you would do me the honour to stop with me.'

'I rather agree with your *beau-frère*,' said Anna, 'though not quite on the same ground as he,' she added with a smile. 'I'm afraid that we have too many of these public duties in these latter days. Just as in old days there were so many government functionaries that one had to call in a functionary for every single thing, so now everyone's doing some sort of public duty. Alexey has been here now six months, and he's a member, I do believe, of five or six different public bodies. *Du train que cela va*, the whole time will be wasted on it. And I'm afraid that with such a multiplicity of these bodies, they'll end in being a mere form. How many are you a member of, Nikolay Ivanitch?' she turned to Sviazhsky—'over twenty, I fancy.'

Anna spoke lightly, but irritation could be discerned in her tone. Darya Alexandrovna, watching Anna and Vronsky, attentively, detected it instantly. She noticed, too, that as she spoke Vronsky's face had immediately taken a serious and obstinate expression. Noticing this, and that Princess Varvara at once made haste to change the conversation by talking of Petersburg acquaintances, and remembering what Vronsky had without apparent connection said in the garden of his work in the country, Dolly surmised that this question of public activity was connected with some deep private disagreement between Anna and Vronsky.

The dinner, the wine, the decoration of the table, was all very good; but it was all like what Darya Alexandrovna had seen at formal dinners and balls which of late years had become quite unfamiliar to her; it all had the same impersonal and constrained character, and so on an ordinary day and in a little circle of friends it made a disagreeable impression on her.

After dinner they sat on the terrace, then they proceeded to play lawn tennis. The players, divided into two parties, stood on opposite sides of a tightly drawn net with gilt poles on the carefully levelled and rolled croquet-ground. Darya Alexandrovna made an attempt to play, but it was a long time before she could understand the game, and by the time she did understand it, she was so tired that she sat down with Princess Varvara and simply looked on at the players. Her partner, Tushkevitch, gave up playing too, but the others kept the game up for a long time. Sviazsky and Vronsky both played very well and seriously. They kept a sharp lookout on the balls served to them, and without haste or getting in each other's way, they ran adroitly up to them, waited for the rebound, and neatly and accurately returned them over the net. Veslovsky played worse than the others. He was too eager, but he kept the players lively with his high spirits. His laughter and outcries never paused. Like the other men of the party, with the ladies' permission, he took off his coat, and his solid, comely figure in his white shirt-sleeves, with his red perspiring face and his impulsive movements, made a picture that imprinted itself vividly on the memory.

When Darya Alexandrovna lay in bed that night, as soon as she closed her eyes, she saw Vassenka Veslovsky flying about the croquet-ground.

During the game Darya Alexandrovna was not enjoying herself. She did not like the light tone of raillery that was kept up all the time between Vassenka Veslovsky and Anna, and the unnaturalness altogether of grown-up people, all alone without children, playing at a child's game. But to avoid breaking up the party and to get through the time somehow, after a rest she joined the game again, and pretended to be enjoying it. All that day it seemed to her as though she were acting in a theatre with actors cleverer than she, and that her bad acting was spoiling the whole performance. She had come with the intention of staying two days, if all went well. But in the evening, during the game, she made up her mind that she would go home next day. The maternal cares and worries, which she had so hated on the way, now, after a day spent without them, struck her in quite another light, and tempted her back to them.

When, after evening tea and a row by night in the boat, Darya Alexandrovna went alone to her room, took off her dress, and began arranging her thin hair for the night, she had a great sense of relief.

It was positively disagreeable to her to think that Anna was coming to see her immediately. She longed to be alone with her own thoughts.

XXIII

DOLLY was wanting to go to bed when Anna came in to see her, attired for the night. In the course of the day Anna had several times begun to speak of matters near her heart, and every time after a few words she had stopped: 'Afterwards, by ourselves, we'll talk about everything. I've got so much I want to tell you,' she said.

Now they were by themselves, and Anna did not know what to talk about. She sat in the window looking at Dolly, and going over in her own mind all the stores of intimate talk which had seemed so inexhaustible beforehand, and she found nothing. At that moment it seemed to her that everything had been said already.

'Well, what of Kitty?' she said with a heavy sigh, looking penitently at Dolly. 'Tell me the truth, Dolly: isn't she angry with me?'

'Angry? Oh no!' said Darya Alexandrovna, smiling.

'But she hates me, despises me?'

'Oh no! But you know that sort of thing isn't forgiven.'

'Yes, yes,' said Anna, turning away and looking out of the open window. 'But I was not to blame. And who is to blame? What's the meaning of being to blame? Could it have been otherwise? What do you think? Could it possibly have happened that you didn't become the wife of Stiva?'

'Really I don't know. But this is what I want you to tell me . . .'

'Yes, yes, but we've not finished about Kitty. Is she happy? He's a very nice man, they say.'

'He's much more than very nice. I don't know a better man.'

'Ah, how glad I am! I'm so glad! Much more than very nice,' she repeated.

Dolly smiled.

'But tell me about yourself. We've a great deal to talk about. And I've had a talk with . . .' Dolly did not know what to call him. She felt it awkward to call him either the count or Alexey Kirillovitch.

'With Alexey,' said Anna, 'I know what you talked about. But I wanted to ask you directly what you think of me, of my life?'

'How am I to say like that straight off? I really don't know.'

'No, tell me all the same.... You see my life. But you mustn't forget that you're seeing us in the summer, when you have come to us and we are not alone. . . . But we came here early in the spring, lived quite alone, and shall be alone again, and I desire nothing better. But imagine me living alone without him, alone, and that will be ... I see by everything that it will often be repeated, that he will be half the time away from home,' she said, getting up and sitting down close by Dolly.

'Of course,' she interrupted Dolly, who would have answered, 'of course I won't try to keep him by force. I don't keep him indeed. The races are just coming, his horses are running, he will go. I'm very glad. But think of me, fancy my position. . . . But what's the use of talking about it?' she smiled. 'Well, what did he talk about with you?'

'He spoke of what I want to speak about of myself, and it's easy for me to be his advocate; of whether there is not a possibility . . . whether you could not . . .' (Darya Alexandrovna hestitated) 'correct, improve your position. . . . You know how I look at it. . . . But all the same, if possible, you should get married. . . .'

'Divorce, you mean?' said Anna. 'Do you know, the only woman who came to see me in Petersburg was Betsy Tverskoy? You know her, of course? *Au fond, c'est la femme la plus depravée qui existe.* She had an intrigue with Tushkevitch, deceiving her husband in the basest way. And she told me that she did not care to know me so long as my position was irregular. Don't imagine I would compare . . . I know you, darling. But I could not help remembering . . . Well, so what did he say to you?' she repeated.

'He said that he was unhappy on your account and his own. Perhaps you will say that it's egoism, but what a legitimate and noble egoism. He wants first of all to legitimise his daughter, and to be your husband, to have a legal right to you.'

'What wife, what slave can be so utterly a slave as I, in my position?' she put in gloomily.

'The chief thing he desires . . . he desires that you should not suffer.'

'That's impossible. Well?'

'Well, and the most legitimate desire—he wishes that your children should have a name.'

'What children?' Anna said, not looking at Dolly, and half closing her eyes.

'Annie and those to come . . .'

'He need not trouble on that score; I shall have no more children.'

'How can you tell that you won't?'

'I shall not, because I don't wish it.' And, in spite of all her emotion, Anna smiled, as she caught the naïve expression of curiosity, wonder, and horror on Dolly's face.

'The doctor told me after my illness . . .'

. . . . . .

'Impossible!' said Dolly, opening her eyes wide.

For her this was one of those discoveries the consequences and deductions from which are so immense that all that one feels for the first instant is that it is impossible to take it all in, and that one will have to reflect a great, great deal upon it.

This discovery, suddenly throwing light on all those families of one or two children, which had hitherto been so incomprehensible to her, aroused so many ideas, reflections, and contradictory emotions, that she had nothing to say, and simply gazed with wide-open eyes of wonder at Anna. This was the very thing she had been dreaming of, but now learning that it was possible, she was horrified. She felt that it was too simple a solution of too complicated a problem.

'*N'est-ce pas immoral?*' was all she said, after a brief pause.

'Why so? Think, I have a choice between two alternatives: either to be with child, that is an invalid, or to be the friend and companion of my husband—practically my husband,' Anna said in a tone intentionally superficial and frivolous.

'Yes, yes,' said Darya Alexandrovna, hearing the very arguments she had used to herself, and not finding the same force in them as before.

'For you, for other people,' said Anna, as though divining her thoughts, 'there may be reason to hestitate; but for me . . . You must consider, I am not his wife; he loves me as long as he loves me. And how am I to keep his love? Not like this!'

She moved her white hands in a curve before her waist with extraordinary rapidity, as happens during moments of excitement; ideas and memories rushed into Darya Alexandrovna's head. 'I' she thought, 'did not keep my attraction for Stiva; he left me for others, and the first woman for whom he betrayed me did not keep him by being always pretty and lively. He deserted her and took another. And can Anna attract and keep Count Vronsky in that way? If that is what he looks for, he will find dresses and manners still more attractive and charming. And however white and beautiful her bare arms are, however beautiful her full figure and her eager face under her black curls, he will find something better still, just as my disgusting, pitiful, and charming husband does.'

Dolly made no answer, she merely sighed. Anna noticed this sigh, indicating dissent, and she went on. In her armoury she had other arguments so strong that no answer could be made to them.

'Do you say that it's not right? But you must consider,' she went on; 'you forget my position. How can I desire children? I'm not speaking of the suffering, I'm not afraid of that. Think only, what are my children to be? Ill-fated children, who will have to bear a stranger's name. For the very fact of their birth they will be forced to be ashamed of their mother, their father, their birth.'

'But that is just why a divorce is necessary.' But Anna did not hear her. She longed to give utterance to all the arguments with which she had so many times convinced herself.

'What is reason given me for, if I am not to use it to avoid bringing unhappy beings into the world?' She looked at Dolly, but without waiting for a reply she went on—

'I should always feel I had wronged these unhappy children,' she said. 'If they are not, at any rate they are not unhappy; while if they are unhappy, I alone should be to blame for it.'

These were the very arguments Darya Alexandrovna had used in her own reflections; but she heard them without understanding them. 'How can one wrong creatures that don't exist?' she thought. And all at once the idea struck her: could it possibly, under any circumstances, have been better for her favourite Grisha if he had never existed? And this seemed to her so wild, so strange, that she shook her head to drive away this tangle of whirling, mad ideas.

'No, I don't know; it's not right,' was all she said, with an expression of disgust on her face.

'Yes, but you mustn't forget that you and I . . . And besides that,' added Anna, in spite of the wealth of her arguments and the poverty of Dolly's objections, seeming still to admit that it was not right, 'don't forget the chief point, that I am not now in the same position as you. For you the question is: do you desire not to have any more children; while for me it is: do I desire to have them. And that's a great difference. You must see that I can't desire it in my position.'

Darya Alexandrovna made no reply. She suddenly felt that she had got far away from Anna; that there lay between them a barrier of questions on which they could never agree, and about which it was better not to speak.

XXIV

'THEN there is all the more reason for you to legalise your position, if possible,' said Dolly.

'Yes, if possible,' said Anna, speaking all at once in an utterly different tone, subdued and mournful.

'Surely you don't mean a divorce is impossible? I was told your husband had consented to it.'

'Dolly, I don't want to talk about that.'

'Oh, we won't then,' Darya Alexandrovna hastened to say, noticing the expression of suffering on Anna's face. 'All I see is that you take too gloomy a view of things.'

'I? Not at all! I'm always bright and happy. You see, *je fais des passions*. Veslovsky . . .'

'Yes, to tell the truth, I don't like Veslovsky's tone,' said Darya Alexandrovna, anxious to change the subject.

'Oh, that's nonsense! It amuses Alexey, and that's all; but he's a boy, and quite under my control. You know, I turn him as I please. It's just as it might be with your Grisha. . . . Dolly!'—she suddenly changed the subject—'you say I take too gloomy a view of things. You can't understand. It's too awful! I try not to take any view of it at all.'

'But I think you ought to. You ought to do all you can.'

'But what can I do? Nothing. You tell me to marry Alexey, and say I don't think about it. I don't think about it!' she repeated, and a flush rose into her face. She got up, straightening her chest, and sighed heavily. With her light step she began pacing up and down the room, stopping now and then. 'I don't think of it? Not a day, not an hour passes that I don't think of it, and blame myself for thinking of it . . . because thinking of that may drive me mad. Drive me mad!' she repeated. 'When I think of it, I can't sleep without morphine. But never mind. Let us talk quietly. They tell me, divorce. In the first place, he won't give me a divorce. He's under the influence of Countess Lidia Ivanovna now.'

Darya Alexandrovna, sitting erect on a chair, turned her head, following Anna with a face of sympathetic suffering.

'You ought to make the attempt,' she said softly.

'Suppose I make the attempt. What does it mean?' she said, evidently giving utterance to a thought, a thousand times thought over and learned by heart. 'It means that I, hating him, but still recognising that I have wronged him—and I consider him magnanimous—that I humiliate myself to write to him . . . Well, suppose I make the effort; I do it. Either I receive a humiliating refusal or consent . . . Well, I have received his consent, say . . .' Anna was at that moment at the furthest end of the room, and she stopped there, doing something to the curtain at the window . . . 'I receive his consent, but my . . . my son? They won't give him up to me. He will grow up despising me, with his father, whom I've abandoned. Do you see, I love . . . equally, I think, but both more than myself—two creatures, Seryozha and Alexey.'

She came out into the middle of the room and stood facing Dolly, with her arms pressed tightly across her chest. In her white dressing-gown her figure seemed more than usually grand and broad. She bent her head, and with shining, wet eyes looked from under her brows at Dolly, a thin little pitiful figure in her patched dressing-jacket and night-cap, shaking all over with emotion.

‘It is only those two creatures that I love, and one excludes the other. I can’t have them together, and that’s the only thing I want. And since I can’t have that, I don’t care about the rest. I don’t care about anything, anything. And it will end one way or another, and so I can’t, I don’t like to talk of it. So don’t blame me, don’t judge me for anything. You can’t with your pure heart understand all that I’m suffering.’ She went up, sat down beside Dolly, and with a guilty look, peeped into her face and took her hand.

‘What are you thinking? What are you thinking about me? Don’t despise me. I don’t deserve contempt. I’m simply unhappy. If any one is unhappy, I am,’ she articulated, and turning away, she burst into tears.

Left alone, Darya Alexandrovna said her prayers and went to bed. She had felt for Anna with all her heart while she was speaking to her, but now she could not force herself to think of her. The memories of home and of her children rose up in her imagination with a peculiar charm quite new to her, with a sort of new brilliance. That world of her own seemed to her now so sweet and precious that she would not on any account spend an extra day outside it, and she made up her mind that she would certainly go back next day.

Anna meantime went back to her boudoir, took a wine-glass and dropped into it several drops of a medicine, of which the principal ingredient was morphine. After drinking it off and sitting still a while, she went into her bedroom in a soothed and more cheerful frame of mind.

When she went into the bedroom, Vronsky looked intently at her. He was looking for traces of the conversation which he knew that, staying so long in Dolly’s room, she must have had with her. But in her expression of restrained excitement, and of a sort of reserve, he could find nothing but the beauty that always bewitched him afresh though he was used to it, the consciousness of it, and the desire that it should affect him. He did not want to ask her what they had been talking of, but he hoped that she would tell him something of her own accord. But she only said—

‘I am so glad you like Dolly. You do, don’t you?’

‘Oh, I’ve known her a long while, you know. She’s very good-hearted, I suppose, *mais excessivement terre-à-terre.* Still, I’m very glad to see her.’

He took Anna’s hand and looked inquiringly into her eyes.

Misinterpreting the look, she smiled at him. Next morning, in spite of the protests of her hosts, Darya Alexandrovna prepared for her homeward journey. Levin’s coachman, in his by no means new coat and shabby hat, with his ill-matched horses and his coach with the patched mudguards, drove with gloomy determination into the covered gravel approach.

Darya Alexandrovna disliked taking leave of Princess Varvara and the gentlemen of the party. After a day spent together, both she and her hosts were distinctly aware that they did not get on together, and that it was better for them not to meet. Only Anna was sad. She knew that now, from Dolly's departure, no one again would stir up within her soul the feelings that had been roused by their conversation. It hurt her to stir up these feelings, but yet she knew that that was the best part of her soul, and that that part of her soul would quickly be smothered in the life she was leading.

As she drove out into the open country, Darya Alexandrovna had a delightful sense of relief, and she felt tempted to ask the two men how they had liked being at Vronsky's, when suddenly the coachman, Philip, expressed himself unasked—

'Rolling in wealth they may be, but three pots of oats was all they gave us. Everything cleared up till there wasn't a grain left by cockcrow. What are three pots? A mere mouthful! And oats now down to forty-five kopecks. At our place, no fear, all comers may have as much as they can eat.'

'The master's a screw,' put in the counting-house clerk.

'Well, did you like their horses?' asked Dolly.

'The horses!—there's no two opinions about them. And the food was good. But it seemed to me sort of dreary there, Darya Alexandrovna. I don't know what you thought,' he said, turning his handsome, good-natured face to her.

'I thought so too. Well, shall we get home by evening?'

'Eh, we must!'

On reaching home and finding everyone entirely satisfactory and particularly charming, Darya Alexandrovna began with great liveliness telling them how she had arrived, how warmly they had received her, of the luxury and good taste in which the Vronskys lived, and of their recreations, and she would not allow a word to be said against them.

'One has to know Anna and Vronsky—I have got to know him better now—to see how nice they are, and how touching,' she said, speaking now with perfect sincerity, and forgetting the vague feeling of dissatisfaction and awkwardness she had experienced there.

XXV

VRONSKY and Anna spent the whole summer and part of the winter in the country, living in just the same conditions, and still taking no steps to obtain a divorce. It was an understood thing between them that they should not go away anywhere; but both felt, the longer they lived alone, especially in the autumn, without guests in the house, that they could not stand this existence, and that they would have to alter it.

Their life was apparently such that nothing better could be desired. They had the fullest abundance of everything; they had a child, and both had occupation. Anna devoted just as much care to her appearance when they had no visitors, and she did a great deal of reading, both of novels and of what serious literature was in fashion. She ordered all the books that were praised in the foreign papers and reviews she received, and read them with that concentrated attention which is only given to what is read in seclusion. Moreover, every subject that was of interest to Vronsky, she studied in books and special journals, so that he often went straight to her with questions relating to agriculture or architecture, sometimes even with questions relating to horse-breeding or sport. He was amazed at her knowledge, her memory, and at first was disposed to doubt it, to ask for confirmation of her facts; and she would find what he asked for in some book, and show it him.

The building of the hospital, too, interested her. She did not merely assist, but planned and suggested a great deal herself. But her chief thought was still of herself—how far she was dear to Vronsky, how far she could make up to him for all he had given up. Vronsky appreciated this desire not only to please, but to serve him, which had become the sole aim of her existence, but at the same time he wearied of the loving snares in which she tried to hold him fast. As time went on, and he saw himself more and more often held fast in these snares, he had an ever-growing desire, not so much to escape from them, as to try whether they hindered his freedom. Had it not been for this growing desire to be free, not to have scenes every time he wanted to go to the town to a meeting or a race, Vronsky would have been perfectly satisfied with his life. The rôle he had taken up, the rôle of a wealthy landowner, one of that class which ought to be the very heart of the Russian aristocracy, was entirely to his taste; and now, after spending six months in that character, he derived even greater satisfaction from it. And his management of his estate, which occupied and absorbed him more and more, was most successful. In spite of the immense sums cost him by the hospital, by machinery, by cows ordered from Switzerland, and many other things, he was convinced that he was not wasting, but increasing his substance. In all matters affecting income, the sales of timber, wheat, and wool, the letting of lands, Vronsky was hard as a rock, and knew well how to keep up prices. In all operations on a large scale on this and on his other estates, he kept to the simplest methods involving no risk, and in trifling details he was careful and exacting to an extreme degree. In spite of all the cunning and ingenuity of the German steward, who would try to tempt him into purchases by making his original estimate always far larger than really required, and then representing to Vronsky that he might get the thing cheaper, and so make a profit, Vronsky did not give in. He listened to his steward, cross-examined him, and only agreed to his suggestions when the implement to be ordered or constructed was the very newest, not yet known in Russia, and likely to excite wonder. Apart from such exceptions, he resolved upon an increased outlay only where there was a surplus, and in making such an outlay he went into the minutest details, and insisted on getting the very best for his money; so that by the method on which he managed his affairs, it was clear that he was not wasting, but increasing his substance.

In October there were the provincial elections in the Kashinsky province, where were the estates of Vronsky, Sviazhsky, Koznishev, Oblonsky, and a small part of Levin's land.

These elections were attracting public attention from several circumstances connected with them, and also from the people taking part in them. There had been a great deal of talk about them, and great preparations were being made for them. Persons who never attended the elections were coming from Moscow, from Petersburg, and from abroad to attend these. Vronsky had long before promised Sviazhsky to go to them. Before the elections Sviazhsky, who often visited Vozdvizhenskoe, drove over to fetch Vronsky. On the day before there had been almost a quarrel between Vronsky and Anna over this proposed expedition. It was the very dullest autumn weather, which is so dreary in the country, and so, preparing himself for a struggle, Vronsky, with a hard and cold expression, informed Anna of his departure as he had never spoken to her before. But, to his surprise, Anna accepted the information with great composure, and merely asked when he would be back. He looked intently at her, at a loss to explain this composure. She smiled at his look. He knew that way she had of withdrawing into herself, and knew that it only happened when she had determined upon something without letting him know her plans. He was afraid of this; but he was so anxious to avoid a scene that he kept up appearances, and half sincerely believed in what he longed to believe in—her reasonableness.

'I hope you won't be dull?'

'I hope not,' said Anna. 'I got a box of books yesterday from Gautier's. No, I shan't be dull.'

'She's trying to take that tone, and so much the better,' he thought, 'or else it would be the same thing over and over again.'

And he set off for the elections without appealing to her for a candid explanation. It was the first time since the beginning of their intimacy that he had parted from her without a full explanation. From one point of view this troubled him, but on the other side he felt that it was better so. 'At first there will be, as this time, something undefined kept back, and then she will get used to it. In any case I can give up anything for her, but not my masculine independence,' he thought.

XXVI

IN September Levin moved to Moscow for Kitty's confinement. He had spent a whole month in Moscow with nothing to do, when Sergey Ivanovitch, who had property in the Kashinsky province, and took great interest in the question of the approaching elections, made ready to set off to the elections. He invited his brother, who had a vote in the Seleznevsky district, to come with him. Levin had, moreover, to transact in Kashin some extremely important business relating to the wardship of land and to the receiving of certain redemption-money for his sister, who was abroad.

Levin still hesitated, but Kitty, who saw that he was bored in Moscow, and urged him to go, on her own authority ordered him the proper nobleman's uniform, costing seven pounds. And that seven pounds paid for the uniform was the chief cause that finally decided Levin to go. He went to Kashin. . . .

Levin had been six days in Kashin, visiting the assembly each day, and busily engaged about his sister's business, which still dragged on. The district marshals of nobility were all occupied with the elections, and it was impossible to get the simplest thing done that depended upon the court of wardship. The other matter, the payment of the sums due, was met too by difficulties. After long negotiations over the legal details, the money was at last ready to be paid; but the notary, a most obliging person, could not hand over the order, because it must have the signature of the president, and the president, though he had not given over his duties to a deputy, was at the elections. All these worrying negotiations, this endless going from place to place, and talking with pleasant and excellent people, who quite saw the unpleasantness of the petitioner's position, but were powerless to assist him—all these efforts that yielded no result, led to a feeling of misery in Levin akin to the mortifying helplessness one experiences in dreams when one tries to use physical force. He felt this frequently as he talked to his most good-natured solicitor. This solicitor did, it seemed, everything possible, and strained every nerve to get him out of his difficulties. 'I tell you what you might try,' he said more than once; 'go to so-and-so and so-and-so,' and the solicitor drew up a regular plan for getting round the fatal point that hindered everything. But he would add immediately, 'It'll mean some delay, anyway, but you might try it.' And Levin did try, and did go. Everyone was kind and civil, but the point evaded seemed to crop up again in the end, and again to bar the way. What was particularly trying, was that Levin could not make out with whom he was struggling, to whose interest it was that his business should not be done. That no one seemed to know; the solicitor certainly did not know. If Levin could have understood why, just as he saw why one can only approach the booking-office of a railway station in single file, it would not have been so vexatious and tiresome to him. But with the hindrances that confronted him in his business, no one could explain why this existed.

But Levin had changed a good deal since his marriage; he was patient, and if he could not see why it was all arranged like this, he told himself that he could not judge without knowing all about it, and that most likely it must be so, and he tried not to fret.

In attending the elections, too, and taking part in them, he tried now not to judge, not to fall foul of them, but to comprehend as fully as he could the question which was so earnestly and ardently absorbing honest and excellent men whom he respected. Since his marriage there had been revealed to Levin so many new and serious aspects of life that had previously, through his frivolous attitude to them, seemed of no importance, that in the question of the elections too he assumed and tried to find some serious significance.

Sergey Ivanovitch explained to him the meaning and object of the proposed revolution at the elections. The marshal of the province in whose hands the law had placed the control of so many important public functions—the guardianship of wards (the very department which was giving Levin so much trouble just now), the disposal of large sums subscribed by the nobility of the province, the high schools, female, male, and military, and popular instruction on the new model, and finally, the district council—the marshal of the province, Snetkov, was a nobleman of the old school,—dissipating an immense fortune, a good-hearted man, honest after his own fashion, but utterly without any comprehension of the needs of modern days. He always took, in every question, the side of the nobility; he was positively antagonistic to the spread of popular education, and he succeeded in giving a purely party character to the district council which ought by rights to be of such an immense importance. What was needed was to put in his place a fresh, capable, perfectly modern man, of contemporary ideas, and to frame their policy so as from the rights conferred upon the nobles, not as the nobility, but as an element of the district council, to extract all the powers of self-government that could possibly be derived from them. In the wealthy Kashinsky province, which always took the lead of other provinces in everything, there was now such a preponderance of forces that this policy once carried through properly there, might serve as a model for other provinces for all Russia. And hence the whole question was of the greatest importance. It was proposed to elect as marshal in place of Snetkov either Sviazhsky, or, better still, Nevyedovsky, a former university professor, a man of remarkable intelligence and a great friend of Sergey Ivanovitch.

The meeting was opened by the governor, who made a speech to the nobles, urging them to elect the public functionaries, not from regard for persons, but for the service and welfare of their fatherland, and hoping that the honourable nobility of the Kashinsky province would, as at all former elections, hold their duty as sacred, and vindicate the exalted confidence of the monarch.

When he had finished his speech, the governor walked out of the hall, and the noblemen noisily and eagerly—some even enthusiastically—followed him and thronged round him while he put on his fur-coat and conversed amicably with the marshal on the province. Levin, anxious to see into everything and not to miss anything, stood there too in the crowd, and heard the governor say: 'Please tell Marya Ivanovna my wife is very sorry she couldn't come to the Home.' And thereupon the nobles in high good humour sorted out their fur-coats and all drove off to the cathedral.

In the cathedral Levin, lifting his hand like the rest and repeating the words of the archdeacon, swore with the most terrible oaths to do all the governor had hoped they would do. Church services always affected Levin, and as he uttered the words 'I kiss the cross,' and glanced round at the crowd of young and old men repeating the same, he felt touched.

On the second and third days there was business relating to the finances of the nobility and the female high school, of no importance whatever, as Sergey Ivanovitch explained, and Levin, busy seeing after his own affairs, did not attend the meetings. On the fourth day the auditing of the marshal's accounts took place at the high table of the marshal of the province. And then there occurred the first skirmish between the new party and the old. The committee who had been deputed to verify the accounts reported to the meeting that all was in order. The marshal of the province got up, thanked the nobility for their confidence, and shed tears. The nobles gave him a loud welcome, and shook hands with him. But at that instant a nobleman of Sergey Ivanovitch's party said that he had heard that the committee had not verified the accounts, considering such a verification an insult to the marshal of the province. One of the members of the committee incautiously admitted this. Then a small gentleman, very young-looking but very malignant, began to say that it would probably be agreeable to the marshal of the province to give an account of his expenditure of the public moneys, and that the misplaced delicacy of the members of the committee was depriving him of this moral satisfaction. Then the members of the committee tried to withdraw their admission, and Sergey Ivanovitch began to prove that they must logically admit either that they had verified the accounts or that they had not, and he developed this dilemma in detail. Sergey Ivanovitch was answered by the spokesman of the opposite party. Then Sviazhsky spoke, and then the malignant gentleman again. The discussion lasted a long time and ended in nothing. Levin was surprised that they should dispute upon this subject so long, especially as, when he asked Sergey Ivanovitch whether he supposed that money had been misappropriated, Sergey Ivanovitch answered—

'Oh no! He's an honest man. But those old-fashioned methods of paternal family arrangements in the management of provincial affairs must be broken down.'

On the fifth day came the elections of the district marshals. It was rather a stormy day in several districts. In the Seleznevsky district Sviazhsky was elected unanimously without a ballot, and he gave a dinner that evening.

XXVII

THE sixth day was fixed for the election of the marshal of the province. The rooms, large and small, were full of noblemen in all sorts of uniforms. Many had come only for that day. Men who had not seen each other for years, some from the Crimea, some from Petersburg, some from abroad, met in the rooms of the Hall of Nobility. There was much discussion around the governor's table under the portrait of the Tsar.

The nobles, both in the larger and the smaller rooms, grouped themselves in camps, and from their hostile and suspicious glances, from the silence that fell upon them when outsiders approached a group, and from the way that some, whispering together, retreated to the further corridor, it was evident that each side had secrets from the other.

In appearance the noblemen were sharply divided into two classes: the old and the new. The old were for the most part either in old uniforms of the nobility, buttoned up closely, with spurs and hats, or in their own special naval, cavalry, infantry, or official uniforms. The uniforms of the older men were embroidered in the old-fashioned way with epaulettes on their shoulders; they were unmistakably tight and short in the waists, as though their wearers had grown out of them. The younger men wore the uniform of the nobility with long waists and broad shoulders, unbuttoned over white waistcoats, or uniforms with black collars and with the embroidered badges of justices of the peace. To the younger men belonged the court uniforms that here and there brightened up the crowd.

But the division into young and old did not correspond with the division of parties. Some of the young men, as Levin observed, belonged to the old party; and some of the very oldest noblemen, on the contrary, were whispering with Sviazhsky, and were evidently ardent partisans of the new party.

Levin stood in the smaller room, where they were smoking and taking light refreshments, close to his own friends, and listening to what they were saying, he conscientiously exerted all his intelligence trying to understand what was said. Sergey Ivanovitch was the centre round which the others grouped themselves. He was listening at that moment to Sviazhsky and Hliustov, the marshal of another district, who belonged to their party. Hliustov would not agree to go with his district to ask Snetkov to stand, while Sviazhsky was persuading him to do so, and Sergey Ivanovitch was approving of the plan. Levin could not make out why the opposition was to ask the marshal to stand whom they wanted to supersede.

Stepan Arkadyevitch, who had just been drinking and taking some lunch, came up to them in his uniform of a gentleman of the bedchamber, wiping his lips with a perfumed handkerchief of bordered batiste.

'We are placing our forces,' he said, pulling out his whiskers, 'Sergey Ivanovitch!'

And listening to the conversation, he supported Sviazhsky's contention.

'One district's enough, and Sviazhsky's obviously of the opposition,' he said, words evidently intelligible to all except Levin.

'Why, Kostya, you here too! I suppose you're converted, eh?' he added, turning to Levin and drawing his arm through his. Levin would have been glad indeed to be converted, but could not make out what the point was, and retreating a few steps from the speakers, he explained to

Stepan Arkadyevitch his inability to understand why the marshal of the province should be asked to stand.

'*O sancta simplicitas!*' said Stepan Arkadyevitch, and briefly and clearly he explained it to Levin. If, as at previous elections, all the districts asked the marshal of the province to stand, then he would be elected without a ballot. That must not be. Now eight districts had agreed to call upon him: if two refused to do so, Snetkov might decline to stand at all; and then the old party might choose another of their party, which would throw them completely out in their reckoning. But if only one district, Sviazhsky's, did not call upon him to stand, Snetkov would let himself be balloted for. They were even, some of them, going to vote for him, and purposely to let him get a good many votes, so that the enemy might be thrown off the scent, and when a candidate of the other side was put up, they too might give him some votes. Levin understood to some extent, but not fully, and would have put a few more questions, when suddenly everyone began talking and making a noise and they moved towards the big room.

'What is it? eh? whom?' 'No guarantee? whose? what?' 'They won't pass him?' 'No guarantee?' 'They won't let Flerov in?' 'Eh, because of the charge against him?' 'Why, at this rate, they won't admit anyone. It's a swindle!' 'The law!' Levin heard exclamations on all sides, and he moved into the big room together with the others, all hurrying somewhere and afraid of missing something. Squeezed by the crowding noblemen, he drew near the high table where the marshal of the province, Sviazhsky, and the other leaders were hotly disputing about something.

XXVIII

LEVIN was standing rather far off. A nobleman breathing heavily and hoarsely at his side, and another whose thick boots were creaking, prevented him from hearing distinctly. He could only hear the soft voice of the marshal faintly, then the shrill voice of the malignant gentleman, and then the voice of Sviazhsky. They were disputing, as far as he could make out, as to the interpretation to be put on the act and the exact meaning of the words: 'liable to be called up for trial.'

The crowd parted to make way for Sergey Ivanovitch approaching the table. Sergey Ivanovitch, waiting till the malignant gentleman had finished speaking, said that he thought the best solution would be to refer to the act itself, and asked the secretary to find the act. The act said that in case of difference of opinion, there must be a ballot.

Sergey Ivanovitch read the act and began to explain its meaning, but at that point a tall, stout, round-shouldered landowner, with dyed whiskers, in a tight uniform that cut the back of his neck, interrupted him. He went up to the table, and striking it with his finger-ring, he shouted loudly: 'A ballot! Put it to the vote! No need for more talking!' Then several voices began to talk all at once, and the tall nobleman with the ring, getting more and more exasperated, shouted more and more loudly. But it was impossible to make out what he said.

He was shouting for the very course Sergey Ivanovitch had proposed; but it was evident that he hated him and all his party, and this feeling of hatred spread through the whole party and roused in opposition to it the same vindictiveness, though in a more seemly form, on the other side. Shouts were raised, and for a moment all was confusion, so that the marshal of the province had to call for order.

'A ballot! A ballot! Every nobleman sees it! We shed our blood for our country! . . . The confidence of the monarch. . . . No checking the accounts of the marshal; he's not a cashier. . . . But that's not the point. . . . Votes, please! Beastly! . . .' shouted furious and violent voices on all sides. Looks and faces were even more violent and furious than their words. They expressed the most implacable hatred. Levin did not in the least understand what was the matter, and he marvelled at the passion with which it was disputed whether or not the decision about Flerov should be put to the vote. He forgot, as Sergey Ivanovitch explained to him afterwards, this syllogism: that it was necessary for the public good to get rid of the marshal of the province; that to get rid of the marshal it was necessary to have a majority of votes; that to get a majority of votes it was necessary to secure Flerov's right to vote; that to secure the recognition of Flerov's right to vote they must decide on the interpretation to be put on the act.

'And one vote may decide the whole question, and one must be serious and consecutive, if one wants to be of use in public life,' concluded Sergey Ivanovitch. But Levin forgot all that, and it was painful to him to see all these excellent persons, for whom he had a respect, in such an unpleasant and vicious state of excitement. To escape from this painful feeling he went away into the other room where there was nobody except the waiters at the refreshment-bar. Seeing the waiters busy over washing up the crockery and setting in order their plates and wine-glasses, seeing their calm and cheerful faces, Levin felt an unexpected sense of relief as though he had come out of a stuffy room into the fresh air. He began walking up and down, looking with pleasure at the waiters. He particularly liked the way one grey-whiskered waiter, who showed his scorn for the other younger ones and was jeered at by them, was teaching them how to fold up napkins properly. Levin was just about to enter into conversation with the old waiter, when the secretary of the court of wardship, a little old man whose speciality it was to know all the noblemen of the province by name and patronymic, drew him away.

'Please come, Konstantin Dmitrich,' he said, 'your brother's looking for you. They are voting on the legal point.'

Levin walked into the room, received a white ball, and followed his brother, Sergey Ivanovitch, to the table where Sviazhsky was standing with a significant and ironical face, holding his beard in his fist and sniffing at it. Sergey Ivanovitch put his hand into the box, put the ball somewhere, and making room for Levin, stopped. Levin advanced, but utterly forgetting what he was to do, and much embarrassed, he turned to Sergey Ivanovitch with the question, 'Where am I to put it?' He asked this softly, at a moment when there was talking going on near, so that he had hoped his question would not be overheard. But the persons speaking paused, and his improper question was overheard. Sergey Ivanovitch frowned.

'That is a matter for each man's own decision,' he said severely.

Several people smiled. Levin crimsoned, hurriedly thrust his hand under the cloth, and put the ball to the right as it was in his right hand. Having put it in, he recollected that he ought to have thrust his left hand in too, and so he thrust it in though too late, and, still more overcome with confusion, he beat a hasty retreat into the background.

'A hundred and twenty-six for admission! Ninety-eight against!' sang out the voice of the secretary, who could not pronounce the letter *r*. Then there was a laugh; a button and two nuts were found in the box. The nobleman was allowed the right to vote, and the new party had conquered.

But the old party did not consider themselves conquered. Levin heard that they were asking Snetkov to stand, and he saw that a crowd of noblemen were surrounding the marshal, who was saying something. Levin went nearer. In reply Snetkov spoke of the trust the noblemen of the province had placed in him, the affection they had shown him, which he did not deserve, as his only merit had been his attachment to the nobility, to whom he had devoted twelve years of service. Several times he repeated the words: 'I have served to the best of my powers with truth and good faith, I value your goodness and thank you,' and suddenly he stopped short from the tears that choked him, and went out of the room. Whether these tears came from a sense of the injustice being done him, from his love for the nobility, or from the strain of the position he was placed in, feeling himself surrounded by enemies, his emotion infected the assembly, the majority were touched, and

Levin felt a tenderness for Snetkov.

In the doorway the marshal of the province jostled against Levin.

'Beg pardon, excuse me, please,' he said as to a stranger, but recognising Levin, he smiled timidly. It seemed to Levin that he would have liked to say something, but could not speak for emotion. His face and his whole figure in his uniform with the crosses, and white trousers striped with braid, as he moved hurriedly along, reminded Levin of some hunted beast who sees that he is in evil case. This expression in the marshal's face was particularly touching to Levin, because, only the day before, he had been at his house about his trustee business and had seen him in all his grandeur, a kind-hearted, fatherly man. The big house with the old family furniture; the rather dirty, far from stylish, but respectful footmen, unmistakably old house serfs who had stuck to their master; the stout, good-natured wife in a cap with lace and a Turkish shawl, petting her pretty grandchild, her daughter's daughter; the young son, a sixth form high school boy, coming home from school, and greeting his father, kissing his big hand; the genuine, cordial words and gestures of the old man—all this had the day before roused an instinctive feeling of respect and sympathy in Levin. This old man was a touching and pathetic figure to Levin now, and he longed to say something pleasant to him.

'So you're sure to be our marshal again,' he said.

'It's not likely,' said the marshal, looking round with a scared expression. 'I'm worn out, I'm old. If there are men younger and more deserving than I, let them serve.'

And the marshal disappeared through a side-door.

The most solemn moment was at hand. They were to proceed immediately to the election. The leaders of both parties were reckoning white and black on their fingers.

The discussion upon Flerov had given the new party not only Flerov's vote, but had also gained time for them, so that they could send to fetch three noblemen who had been rendered unable to take part in the elections by the wiles of the other party. Two noble gentlemen, who had a weakness for strong drink, had been made drunk by the partisans of Snetkov, and a third had been robbed of his uniform.

On learning this, the new party had made haste, during the dispute about Flerov, to send some of their men in a sledge to clothe the stripped gentleman, and to bring along one of the intoxicated to the meeting.

'I've brought one, drenched him with water,' said the landowner, who had gone on this errand to Sviazhsky. 'He's all right; he'll do.'

'Not too drunk, he won't fall down?' said Sviazhsky, shaking his head.

'No, he's first-rate. If only they don't give him any more here . . . I've told the waiter not to give him anything on any account.'

XXIX

THE narrow room, in which they were smoking and taking refreshments, was full of noblemen. The excitement grew more intense, and every face betrayed some uneasiness. The excitement was specially keen for the leaders of each party, who knew every detail, and had reckoned up every vote. They were the generals organising the approaching battle. The rest, like the rank and file before an engagement, though they were getting ready for the fight, sought for other distractions in the interval. Some were lunching, standing at the bar, or sitting at the table; others were walking up and down the long room, smoking cigarettes, and talking with friends whom they had not seen for a long while.

Levin did not care to eat, and he was not smoking; he did not want to join his own friends, that is Sergey Ivanovitch, Stepan Arkadyevitch, Sviazhsky and the rest, because Vronsky in his equerry's uniform was standing with them in eager conversation. Levin had seen him already at the meeting on the previous day, and he had studiously avoided him, not caring to greet him. He went to the window and sat down, scanning the groups, and listening to what was being said around him. He felt depressed, especially because everyone else was, as he saw, eager, anxious, and interested, and he alone, with an old, toothless little man with mumbling lips wearing a naval uniform, sitting beside him, had no interest in it and nothing to do.

'He's such a blackguard! I have told him so, but it makes no difference. Only think of it! He couldn't collect it in three years!' he heard vigorously uttered by a round-shouldered short country gentleman, who had pomaded hair hanging on his embroidered collar, and new boots, obviously put on for the occasion, with heels that tapped energetically as he spoke. Casting a displeased glance at Levin, this gentleman sharply turned his back.

'Yes, it's a dirty business, there's no denying,' a small gentleman assented in a high voice.

Next a whole crowd of country gentlemen, surrounding a stout general, hurriedly came near Levin. These persons were unmistakably seeking a place where they could talk without being overheard.

'How dare he say I had his breeches stolen! Pawned them for drink,

I expect. Damn the fellow, prince indeed! He'd better not say it, the beast!'

'But excuse me! They take their stand on the act,' was being said in another group; 'the wife must be registered as noble.'

'Oh, damn your acts! I speak from my heart. We're all gentlemen, aren't we? Above suspicion.'

'Shall we go on, your excellency, *fine champagne*?'

Another group was following a nobleman, who was shouting something in a loud voice; it was one of the three intoxicated gentlemen.

'I always advised Marya Semyonovna to let for a fair rent, for she can never save a profit,' he heard a pleasant voice say. The speaker was a country gentleman with grey whiskers, wearing the regimental uniform of an old general staff-officer. It was the very landowner Levin had met at Sviazhsky's. He knew him at once. The landowner too stared at Levin, and they exchanged greetings.

'Very glad to see you! To be sure! I remember you very well. Last year at our district marshal, Nikolay Ivanovitch's.'

'Well, and how is your land doing?' asked Levin.

'Oh, still just the same, always at a loss,' the landowner answered with a resigned smile, but with an expression of serenity and conviction that so it must be. 'And how do you come to be in our province?' he asked. 'Come to take part in our *coup d'état*?' he said, confidently pronouncing the French words with a bad accent. 'All Russia's here—gentlemen of the bedchamber, and everything short of the ministry.' He pointed to the imposing figure of Stepan Arkadyevitch in white trousers and his court uniform, walking by with a general.

'I ought to own that I don't very well understand the drift of the provincial elections,' said Levin.

The landowner looked at him.

'Why, what is there to understand? There's no meaning in it at all. It's a decaying institution that goes on running only by the force of inertia. Just look, the very uniforms tell you that it's an assembly of justices of the peace, permanent members of the court, and so on, but not of noblemen.'

'Then why do you come?' asked Levin.

'From habit, nothing else. Then, too, one must keep up connections. It's a moral obligation of a sort. And then, to tell the truth, there's one's own interests. My son-in-law wants to stand as a permanent member; they're not rich people, and he must be brought forward. These gentlemen, now, what do they come for?' he said, pointing to the malignant gentleman, who was talking at the high table.

'That's the new generation of nobility.'

'New it may be, but nobility it isn't. They're proprietors of a sort, but we're the landowners. As noblemen, they're cutting their own throats.'

'But you say it's an institution that's served its time.'

'That it may be, but still it ought to be treated a little more respectfully. Snetkov, now . . . We may be of use, or we may not, but we're the growth of a thousand years. If we're laying out a garden, planning one before the house, you know, and there you've a tree that's stood for centuries in the very spot. . . . Old and gnarled it may be, and yet you don't cut down the old fellow to make room for flower-beds, but lay out your beds so as to take advantage of the tree. You won't grow him again in a year,' he said cautiously, and he immediately changed the conversation. 'Well, and how is your land doing?'

'Oh, not very well. I make five per cent.'

'Yes, but you don't reckon your own work. Aren't you worth something too? I'll tell you my own case. Before I took to seeing after the land, I had a salary of three hundred pounds from the service. Now I do more work than I did in the service, and like you I get five per cent on the land, and thank God for that. But one's work is thrown in for nothing.'

'Then why do you do it, if it's a clear loss?'

'Oh, well, one does it! What would you have? It's habit, and one knows it's how it should be. And what's more,' the landowner went on, leaning his elbows on the window and chatting on, 'my son, I must tell you, has no taste for it. There's no doubt he'll be a scientific man. So there'll be no one to keep it up. And yet one does it. Here this year I've planted an orchard.'

'Yes, yes,' said Levin, 'that's perfectly true. I always feel there's no real balance of gain in my work on the land, and yet one does it. . . . It's a sort of duty one feels to the land.'

'But I tell you what,' the landowner pursued; 'a neighbour of mine, a merchant, was at my place. We walked about the fields and the garden. "No," said he, "Stepan Vassilievitch, everything's well looked after, but your garden's neglected." But, as a fact, it's well kept up. "To my thinking, I'd cut down that lime-tree. Here you've thousands of limes, and each would make two good bundles of bark. And nowadays that bark's worth something. I'd cut down the lot." '

'And with what he made he'd increase his stock, or buy some land for a trifle, and let it out in lots to the peasants,' Levin added, smiling. He had evidently more than once come across those commercial calculations. 'And he'd make his fortune. But you and I must thank God if we keep what we've got and leave it to our children.'

'You're married, I've heard?' said the landowner.

'Yes,' Levin answered, with proud satisfaction. 'Yes, it's rather strange,' he went on. 'So we live without making anything, as though we were ancient vestals set to keep in a fire.'

The landowner chuckled under his white moustaches.

'There are some among us, too, like our friend Nikolay Ivanovitch, or Count Vronsky, that's settled here lately, who try to carry on their husbandry as though it were a factory; but so far it leads to nothing but making away with capital on it.'

'But why is it we don't do like the merchants? Why don't we cut down our parks for timber?' said Levin, returning to a thought that had struck him.

'Why, as you said, to keep the fire in. Besides, that's not work for a nobleman. And our work as noblemen isn't done here at the elections, but yonder, each in our corner. There's a class instinct, too, of what one ought and oughtn't to do. There's the peasants, too, I wonder at them sometimes; any good peasant tries to take all the land he can. However bad the land is, he'll work it. Without a return too. At a simple loss.'

'Just as we do,' said Levin. 'Very, very glad to have met you,' he added, seeing Sviazhsky approaching him.

'And here we've met for the first time since we met at your place,' said the landowner to Sviazhsky, 'and we've had a good talk too.'

'Well, have you been attacking the new order of things?' said Sviazhsky with a smile.

'That we're bound to do.'

'You've relieved your feelings?'

XXX

SVIAZHSKY took Levin's arm, and went with him to his own friends.

This time there was no avoiding Vronsky. He was standing with Stepan Arkadyevitch and Sergey Ivanovitch, and looking straight at Levin as he drew near.

'Delighted! I believe I've had the pleasure of meeting you . . . at Princess Shtcherbatsky's,' he said, giving Levin his hand.

'Yes, I quite remember our meeting,' said Levin, and blushing crimson, he turned away immediately, and began talking to his brother.

With a slight smile Vronsky went on talking to Sviazhsky, obviously without the slightest inclination to enter into conversation with Levin. But Levin, as he talked to his brother, was continually looking round at Vronsky, trying to think of something to say to him to gloss over his rudeness.

'What are we waiting for now?' asked Levin, looking at Sviazhsky and Vronsky.

'For Snetkov. He has to refuse or to consent to stand,' answered Sviazhsky.

'Well, and what has he done, consented or not?'

'That's the point, that he's done neither,' said Vronsky.

'And if he refuses, who will stand then?' asked Levin, looking at Vronsky.

'Whoever chooses to,' said Sviazhsky.

'Shall you?' asked Levin.

'Certainly not I,' said Sviazhsky, looking confused, and turning an alarmed glance at the malignant gentleman, who was standing beside Sergey Ivanovitch.

'Who then? Nevyedovsky?' said Levin, feeling he was putting his foot into it.

But this was worse still. Nevyedovsky and Sviazhsky were the two candidates.

'I certainly shall not, under any circumstances,' answered the malignant gentleman.

This was Nevyedovsky himself. Sviazhsky introduced him to Levin.

'Well, you find it exciting too?' said Stepan Arkadyevitch, winking at Vronsky. 'It's something like a race. One might bet on it.'

'Yes, it is keenly exciting,' said Vronsky. 'And once taking the thing up, one's eager to see it through. It's a fight!' he said, scowling and setting his powerful jaws.

'What a capable fellow Sviazhsky is! Sees it all so clearly.'

'Oh yes!' Vronsky assented indifferently.

A silence followed, during which Vronsky—since he had to look at something—looked at Levin, at his feet, at his uniform, then at his face, and noticing his gloomy eyes fixed upon him, he said, in order to say something—

'How is it that you, living constantly in the country, are not a justice of the peace? You are not in the uniform of one.'

'It's because I consider that the justice of the peace is a silly institution,' Levin answered gloomily. He had been all the time looking for an opportunity to enter into conversation with Vronsky, so as to smooth over his rudeness at their first meeting.

'I don't think so, quite the contrary,' Vronsky said, with quiet surprise.

'It's a plaything,' Levin cut him short. 'We don't want justices of the peace. I've never had a single thing to do with them during eight years. And what I have had was decided wrongly by them. The justice of the peace is over thirty miles from me. For some matter of two roubles I should have to send a lawyer; who costs me fifteen.'

And he related how a peasant had stolen some flour from the miller, and when the miller told him of it, had lodged a complaint for slander. All this was utterly uncalled for and stupid, and Levin felt it himself as he said it.

'Oh, this is such an original fellow!' said Stepan Arkadyevitch with his most soothing, almond-oil smile. 'But come along; I think they're voting . . .'

And they separated.

'I can't understand,' said Sergey Ivanovitch, who had observed his brother's clumsiness, 'I can't understand how anyone can be so absolutely devoid of political tact. That's where we Russians are so deficient. The marshal of the province is our opponent, and with him you're *ami cochon*, and you beg him to stand. Count Vronsky, now . . . I'm not making a friend of him; he's asked me to dinner, and I'm not going; but he's one of our side—why make an enemy of him? Then you ask Nevyedovsky if he's going to stand. That's not a thing to do.'

'Oh, I don't understand it at all! And it's all such nonsense,' Levin answered gloomily.

'You say it's all such nonsense, but as soon as you have anything to do with it, you make a muddle.'

Levin did not answer, and they walked together into the big room.

The marshal of the province, though he was vaguely conscious in the air of some trap being prepared for him, and though he had not been called upon by all to stand, had still made up his mind to stand. All was silence in the room. The secretary announced in a loud voice that the captain of the guards, Mihail Stepanovitch Snetkov, would now be balloted for as marshal of the province.

The district marshals walked carrying plates, on which were balls, from their tables to the high table, and the election began.

'Put it in the right side,' whispered Stepan Arkadyevitch, as with his brother Levin followed the marshal of his district to the table. But Levin had forgotten by now the calculations that had been explained to him, and was afraid Stepan Arkadyevitch might be mistaken in saying 'the right side'. Surely Snetkov was the enemy. As he went up, he held the ball in his right hand, but thinking he was wrong, just at the box he changed to the left hand, and undoubtedly put the ball to the left. An adept in the business, standing at the box and seeing by the mere action of the elbow where each put his ball, scowled with annoyance. It was no good for him to use his insight.

Everything was still, and the counting of the balls was heard. Then a single voice rose and proclaimed the numbers for and against. The marshal had been voted for by a considerable majority. All was noise and eager movement towards the doors. Snetkov came in, and the nobles thronged round him, congratulating him.

'Well, now is it over?' Levin asked Sergey Ivanovitch.

'It's only just beginning,' Sviazhsky said, replying for Sergey Ivanovitch with a smile. 'Some other candidate may receive more votes than the marshal.'

Levin had quite forgotten about that. Now he could only remember that there was some sort of trickery in it, but he was too bored to think what it was exactly. He felt depressed, and longed to get out of the crowd.

As no one was paying any attention to him, and no one apparently needed him, he quietly slipped away into the little room where the refreshments were, and again had a great sense of comfort when he saw the waiters. The little old waiter pressed him to have something, and Levin agreed. After eating a cutlet with beans and talking to the waiters of their former masters, Levin, not wishing to go back to the hall, where it was all so distasteful to him, proceeded to walk through the galleries. The galleries were full of fashionably dressed ladies, leaning over the balustrade and trying not to lose a single word of what was being said below. With the ladies were sitting and standing smart lawyers, high school teachers in spectacles, and officers. Everywhere they were talking of the election, and of how worried the marshal was, and how splendid the discussions had been. In one group Levin heard his brother's praises. One lady was telling a lawyer—

'How glad I am I heard Koznishev! It's worth losing one's dinner. He's exquisite! So clear and distinct all of it! There's not one of you in the law-courts that speaks like that. The only one is Meidel, and he's not so eloquent by a long way.'

Finding a free place, Levin leaned over the balustrade and began looking and listening.

All the noblemen were sitting railed off behind barriers according to their districts. In the middle of the room stood a man in a uniform, who shouted in a loud high voice—

'As candidate for the marshalship of the nobility of the province we call upon staff-captain Yevgeney Ivanovitch Apuhtin!' A dead silence followed, and then a weak old voice was heard: 'Declined!'

'We call upon the privy councillor Pyotr Petrovitch Bol,' the voice began again.

'Declined!' a high boyish voice replied.

Again it began, and again 'Declined'. And so it went on for about an hour. Levin, with his elbows on the balustrade, looked and listened. At first he wondered and wanted to know what it meant; then feeling sure that he could not make it out he began to be bored. Then recalling all the excitement and vindictiveness he had seen on all the faces, he felt sad; he made up his mind to go, and went downstairs. As he passed through the entry to the galleries he met a dejected high-school boy walking up and down with tired-looking eyes. On the stairs he met a couple—a lady running quickly on her high heels and the jaunty deputy prosecutor.

'I told you you weren't late,' the deputy prosecutor was saying at the moment when Levin moved aside to let the lady pass.

Levin was on the stairs to the way out, and was just feeling in his waistcoat pocket for the number of his overcoat, when the secretary overtook him.

'This way, please, Konstantin Dmitrievitch; they are voting.'

The candidate who was being voted on was Nevyedovsky, who had so stoutly denied all idea of standing. Levin went up to the door of the room; it was locked. The secretary knocked, the door opened, and Levin was met by two red-faced gentlemen, who darted out.

'I can't stand any more of it,' said one red-faced gentleman.

After them the face of the marshal of the province was poked out. His face was dreadful-looking from exhaustion and dismay.

'I told you not to let anyone out!' he cried to the doorkeeper.

'I let someone in, your excellency!'

'Mercy on us!' and with a heavy sigh the marshal of the province walked with downcast head to the high table in the middle of the room, his legs staggering in his white trousers.

Nevyedovsky had scored a higher majority, as they had planned, and he was the new marshal of the province. Many people were amused, many were pleased and happy, many were in ecstasies, many were disgusted and unhappy. The former marshal of the province was in a state of despair, which he could not conceal. When Nevyedovsky went out of the room, the crowd thronged round him and followed him enthusiastically, just as they had followed the governor who had opened the meetings, and just as they had followed Snetkov when he was elected.

XXXI

THE newly elected marshal and many of the successful party dined that day with Vronsky.

Vronsky had come to the elections partly because he was bored in the country and wanted to show Anna his right to independence, and also to repay Sviazhsky by his support at the election for all the trouble he had taken for Vronsky at the district council election, but chiefly in order strictly to perform all those duties of a nobleman and landowner which he had taken upon himself. But he had not in the least expected that the election would so interest him, so keenly excite him, and that he would be so good at this kind of thing. He was quite a new man in the circle of the nobility of the province, but his success was unmistakable, and he was not wrong in supposing that he had already obtained a certain influence. This influence was due to his wealth and reputation, the capital house in the town lent him by his old friend Shirkov, who had a post in the department of finances and was director of a flourishing bank in Kashin; the excellent cook Vronsky had brought from the country, and his friendship with the governor, who was a schoolfellow of Vronsky's—a schoolfellow he had patronised and protected indeed. But what contributed more than all to his success was his direct, equable manner with everyone, which very quickly made the majority of the noblemen reverse the current opinion of his supposed haughtiness. He was himself conscious that, except that whimsical gentleman married to Kitty Shtcherbatsky, who had *à propos de bottes* poured out a stream of irrelevant absurdities with such spiteful fury, every nobleman with whom he had made acquaintance had become his adherent. He saw clearly, and other people recognised it too, that he had done a great deal to secure the success of Nevyedovsky. And now at his own table, celebrating Nevyedovsky's election, he was experiencing an agreeable sense of triumph over the success of his candidate. The election itself had so fascinated him that, if he could succeed in getting married during the next three years, he began to think of standing himself—much as after winning a race ridden by a jockey, he had longed to ride a race himself.

Today he was celebrating the success of his jockey. Vronsky sat at the head of the table, on his right hand sat the young governor, a general of high rank. To all the rest he was the chief man in the province, who had solemnly opened the elections with his speech, and aroused a feeling of respect and even of awe in many people, as Vronsky saw; to Vronsky he was little Katka Maslov—that had been his nickname in the Pages' Corps—whom he felt to be shy and tried to *mettre à son aise*. On the left hand sat Nevyedovsky with his youthful, stubborn, and malignant face. With him Vronsky was simple and deferential.

Sviazhsky took his failure very light-heartedly. It was indeed no failure in his eyes, as he said himself, turning, glass in hand, to Nevyedovsky; they could not have found a better representative of the new movement, which the nobility ought to follow. And so every honest person, as he said, was on the side of today's success and was rejoicing over it.

Stepan Arkadyevitch was glad, too, that he was having a good time, and that everyone was pleased. The episode of the elections served as a good occasion for a capital dinner. Sviazhsky comically imitated the tearful discourse of the marshal, and observed, addressing Nevyedovsky, that his excellency would have to select another more complicated method of auditing the accounts than tears. Another nobleman jocosely described how footmen in stockings had been ordered for the marshal's ball, and how now they would have to be sent back unless the new marshal would give a ball with footmen in stockings.

Continually during dinner they said of Nevyedovsky: 'Our marshal,' and 'your excellency.'

This was said with the same pleasure with which a bride is called 'Madame' and her husband's name. Nevyedovsky affected to be not merely indifferent but scornful of this appellation, but it was obvious that he was highly delighted, and had to keep a curb on himself not to betray the triumph which was unsuitable to their new liberal tone.

After dinner several telegrams were sent to people interested in the result of the election. And Stepan Arkadyevitch, who was in high good-humour, sent Darya Alexandrovna a telegram: 'Nevyedovsky elected by twenty votes. Congratulations. Tell people.' He dictated it aloud, saying: 'we must let them share our rejoicing.' Darya Alexandrovna, getting the message, simply sighed over the rouble wasted on it, and understood that it was an after-dinner affair. She knew Stiva had a weakness after dining for *faire jouer le télégraphe*.

Everything, together with the excellent dinner and the wine, not from Russian merchants, but imported direct from abroad, was extremely dignified, simple, and enjoyable. The party—some twenty—had been selected by Sviazhsky from among the more active new liberals, all of the same way of thinking, who were at the same time clever and well bred. They drank, also half in jest, to the health of the new marshal of the province, of the governor, of the bank director, and of 'our amiable host'.

Vronsky was satisfied. He had never expected to find so pleasant a tone in the provinces.

Towards the end of dinner it was still more lively. The governor asked Vronsky to come to a concert for the benefit of the Servians which his wife, who was anxious to make his acquaintance, had been getting up.

'There'll be a ball, and you'll see the belle of the province. Worth seeing, really.'

'Not in my line,' Vronsky answered. He liked that English phrase.

But he smiled, and promised to come.

Before they rose from the table, when all of them were smoking, Vronsky's valet went up to him with a letter on a tray.

'From Vozdvizhenskoe by special messenger,' he said with a significant expression.

'Astonishing! how like he is to the deputy prosecutor Sventitsky,' said one of the guests in French of the valet, while Vronsky, frowning, read the letter.

The letter was from Anna. Before he read the letter, he knew its contents. Expecting the elections to be over in five days, he had promised to be back on Friday. Today was Saturday, and he knew that the letter contained reproaches for not being back at the time fixed. The letter he had sent the previous evening had probably not reached yet.

The letter was what he had expected, but the form of it was unexpected, and particularly disagreeable to him. 'Annie is very ill, the doctor says it may be inflammation. I am losing my head all alone. Princess Varvara is no help, but a hindrance. I expected you the day before yesterday, and yesterday, and now I am sending to find out where you are and what you are doing. I wanted to come myself, but thought better of it, knowing you would dislike it. Send some answer, that I may know what to do.'

The child ill, yet she had thought of coming herself. Their daughter ill, and this hostile tone.

The innocent festivities over the election, and this gloomy, burdensome love to which he had to return struck Vronsky by their contrast. But he had to go, and by the first train that night he set off home.

XXXII

BEFORE Vronsky's departure for the elections, Anna had reflected that the scenes constantly repeated between them each time he left home, might only make him cold to her instead of attaching him to her, and resolved to do all she could to control herself so as to bear the parting with composure. But the cold, severe glance with which he had looked at her when he came to tell her he was going had wounded her, and before he had started her peace of mind was destroyed.

In solitude afterwards, thinking over that glance which had expressed his right to freedom, she came, as she always did, to the same point—the sense of her own humiliation. 'He has the right to go away when and where he chooses. Not simply to go away, but to leave me. He has every right, and I have none. But knowing that, he ought not to do it. What has he done, though? . . . He looked at me with a cold, severe expression. Of course that is something indefinable, impalpable, but it has never been so before, and that glance means a great deal,' she thought. 'That glance shows the beginning of indifference.'

And though she felt sure that a coldness was beginning, there was nothing she could do, she could not in any way alter her relations to him. Just as before, only by love and by charm could she keep him. And so, just as before, only by occupation in the day, by morphine at night, could she stifle the fearful thought of what would be if he ceased to love her. It is true there was still one means; not to keep him—for that she wanted nothing more than his love—but to be nearer to him, to be in such a position that he would not leave her. That means was divorce and marriage. And she began to long for that, and made up her mind to agree to it the first time he or Stiva approached her on the subject.

Absorbed in such thoughts, she passed five days without him, the five days that he was to be at the elections.

Walks, conversation with Princess Varvara, visits to the hospital, and, most of all, reading—reading of one book after another—filled up her time. But on the sixth day, when the coachman came back without him, she felt that now she was utterly incapable of stifling the thought of him and of what he was doing there, just at that time her little girl was taken ill. Anna began to look after her, but even that did not distract her mind, especially as the illness was not serious. However hard she tried, she could not love this little child, and to feign love was beyond her powers. Towards the evening of that day, still alone, Anna was in such a panic about him, that she decided to start for the town, but on second thoughts wrote him the contradictory letter that Vronsky received, and, without reading it through, sent it off by a special messenger. The next morning she received his letter and regretted her own. She dreaded a repetition of the severe look he had flung at her at parting, especially when he knew that the baby was not dangerously ill. But still she was glad she had written to him. At this moment Anna was positively admitting to herself that she was a burden to him, that he would relinquish his freedom regretfully to return to her, and in spite of that she was glad he was coming. Let him weary of her, but he would be here with her, so that she would see him, would know of every action he took.

She was sitting in the drawing-room near a lamp, with a new volume of Taine, and as she read, listening to the sound of the wind outside, and every minute expecting the carriage to arrive. Several times she had fancied she heard the sound of wheels, but she had been mistaken. At last she heard not the sound of wheels, but the coachman's shout and the dull rumble in the covered entry. Even Princess Varvara, playing patience, confirmed this, and Anna, flushing hotly, got up; but instead of going down, as she had done twice before, she stood still. She suddenly felt ashamed of her duplicity, but even more she dreaded how he might meet her. All feeling of wounded pride had passed now; she was only afraid of the expression of his displeasure. She remembered that her child had been perfectly well again for the last two days. She felt positively vexed with her for getting better from the very moment her letter was sent off. Then she thought of him, that he was here, all of him, with his hands, his eyes. She heard his voice. And forgetting everything, she ran joyfully to meet him.

'Well, how is Annie?' he said timidly from below, looking up to Anna as she ran down to him.

He was sitting on a chair, and a footman was pulling off his warm over-boot.

'Oh, she is better.'

'And you?' he said, shaking himself.

She took his hand in both of hers, and drew it to her waist, never taking her eyes off him.

'Well, I'm glad,' he said, coldly scanning her, her hair, her dress, which he knew she had put on for him. All was charming, but how many times it had charmed him! And the stern, stony expression that she so dreaded settled upon his face.

'Well, I'm glad. And are you well?' he said, wiping his damp beard with his handkerchief and kissing her hand.

'Never mind,' she thought, 'only let him be here, and so long as he's here he cannot, he dare not, cease to love me.'

The evening was spent happily and gaily in the presence of Princess Varvara, who complained to him that Anna had been taking morphine in his absence.

'What am I to do? I couldn't sleep . . . My thoughts prevented me. When he's here I never take it—hardly ever.'

He told her about the election, and Anna knew how by adroit questions to bring him to what gave him most pleasure—his own success. She told him of everything that interested him at home; and all that she told him was of the most cheerful description.

But late in the evening, when they were alone, Anna, seeing that she had regained complete possession of him, wanted to erase the painful impression of the glance he had given her for her letter. She said—

'Tell me frankly, you were vexed at getting my letter, and you didn't believe me?'

As soon as she had said it, she felt that however warm his feelings were to her, he had not forgiven her for that.

'Yes,' he said, 'the letter was so strange. First, Annie ill, and then you thought of coming yourself.'

'It was all the truth.'

'Oh, I don't doubt it.'

'Yes, you do doubt it. You are vexed, I see.'

'Not for one moment. I'm only vexed, that's true, that you seem somehow unwilling to admit that there are duties . . .'

'The duty of going to a concert . . .'

'But we won't talk about it,' he said.

'Why not talk about it?' she said.

'I only meant to say that matters of real importance may turn up. Now, for instance, I shall have to go to Moscow to arrange about the house. . . . Oh, Anna, why are you so irritable? Don't you know that I can't live without you?'

'If so,' said Anna, her voice suddenly changing, 'it means that you are sick of this life . . . Yes, you will come for a day and go away, as men do . . .'

'Anna, that's cruel. I am ready to give up my whole life.'

But she did not hear him.

'If you go to Moscow, I will go too. I will not stay here. Either we must separate or else live together.'

'Why, you know, that's my one desire. But for that . . .'

'We must get a divorce. I will write to him. I see I cannot go on like this . . . But I will come with you to Moscow.'

'You talk as if you were threatening me. But I desire nothing so much as never to be parted from you,' said Vronsky, smiling.

But as he said these words there gleamed in his eyes not merely a cold look, but the vindictive look of a man persecuted and made cruel.

She saw the look and correctly divined its meaning.

'If so, it's a calamity!' that glance told her. It was a moment's impression, but she never forgot it.

Anna wrote to her husband asking him about a divorce, and towards the end of November, taking leave of Princess Varvara, who wanted to go to Petersburg, she went with Vronsky to Moscow. Expecting every day an answer from Alexey Alexandrovitch, and after that the divorce, they now established themselves together like married people.

PART VII

I

THE Levins had been three months in Moscow. The date had long passed on which, according to the most trustworthy calculations of people learned in such matters, Kitty should have been confined. But she was still about, and there was nothing to show that her time was any nearer than two months ago. The doctor, the monthly nurse, and Dolly and her mother, and most of all Levin, who could not think of the approaching event without terror, began to be impatient and uneasy. Kitty was the only person who felt perfectly calm and happy.

She was distinctly conscious now of the birth of a new feeling of love for the future child, for her to some extent actually existing already, and she brooded blissfully over this feeling. He was not by now altogether a part of herself, but sometimes lived his own life independently of her. Often this separate being gave her pain, but at the same time she wanted to laugh with a strange new joy.

All the people she loved were with her, and all were so good to her, so attentively caring for her, so entirely pleasant was everything presented to her, that if she had not known and felt that it must all soon be over, she could not have wished for a better and pleasanter life. The only thing that spoiled the charm of this manner of life was that her husband was not here as she loved him to be, and as he was in the country.

She liked his serene, friendly, and hospitable manner in the country. In the town he seemed continually uneasy and on his guard, as though he were afraid someone would be rude to him, and still more to her. At home in the country, knowing himself distinctly to be in his right place, he was never in haste to be off elsewhere. He was never unoccupied. Here in town he was in a continual hurry, as though afraid of missing something, and yet he had nothing to do. And she felt sorry for him. To others, she knew, he did not appear an object of pity. On the contrary, when Kitty looked at him in society, as one sometimes looks at those one loves, trying to see him as if he were a stranger, so as to catch the impression he must make on others, she saw with a panic even of jealous fear that he was far indeed from being a pitiable figure, that he was very attractive with his fine breeding, his rather old-fashioned, reserved courtesy with women, his powerful figure, and striking, as she thought, and expressive face. But she saw him not from without, but from within; she saw that here he was not himself; that was the only way she could define his condition to herself. Sometimes she inwardly reproached him for his inability to live in the town; sometimes she recognised that it was really hard for him to order his life here so that he could be satisfied with it.

What had he to do, indeed? He did not care for cards; he did not go to a club. Spending the time with jovial gentlemen of Oblonsky's type—she knew now what that meant . . . it meant drinking and going somewhere after drinking. She could not think without horror of where men went on such occasions. Was he to go into society? But she knew he could only find satisfaction in that if he took pleasure in the society of young women, and that she could not wish for. Should he stay at home with her, her mother and her sisters? But much as she liked and enjoyed their conversations for ever on the same subjects—'Aline-Nadine,' as the old prince called the sisters' talks—she knew it must bore him. What was there left for him to do? To go on writing at his book he had indeed attempted, and at first he used to go to the library and make extracts and look up references for his book. But, as he told her, the more he did nothing, the less time he had to do anything. And besides, he complained that he had talked too much about his book here, and that consequently all his ideas about it were muddled and had lost their interest for him.

One advantage in this town life was that quarrels hardly ever happened between them here in town. Whether it was that their conditions were different, or that they had both become more careful and sensible in that respect, they had no quarrels in Moscow from jealousy, which they had so dreaded when they moved from the country.

One event, an event of great importance to both from that point of view, did indeed happen—that was Kitty's meeting with Vronsky.

The old Princess Marya Borissovna, Kitty's godmother, who had always been very fond of her, had insisted on seeing her. Kitty, though she did not go into society at all on account of her condition, went with her father to see the venerable old lady, and there met Vronsky.

The only thing Kitty could reproach herself for at this meeting was that at the instant when she recognised in his civilian dress the features once so familiar to her, her breath failed her, the blood rushed to her heart, and a vivid blush—she felt it—overspread her face. But this lasted only a few seconds. Before her father, who purposely began talking in a loud voice to Vronsky, had finished, she was perfectly ready to look at Vronsky, to speak to him, if necessary, exactly as she spoke to Princess Marya Borissovna, and more than that, to do so in such a way that everything to the faintest intonation and smile would have been approved by her husband, whose unseen presence she seemed to feel about her at that instant.

She said a few words to him, even smiled serenely at his joke about the elections, which he called 'our parliament.' (She had to smile to show she saw the joke.) But she turned away immediately to Princess Marya Borrissovna, and did not once glance at him till he got up to go; then she looked at him, but evidently only because it would be uncivil not to look at a man when he is saying good-bye.

She was grateful to her father for saying nothing to her about their meeting Vronsky, but she saw by his special warmth to her after the visit during their usual walk that he was pleased with her. She was pleased with herself. She had not expected she would have had the power, while keeping somewhere in the bottom of her heart all the memories of her old feeling for Vronsky, not only to seem but to be perfectly indifferent and composed with him.

Levin flushed a great deal more than she when she told him she had met Vronsky at Princess Marya Borissovna's. It was very hard for her to tell him this, but still harder to go on speaking of the details of the meeting, as he did not question her, but simply gazed at her with a frown.

'I am very sorry you weren't there,' she said. 'Not that you weren't in the room . . . I couldn't have been so natural in your presence . . . I am blushing now much more, much, much more,' she said, blushing till the tears came into her eyes. 'But that you couldn't see through a crack.'

The truthful eyes told Levin that she was satisfied with herself, and in spite of her blushing he was quickly reassured and began questioning her, which was all she wanted. When he had heard everything, even to the detail that for the first second she could not help flushing, but that afterwards she was just as direct and as much at her ease as with any chance acquaintance, Levin was quite happy again and said he was glad of it, and would not now behave as stupidly as he had done at the election, but would try the first time he met Vronsky to be as friendly as possible.

'It's so wretched to feel that there's a man almost an enemy whom it's painful to meet,' said Levin. 'I'm very, very glad.'

II

'Do, please, go then and call on the Bols,' Kitty said to her husband, when he came in to see her at eleven o'clock before going out. 'I know you are dining at the club; papa put down your name. But what are you going to do in the morning?'

'I am only going to Katavasov,' answered Levin.

'Why so early?'

'He promised to introduce me to Metrov. I wanted to talk to him about my work. He's a distinguished scientific man from Petersburg,' said Levin.

'Yes; wasn't it his article you were praising so? Well, and after that?' said Kitty.

'I shall go to the court, perhaps, about my sister's business.'

'And the concert?' she queried.

'I shan't go there all alone.'

'No? do go; there are going to be some new things. . . . That interested you so. I should certainly go.'

'Well, anyway, I shall come home before dinner,' he said, looking at his watch.

'Put on your frock-coat, so that you can go straight to call on Countess Bol.'

'But is it absolutely necessary?'

'Oh, absolutely! He has been to see us. Come, what is it? You go in, sit down, talk for five minutes of the weather, get up and go away.'

'Oh, you wouldn't believe it! I've got so out of the way of all this that it makes me feel positively ashamed. It's such a horrible thing to do! A complete outsider walks in, sits down, stays on with nothing to do, wastes their time and worries himself, and walks away!'

Kitty laughed.

'Why, I suppose you used to pay calls before you were married, didn't you?'

'Yes, I did, but I always felt ashamed, and now I'm so out of the way of it that, by Jove! I'd sooner go two days running without my dinner than pay this call! One's so ashamed! I feel all the while that they're annoyed, that they're saying, "What has he come for?"'

'No, they won't. I'll answer for that,' said Kitty, looking into his face with a laugh. She took his hand. 'Well, good-bye. . . . Do go, please.'

He was just going out after kissing his wife's hand, when she stopped him.

'Kostya, do you know I've only fifty roubles left?'

'Oh, all right, I'll go to the bank and get some. How much?' he said, with the expression of dissatisfaction she knew so well.

'No, wait a minute.' She held his hand. 'Let's talk about it, it worries me. I seem to spend nothing unnecessary, but money seems to fly away simply. We don't manage well, somehow.'

'Oh, it's all right,' he said, with a little cough, looking at her from under his brows.

That cough she knew well. It was a sign of intense dissatisfaction, not with her, but with himself. He certainly was displeased not at so much money being spent, but at being reminded of what he, knowing something was unsatisfactory, wanted to forget.

'I have told Sokolov to sell the wheat, and to borrow an advance on the mill. We shall have money enough in any case.'

'Yes, but I'm afraid that altogether . . .'

'Oh, it's all right, all right,' he repeated. 'Well, good-bye darling.'

'No, I'm really sorry sometimes that I listened to mamma. How nice it would have been in the country! As it is, I'm worrying you all, and we're wasting our money.'

'Not at all, not at all. Not since I've been married have I said that things could have been better than they are. . . .'

'Truly?' she said, looking into his eyes.

He said it without thinking, simply to console her. But when he glanced at her and saw those sweet truthful eyes fastened questioningly on him, he repeated it with his whole heart. 'I was positively forgetting her,' he thought. And he remembered what was before them, so soon to come.

'Will it be soon? How do you feel?' he whispered, taking her two hands.

'I have so often thought so, that now I don't think about it or know anything about it.'

'And you're not frightened?'

She smiled contemptuously.

'Not the least little bit,' she said.

'Well, if anything happens, I shall be at Katavasov's.'

'No, nothing will happen, and don't think about it. I'm going for a walk on the boulevard with papa. We're going to see Dolly. I shall expect you before dinner. Oh yes! Do you know that Dolly's position is becoming utterly impossible? She's in debt all round; she hasn't a penny. We were talking yesterday with mamma and Arseny' (this was her sister's husband Lvov), 'and we determined to send you with him to talk to Stiva. It's really unbearable. One can't speak to papa about it . . . But if you and he . . .'

'Why, what can we do?' said Levin.

'You'll be at Arseny's, anyway; talk to him, he will tell what we decided.

'Oh, I agree to everything Arseny thinks beforehand. I'll go and see him. By the way, if I do go to the concert, I'll go with Natalie. Well, good-bye.'

On the steps Levin was stopped by his old servant Kouzma, who had been with him before his marriage, and now looked after their household in town.

'Beauty' (that was the left shaft-horse brought up from the country) 'has been badly shod and is quite lame,' he said. 'What does your honour wish to be done?'

During the first part of their stay in Moscow, Levin had used his own horses brought up from the country. He had tried to arrange this part of their expenses in the best and cheapest way possible; but it appeared that their own horses came dearer than hired horses, and they still hired too.

'Send for the veterinary, there may be a bruise.'

'And for Katerina Alexandrovna?' asked Kouzma.

Levin was not by now struck as he had been at first by the fact that to get from one end of Moscow to the other he had to have two powerful horses put into a heavy carriage, to take the carriage three miles through the snowy slush and to keep it standing there four hours, paying five roubles every time. Now it seemed quite natural.

'Hire a pair for our carriage from the jobmaster,' said he.

'Yes, sir.'

And so, simply and easily, thanks to the facilities of town life, Levin settled a question which, in the country, would have called for so much personal trouble and exertion, and going out on to the steps, he called a sledge, sat down, and drove to Nikitsky. On the way he thought no more of money, but mused on the introduction that awaited him to the Petersburg savant, a writer on sociology, and what he would say to him about his book.

Only during the first day of his stay in Moscow Levin had been struck by the expenditure, strange to one living in the country, unproductive but inevitable, that was expected of him on every side. But by now he had grown used to it. That had happened to him in this matter which is said to happen to drunkards—the first glass sticks in the throat, the second flies down like a hawk, but after the third they're like tiny little birds. When Levin had changed his first hundred-rouble note to pay for liveries for his footmen and hall-porter, he could not help reflecting that these liveries were of no use to anyone—but they were indubitably necessary, to judge by the amazement of the princess and Kitty when he suggested that they might do without liveries,—that these liveries would cost the wages of two labourers for the summer, that is, would pay for about three hundred working days from Easter to Ash-Wednesday, and each day of hard work from early morning to late evening—and that hundred-rouble note did stick in his throat. But the next note, changed to pay for providing a dinner for their relations, that cost twenty-eight roubles, though it did excite in Levin the reflection that twenty-eight roubles meant nine measures of oats, which men would with groans and sweat have reaped and bound and threshed and winnowed and sifted and sown,—this next one he parted with more easily. And now the notes he changed no longer aroused such reflections, and they flew off like little birds. Whether the labour devoted to obtaining the money corresponded to the pleasure given by what was bought with it, was a consideration he had long ago dismissed. His business calculation that there was a certain price below which he could not sell certain grain was forgotten too. The rye, for the price of which he had so long held out, had been sold for fifty kopecks a measure cheaper than it had been fetching a month ago. Even the consideration that with such an expenditure he could not go on living for a year without debt, that even had no force. Only one thing was essential: to have money in the bank, without inquiring where it came from, so as to know that one had the wherewithal to buy meat for tomorrow. And this condition had hitherto been fulfilled; he had always had the money in the bank. But now the money in the bank had gone, and he could not quite tell where to get the next instalment. And this it was which, at the moment when Kitty had mentioned money, had disturbed him; but he had no time to think about it. He drove off, thinking of Katavasov and the meeting with Metrov that was before him.

III

LEVIN had on this visit to town seen a great deal of his old friend at the university, Professor Katavasov, whom he had not seen since his marriage. He liked in Katavasov the clearness and simplicity of his conception of life. Levin thought that the clearness of Katavasov's conception of life was due to the poverty of his nature; Katavasov thought that the disconnectedness of Levin's ideas was due to his lack of intellectual discipline; but Levin enjoyed Katavasov's clearness, and Katavasov enjoyed the abundance of Levin's untrained ideas, and they liked to meet and to discuss.

Levin had read Katavasov some parts of his book, and he had liked them. On the previous day Katavasov had met Levin at a public lecture and told him that the celebrated Metrov, whose article Levin had so much liked, was in Moscow, that he had been much interested by what Katavasov had told him about Levin's work, and that he was coming to see him tomorrow at eleven, and would be very glad to make Levin's acquaintance.

'You're positively a reformed character, I'm glad to see,' said Katavasov, meeting Levin in the little drawing-room. 'I heard the bell and thought: Impossible that it can be he at the exact time! . . . Well, what do you say to the Montenegrins now? They're a race of warriors.'

'Why, what's happened?' asked Levin.

Katavasov in few words told him the last piece of news from the war, and going into his study, introduced Levin to a short, thick-set man of pleasant appearance. This was Metrov. The conversation touched for a brief space on politics and on how recent events were looked at in the higher spheres in Petersburg. Metrov repeated a saying that had reached him through a most trustworthy source, reported as having been uttered on this subject by the Tsar and one of the ministers. Katavasov had heard also on excellent authority that the Tsar had said something quite different. Levin tried to imagine circumstances in which both sayings might have been uttered, and the conversation on that topic dropped.

'Yes, here he's written almost a book on the natural conditions of the labourer in relation to the land,' said Katavasov; 'I'm not a specialist, but I, as a natural science man, was pleased at his not taking mankind as something outside biological laws; but, on the contrary, seeing his dependence on his surroundings, and in that dependence seeking the laws of his development.'

'That's very interesting,' said Metrov.

'What I began precisely was to write a book on agriculture; but studying the chief instrument of agriculture, the labourer,' said Levin, reddening, 'I could not help coming to quite unexpected results.'

And Levin began carefully, as it were, feeling his ground, to expound his views. He knew Metrov had written an article against the generally accepted theory of political economy, but to what extent he could reckon on his sympathy with his own new views he did not know and could not guess from the clever and serene face of the learned man.

'But in what do you see the special characteristics of the Russian labourer?' said Metrov; 'in his biological characteristics, so to speak, or in the condition in which he is placed?'

Levin saw that there was an idea underlying this question with which he did not agree. But he went on explaining his own idea that the Russian labourer has a quite special view of the land, different from that of other people; and to support this proposition he made haste to add that in his opinion this attitude of the Russian peasants was due to the consciousness of his vocation to people vast unoccupied expanses in the East.

'One may easily be led into error in basing any conclusion on the general vocation of a people,' said Metrov, interrupting Levin. 'The condition of the labourer will always depend on his relation to the land and to capital.'

And without letting Levin finish explaining his idea, Metrov began expounding to him the special point of his own theory.

In what the point of his theory lay, Levin did not understand, because he did not take the trouble to understand. He saw that Metrov, like other people, in spite of his own article, in which he had attacked the current theory of political economy, looked at the position of the Russian peasant simply from the point of view of capital, wages and rent. He would indeed have been obliged to admit that in the eastern—much the larger—part of Russia rent was as yet *nil*, that for nine-tenths of the Russian peasants wages took the form simply of food provided for themselves, and that capital does not so far exist except in the form of the most primitive tools. Yet it was only from that point of view that he considered every labourer, though in many points he differed from the economists and had his own theory of the wage-fund, which he expounded to Levin.

Levin listened reluctantly, and at first made objections. He would have liked to interrupt Metrov, to explain his own thought, which in his opinion would have rendered further exposition of Metrov's theories superfluous. But later on, feeling convinced that they looked at the matter so differently, that they could never understand one another, he did not even oppose his statements, but simply listened. Although what Metrov was saying was by now utterly devoid of interest for him, he yet experienced a certain satisfaction in listening to him. It flattered his vanity that such a learned man should explain his ideas to him so eagerly, with such intensity and confidence in Levin's understanding of the subject, sometimes with a mere hint referring him to a whole aspect of the subject. He put this down to his own credit, unaware that Metrov, who had already discussed his theory over and over again with all his intimate friends, talked of it with special eagerness to every new person, and in general was eager to talk to anyone of any subject that interested him, even if still obscure to himself.

'We are late though,' said Katavasov, looking at his watch directly Metrov had finished his discourse.

'Yes, there's a meeting of the Society of Amateurs today in commemoration of the jubilee of Svintitch,' said Katavasov in answer to Levin's inquiry. 'Pyotr Ivanovitch and I were going. I've promised to deliver an address on his labours in zoology. Come along with us, it's very interesting.'

'Yes, and indeed it's time to start,' said Metrov. 'Come with us, and from there, if you care to, come to my place. I should very much like to hear your work.'

'Oh, no! It's no good yet, it's unfinished. But I shall be very glad to go to the meeting.'

'I say, friends, have you heard? He has handed in the separate report,' Katavasov called from the room, where he was putting on his frock-coat.

And a conversation sprang up upon the university question, which was a very important event that winter in Moscow. Three old professors in the council had not accepted the opinion of the younger professors. The young ones had registered a separate resolution. This, in the judgment of some people, was monstrous, in the judgment of others it was the simplest and most just thing to do, and the professors were split up into two parties.

One party, to which Katavasov belonged, saw in the opposite party a scoundrelly betrayal and treachery, while the opposite party saw in them childishness and lack of respect for the authorities. Levin, though he did not belong to the university, had several times already during his stay in Moscow heard and talked about this matter, and had his own opinion on the subject. He took part in the conversation that was continued in the street, as they all three walked to the buildings of the old university.

The meeting had already begun. Round the cloth-covered table, at which Katavasov and Metrov seated themselves, there were some half-dozen persons, and one of these was bending close over a manuscript, reading something aloud. Levin sat down in one of the empty chairs that were standing round the table, and in a whisper asked a student sitting near what was being read. The student, eyeing Levin with displeasure, said—

'Biography.'

Though Levin was not interested in the biography, he could not help listening, and learned some new and interesting facts about the life of the distinguished man of science.

When the reader had finished, the chairman thanked him and read some verses of the poet Ment sent him on the jubilee, and said a few words by way of thanks to the poet. Then Katavasov in his loud, ringing voice read his address on the scientific labours of the man whose jubilee was being kept.

When Katavasov had finished, Levin looked at his watch, saw it was past one, and thought that there would not be time before the concert to read Metrov his book, and indeed, he did not now care to do so. During the reading he had thought over their conversation. He saw distinctly now that though Metrov's ideas might perhaps have value, his own ideas had a value too, and their ideas could only be made clear and lead to something if each worked separately in his chosen path, and that nothing would be gained by putting their ideas together. And having made up his mind to refuse Metrov's invitation, Levin went up to him at the end of the meeting. Metrov introduced Levin to the chairman, with whom he was talking of the political news. Metrov told the chairman what he had already told Levin, and Levin made the same remarks on his news that he had already made that morning, but for the sake of variety he expressed also a new opinion which had only just struck him. After that the conversation turned again on the university question. As Levin had already heard it all, he made haste to tell Metrov that he was sorry he could not take advantage of his invitation, took leave, and drove to Lvov's.

IV

Lvov, the husband of Natalie, Kitty's sister, had spent all his life in foreign capitals, where he had been educated, and had been in the diplomatic service.

During the previous year he had left the diplomatic service, not owing to any 'unpleasantness' (he never had any 'unpleasantness' with anyone), and was transferred to the department of the court of the palace in Moscow, in order to give his two boys the best education possible.

In spite of the striking contrast in their habits and views, and the fact that Lvov was older than Levin, they had seen a great deal of one another that winter, and had taken a great liking to each other.

Lvov was at home, and Levin went in to him unannounced.

Lvov, in a house coat with a belt and in chamois leather shoes, was sitting in an arm-chair, and with a pince-nez with blue glasses he was reading a book that stood on a reading-desk, while in his beautiful hand he held a half-burned cigarette daintily away from him.

His handsome, delicate, and still youthful-looking face, to which his curly, glistening silvery hair gave a still more aristocratic air, lighted up with a smile when he saw Levin.

'Capital! I was meaning to send to you. How's Kitty? Sit here, it's more comfortable.' He got up and pushed up a rocking-chair. 'Have you read the last circular in the *Journal de St. Pétersbourg*? I think it's excellent,' he said, with a slight French accent.

Levin told him what he had heard from Katavasov was being said in Petersburg, and after talking a little about politics, he told him of his interview with Metrov, and the learned society's meeting. To Lvov it was very interesting.

'That's what I envy you, that you are able to mix in these interesting scientific circles,' he said. And as he talked, he passed as usual into French, which was easier to him. 'It's true I haven't the time for it. My official work and the children leave me no time; and then I'm not ashamed to own that my education has been too defective.'

'That I don't believe,' said Levin with a smile, feeling, as he always did, touched at Lvov's low opinion of himself, which was not in the least put on from a desire to seem or to be modest, but was absolutely sincere.

'Oh, yes, indeed! I feel now how badly educated I am. To educate my children I positively have to look up a great deal, and in fact simply to study myself. For it's not enough to have teachers, there must be someone to look after them, just as on your land you want labourers and an overseer. See what I'm reading'—he pointed to Buslaev's *Grammar* on the desk—'it's expected of Misha, and it's so difficult . . . Come, explain to me . . . Here he says . . .'

Levin tried to explain to him that it couldn't be understood, but that it had to be taught; but Lvov would not agree with him.

'Oh, you're laughing at it!'

'On the contrary, you can't imagine how, when I look at you, I'm always learning the task that lies before me, that is the education of one's children.'

'Well, there's nothing for you to learn,' said Lvov.

'All I know,' said Levin, 'is that I have never seen better brought-up children than yours, and I wouldn't wish for children better than yours.'

Lvov visibly tried to restrain the expression of his delight, but he was positively radiant with smiles.

'If only they're better than me! That's all I desire. You don't know yet all the work,' he said, 'with boys who've been left like mine to run wild abroad.'

'You'll catch all that up. They're such clever children. The great thing is the education of character. That's what I learn when I look at your children.'

'You talk of the education of character. You can't imagine how difficult that is! You have hardly succeeded in combating one tendency when others crop up, and the struggle begins again. If one had not a support in religion—you remember we talked about that—no father could bring children up relying on his own strength alone without that help.'

This subject, which always interested Levin, was cut short by the entrance of the beauty Natalie Alexandrovna, dressed to go out.

'I didn't know you were here,' she said, unmistakably feeling no regret, but a positive pleasure, in interrupting this conversation on a topic she had heard so much of that she was by now weary of it. 'Well, how is Kitty? I am dining with you today. I tell you what, Arseny,' she turned to her husband, 'you take the carriage.'

And the husband and wife began to discuss their arrangements for the day. As the husband had to drive to meet someone on official business, while the wife had to go to the concert and some public meeting of a committee on the Eastern Question, there was a great deal to consider and settle. Levin had to take part in their plans as one of themselves. It was settled that Levin should go with Natalie to the concert and the meeting, and that from there they should send the carriage to the office for Arseny, and he should call for her and take her to Kitty's; or that, if he had not finished his work, he should send the carriage back and Levin would go with her.

'He's spoiling me,' Lvov said to his wife; 'he assures me that our children are splendid, when I know how much that's bad there is in them.'

'Arseny goes to extremes, I always say,' said his wife. 'If you look for perfection, you will never be satisfied. And it's true, as papa says, that when we were brought up there was one extreme—we were kept in the basement, while our parents lived in the best rooms; now it's just the other way—the parents are in the wash-house, while the children are in the best rooms. Parents now are not expected to live at all, but to exist altogether for their children.'

'Well, what if they like it better?' Lvov said, with his beautiful smile, touching her hand. 'Anyone who didn't know you would think you were a stepmother, not a true mother.'

'No, extremes are not good in anything,' Natalie said serenely, putting his paper-knife straight in its proper place on the table.

'Well, come here, you perfect children,' Lvov said to the two handsome boys who came in, and after bowing to Levin, went up to their father, obviously wishing to ask him about something.

Levin would have liked to talk to them, to hear what they would say to their father, but Natalie began talking to him, and then Lvov's colleague in the service, Mahotin, walked in, wearing his court uniform, to go with him to meet someone, and a conversation was kept up without a break upon Herzegovina, Princess Korzinsky, the town council, and the sudden death of Madame Apraksin.

Levin even forgot the commission intrusted to him. He recollected it as he was going into the hall.

'Oh, Kitty told me to talk to you about Oblonsky,' he said, as Lvov was standing on the stairs, seeing his wife and Levin off.

'Yes, yes, maman wants us, *les beaux-frères*, to attack him,' he said, blushing. 'But why should I?'

'Well, then, I will attack him,' said Madame Lvov, with a smile, standing in her white sheepskin cape, waiting till they had finished speaking. 'Come, let us go.'

V

AT the concert in the afternoon two very interesting things were performed. One was a fantasia, *King Lear*; the other was a quartette dedicated to the memory of Bach. Both were new and in the new style, and Levin was eager to form an opinion of them. After escorting his sister-in-law to her stall, he stood against a column and tried to listen as attentively and conscientiously as possible. He tried not to let his attention be distracted, and not to spoil his impression by looking at the conductor in a white tie, waving his arms, which always disturbed his enjoyment of music so much, or the ladies in bonnets, with strings carefully tied over their ears, and all these people either thinking of nothing at all or thinking of all sorts of things except the music. He tried to avoid meeting musical connoisseurs or talkative acquaintances, and stood looking at the floor straight before him, listening.

But the more he listened to the fantasia of *King Lear* the further he felt from forming any definite opinion of it. There was, as it were, a continual beginning, a preparation of the musical expression of some feeling, but it fell to pieces again directly, breaking into new musical motives, or simply nothing but the whims of the composer, exceedingly complex but disconnected sounds. And these fragmentary musical expressions, though sometimes beautiful, were disagreeable, because they were utterly unexpected and not led up to by anything. Gaiety and grief and despair and tenderness and triumph followed one another without any connection, like the emotions of a madman. And those emotions, like a madman's, sprang up quite unexpectedly.

During the whole of the performance Levin felt like a deaf man watching people dancing, and was in a state of complete bewilderment when the fantasia was over, and felt a great weariness from the fruitless strain on his attention. Loud applause resounded on all sides. Everyone got up, moved about, and began talking. Anxious to throw some light on his own perplexity from the impressions of others, Levin began to walk about, looking for connoisseurs, and was glad to see a well-known musical amateur in conversation with Pestsov, whom he knew.

'Marvellous!' Pestsov was saying in his mellow bass. 'How are you, Konstantin Dmitritch? Particularly sculpturesque and plastic, so to say, and richly coloured is that passage where you feel Cordelia's approach, where woman, *das ewig Weibliche*, enters into conflict with fate. Isn't it?'

'You mean . . . what has Cordelia to do with it?' Levin asked timidly, forgetting the fantasia was supposed to represent King Lear.

'Cordelia comes in . . . see here!' said Pestsov, tapping his finger on the satiny surface of the programme he held in his hand and passing it to Levin.

Only then Levin recollected the title of the fantasia, and made haste to read in the Russian translation the lines from Shakespeare that were printed on the back of the programme.

'You can't follow it without that,' said Pestsov, addressing Levin, as the person he had been speaking to had gone away, and he had no one to talk to.

In the *entr'acte* Levin and Pestsov fell into an argument upon the merits and defects of music of the Wagner school. Levin maintained that the mistake of Wagner and all his followers lay in their trying to take music into the sphere of another art, just as poetry goes wrong when it tries to paint a face as the art of painting ought to do, and as an instance of this mistake he cited the sculptor who carved in marble certain poetic phantasms flitting round the figure of the poet on the pedestal. 'These phantoms were so far from being phantoms that they were positively clinging on the ladder,' said Levin. The comparison pleased him, but he could not remember whether he had not used the same phrase before, and to Pestsov, too, and as he said it he felt confused.

Pestsov maintained that art is one, and that it can attain its highest manifestations only by conjunction with all kinds of art.

The second piece that was performed Levin could not hear. Pestsov, who was standing beside him, was talking to him almost all the time, condemning the music for its excessive affected assumption of simplicity, and comparing it with the simplicity of the Pre-Raphaelites in painting. As he went out Levin met many more acquaintances, with whom he talked of politics, of music, and of common acquaintances. Among others he met Count Bol, whom he had utterly forgotten to call upon.

'Well, go at once then,' Madame Lvov said, when he told her; 'perhaps they'll not be at home, and then you can come to the meeting to fetch me. You'll find me still there.'

VI

'PERHAPS they're not at home?' said Levin, as he went into the hall of Countess Bol's house.

'At home; please walk in,' said the porter, resolutely removing his overcoat.

'How annoying!' thought Levin with a sigh, taking off one glove and stroking his hat. 'What did I come for? What have I to say to them?'

As he passed through the first drawing-room Levin met in the doorway Countess Bol, giving some order to a servant with a careworn and severe face. On seeing Levin she smiled, and asked him to come into the little drawing-room, where he heard voices. In this room there were sitting in arm-chairs the two daughters of the countess, and a Moscow colonel, whom Levin knew. Levin went up, greeted them, and sat down beside the sofa with his hat on his knees.

'How is your wife? Have you been at the concert? We couldn't go. Mamma had to be at the funeral service.'

'Yes, I heard . . . What a sudden death!' said Levin.

The countess came in, sat down on the sofa, and she too asked after his wife and inquired about the concert.

Levin answered, and repeated an inquiry about Madame Apraksin's sudden death.

'But she was always in weak health.'

'Were you at the opera yesterday?'

'Yes, I was.'

'Lucca was very good.'

'Yes, very good,' he said, and as it was utterly of no consequence to him what they thought of him, he began repeating what they had heard a hundred times about the characteristics of the singer's talent. Countess Bol pretended to be listening. Then, when he had said enough and paused, the colonel, who had been silent till then, began to talk. The colonel too talked of the opera, and about culture. At last, after speaking of the proposed *folle journée* at Turin's, the colonel laughed, got up noisily, and went away. Levin too rose, but he saw by the face of the countess that it was not yet time for him to go. He must stay two minutes longer. He sat down.

But as he was thinking all the while how stupid it was, he could not find a subject for conversation, and sat silent.

'You are not going to the public meeting? They say it will be very interesting,' began the countess.

'No, I promised my *belle-sœur* to fetch her from it,' said Levin.

A silence followed. The mother once more exchanged glances with a daughter.

'Well, now I think the time has come,' thought Levin, and he got up. The ladies shook hands with him, and begged him to say *mille choses* to his wife for them.

The porter asked him, as he gave him his coat, 'Where is your honour staying?' and immediately wrote down his address in a big handsomely-bound book.

'Of course I don't care, but still I feel ashamed and awfully stupid,' thought Levin, consoling himself with the reflection that everyone does it. He drove to the public meeting, where he was to find his sister-in-law, so as to drive home with her.

At the public meeting of the committee there were a great many people, and almost all the highest society. Levin was in time for the report which, as everyone said, was very interesting. When the reading of the report was over, people moved about, and Levin met Sviazhsky, who invited him very pressingly to come that evening to a meeting of the Society of Agriculture, where a celebrated lecture was to be delivered, and Stepan Arkadyevitch, who had only just come from the races, and many other acquaintances; and Levin heard and uttered various criticisms on the meeting, on the new fantasia, and on a public trial. But, probably from the mental fatigue he was beginning to feel, he made a blunder in speaking of the trial, and this blunder he recalled several times with vexation. Speaking of the sentence upon a foreigner who had been condemned in Russia, and of how unfair it would be to punish him by exile abroad, Levin repeated what he had heard the day before in conversation from an acquaintance.

'I think sending him abroad is much the same as punishing a carp by putting it into the water,' said Levin. Then he recollected that this idea, which he had heard from an acquaintance and uttered as his own, came from a fable of Krilov's, and that the acquaintance had picked it up from a newspaper article.

After driving home with his sister-in-law, and finding Kitty in good spirits and quite well, Levin drove to the club.

VII

LEVIN reached the club just at the right time. Members and visitors were driving up as he arrived. Levin had not been at the club for a very long while—not since he lived in Moscow, when he was leaving the university and going into society. He remembered the club, the external details of its arrangement, but he had completely forgotten the impression it had made on him in old days. But as soon as, driving into the wide semi-circular court and getting out of the sledge, he mounted the steps, and the hall-porter, adorned with a cross-way scarf, noiselessly opened the door to him with a bow; as soon as he saw in the porter's room the cloaks and goloshes of members who thought it less trouble to take them off downstairs; as soon as he heard the mysterious ringing bell that preceded him as he ascended the easy, carpeted staircase, and saw the statue on the landing, and the third porter at the top doors, a familiar figure grown older, in the club livery, opening the door without haste or delay, and scanning the visitors as they passed in—Levin felt the old impression of the club come back in a rush, an impression of repose, comfort, and propriety.

'Your hat, please,' the porter said to Levin, who forgot the club rule to leave his hat in the porter's room. 'Long time since you've been. The prince put your name down yesterday. Prince Stepan Arkadyevitch is not here yet.'

The porter did not only know Levin, but also all his ties and relationships, and so immediately mentioned his intimate friends.

Passing through the outer hall, divided up by screens, and the room partitioned on the right, where a man sits at the fruit-buffet, Levin overtook an old man walking slowly in, and entered the dining-room full of noise and people.

He walked along the tables, almost all full, and looked at the visitors. He saw people of all sorts, old and young; some he knew a little, some intimate friends. There was not a single cross or worried-looking face. All seemed to have left their cares and anxieties in the porter's room with their hats, and were all deliberately getting ready to enjoy the material blessings of life. Sviazhsky was here and Shtcherbatsky, Nevyedovsky and the old prince, and Vronsky and Sergey Ivanovitch.

'Ah! why are you late?' the prince said smiling, and giving him his hand over his own shoulder. 'How's Kitty?' he added, smoothing out the napkin he had tucked in at his waistcoat buttons.

'All right; they are dining at home, all the three of them.'

'Ah, "Aline-Nadine," to be sure! There's no room with us. Go to that table, and make haste and take a seat,' said the prince, and turning away he carefully took a plate of eel soup.

'Levin, this way!' a good-natured voice shouted a little further on. It was Turovtsin. He was sitting with a young officer, and beside them were two chairs turned upside down. Levin gladly went up to them. He had always liked the good-hearted rake, Turovtsin—he was associated in his mind with memories of his courtship—and at that moment, after the strain of intellectual conversation, the sight of Turovtsin's good-natured face was particularly welcome.

'For you and Oblonsky. He'll be here directly.'

The young man, holding himself very erect, with eyes for ever twinkling with enjoyment, was an officer from Petersburg, Gagin. Turovtsin introduced them.

'Oblonsky's always late.'

'Ah, here he is!'

'Have you only just come,' said Oblonsky, coming quickly towards them. 'Good-day. Had some vodka? Well, come along then.'

Levin got up and went with him to the big table spread with spirits and appetisers of the most various kinds. One would have thought that out of two dozen delicacies one might find something to one's taste, but Stepan Arkadyevitch asked for something special, and one of the liveried waiters standing by immediately brought what was required. They drank a wineglassful and returned to their table.

At once, while they were still at the soup, Gagin was served with champagne, and told the waiter to fill four glasses. Levin did not refuse the wine, and asked for a second bottle. He was very hungry, and ate and drank with great enjoyment, and with still greater enjoyment took part in the lively and simple conversation of his companions. Gagin, dropping his voice, told the last good story from Petersburg, and the story, though improper and stupid, was so ludicrous that Levin broke into roars of laughter so loud that those near looked round.

'That's in the same style as, "that's a thing I can't endure!" You know the story?' said Stepan Arkadyevitch. 'Ah, that's exquisite! Another bottle,' he said to the waiter, and he began to relate his good story.

'Pyotr Ilyitch Vinovsky invites you to drink with him,' a little old waiter interrupted Stepan Arkadyevitch, bringing two delicate glasses of sparkling champagne, and addressing Stepan Arkadyevitch and Levin. Stepan Arkadyevitch took the glass, and looking towards a bald man with red moustaches at the other end of the table, he nodded to him, smiling.

'Who's that?' asked Levin.

'You met him once at my place, don't you remember? A good-natured fellow.'

Levin did the same as Stepan Arkadyevitch and took the glass.

Stepan Arkadyevitch's anecdote too was very amusing. Levin told his story, and that too was successful. Then they talked of horses, of the races, of what they had been doing that day, and of how smartly Vronsky's Atlas had won the first prize. Levin did not notice how the time passed at dinner.

'Ah! and here they are!' Stepan Arkadyevitch said towards the end of dinner, leaning over the back of his chair and holding out his hand to Vronsky, who came up with a tall officer of the Guards. Vronsky's face too beamed with the look of good-humoured enjoyment that was general in the club. He propped his elbow playfully on Stepan Arkadyevitch's shoulder, whispering something to him, and he held out his hand to Levin with the same good-humoured smile.

'Very glad to meet you,' he said. 'I looked out for you at the election, but I was told you had gone away.'

'Yes, I left the same day. We've just been talking of your horse. I congratulate you,' said Levin. 'It was very rapidly run.'

'Yes; you've race-horses too, haven't you?'

'No, my father had; but I remember and know something about it.'

'Where have you dined?' asked Stepan Arkadyevitch.

'We were at the second table, behind the columns.'

'We've been celebrating his success,' said the tall colonel. 'It's his second Imperial prize. I wish I might have the luck at cards he has with horses. Well, why waste the precious time? I'm going to the "infernal regions",' added the colonel, and he walked away.

'That's Yashvin,' Vronsky said in answer to Turovtsin, and he sat down in the vacated seat beside them. He drank the glass offered him, and ordered a bottle of wine. Under the influence of the club atmosphere or the wine he had drunk, Levin chatted away to Vronsky of the best breeds of cattle, and was very glad not to feel the slightest hostility to this man. He even told him, among other things, that he had heard from his wife that she had met him at Princess Marya Borissovna's.

'Ah, Princess Marya Borissovna, she's exquisite!' said Stepan Arkadyevitch, and he told an anecdote about her which set them all laughing. Vronsky particularly laughed with such simple-hearted amusement that Levin felt quite reconciled to him.

'Well, have we finished?' said Stepan Arkadyevitch, getting up with a smile. 'Let us go.'

VIII

GETTING up from the table, Levin walked with Gagin through the lofty room to the billiard-room, feeling his arms swing as he walked with a peculiar lightness and ease. As he crossed the big room, he came upon his father-in-law.

'Well, how do you like our Temple of Indolence?' said the prince, taking his arm. 'Come along, come along!'

'Yes, I wanted to walk about and look at everything. It's interesting.'

'Yes, it's interesting for you. But its interest for me is quite different.

You look at those little old men now,' he said, pointing to a club member with bent back and projecting lip, shuffling towards them in his soft boots, 'and imagine that they were *shlupiks* like that from their birth up.'

'How *shlupiks*?'

'I see you don't know that name. That's our club designation. You know the game of rolling eggs: when one's rolled a long while it becomes a *shlupik*. So it is with us; one goes on coming and coming to the club, and ends by becoming a *shlupik*. Ah, you laugh! but we look out, for fear of dropping into it ourselves. You know Prince Tchetchensky?' inquired the prince; and Levin saw by his face that he was just going to relate something funny.

'No, I don't know him.'

'You don't say so! Well, Prince Tchetchensky is a well-known figure. No matter, though. He's always playing billiards here. Only three years ago he was not a *shlupik* and kept up his spirits and even used to call other people *shlupiks*. But one day he turns up, and our porter . . . you know Vassily? Why, that fat one! He's famous for his *bon mots*. And so Prince Tchetchensky asks him, "Come, Vassily, who's here? Any *shlupiks* here yet?" And he says, "You're the third." Yes, my dear boy, that he did!'

Talking and greeting the friends they met, Levin and the prince walked through all the rooms: the great room where tables had already been set, and the usual partners were playing for small stakes; the divan-room, where they were playing chess, and Sergey Ivanovitch was sitting talking to somebody; the billiard-room, where, about a sofa in a recess, there was a lively party drinking champagne—Gagin was one of them. They peeped into the 'infernal regions', where a good many men were crowding round one table, at which Yashvin was sitting. Trying not to make a noise, they walked into the dark reading-room, where under the shaded lamps there sat a young man with a wrathful countenance, turning over one journal after another, and a bald general buried in a book. They went, too, into what the prince called the intellectual room, where three gentlemen were engaged in a heated discussion of the latest political news.

'Prince, please come, we're ready,' said one of his card-party, who had come to look for him, and the prince went off. Levin sat down and listened, but recalling all the conversation of the morning he felt all of a sudden fearfully bored. He got up hurriedly, and went to look for Oblonsky and Turovtsin, with whom it had been so pleasant.

Turovtsin was one of the circle drinking in the billiard-room, and Stepan Arkadyevitch was talking with Vronsky near the door at the farther corner of the room.

'It's not that she's dull; but this undefined, this unsettled position,' Levin caught, and he was hurrying away, but Stepan Arkadyevitch called to him.

'Levin!' said Stepan Arkadyevitch; and Levin noticed that his eyes were not full of tears exactly, but moist, which always happened when he had been drinking, or when he was touched. Just now it was due to both causes. 'Levin, don't go,' he said, and he warmly squeezed his arm above the elbow, obviously not at all wishing to let him go.

'This is a true friend of mine—almost my greatest friend,' he said to Vronsky. 'You have become even closer and dearer to me. And I want you, and I know you ought, to be friends, and great friends, because you're both splendid fellows.'

'Well, there's nothing for us now but to kiss and be friends,' Vronsky said, with good-natured playfulness, holding out his hand.

Levin quickly took the offered hand, and pressed it warmly.

'I'm very, very glad,' said Levin.

'Waiter, a bottle of champagne,' said Stepan Arkadyevitch.

'And I'm very glad,' said Vronsky.

But in spite of Stepan Arkadyevitch's desire, and their own desire, they had nothing to talk about, and both felt it.

'Do you know, he has never met Anna?' Stepan Arkadyevitch said to Vronsky. 'And I want above everything to take him to see her. Let us go, Levin!'

'Really?' said Vronsky. 'She will be very glad to see you. I should be going home at once,' he added, 'but I'm worried about Yashvin, and I want to stay on till he finishes.'

'Why, is he losing?'

'He keeps losing, and I'm the only friend that can restrain him.'

'Well, what do you say to pyramids? Levin, will you play? Capital!' said Stepan Arkadyevitch. 'Get the table ready,' he said to the marker.

'It has been ready for a long while,' answered the marker, who had already set the balls in a triangle, and was knocking the red one about for his own diversion.

'Well, let us begin.'

After the game Vronsky and Levin sat down at Gagin's table, and at Stepan Arkadyevitch's suggestion Levin took a hand in the game.

Vronsky sat down at the table, surrounded by friends, who were incessantly coming up to him. Every now and then he went to the 'infernal' to keep an eye on Yashvin. Levin was enjoying a delightful sense of repose after the mental fatigue of the morning. He was glad that all hostility was at an end with Vronsky, and the sense of peace, decorum, and comfort never left him.

When the game was over, Stepan Arkadyevitch took Levin's arm.

'Well, let us go to Anna's, then. At once? Eh? She is at home. I promised her long ago to bring you. Where were you meaning to spend the evening?'

'Oh, nowhere specially. I promised Sviazhsky to go to the Society of Agriculture. By all means, let us go,' said Levin.

'Very good; come along. Find out if my carriage is here,' Stepan Arkadyevitch said to the waiter.

Levin went up to the table, paid the forty roubles he had lost; paid his bill, the amount of which was in some mysterious way ascertained by the little old waiter who stood at the counter, and swinging his arms he walked through all the rooms to the way out.

IX

'OBLONSKY'S carriage!' the porter shouted in an angry bass. The carriage drove up and both got in. It was only for the first few moments, while the carriage was driving out of the club-house gates, that Levin was still under the influence of the club atmosphere of repose, comfort, and unimpeachable good form. But as soon as the carriage drove out into the street, and he felt it jolting over the uneven road, heard the angry shout of a sledge-driver coming towards them, saw in the uncertain light the red blind of a tavern and the shops, this impression was dissipated, and he began to think over his actions, and to wonder whether he was doing right in going to see Anna. What would Kitty say? But Stepan Arkadyevitch gave him no time for reflection, and, as though divining his doubts, he scattered them.

'How glad I am,' he said, 'that you should know her! You know Dolly has long wished for it. And Lvov's been to see her, and often goes. Though she is my sister,' Stepan Arkadyevitch pursued, 'I don't hesitate to say that she's a remarkable woman. But you will see. Her position is very painful, especially now.'

'Why especially now?'

'We are carrying on negotiations with her husband about a divorce. And he's agreed; but there are difficulties in regard to the son, and the business, which ought to have been arranged long ago, has been dragging on for three months past. As soon as the divorce is over, she will marry Vronsky. How stupid these old ceremonies are, that no one believes in, and which only prevent people being comfortable!' Stepan Arkadyevitch put in. 'Well, then their position will be as regular as mine, as yours.'

'What is the difficulty?' said Levin.

'Oh, it's a long and tedious story! The whole business is in such an anomalous position with us. But the point is she has been for three months in Moscow, where everyone knows her, waiting for the divorce; she goes out nowhere, sees no woman except Dolly, because, do you understand, she doesn't care to have people come as a favour. That fool Princess Varvara, even she has left her, considering this a breach of propriety. Well, you see, in such a position any other woman would not have found resources in herself. But you'll see how she has arranged her life—how calm, how dignified she is. To the left, in the crescent opposite the church!' shouted Stepan Arkadyevitch, leaning out of the window. 'Phew! how hot it is!' he said, in spite of twelve degrees of frost, flinging his open overcoat still wider open.

'But she has a daughter: no doubt she's busy looking after her?' said Levin.

'I believe you picture every woman simply as a female, *une couveuse*,' said Stepan Arkadyevitch. 'If she's occupied, it must be with her children. No, she brings her up capitally, I believe, but one doesn't hear about her. She's busy, in the first place, with what she writes. I see you're smiling ironically, but you're wrong. She's writing a children's book, and doesn't talk about it to anyone, but she read it to me and I gave the manuscript to Vorkuev . . . you know the publisher . . . and he's an author himself too, I fancy. He understands those things, and he says it's a remarkable piece of work. But are you fancying she's an authoress? —not a bit of it. She's a woman with a heart, before everything, but you'll see. Now she has a little English girl with her, and a whole family she's looking after.'

'Oh, something in a philanthropic way?'

'Why, you will look at everything in the worst light. It's not from philanthropy, it's from the heart. They—that is, Vronsky—had a trainer, an Englishman, first-rate in his own line, but a drunkard. He's completely given up to drink—delirium tremens—and the family were cast on the world. She saw them, helped them, got more and more interested in them, and now the whole family is on her hands. But not by way of patronage, you know, helping with money; she's herself preparing the boys in Russian for the high school, and she's taken the little girl to live with her. But you'll see her for yourself.'

The carriage drove into the courtyard, and Stepan Arkadyevitch rang loudly at the entrance where sledges were standing.

And without asking the servant who opened the door whether the lady were at home, Stepan Arkadyevitch walked into the hall. Levin followed him, more and more doubtful whether he was doing right or wrong.

Looking at himself in the glass, Levin noticed that he was red in the face, but he felt certain he was not drunk, and he followed Stepan Arkadyevitch up the carpeted stairs. At the top Stepan Arkadyevitch inquired of the footman, who bowed to him as to an intimate friend, who was with Anna Arkadyevna, and received the answer that it was M. Vorkuev.

'Where are they?'

'In the study.'

Passing through the dining-room, a room not very large, with dark panelled walls, Stepan Arkadyevitch and Levin walked over the soft carpet to the half-dark study, lighted up by a single lamp with a big dark shade. Another lamp with a reflector was hanging on the wall, lighting up a big full-length portrait of a woman, which Levin could not help looking at. It was the portrait of Anna, painted in Italy by Mihailov. While Stepan Arkadyevitch went behind the *treillage*, and the man's voice which had been speaking paused, Levin gazed at the portrait, which stood out from the frame in the brilliant light thrown on it, and he could not tear himself away from it. He positively forgot where he was, and not even hearing what was said, he could not take his eyes off the marvellous portrait. It was not a picture, but a living, charming woman, with black curling hair, with bare arms and shoulders, with a pensive smile on the lips, covered with soft down; triumphantly and softly she looked at him with eyes that baffled him. She was not living only because she was more beautiful than a living woman can be.

'I am delighted!' He heard suddenly near him a voice, unmistakably addressing him, the voice of the very woman he had been admiring in the portrait. Anna had come from behind the *treillage* to meet him, and Levin saw in the dim light of the study the very woman in the portrait, in a dark blue shot gown, not in the same position nor with the same expression, but with the same perfection of beauty which the artist had caught in the portrait. She was less dazzling in reality, but, on the other hand, there was something fresh and seductive in the living woman which was not in the portrait.

X

SHE had risen to meet him, not concealing her pleasure at seeing him; and in the quiet ease with which she held out her little vigorous hand, introduced him to Vorkuev and indicated a red-haired, pretty little girl who was sitting at work, calling her her pupil, Levin recognised and liked the manners of a woman of the great world, always self-possessed and natural.

'I am delighted, delighted,' she repeated, and on her lips these simple words took for Levin's ears a special significance. 'I have known you and liked you a long while, both from your friendship with Stiva and for your wife's sake. . . . I knew her for a very short time, but she left on me the impression of an exquisite flower, simply a flower. And to think she will soon be a mother!'

She spoke easily and without haste, looking now and then from Levin to her brother, and Levin felt that the impression he was making was good, and he felt immediately at home, simple and happy with her, as though he had known her from childhood.

'Ivan Petrovitch and I settled in Alexey's study,' she said in answer to Stepan Arkadyevitch's question whether he might smoke, 'just so as to be able to smoke'—and glancing at Levin, instead of asking whether he would smoke, she pulled closer a tortoiseshell cigar-case and took a cigarette.

'How are you feeling today?' her brother asked her.

'Oh, nothing. Nerves, as usual.'

'Yes, isn't it extraordinarily fine,' said Stepan Arkadyevitch, noticing that Levin was scrutinising the picture.

'I have never seen a better portrait.'

'And extraordinarily like, isn't it?' said Vorkuev.

Levin looked from the portrait to the original. A peculiar brilliance lighted up Anna's face when she felt his eyes on her. Levin flushed, and to cover her confusion would have asked whether she had seen Darya Alexandrovna lately; but at that moment Anna spoke. 'We were just talking, Ivan Petrovitch and I, of Vashtchenkov's last pictures. Have you seen them?'

'Yes, I have seen them,' answered Levin.

'But, I beg your pardon, I interrupted you . . . you were saying? . . .'

Levin asked if she had seen Dolly lately.

'She was here yesterday. She was very indignant with the high school people on Grisha's account. The Latin teacher, it seems, had been unfair to him.'

'Yes, I have seen his pictures. I didn't care for them very much,' Levin went back to the subject she had started.

Levin talked now not at all with that purely businesslike attitude to the subject with which he had been talking all the morning. Every word in his conversation with her had a special significance. And talking to her was pleasant; still pleasanter it was to listen to her.

Anna talked not merely naturally and cleverly, but cleverly and carelessly, attaching no value to her own ideas and giving great weight to the ideas of the person she was talking to.

The conversation turned on the new movement in art, on the new illustrations of the Bible by a French artist. Vorkuev attacked the artist for a realism carried to the point of coarseness.

Levin said that the French had carried conventionality further than anyone, and that consequently they see a great merit in the return to realism. In the fact of not lying they see poetry.

Never had anything clever said by Levin given him so much pleasure as this remark. Anna's face lighted up at once, as at once she appreciated the thought. She laughed.

'I laugh,' she said, 'as one laughs when one sees a very true portrait. What you said so perfectly hits off French art now, painting and literature too, indeed—Zola, Daudet. But perhaps it is always so, that men form their conceptions from fictitious, conventional types, and then—all the *combinaisons* made—they are tired of the fictitious figures and begin to invent more natural, true figures.'

'That's perfectly true,' said Vorkuev.

'So you've been at the club?' she said to her brother.

'Yes, yes, this is a woman!' Levin thought, forgetting himself and staring persistently at her lovely, mobile face, which at that moment was all at once completely transformed. Levin did not hear what she was talking of as she leaned over to her brother, but he was struck by the change of her expression. Her face—so handsome a moment before in its repose—suddenly wore a look of strange curiosity, anger, and pride. But this lasted only an instant. She dropped her eyelids, as though recollecting something.

'Oh, well, but that's of no interest to anyone,' she said, and she turned to the English girl.

'Please order the tea in the drawing-room,' she said in English.

The girl got up and went out.

'Well, how did she get through her examination?' asked Stepan Arkadyevitch.

'Splendidly! She's a very gifted child and a sweet character.'

'It will end in your loving her more than your own.'

'There a man speaks. In love there's no more nor less. I love my daughter with one love, and her with another.'

'I was just telling Anna Arkadyevna,' said Vorkuev, 'that if she were to put a hundredth part of the energy she devotes to this English girl to the public question of the education of Russian children, she would be doing a great and useful work.'

'Yes, but I can't help it; I couldn't do it. Count Alexey Kirillovitch urged me very much' (as she uttered the words *Count Alexey Kirillo-*

vitch she glanced with appealing timidity at Levin, and he unconsciously responded with a respectful and reassuring look), 'he urged me to take up the school in the village. I visited it several times. The children were very nice, but I could not feel drawn to the work. You speak of energy. Energy rests upon love; and come as it will, there's no forcing it. I took to this child—I could not myself say why.'

And she glanced again at Levin. And her smile and her glance—all told him that it was to him only she was addressing her words, valuing his good opinion, and at the same time sure beforehand that they understood each other.

'I quite understand that,' Levin answered. 'It's impossible to give one's heart to a school or such institutions in general, and I believe that that's just why philanthropic institutions always give such poor results.'

She was silent for a while, then she smiled.

'Yes, yes,' she agreed; 'I never could. *Je n'ai pas le cœur assez large* to love a whole asylum of horrid little girls. *Cela ne m'a jamais réussi.* There are so many women who have made themselves *une position sociale* in that way. And now more than ever,' she said with a mournful, confiding expression, ostensibly addressing her brother, but unmistakably intending her words only for Levin, 'now when I have such need of some occupation, I cannot.' And suddenly frowning (Levin saw that she was frowning at herself for talking about herself) she changed the subject. 'I know about you,' she said to Levin; 'that you're not a public-spirited citizen, and I have defended you to the best of my ability.'

'How have you defended me?'

'Oh, according to the attacks made on you. But won't you have some tea?' She rose and took up a book bound in morocco.

'Give it to me, Anna Arkadyevna,' said Vorkuev, indicating the book. 'It's well worth taking up.'

'Oh, no, it's all so sketchy.'

'I told him about it,' Stepan Arkadyevitch said to his sister, nodding at Levin.

'You shouldn't have. My writing is something after the fashion of those little baskets and carving which Liza Mertsalov used to sell me from the prisons. She had the direction of the prison department in that society,' she turned to Levin; 'and they were miracles of patience, the work of those poor wretches.'

And Levin saw a new trait in this woman, who attracted him so extraordinarily. Besides wit, grace, and beauty, she had truth. She had no wish to hide from him all the bitterness of her position. As she said that she sighed, and her face suddenly taking a hard expression, looked as it were turned to stone. With that expression on her face she was more beautiful than ever; but the expression was new; it was utterly unlike that expression, radiant with happiness and creating happiness, which had been caught by the painter in her portrait. Levin looked more than once at the portrait and at her figure, as taking her brother's arm she walked with him to the high doors, and he felt for her a tenderness and pity at which he wondered himself.

She asked Levin and Vorkuev to go into the drawing-room, while she stayed behind to say a few words to her brother. 'About her divorce, about Vronsky, and what he's doing at the club, about me?' wondered Levin. And he was so keenly interested by the question of what she was saying to Stepan Arkadyevitch, that he scarcely heard what Vorkuev was telling him of the qualities of the story for children Anna Arkadyevna had written.

At tea the same pleasant sort of talk, full of interesting matter, continued. There was not a single instant when a subject for conversation was to seek; on the contrary, it was felt that one had hardly time to say what one had to say, and eagerly held back to hear what the others were saying. And all that was said, not only by her, but by Vorkuev and Stepan Arkadyevitch—all, so it seemed to Levin, gained peculiar significance from her appreciation and her criticism. While he followed this interesting conversation, Levin was all the time admiring her—her beauty, her intelligence, her culture, and at the same time her directness and genuine depth of feeling. He listened and talked, and all the while he was thinking of her inner life, trying to divine her feelings. And though he had judged her so severely hitherto, now by some strange chain of reasoning he was justifying her and also sorry for her, and afraid that Vronsky did not fully understand her. At eleven o'clock, when Stepan Arkadyevitch got up to go (Vorkuev had left earlier), it seemed to Levin that he had only just come. Regretfully Levin too rose.

'Good-bye,' she said, holding his hand and glancing into his face with a winning look. 'I am very glad *que la glace est rompue.*'

She dropped his hand, and half closed her eyes.

'Tell your wife that I love her as before, and that if she cannot pardon me my position, then my wish for her is that she may never pardon it. To pardon it, one must go through what I have gone through, and may God spare her that.'

'Certainly, yes, I will tell her . . .' Levin said, blushing.

XI

'WHAT a marvellous, sweet, and unhappy woman!' he was thinking, as he stepped out into the frosty air with Stepan Arkadyevitch.

'Well, didn't I tell you?' said Stepan Arkadyevitch, seeing that Levin had completely won over.

'Yes,' said Levin dreamily, 'an extraordinary woman! It's not her cleverness, but she has such wonderful depth of feeling. I'm awfully sorry for her!'

'Now, please God, everything will soon be settled. Well, well, don't be hard on people in future,' said Stepan Arkadyevitch, opening the carriage door. 'Good-bye; we don't go the same way.'

Still thinking of Anna, of everything, even the simplest phrase in their conversation with her, and recalling the minutest changes in her expression, entering more and more into her position, and feeling sympathy for her, Levin reached home.

At home Kouzma told Levin that Katerina Alexandrovna was quite well, and that her sisters had not long been gone, and he handed him two letters. Levin read them at once in the hall, that he might not overlook them later. One was from Sokolov, his bailiff. Sokolov wrote that the corn could not be sold, that it was fetching only five and a half roubles, and that more than that could not be got for it. The other letter was from his sister. She scolded him for her business being still unsettled.

'Well, we must sell it at five and a half if we can't get more,' Levin decided the first question, which had always before seemed such a weighty one, with extraordinary facility on the spot. 'It's extraordinary how all one's time is taken up here,' he thought, considering the second letter. He felt himself to blame for not having got done what his sister had asked him to do for her. 'Today, again, I've not been to the court, but today I've certainly not had time.' And resolving that he would not fail to do it next day, he went up to his wife. As he went in, Levin rapidly ran through mentally the day he had spent. All the events of the day were conversations, conversations he had heard and taken part in. All the conversations were upon subjects which, if he had been alone at home, he would never have taken up, but here they were very interesting. And all these conversations were right enough, only in two places there was something not quite right. One was what he had said about the carp, the other was something not 'quite the thing' in the tender sympathy he was feeling for Anna.

Levin found his wife low-spirited and dull. The dinner of the three sisters had gone off very well, but then they had waited and waited for him, all of them had felt dull, the sisters had departed, and she had been left alone.

'Well, and what have you been doing?' she asked him, looking straight into his eyes, which shone with rather a suspicious brightness. But that she might not prevent his telling her everything, she concealed her close scrutiny of him, and with an approving smile listened to his account of how he had spent the evening.

'Well, I'm very glad I met Vronsky. I felt quite at ease and natural with him. You understand, I shall try not to see him, but I'm glad that this awkwardness is all over,' he said, and remembering that by way of trying not to see him, he had immediately gone to call on Anna, he blushed. 'We talk about the peasants drinking; I don't know which drinks most, the peasantry or our own class: the peasants do on holidays, but . . .'

But Kitty took not the slightest interest in discussing the drinking habits of the peasants. She saw that he blushed, and she wanted to know why.

'Well, and then where did you go?'

'Stiva urged me awfully to go and see Anna Arkadyevna.'

And as he said this, Levin blushed even more, and his doubts as to whether he had done right in going to see Anna were settled once for all. He knew now that he ought not to have done so.

Kitty's eyes opened in a curious way and gleamed at Anna's name, but controlling herself with an effort, she concealed her emotion and deceived him.

'Oh!' was all she said.

'I'm sure you won't be angry at my going. Stiva begged me to, and Dolly wished it,' Levin went on.

'Oh no!' she said, but he saw in her eyes a constraint that boded him no good.

'She is a very sweet, very, very unhappy, good woman,' he said, telling her about Anna, her occupations, and what she had told him to say to her.

'Yes, of course, she is very much to be pitied,' said Kitty, when he had finished. 'Whom was your letter from?'

He told her, and believing in her calm tone, he went to change his coat.

Coming back, he found Kitty in the same easy-chair. When he went up to her, she glanced at him and broke into sobs.

'What? what is it?' he asked, knowing beforehand what.

'You're in love with that hateful woman; she has bewitched you! I saw it in your eyes. Yes, yes! What can it all lead to? You were drinking at the club, drinking and gambling, and then you went . . . to her of all people! No, we must go away. . . . I shall go away tomorrow.'

It was a long while before Levin could soothe his wife. At last he succeeded in calming her, only by confessing that a feeling of pity, in conjunction with the wine he had drunk, had been too much for him, that he had succumbed to Anna's artful influence, and that he would avoid her. One thing he did with more sincerity confess to was that living so long in Moscow, a life of nothing but conversation, eating and drinking, he was degenerating. They talked till three o'clock in the morning. Only at three o'clock they were sufficiently reconciled to be able to go to sleep.

XII

AFTER taking leave of her guests, Anna did not sit down, but began walking up and down the room. She had unconsciously the whole evening done her utmost to arouse in Levin a feeling of love—as of late she had fallen into doing with all young men—and she knew she had attained her aim, as far as was possible in one evening, with a married and conscientious man. She liked him indeed extremely, and, in spite of the striking difference, from the masculine point of view, between Vronsky and Levin, as a woman she saw something they had in common, which had made Kitty able to love both. Yet as soon as he was out of the room, she ceased to think of him.

One thought, and one only, pursued her in different forms, and refused to be shaken off. 'If I have so much effect on others, on this man, who loves his home and his wife, why is it *he* is so cold to me? . . . not cold exactly, he loves me, I know that! But something new is drawing us apart now. Why wasn't he here all the evening? He told Stiva to say he could not leave Yashvin, and must watch over his play. Is Yashvin a child? But supposing it's true. He never tells a lie. But there's something else in it if it's true. He is glad of an opportunity of showing me that he has other duties; I know that, I submit to that. But why prove that to me? He wants to show me that his love for me is not to interfere with his freedom. But I need no proofs, I need love. He ought to understand all the bitterness of his life for me here in Moscow. Is this life? I am not living, but waiting for an event, which is continually put off and put off. No answer again! And Stiva says he cannot go to Alexey Alexandrovitch. And I can't write again. I can do nothing, can begin nothing, can alter nothing; I hold myself in, I wait, inventing amusements for myself—the English family, writing, reading—but it's all nothing but a sham, it's all the same as morphine. He ought to feel for me,' she said, feeling tears of self-pity coming into her eyes.

She heard Vronsky's abrupt ring and hurriedly dried her tears—not only dried her tears, but sat down by a lamp and opened a book, affecting composure. She wanted to show him that she was displeased that he had not come home as he had promised—displeased only, and not on any account to let him see her distress, and least of all, her self-pity. She might pity herself, but he must not pity her. She did not want strife, she blamed him for wanting to quarrel, but unconsciously put herself into an attitude of antagonism.

'Well, you've not been dull?' he said, eagerly and good-humouredly, going up to her. 'What a terrible passion it is—gambling!'

'No, I've not been dull; I've learned long ago not to be dull. Stiva has been here and Levin.'

'Yes, they meant to come and see you. Well, how did you like Levin?' he said, sitting down beside her.

'Very much. They have not long been gone. What was Yashvin doing?'

'He was winning—seventeen thousand. I got him away. He had really started home, but he went back again, and now he's losing.'

'Then what did you stay for?' she asked, suddenly lifting her eyes to him. The expression of her face was cold and ungracious. 'You told Stiva you were saying on to get Yashvin away. And you have left him there.'

The same expression of cold readiness for the conflict appeared on his face too.

'In the first place, I did not ask him to give you any message; and secondly, I never tell lies. But what's the chief point, I wanted to stay, and I stayed,' he said, frowning. 'Anna, what is it for, why will you?' he said after a moment's silence, bending over towards her, and he opened his hand, hoping she would lay hers in it.

She was glad of this appeal for tenderness. But some strange force of evil would not let her give herself up to her feelings, as though the rules of warfare would not permit her to surrender.

'Of course you wanted to stay, and you stayed. You do everything you want to. But what do you tell me that for? With what object?' she said, getting more and more excited. 'Does anyone contest your rights? But you want to be right, and you're welcome to be right.'

His hand closed, he turned away, and his face wore a still more obstinate expression.

'For you it's a matter of obstinacy,' she said, watching him intently and suddenly finding the right word for that expression that irritated her, 'simply obstinacy. For you it's a question of whether you keep the upper hand of me, while for me . . .' Again she felt sorry for herself, and she almost burst into tears. 'If you knew what it is for me! When I feel as I do now that you are hostile, yes, hostile to me, if you knew what this means for me! If you knew how I feel on the brink of calamity at this instant, how afraid I am of myself!' And she turned away, hiding her sobs.

'But what are you talking about?' he said, horrified at her expression of despair, and again bending over her, he took her hand and kissed it. 'What is it for? Do I seek amusements outside our home? Don't I avoid the society of women?'

'Well, yes! If that were all!' she said.

'Come, tell me what I ought to do to give you peace of mind? I am ready to do anything to make you happy,' he said, touched by her expression of despair; 'what wouldn't I do to save you from distress of any sort, as now, Anna!' he said.

'It's nothing, nothing!' she said. 'I don't know myself whether it's the solitary life, my nerves . . . Come, don't let us talk of it. What about the race? You haven't told me!' she inquired, trying to conceal her triumph at the victory, which had anyway been on her side.

He asked for supper, and began telling her about the races; but in his tone, in his eyes, which became more and more cold, she saw that he did not forgive her for her victory, that the feeling of obstinacy with which she had been struggling had asserted itself again in him. He was colder to her than before, as though he were regretting his surrender. And she, remembering the words that had given her the victory, 'how I feel on the brink of calamity, how afraid I am of myself,' saw that this weapon was a dangerous one, and that it could not be used a second time. And she felt that beside the love that bound them together there had grown up between them some evil spirit of strife, which she could not exorcise from his, and still less from her own heart.

XIII

THERE are no conditions to which a man cannot become used, especially if he sees that all around him are living in the same way. Levin could not have believed three months before that he could have gone quietly to sleep in the condition in which he was that day, that leading an aimless, irrational life, living too beyond his means, after drinking to excess (he could not call what happened at the club anything else), forming inappropriately friendly relations with a man with whom his wife had once been in love, and a still more inappropriate call upon a woman who could only be called a lost woman, after being fascinated by that woman and causing his wife distress—he could still go quietly to sleep. But under the influence of fatigue, a sleepless night, and the wine he had drunk, his sleep was sound and untroubled.

At five o'clock the creak of a door opening waked him. He jumped up and looked round. Kitty was not in bed beside him. But there was a light moving behind the screen, and he heard her steps.

'What is it? . . .what is it?' he said, half-asleep. 'Kitty! What is it?'

'Nothing,' she said, coming from behind the screen with a candle in her hand. 'I felt unwell,' she said, smiling a particularly sweet and meaning smile.

'What? has it begun?' he said in terror. 'We ought to send . . .' and hurriedly he reached after his clothes.

'No, no,' she said, smiling and holding his hand. 'It's sure to be nothing. I was rather unwell, only a little. It's all over now.'

And getting into bed, she blew out the candle, lay down and was still. Though he thought her stillness suspicious, as though she were holding her breath, and still more suspicious the expression of peculiar tenderness and excitement with which, as she came from behind the screen, she said 'nothing', he was so sleepy that he fell asleep at once. Only later he remembered the stillness of her breathing, and understood all that must have been passing in her sweet, precious heart while she lay beside him, not stirring, in anticipation of the greatest event in a woman's life. At seven o'clock he was waked by the touch of her hand on his shoulder, and a gentle whisper. She seemed struggling between regret at waking him, and the desire to talk to him.

'Kostya, don't be frightened. It's all right. But I fancy . . . We ought to send for Lizaveta Petrovna.'

The candle was lighted again. She was sitting up in bed, holding some knitting, which she had been busy upon during the last few days.

'Please, don't be frightened, it's all right. I'm not a bit afraid,' she said, seeing his scared face, and she pressed his hand to her bosom and then to her lips.

He hurriedly jumped up, hardly awake, and kept his eyes fixed on her, as he put on his dressing-gown; then he stopped, still looking at her. He had to go, but he could not tear himself from her eyes. He thought he loved her face, knew her expression, her eyes, but never had he seen it like this. How hateful and horrible he seemed to himself, thinking of the distress he had caused her yesterday. Her flushed face, fringed with soft curling hair under her night-cap, was radiant with joy and courage.

Though there was so little that was complex or artificial in Kitty's character in general, Levin was struck by what was revealed now, when suddenly all disguises were thrown off and the very kernel of her soul shone in her eyes. And in this simplicity and nakedness of her soul, she, the very woman he loved in her, was more manifest than ever. She looked at him, smiling; but all at once her brows twitched, she threw up her head, and going quickly up to him, clutched his hand and pressed close up to him, breathing her hot breath upon him. She was in pain and was, as it were, complaining to him of her suffering. And for the first minute, from habit, it seemed to him that he was to blame. But in her eyes there was a tenderness that told him that she was far from reproaching him, that she loved him for her sufferings. 'If not I, who is to blame for it?' he thought unconsciously, seeking someone responsible for this suffering for him to punish; but there was no one responsible. She was suffering, complaining, and triumphing in her sufferings, and rejoicing in them, and loving them. He saw that something sublime was being accomplished in her soul, but what? He could not make it out. It was beyond his understanding.

'I have sent to mamma. You go quickly to fetch Lizaveta Petrovna ... Kostya! ... Nothing, it's over.'

She moved away from him and rang the bell.

'Well, go now; Pasha's coming. I am all right.'

And Levin saw with astonishment that she had taken up the knitting she had brought in in the night and had begun working at it again.

As Levin was going out of one door, he heard the maid-servant come in at the other. He stood at the door and heard Kitty giving exact directions to the maid, and beginning to help her move the bedstead.

He dressed, and while they were putting in his horses, as a hired sledge was not to be seen yet, he ran again up to the bedroom, not on tiptoe, it seemed to him, but on wings. Two maid-servants were carefully moving something in the bedroom.

Kitty was walking about knitting rapidly and giving directions.

'I'm going for the doctor. They have sent for Lizaveta Petrovna, but I'll go on there too. Isn't there anything wanted? Yes, shall I go to Dolly's?'

She looked at him, obviously not hearing what he was saying.

'Yes, yes. Do go,' she said quickly, frowning and waving her hand to him.

He had just gone into the drawing-room, when suddenly a plaintive moan sounded from the bedroom, smothered instantly. He stood still, and for a long while he could not understand.

'Yes, that is she,' he said to himself, and clutching at his head he ran downstairs.

'Lord have mercy on us! pardon us! aid us!' he repeated the words that for some reason came suddenly to his lips. And he, an unbeliever, repeated these words not with his lips only. At that instant he knew that all his doubts, even the impossibility of believing with his reason, of which he was aware in himself, did not in the least hinder his turning to God. All of that now floated out of his soul like dust. To whom was he to turn if not to Him in whose hands he felt himself, his soul, and his love?

The horse was not yet ready, but feeling a peculiar concentration of his physical forces and his intellect on what he had to do, he started off on foot without waiting for the horse, and told Kouzma to overtake him.

At the corner he met a night cabman driving hurriedly. In the little sledge, wrapped in a velvet cloak, sat Lizaveta Petrovna with a kerchief round her head. 'Thank God! thank God!' he said, overjoyed to recognise her little fair face which wore a peculiarly serious, even stern expression. Telling the driver not to stop, he ran along beside her.

'For two hours, then? Not more?' she inquired. 'You should let Pyotr Dmitrievitch know, but don't hurry him. And get some opium at the chemist's.'

'So you think that it may go on well? Lord have mercy on us and help us!' Levin said, seeing his own horse driving out of the gate. Jumping into the sledge beside Kouzma, he told him to drive to the doctor's.

XIV

THE doctor was not yet up, and the footman said that 'he had been up late, and had given orders not to be waked, but would get up soon.' The footman was cleaning the lamp-chimneys, and seemed very busy about them. This concentration of the footman upon his lamps, and his indifference to what was passing in Levin, at first astounded him, but immediately on considering the question he realised that no one knew or was bound to know his feelings, and that it was all the more necessary to act calmly, sensibly, and resolutely to get through this wall of indifference and attain his aim.

'Don't be in a hurry or let anything slip,' Levin said to himself, feeling a greater and greater flow of physical energy and attention to all that lay before him to do.

Having ascertained that the doctor was not getting up, Levin considered various plans, and decided on the following one; that Kouzma should go for another doctor, while he himself should go to the chemist's for opium, and if when he came back the doctor had not yet begun to get up, he would either by tipping the footman, or by force, wake the doctor at all hazards.

At the chemist's the lank shopman sealed up a packet of powders for a coachman who stood waiting, and refused him opium with the same callousness with which the doctor's footman had cleaned his lamp-chimneys. Trying not to get flurried or out of temper, Levin mentioned the names of the doctor and midwife, and explaining what the opium was needed for, tried to persuade him. The assistant inquired in German whether he should give it, and receiving an affirmative reply from behind the partition, he took a bottle and a funnel, deliberately poured the opium from a bigger bottle into a little one, stuck on a label, sealed it up, in spite of Levin's request that he would not do so, and was about to wrap it up too. This was more than Levin could stand; he took the bottle firmly out of his hands, and ran to the big glass doors. The doctor was not even now getting up, and the footman, busy now in putting down the rugs, refused to wake him. Levin deliberately took out a ten-rouble note, and careful to speak slowly, though losing no time over the business, he handed him the note, and explained that Pyotr Dmitrievitch (what a great and important personage he seemed to Levin now, this Pyotr Dmitrievitch, who had been of so little consequence in his eyes before!) had promised to come at any time; that he would certainly not be angry; and that he must therefore wake him at once.

The footman agreed, and went upstairs, taking Levin into the waiting-room.

Levin could hear through the door the doctor coughing, moving about, washing, and saying something. Three minutes passed; it seemed to Levin that more than an hour had gone by. He could not wait any longer.

'Pyotr Dmitrievitch, Pyotr Dmitrievitch!' he said in an imploring voice at the open door. 'For God's sake, forgive me! See me as you are. It's been going on more than two hours already.'

'In a minute; in a minute!' answered a voice, and to his amazement Levin heard the doctor was smiling as he spoke.

'For one instant.'

'In a minute.'

Two minutes more passed while the doctor was putting on his boots, and two minutes more while the doctor put on his coat and combed his hair.

'Pyotr Dmitrievitch!' Levin was beginning again in a plaintive voice, just as the doctor came in dressed and ready. 'These people have no conscience,' thought Levin. 'Combing his hair, while we're dying!'

'Good-morning!' the doctor said to him, shaking hands, and, as it were, teasing him with his composure. 'There's no hurry. Well now?'

Trying to be as accurate as possible, Levin began to tell him every unnecessary detail of his wife's condition, interrupting his account repeatedly with entreaties that the doctor would come with him at once.

'Oh, you needn't be in any hurry. You don't understand, you know. I'm certain I'm not wanted, still I've promised, and if you like, I'll come. But there's no hurry. Please sit down; won't you have some coffee?'

Levin stared at him with eyes that asked whether he was laughing at him; but the doctor had no notion of making fun of him.

'I know, I know,' the doctor said, smiling; 'I'm a married man myself; and at these moments we husbands are very much to be pitied. I've a patient whose husband always takes refuge in the stables on such occasions.'

'But what do you think, Pyotr Dmitrievitch? Do you suppose it may go all right?'

'Everything points to a favourable issue.'

'So you'll come immediately?' said Levin, looking wrathfully at the servant who was bringing in the coffee.

'In an hour's time.'

'Oh, for mercy's sake!'

'Well, let me drink my coffee, anyway.'

The doctor started upon his coffee. Both were silent.

'The Turks are really getting beaten, though. Did you read yesterday's telegrams?' said the doctor, munching some roll.

'No, I can't stand it!' said Levin, jumping up. 'So you'll be with us in a quarter of an hour?'

'In half an hour.'

'On your honour?'

When Levin got home, he drove up at the same time as the princess, and they went up to the bedroom door together. The princess had tears in her eyes, and her hands were shaking. Seeing Levin, she embraced him, and burst into tears.

'Well, my dear Lizaveta Petrovna?' she queried, clasping the hand of the midwife, who came out to meet them with a beaming and anxious face.

'She's going on well,' she said; 'persuade her to lie down. She will be easier so.'

From the moment when he had waked up and understood what was going on, Levin had prepared his mind to bear resolutely what was before him, and without considering or anticipating anything, to avoid upsetting his wife, and on the contrary to soothe her and keep up her courage. Without allowing himself even to think of what was to come, of how it would end, judging from his inquiries as to the usual duration of these ordeals, Levin had in his imagination braced himself to bear up and to keep a tight rein on his feelings for five hours, and it had seemed to him he could do this. But when he came back from the doctor's and saw her sufferings again, he fell to repeating more and more frequently: 'Lord, have mercy on us, and succour us!' He sighed, and flung his head up, and began to feel afraid he could not bear it, that he would burst into tears or run away. Such agony it was to him. And only one hour had passed.

But after that hour there passed another hour, two hours, three, the full five hours he had fixed as the furthest limit of his sufferings, and the position was still unchanged; and he was still bearing it because there was nothing to be done but bear it; every instant feeling that he had reached the utmost limits of his endurance, and that his heart would break with sympathy and pain.

But still the minutes passed by and the hours, and still hours more, and his misery and horror grew and were more and more intense.

All the ordinary conditions of life, without which one can form no conception of anything, had ceased to exist for Levin. He lost all sense of time. Minutes—those minutes when she sent for him and he held her moist hand, that would squeeze his hand with extraordinary violence and then push it away—seemed to him hours, and hours seemed to him minutes. He was surprised when Lizaveta Petrovna asked him to light a candle behind a screen, and he found that it was five o'clock in the afternoon. If he had been told it was only ten o'clock in the morning, he would not have been more surprised. Where he was all this time, he knew as little as the time of anything. He saw her swollen face, sometimes bewildered and in agony, sometimes smiling and trying to reassure him. He saw the old princess too, flushed and overwrought, with her grey curls in disorder, forcing herself to gulp down her tears, biting her lips; he saw Dolly too and the doctor, smoking fat cigarettes, and Lizaveta Petrovna with a firm, resolute, reassuring face, and the old prince walking up and down the hall with a frowning face. But why they came in and went out, where they were, he did not know. The princess was with the doctor in the bedroom, then in the study, where a table set for dinner suddenly appeared; then she was not there, but Dolly was. Then Levin remembered he had been sent somewhere. Once he had been sent to move a table and sofa. He had done this eagerly, thinking it had to be done for her sake, and only later on he found it was his own bed he had been getting ready. Then he had been sent to the study to ask the doctor something. The doctor had answered and then had said something about the irregularities in the municipal council. Then he had been sent to the bedroom to help the old princess to move the holy picture in its silver and gold setting, and with the princess's old waiting-maid he had clambered on a shelf to reach it and had broken the little lamp, and the old servant had tried to reassure him about the lamp and about his wife, and he carried the holy picture and set it at Kitty's head, carefully tucking it in behind the pillow. But where, when, and why all this had happened, he could not tell. He did not understand why the old princess took his hand, and looking compassionately at him, begged him not to worry himself, and Dolly persuaded him to eat something and led him out of the room, and even the doctor looked seriously and with commiseration at him and offered him a drop of something.

All he knew and felt was that what was happening was what had happened nearly a year before in the hotel of the country town at the deathbed of his brother Nikolay. But that had been grief—this was joy. Yet that grief and this joy were alike outside all the ordinary conditions of life; they were loop-holes, as it were, in that ordinary life through which there came glimpses of something sublime. And in the contemplation of this sublime something the soul was exalted to inconceivable heights of which it had before had no conception, while reason lagged behind, unable to keep up with it.

'Lord, have mercy on us, and succour us!' he repeated to himself incessantly, feeling, in spite of his long and, as it seemed, complete alienation from religion, that he turned to God just as trustfully and simply as he had in his childhood and first youth.

All this time he had two distinct spiritual conditions. One was away from her, with the doctor, who kept smoking one fat cigarette after another and extinguishing them on the edge of a full ash-tray, with Dolly, and with the old prince, where there was talk about dinner, about politics, about Marya Petrovna's illness, and where Levin suddenly forgot for a minute what was happening, and felt as though he had waked up from sleep; the other was in her presence, at her pillow, where his heart seemed breaking and still did not break from sympathetic suffering, and he prayed to God without ceasing. And every time he was brought back from a moment of oblivion by a scream reaching him from the bedroom, he fell into the strange error that had come upon him the first minute. Every time he heard a shriek, he jumped up, ran to justify himself, remembered on the way that he was not to blame, and he longed to defend her, to help her. But as he looked at her, he saw again that help was impossible, and he was filled with terror and prayed: 'Lord, have mercy on us, and help us!' And as time went on, both these conditions became more intense; the calmer he became away from her, completely forgetting her, the more agonising became both her sufferings and his feeling of helplessness before them. He jumped up, would have liked to run away, but ran to her.

Sometimes, when again and again she called upon him, he blamed her; but seeing her patient, smiling face, and hearing the words, 'I am worrying you,' he threw the blame on God; but thinking of God, at once he fell to beseeching God to forgive him and have mercy.

XV

HE did not know whether it was late or early. The candles had all burned out. Dolly had just been in the study and had suggested to the doctor that he should lie down. Levin sat listening to the doctor's stories of a quack mesmeriser and looking at the ashes of his cigarette. There had been a period of repose, and he had sunk into oblivion. He had completely forgotten what was going on now. He heard the doctor's chat and understood it. Suddenly there came an unearthly shriek. The shriek was so awful that Levin did not even jump up, but holding his breath, gazed in terrified inquiry at the doctor. The doctor put his head on one side, listened, and smiled approvingly. Everything was so extraordinary that nothing could strike Levin as strange. 'I suppose it must be so,' he thought, and still sat where he was. Whose scream was this? He jumped up, ran on tip-toe to the bedroom, edged round Lizaveta Petrovna and the princess, and took up his position at Kitty's pillow. The scream had subsided, but there was some change now. What it was he did not see and did not comprehend, and he had no wish to see or comprehend. But he saw it by the face of Lizaveta Petrovna. Livaveta Petrovna's face was stern and pale, and still as resolute, though her jaws were twitching, and her eyes were fixed intently on Kitty. Kitty's swollen and agonised face, a tress of hair clinging to her moist brow, was turned to him and sought his eyes. Her lifted hands asked for his hands. Clutching his chill hands in her moist ones, she began squeezing them to her face.

'Don't go, don't go! I'm not afraid, I'm not afraid!' she said rapidly. 'Mamma, take my earrings. They bother me. You're not afraid? Quick, quick, Lizaveta Petrovna . . .'

She spoke quickly, very quickly, and tried to smile. But suddenly her face was drawn, she pushed him away.

'Oh, this is awful! I'm dying, I'm dying! Go away!' she shrieked, and again he heard that unearthly scream.

Levin clutched at his head and ran out of the room.

'It's nothing, it's nothing, it's all right,' Dolly called after him.

But they might say what they liked, he knew now that all was over. He stood in the next room, his head leaning against the doorpost, and heard shrieks, howls such as he had never heard before, and he knew that what had been Kitty was uttering these shrieks. He had long ago ceased to wish for the child. By now he loathed this child. He did not even wish for her life now, all he longed for was the end of this awful anguish.

'Doctor! What is it? What is it? By God!' he said, snatching at the doctor's hand as he came up.

'It's the end,' said the doctor. And the doctor's face was so grave as he said it that Levin took *the end* as meaning her death.

Beside himself, he ran into the bedroom. The first thing he saw was the face of Lizaveta Petrovna. It was even more frowning and stern. Kitty's face he did not know. In the place where it had been was something that was fearful in its strained distortion and in the sounds that came from it. He fell down with his head on the wooden framework of the bed, feeling that his heart was bursting. The awful scream never paused, it became still more awful, and as though it had reached the utmost limit of terror, suddenly it ceased. Levin could not believe his ears, but there could be no doubt; the scream had ceased and he heard a subdued stir and bustle, and hurried breathing, and her voice, gasping, alive, tender, and blissful, uttered softly, 'It's over!'

He lifted his head. With her hands hanging exhausted on the quilt, looking extraordinarily lovely and serene, she looked at him in silence and tried to smile, and could not.

And suddenly, from the mysterious and awful far-away world in which he had been living for the last twenty-two hours, Levin felt himself all in an instant borne back to the old everyday world, glorified though now, by such a radiance of happiness that he could not bear it. The strained chords snapped, sobs and tears of joy which he had never foreseen rose up with such violence that his whole body shook, that for long they prevented him from speaking.

Falling on his knees before the bed, he held his wife's hand before his lips and kissed it, and the hand, with a weak movement of the fingers, responded to his kiss. And meanwhile, there at the foot of the bed, in the deft hands of Lizaveta Petrovna, like a flickering light in a lamp, lay the life of a human creature, which had never existed before, and which would now with the same right, with the same importance to itself, live and create in its own image.

'Alive! alive! And a boy too! Set your mind at rest!' Levin heard Lizaveta Petrovna saying, as she slapped the baby's back with a shaking hand.

'Mamma, is it true?' said Kitty's voice.

The princess's sobs were all the answer she could make. And in the midst of the silence there came in unmistakable reply to the mother's question, a voice quite unlike the subdued voices speaking in the room. It was the bold, clamorous, self-assertive squall of the new human being, who had so incomprehensibly appeared.

If Levin had been told before that Kitty was dead, and that he had died with her, and that their children were angels, and that God was standing before him, he would have been surprised at nothing. But now, coming back to the world of reality, he had to make great mental efforts to take in that she was alive and well, and that the creature squalling so desperately was his son. Kitty was alive, her agony was over. And he was unutterably happy. That he understood; he was completely happy in it. But the baby? Whence, why, who was he? . . . He could not get used to the idea. It seemed to him something extraneous, superfluous, to which he could not accustom himself.

XVI

At ten o'clock the old prince, Sergey Ivanovitch, and Stepan Arkadyevitch were sitting at Levin's. Having inquired after Kitty, they had dropped into conversation upon other subjects. Levin heard them, and unconsciously, as they talked, going over the past, over what had been up to that morning, he thought of himself as he had been yesterday till that point. It was as though a hundred years had passed since then. He felt himself exalted to unattainable heights, from which he studiously lowered himself so as not to wound the people he was talking to. He talked, and was all the time thinking of his wife, of her condition now, of his son, in whose existence he tried to school himself into believing. The whole world of woman, which had taken for him since his marriage a new value he had never suspected before, was now so exalted that he could not take it in in his imagination. He heard them talk of yesterday's dinner at the club, and thought: 'What is happening with her now? Is she asleep? How is she? What is she thinking of? Is he crying, my son Dmitri?' And in the middle of the conversation, in the middle of a sentence, he jumped up and went out of the room.

'Send me word if I can see her,' said the prince.

'Very well, in a minute,' answered Levin, and without stopping, he went to her room.

She was not asleep, she was talking gently with her mother, making plans about the christening.

Carefully set to rights, with hair well-brushed, in a smart little cap with some blue in it, her arms out on the quilt, she was lying on her back. Meeting his eyes, her eyes drew him to her. Her face, bright before, brightened still more as he drew near her. There was the same change in it from earthly to unearthly that is seen in the face of the dead. But then it means farewell, here it meant welcome. Again a rush of emotion, such as he had felt at the moment of the child's birth, flooded his heart. She took his hand and asked him if he had slept. He could not answer, and turned away, struggling with his weakness.

'I have had a nap, Kostya!' she said to him; 'and I am so comfortable now.'

She looked at him, but suddenly her expression changed.

'Give him to me,' she said, hearing the baby's cry. 'Give him to me, Lizaveta Petrovna, and he shall look at him.'

'To be sure, his papa shall look at him,' said Lizaveta Petrovna, getting up and bringing something red, and queer, and wriggling. 'Wait a minute, we'll make him tidy first,' and Lizaveta Petrovna laid the red wobbling thing on the bed, began untrussing and trussing up the baby, lifting it up and turning it over with one finger and powdering it with something.

Levin, looking at the tiny, pitiful creature, made strenuous efforts to discover in his heart some traces of fatherly feeling for it. He felt nothing towards it but disgust. But when it was undressed and he caught a glimpse of wee, wee, little hands, little feet, saffron-coloured, with little toes, too; and positively with a little big toe different from the rest, and when he saw Lizaveta Petrovna closing the wide-open little hands, as though they were soft springs, and putting them into linen garments, such pity for the little creature came upon him, and such terror that she would hurt it, that he held her hand back.

Lizaveta Petrovna laughed.

'Don't be frightened, don't be frightened!'

When the baby had been put to rights and transformed into a firm doll, Lizaveta Petrovna dandled it as though proud of her handiwork, and stood a little away so that Levin might see his son in all his glory.

Kitty looked sideways in the same direction, never taking her eyes off the baby. 'Give him to me! give him to me!' she said, and even made as though she would sit up.

'What are you thinking of, Katerina Alexandrovna, you mustn't move like that! Wait a minute. I'll give him to you. Here we're showing papa what a fine fellow we are!'

And Lizaveta Petrovna, with one hand supporting the wobbling head, lifted up on the other arm the strange, limp, red creature, whose head was lost in its swaddling-clothes. But it had a nose, too, and slanting eyes and smacking lips.

'A splendid baby!' said Lizaveta Petrovna.

Levin sighed with mortification. This splendid baby excited in him no feeling but disgust and compassion. It was not at all the feeling he had looked forward to.

He turned away while Lizaveta Petrovna put the baby to the unaccustomed breast.

Suddenly laughter made him look round. The baby had taken the breast.

'Come, that's enough, that's enough!' said Lizaveta Petrovna, but Kitty would not let the baby go. He fell asleep in her arms.

'Look, now,' said Kitty, turning the baby so that he could see it. The aged-looking little face suddenly puckered up still more and the baby sneezed.

Smiling, hardly able to restrain his tears, Levin kissed his wife and went out of the dark room. What he felt towards this little creature was utterly unlike what he had expected. There was nothing cheerful and joyous in the feeling; on the contrary, it was a new torture of apprehension. It was the consciousness of a new sphere of liability to pain. And this sense was so painful at first, the apprehension lest this helpless creature should suffer was so intense, that it prevented him from noticing the strange thrill of senseless joy and even pride that he had felt when the baby sneezed.

XVII

STEPAN ARKADYEVITCH'S affairs were in a very bad way.

The money for two-thirds of the forest had all been spent already, and he had borrowed from the merchant in advance at ten per cent discount almost all the remaining third. The merchant would not give more, especially as Darya Alexandrovna, for the first time that winter insisting on her right to her own property, had refused to sign the receipt for the payment of the last third of the forest. All his salary went on household expenses and in payment of petty debts that could not be put off. There was positively no money.

This was unpleasant and awkward, and in Stepan Arkadyevitch's opinion things could not go on like this. The explanation of the position was, in his view, to be found in the fact that his salary was too small. The post he filled had been unmistakably very good five years ago, but it was so no longer.

Petrov, the bank director, had twelve thousand; Sventitsky, a company director, had seventeen thousand; Mitin, who had founded a bank, received fifty thousand.

'Clearly I've been napping, and they've overlooked me,' Stepan Arkadyevitch thought about himself. And he began keeping his eyes and ears open, and towards the end of the winter he had discovered a very good berth and had formed a plan of attack upon it, at first from Moscow through aunts, uncles, and friends, and then, when the matter was well advanced, in the spring, he went himself to Petersburg. It was one of those snug, lucrative berths of which there are so many more nowadays than there used to be, with incomes ranging from one thousand to fifty thousand roubles. It was the post of secretary of the committee of the amalgamated agency of the southern railways, and of certain banking companies. This position, like all such appointments, called for such immense energy and such varied qualifications, that it was difficult for them to be found united in any one man. And since a man combining all the qualifications was not to be found, it was at least better that the post be filled by an honest than by a dishonest man. And Stepan Arkadyevitch was not merely an honest man—unemphatically—in the common acceptation of the words, he was an honest man—emphatically—in that special sense which the word has in Moscow, when they talk of an 'honest' politician, an 'honest' writer, an 'honest' newspaper, an 'honest' institution, an 'honest' tendency, meaning not simply that the man or the institution is not dishonest, but that they are capable on occasion of taking a line of their own in opposition to the authorities.

Stepan Arkadyevitch moved in those circles in Moscow in which that expression had come into use, was regarded there as an honest man, and so had more right to this appointment than others.

The appointment yielded an income from seven to ten thousand a year, and Oblonsky could fill it without giving up his government position. It was in the hands of two ministers, one lady, and two Jews, and all these people, though the way had been paved already with them, Stepan Arkadyevitch had to see in Petersburg. Besides this business, Stepan Arkadyevitch had promised his sister Anna to obtain from Karenin a definite answer on the question of divorce. And begging fifty roubles from Dolly, he set off for Petersburg.

Stepan Arkadyevitch sat in Karenin's study listening to his report on the causes of the unsatisfactory position of Russian finance, and only waiting for the moment when he would finish to speak about his own business or about Anna.

'Yes, that's very true,' he said, when Alexey Alexandrovitch took off the pince-nez, without which he could not read now, and looked inquiringly at his former brother-in-law, 'that's very true in particular cases, but still the principle of our day is freedom.'

'Yes, but I lay down another principle, embracing the principle of freedom,' said Alexey Alexandrovitch, with emphasis on the word 'embracing', and he put on his pince-nez again, so as to read the passage in which this statement was made. And turning over the beautifully written wide-margined manuscript, Alexey Alexandrovitch read aloud over again the conclusive passage.

'I don't advocate protection for the sake of private interests, but for the public weal, and for the lower and upper classes equally,' he said, looking over his pince-nez at Oblonsky. 'But *they* cannot grasp that, *they* are taken up now with personal interests, and carried away by phrases.'

Stepan Arkadyevitch knew that when Karenin began to talk of what *they* were doing and thinking, the persons who would not accept his report and were the cause of everything wrong in Russia, that it was coming near the end. And so now he eagerly abandoned the principle of free-trade, and fully agreed. Alexey Alexandrovitch paused, thoughtfully turning over the pages of his manuscript.

'Oh, by the way,' said Stepan Arkadyevitch, 'I wanted to ask you, some time when you see Pomorsky, to drop him a hint that I should be very glad to get that new appointment of secretary of the committee of the amalgamated agency of the Southern Railways and banking companies.' Stepan Arkadyevitch was familiar by now with the title of the post he coveted, and he brought it out rapidly without mistake.

Alexey Alexandrovitch questioned him as to the duties of this new committee, and pondered. He was considering whether the new committee would not be acting in some way contrary to the views he had been advocating. But as the influence of the new committee was of a very complex nature, and his views were of very wide application, he could not decide this straight off, and taking off his pince-nez, he said—

'Of course, I can mention it to him; but what is your reason precisely for wishing to obtain the appointment?'

'It's a good salary, rising to nine thousand, and my means . . .'

'Nine thousand!' repeated Alexey Alexandrovitch, and he frowned. The high figure of the salary made him reflect that on that side Stepan Arkadyevitch's proposed position ran counter to the main tendency of his own projects of reform, which always leaned towards economy.

'I consider, and I have embodied my views in a note on the subject, that in our day these immense salaries are evidence of the unsound economic *assiette* of our finances.'

'But what's to be done?' said Stepan Arkadyevitch. 'Suppose a bank director gets ten thousand—well, he's worth it; or an engineer gets twenty thousand—after all, it's a growing thing, you know!'

'I assume that a salary is the price paid for a commodity, and it ought to conform with the law of supply and demand. If the salary is fixed without any regard for that law, as, for instance, when I see two engineers leaving college together, both equally well trained and efficient, and one getting forty thousand while the other is satisfied with two; or when I see lawyers and hussars, having no special qualifications, appointed directors of banking companies with immense salaries, I conclude that the salary is not fixed in accordance with the law of supply and demand, but simply through personal interest. And this is an abuse of great gravity in itself, and one that reacts injuriously on the government service. I consider . . .'

Stepan Arkadyevitch made haste to interrupt his brother-in-law.

'Yes; but you must agree that it's a new institution of undoubted utility that's being started. After all, you know, it's a growing thing! What they lay particular stress on is the thing being carried on honestly,' said Stepan Arkadyevitch with emphasis.

But the Moscow significance of the word 'honest' was lost on Alexey Alexandrovitch.

'Honesty is only a negative qualification,' he said.

'Well, you'll do me a great service, anyway,' said Stepan Arkadyevitch, 'by putting in a word to Pomorsky—just in the way of conversation. . . .'

'But I fancy it's more in Volgarinov's hands,' said Alexey Alexandrovitch.

'Volgarinov has fully assented, as far as he's concerned,' said Stepan Arkadyevitch, turning red. Stepan Arkadyevitch reddened at the mention of that name, because he had been that morning at the Jew Volgarinov's, and the visit had left an unpleasant recollection.

Stepan Arkadyevitch believed most positively that the committee in which he was trying to get an appointment was a new, genuine, and honest public body, but that morning when Volgarinov had—intentionally, beyond a doubt—kept him two hours waiting with other petitioners in his waiting-room, he had suddenly felt uneasy.

Whether he was uncomfortable that he, a descendant of Rurik, Prince Oblonsky, had been kept for two hours waiting to see a Jew, or that for the first time in his life he was not following the example of his ancestors in serving the government, but was turning off into a new career, anyway he was very uncomfortable. During these two hours in Volgarinov's waiting-room Stepan Arkadyevitch, stepping jauntily about the room, pulling his whiskers, entering into conversation with the other petitioners, and inventing an epigram on his position, assiduously concealed from others, and even from himself, the feeling he was experiencing.

But all the time he was uncomfortable and angry, he could not have said why—whether because he could not get his epigram just right, or from some other reason. When at last Volgarinov had received him with exaggerated politeness and unmistakable triumph at his humiliation, and had all but refused the favour asked of him, Stepan Arkadyevitch had made haste to forget it all as soon as possible. And now, at the mere recollection, he blushed.

XVIII

'NOW there is something I want to talk about, and you know what it is. About Anna,' Stepan Arkadyevitch said, pausing for a brief space, and shaking off the unpleasant impression.

As soon as Oblonsky uttered Anna's name, the face of Alexey Alexandrovitch was completely transformed; all the life was gone out of it, and it looked weary and dead.

'What is it exactly that you want from me?' he said, moving in his chair and snapping his pince-nez.

'A definite settlement, Alexey Alexandrovitch, some settlement of the position. I'm appealing to you' ('not as an injured husband,' Stepan Arkadyevitch was going to say, but afraid of wrecking his negotiation by this, he changed the words) 'not as a statesman' (which did not sound *à propos*), 'but simply as a man, and a good-hearted man and a Christian. You must have pity on her,' he said.

'That is, in what way precisely?' Karenin said softly.

'Yes, pity on her. If you had seen her as I have!—I have been spending all the winter with her—you would have pity on her. Her position is awful, simply awful!'

'I had imagined,' answered Alexey Alexandrovitch in a higher, almost shrill voice, 'that Anna Arkadyevna had everything she had desired for herself.'

'Oh, Alexey Alexandrovitch, for heaven's sake, don't let us indulge in recriminations! What is past is past, and you know what she wants and is waiting for—divorce.'

'But I believe Anna Arkadyevna refuses a divorce, if I make it a condition to leave me my son. I replied in that sense, and supposed that the matter was ended. I consider it at an end,' shrieked Alexey Alexandrovitch.

'But, for heaven's sake, don't get hot!' said Stepan Arkadyevitch, touching his brother-in-law's knee. 'The matter is not ended. If you will allow me to recapitulate, it was like this: when you parted, you were as magnanimous as could possibly be; you were ready to give her everything—freedom, divorce even. She appreciated that. No, don't think that. She did appreciate it—to such a degree that at the first moment, feeling how she had wronged you, she did not consider and could not consider everything. She gave up everything. But experience, time, have shown that her position is unbearable, impossible.'

'The life of Anna Arkadyevna can have no interest for me,' Alexey Alexandrovitch put in, lifting his eyebrows.

'Allow me to disbelieve that,' Stepan Arkadyevitch replied gently. 'Her position is intolerable for her, and of no benefit to anyone whatever. She has deserved it, you will say. She knows that and asks you for nothing; she says plainly that she dare not ask you. But I, all of us, her relatives, all who love her, beg you, entreat you. Why should she suffer? Who is any the better for it?'

'Excuse me, you seem to put me in the position of the guilty party,' observed Alexey Alexandrovitch.

'Oh no, oh no, not at all! please understand me,' said Stepan Arkadyevitch, touching his hand again, as though feeling sure this physical contact would soften his brother-in-law. 'All I say is this: her position is intolerable, and it might be alleviated by you, and you will lose nothing by it. I will arrange it all for you, so that you'll not notice it. You did promise it, you know.'

'The promise was given before. And I had supposed that the question of my son had settled the matter. Besides, I had hoped that Anna Arkadyevna had enough generosity . . .' Alexey Alexandrovitch articulated with difficulty, his lips twitching and his face white.

'She leaves it all to your generosity. She begs, she implores one thing of you—to extricate her from the impossible position in which she is placed. She does not ask for her son now. Alexey Alexandrovitch, you are a good man. Put yourself in her position for a minute. The question of divorce for her in her position is a question of life and death. If you had not promised it once, she would have reconciled herself to her position, she would have gone on living in the country. But you promised it, and she wrote to you, and moved to Moscow. And here she's been for six months in Moscow, where every chance meeting cuts her to the heart, every day expecting an answer. Why, it's like keeping a condemned criminal for six months with the rope round his neck, promising him perhaps death, perhaps mercy. Have pity on her, and I will undertake to arrange everything. *Vos scrupules* . . .'

'I am not talking about that, about that . . .' Alexey Alexandrovitch interrupted with disgust. 'But, perhaps, I promised what I had no right to promise.'

'So you go back from your promise.'

'I have never refused to do all that is possible, but I want time to consider how much of what I promised is possible.'

'No, Alexey Alexandrovitch!' cried Oblonsky, jumping up, 'I won't believe that! She's unhappy as only an unhappy woman can be, and you cannot refuse in such . . .'

'As much of what I promised as is possible. *Vous professez d'être libre penseur.* But I as a believer cannot, in a matter of such gravity, act in opposition to the Christian law.'

'But in Christian societies and among us, as far as I'm aware, divorce is allowed,' said Stepan Arkadyevitch. 'Divorce is sanctioned even by our church. And we see . . .'

'It is allowed, but not in the sense . . .'

'Alexey Alexandrovitch, you are not like yourself,' said Oblonsky, after a brief pause. 'Wasn't it you (and didn't we all appreciate it in you?) who forgave everything, and moved simply by Christian feeling was ready to make any sacrifice? You said yourself: if a man take thy coat, give him thy cloak also, and now . . .'

'I beg,' said Alexey Alexandrovitch shrilly, getting suddenly on to his feet, white and his jaws twitching, 'I beg you to drop this . . . to drop . . . this subject!'

'Oh no! Oh, forgive me, forgive me if I have wounded you,' said Stepan Arkadyevitch, holding out his hand with a smile of embarrassment; 'but like a messenger I have simply performed the commission given me.'

Alexey Alexandrovitch gave him his hand, pondered a little, and said—

'I must think it over and seek for guidance. The day after tomorrow I will give you a final answer,' he said, after considering a moment.

XIX

STEPAN ARKADYEVITCH was about to go away when Korney came in to announce—

'Sergey Alexyevitch!'

'Who's Sergey Alexyevitch?' Stepan Arkadyevitch was beginning, but he remembered immediately.

'Ah, Seryozha!' he said aloud. 'Sergey Alexyevitch! I thought it was the director of a department. Anna asked me to see him too,' he thought.

And he recalled the timid, piteous expression with which Anna had said to him at parting: 'Anyway, you will see him. Find out exactly where he is, who is looking after him. And Stiva . . . if it were possible! Could it be possible?' Stepan Arkadyevitch knew what was meant by that 'if it were possible,'—if it were possible to arrange the divorce so as to let her have her son. . . . Stepan Arkadyevitch saw now that it was no good to dream of that, but still he was glad to see his nephew.

Alexey Alexandrovitch reminded his brother-in-law that they never spoke to the boy of his mother, and he begged him not to mention a single word about her.

'He was very ill after that interview with his mother, which we had not foreseen,' said Alexey Alexandrovitch. 'Indeed, we feared for his life. But with rational treatment, and sea-bathing in the summer, he regained his strength, and now, by the doctor's advice, I have let him go to school. And certainly the companionship of school has had a good effect on him, and he is perfectly well, and making good progress.'

'What a fine fellow he's grown! He's not Seryozha now, but quite full-fledged Sergey Alexyevitch!' said Stepan Arkadyevitch, smiling, as he looked at the handsome, broad-shouldered lad in blue coat and long trousers, who walked in alertly and confidently. The boy looked healthy and good-humoured. He bowed to his uncle as to a stranger, but recognising him, he blushed and turned hurriedly away from him, as though offended and irritated at something. The boy went up to his father and handed him a note of the marks he had gained in school.

'Well, that's very fair,' said his father, 'you can go.'

'He's thinner and taller, and has grown out of being a child into a boy; I like that,' said Stepan Arkadyevitch. 'Do you remember me?'

The boy looked back quickly at his uncle.

'Yes, *mon uncle*,' he answered, glancing at his father, and again he looked downcast.

His uncle called him to him, and took his hand.

'Well, and how are you getting on?' he said, wanting to talk to him, and not knowing what to say.

The boy, blushing and making no answer, cautiously drew his hand away. As soon as Stepan Arkadyevitch let go his hand, he glanced doubtfully at his father, and like a bird set free he darted out of the room.

A year had passed since the last time Seryozha had seen his mother. Since then he had heard nothing more of her. And in the course of that year he had gone to school, and made friends among his schoolfellows. The dreams and memories of his mother, which had made him ill after seeing her, did not occupy his thoughts now. When they came back to him, he studiously drove them away, regarding them as shameful and girlish, below the dignity of a boy and a schoolboy. He knew that his father and mother were separated by some quarrel, he knew that he had to remain with his father, and he tried to get used to the idea.

He disliked seeing his uncle, so like his mother, for it called up those memories which he was ashamed of. He disliked it all the more as from some words he had caught as he waited at the study door, and still more from the faces of his father and uncle, he guessed that they must have been talking of his mother. And to avoid condemning the father with whom he lived and on whom he was dependent, and, above all, to avoid giving way to sentimentality, which he considered so degrading, Seryozha tried not to look at this uncle who had come to disturb his peace of mind, and not to think of what he recalled to him.

But when Stepan Arkadyevitch, going out after him, saw him on the stairs, and calling to him, asked him how he spent his playtime at school, Seryozha talked more freely to him away from his father's presence.

'We have a railway now,' he said in answer to his uncle's question. 'It's like this, do you see: two sit on a bench—they're the passengers; and one stands up straight on the bench. And all are harnessed to it by their arms or by their belts, and they run through all the rooms—the doors are left open beforehand. Well, and it's pretty hard work being the conductor!'

'That's the one that stands?' Stepan Arkadyevitch inquired, smiling.

'Yes, you want pluck for it, and cleverness too, especially when they stop all of a sudden, or someone falls down.'

'Yes, that must be a serious matter,' said Stepan Arkadyevitch, watching with mournful interest the eager eyes, like his mother's; not childish now—no longer fully innocent. And though he had promised Alexey Alexandrovitch not to speak of Anna, he could not restrain himself.

'Do you remember your mother?' he asked suddenly.

'No, I don't,' Seryozha said quickly. He blushed crimson, and his face clouded over. And his uncle could get nothing more out of him. His tutor found his pupil on the staircase half an hour later, and for a long while he could not make out whether he was ill-tempered or crying.

'What is it? I expect you hurt yourself when you fell down?' said the tutor. 'I told you it was a dangerous game. And we shall have to speak to the director.'

'If I had hurt myself, nobody should have found it out, that's certain.'

'Well, what is it, then?'

'Leave me alone! If I remember, or if I don't remember . . . what business is it of his? Why should I remember? Leave me in peace!' he said, addressing not his tutor, but the whole world.

XX

STEPAN ARKADYEVITCH, as usual, did not waste his time in Petersburg. In Petersburg, besides business, his sister's divorce, and his coveted appointment, he wanted, as he always did, to freshen himself up, as he said, after the mustiness of Moscow.

In spite of its *cafés chantants* and its omnibuses, Moscow was yet a stagnant bog. Stepan Arkadyevitch always felt it. After living for some time in Moscow, especially in close relations with his family, he was conscious of a depression of spirits. After being a long time in Moscow without a change, he reached a point when he positively began to be worrying himself over his wife's ill-humour and reproaches, over his children's health and education, and the petty details of his official work; even the fact of being in debt worried him. But he had only to go and stay a little while in Petersburg, in the circle there in which he moved, where people lived—really lived—instead of vegetating as in Moscow, and all such ideas vanished and melted away at once, like wax before the fire. His wife? . . . Only that day he had been talking to Prince Tchetchensky. Prince Tchetchensky had a wife and family, grown-up pages in the corps, . . . and he had another illegitimate family of children also. Though the first family was very nice too, Prince Tchetchensky felt happier in his second family; and he used to take his eldest son with him to his second family, and told Stepan Arkadyevitch that he thought it good for his son, enlarging his ideas. What would have been said to that in Moscow?

His children? In Petersburg children did not prevent their parents from enjoying life. The children were brought up in schools, and there was no trace of the wild idea that prevailed in Moscow, in Lvov's household, for instance, that all the luxuries of life were for the children, while the parents have nothing but work and anxiety. Here people understand that a man is in duty bound to live for himself, as every man of culture should live.

His official duties? Official work here was not the stiff, hopeless drudgery that it was in Moscow. Here there was some interest in official life. A chance meeting, a service rendered, a happy phrase, a knack of facetious mimicry, and a man's career might be made in a trice. So it had been with Bryantsev, whom Stepan Arkadyevitch had met the previous day, and who was one of the highest functionaries in government now. There was some interest in official work like that.

The Petersburg attitude on pecuniary matters had an especially soothing effect on Stepan Arkadyevitch. Bartnyansky, who must spend at least fifty thousand to judge by the style he lived in, had made an interesting comment the day before on that subject.

As they were talking before dinner, Stepan Arkadyevitch said to Bartnyansky—

'You're friendly, I fancy, with Mordvinsky; you might do me a favour: say a word to him, please, for me. There's an appointment I should like to get—secretary of the agency . . .'

'Oh, I shan't remember all that, if you tell me . . . But what possesses you to have to do with railways and Jews? . . . Take it as you will, it's a low business.'

Stepan Arkadyevitch did not say to Bartnyansky that it was a 'growing thing'—Bartnyansky would not have understood that.

'I want the money, I've nothing to live on.'

'You're living, aren't you?'

'Yes, but in debt.'

'Are you, though? Heavily?' said Bartnyansky sympathetically.

'Very heavily: twenty thousand.'

Bartnyansky broke into good-humoured laughter.

'Oh, lucky fellow!' said he. 'My debts mount up to a million and a half, and I've nothing, and still I can live, as you see!'

And Stepan Arkadyevitch saw the correctness of this view not in words only but in actual fact. Zhivahov owed three hundred thousand, and hadn't a farthing to bless himself with, and he lived, and in style too! Count Krivtsov was considered a hopeless case by everyone, and yet he kept two mistresses. Petrovsky had run through five millions, and still lived in just the same style, and was even a manager in the financial department with a salary of twenty thousand. But besides this, Petersburg had physically an agreeable effect on Stepan Arkadyevitch. It made him younger. In Moscow he sometimes found a grey hair in his head, dropped asleep after dinner, stretched, walked slowly upstairs, breathing heavily, was bored by the society of young women, and did not dance at balls. In Petersburg he always felt ten years younger.

His experience in Petersburg was exactly what had been described to him on the previous day by Prince Pyotr Oblonsky, a man of sixty, who had just come back from aboard—

'We don't know the way to live here,' said Pyotr Oblonsky. 'I spent the summer in Baden, and you wouldn't believe it, I felt quite a young man. At a glimpse of a pretty woman, my thoughts . . .One dines and drinks a glass of wine, and feels strong and ready for anything. I came home to Russia—had to see my wife, and, what's more, go to my country place; and there, you'd hardly believe it, in a fortnight I'd got into a dressing-gown and given up dressing for dinner. Needn't say I had no thoughts left for pretty women. I became quite an old gentleman. There was nothing left for me but to think of my eternal salvation. I went off to Paris—I was as right as could be at once.'

Stepan Arkadyevitch felt exactly the difference that Pyotr Oblonsky described. In Moscow he degenerated so much that if he had had to be there for long together, he might in good earnest have come to considering his salvation; in Petersburg he felt himself a man of the world again.

Between Princess Betsy Tverskoy and Stepan Arkadyevitch there had long existed rather curious relations. Stepan Arkadyevitch always flirted with her in jest, and used to say to her, also in jest, the most unseemly things, knowing that nothing delighted her so much. The day after his conversation with Karenin, Stepan Arkadyevitch went to see her, and felt so youthful that in this jesting flirtation and nonsense he recklessly went so far that he did not know how to extricate himself, as unluckily he was so far from being attracted by her that he thought her positively disagreeable. What made it hard to change the conversation was the fact that he was very attractive to her. So that he was considerably relieved at the arrival of Princess Myaky, which cut short their *tête-à-tête*.

'Ah, so you're here!' said she when she saw him. 'Well, and what news of your poor sister? You needn't look at me like that,' she added. 'Ever since they've all turned against her, all those who're a thousand times worse than she, I've thought she did a very fine thing. I can't forgive Vronsky for not letting me know when she was in Petersburg. I'd have gone to see her and gone about with her everywhere. Please give her my love. Come, tell me about her.'

'Yes, her position is very difficult; she . . .' began Stepan Arkadyevitch, in the simplicity of his heart accepting as sterling coin Princess Myaky's words 'tell me about her'. Princess Myaky interrupted him immediately, as she always did, and began talking herself.

'She's done what they all do, except me—only they hide it. But she wouldn't be deceitful, and she did a fine thing. And she did better still in throwing up that crazy brother-in-law of yours. You must excuse me. Everybody used to say he was so clever, so very clever; I was the only one that said he was a fool. Now that he's so thick with Lidia Ivanovna and Landau, they all say he's crazy, and I should prefer not to agree with everybody, but this time I can't help it.'

'Oh, do please explain,' said Stepan Arkadyevitch; 'what does it mean? Yesterday I was seeing him on my sister's behalf, and I asked him to give me a final answer. He gave me no answer, and said he would think it over. But this morning, instead of an answer, I received an invitation from Countess Lidia Ivanovna for this evening.'

'Ah, so that's it, that's it!' said Princess Myaky gleefully, 'they're going to ask Landau what he's to say.'

'Ask Landau? What for? Who or what's Landau?'

'What! you don't know Jules Landau, *le fameux Jules Landau, le clairvoyant*? He's crazy too, but on him your sister's fate depends. See what comes of living in the provinces—you know nothing about anything. Landau, do you see, was a *commis* in a shop in Paris, and he went to a doctor's; and in the doctor's waiting-room he fell asleep, and in his sleep he began giving advice to all the patients. And wonderful advice it was! Then the wife of Yury Meledinsky—you know, the invalid?—heard of this Landau, and had him to see her husband. And he cured her husband, though I can't say that I see he did much good, for he's just as feeble a creature as ever he was, but they believed in him, and took him along with them and brought him to Russia. Here there's been a general rush to him, and he's begun doctoring everyone. He cured Countess Bezzubov, and she took a fancy to him that she adopted him.'

'Adopted him?'

'Yes, as her son. He's not Landau any more now, but Count Bezzubov. That's neither here nor there, though; but Lidia—I'm very fond of her, but she has a screw loose somewhere—has lost her heart to this Landau now, and nothing is settled now in her house or Alexey Alexandrovitch's without him, and so your sister's fate is now in the hands of Landau, *alias* Count Bezzubov.'

XXI

AFTER a capital dinner and a great deal of cognac drunk at Bartnyansky's, Stepan Arkadyevitch, only a little later than the appointed time, went into Countess Lidia Ivanovna's.

'Who else is with the countess?—a Frenchman?' Stepan Arkadyevitch asked the hall-porter, as he glanced at the familiar overcoat of Alexey Alexandrovitch and a queer, rather artless-looking overcoat with clasps.

'Alexey Alexandrovitch Karenin and Count Bezzubov,' the porter answered severely.

'Princess Myaky guessed right,' thought Stepan Arkadyevitch, as he went upstairs. 'Curious! It would be quite as well, though, to get on friendly terms with her. She has immense influence. If she would say a word to Pomorsky, the thing would be a certainty.'

It was still quite light out of doors, but in Countess Lidia Ivanovna's little drawing-room the blinds were drawn and the lamps lighted. At a round table under a lamp sat the countess and Alexey Alexandrovitch, talking softly. A short, thinnish man, very pale and handsome, with feminine hips and knock-kneed legs, with fine brilliant eyes and long hair lying on the collar of his coat, was standing at the other end of the room gazing at the portraits on the wall. After greeting the lady of the house and Alexey Alexandrovitch, Stepan Arkadyevitch could not resist glancing once more at the unknown man.

'Monsieur Landau!' the countess addressed him with a softness and caution that impressed Oblonsky. And she introduced them.

Landau looked round hurriedly, came up, and smiling, laid his moist, lifeless hand in Stepan Arkadyevitch's outstretched hand and immediately walked away and fell to gazing at the portraits again. The countess and Alexey Alexandrovitch looked at each other significantly.

'I am very glad to see you, particularly today,' said Countess Lidia Ivanovna, pointing Stepan Arkadyevitch to a seat beside Karenin.

'I introduced you to him as Landau,' she said in a soft voice, glancing at the Frenchman, and again immediately after at Alexey Alexandrovitch, 'but he is really Count Bezzubov, as you're probably aware. Only he does not like the title.'

'Yes, I heard so,' answered Stepan Arkadyevitch; 'they say he completely cured Countess Bezzubov.'

'She was here today, poor thing!' the countess said, turning to Alexey Alexandrovitch. 'This separation is awful for her. It's such a blow to her!'

'And he positively is going?' queried Alexey Alexandrovitch.

'Yes, he's going to Paris. He heard a voice yesterday,' said Countess Lidia Ivanovna, looking at Stepan Arkadyevitch.

'Ah, a voice!' repeated Oblonsky, feeling that he must be as circumspect as he possibly could in this society, where something peculiar was going on, or was to go on, to which he had not the key.

A moment's silence followed, after which Countess Lidia Ivanovna, as though approaching the main topic of conversation, said with a fine smile to Oblonsky—

'I've known you for a long while, and am very glad to make a closer acquaintance with you. *Les amis de nos amis sont nos amis.* But to be a true friend, one must enter into the spiritual state of one's friend, and I fear that you are not doing so in the case of Alexey Alexandrovitch. You understand what I mean?' she said, lifting her fine pensive eyes.

'In part, countess, I understand the position of Alexey Alexandrovitch . . .' said Oblonsky. Having no clear idea what they were talking about, he wanted to confine himself to generalities.

'The change is not in his external position,' Countess Lidia Ivanovna said sternly, following with eyes of love the figure of Alexey Alexandrovitch as he got up and crossed over to Landau; 'his heart is changed, a new heart has been vouchsafed him, and I fear you don't fully apprehend the change that has taken place in him.'

'Oh, well, in general outlines I can conceive the change. We have always been friendly, and now . . .' said Stepan Arkadyevitch, responding with a sympathetic glance to the expression of the countess, and mentally balancing the question with which of the two ministers she was not intimate, so as to know about which to ask her to speak for him.

'The change that has taken place in him cannot lessen his love for his neighbours; on the contrary, that change can only intensify love in his heart. But I am afraid you do not understand me. Won't you have some tea?' she said, with her eyes indicating the footman, who was handing round tea on a tray.

'Not quite, countess. Of course, his misfortune . . .'

'Yes, a misfortune which has proved the highest happiness, when his heart was made new, was filled full of it,' she said, gazing with eyes full of love at Stepan Arkadyevitch.

'I do believe I might ask her to speak to both of them,' thought Stepan Arkadyevitch.

'Oh, of course, countess,' he said; 'but I imagine such changes are a matter so private that no one, even the most intimate friend, would care to speak of them.'

'On the contrary! We ought to speak freely and help one another.'

'Yes, undoubtedly so, but there is such a difference of convictions, and besides . . .' said Oblonsky with a soft smile.

'There can be no difference where it is a question of holy truth.'

'Oh no, of course; but . . .' and Stepan Arkadyevitch paused in confusion. He understood at last that they were talking of religion.

'I fancy he will fall asleep immediately,' said Alexey Alexandrovitch in a whisper full of meaning, going up to Lidia Ivanovna.

Stepan Arkadyevitch looked round. Landau was sitting at the window, leaning on his elbow and the back of his chair, his head drooping. Noticing that all eyes were turned on him he raised his head and smiled a smile of childlike artlessness.

'Don't take any notice,' said Lidia Ivanovna, and she lightly moved a chair up for Alexey Alexandrovitch. 'I have observed . . .' she was beginning, when a footman came into the room with a letter. Lidia Ivanovna rapidly ran her eyes over the note, and excusing herself, wrote an answer with extraordinary rapidity, handed it to the man, and came back to the table. 'I have observed,' she went on, 'that Moscow people, especially the men, are more indifferent to religion than anyone.'

'Oh no, countess, I thought Moscow people had the reputation of being the firmest in the faith,' answered Stepan Arkadyevitch.

'But as far as I can make out, you are unfortunately one of the indifferent ones,' said Alexey Alexandrovitch, turning to him with a weary smile.

'How anyone can be indifferent!' said Lidia Ivanovna.

'I am not so much indifferent on that subject as I am waiting in suspense,' said Stepan Arkadyevitch, with his most deprecating smile. 'I hardly think that the time for such questions has come yet for me.'

Alexey Alexandrovitch and Lidia Ivanovna looked at each other.

'We can never tell whether the time has come for us or not,' said Alexey Alexandrovitch severely. 'We ought not to think whether we are ready or not ready. God's grace is not guided by human considerations: sometimes it comes not to those that strive for it, and comes to those that are unprepared, like Saul.'

'No, I believe it won't be just yet,' said Lidia Ivanovna, who had been meanwhile watching the movements of the Frenchman. Landau got up and came to them.

'Do you allow me to listen?' he asked.

'Oh yes; I did not want to disturb you,' said Lidia Ivanovna, gazing tenderly at him; 'sit here with us.'

'One has only not to close one's eyes to shut out the light,' Alexey Alexandrovitch went on.

'Ah, if you know the happiness we know, feeling His presence ever in our hearts!' said Countess Lidia Ivanovna with a rapturous smile.

'But a man may feel himself unworthy sometimes to rise to that height,' said Stepan Arkadyevitch, conscious of hypocrisy in admitting this religious height, but at the same time unable to bring himself to acknowledge his free-thinking views before a person who, by a single word to Pomorsky, might procure him the coveted appointment.

'That is, you mean that sin keeps him back?' said Lidia Ivanovna. 'But that is a false idea. There is no sin for believers, their sin has been atoned for. *Pardon,*' she added, looking at the footman, who came in again with another letter. She read it and gave a verbal answer: 'To-morrow at the Grand Duchess's say. For the believer sin is not,' she went on.

'Yes, but faith without works is dead,' said Stepan Arkadyevitch, recalling the phrase from the catechism, and only by his smile clinging to his independence.

'There you have it—from the epistle of St. James,' said Alexey Alexandrovitch, addressing Lidia Ivanovna, with a certain reproachfulness in his tone. It was unmistakably a subject they had discussed more than once before. 'What harm has been done by the false interpretation of that passage! Nothing holds men back from belief like that misinterpretation. "I have not works, so I cannot believe," though all the while that is not said. But the very opposite is said.'

'Striving for God, saving the soul by fasting,' said Countess Lidia Ivanovna, with disgusted contempt, 'those are the crude ideas of our monks. . . . Yet that is nowhere said. It is far simpler and easier,' she added, looking at Oblonsky with the same encouraging smile with which at court she encouraged youthful maids of honour, disconcerted by the new surroundings of the court.

'We are saved by Christ who suffered for us. We are saved by faith,' Alexey Alexandrovitch chimed in, with a glance of approval at her words.

'*Vous comprenez l'anglais?*' asked Lidia Ivanovna, and receiving a reply in the affirmative, she got up and began looking through a shelf of books.

'I want to read him "Safe and Happy," or "Under the Wing,"' she said, looking inquiringly at Karenin. And finding the book, and sitting down again in her place, she opened it. 'It's very short. In it is described the way by which faith can be reached, and the happiness, above all earthly bliss, with which it fills the soul. The believer cannot be unhappy because he is not alone. But you will see.' She was just settling herself to read when the footman came in again. 'Madame Borozdin? Tell her, tomorrow at two o'clock. Yes,' she said, putting her finger in the place in the book, and gazing before her with her fine pensive eyes, 'that is how true faith acts. You know Marie Sanin? You know about her trouble? She lost her only child. She was in despair. And what happened? She found this comforter, and she thanks God now for the death of her child. Such is the happiness faith brings!'

'Oh yes, that is most . . .' Stepan Arkadyevitch, glad they were going to read, and let him have a chance to collect his faculties. 'No, I see I'd better not ask her about anything today,' he thought. 'If only I can get out of this without putting my foot in it!'

'It will be dull for you,' said Countess Lidia Ivanovna, addressing Landau; 'you don't know English, but it's short.'

'Oh, I shall understand,' said Landau, with the same smile, and he closed his eyes. Alexey Alexandrovitch and Lidia Ivanovna exchanged meaning glances, and the reading began.

XXII

STEPAN ARKADYEVITCH felt completely nonplussed by the strange talk which he was hearing for the first time. The complexity of Petersburg, as a rule, had a stimulating effect on him, rousing him out of his Moscow stagnation. But he liked these complications, and understood them only in the circles he knew and was at home in. In these unfamiliar surroundings he was puzzled and disconcerted, and could not get his bearings. As he listened to Countess Lidia Ivanovna, aware of the beautiful, artless—or perhaps artful, he could not decide which—eyes of Landau fixed upon him, Stepan Arkadyevitch began to be conscious of a peculiar heaviness in his head.

The most incongruous ideas were in confusion in his head. 'Marie Sanin is glad her child's dead . . . How good a smoke would be now! . . . To be saved, one need only believe, and the monks don't know how the thing's to be done, but Countess Lidia Ivanovna does know . . . And why is my head so heavy? Is it the cognac, or all this being so queer? Anyway, I fancy I've done nothing unsuitable so far. But, anyway, it won't do to ask her now. They say they make one say one's prayers. I only hope they won't make me! That'll be too imbecile. And what stuff it is she's reading! but she has a good accent. Landau—Bezzubov—what's he Bezzubov for?' All at once Stepan Arkadyevitch became aware that his lower jaw was uncontrollably forming a yawn. He pulled his whiskers to cover the yawn, and shook himself together. But soon after he became aware that he was dropping asleep and on the very point of snoring. He recovered himself at the very moment when the voice of Countess Lidia Ivanovna was saying 'he's asleep'. Stepan Arkadyevitch started with dismay, feeling guilty and caught. But he was reassured at once by seeing that the words 'he's asleep' referred not to him, but to Landau. The Frenchman was asleep as well as Stepan Arkadyevitch. But Stepan Arkadyevitch's being asleep would have offended them, as he thought (though even this, he thought, might not be so, as everything seemed so queer), while Landau's being asleep delighted them extremely, especially Countess Lidia Ivanovna.

'*Mon ami*,' said Lidia Ivanovna, carefully holding the folds of her silk gown so as not to rustle, and in her excitement calling Karenin not Alexey Alexandrovitch, but '*mon ami*,' '*donnez-lui la main. Vous voyez?* Sh!' she hissed at the footman as he came in again. 'Not at home.'

The Frenchman was asleep, or pretending to be asleep, with his head on the back of his chair, and his moist hand, as it lay on his knee, made faint movements, as though trying to catch something. Alexey Alexandrovitch got up, tried to move carefully, but stumbled against the table, went up and laid his hand in the Frenchman's hand. Stepan Arkadyevitch got up too, and opening his eyes wide, trying to wake himself up if he was asleep, he looked first at one and then at the other. It was all real. Stepan Arkadyevitch felt that his head was getting worse and worse.

'*Que la personne qui est arrivée la dernière, celle qui demande, qu'elle sorte! Qu'elle sorte!*' articulated the Frenchman, without opening his eyes.

'*Vous m'excuserez, mais vous voyez . . . Revenez vers dix heures, encore mieux demain.*'

'*Qu'elle sorte!*' repeated the Frenchman impatiently.

'*C'est moi, n'est-ce pas?*' And receiving an answer in the affirmative, Stepan Arkadyevitch, forgetting the favour he had meant to ask of Lidia Ivanovna, and forgetting his sister's affairs, caring for nothing, but filled with the sole desire to get away as soon as possible, went out on tiptoe and ran out into the street as though from a plague-stricken house. For a long while he chatted and joked with his cabdriver, trying to recover his spirits.

At the French theatre where he arrived for the last act, and afterwards at the Tatar restaurant after his champagne, Stepan Arkadyevitch felt a little refreshed in the atmosphere he was used to. But still he felt quite unlike himself all that evening.

On getting home to Pyotr Oblonsky's, where he was staying, Stepan Arkadyevitch found a note from Betsy. She wrote to him that she was very anxious to finish their interrupted conversation, and begged him to come next day. He had scarcely read this note, and frowned at its contents, when he heard below the ponderous tramp of the servants, carrying something heavy.

Stepan Arkadyevitch went out to look. It was the rejuvenated Pyotr Oblonsky. He was so drunk that he could not walk upstairs; but he told them to set him on his legs when he saw Stepan Arkadyevitch, and clinging to him, walked with him into his room and there began telling him how he had spent the evening, and fell asleep doing so.

Stepan Arkadyevitch was in very low spirits, which happened rarely with him, and for a long while he could not go to sleep. Everything he could recall to his mind, everything was disgusting; but most disgusting of all, as if it were something shameful, was the memory of the evening he had spent at Countess Lidia Ivanovna's.

Next day he received from Alexey Alexandrovna a final answer, refusing to grant Anna's divorce, and he understood that this decision was based on what the Frenchman had said in his real or pretended trance.

XXIII

IN order to carry through any undertaking in family life, there must necessarily be either complete division between the husband and wife, or loving agreement. When the relations of a couple are vacillating and neither one thing nor the other, no sort of enterprise can be undertaken.

Many families remain for years in the same place, though both husband and wife are sick of it, simply because there is neither complete division nor agreement between them.

Both Vronsky and Anna felt life in Moscow insupportable in the heat and dust, when the spring sunshine was followed by the glare of summer, and all the trees in the boulevards had long since been in full leaf, and the leaves were covered with dust. But they did not go back to Vozdvizhenskoe, as they had arranged to do long before; they went staying on in Moscow, though they both loathed it, because of late there had been no agreement between them.

The irritability that kept them apart had no external cause, and all efforts to come to an understanding intensified it, instead of removing it. It was an inner irritation, grounded in her mind on the conviction that his love had grown less; in his, on regret that he had put himself for her sake in a difficult position, which she, instead of lightening, made still more difficult. Neither of them gave full utterance to their sense of grievance, but they considered each other in the wrong, and tried on every pretext to prove this to one another.

In her eyes the whole of him, with all his habits, ideas, desires, with all his spiritual and physical temperament, was one thing—love for women, and that love, she felt, ought to be entirely concentrated on her alone. That love was less; consequently, as she reasoned, he must have transferred part of his love to other women or to another woman—and she was jealous. She was jealous not of any particular woman but of the decrease of his love. Not having got an object for her jealousy, she was on the lookout for it. At the slightest hint she transferred her jealousy from one object to another. At one time she was jealous of those low women with whom he might so easily renew his old bachelor ties; then she was jealous of the society women he might meet; then she was jealous of the imaginary girl whom he might want to marry, for whose sake he would break with her. And this last form of jealousy tortured her most of all, especially as he had unwarily told her, in a moment of frankness, that his mother knew him so little that she had had the audacity to try and persuade him to marry the young Princess Sorokin.

And being jealous of him, Anna was indignant against him and found grounds for indignation in everything. For everything that was difficult in her position she blamed him. The agonising condition of suspense she had passed at Moscow, the tardiness and indecision of Alexey Alexandrovitch, her solitude—she put it all down to him. If he had loved her, he would have seen all the bitterness of her position, and would have rescued her from it. For her being in Moscow and not in the country, he was to blame too. He could not live buried in the country as she would have liked to do. He must have society, and he had put her in this awful position, the bitterness of which he would not see. And again, it was his fault that she was for ever separated from her son.

Even the rare moments of tenderness that came from time to time did not soothe her; in his tenderness now she saw a shade of complacency, of self-confidence, which had not been of old, and which exasperated her.

It was dusk. Anna was alone, and waiting for him to come back from a bachelor dinner. She walked up and down in his study (the room where the noise from the street was least heard), and thought over every detail of their yesterday's quarrel. Going back from the well-remembered, offensive words of the quarrel to what had been the ground of it, she arrived at last at its origin. For a long while she could hardly believe that their dissension had arisen from a conversation so inoffensive, of so little moment to either. But so it actually had been. It all arose from his laughing at the girls' high schools, declaring they were useless, while she defended them. He had spoken slightingly of women's education in general, and had said that Hannah, Anna's English protégée, had not the slightest need to know anything of physics.

This irritated Anna. She saw in this a contemptuous reference to her occupations. And she bethought her of a phrase to pay him back for the pain he had given her. 'I don't expect you to understand me, my feelings, as anyone who loved me might, but simple delicacy I did expect,' she said.

And he had actually flushed with vexation, and had said something unpleasant. She could not recall her answer, but at that point, with an unmistakable desire to wound her too, he had said—

'I feel no interest in your infatuation over this girl, that's true, because I see it's unnatural.'

The cruelty with which he shattered the world she had built up for herself so laboriously to enable her to endure her hard life, the injustice with which he had accused her of affectation, of artificiality, aroused her.

'I am very sorry that nothing but what's coarse and material is comprehensible and natural to you,' she said, and walked out of the room.

When he had come in to her yesterday evening, they had not referred to the quarrel, but both felt that the quarrel had been smoothed over, but was not at an end.

Today he had not been at home all day, and she felt so lonely and wretched in being on bad terms with him that she wanted to forget it all, to forgive him, and be reconciled with him; she wanted to throw the blame on herself and to justify him.

'I am myself to blame. I'm irritable, I'm insanely jealous. I will make it up with him, and we'll go away to the country, there I shall be more at peace.'

'Unnatural!' She suddenly recalled the word that had stung her most of all, not so much the word itself as the intent to wound her with which it was said. 'I know what he meant; he meant—unnatural, not loving my own daughter, to love another person's child. What does he know of love for children, of my love for Seryozha, whom I've sacrificed for him? But that wish to wound me! No, he loves another woman, it must be so.'

And perceiving that, while trying to regain her peace of mind, she had gone round the same circle that she had been round so often before, and had come back to her former state of exasperation, she was horrified at herself. 'Can it be impossible? Can it be beyond me to control myself?' she said to herself, and began again from the beginning. 'He's truthful, he's honest, he loves me. I love him, and in a few days the divorce will come. What more do I want? I want peace of mind and trust, and I will take the blame on myself. Yes, now when he comes in, I will tell him I was wrong, though I was not wrong, and we will go away tomorrow.'

And to escape thinking any more, and being overcome by irritability, she rang, and ordered the boxes to be brought up for packing their things for the country.

At ten o'clock Vronsky came in.

XXIV

'WELL, was it nice?' she asked, coming out to meet him with a penitent and meek expression.

'Just as usual,' he answered, seeing at a glance that she was in one of her good moods. He was used by now to these transitions, and he was particularly glad to see it today, as he was in a specially good humour himself.

'What do I see? Come, that's good!' he said, pointing to the boxes in the passage.

'Yes, we must go. I went out for a drive, and it was so fine I longed to be in the country. There's nothing to keep you, is there?'

'It's the one thing I desire. I'll be back directly, and we'll talk it over; I only want to change my coat. Order some tea.'

And he went into his room.

There was something mortifying in the way he had said 'Come, that's good,' as one says to a child when it leaves off being naughty, and still more mortifying was the contrast between her penitent and his self-confident tone; and for one instant she felt the lust of strife rising up in her again, but making an effort she conquered it, and met Vronsky as good-humouredly as before.

When he came in she told him, partly repeating phrases she had prepared beforehand, how she had spent the day, and her plans for going away.

'You know it came to me almost like an inspiration,' she said. 'Why wait here for the divorce? Won't it be just the same in the country? I can't wait any longer! I don't want to go on hoping, I don't want to hear anything about the divorce. I have made up my mind it shall not have any more influence on my life. Do you agree?'

'Oh yes!' he said, glancing uneasily at her excited face.

'What did you do? Who was there?' she said, after a pause.

Vronsky mentioned the names of the guests. 'The dinner was first-rate, and the boat race, and it was all pleasant enough, but in Moscow they can never do anything without something *ridicule*. A lady of a sort appeared on the scene, teacher of swimming to the Queen of Sweden, and gave us an exhibition of her skill.'

'How? did she swim?' asked Anna, frowning.

'In an absurd red *costume de natation*; she was old and hideous too. So when shall we go?'

'What an absurd fancy! Why, did she swim in some special way, then?' said Anna, not answering.

'There was absolutely nothing in it. That's just what I say, it was awfully stupid. Well, then, when do you think of going?'

Anna shook her head as though trying to drive away some unpleasant idea.

'When? Why, the sooner the better! By tomorrow we shan't be ready. The day after tomorrow.'

'Yes . . . oh no, wait a minute! The day after tomorrow's Sunday, I have to be at maman's,' said Vronsky, embarrassed, because as soon as he uttered his mother's name he was aware of her intent, suspicious eyes. His embarrassment confirmed her suspicion. She flushed hotly and drew away from him. It was now not the Queen of Sweden's swimming-mistress who filled Anna's imagination, but the young Princess Sorokin.

She was staying in a village near Moscow with Countess Vronsky.

'Can't you go tomorrow?' she said.

'Well, no! The deeds and the money for the business I'm going there for I can't get by tomorrow,' he answered.

'If so, we won't go at all.'

'But why so?'

'I shall not go later. Monday or never!'

'What for?' said Vronsky, as though in amazement. 'Why there's no meaning in it!'

'There's no meaning in it to you, because you care nothing for me. You don't care to understand my life. The one thing that I cared for here was Hannah. You say it's affectation. Why, you said yesterday that I don't love my daughter, that I love this English girl, that it's unnatural. I should like to know what life there is for me that could be natural!'

For an instant she had a clear vision of what she was doing, and was horrified at how she had fallen away from her resolution. But even though she knew it was her own ruin, she could not restrain herself, could not keep herself from proving to him that he was wrong, could not give way to him.

'I never said that; I said I did not sympathise with this sudden passion.'

'How is it, though you boast of your straightforwardness, you don't tell the truth?'

'I never boast, and I never tell lies,' he said slowly, restraining his rising anger. 'It's a great pity if you can't respect . . .'

'Respect was invented to cover the empty place where love should be. And if you don't love me any more, it would be better and more honest to say so.

'No, this is becoming unbearable!' cried Vronsky, getting up from his chair; and stopping short, facing her, he said, speaking deliberately: 'What do you try my patience for?' looking as though he might have said much more, but was restraining himself. 'It has limits.'

'What do you mean by that?' she cried, looking with terror at the undisguised hatred in his whole face, and especially in his cruel, menacing eyes.

'I mean to say . . .' he was beginning, but he checked himself. 'I must ask what it is you want of me?'

'What I can want? All I can want is that you should not desert me, as you think of doing,' she said, understanding all he had not uttered. 'But that I don't want; that's secondary. I want love, and there is none. So then all is over.'

She turned towards the door.

'Stop! st—op!' said Vronsky, with no change in the gloomy lines of his brows, though he held her by the hand. 'What is it all about! I said that we must put off going for three days, and on that you told me I was lying, that I was not an honourable man.'

'Yes, and I repeat that the man who reproaches me with having sacrificed everything for me,' she said, recalling the words of a still earlier quarrel, 'that he's worse than a dishonourable man—he's a heartless man.'

'Oh, there are limits to endurance!' he cried, and hastily let go her hand.

'He hates me, that's clear,' she thought, and in silence, without looking round, she walked with faltering steps out of the room. 'He loves another woman, that's even clearer,' she said to herself as she went into her own room. 'I want love, and there is none. So, then, all is over.' She repeated the words she had said, 'and it must be ended.'

'But how?' she asked herself, and she sat down in a low chair before the looking-glass.

Thoughts of where she would go now, whether to the aunt who had brought her up, to Dolly, or simply alone abroad, and of what *he* was doing now alone in his study; whether this was the final quarrel, or whether reconciliation were still possible; and of what all her old friends at Petersburg would say of her now; and of how Alexey Alexandrovitch would look at it, and many other ideas of what would happen now after the rupture, came into her head; but she did not give herself up to them with all her heart. At the bottom of her heart was some obscure idea that alone interested her, but she could not get clear sight of it. Thinking once more of Alexey Alexandrovitch, she recalled the time of her illness after her confinement, and the feeling which never left her at that time. 'Why didn't I die!' and the words and the feeling of that time came back to her. And all at once she knew what was in her soul. Yes, it was that idea which alone solved all. 'Yes, to die! . . . And the shame and disgrace of Alexey Alexandrovitch and of Seryozha, and my awful shame, it will all be saved by death. To die! and he will feel remorse; will be sorry; will love me; he will suffer on my account.' With the trace of a smile of commiseration for herself she sat down in the arm-chair, taking off and putting on the rings on her left hand, vividly picturing from different sides his feelings after her death.

Approaching footsteps—his steps—distracted her attention. As though absorbed in the arrangement of her rings, she did not even turn to him.

He went up to her, and taking her by the hand, said softly—

'Anna, we'll go the day after tomorrow, if you like. I agree to everything.'

She did not speak.

'What is it?' he urged.

'You know,' she said, and at the same instant, unable to restrain herself any longer, she burst into sobs.

'Cast me off!' she articulated between her sobs. 'I'll go away tomorrow . . . I'll do more. What am I? An immoral woman! A stone round your neck. I don't want to make you wretched; I don't want to! I'll set you free. You don't love me; you love someone else!'

Vronsky besought her to be calm, and declared that there was no trace of foundation for her jealousy; that he had never ceased, and never would cease, to love her; that he loved her more than ever.

'Anna, why distress yourself and me so?' he said to her, kissing her hands. There was tenderness now in his face, and she fancied she caught the sound of tears in his voice, and she felt them wet on her hand. And instantly Anna's despairing jealousy changed to a despairing passion of tenderness. She put her arms round him, and covered with kisses his head, his neck, his hands.

XXV

FEELING that the reconciliation was complete, Anna set eagerly to work in the morning preparing for their departure. Though it was not settled whether they should go on Monday or Tuesday, as they had each given way to the other, Anna packed busily, feeling absolutely indifferent whether they went a day earlier or later. She was standing in her room over an open box, taking things out of it, when he came in to see her earlier than usual, dressed to go out.

'I'm going off at once to see maman, she can send me the money by Yegorov. And I shall be ready to go tomorrow,' he said.

Though she was in such a good mood, the thought of his visit to his mother's gave her a pang.

'No, I shan't be ready by then myself,' she said; and at once reflected, 'so then it was possible to arrange to do as I wished.' 'No, do as you meant to do. Go into the dining-room, I'm coming directly. It's only to turn out those things that aren't wanted,' she said, putting something more on the heap of frippery that lay in Annushka's arms.

Vronsky was eating his beefsteak when she came into the dining-room.

'You wouldn't believe how distasteful these rooms have become to me,' she said, sitting down beside him to her coffee. 'There's nothing more awful than these *chambres garnies*. There's no individuality in them, no soul. These clocks, and curtains, and, worst of all, the wall-papers—

they're a nightmare. I think of Vozdvizhenskoe as the promised land. You're not sending the horses off yet?'

'No, they will come after us. Where are you going to?

'I wanted to go to Wilson's to take some dresses for her. So it's really to be tomorrow?' she said in a cheerful voice; but suddenly her face changed.

Vronsky's valet came in to ask him to sign a receipt for a telegram from Petersburg. There was nothing out of the way in Vronsky's getting a telegram, but he said, as though anxious to conceal something from her, that the receipt was in his study, and he turned hurriedly to her.

'By tomorrow, without fail, I will finish it all.'

'From whom is the telegram?' she asked, not hearing him.

'From Stiva,' he answered reluctantly.

'Why didn't you show it to me? What secret can there be between Stiva and me?'

Vronsky called the valet back, and told him to bring the telegram.

'I didn't want to show it you, because Stiva has such a passion for telegraphing: why telegraph when nothing is settled?'

'About the divorce?'

'Yes; but he says he has not been able to come at anything yet. He has promised a decisive answer in a day or two. But here it is; read it.'

With trembling hands Anna took the telegram, and read what Vronsky had told her. At the end was added: 'little hope; but I will do everything possible and impossible.'

'I said yesterday that it's absolutely nothing to me when I get, or whether I never get, a divorce,' she said, flushing crimson. 'There was not the slightest necessity to hide it from me.' 'So he may hide and does hide his correspondence with women from me,' she thought.

'Yashvin meant to come this morning with Voytov,' said Vronsky; 'I believe he's won from Pyevtsov all and more than he can pay, about sixty thousand.'

'No,' she said, irritated by his so obviously showing by this change of subject that he was irritated, 'why did you suppose that this news would affect me so, that you must even try to hide it? I said I don't want to consider it, and I should have liked you to care as little about it as I do.'

'I care about it because I like definiteness,' he said.

'Definiteness is not in the form but the love,' she said, more and more irritated, not by his words, but by the tone of cool composure in which he spoke. 'What do you want it for?'

'My God! love again,' he thought, frowning.

'Oh, you know what for; for your sake and your children's in the future.'

'There won't be children in the future.'

'That's a great pity,' he said.

'You want it for the children's sake, but you don't think of me?' she said, quite forgetting or not having heard that he had said, '*For your sake* and the children's.'

The question of the possibility of having children had long been a subject of dispute and irritation to her. His desire to have children she interpreted as a proof he did not prize her beauty.

'Oh, I said: for your sake. Above all for your sake,' he repeated, frowning as though in pain, 'because I am certain that the greater part of your irritability comes from the indefiniteness of the position.'

'Yes, now he has laid aside all pretence, and all his cold hatred for me is apparent,' she thought, not hearing his words, but watching with terror the cold, cruel judge who looked mocking her out of his eyes.

'The cause is not that,' she said, 'and, indeed, I don't see how the cause of my irritability, as you call it, can be that I am completely in your power. What indefiniteness is there in the position? on the contrary . . .'

'I am very sorry that you don't care to understand,' he interrupted, obstinately anxious to give utterance to his thought. 'The indefiniteness consists in your imagining that I am free.'

'On that score you can set your mind quite at rest,' she said, and turning away from him, she began drinking her coffee.

She lifted her cup, with her little finger held apart, and put it to her lips. After drinking a few sips she glanced at him, and by his expression, she saw clearly that he was repelled by her hand, and her gesture, and the sound made by her lips.

'I don't care in the least what your mother thinks, and what match she wants to make for you,' she said, putting the cup down with a shaking hand.

'But we are not talking about that.'

'Yes, that's just what we are talking about. And let me tell you that a heartless woman, whether she's old or not old, your mother or anyone else, is of no consequence to me, and I would not consent to know her.'

'Anna, I beg you not to speak disrespectfully of my mother.'

'A woman whose heart does not tell her where her son's happiness and honour lie has no heart.'

'I repeat my request that you will not speak disrespectfully of my mother, whom I respect,' he said, raising his voice and looking sternly at her.

She did not answer. Looking intently at him, at his face, his hands, she recalled all the details of their reconciliation the previous day, and his passionate caresses. 'There, just such caresses he has lavished, and will lavish, and longs to lavish on other women!' she thought.

'You don't love your mother. That's all talk, and talk, and talk!' she said, looking at him with hatred in her eyes.

'Even if so, you must . . .'

'Must decide, and I have decided,' she said, and she would have gone away, but at that moment Yashvin walked into the room. Anna greeted him and remained.

Why, when there was a tempest in her soul, and she felt she was standing at a turning-point in her life, which might have fearful consequences—why, at that minute, she had to keep up appearances before an outsider, who sooner or later must know it all—she did not know. But at once quelling the storm within her, she sat down and began talking to their guest.

'Well, how are you getting on? Has your debt been paid you?' she asked Yashvin.

'Oh, pretty fair; I fancy I shan't get it all, but I shall get a good half. And when are you off?' said Yashvin, looking at Vronsky, and unmistakably guessing at a quarrel.

'The day after tomorrow, I think,' said Vronsky.

'You've been meaning to go so long, though.'

'But now it's quite decided,' said Anna, looking Vronsky straight in the face with a look which told him not to dream of the possibility of reconciliation.

'Don't you feel sorry for that unlucky Pyevtsov?' she went on, talking to Yashvin.

'I've never asked myself the question, Anna Arkadyevna, whether I'm sorry for him or not. You see, all my fortune's here'—he touched his breast-pocket—'and just now I'm a wealthy man. But today I'm going to the club, and I may come out a beggar. You see, whoever sits down to play with me—he wants to leave me without a shirt to my back, and so do I him. And so we fight it out, and that's the pleasure of it.'

'Well, but suppose you were married,' said Anna, 'how would it be for your wife?'

Yashvin laughed.

'That's why I'm not married, and never mean to be.'

'And Helsingfors?' said Vronsky, entering into the conversation and glancing at Anna's smiling face. Meeting his eyes, Anna's face instantly took a coldly severe expression as though she were saying to him: 'It's not forgotten. It's all the same.'

'Were you really in love?' she said to Yashvin.

'Oh heavens! ever so many times! But you see, some men can play but only so that they can always lay down their cards when the hour comes of a *rendezvous*, while I can take up love, but only so as not to be late for my cards in the evening. That's how I manage things.'

'No, I didn't mean that, but the real thing.' She would have said *Helsingfors*, but would not repeat the word used by Vronsky.

Voytov, who was buying the horse, came in. Anna got up and went out of the room.

Before leaving the house, Vronsky went into her room. She would have pretended to be looking for something on the table, but ashamed of making a pretence, she looked straight in his face with cold eyes.

'What do you want?' she asked in French.

'To get the guarantee for Gambetta, I've sold him,' he said, in a tone which said more clearly than words, 'I've no time for discussing things, and it would lead to nothing.'

'I'm not to blame in any way,' he thought. 'If she will punish herself, *tant pis pour elle*.' But as he was going he fancied that she said something, and his heart suddenly ached with pity for her.

'Eh, Anna?' he queried.

'I said nothing,' she answered just as coldly and calmly.

'Oh nothing, *tant pis* then,' he thought, feeling cold again, and he turned and went out. As he was going out he caught a glimpse in the looking-glass of her face, white, with quivering lips. He even wanted to stop and to say some comforting word to her, but his legs carried him out of the room before he could think what to say. The whole of that day he spent away from home, and when he came in late in the evening the maid told him that Anna Arkadyevna had a headache and begged him not to go in to her.

XXVI

NEVER before had a day been passed in quarrel. Today was the first time. And this was not a quarrel. It was the open acknowledgment of complete coldness. Was it possible to glance at her as he had glanced when he came into the room for the guarantee?—to look at her, see her heart was breaking with despair, and go out without a word with that face of callous composure? He was not merely cold to her, he hated her because he loved another woman—that was clear.

And remembering all the cruel words he had said, Anna supplied, too, the words that he had unmistakably wished to say and could have said to her, and she grew more and more exasperated.

'I won't prevent you,' he might say. 'You can go where you like.

You were unwilling to be divorced from your husband, no doubt so that you might go back to him. Go back to him. If you want money, I'll give it you. How many roubles do you want?'

All the most cruel words that a brutal man could say, he said to her in her imagination, and she could not forgive him for them, as though he had actually said them.

'But didn't he only yesterday swear he loved me, he, a truthful and sincere man? Haven't I despaired for nothing many times already?' she said to herself afterwards.

All that day, except for the visit to Wilson's which occupied two hours, Anna spent in doubts whether everything were over or whether there were still hope of reconciliation, whether she should go away at once or see him once more. She was expecting him the whole day, and in the evening, as she went to her own room, leaving a message for him that she had a headache, she said to herself, 'If he comes in spite of what the maid says, it means that he loves me still. If not, it means that all is over, and then I will decide what I'm to do! . . .'

In the evening she heard the rumbling of his carriage stop at the entrance, his ring, his steps and his conversation with the servant; he believed what was told him, did not care to find out more, and went to his own room. So then everything was over.

And death rose clearly and vividly before her mind as the sole means of bringing back love for her in his heart, of punishing him and of gaining the victory in that strife which the evil spirit in possession of her heart was waging with him.

Now nothing mattered: going or not going to Vozdvizhenskoe, getting or not getting a divorce from her husband—all that did not matter. The one thing that mattered was punishing him. When she poured herself out her usual dose of opium, and thought that she had only to drink off the whole bottle to die, it seemed to her so simple and easy, that she began musing with enjoyment on how he would suffer, and repent and love her memory when it would be too late. She lay in bed with open eyes, by the light of a single burned-down candle, gazing at the carved cornice of the ceiling and at the shadow of the screen that covered part of it, while she vividly pictured to herself how he would feel when she would be no more, when she would be only a memory to him. 'How could I say such cruel things to her?' he would say. 'How could I go out of the room without saying anything to her? But now she is no more. She has gone away from us for ever. She is . . .' Suddenly the shadow of the screen wavered, pounced on the whole cornice, the whole ceiling; other shadows from the other side swooped to meet it, for an instant the shadows flitted back, but then with fresh swiftness they darted forward, wavered, mingled, and all was darkness. 'Death!' she thought. And such horror came upon her that for a long while she could not realise where she was, and for a long while her trembling hands could not find the matches and light another candle, instead of the one that had burned down and gone out. 'No, anything—only to live! Why, I love him! Why, he loves me! This has been before and will pass,' she said, feeling that tears of joy at the return to life were trickling down her cheeks. And to escape from her panic she went hurriedly to his room.

He was asleep there, and sleeping soundly. She went up to him, and holding the light above his face, she gazed a long while at him. Now when he was asleep, she loved him so that at the sight of him she could not keep back tears of tenderness. But she knew that if he waked up he would look at her with cold eyes, convinced that he was right, and that before telling him of her love, she would have to prove to him that he had been wrong in his treatment of her. Without waking him, she went back, and after a second dose of opium she fell towards morning into a heavy, incomplete sleep, during which she never quite lost consciousness.

In the morning she was waked by a horrible nightmare, which had recurred several times in her dreams, even before her connection with Vronsky. A little old man with unkempt beard was doing something bent down over some iron, muttering meaningless French words, and she, as she always did in this nightmare (it was what made the horror of it), felt that this peasant was taking no notice of her, but was doing something horrible with the iron—over her. And she waked up in a cold sweat.

When she got up, the previous day came back to her as though veiled in mist.

'There was a quarrel. Just what has happened several times. I said I had a headache, and he did not come in to see me. Tomorrow we're going away, I must see him and get ready for the journey,' she said to herself. And learning that he was in his study, she went down to him. As she passed through the drawing-room she heard a carriage stop at the entrance, and looking out of window she saw the carriage, from which a young girl in a lilac hat was leaning out giving some direction to the footman ringing the bell. After a parley in the hall, someone came upstairs, and Vronsky's steps could be heard passing the drawing-room. He went rapidly downstairs. Anna went again to the window. She saw him come out on to the steps without his hat and go up to the carriage. The young girl in the lilac hat handed him a parcel. Vronsky, smiling, said something to her. The carriage drove away; he ran rapidly upstairs again.

The mists that had shrouded everything in her soul parted suddenly. The feelings of yesterday pierced the sick heart with a fresh pang. She could not understand now how she could have lowered herself by spending a whole day with him in his house. She went into his room to announce her determination.

'That was Madame Sorokin and her daughter. They came and brought me the money and the deeds from maman. I couldn't get them yesterday. How is your head, better?' he said quietly, not wishing to see and to understand the gloomy and solemn expression of her face.

She looked silently, intently at him, standing in the middle of the room. He glanced at her, frowned for a moment, and went on reading a letter. She turned, and went deliberately out of the room. He still might have turned her back, but she had reached the door, he was still silent, and the only sound audible was the rustling of the notepaper as he turned it.

'Oh, by the way,' he said at the very moment she was in the doorway, 'we're going tomorrow for certain, aren't we?'

'You, but not I,' she said, turning round to him.

'Anna, we can't go on like this . . .'

'You, but not I,' she repeated.

'This is getting unbearable!'

'You . . . you will be sorry for this,' she said, and went out. Frightened by the desperate expression with which these words were uttered, he jumped up and would have run after her, but on second thoughts he sat down and scowled, setting his teeth. This vulgar—as he thought it—threat of something vague exasperated him. 'I've tried everything,' he thought; 'the only thing left is not to pay attention,' and he began to get ready to drive into town, and again to his mother's to get her signature to the deeds.

She heard the sound of his steps about the study and the dining-room. At the drawing-room he stood still. But he did not turn in to see her, he merely gave an order that the horse should be given to Voytov if he came while he was away. Then she heard the carriage brought round, the door opened, and he came out again. But he went back into the porch again, and someone was running upstairs. It was the valet running up for his gloves that had been forgotten. She went to the window and saw him take the gloves without looking, and touching the coachman on the back he said something to him. Then without looking up at the window he settled himself in his usual attitude in the carriage, with his legs crossed, and drawing on his gloves he vanished round the corner.

XXVII

'HE has gone! It is over!' Anna said to herself, standing at the window; and in answer to this question the impressions of the darkness when the candle had flickered out, and of her fearful dream mingling into one, filled her heart with cold terror.

'No, that cannot be!' she cried, and crossing the room she rang the bell. She was so afraid now of being alone, that without waiting for the servant to come in, she went out to meet him.

'Inquire where the count has gone,' she said. The servant answered that the count had gone to the stable.

'His honour left word that if you cared to drive out, the carriage would be back immediately.'

'Very good. Wait a minute. I'll write a note at once. Send Mihail with the note to the stables. Make haste.'

She sat down and wrote—

'I was wrong. Come back home; I must explain. For God's sake come! I'm afraid.'

She sealed it up and gave it to the servant.

She was afraid of being left alone now, she followed the servant out of the room, and went to the nursery.

'Why, this isn't it, this isn't he! Where are his blue eyes, his sweet shy smile?' was her first thought when she saw her chubby, rosy little girl with her black, curly hair instead of Seryozha, whom in the tangle of her ideas she had expected to see in the nursery. The little girl sitting at the table was obstinately and violently battering on it with a cork, and staring aimlessly at her mother with her pitch-black eyes. Answering the English nurse that she was quite well, and that she was going to the country tomorrow, Anna sat down by the little girl and began spinning the cork to show her. But the child's loud, ringing laugh, and the motion of her eyebrows, recalled Vronsky so vividly that she got up hurriedly, restraining her sobs, and went away. 'Can it be all over? No, it cannot be!' she thought. 'He will come back. But how can he explain that smile, that excitement after he had been talking to her? But even if he doesn't explain, I will believe. If I don't believe, there's only one thing left for me, and I can't.'

She looked at her watch. Twenty minutes had passed. 'By now he has received the note and is coming back. Not long, ten minutes more.... But what if he doesn't come? No, that cannot be. He mustn't see me with tear-stained eyes. I'll go and wash. Yes, yes; did I do my hair or not?' she asked herself. And she could not remember. She felt her head with her hand. 'Yes, my hair has been done, but when I did it I can't in the least remember.' She could not believe the evidence of her hand, and went up to the pier-glass to see whether she really had done her hair. She certainly had, but she could not think when she had done it. 'Who's that?' she thought, looking in the looking-glass at the swollen face with strangely glittering eyes, that looked in a scared way at her. 'Why, it's I!' she suddenly understood, and looking round, she seemed all at once to feel his kisses on her, and twitched her shoulders, shuddering. Then she lifted her hand to her lips and kissed it.

'What is it? Why, I'm going out of my mind!' and she went into her bedroom, where Annushka was tidying the room.

'Annushka,' she said, coming to a standstill before her, and she stared at the maid, not knowing what to say to her.

'You meant to go and see Darya Alexandrovna,' said the girl, as though she understood.

'Darya Alexandrovna? Yes, I'll go.'

'Fifteen minutes there, fifteen minutes back. He's coming, he'll be here soon.' She took out her watch and looked at it. 'But how could he go away, leaving me in such a state? How can he live, without making it up with me?' She went to the window and began looking into the street. Judging by the time, he might be back now. But her calculations might be wrong, and she began once more to recall when he had started and to count the minutes.

At the moment when she had moved away to the big clock to compare it with her watch, some one drove up. Glancing out of window, she saw his carriage. But no one came upstairs, and voices could be heard below. It was the messenger who had come back in the carriage. She went down to him.

'We didn't catch the count. The count had driven off on the lower city road.'

'What do you say? What! . . .' she said to the rosy, good-humoured Mihail, as he handed her back her note.

'Why, then, he has never received it!' she thought.

'Go with this note to Countess Vronsky's place, you know? and bring an answer back immediately,' she said to the messenger.

'And I, what am I going to do?' she thought. 'Yes, I'm going to Dolly's, that's true, or else I shall go out of my mind. Yes, and I can telegraph, too.' And she wrote a telegram. 'I absolutely must talk to you; come at once.' After sending off the telegram, she went to dress. When she was dressed and in her hat, she glanced again into the eyes of the plump, comfortable-looking Annushka. There was unmistakable sympathy in those good-natured little grey eyes.

'Annushka, dear, what am I to do?' said Anna, sobbing and sinking helplessly into a chair.

'Why fret yourself so, Anna Arkadyevna? Why, there's nothing out of the way. You drive out a little, and it'll cheer you up,' said the maid.

'Yes, I'm going,' said Anna, rousing herself and getting up. 'And if there's a telegram while I'm away, send it on to Darya Alexandrovna's . . . but no, I shall be back myself.'

'Yes, I mustn't think, I must do something, drive somewhere, and, most of all, get out of this house,' she said, feeling with terror the strange turmoil going on in her own heart, and she made haste to go out and get into the carriage.

'Where to?' asked Pyotr before getting on to the box.

'To Znamenka, the Oblonskys'.'

XXVIII

IT was bright and sunny. A fine rain had been falling all the morning, and now it had not long cleared up. The iron roofs, the flags of the roads, the flints of the pavements, the wheels and leather, the brass and the tinplate of the carriages—all glistened brightly in the May sunshine. It was three o'clock, and the very liveliest time in the streets.

As she sat in a corner of the comfortable carriage, that hardly swayed on its supple springs, while the greys trotted swiftly, in the midst of the unceasing rattle of wheels and the changing impressions in the pure air, Anna ran over the events of the last days, and she saw her position quite differently from how it had seemed at home. Now the thought of death seemed no longer so terrible and so clear to her, and death itself no longer seemed so inevitable. Now she blamed herself for the humiliation to which she had lowered herself. 'I entreat him to forgive me. I have given in to him. I have owned myself in fault. What for? Can't I live without him?' And leaving unanswered the question how she was going to live without him, she fell to reading the signs on the shops. 'Office and warehouse. Dental surgeon. Yes, I'll tell Dolly all about it. She doesn't like Vronsky. I shall be sick and ashamed, but I'll tell her. She loves me, and I'll follow her advice. I won't give in to him; I won't let him train me as he pleases. Filippov, bun-shop. They say they send their dough to Petersburg. The Moscow water is so good for it. Ah, the springs at Mitishtchen, and the pancakes!'

And she remembered how, long, long ago, when she was a girl of seventeen, she had gone with her aunt to Troitsa. 'Riding, too. Was that really me, with red hands? How much that seemed to me then splendid and out of reach has become worthless, while what I had then has gone out of my reach for ever! Could I ever have believed then that I could come to such humiliation? How conceited and self-satisfied he will be when he gets my note! But I will show him. . . . How horrid that paint smells! Why is it they're always painting and building? *Modes et robes*,' she read. A man bowed to her. It was Annushka's husband. 'Our parasites'; she remembered how Vronsky had said that. 'Our? Why our? What's so awful is that one can't tear up the past by its roots. One can't tear it out, but one can hide one's memory of it. And I'll hide it.' And then she thought of her past with Alexey Alexandrovitch, of how she had blotted the memory of it out of her life. 'Dolly will think I'm leaving my second husband, and so I certainly must be in the wrong. As if I cared to be right! I can't help it!' she said, and she wanted to cry. But at once she fell to wondering what those two girls could be smiling about. 'Love, most likely. They don't know how dreary it is, how low . . . The boulevard and the children. Three boys running, playing at horses. Seryozha! And I'm losing everything and not getting him back. Yes, I'm losing everything, if he doesn't return. Perhaps he was late for the train and has come back by now. Longing for humiliation again!' she said to herself. 'No, I'll go to Dolly, and say straight out to her, I'm unhappy, I deserve this, I'm to blame, but still I'm unhappy, help me. These horses, this carriage—how loathsome I am to myself in this carriage—all his; but I won't see them again.'

Thinking over the words in which she would tell Dolly, and mentally working her heart up to great bitterness, Anna went upstairs.

'Is there anyone with her?' she asked in the hall.

'Katerina Alexandrovna Levin,' answered the footman.

'Kitty! Kitty, whom Vronsky was in love with!' thought Anna, 'the girl he thinks of with love. He's sorry he didn't marry her. But me he thinks of with hatred, and is sorry he had anything to do with me.'

The sisters were having a consultation about nursing when Anna called. Dolly went down alone to see the visitor who had interrupted their conversation.

'Well, so you've not gone away yet? I meant to have come to you,' she said; 'I had a letter from Stiva today.'

'We had a telegram too,' answered Anna, looking round for Kitty.

'He writes that he can't make out quite what Alexey Alexandrovitch wants, but he won't go away without a decisive answer.'

'I thought you had someone with you. Can I see the letter?'

'Yes; Kitty,' said Dolly, embarrassed. 'She stayed in the nursery. She has been very ill.'

'So I heard. May I see the letter?'

'I'll get it directly. But he doesn't refuse; on the contrary, Stiva has hopes,' said Dolly, stopping in the doorway.

'I haven't, and indeed I don't wish it,' said Anna.

'What's this? Does Kitty consider it degrading to meet me?' thought Anna when she was alone. 'Perhaps she's right, too. But it's not for her, the girl who was in love with Vronsky, it's not for her to show me that, even if it is true. I know that in my position I can't be received by any decent woman. I knew that from the first moment I sacrificed everything to him. And this is my reward! Oh, how I hate him! And what did I come here for? I'm worse here, more miserable.' She heard from the next room the sister's voices in consultation. 'And what am I going to say to Dolly now? Amuse Kitty by the sight of my wretchedness, submit to her patronising? No; and besides, Dolly wouldn't understand. And it would be no good my telling her. It would only be interesting to see Kitty, to show her how I despise everyone and everything, how nothing matters to me now.'

Dolly came in with the letter. Anna read it and handed it back in silence.

'I knew all that,' she said, 'and it doesn't interest me in the least.'

'Oh, why so? On the contrary, I have hopes,' said Dolly, looking inquisitively at Anna. She had never seen her in such a strangely irritable condition. 'When are you going away?' she asked.

Anna, half-closing her eyes, looked straight before her and did not answer.

'Why does Kitty shrink from me?' she said, looking at the door and flushing red.

'Oh, what nonsense! She's nursing, and things aren't going right with her, and I've been advising her. . . . She's delighted. She'll be here in a minute,' said Dolly awkwardly, not clever at lying. 'Yes, here she is.'

Hearing that Anna had called, Kitty had wanted not to appear, but Dolly persuaded her. Rallying her forces, Kitty went in, walked up to her, blushing, and shook hands.

'I am so glad to see you,' she said with a trembling voice.

Kitty had been thrown into confusion by the inward conflict between her antagonism to this bad woman and her desire to be nice to her. But as soon as she saw Anna's lovely and attractive face, all feeling of antagonism disappeared.

'I should not have been surprised if you had not cared to meet me. I'm used to everything. You have been ill? Yes, you are changed,' said Anna.

Kitty felt that Anna was looking at her with hostile eyes. She ascribed this hostility to the awkward position in which Anna, who had once patronised her, must feel with her now, and she felt sorry for her.

They talked of Kitty's illness, of the baby, of Stiva, but it was obvious that nothing interested Anna.

'I came to say good-bye,' she said, getting up.

'Oh, when are you going?'

But again not answering, Anna turned to Kitty.

'Yes, I am very glad to have seen you,' she said with a smile. 'I have heard so much of you from everyone, even from your husband. He came to see me, and I liked him exceedingly,' she said, unmistakably with malicious intent. 'Where is he?'

'He has gone back to the country,' said Kitty, blushing.

'Remember me to him, be sure you do.'

'I'll be sure to!' Kitty said naïvely, looking compassionately into her eyes.

'So good-bye, Dolly.' And kissing Dolly and shaking hands with Kitty, Anna went out hurriedly.

'She's just the same and just as charming! She's very lovely!' said Kitty, when she was alone with her sister. 'But there's something piteous about her. Awfully piteous!'

'Yes, there's something unusual about her today,' said Dolly. 'When I went with her into the hall, I fancied she was almost crying.'

XXIX

ANNA got into the carriage again in an even worse frame of mind than when she set out from home. To her previous tortures was added now that sense of mortification and of being an outcast which she had felt so distinctly on meeting Kitty.

'Where to? Home?' asked Pyotr.

'Yes, home,' she said, not even thinking now where she was going.

'How they looked at me as something dreadful, incomprehensible, and curious! What can he be telling the other with such warmth?' she thought, staring at two men who walked by. 'Can one ever tell anyone what one is feeling? I meant to tell Dolly, and it's a good thing I didn't tell her. How pleased she would have been at my misery! She would have concealed it, but her chief feeling would have been delight at my being punished for the happiness she envied me for. Kitty, she would have been even more pleased. How I can see through her! She knows I was more than usually sweet to her husband. And she's jealous and hates me. And she despises me. In her eyes I'm an immoral woman. If I were an immoral woman I could have made her husband fall in love with me . . . If I'd cared to. And, indeed, I did care to. There's someone who's pleased with himself,' she thought, as she saw a fat, rubicund gentleman coming towards her. He took her for an acquaintance, and lifted his glossy hat above his bald, glossy head, and then perceived his mistake. 'He thought he knew me. Well, he knows me as well as anyone in the world knows me. I don't know myself. I know my appetites, as the French say. They want that dirty ice-cream, that they do know for certain,' she thought, looking at two boys stopping an ice-cream seller, who took a barrel off his head and began wiping his perspiring face with a towel. 'We all want what is sweet and nice. If not sweetmeats, then a dirty ice. And Kitty's the same—if not Vronsky, then Levin. And she envies me, and hates me. And we shall all hate each other. I Kitty, Kitty me. Yes, that's the truth. "*Tiutkin, coiffeur.*" *Je me fais coiffer par Tiutkin.* . . . I'll tell him that when he comes,' she thought and smiled. But the same instant she remembered that she had no one now to tell anything amusing to. 'And there's nothing amusing, nothing mirthful, really. It's all hateful. They're singing for vespers, and how carefully that merchant crosses himself! as if he were afraid of missing something. Why these churches and this singing and this humbug? Simply to conceal that we all hate each other like these cab-drivers who are abusing each other so angrily. Yashvin says, "He wants to strip me of my shirt, and I him of his." Yes, that's the truth!'

She was plunged in these thoughts, which so engrossed her that she left off thinking of her own position, when the carriage drew up at the steps of her house. It was only when she saw the porter running out to meet her that she remembered she had sent the note and the telegram.

'Is there an answer?' she inquired.

'I'll see this minute,' answered the porter, and glancing into his room, he took out and gave her the thin square envelope of a telegram. 'I can't come before ten o'clock.—Vronsky,' she read.

'And hasn't the messenger come back?'

'No,' answered the porter.

'Then, since it's so, I know what I must do,' she said, and feeling a vague fury and craving for revenge rising up within her, she ran upstairs. 'I'll go to him myself. Before going away for ever, I'll tell him all. Never have I hated anyone as I hate that man!' she thought. Seeing his hat on the rack, she shuddered with aversion. She did not consider that his telegram was an answer to her telegram and that he had not yet received her note. She pictured him to herself as talking calmly to his mother and Princess Sorokin and rejoicing at her sufferings. 'Yes, I must go quickly,' she said, not knowing yet where she was going. She longed to get away as quickly as possible from the feelings she had gone through in that awful house. The servants, the walls, the things in that house—all aroused repulsion and hatred in her and lay like a weight upon her.

'Yes, I must go to the railway station, and if he's not there, then go there and catch him.' Anna looked at the railway time-table in the newspapers. An evening train went at two minutes past eight. 'Yes, I shall be in time.' She gave orders for the other horses to be put in the carriage, and packed in a travelling-bag the things needed for a few days. She knew she would never come back here again.

Among the plans that came into her head she vaguely determined that after what would happen at the station or at the countess's house, she would go as far as the first town on the Nizhigorod road and stop there.

Dinner was on the table; she went up, but the smell of the bread and cheese was enough to make her feel that all food was disgusting. She ordered the carriage and went out. The house threw a shadow now right across the street, but it was a bright evening and still warm in the sunshine. Annushka, who came down with her things, and Pyotr, who put the things in the carriage, and the coachman, evidently out of humour, were all hateful to her, and irritated her by their words and actions.

'I don't want you, Pyotr.'

'But how about the ticket?'

'Well, as you like, it doesn't matter,' she said crossly.

Pyotr jumped on the box, and putting his arms akimbo, told the coachman to drive to the booking-office.

XXX

'HERE it is again! Again I understand it all!' Anna said to herself, as soon as the carriage had started, and swaying lightly, rumbled over the tiny cobbles of the paved road, and again one impression followed rapidly upon another.

'Yes; what was the last thing I thought of so clearly?' she tried to recall it. '"*Tiutkin, coiffeur?*"—no, not that. Yes, of what Yashvin says, the struggle for existence and hatred is the one thing that holds men together. No, it's a useless journey you're making,' she said, mentally addressing a party in a coach and four, evidently going for an excursion into the country. 'And the dog you're taking with you will be no help to you. You can't get away from yourselves.' Turning her eyes in the direction Pyotr had turned to look, she saw a factory-hand almost dead-drunk, with hanging head, being led away by a policeman. 'Come, he's found a quicker way,' she thought. 'Count Vronsky and I did not find that happiness either, though we expected so much from it.' And now for the first time Anna turned that glaring light in which she was seeing everything on to her relations with him, which she had hitherto avoided thinking about. 'What was it he sought in me? Not love so much as the satisfaction of vanity.' She remembered his words, the expression of his face that recalled an abject setter-dog, in the early days of their connection. And everything now confirmed this. 'Yes, there was the triumph of success in him. Of course there was love too, but the chief element was the pride of success. He boasted of me. Now that's over. There's nothing to be proud of. Not to be proud of, but to be ashamed of. He has taken from me all he could, and now I am no use to him. He is weary of me and is trying not to be dishonourable in his behaviour to me. He let that out yesterday—he wants divorce and marriage so as to burn his ships. He loves me, but how? The zest is gone, as the English say. That fellow wants everyone to admire him and is very much pleased with himself,' she thought, looking at a red-faced clerk, riding on a riding-school horse. 'Yes, there's not the same flavour about me for him now. If I go away from him, at the bottom of his heart he will be glad.'

This was not mere supposition, she saw it distinctly in the piercing light, which revealed to her now the meaning of life and human relations.

'My love keeps growing more passionate and egoistic, while his is waning and waning, and that's why we're drifting apart.' She went on musing. 'And there's no help for it. He is everything for me, and I want him more and more to give himself up to me entirely. And he wants more and more to get away from me. We walked to meet each other up to the time of our love, and then we have been irresistibly drifting in different directions. And there's no altering that. He tells me I'm insanely jealous, and I have told myself that I am insanely jealous; but it's not true. I'm not jealous, but I'm unsatisfied. But . . .' she opened her lips, and shifted her place in the carriage in the excitement, aroused by the thought that suddenly struck her. 'If I could be anything but a mistress, passionately caring for nothing but his caresses; but I can't and I don't care to be anything else. And by that desire I rouse aversion in him, and he rouses fury in me, and it cannot be different. Don't I know that he wouldn't deceive me, that he has no schemes about Princess Sorokin, that he's not in love with Kitty, that he won't desert me! I know all that, but it makes it no better for me. If without loving me, from *duty* he'll be good and kind to me, without what I want, that's a thousand times worse than unkindness! That's—hell! And that's just how it is. For a long while now he hasn't loved me. And where love ends, hate begins. I don't know these streets at all. Hills it seems, and still houses, and houses . . . And in the houses always people and people . . . How many of them, no end, and all hating each other! Come, let me try and think what I want, to make me happy. Well? Suppose I am divorced, and Alexey Alexandrovitch lets me have Seryozha, and I marry Vronsky.' Thinking of Alexey Alexandrovitch, she at once pictured him with extraordinary vividness as though he were alive before her, with his mild, lifeless, dull eyes, the blue veins in his white hands, his intonations and the cracking of his fingers, and remembering the feeling which had existed between them, and which was also called love, she shuddered with loathing. 'Well, I'm divorced, and become Vronsky's wife. Well, will Kitty cease looking at me as she looked at me today? No. And will Seryozha leave off asking and wondering about my two husbands? And is there any new feeling I can awaken between Vronsky and me? Is there possible, if not happiness, some sort of ease from misery? No, no!' she answered now without the slightest hesitation. 'Impossible! We are drawn apart by life, and I make his unhappiness, and he mine, and there's no altering him or me. Every attempt has been made, the screw has come unscrewed. Oh, a beggar-woman with a baby. She thinks I'm sorry for her. Aren't we all flung into the world only to hate each other, and so to torture ourselves and each other? Schoolboys coming—laughing—Seryozha?' she thought. 'I thought, too, that I loved him, and used to be touched by my own tenderness. But I have lived without him, I gave him up for another love, and did not regret the exchange till that love was satisfied.' And with loathing she thought of what she meant by that love. And the clearness with which she saw life now, her own and all men's, was a pleasure to her. 'It's so with me and Pyotr, and the coachman, Fyodor, and that merchant, and all the people living along the Volga, where those placards invite one to go, and everywhere and always,' she thought when she had driven under the low-pitched roof af the Nizhigorod station, and the porters ran to meet her.

'A ticket for Obiralovka?' said Pyotr.

She had utterly forgotten where and why she was going, and only by a great effort she understood the question.

'Yes,' she said, handing him her purse, and taking a little red bag in her hand, she got out of the carriage.

Making her way through the crowd to the first-class waiting-room, she gradually recollected all the details of her position, and the plans between which she was hesitating. And again at the old sore places, hope and then despair poisoned the wounds of her tortured, fearfully throbbing heart. As she sat on the star-shaped sofa waiting for the train, she gazed with aversion at the people coming and going (they were all hateful to her), and thought how she would arrive at the station, would write him a note, and what she would write to him, and how he was at this moment complaining to his mother of his position, not understanding her sufferings, and how she would go into the room, and what she would say to him. Then she thought that life might still be happy, and how miserably she loved and hated him, and how fearfully her heart was beating.

XXXI

A BELL rang, some young men, ugly and impudent, and at the same time careful of the impression they were making, hurried by. Pyotr, too, crossed the room in his livery and top-boots, with his dull, animal face, and came up to her to take her to the train. Some noisy men were quiet as she passed them on the platform, and one whispered something about her to another—something vile, no doubt. She stepped up on the high step, and sat down in a carriage by herself on a dirty seat that had been white. Her bag lay beside her, shaken up and down by the springiness of the seat. With a foolish smile Pyotr raised his hat, with its coloured band, at the window, in token of farewell, an impudent conductor slammed the door and the latch. A grotesque-looking lady wearing a bustle (Anna mentally undressed the woman, and was appalled at her hideousness), and a little girl laughing affectedly ran down the platform.

'Katerina Andreevna, she's got them all, *ma tante*!' cried the girl.

'Even the child's hideous and affected,' thought Anna. To avoid seeing anyone, she got up quickly and seated herself at the opposite window of the empty carriage. A misshapen-looking peasant covered with dirt, in a cap from which his tangled hair stuck out all round, passed by that window, stooping down to the carriage wheels. 'There's something familiar about that hideous peasant,' thought Anna. And remembering her dream, she moved away to the opposite door, shaking with terror. The conductor opened the door and let in a man and his wife.

'Do you wish to get out?'

Anna made no answer. The conductor and her two fellow-passengers did not notice under her veil her panic-stricken face. She went back to her corner and sat down. The couple seated themselves on the opposite side, and intently but surreptitiously scrutinised her clothes. Both husband and wife seemed repulsive to Anna. The husband asked, would she allow him to smoke, obviously not with a view to smoking but to getting into conversation with her. Receiving her assent, he said to his wife in French something about caring less to smoke than to talk. They made inane and affected remarks to one another, entirely for her benefit. Anna saw clearly that they were sick of each other, and hated each other. And no one could have helped hating such miserable monstrosities.

A second bell sounded, and was followed by moving of luggage, noise, shouting and laughter. It was so clear to Anna that there was nothing for anyone to be glad of, that this laughter irritated her agonisingly, and she would have liked to stop up her ears not to hear it. At last the third bell rang, there was a whistle and a hiss of steam, and a clank of chains, and the man in her carriage crossed himself. 'It would be interesting to ask him what meaning he attaches to that,' thought Anna, looking angrily at him. She looked past the lady out of window at the people who seemed whirling by as they ran beside the train or stood on the platform. The train, jerking at regular intervals at the junctions of the rails, rolled by the platform, past a stone wall, a signal-box, past other trains; the wheels, moving more smoothly and evenly, resounded with a slight clang on the rails. The window was lighted up by the bright evening sun, and a slight breeze fluttered the curtain. Anna forgot her fellow-passengers, and to the light swaying of the train she fell to thinking again, as she breathed the fresh air.

'Yes, what did I stop at? That I couldn't conceive a position in which life would not be a misery, that we are all created to be miserable, and that we all know it, and all invent means of deceiving each other. And when one sees the truth, what is one to do?'

'That's what reason is given man for, to escape from what worries him,' said the lady in French, lisping affectedly, and obviously pleased with her phrase.

The words seemed an answer to Anna's thoughts.

'To escape from what worries him,' repeated Anna. And glancing at the red-cheeked husband and the thin wife, she saw that the sickly wife considered herself misunderstood, and the husband deceived her and encouraged her in that idea of herself. Anna seemed to see all their history and all the crannies of their souls, as it were turning a light upon them. But there was nothing interesting in them, and she pursued her thought.

'Yes, I'm very much worried, and that's what reason was given me for, to escape; so then one must escape: why not put out the light when there's nothing more to look at, when it's sickening to look at it all? But how? Why did the conductor run along the footboard, why are they shrieking, those young men in that train? why are they talking? why are they laughing? It's all falsehood, all lying, all humbug, all cruelty! . . .'

When the train came into the station, Anna got out into the crowd of passengers, and moving apart from them as if they were lepers, she stood on the platform, trying to think what she had come here for, and what she meant to do. Everything that had seemed to her possible before was now so difficult to consider, especially in this noisy crowd of hideous people who would not leave her alone. At one moment porters ran up to her proffering their services, then young men clacking their heels on the planks of the platform and talking loudly, stared at her, then people meeting her dodged past on the wrong side. Remembering that she had meant to go on further if there was no answer, she stopped a porter and asked if her coachman were not here with a note from Count Vronsky.

'Count Vronsky? They sent up here from the Vronskys just this minute, to meet Princess Sorokin and her daughter. And what is the coachman like?'

Just as she was talking to the porter, the coachman Mihail, red and cheerful in his smart blue coat and chain, evidently proud of having so successfully performed his commission, came up to her and gave her a letter. She broke it open, and her heart ached before she had read it.

'I am very sorry your note did not reach me. I will be home at ten,' Vronsky had written carelessly....

'Yes, that's what I expected!' she said to herself with an evil smile.

'Very good, you can go home then,' she said softly, addressing Mihail. She spoke softly because the rapidity of her heart's beating hindered her breathing. 'No, I won't let you make me miserable,' she thought menacingly, addressing not him, not herself, but the power that made her suffer, and she walked along the platform.

Two maid-servants walking along the platform turned their heads, staring at her and making some remarks about her dress. 'Real,' they said of the lace she was wearing. The young men would not leave her in peace. Again they passed by, peering into her face, and with a laugh shouting something in an unnatural voice. The stationmaster coming up asked her whether she was going by train. A boy selling kvas, never took his eyes off her. 'My God! where am I to go?' she thought, going farther and farther along the platform. At the end she stopped. Some ladies and children, who had come to meet a gentleman in spectacles, paused in their loud laughter and talking, and stared at her as she reached them. She quickened her pace and walked away from them to the edge of the platform. A luggage train was coming in. The platform began to sway, and she fancied she was in the train again.

And all at once she thought of the man crushed by the train the day she had first met Vronsky, and she knew what she had to do. With a rapid, light step she went down the steps that led from the tank to the rails and stopped quite near the approaching train.

She looked at the lower part of the carriages, at the screws and chains, and the tall cast-iron wheel of the first carriage slowly moving up, and trying to measure the middle between the front and back wheels, and the very minute when that middle point would be opposite her.

'There,' she said to herself, looking into the shadow of the carriage, at the sand and coal-dust which covered the sleepers—'there, in the very middle, and I will punish him and escape from everyone and from myself.'

She tried to fling herself below the wheels of the first carriage as it reached her; but the red bag which she tried to drop out of her hand delayed her, and she was too late; she missed the moment. She had to wait for the next carriage. A feeling such as she had known when about to take the first plunge in bathing came upon her, and she crossed herself. That familiar gesture brought back into her soul a whole series of girlish and childish memories, and suddenly the darkness that had covered everything for her was torn apart, and life rose up before her for an instant with all its bright past joys. But she did not take her eyes from the wheels of the second carriage. And exactly at the moment when the space between the wheels came opposite her, she dropped the red bag, and drawing her head back into her shoulders, fell on her hands under the carriage, and lightly, as though she would rise again at once, dropped on to her knees. And at the same instant she was terror-stricken at what she was doing. 'Where am I? What am I doing? What for?' She tried to get up, to drop backwards; but something huge and merciless struck her on the head and rolled her on her back. 'Lord, forgive me all!' she said, feeling it impossible to struggle. A peasant muttering something was working at the iron above her. And the light by which she had read the book filled with troubles, falsehoods, sorrow, and evil, flared up more brightly than ever before, lighted up for her all that had been in darkness, flickered, began to grow dim, and was quenched for ever.

PART VIII

I

ALMOST two months had passed. The hot summer was half over, but Sergey Ivanovitch was only just preparing to leave Moscow.

Sergey Ivanovitch's life had not been uneventful during this time. A year ago he had finished his book, the fruit of six years' labour, 'Sketch of a Survey of the Principles and Forms of Government in Europe and Russia.' Several sections of this book and its introduction had appeared in periodical publications, and other parts had been read by Sergey Ivanovitch to persons of his circle, so that the leading ideas of the work could not be completely novel to the public. But still Sergey Ivanovitch had expected that on its appearance his book would be sure to make a serious impression on society, and if it did not cause a revolution in social science it would, at any rate, make a great stir in the scientific world.

After the most conscientious revision the book had last year been published, and had been distributed among the booksellers.

Though he asked no one about it, reluctantly and with feigned indifference answered his friends' inquiries as to how the book was going, and did not even inquire of the booksellers how the book was selling, Sergey Ivanovitch was all on the alert, with strained attention, watching for the first impression his book would make in the world and in literature.

But a week passed, a second, a third, and in society no impression whatever could be detected. His friends who were specialists and savants, occasionally—unmistakably from politeness—alluded to it. The rest of his acquaintances, not interested in a book on a learned subject, did not talk of it at all. And society generally—just now especially absorbed in other things—was absolutely indifferent. In the press, too, for a whole month there was not a word about his book.

Sergey Ivanovitch had calculated to a nicety the time necessary for writing a review, but a month passed, and a second, and still there was silence.

Only in the *Northern Beetle*, in a comic article on the singer Drabanti, who had lost his voice, there was a contemptuous allusion to Koznishev's book, suggesting that the book had been long ago seen through by everyone, and was a subject of general ridicule.

At last in the third month, a critical article appeared in a serious review. Sergey Ivanovitch knew the author of the article. He had met him once at Golubtsov's.

The author of the article was a young man, an invalid, very bold as a writer, but extremely deficient in breeding and shy in personal relations.

In spite of his absolute contempt for the author, it was with complete respect that Sergey Ivanovitch set about reading the article. The article was awful.

The critic had undoubtedly put an interpretation upon the book which could not possibly be put on it. But he had selected quotations so adroitly that for people who had not read the book (and obviously scarcely anyone had read it) it seemed absolutely clear that the whole book was nothing but a medley of high-flown phrases, not even—as suggested by marks of interrogation—used appropriately, and that the author of the book was a person absolutely without knowledge of the subject. All this was so wittily done that Sergey Ivanovitch would not have disowned such wit himself. But that was just what was so awful.

In spite of the scrupulous conscientiousness with which Sergey Ivanovitch verified the correctness of the critic's arguments, he did not for a minute stop to ponder over the faults and mistakes which were ridiculed; but unconsciously he began immediately trying to recall every detail of his meeting and conversation with the author of the article.

'Didn't I offend him in some way?' Sergey Ivanovitch wondered.

And remembering that when they met he had corrected the young man about something he had said that betrayed ignorance, Sergey Ivanovitch found the clue to explain the article.

This article was followed by a deadly silence about the book both in the press and in conversation, and Sergey Ivanovitch saw that his six years' task, toiled at with such love and labour, had gone, leaving no trace.

Sergey Ivanovitch's position was still more difficult from the fact that, since he had finished his book, he had had no more literary work to do, such as had hitherto occupied the greater part of his time.

Sergey Ivanovitch was clever, cultivated, healthy, and energetic, and he did not know what use to make of his energy. Conversations in drawing-rooms, in meetings, assemblies, and committees—everywhere where talk was possible—took up part of his time. But being used for years to town life, he did not waste all his energies in talk, as his less experienced younger brother did, when he was in Moscow. He had a great deal of leisure and intellectual energy still to dispose of.

Fortunately for him, at this period so difficult for him from the failure of his book, the various public questions of the dissenting sects, of the American alliance, of the Samara famine, of exhibitions, and of spiritualism, were definitely replaced in public interest by the Slavonic question, which had hitherto rather languidly interested society, and Sergey Ivanovitch, who had been one of the first to raise this subject, threw himself into it heart and soul.

In the circle to which Sergey Ivanovitch belonged, nothing was talked of or written about just now but the Servian War. Everything that the idle crowd usually does to kill time was done now for the benefit of the Slavonic States. Balls, concerts, dinners, matchboxes, ladies' dresses, beer, restaurants—everything testified to sympathy with the Slavonic peoples.

From much of what was spoken and written on the subject, Sergey Ivanovitch differed on various points. He saw that the Slavonic question had become one of those fashionable distractions which succeed one another in providing society with an object and an occupation. He saw, too, that a great many people were taking up the subject from motives of self-interest and self-advertisement. He recognised that the newspapers published a great deal that was superfluous and exaggerated, with the sole aim of attracting attention and outbidding one another. He saw that in this general movement those who thrust themselves most forward and shouted the loudest were men who had failed and were smarting under a sense of injury—generals without armies, ministers not in the ministry, journalists not on any paper, party leaders without followers. He saw that there was a great deal in it that was frivolous and absurd. But he saw and recognised an unmistakable growing enthusiasm, uniting all classes, with which it was impossible not to sympathise. This massacre of men who were fellow-Christians, and of the same Slavonic race, excited sympathy for the sufferers and indignation against the oppressors. And the heroism of the Servians and Montenegrins struggling for a great cause begot in the whole people a longing to help their brothers not in word but in deed.

But in this there was another aspect that rejoiced Sergey Ivanovitch. That was the manisfestation of public opinion. The public had definitely expressed its desire. The soul of the people had, as Sergey Ivanovitch said, found expression. And the more he worked in this cause, the more incontestable it seemed to him that it was a cause destined to assume vast dimensions, to create an epoch.

He threw himself heart and soul into the service of this great cause, and forgot to think about his book. His whole time now was engrossed by it, so that he could scarcely manage to answer all the letters and appeals addressed to him. He worked the whole spring and part of the summer, and it was only in July that he prepared to go away to his brother's in the country.

He was going both to rest for a fortnight, and in the very heart of the people, in the farthest wilds of the country, to enjoy the sight of that uplifting of the spirit of the people, of which, like all residents in the capital and big towns, he was fully persuaded. Katavasov had long been meaning to carry out his promise to stay with Levin, and so he was going with him.

II

SERGEY IVANOVITCH and Katavasov had only just reached the station of the Kursk line, which was particularly busy and full of people that day, when, looking round for the groom who was following with their things, they saw a party of volunteers driving up in four cabs. Ladies met them with bouquets of flowers, and followed by the rushing crowd they went into the station.

One of the ladies, who had met the volunteers, came out of the hall and addressed Sergey Ivanovitch.

'You too come to see them off?' she asked in French.

'No, I'm going away myself, princess. To my brother's for a holiday. Do you always see them off?' said Sergey Ivanovitch with a hardly perceptible smile.

'Oh, that would be impossible!' answered the princess. 'Is it true that eight hundred have been sent from us already? Malvinsky wouldn't believe me.'

'More than eight hundred. If you reckon those who have been sent not directly from Moscow, over a thousand,' answered Sergey Ivanovitch.

'There! That's just what I said!' exclaimed the lady. 'And it's true too, I suppose, that more than a million has been subscribed?'

'Yes, princess.'

'What do you say to today's telegram? Beaten the Turks again.'

'Yes, so I saw,' answered Sergey Ivanovitch. They were speaking of the last telegram stating that the Turks had been for three days in succession beaten at all points and put to flight, and that tomorrow a decisive engagement was expected.

'Ah, by the way, a splendid young fellow has asked leave to go, and they've made some difficulty, I don't know why. I meant to ask you; I know him, please write a note about his case. He's being set by

Countess Lidia Ivanovna.'

Sergey Ivanovitch asked for all the details the princess knew about the young man, and going into the first-class waiting-room, wrote a note to the person on whom the granting of leave of absence depended, and handed it to the princess.

'You know Count Vronsky, the notorious one . . . is going by this train?' said the princess with a smile full of triumph and meaning, when he found her again and gave her the letter.

'I had heard he was going, but I did not know when. By this train?'

'I've seen him. He's here: there's only his mother seeing him off. It's the best thing, anyway, that he could do.'

'Oh yes, of course.'

While they were talking the crowd streamed by them into the dining-room. They went forward too, and heard a gentleman with a glass in his hand delivering a loud discourse to the volunteers. 'In the service of religion, humanity, and our brothers,' the gentleman said, his voice growing louder and louder; 'to this great cause mother Moscow dedicates you with her blessing. *Jivio!*' he concluded, loudly and tearfully.

Every one shouted *Jivio!* and a fresh crowd dashed into the hall, almost carrying the princess off her legs.

'Ah, princess! that was something like!' said Stepan Arkadyevitch, suddenly appearing in the middle of the crowd and beaming upon them with a delighted smile. 'Capitally, warmly said, wasn't it? Bravo! And Sergey Ivanovitch! Why, you ought to have said something—just a few words, you know, to encourage them; you do that so well,' he added with a soft, respectful, and discreet smile, moving Sergey Ivanovitch forward a little by the arm.

'No, I'm just off.'

'Where to?'

'To the country, to my brother's,' answered Sergey Ivanovitch.

'Then you'll see my wife. I've written to her, but you'll see her first. Please tell her that they've seen me and that it's "all right," as the English say. She'll understand. Oh, and be so good as to tell her I'm appointed secretary of the committee. . . . But she'll understand! You know, *les petites misères de la vie humaine*,' he said, as it were apologising to the princess. 'And Princess Myaky—not Liza, but Bibish—is sending a thousand guns and twelve nurses. Did I tell you?'

'Yes, I heard so,' answered Koznishev indifferently.

'It's a pity you're going away,' said Stepan Arkadyevitch. 'Tomorrow we're giving a dinner to two who're setting off—Dimer-Bartnyansky from Petersburg and our Veslovsky, Grisha. They're both going. Veslovsky's only lately married. There's a fine fellow for you! Eh, princess?' he turned to the lady.

The princess looked at Koznishev without replying. But the fact that Sergey Ivanovitch and the princess seemed anxious to get rid of him did not in the least disconcert Stepan Arkadyevitch. Smiling, he stared at the feather in the princess's hat, and then about him as though he were going to pick something up. Seeing a lady approaching with a collecting-box, he beckoned her up and put in a five-rouble note.

'I can never see these collecting-boxes unmoved while I've money in my pocket,' he said. 'And how about today's telegram? Fine chaps those Montenegrins!'

'You don't say so!' he cried, when the princess told him that Vronsky was going by this train. For an instant Stepan Arkadyevitch's face looked sad, but a minute later, when, stroking his moustaches and swinging as he walked, he went into the hall where Vronsky was, he had completely forgotten his own despairing sobs over his sister's corpse, and he saw in Vronsky only a hero and an old friend.

'With all his faults one can't refuse to do him justice,' said the princess to Sergey Ivanovitch as soon as Stepan Arkadyevitch had left them. 'What a typically Russian, Slav nature! Only, I'm afraid it won't be pleasant for Vronsky to see him. Say what you will, I'm touched by that man's fate. Do talk to him a little on the way,' said the princess.

'Yes, perhaps, if it happens so.'

'I never liked him. But this atones for a great deal. He's not merely going himself, he's taking a squadron at his own expense.'

'Yes, so I heard.'

A bell sounded. Everyone crowded to the doors. 'Here he is!' said the princess, indicating Vronsky, who with his mother on his arm walked by, wearing a long overcoat and wide-brimmed black hat. Oblonsky was walking beside him, talking eagerly of something.

Vronsky was frowning and looking straight before him, as though he did not hear what Stepan Arkadyevitch was saying.

Probably on Oblonsky's pointing them out, he looked round in the direction where the princess and Sergey Ivanovitch were standing, and without speaking lifted his hat. His face, aged and worn by suffering, looked stony.

Going on to the platform, Vronsky left his mother and disappeared into a compartment.

On the platform there rang out 'God save the Tsar,' then shouts of 'hurrah!' and '*jivio!*' One of the volunteers, a tall, very young man with a hollow chest, was particularly conspicuous, bowing and waving his felt hat and a nosegay over his head. Then two officers emerged, bowing too, and a stout man with a big beard, wearing a greasy forage-cap.

III

SAYING good-bye to the princess, Sergey Ivanovitch was joined by Katavasov; together they got into a carriage full to overflowing, and the train started.

At Tsaritsino station the train was met by a chorus of young men singing 'Hail to Thee!' Again the volunteers bowed and poked their heads out, but Sergey Ivanovitch paid no attention to them. He had had so much to do with the volunteers that the type was familiar to him and did not interest him. Katavasov, whose scientific work had prevented his having a chance of observing them hitherto, was very much interested in them and questioned Sergey Ivanovitch.

Sergey Ivanovitch advised him to go into the second-class and talk to them himself. At the next station Katavasov acted on this suggestion.

At the first stop he moved into the second-class and made the acquaintance of the volunteers. They were sitting in a corner of the carriage, talking loudly and obviously aware that the attention of the passengers and Katavasov as he got in was concentrated upon them. More loudly than all talked the tall, hollow-chested young man. He was unmistakably tipsy, and was relating some story that had occurred at his school. Facing him sat a middle-aged officer in the Austrian military jacket of the Guards uniform. He was listening with a smile to the hollow-chested youth, and occasionally pulling him up. The third, in an artillery uniform, was sitting on a box beside them. A fourth was asleep.

Entering into conversation with the youth, Katavasov learned that he was a wealthy Moscow merchant who had run through a large fortune before he was two-and-twenty. Katavasov did not like him, because he was unmanly and effeminate and sickly. He was obviously convinced, especially now after drinking, that he was performing a heroic action, and he bragged of it in the most unpleasant way.

The second, the retired officer, made an unpleasant impression too upon Katavasov. He was, it seemed, a man who had tried everything. He had been on a railway, had been a land-steward, and had started factories, and he talked, quite without necessity, of all he had done, and used learned expressions quite inappropriately.

The third, the artilleryman, on the contrary, struck Katavasov very favourably. He was a quiet, modest fellow, unmistakably impressed by the knowledge of the officer and the heroic self-sacrifice of the merchant and saying nothing about himself. When Katavasov asked him what had impelled him to go to Servia, he answered modestly—

'Oh, well, everyone's going. The Servians want help, too. I'm sorry for them.'

'Yes, you artillerymen especially are scarce there,' said Katavasov.

'Oh, I wasn't long in the artillery; maybe they'll put me into the infantry or the cavalry.'

'Into the infantry when they need artillery more than anything?' said Katavasov, fancying from the artilleryman's apparent age that he must have reached a fairly high grade.

'I wasn't long in the artillery, I'm a cadet retired,' he said, and he began to explain how he had failed in his examination.

All of this together made a disagreeable impression on Katavasov, and when the volunteers got out at a station for a drink, Katavasov would have liked to compare his unfavourable impression in conversation with someone. There was an old man in the carriage, wearing a military overcoat, who had been listening all the while to Katavasov's conversation with the volunteers. When they were left alone, Katavasov addressed him.

'What different positions they come from, all those fellows who are going off there,' Katavasov said vaguely, not wishing to express his own opinion, and at the same time anxious to find out the old man's views.

The old man was an officer who had served on two campaigns. He knew what makes a soldier, and judging by the appearance and the talk of those persons, by the swagger with which they had recourse to the bottle on the journey, he considered them poor soldiers. Moreover, he lived in a district town, and he was longing to tell how one soldier had volunteered from his town, a drunkard and a thief whom no one would employ as a labourer. But knowing by experience that in the present condition of the public temper it was dangerous to express an opinion opposed to the general one, and especially to criticise the volunteers unfavourably, he too watched Katavasov without committing himself.

'Well, men are wanted there,' he said, laughing with his eyes. And they fell to talking of the last war news, and each concealed from the other his perplexity as to the engagement expected next day, since the Turks had been beaten, according to the latest news, at all points. And so they parted, neither giving expression to his opinion.

Katavasov went back to his own carriage, and with reluctant hypocrisy reported to Sergey Ivanovitch his observations of the volunteers, from which it would appear that they were capital fellows.

At the big station at a town the volunteers were again greeted with shouts and singing, again men and women with collecting-boxes appeared, and provincial ladies brought bouquets to the volunteers and followed them into the refreshment-room; but all this was on a much smaller and feebler scale than in Moscow.

IV

WHILE the train was stopping at the provincial town, Sergey Ivanovitch did not go to the refreshment-room, but walked up and down the platform.

The first time he passed Vronsky's compartment he noticed that the curtain was drawn over the window; but as he passed it the second time he saw the old countess at the window. She beckoned to Koznishev.

'I'm going, you see, taking him as far as Kursk,' she said.

'Yes, so I heard,' said Sergey Ivanovitch, standing at her window and peeping in. 'What a noble act on his part!' he added, noticing that Vronsky was not in the compartment.

'Yes, after his misfortune, what was there for him to do?'

'What a terrible thing it was!' said Sergey Ivanovitch.

'Ah, what I have been through! But do get in. . . . Ah, what I have been through!' she repeated, when Sergey Ivanovitch had got in and sat down beside her. 'You can't conceive it! For six weeks he did not speak to anyone, and would not touch food except when I implored him. And not for one minute could we leave him alone. We took away everything he could have used against himself. We lived on the ground-floor, but there was no reckoning on anything. You know, of course, that he had shot himself once already on her account,' she said, and the old lady's eyelashes twitched at the recollection. 'Yes, hers was the fitting end for such a woman. Even the death she chose was low and vulgar.'

'It's not for us to judge, countess,' said Sergey Ivanovitch; 'but I can understand that it has been very hard for you.'

'Ah, don't speak of it! I was staying on my estate, and he was with me. A note was brought him. He wrote an answer and sent it off. We hadn't an idea that she was close by at the station. In the evening I had only just gone to my room, when my Mary told me a lady had thrown herself under the train. Something seemed to strike me at once. I knew it was she. The first thing I said was, he was not to be told. But they'd told him already. His coachman was there and saw it all. When I ran into his room, he was beside himself—it was fearful to see him. He didn't say a word, but galloped off there. I don't know to this day what happened there, but he was brought back at death's-door. I shouldn't have known him. *Prostration complète*, the doctor said. And that was followed almost by madness. Oh, why talk of it!' said the countess with a wave of her hand. 'It was an awful time! No, say what you will, she was a bad woman. Why, what is the meaning of such desperate passions? It was all to show herself something out of the way. Well, and that she did do. She brought herself to ruin and two good men—her husband and my unhappy son.'

'And what did her husband do?' asked Sergey Ivanovitch.

'He has taken her daughter. Alexey was ready to agree to anything at first. Now it worries him terribly that he should have given his own child away to another man. But he can't take back his word. Karenin came to the funeral. But we tried to prevent his meeting Alexey. For him, for her husband, it was easier, anyway. She had set him free. But my poor son was utterly given up to her. He had thrown up everything, his career, me, and even then she had no mercy on him, but of set purpose she made his ruin complete. No, say what you will, her very death was the death of a vile woman, of no religious feeling. God forgive me, but I can't help hating the memory of her, when I look at my son's misery!'

'But how is he now?'

'It was a blessing from Providence for us—this Servian war. I'm old, and I don't understand the rights and wrongs of it, but it's come as a providential blessing to him. Of course for me, as his mother, it's terrible; and what's worse, they say *ce n'est pas très bien vu à Pétersbourg*. But it can't be helped! It was the one thing that could rouse him. Yashvin—a friend of his—he had lost all he had at cards and he was going to Servia. He came to see him and persuaded him to go. Now it's an interest for him. Do please talk to him a little. I want to distract his mind. He's so low-spirited. And as bad luck would have it, he has toothache too. But he'll be delighted to see you. Please do talk to him; he's walking up and down on that side.'

Sergey Ivanovitch said he would be very glad to, and crossed over to the other side of the station.

V

IN the slanting evening shadows cast by the baggage piled up on the platform, Vronsky in his long overcoat and slouch hat, with his hands in his pockets, strode up and down, like a wild beast in a cage, turning sharply after twenty paces. Sergey Ivanovitch fancied, as he approached him, that Vronsky saw him but was pretending not to see. This did not affect Sergey Ivanovitch in the slightest. He was above all personal considerations with Vronsky.

At that moment Sergey Ivanovitch looked upon Vronsky as a man taking an important part in a great cause, and Koznishev thought it his duty to encourage him and express his approval. He went up to him.

Vronsky stood still, looked intently at him, recognised him, and going a few steps forward to meet him, shook hands with him very warmly.

'Possibly you didn't wish to see me,' said Sergey Ivanovitch, 'but couldn't I be of use to you?'

'There's no one I should less dislike seeing than you,' said Vronsky. 'Excuse me; and there's nothing in life for me to like.'

'I quite understand, and I merely meant to offer you my services,' said Sergey Ivanovitch, scanning Vronsky's face, full of unmistakable suffering. 'Wouldn't it be of use to you to have a letter to Ristitch—to Milan?'

'Oh no!' Vronsky said, seeming to understand him with difficulty. 'If you don't mind, let's walk on. It's so stuffy among the carriages. A letter? No, thank you; to meet death one needs no letters of introduction. Nor for the Turks . . .' he said, with a smile that was merely of the lips. His eyes still kept their look of angry suffering.

'Yes; but you might find it easier to get into relations, which are after all essential, with anyone prepared to see you. But that's as you like. I was very glad to hear of your intention. There have been so many attacks made on the volunteers, and a man like you raises them in public estimation.'

'My use as a man,' said Vronsky, 'is that life's worth nothing to me. And that I've enough bodily energy to cut my way into their ranks, and to trample on them or fall—I know that. I'm glad there's something to give my life for, for it's not simply useless but loathsome to me. Anyone's welcome to it.' And his jaw twitched impatiently from the incessant gnawing toothache, that prevented him from even speaking with a natural expression.

'You will become another man, I predict,' said Sergey Ivanovitch, feeling touched. 'To deliver one's brother-men from bondage is an aim worth death and life. God grant you success outwardly—and inwardly peace,' he added, and he held out his hand. Vronsky warmly pressed his outstretched hand.

'Yes, as a weapon I may be of some use. But as a man, I'm a wreck,' he jerked out.

He could hardly speak for the throbbing ache in his strong teeth, that were like rows of ivory in his mouth. He was silent, and his eyes rested on the wheels of the tender, slowly and smoothly rolling along the rails.

And all at once a different pain, not an ache, but an inner trouble, that set his whole being in anguish, made him for an instant forget his toothache. As he glanced at the tender and the rails, under the influence of the conversation with a friend he had not met since his misfortune, he suddenly recalled *her*—that is, what was left of her when he had run like one distraught into the cloak-room of the railway station—on the table, shamelessly sprawling out among strangers, the blood-stained body so lately full of life; the head unhurt dropping back with its weight of hair, and the curling tresses about the temples, and the exquisite face, with red, half-opened mouth, the strange, fixed expression, piteous on the lips and awful in the still open eyes, that seemed to utter that fearful phrase—that he would be sorry for it—that she had said when they were quarrelling.

And he tried to think of her as she was when he met her the first time, at a railway-station too, mysterious, exquisite, loving, seeking and giving happiness, and not cruelly revengeful as he remembered her on that last moment. He tried to recall his best moments with her, but those moments were poisoned for ever. He could only think of her as triumphant, successful in her menace of a wholly useless remorse never to be effaced. He lost all consciousness of toothache, and his face worked with sobs.

Passing twice up and down beside the baggage in silence and regaining his self-possession, he addressed Sergey Ivanovitch calmly—

'You have had no telegrams since yesterday's? Yes, driven back for a third time, but a decisive engagement expected for tomorrow.'

And after talking a little more of King Milan's proclamation, and the immense effect it might have, they parted, going to their carriages on hearing the second bell.

VI

SERGEY IVANOVITCH had not telegraphed to his brother to send to meet him, as he did not know when he should be able to leave Moscow. Levin was not at home when Katavasov and Sergey Ivanovitch in a fly hired at the station drove up to the steps of the Pokrovskoe house, as black as niggers from the dust of the road. Kitty, sitting on the balcony with her father and sister, recognised her brother-in-law, and ran down to meet him.

'What a shame not to have let us know,' she said, giving her hand to Sergey Ivanovitch, and putting her forehead up for him to kiss.

'We drove here capitally, and have not put you out,' answered Sergey Ivanovitch. 'I'm so dirty, I'm afraid to touch you. I've been so busy, I didn't know when I should be able to tear myself away. And so you're still as ever enjoying your peaceful, quiet happiness,' he said, smiling, 'out of the reach of the current in your peaceful backwater. Here's our friend Fyodor Vassilievitch has succeeded in getting here at last.'

'But I'm not a negro, I shall look like a human being when I wash,' said Katavasov in his jesting fashion, and he shook hands and smiled, his teeth flashing white in his black face.

'Kostya will be delighted. He has gone to his settlement. It's time he should be home.

'Busy as ever with his farming. It really is a peaceful backwater,' said Katavasov; 'while we in town think of nothing but the Servian war. Well, how does our friend look at it? He's sure not to think like other people.'

'Oh, I don't know, like everybody else,' Kitty answered, a little embarrassed, looking round at Sergey Ivanovitch. 'I'll send to fetch him. Papa's staying with us. He's only just come home from abroad.'

And making arrangements to send for Levin and for the guests to wash, one in his room and the other in what had been Dolly's, and giving orders for their luncheon, Kitty ran out on to the balcony, enjoying the freedom and rapidity of movement, of which she had been deprived during the months of her pregnancy.

'It's Sergey Ivanovitch and Katavasov, a professor,' she said.

'Oh, that's a bore in this heat,' said the prince.

'No, papa, he's very nice, and Kostya's very fond of him,' Kitty said, with a deprecating smile, noticing the irony on her father's face.

'Oh, I didn't say anything.'

'You go to them, darling,' said Kitty to her sister, 'and entertain them. They saw Stiva at the station; he was quite well. And I must run to Mitya. As ill-luck would have it, I haven't fed him since tea. He's awake now, and sure to be screaming.' And feeling a rush of milk, she hurried to the nursery.

This was not a mere guess; her connection with the child was still so close, that she could gauge by the flow of her milk his need of food, and knew for certain he was hungry.

She knew he was crying before she reached the nursery. And he was indeed crying. She heard him and hastened. But the faster she went, the louder he screamed. It was a fine healthy scream, hungry and impatient.

'Has he been screaming long, nurse, very long?' said Kitty hurriedly, seating herself on a chair, and preparing to give the baby the breast. 'But give me him quickly. Oh, nurse, how tiresome you are! There, tie the cap afterwards, do!'

The baby's greedy scream was passing into sobs.

'But you can't manage so, ma'am,' said Agafea Mihalovna, who was almost always to be found in the nursery. 'He must be put straight. A-oo! a-oo!' she chanted over him, paying no attention to the mother.

The nurse brought the baby to his mother. Agafea Mihalovna followed him with a face dissolving with tenderness.

'He knows me, he knows me. In God's faith, Katerina Alexandrovna, ma'am, he knew me!' Agafea Mihalovna cried above the baby's screams.

But Kitty did not heed her words. Her impatience kept growing, like the baby's.

Their impatience hindered things for a while. The baby could not get hold of the breast right, and was furious.

At last, after despairing, breathless screaming, and vain sucking, things went right, and mother and child felt simultaneously soothed, and both subsided into calm.

'But poor darling, he's all in perspiration!' said Kitty in a whisper, touching the baby.

'What makes you think he knows you?' she added, with a sidelong glance at the baby's eyes, that peered roguishly, as she fancied, from under his cap, at his rhythmically puffing cheeks, and the little red-palmed hand he was waving.

'Impossible! If he knew anyone, he would have known me,' said Kitty, in response to Agafea Mihalovna's statement, and she smiled.

She smiled because, though she said he could not know her, in her heart she was sure that he knew not merely Agafea Mihalovna, but that he knew and understood everything, and knew and understood a great deal too that no one else knew, and that she, his mother, had learned and come to understand only through him. To Agafea Mihalovna, to the nurse, to his grandfather, to his father even, Mitya was a living being, requiring only material care, but for his mother he had long been a moral being, with whom there had been a whole series of spiritual relations already.

'When he wakes up, please God, you shall see for yourself. Then when I do like this, he simply beams on me, the darling! Simply beams like a sunny day!' said Agafea Mihalovna.

'Well, well; then we shall see,' whispered Kitty. 'But now go away, he's going to sleep.'

VII

AGAFEA MIHALOVNA went out on tiptoe; the nurse let down the blind, chased a fly out from under the muslin canopy of the crib, and a humble-bee struggling on the window-frame, and sat waving a faded branch of birch over the mother and the baby.

'How hot it is! if God would send a drop of rain,' she said.

'Yes, yes, sh—sh—sh—' was all Kitty answered, rocking a little, and tenderly squeezing the plump little arm, with rolls of fat at the wrist, which Mitya still waved feebly as he opened and shut his eyes. That hand worried Kitty; she longed to kiss the little hand, but was afraid to for fear of waking the baby. At last the little hand ceased waving, and the eyes closed. Only from time to time, as he went on sucking, the baby raised his long, curly eyelashes and peeped at his mother with wet eyes, that looked black in the twilight. The nurse had left off fanning, and was dozing. From above came the peals of the old prince's voice, and the chuckle of Katavasov.

'They have got into talk without me,' thought Kitty, 'but still it's vexing that Kostya's out. He's sure to have gone to the bee-house again. Though it's a pity he's there so often, still I'm glad. It distracts his mind. He's become altogether happier and better now than in the spring. He used to be so gloomy and worried that I felt frightened for him. And how absurd he is!' she whispered, smiling.

She knew what worried her husband. It was his unbelief. Although, if she had been asked whether she supposed that in the future life, if he did not believe, he would be damned, she would have had to admit that he would be damned, his unbelief did not cause her unhappiness. And she, confessing that for an unbeliever there can be no salvation, and loving her husband's soul more than anything in the world, thought with a smile of his unbelief, and told herself that he was absurd.

'What does he keep reading philosophy of some sort for all this year?' she wondered. 'If it's all written in those books, he can understand them. If it's all wrong, why does he read them? He says himself that he would like to believe. Then why is it he doesn't believe? Surely from his thinking so much? And he thinks so much from being solitary. He's always alone, alone. He can't talk about it all to us. I fancy he'll be glad of these visitors, especially Katavasov. He likes discussions with them,' she thought, and passed instantly to the consideration of where it would be more convenient to put Katavasov, to sleep alone or to share Sergey Ivanovitch's room. And then an idea suddenly struck her, which made her shudder and even disturb Mitya, who glanced severely at her. 'I do believe the laundress hasn't sent the washing yet, and all the best sheets are in use. If I don't see to it, Agafea Mihalovna will give Sergey Ivanovitch the wrong sheets,' and at the very idea of this the blood rushed to Kitty's face.

'Yes, I will arrange it,' she decided, and going back to her former thoughts, she remembered that some spiritual question of importance had been interrupted, and she began to recall what. 'Yes, Kostya, an unbeliever,' she thought again with a smile.

'Well, an unbeliever then! Better let him always be one than like Madame Stahl, or what I tried to be in those days abroad. No, he won't ever sham anything.'

And a recent instance of his goodness rose vividly to her mind. A fortnight ago a penitent letter had come from Stepan Arkadyevitch to Dolly. He besought her to save his honour, to sell her estate to pay his debts. Dolly was in despair, she detested her husband, despised him, pitied him, resolved on a separation, resolved to refuse, but ended by agreeing to sell part of her property. After that, with an irrepressible smile of tenderness, Kitty recalled her husband's shamefaced embarrassment, his repeated, awkward efforts to approach the subject, and how at last, having thought of the one means of helping Dolly without wounding her pride, he had suggested to Kitty—what had not occurred to her before—that she should give up her share of the property.

'He an unbeliever indeed! With his heart, his dread of offending anyone, even a child! Everything for others, nothing for himself. Sergey Ivanovitch simply considers it as Kostya's duty to be his steward. And it's the same with his sister. Now Dolly and her children are under his guardianship; all these peasants who come to him every day, as though he were bound to be at their service.'

'Yes, only be like your father, only like him,' she said, handing Mitya over to the nurse, and putting her lips to his cheek.

VIII

EVER since, by his beloved brother's deathbed, Levin had first glanced into the questions of life and death in the light of these new convictions, as he called them, which had during the period from his twentieth to his thirty-fourth year imperceptibly replaced his childish and youthful beliefs—he had been stricken with horror, not so much of death, as of life, without any knowledge of whence, and why, and how, and what it was. The physical organisation, its decay, the indestructibility of matter, the law of the conservation of energy, evolution, were the words which usurped the place of his old belief. These words and the ideas associated with them were very well for intellectual purposes. But for life they yielded nothing, and Levin felt suddenly like a man who has changed his warm fur cloak for a muslin garment, and going for the first time into the frost is immediately convinced, not by reason, but by his whole nature, that he is as good as naked, and that he must infallibly perish miserably.

From that moment, though he did not distinctly face it, and still went on living as before, Levin had never lost this sense of terror at his lack of knowledge.

He vaguely felt, too, that what he called his new convictions were not merely lack of knowledge, but that they were part of a whole order of ideas, in which no knowledge of what he needed was possible.

At first, marriage, with the new joys and duties bound up with it, had completely crowded out these thoughts. But of late, while he was staying in Moscow after his wife's confinement, with nothing to do, the question that clamoured for solution had more and more often, more and more insistently, haunted Levin's mind.

The question was summed up for him thus; 'If I do not accept the answers Christianity gives to the problems of my life, what answers do I accept?' And in the whole arsenal of his convictions, so far from finding any satisfactory answers, he was utterly unable to find anything at all like an answer.

He was in the position of a man seeking food in toy-shops and tool-shops.

Instinctively, unconsciously, with every book, with every conversation, with every man he met, he was on the lookout for light on these questions and their solution.

What puzzled and distracted him above everything was that the majority of men of his age and circle had, like him, exchanged their old beliefs for the same new convictions, and yet saw nothing to lament in this, and were perfectly satisfied and serene. So that, apart from the principal question, Levin was tortured by other questions too. Were these people sincere? he asked himself, or were they playing a part? or was it that they understood the answers science gave to these problems in some different, clearer sense than he did? And he assiduously studied both these men's opinions and the books which treated of these scientific explanations.

One fact he had found out since these questions had engrossed his mind, was that he had been quite wrong in supposing from the recollections of the circle of his young days at college, that religion had outlived its day, and that it was now practically non-existent. All the people nearest to him who were good in their lives were believers. The old prince, and Lvov, whom he liked so much, and Sergey Ivanovitch, and all the women believed, and his wife believed as simply as he had believed in his earliest childhood, and ninety-nine hundredths of the Russian people, all the working-people for whose life he felt the deepest respect, believed.

Another fact of which he became convinced, after reading many scientific books, was that the men who shared his views had no other construction to put on them, and that they gave no explanation of the questions which he felt he could not live without answering, but simply ignored their existence and attempted to explain other questions of no possible interest to him, such as the evolution of organisms, the materialistic theory of consciousness, etc.

Moreover, during his wife's confinement, something had happened that seemed extraordinary to him. He, an unbeliever, had fallen into praying, and at the moment he prayed, he believed. But that moment had passed, and he could not make his state of mind at that moment fit into the rest of his life.

He could not admit that at that moment he knew the truth, and that now he was wrong; for as soon as he began thinking calmly about it, it all fell to pieces. He could not admit that he was mistaken then, for his spiritual condition then was precious to him, and to admit that it was a proof of weakness would have been to desecrate those moments. He was miserably divided against himself, and strained all his spiritual forces to the utmost to escape from this condition.

IX

THESE doubts fretted and harassed him, growing weaker or stronger from time to time, but never leaving him. He read and thought, and the more he read and the more he thought, the further he felt from the aim he was pursuing.

Of late in Moscow and in the country, since he had become convinced that he would find no solution in the materialists, he had read and re-read thoroughly Plato, Spinoza, Kant, Schelling, Hegel, and Schopenhauer, the philosophers who gave a non-materialistic explanation of life.

Their ideas seemed to him fruitful when he was reading or was himself seeking arguments to refute other theories, especially those of the materialists; but as soon as he began to read or sought for himself a solution of problems, the same thing always happened. As long as he followed the fixed definition of obscure words such as *spirit, will, freedom, essence*, purposely letting himself go into the snare of words the philosophers set for him, he seemed to comprehend something. But he had only to forget the artificial train of reasoning, and to turn from life itself to what had satisfied him while thinking in accordance with the fixed definitions, and all this artificial edifice fell to pieces at once like a house of cards, and it became clear that the edifice had been built up out of those transposed words, apart from anything in life more important than reason.

At one time, reading Schopenhauer, he put in place of his *will* the word *love*, and for a couple of days this new philosophy charmed him, till he removed a little away from it. But then, when he turned from life itself to glance at it again, it fell away too, and proved to be the same muslin garment with no warmth in it.

His brother Sergey Ivanovitch advised him to read the theological works of Homiakov. Levin read the second volume of Homiakov's works, and in spite of the elegant, epigrammatic, argumentative style which at first repelled him, he was impressed by the doctrine of the church he found in them. He was struck at first by the idea that the apprehension of divine truths has not been vouchsafed to man, but to a corporation of men bound together by love—to the church. What delighted him was the thought how much easier it was to believe in a still existing living church, embracing all the beliefs of men, and having God at its head, and therefore holy and infallible, and from it to accept the faith in God, in the creation, the fall, the redemption, than to begin with God, a mysterious, far-away God, the creation, etc. But afterwards, on reading a Catholic writer's history of the church, and then a Greek Orthodox writer's history of the church, and seeing that the two churches, in their very conception infallible, each deny the authority of the other, Homiakov's doctrine of the church lost all its charm for him, and this edifice crumbled into dust like the philosophers' edifices.

All that spring he was not himself, and went through fearful moments of horror.

'Without knowing what I am and why I am here, life's impossible; and that I can't know, and so I can't live,' Levin said to himself.

'In infinite time, in infinite matter, in infinite space, is formed a bubble-organism, and that bubble lasts a while and bursts, and that bubble is Me.'

It was an agonising error, but it was the sole logical result of ages of human thought in that direction.

This was the ultimate belief on which all the systems elaborated by human thought in almost all their ramifications rested. It was the prevalent conviction, and of all other explanations Levin had unconsciously, not knowing when or how, chosen it, as anyway the clearest, and made it his own.

But it was not merely a falsehood, it was the cruel jeer of some wicked power, some evil, hateful power, to whom one could not submit.

He must escape from this power. And the means of escape every man had in his own hands. He had but to cut short this dependence on evil. And there was one means—death.

And Levin, a happy father and husband, in perfect health, was several times so near suicide that he hid the cord that he might not be tempted to hang himself, and was afraid to go out with his gun for fear of shooting himself.

But Levin did not shoot himself, and did not hang himself; he went on living.

X

WHEN Levin thought what he was and what he was living for, he could find no answer to the questions and was reduced to despair, but he left off questioning himself about it. It seemed as though he knew both what he was and for what he was living, for he acted and lived resolutely and without hesitation. Indeed, in these latter days he was far more decided and unhesitating in life than he had ever been.

When he went back to the country at the beginning of June, he went back also to his usual pursuits. The management of the estate, his relations with the peasants and the neighbours, the care of his household, the management of his sister's and brother's property, of which he had the direction, his relations with his wife and kindred, the care of his child, and the new beekeeping hobby he had taken up that spring, filled all his time.

These things occupied him now, not because he justified them to himself by any sort of general principles, as he had done in former days; on the contrary, disappointed by the failure of his former efforts for the general welfare, and too much occupied with his own thought and the mass of business with which he was burdened from all sides, he had completely given up thinking of the general good, and he busied himself with all this work simply because it seemed to him that he must do what he was doing—that he could not do otherwise. In former days—almost from childhood, and increasingly up to full manhood—when he had tried to do anything that would be good for all, for humanity, for Russia, for the whole village, he had noticed that the idea of it had been pleasant, but the work itself had always been incoherent, that then he had never had a full conviction of its absolute necessity, and that the work that had begun by seeming so great, had grown less and less, till it vanished into nothing. But now, since his marriage, when he had begun to confine himself more and more to living for himself, though he experienced no delight at all at the thought of the work he was doing, he felt a complete conviction of its necessity, saw that it succeeded far better than in old days, and that it kept on growing more and more.

Now, involuntarily it seemed, he cut more and more deeply into the soil like a plough, so that he could not be drawn out without turning aside the furrow.

To live the same family life as his father and forefathers—that is, in the same condition of culture—and to bring up his children in the same, was incontestably necessary. It was as necessary as dining when one was hungry. And to do this, just as it was necessary to cook dinner, it was necessary to keep the mechanism of agriculture at Pokrovskoe going so as to yield an income. Just as incontestably as it was necessary to repay a debt was it necessary to keep the property in such a condition that his son, when he received it as heritage, would say 'thank you' to his father as Levin had said 'thank you' to his grandfather for all he built and planted. And to do this it was necessary to look after the land himself, not to let it, and to breed cattle, manure the fields, and plant timber.

It was impossible not to look after the affairs of Sergey Ivanovitch, of his sister, of the peasants who came to him for advice and were accustomed to do so—as impossible as to fling down a child one is carrying in one's arms. It was necessary to look after the comfort of his sister-in-law and her children, and of his wife and baby, and it was impossible not to spend with them at least a short time each day.

And all this, together with shooting and his new beekeeping, filled up the whole of Levin's life, which had no meaning at all for him, when he began to think.

But besides knowing thoroughly what he had to do, Levin knew in just the same way *how* he had to do it all, and what was more important than the rest.

He knew he must hire labourers as cheaply as possible; but to hire men under bond, paying them in advance at less than the current rate of wages, was what he must not do, even though it was very profitable. Selling straw to the peasants in times of scarcity of provender was what he might do, even though he felt sorry for them; but the tavern and the pot-house must be put down, though they were a source of income. Felling timber must be punished as severely as possible, but he could not exact forfeits for cattle being driven on to his fields; and though it annoyed the keeper and made the peasants not afraid to graze their cattle on his land, he could not keep their cattle as a punishment.

To Pyotr, who was paying a money-lender ten per cent a month, he must lend a sum of money to set him free. But he could not let off peasants who did not pay their rent, nor let them fall in arrears. It was impossible to overlook the bailiff's not having mown the meadows and letting the hay spoil; and it was equally impossible to mow those acres where a young copse had been planted. It was impossible to excuse a labourer who had gone home in the busy season because his father was dying, however sorry he might feel for him, and he must subtract from his pay those costly months of idleness. But it was impossible not to allow monthly rations to the old servants who were of no use for anything.

Levin knew that when he got home he must first of all go to his wife, who was unwell, and that the peasants who had been waiting for three hours to see him could wait a little longer. He knew too that, regardless of all the pleasure he felt in taking a swarm, he must forgo that pleasure, and leave the old man to see to the bees alone, while he talked to the peasants who had come after him to the bee-house.

Whether he were acting rightly or wrongly he did not know, and far from trying to prove that he was, nowadays he avoided all thought or talk about it.

Reasoning had brought him to doubt, and prevented him from seeing what he ought to do and what he ought not. When he did not think, but simply lived, he was continually aware of the presence of an infallible judge in his soul, determining which of two possible courses of action was the better and which was the worse, and as soon as he did not act rightly, he was at once aware of it.

So he lived, not knowing and not seeing any chance of knowing what he was and what he was living for, and harassed at this lack of knowledge to such a point that he was afraid of suicide, and yet firmly laying down his own individual definite path in life.

XI

THE day on which Sergey Ivanovitch came to Pokrovskoe was one of Levin's most painful days. It was the very busiest working-time, when all the peasantry show an extraordinary intensity of self-sacrifice in labour, such as is never shown in any other conditions of life, and would be highly esteemed if the men who showed these qualities themselves thought highly of them, and if it were not repeated every year, and if the results of this intense labour were not so simple.

To reap and bind the rye and oats and to carry it, to mow the meadows, turn over the fallows, thrash the seed and sow the winter corn—all this seems so simple and ordinary; but to succeed in getting through it all everyone in the village, from the old man to the young child, must toil incessantly for three or four weeks, three times as hard as usual, living on rye-beer, onions, and black bread, thrashing and carrying the sheaves at night, and not giving more than two or three hours in the twenty-four to sleep. And every year this is done all over Russia.

Having lived the greater part of his life in the country and in the closest relations with the peasants, Levin always felt in this busy time that he was infected by this general quickening of energy in the people.

In the early morning he rode over to the first sowing of the rye, and to the oats, which were being carried to the stacks, and returning home at the time his wife and sister-in-law were getting up, he drank coffee with them and walked to the farm, where a new threshing-machine was to be set working to get ready the seed-corn.

He was standing in the cool granary, still fragrant with the leaves of the hazel branches interlaced on the freshly peeled aspen beams of the new thatch roof. He gazed through the open door in which the dry bitter dust of the threshing whirled and played, at the grass of the threshing-floor in the sunlight and the fresh straw that had been brought in from the barn, then at the speckly-headed, white-breasted swallows that flew chirping in under the roof and, fluttering their wings, settled in the crevices of the doorway, then at the peasants bustling in the dark, dusty barn, and he thought strange thoughts—

'Why is it all being done?' he thought. 'Why am I standing here, making them work? What are they all so busy for, trying to show their zeal before me? What is that old Matrona, my old friend, toiling for? (I doctored her, when the beam fell on her in the fire)' he thought, looking at a thin old woman who was raking up the grain, moving painfully with her bare, sun-blackened feet over the uneven, rough floor. 'Then she recovered, but today or tomorrow or in ten years she won't; they'll bury her, and nothing will be left either of her or of that smart girl in the red jacket, who with that skilful, soft action shakes the ears out of their husks. They'll bury her and this piebald horse, and very soon too,' he thought, gazing at the heavily moving, panting horse that kept walking up the wheel that turned under him. 'And they will bury her and Fyodor the thresher with his curly beard full of chaff and his shirt torn on his white shoulders—they will bury him. He's untying the sheaves, and giving orders, and shouting to the women, and quickly setting straight the strap on the moving wheel. And what's more, it's not them alone—me they'll bury too, and nothing will be left. What for?'

He thought this, and at the same time looked at his watch to reckon how much they threshed in an hour. He wanted to know this so as to judge by it the task to set for the day.

'It'll soon be one, and they're only beginning the third sheaf,' thought Levin. He went up to the man that was feeding the machine, and shouting over the roar of the machine he told him to put it in more slowly. 'You put in too much at a time, Fyodor. Do you see—it gets choked, that's why it isn't getting on. Do it evenly.'

Fyodor, black with the dust that clung to his moist face, shouted something in response, but still went on doing it as Levin did not want him to.

Levin, going up to the machine, moved Fyodor aside, and began feeding the corn in himself. Working on till the peasants' dinner-hour, which was not long in coming, he went out of the barn with Fyodor and fell into talk with him, stopping beside a neat yellow sheaf of rye laid on the threshing-floor for seed.

Fyodor came from a village at some distance from the one in which Levin had once allotted land to his co-operative association. Now it had been let to a former house-porter.

Levin talked to Fyodor about this land and asked whether Platon, a well-to-do peasant of good character belonging to the same village, would not take the land for the coming year.

'It's a high rent; it wouldn't pay Platon, Konstantin Dmitrievitch,' answered the peasant, picking the ears off his sweat-drenched shirt.

'But how does Kirillov make it pay?'

'Mituh!' (so the peasant called the house-porter, in a tone of contempt), 'you may be sure he'll make it pay, Konstantin Dmitrievitch! He'll get his share, however he has to squeeze to get it! He's no mercy on a Christian. But Uncle Fokanitch' (so he called the old peasant Platon), 'do you suppose he'd flay the skin off a man? Where there's debt, he'll let anyone off. And he'll not wring the last penny out. He's a man too.'

'But why will he let anyone off?'

'Oh, well, of course, folks are different. One man lives for his own wants and nothing else, like Mituh; he only thinks of filling his belly, but Fokanitch is a righteous man. He lives for his soul. He does not forget God.'

'How thinks of God? How does he live for his soul?' Levin almost shouted.

'Why, to be sure, in truth, in God's way. Folks are different. Take you now, you wouldn't wrong a man. . . .'

'Yes, yes, good-bye!' said Levin, breathless with excitement, and turning round he took his stick and walked quickly away towards home. At the peasant's words that Fokanitch lived for his soul, in truth, in God's way, undefined but significant ideas seemed to burst out as though they had been locked up, and all striving towards one goal, they thronged whirling through his head, blinding him with their light.

XII

LEVIN strode along the highroad, absorbed not so much in his thoughts (he could not yet disentangle them) as in his spiritual condition, unlike anything he had experienced before.

The words uttered by the peasant had acted on his soul like an electric shock, suddenly transforming and combining into a single whole the whole swarm of disjointed, impotent, separate thoughts that incessantly occupied his mind. These thoughts had unconsciously been in his mind even when he was talking about the land.

He was aware of something new in his soul, and joyfully tested this new thing, not yet knowing what it was.

'Not living for his own wants, but for God? For what God? And could one say anything more senseless than what he said? He said that one must not live for one's own wants, that is, that one must not live for what we understand, what we are attracted by, what we desire, but must live for something incomprehensible, for God, whom no one can understand nor even define. What of it? Didn't I understand those senseless words of Fyodor's? And understanding them, did I doubt of their truth? Did I think them stupid, obscure, inexact? No, I understood him, and exactly as he understands the words. I understood them more fully and clearly than I understand anything in life, and never in my life have I doubted nor can I doubt about it. And not only I, but everyone, the whole world understands nothing fully but this, and about this only they have no doubt and are always agreed.

'And I looked out for miracles, complained that I did not see a miracle which would convince me. A material miracle would have persuaded me. And here is a miracle, the sole miracle possible, continually existing, surrounding me on all sides, and I never noticed it!

'Fyodor says that Kirillov lives for his belly. That's comprehensible and rational. All of us as rational beings can't do anything else but live for our belly. And all of a sudden the same Fyodor says that one mustn't live for one's belly, but must live for truth, for God, and at a hint I understand him! And I and millions of men, men who lived ages ago and men living now—peasants, the poor in spirit and the learned, who have thought and written about it, in their obscure words saying the same thing—we are all agreed about this one thing: what we must live for and what is good. I and all men have only one firm, incontestable, clear knowledge, and that knowledge cannot be explained by the reason—it is outside it, and has no causes and can have no effects.

'If goodness has causes, it is not goodness; if it has effects, a reward, it is not goodness either. So goodness is outside the chain of cause and effect.

'And yet I know it, and we all know it.

'What could be a greater miracle than that?

'Can I have found the solution of it all? can my sufferings be over?' thought Levin, striding along the dusty road, not noticing the heat nor his weariness, and experiencing a sense of relief from prolonged suffering. This feeling was so delicious that it seemed to him incredible. He was breathless with emotion and incapable of going farther; he turned off the road into the forest and lay down in the shade of an aspen on the uncut grass. He took his hat off his hot head and lay propped on his elbow in the lush, feathery, woodland grass.

'Yes, I must make it clear to myself and understand,' he thought, looking intently at the untrampled grass before him, and following the movements of a green beetle, advancing along a blade of couch-grass and lifting up in its progress a leaf of goat-weed. 'What have I discovered?' he asked himself, bending aside the leaf of goat-weed out of the beetle's way and twisting another blade of grass above for the beetle to cross over on to it. 'What is it makes me glad? What have I discovered?

'I have discovered nothing. I have only found out what I knew. I understand the force that in the past gave me life, and now too gives me life. I have been set free from falsity, I have found the Master.

'Of old I used to say that in my body, that in the body of this grass and of this beetle (there, she didn't care for the grass, she's opened her wings and flown away), there was going on a transformation of matter in accordance with physical, chemical, and physiological laws. And in all of us, as well as in the aspens and the clouds and the misty patches, there was a process of evolution. Evolution from what? into what—Eternal evolution and struggle.... As though there could be any sort of tendency and struggle in the eternal! And I was astonished that in spite of the utmost effort of thought along that road I could not discover the meaning of life, the meaning of my impulses and yearnings. Now I say that I know the meaning of my life: "To live for God, for my soul." And this meaning, in spite of its clearness, is mysterious and marvellous. Such, indeed, is the meaning of everything existing. Yes, pride,' he said to himself, turning over on his stomach and beginning to tie a noose of blades of grass, trying not to break them.

'And not merely pride of intellect, but dulness of intellect. And most of all, the deceitfulness; yes, the deceitfulness of intellect. The cheating knavishness of intellect, that's it,' he said to himself.

And he briefly went through, mentally, the whole course of his ideas during the last two years, the beginning of which was the clear confronting of death at the sight of his dear brother hopelessly ill.

Then, for the first time, grasping that for every man, and himself too, there was nothing in store but suffering, death, and forgetfulness, he had made up his mind that life was impossible like that, and that he must either interpret life so that it would not present itself to him as the evil jest of some devil, or shoot himself.

But he had not done either, but had gone on living, thinking, and feeling, and had even at that very time married, and had had many joys and had been happy, when he was not thinking of the meaning of his life.

What did this mean? It meant that he had been living rightly, but thinking wrongly.

He had lived (without being aware of it) on those spiritual truths that he had sucked in with his mother's milk, but he had thought, not merely without recognition of these truths, but studiously ignoring them.

Now it was clear to him that he could only live by virtue of the beliefs in which he had been brought up.

'What should I have been, and how should I have spent my life, if I had not had these beliefs, if I had not known that I must live for God and not for my own desires? I should have robbed and lied and killed. Nothing of what makes the chief happiness of my life would have existed for me.' And with the utmost stretch of imagination he could not conceive the brutal creature he would have been himself, if he had not known what he was living for.

'I looked for an answer to my question. And thought could not give an answer to my question—it is incommensurable with my question. The answer has been given me by life itself, in my knowledge of what is right and what is wrong. And that knowledge I did not arrive at in any way, it was given to me as to all men, *given*, because I could not have got it from anywhere.

'Where could I have got it? By reason could I have arrived at knowing that I must love my neighbour and not oppress him? I was told that in my childhood, and I believed it gladly, for they told me what was already in my soul. But who discovered it? Not reason. Reason discovered the struggle for existence, and the law that requires us to oppress all who hinder the satisfaction of our desires. That is the deduction of reason. But loving one's neighbour reason could never discover, because it's irrational.'

XIII

AND Levin remembered a scene he had lately witnessed between Dolly and her children. The children, left to themselves, had begun cooking raspberries over the candles, and squirting milk into each other's mouths with a syringe. Their mother, catching them at these pranks, began reminding them in Levin's presence of the trouble their mischief gave to the grown-up people, and that this trouble was all for their sake, and that if they smashed the cups they would have nothing to drink their tea out of, and that if they wasted the milk, they would have nothing to eat, and die of hunger.

And Levin had been struck by the passive, weary incredulity with which the children heard what their mother said to them. They were simply annoyed that their amusing play had been interrupted, and did not believe a word of what their mother was saying. They could not believe it indeed, for they could not take in the immensity of all they habitually enjoyed, and so could not conceive that what they were destroying was the very thing they lived by.

'That all comes of itself,' they thought, 'and there's nothing interesting or important about it because it has always been so, and always will be so. And it's all always the same. We've no need to think about that, it's all ready. But we want to invent something of our own, and new. So we thought of putting raspberries in a cup, and cooking them over a candle, and squirting milk straight into each other's mouths. That's fun, and something new, and not a bit worse than drinking out of cups.'

'Isn't it just the same that we do, that I did, searching by the aid of reason for the significance of the forces of nature and the meaning of the life of man?' he thought.

'And don't all the theories of philosophy do the same, trying by the path of thought, which is strange and not natural to man, to bring him to a knowledge of what he has known long ago, and knows so certainly that he could not live at all without it? Isn't it distinctly to be seen in the development of each philosopher's theory, that he knows what is the chief significance of life beforehand, just as positively as the peasant Fyodor, and not a bit more clearly than he, and is simply trying by a dubious intellectual path to come back to what everyone knows?

'Now then, leave the children to themselves to get things alone and make their crockery, get the milk from the cows, and so on. Would they be naughty then? Why, they'd die of hunger! Well, then, leave us without passions and thoughts, without any idea of the one God, of the

Creator, or without any idea of what is right, without any idea of moral evil.

'Just try and build up anything without those ideas!

'We only try and destroy them, because we're spiritually provided for. Exactly like the children!

'Whence have I that joyful knowledge, shared with the peasant, that alone gives peace to my soul? Whence did I get it?

'Brought up with an idea of God, a Christian, my whole life filled with the spiritual blessings Christianity has given me, full of them, and living on these blessings, like the children I did not understand them, and destroy, that is try to destroy, what I live by. And as soon as an important moment of life comes, like the children when they are cold and hungry, I turn to Him, and even less than the children when their mother scolds them for their childish mischief, do I feel that my childish efforts at wanton madness are reckoned against me.

'Yes, what I know, I know not by reason, but it has been given to me, revealed to me, and I know it with my heart, by my faith in the chief thing taught by the church.

'The church! the church!' Levin repeated to himself. He turned over on the other side, and leaning on his elbow, fell to gazing into the distance at a herd of cattle crossing over to the river.

'But can I believe in all the church teaches?' he thought, trying himself, and thinking of everything that could destroy his present peace of mind. Intentionally he recalled all those doctrines of the church which had always seemed most strange and had always been a stumbling-block to him.

'The Creation? But how did I explain existence? By existence? By nothing? The devil and sin. But how do I explain evil? . . . The atonement? . . .

'But I know nothing, nothing, and I can know nothing but what has been told to me and all men.'

And it seemed to him that there was not a single article of faith of the church which could destroy the chief thing—faith in God, in goodness, as the one goal of man's destiny.

Under every article of faith of the church could be put the faith in the service of truth instead of one's desires. And each doctrine did not simply leave that faith unshaken, each doctrine seemed essential to complete that great miracle, continually manifest upon earth, that made it possible for each man and millions of different sorts of men, wise men and imbeciles, old men and children—all men, peasants, Lvov, Kitty, beggars and kings to understand perfectly the same one thing, and to build up thereby that life of the soul which alone is worth living, and which alone is precious to us.

Lying on his back, he gazed up now into the high, cloudless sky. 'Do I not know that that is infinite space, and that it is not a round arch? But, however I screw up my eyes and strain my sight, I cannot see it not round and not bounded, and in spite of my knowing about infinite space, I am incontestably right when I see a solid blue dome, and more right than when I strain my eyes to see beyond it.'

Levin ceased thinking, and only, as it were, listened to mysterious voices that seemed talking joyfully and earnestly within him.

'Can this be faith?' he thought, afraid to believe in his happiness. 'My God, I thank Thee!' he said, gulping down his sobs, and with both hands brushing away the tears that filled his eyes.

XIV

LEVIN looked before him and saw a herd of cattle, then he caught sight of his trap with Raven in the shafts, and the coachman, who, driving up to the herd, said something to the herdsman. Then he heard the rattle of the wheels and the snort of the sleek horse close by him. But he was so buried in his thoughts that he did not even wonder why the coachman had come for him.

He only thought of that when the coachman had driven quite up to him and shouted to him. 'The mistress sent me. Your brother has come, and some gentleman with him.'

Levin got into the trap and took the reins. As though just roused out of sleep, for a long while Levin could not collect his faculties. He stared at the sleek horse, flecked with lather between his haunches and on his neck, where the harness rubbed, stared at Ivan the coachman sitting beside him, and remembered that he was expecting his brother, thought that his wife was most likely uneasy at his long absence, and tried to guess who was the visitor who had come with his brother. And his brother and his wife and the unknown guest seemed to him now quite different from before. He fancied that now his relations with all men would be different.

'With my brother there will none of that aloofness there always used to be between us, there will no disputes; with Kitty there shall never be quarrels; with the visitor, whoever he may be, I will be friendly and nice; with the servants, with Ivan, it will all be different.'

Pulling the stiff rein and holding in the good horse that snorted with impatience and seemed begging to be let go, Levin looked round at Ivan sitting beside him, not knowing what to do with his unoccupied hand, continually pressing down his shirt as it puffed out, and he tried to find something to start a conversation about with him. He would have said that Ivan had pulled the saddle-girth up too high, but that was like blame, and he longed for friendly, warm talk. Nothing else occurred to him.

'Your honour must keep to the right and mind that stump,' said the coachman, pulling the rein Levin held.

'Please don't touch and don't teach me!' said Levin, angered by this interference. Now, as always, interference made him angry, and he felt sorrowfully at once how mistaken had been his supposition that his spiritual condition could immediately change him in contact with reality.

He was not a quarter of a mile from home when he saw Grisha and Tanya running to meet him.

'Uncle Kostya! mamma's coming, and grandfather, and Sergey Ivanovitch, and someone else,' they said, clambering up into the trap.

'Who is he?'

'An awfully terrible person! And he does like this with his arms,' said Tanya, getting up in the trap and mimicking Katavasov.

'Old or young?' asked Levin, laughing, reminded of someone, he did not know whom, by Tanya's performance.

'Oh, I hope it's not a tiresome person!' thought Levin.

As soon as he turned, at a bend in the road, and saw the party coming, Levin recognised Katavasov in a straw hat, walking along swinging his arms just as Tanya had shown him. Katavasov was very fond of discussing metaphysics, having derived his notions from natural science writers who had never studied metaphysics, and in Moscow Levin had had many arguments with him of late.

And one of these arguments, in which Katavasov had obviously considered that he came off victorious, was the first thing Levin thought of as he recognised him.

'No, whatever I do, I won't argue and give utterance to my ideas lightly,' he thought.

Getting out of the trap and greeting his brother and Katavasov, Levin asked about his wife.

'She has taken Mitya to Kolok' (a copse near the house). 'She meant to have him out there because it's so hot indoors,' said Dolly. Levin had always advised his wife not to take the baby to the wood, thinking it unsafe, and he was not pleased to hear this.

'She rushes about from place to place with him,' said the prince, smiling. 'I advised her to try putting him in the ice cellar.'

'She meant to come to the bee-house. She thought you would be there. We are going there,' said Dolly.

'Well, and what are you doing?' said Sergey Ivanovitch, falling back from the rest and walking beside him.

'Oh, nothing special. Busy as usual with the land,' answered Levin. 'Well, and what about you? Come for long? We have been expecting you for such a long time.'

'Only for a fortnight. I've a great deal to do in Moscow.'

At these words the brothers' eyes met, and Levin, in spite of the desire he always had, stronger than ever just now, to be an affectionate and still more open terms with his brother, felt an awkwardness in looking at him. He dropped his eyes and did not know what to say.

Casting over the subjects of conversation that would be pleasant to Sergey Ivanovitch, and would keep him off the subject of the Servian war and the Slavonic question, at which he had hinted by the allusion to what he had to do in Moscow, Levin began to talk of Sergey Ivanovitch's book.

'Well, have there been reviews of your book?' he asked.

Sergey Ivanovitch smiled at the intentional character of the question.

'No one is interested in that now, and I less than anyone,' he said. 'Just look, Darya Alexandrovna, we shall have a shower,' he added, pointing with a sunshade at the white rainclouds that showed above the aspen tree-tops.

And these words were enough to re-establish again between the brothers that tone—hardly hostile, but chilly—which Levin had been so longing to avoid.

Levin went up to Katavasov.

'It was jolly of you to make up your mind to come,' he said to him.

'I've been meaning to a long while. Now we shall have some discussion, we'll see to that. Have you been reading Spencer?'

'No, I've not finished reading him,' said Levin. 'But I don't need him now.'

'How's that? that's interesting. Why so?'

'I mean that I'm fully convinced that the solution of the problems that interest me I shall never find in him and his like. Now . . .'

But Katavasov's serene and good-humoured expression suddenly struck him, and he felt such tenderness for his own happy mood, which he was unmistakably disturbing by this conversation, that he remembered his resolution and stopped short.

'But we'll talk later on,' he added. 'If we're going to the bee-house, it's this way, along this little path,' he said, addressing them all.

Going along the narrow path to the little uncut meadow covered on one side with thick clumps of brilliant heart's-ease among which stood up here and there tall, dark green tufts of hellebore, Levin settled his guests in the dense, cool shade of the young aspens on a bench and some stumps purposely put there for visitors to the bee-house who might be afraid of the bees, and he went off himself to the hut to get bread, cucumbers, and fresh honey, to regale them with.

Trying to make his movements as deliberate as possible, and listening to the bees that buzzed more and more frequently past him, he walked along the little path to the hut. In the very entry one bee hummed angrily, caught in his beard, but he carefully extricated it. Going into the shady outer room, he took down from the wall his veil, that hung on a peg, and putting it on, and thrusting his hands into his pockets, he went into the fenced-in bee-garden, where there stood in the midst of a closely mown space in regular rows, fastened with bast on posts, all the hives he knew so well, the old stocks, each with its own history, and along the fences the younger swarms hived that year. In front of the openings of the hives, it made his eyes giddy to watch the bees and drones whirling round and round about the same spot, while among them the working bees flew in and out with spoils or in search of them, always in the same direction into the wood to the flowering lime-trees and back to the hives.

His ears were filled with the incessant hum in various notes, now the busy hum of the working bee flying quickly off, then the blaring of the lazy drone, and the excited buzz of the bees on guard protecting their property from the enemy and preparing to sting. On the farther side of the fence the old beekeeper was shaving a hoop for a tub, and he did not see Levin. Levin stood still in the midst of the beehives and did not call him.

He was glad of a chance to be alone to recover from the influence of ordinary actual life, which had already depressed his happy mood. He thought that he had already had time to lose his temper with Ivan, to show coolness to his brother, and to talk flippantly with Katavasov.

'Can it have been only a momentary mood, and will it pass and leave no trace?' he thought. But the same instant, going back to his mood, he felt with delight that something new and important had happened to him. Real life had only for a time overcast the spiritual peace he had found, but it was still untouched within him.

Just as the bees, whirling round him, now menacing him and distracting his attention, prevented him from enjoying complete physical peace, forced him to restrain his movements to avoid them, so had the petty cares that had swarmed about him from the moment he got into the trap, restricted his spiritual freedom; but that lasted only so long as he was among them. Just as his bodily strength was still unaffected, in spite of the bees, so too was the spiritual strength that he had just become aware of.

XV

'DO you know, Kostya, with whom Sergey Ivanovitch travelled on his way home?' said Dolly, doling out cucumbers and honey to the children; 'with Vronsky! He's going to Servia.'

'And not alone; he's taking a squadron out with him at his own expense,' said Katavasov.

'That's the right thing for him,' said Levin. 'Are volunteers still going out then?' he added, glancing at Sergey Ivanovitch.

Sergey Ivanovitch did not answer. He was carefully with a blunt knife getting a live bee covered with sticky honey out of a cup full of white honeycomb.

'I should think so! You should have seen what was going on at the station yesterday!' said Katavasov, biting with a juicy sound into a cucumber.

'Well, what is one to make of it? For mercy's sake, do explain to me, Sergey Ivanovitch, where are all those volunteers going, whom are they fighting with,' asked the old prince, unmistakably taking up a conversation that had sprung up in Levin's absence.

'With the Turks,' Sergey Ivanovitch answered, smiling serenely, as he extricated the bee, dark with honey and helplessly kicking, and put it with the knife on a stout aspen leaf.

'But who has declared war on the Turks?—Ivan Ivanovitch Ragozov and Countess Lidia Ivanovna, assisted by Madame Stahl?'

'No one has declared war, but people sympathise with their neighbour's sufferings and are eager to help them,' said Sergey Ivanovitch.

'But the prince is not speaking of help,' said Levin, coming to the assistance of his father-in-law, 'but of war. The prince says that private persons cannot take part in war without the permission of the government.'

'Kostya, mind, that's a bee! Really, they'll sting us!' said Dolly, waving away a wasp.

'But that's not a bee, it's a wasp,' said Levin.

'Well now, well, what's your own theory?' Katavasov said to Levin with a smile, distinctly challenging him to a discussion. 'Why have not private persons the right to do so?'

'Oh, my theory's this: war is on one side such a beastly, cruel, and awful thing, that no one man, not to speak of a Christian, can individually take upon himself the responsibility of beginning wars; that can only be done by a government, which is called upon to do this, and is driven inevitably into war. On the other hand, both political science and common sense teach us that in matters of state, and especially in the matter of war, private citizens must forego their personal individual will.'

Sergey Ivanovitch and Katavasov had their replies ready and both began speaking at the same time.

'But the point is, my dear fellow, that there may be cases when the government does not carry out the will of the citizens and then the public asserts its will,' said Katavasov.

But evidently Sergey Ivanovitch did not approve of this answer. His brows contracted at Katavasov's words and he said something else.

'You don't put the matter in its true light. There is no question here of a declaration of war, but simply the expression of a human Christian feeling. Our brothers, one with us in religion and in race, are being massacred. Even supposing they were not our brothers nor fellow-Christians, but simply children, women, old people, feeling is aroused and Russians go eagerly to help in stopping these atrocities. Fancy, if you were going along the street and saw drunken men beating a woman or a child—I imagine you would not stop to inquire whether war had been declared on the men, but would throw yourself on them and protect the victim.'

'But I should not kill them,' said Levin.

'Yes, you would kill them.'

'I don't know. If I saw that, I might give way to my impulse of the moment, but I can't say beforehand. And such a momentary impulse there is not, and there cannot be, in the case of the opposition of the Slavonic peoples.'

'Possibly for you there is not; but for others there is,' said Sergey Ivanovitch, frowning with displeasure. 'There are traditions still extant among the people of Slavs of the true faith suffering under the yoke of the "unclean sons of Hagar." The people have heard of the sufferings of their brethren and have spoken.'

Perhaps so,' said Levin evasively; 'but I don't see it. I'm one of the people myself, and I don't feel it.'

'Here am I too,' said the old prince. 'I've been staying abroad and reading the papers, and I must own, up to the time of the Bulgarian atrocities, I couldn't make out why it was all the Russians were all of a sudden so fond of their Slavonic brethren, while I didn't feel the slightest affection for them. I was very much upset, thought I was a monster, or that it was the influence of Carlsbad on me. But since I have been here, my mind's been set at rest. I see that there are people besides me who're only interested in Russia, and not in their Slavonic brethren. Here's Konstantin too.'

'Personal opinions mean nothing in such a case,' said Sergey Ivanovitch; 'it's not a matter of personal opinions when all Russia—the whole people—has expressed its will.'

'But excuse me, I don't see that. The people don't know anything about it, if you come to that,' said the old prince.

'Oh, papa! . . . how can you say that? And last Sunday in church?' said Dolly, listening to the conversation. 'Please give me a cloth,' she said to the old man, who was looking at the children with a smile. 'Why, it's not possible that all . . .'

'But what was it in church on Sunday? The priest had been told to read that. He read it. They didn't understand a word of it. Then they were told that there was to be a collection for a pious object in church; well, they pulled out their halfpence and gave them, but what for they couldn't say.'

'The people cannot help knowing; the sense of their own destinies is always in the people, and at such moments as the present that sense finds utterance,' said Sergey Ivanovitch with conviction, glancing at the old beekeeper.

The handsome old man, with black grizzled beard and thick silvery hair, stood motionless, holding a cup of honey, looking down from the height of his tall figure with friendly serenity at the gentlefolk, obviously understanding nothing of their conversation and not caring to understand it.

'That's so, no doubt,' he said, with a significant shake of his head at Sergey Ivanovitch's words.

'Here, then, ask him. He knows nothing about it and thinks nothing,' said Levin. 'Have you heard about the war, Mihalitch?' he said, turning to him. 'What they read in the church? What do you think about it? Ought we to fight for the Christians?'

'What should we think? Alexander Nikolaevitch our Emperor has thought for us; he thinks for us indeed in all things. It's clearer for him to see. Shall I bring a bit more bread? Give the little lad some more?' he said addressing Darya Alexandrovna and pointing to Grisha, who had finished his crust.

'I don't need to ask,' said Sergey Ivanovitch; 'we have seen and are seeing hundreds and hundreds of people who give up everything to serve a just cause, come from every part of Russia, and directly and clearly express their thought and aim. They bring their halfpence or go themselves and say directly what for. What does it mean?'

'It means, to my thinking,' said Levin, who was beginning to get warm, 'that among eighty millions of people there can always be found not hundreds, as now, but tens of thousands of people who have lost caste, ne'er-do-wells, who are always ready to go anywhere—to Pogatchev's bands, to Khiva, to Servia . . .'

'I tell you that it's not a case of hundreds or of ne'er-do-wells, but the best representatives of the people!' said Sergey Ivanovitch, with as much irritation as if he were defending the last penny of his fortune. 'And what of the subscriptions? In this case it is a whole people directly expressing their will.'

'That word "people" is so vague,' said Levin. 'Parish clerks, teachers, and one in a thousand of the peasants, maybe, know what it's all about. The rest of the eighty millions, like Mihalitch, far from expressing their will, haven't the faintest idea what there is for them to express their will about. What right have we to say that this is the people's will?'

XVI

SERGEY IVANOVITCH, being practised in argument, did not reply, but at once turned the conversation to another aspect of the subject.

'Oh, if you want to learn the spirit of the people by arithmetical computation, of course it's very difficult to arrive at it. And voting has not been introduced among us and cannot be introduced, for it does not express the will of the people; but there are other ways of reaching that. It is felt in the air, it is felt by the heart. I won't speak of those deep currents which are astir in the still ocean of the people, and which are evident to every unprejudiced man; let us look at society in the narrow sense. All the most diverse sections of the educated public, hostile before, are merged in one. Every division is at an end, all the public organs say the same thing over and over again, all feel the mighty torrent that has overtaken them and is carrying them in one direction.'

'Yes, all the newspapers do say the same thing,' said the prince. 'That's true. But so it is the same thing that all the frogs croak before a storm. One can hear nothing for them.'

'Frogs or no frogs, I'm not the editor of a paper and I don't want to defend them; but I am speaking of the unanimity in the intellectual world,' said Sergey Ivanovitch, addressing his brother. Levin would have answered, but the old prince interrupted him.

'Well, about that unanimity, that's another thing, one may say,' said the prince. 'There's my son-in-law, Stepan Arkadyevitch, you know him. He's got a place now on the committee of a commission and something or other, I don't remember. Only there's nothing to do in it— why, Dolly, it's no secret! – and a salary of eight thousand. You try asking him whether his post is of use, he'll prove to you that it's most necessary. And he's a truthful man too, but there's no refusing to believe in the utility of eight thousand roubles.'

'Yes, he asked me to give a message to Darya Alexandrovna about the post,' said Sergey Ivanovitch reluctantly, feeling the prince's remark to be ill-timed.

'So it is with the unanimity of the press. That's been explained to me: as soon as there's war their incomes are doubled. How can they help believing in the destinies of the people and the Slavonic races . . . and all that?'

'I don't care for many of the papers, but that's unjust,' said Sergey Ivanovitch.

'I would only make one condition,' pursued the old prince. 'Alphonse Karr said a capital thing before the war with Prussia: "You consider war to be inevitable? Very good. Let everyone who advocates war be enrolled in a special regiment of advance-guards, for the front of every storm, of every attack, to lead them all!"'

'A nice lot the editors would make!' said Katavasov, with a loud roar, as he pictured the editors he knew in this picked legion.

'But they'd run,' said Dolly, 'they'd only be in the way.'

'Oh, if they ran away, then we'd have grape-shot or Cossacks with whips behind them,' said the prince.

'But that's a joke, and a poor one too, if you'll excuse me saying so, prince,' said Sergey Ivanovitch.

'I don't see that it was a joke, that . . .' Levin was beginning, but Sergey Ivanovitch interrupted him.

'Every member of society is called upon to do his own special work,' said he. 'And men of thought are doing their work when they express public opinion. And the single-hearted and full expression of public opinion is the service of the press and a phenomenon to rejoice us at the same time. Twenty years ago we should have been silent, but now we have heard the voice of the Russian people, which is ready to rise as one man and ready to sacrifice itself for its oppressed brethren; that is a great step and a proof of strength.'

'But it's not only making a sacrifice, but killing Turks,' said Levin timidly. 'The people make sacrifices and are ready to make sacrifices for their soul, but not for murder,' he added, instinctively connecting the conversation with the ideas that had been absorbing his mind.

'For their soul? That's a most puzzling expression for a natural science man, do you understand? What sort of thing is the soul?' said Katavasov, smiling.

'Oh, you know.'

'No, by God, I haven't the faintest idea!' said Katavasov with a loud roar of laughter.

'"I bring not peace, but a sword," says Christ,' Sergey Ivanovitch rejoined for his part, quoting as simply as though it were the easiest thing to understand the very passage that had always puzzled Levin most.

'That's so, no doubt,' the old man repeated again. He was standing near them and responded to a chance glance turned in his direction.

'Ah, my dear fellow, you're defeated, utterly defeated! cried Katavasov good humouredly.

Levin reddened with vexation, not at being defeated, but at having failed to control himself and being drawn into argument.

'No, I can't argue with them,' he thought; 'they wear impenetrable armour, while I'm naked.'

He saw that it was impossible to convince his brother and Katavasov, and he saw less possibility of himself agreeing with them. What they advocated was the very pride of intellect that had almost been his ruin. He could not admit that some dozens of men, among them his brother, had the right, on the ground of what they were told by some hundreds of glib volunteers swarming to the capital, to say that they and the newspapers were expressing the will and feeling of the people, and a feeling which was expressed in vengeance and murder. He could not admit this, because he neither saw the expression of such feelings in the people among whom he was living, nor found them in himself (and he could not but consider himself one of the persons making up the Russian people), and most of all because he, like the people, did not know and could not know what is for the general good, though he knew beyond a doubt that this general good could be attained only by the strict observance of that law of right and wrong which has been revealed to every man, and therefore he could not wish for war or advocate war for any general objects whatever. He said as Mihalitch did and the people, who had expressed their feeling in the traditional invitations of the Varyagi: 'Be princes and rule over us. Gladly we promise complete submission. All the labour, all humiliations, all sacrifices we take upon ourselves; but we will not judge and decide.' And now, according to Sergey Ivanovitch's account, the people had foregone this privilege they had bought at such a costly price.

He wanted to say too that if public opinion were an infallible guide, then why were not revolutions and the commune as lawful as the movement in favour of the Slavonic peoples? But these were merely thoughts that could settle nothing. One thing could be seen beyond doubt—that was that at the actual moment the discussion was irritating Sergey Ivanovitch, and so it was wrong to continue it. And Levin ceased speaking and then called the attention of his guests to the fact that the storm-clouds were gathering, and that they had better be going home before it rained.

XVII

THE old prince and Sergey Ivanovitch got into the trap and drove off; the rest of the party hastened homewards on foot.

But the storm-clouds, turning white and then black, moved down so quickly that they had to quicken their pace to get home before the rain. The foremost clouds, lowering and black as soot-laden smoke, rushed with extraordinary swiftness over the sky. They were still two hundred paces from home and a gust of wind had already blown up, and every second the downpour might be looked for.

The children ran ahead with frightened and gleeful shrieks. Darya Alexandrovna, struggling painfully with her skirts that clung round her legs, was not walking, but running, her eyes fixed on the children. The men of the party, holding their hats on, strode with long steps beside her. They were just at the steps when a big drop fell splashing on the edge of the iron guttering. The children and their elders after them ran into the shelter of the house, talking merrily.

'Katerina Alexandrovna?' Levin asked of Agafea Mihalovna, who met them with kerchiefs and rugs in the hall.

'We thought she was with you,' she said.

'And Mitya?'

'In the copse, he must be, and the nurse with him.'

Levin snatched up the rugs and ran towards the copse.

In that brief interval of time the storm-clouds had moved on, covering the sun so completely that it was dark as an eclipse. Stubbornly, as though insisting on its right, the wind stopped Levin, and tearing the leaves and flowers off the lime-trees and stripping the white birch branches into strange unseemly nakedness, it twisted everything on one side—acacias, flowers, burdocks, long grass, and tall tree-tops. The peasant girls working in the garden ran shrieking into shelter in the servants' quarters. The streaming rain had already flung its white veil over all the distant forest and half the fields close by, and was rapidly swooping down upon the copse. The wet of the rain spirting up in tiny drops could be smelt in the air.

Holding his head bent down before him, and struggling with the wind that strove to tear the wraps away from him, Levin was moving up to the copse and had just caught sight of something white behind the oak-tree, when there was a sudden flash, the whole earth seemed on fire, and the vault of heaven seemed crashing overhead. Opening his blinded eyes, Levin gazed through the thick veil of rain that separated him now from the copse, and to his horror the first thing he saw was the green crest of the familiar oak-tree in the middle of the copse uncannily changing its position. 'Can it have been struck?' Levin hardly had time to think when, moving more and more rapidly, the oak-tree vanished behind the other trees, and he heard the crash of the great tree falling upon the others.

The flash of lightning, the crash of thunder, and the instantaneous chill that ran through him were all merged for Levin in one sense of terror.

'My God! my God! not on them!' he said.

And though he thought at once how senseless was his prayer that they should not have been killed by the oak which had fallen now, he repeated it, knowing that he could do nothing better than utter this senseless prayer.

Running up to the place where they usually went, he did not find them there.

They were at the other end of the copse under an old lime-tree; they were calling him. Two figures in dark dresses (they had been light summer dresses when they started out) were standing bending over something. It was Kitty with the nurse. The rain was already ceasing, and it was beginning to get light when Levin reached them. The nurse was not wet on the lower part of her dress, but Kitty was drenched through, and her soaked clothes clung to her. Though the rain was over, they still stood in the same position in which they had been standing when the storm broke. Both stood bending over a perambulator with a green umbrella.

'Alive? Unhurt? Thank God!' he said, splashing with his soaked boots through the standing water and running up to them.

Kitty's rosy wet face was turned towards him, and she smiled timidly under her shapeless sopped hat.

'Aren't you ashamed of yourself? I can't think how you can be so reckless!' he said angrily to his wife.

'It wasn't my fault, really. We were just meaning to go, when he made such a to-do that we had to change him. We were just . . .' Kitty began defending herself.

Mitya was unharmed, dry, and still fast asleep.

'Well, thank God! I don't know what I'm saying!'

They gathered up the baby's wet belongings; the nurse picked up the baby and carried it. Levin walked beside his wife, and, penitent for having been angry, he squeezed her hand when the nurse was not looking.

XVIII

DURING the whole of that day, in the extremely different conversations in which he took part, only as it were with the top layer of his mind, in spite of the disappointment of not finding the change he expected in himself, Levin had been all the while joyfully conscious of the fulness of his heart.

After the rain it was too wet to go for a walk; besides, the storm-clouds still hung about the horizon, and gathered here and there, black and thundery, on the rim of the sky. The whole party spent the rest of the day in the house.

No more discussions sprang up; on the contrary, after dinner everyone was in the most amiable frame of mind.

At first Katavasov amused the ladies by his original jokes, which always pleased people on their first acquaintance with him. Then Sergey Ivanovitch induced him to tell them about the very interesting observations he had made on the habits and characteristics of common house-flies, and their life. Sergey Ivanovitch, too, was in good spirits, and at tea his brother drew him on to explain his views of the future of the Eastern question, and he spoke so simply and so well, that everyone listened eagerly.

Kitty was the only one who did not hear it all—she was summoned to give Mitya his bath.

A few minutes after Kitty had left the room she sent for Levin to come to the nursery.

Leaving his tea, and regretfully interrupting the interesting conversation, and at the same time uneasily wondering why he had been sent for, as this only happened on important occasions, Levin went to the nursery.

Although he had been much interested by Sergey Ivanovitch's views of the new epoch in history that would be created by the emancipation of forty millions of men of Slavonic race acting with Russia, a conception quite new to him, and although he was disturbed by uneasy wonder at being sent for by Kitty, as soon as he came out of the drawing-room and was alone, his mind reverted at once to the thoughts of the morning. And all the theories of the significance of the Slav element in the history of the world seemed to him so trivial compared with what was passing in his own soul, that he instantly forgot it all and dropped back into the same frame of mind that he had been in that morning.

He did not, as he had done at other times, recall the whole train of thought—that he did not need. He fell back at once into the feeling which had guided him, which was connected with those thoughts, and he found that feeling in his soul even stronger and more definite than before. He did not, as he had had to do with previous attempts to find comforting arguments, need to revive a whole chain of thought to find the feeling. Now, on the contrary, the feeling of joy and peace was keener than ever, and thought could not keep pace with feeling.

He walked across the terrace and looked at two stars that had come out in the darkening sky, and suddenly he remembered. 'Yes, looking at the sky, I thought that the dome that I see is not a deception, and then I thought something, I shirked facing something,' he mused. 'But whatever it was, there can be no disproving it! I have but to think, and all will come clear!'

Just as he was going into the nursery he remembered what it was he had shirked facing. It was that if the chief proof of the Divinity was His revelation of what is right, how is it this revelation is confined to the Christian church alone? What relation to this revelation have the beliefs of the Buddhists, Mohammedans, who preached and did good too?

It seemed to him that he had an answer to this question; but he had not time to formulate it to himself before he went into the nursery.

Kitty was standing with her sleeves tucked up over the baby in the bath. Hearing her husband's footsteps, she turned towards him, summoning him to her with her smile. With one hand she was supporting the fat baby that lay floating and sprawling on its back, while with the other she squeezed the sponge over him.

'Come, look, look!' she said, when her husband came up to her. 'Agafea Mihalovna's right. He knows us!'

Mitya had on that day given unmistakable, incontestable signs of recognising all his friends.

As soon as Levin approached the bath, the experiment was tried, and it was completely successful. The cook, sent for with this object, bent over the baby. He frowned and shook his head disapprovingly. Kitty bent down to him, he gave her a beaming smile, propped his little hands on the sponge and chirruped, making such a queer little contented sound with his lips, that Kitty and the nurse were not alone in their admiration. Levin, too, was surprised and delighted.

The baby was taken out of the bath, drenched with water, wrapped in towels, dried, and after a piercing scream, handed to his mother.

'Well, I am glad you are beginning to love him,' said Kitty to her husband, when she had settled herself comfortably in her usual place, with the baby at her breast. 'I am so glad! It had begun to distress me. You said you had no feeling for him.'

'No; did I say that? I only said I was disappointed.'

'What! disappointed in him?'

'Not disappointed in him, but in my own feeling; I had expected more. I had expected a rush of new delightful emotion to come as a surprise. And then instead of that—disgust, pity . . .'

She listened attentively, looking at him over the baby, while she put back on her slender fingers the rings she had taken off while giving Mitya his bath.

'And most of all, at there being far more apprehension and pity than pleasure. Today, after that fright during the storm, I understand how I love him.'

Kitty's smile was radiant.

'Were you very much frightened?' she said. 'So was I too, but I feel it more now that it's over. I'm going to look at the oak. How nice Katavasov is! And what a happy day we've had altogether. And you're so nice with Sergey Ivanovitch, when you care to be. . . . Well, go back to them. It's always so hot and steamy here after the bath.'

XIX

GOING out of the nursery and being again alone, Levin went back at once to the thought, in which there was something not clear.

Instead of going into the drawing-room, where he heard voices, he stopped on the terrace, and leaning his elbows on the parapet, he gazed up at the sky.

It was quite dark now, and in the south, where he was looking there were no clouds. The storms had drifted on to the opposite side of the sky, and there were flashes of lightning and distant thunder from that quarter. Levin listened to the monotonous drip from the lime-trees in the garden, and looked at the triangle of stars he knew so well, and the Milky Way with its branches that ran through its midst. At each flash of lightning the Milky Way, and even the bright stars, vanished, but as soon as the lightning died away, they reappeared in their places as though some hand had flung them back with careful aim.

'Well, what is it perplexes me?' Levin said to himself, feeling beforehand that the solution of his difficulties was ready in his soul, though he did not know it yet. 'Yes, the one unmistakable, incontestable manifestation of the Divinity—the law of right and wrong, which has come into the world by revelation, and which I feel in myself, and in the recognition of which—I don't make myself, but whether I will or not—

I am made one with other men in one body of believers, which is called the church. Well, but the Jews, the Mohammedans, the Confucians, the Buddhists—what of them?' he put to himself the question he had feared to face. 'Can these hundreds of millions of men be deprived of that highest blessing without which life has no meaning?' He pondered a moment, but immediately corrected himself. 'But what am I questioning?' he said to himself. 'I am questioning the relation to Divinity of all the different religions of all mankind. I am questioning the universal manifestation of God to all the world with all those misty blurs. What am I about? To me individually, to my heart has been revealed a knowledge beyond all doubt, and unattainable by reason, and here I am obstinately trying to express that knowledge in reason and words.

'Don't I know that the stars don't move?' he asked himself, gazing at the bright planet which had shifted its position up to the topmost twig of the birch-tree. 'But looking at the movements of the stars, I can't picture to myself the rotation of the earth, and I'm right in saying that the stars move.

'And could the astronomers have understood and calculated anything, if they had taken into account all the complicated and varied motions of the earth? All the marvellous conclusions they have reached about the distances, weights, movements, and deflections of the heavenly bodies are only founded on the apparent motions of the heavenly bodies about a stationary earth, on that very motion I see before me now, which has been so for millions of men during long ages, and was and will be always alike, and can always be trusted. And just as the conclusions of the astronomers would have been vain and uncertain if not founded on observations of the seen heavens, in relation to a single meridian and a single horizon, so would my conclusions be vain and uncertain if not founded on that conception of right, which has been and will be always alike for all men, which has been revealed to me as a Christian, and which can always be trusted in my soul. The question of other religions and their relations to Divinity I have no right to decide, and no possibility of deciding.'

'Oh, you haven't gone in then?' he heard Kitty's voice all at once, as she came by the same way to the drawing-room.

'What is it? you're not worried about anything?' she said, looking intently at his face in the starlight.

But she could not have seen his face if a flash of lightning had not hidden the stars and revealed it. In that flash she saw his face distinctly, and seeing him calm and happy, she smiled at him.

'She understands,' he thought; 'she knows what I'm thinking about.

Shall I tell her or not? Yes, I'll tell her.' But at the moment he was about to speak, she began speaking.

'Kostya! do something for me,' she said; 'go into the corner room and see if they've made it all right for Sergey Ivanovitch. I can't very well. See if they've put the new washstand in it.'

'Very well, I'll go directly,' said Levin, standing up and kissing her.

'No, I'd better not speak of it,' he thought, when she had gone in before him. 'It is a secret for me alone, of vital importance for me, and not to be put into words.

'This new feeling has not changed me, has not made me happy and enlightened all of a sudden, as I had dreamed, just like the feeling for my child. There was no surprise in this either. Faith—or not faith—I don't know what it is—but this feeling has come just as imperceptibly through suffering, and has taken firm root in my soul.

'I shall go on in the same way, losing my temper with Ivan the coachman, falling into angry discussions, expressing my opinions tactlessly; there will be still the same wall between the holy of holies of my soul and other people, even my wife; I shall still go on scolding her for my own terror, and being remorseful for it; I shall still be as unable to understand with my reason why I pray, and I shall still go on praying; but my life now, my whole life apart from anything that can happen to me, every minute of it is no more meaningless, as it was before, but it has the positive meaning of goodness, which I have the power to put into it.'

THE END